T3-BWQ-576

ENCYCLOPEDIA
OF THE
AMERICAN THEATRE ORGAN

Colorful and ornate 4/23 Robert Morton console from Loew's Kings Theatre, Brooklyn, New York. Similarly decorated consoles graced several other deluxe Loew houses in New York and New Jersey.

ENCYCLOPEDIA OF THE AMERICAN THEATRE ORGAN

Volume II

DAVID L. JUNCHEN

Pasadena, California

Address all correspondence to:

SHOWCASE PUBLICATIONS
Post Office Box 40165
Pasadena, California 91114

Manufactured in the United States of America

Library of Congress Cataloging in Publication Data
(Revised for volume II)

Junchen, David L., 1946-
Encyclopedia of the American Theatre Organ

Bibliography: v. I, p. 421.
Includes indexes.
1. Organs—United States—Dictionaries. 2. Organbuilders—United States. I. Title.

ML561.J86 786.5′1973 85-51070

ISBN 0-917800-03-6 (set)
ISBN 0-917800-02-8 (v. I)
ISBN 0-917800-04-4 (v II)

CONTENTS

ACKNOWLEDGMENTS 440
L. D. MORRIS & CO. 442
J. H. & C. S. ODELL & CO. 442
THE OPERATORS PIANO COMPANY, INC. 445
THE PAGE ORGAN COMPANY 453
EARL PAVETTE 461
PELOUBET AND COMPANY 462
HENRY PILCHER'S SONS 464
PIPE ORGAN SERVICE CO. 472
POWERS 472
THE REUTER ORGAN COMPANY 473
JAMES N. REYNOLDS 490
ROBERT MORTON ORGAN CO. 491
HILBORNE L. ROOSEVELT 583
SCHAEFER ORGAN CO. 588
A. J. SCHANTZ, SONS & CO. 589
THE WM. SCHUELKE ORGAN CO. 594
J. P. SEEBURG PIANO COMPANY 597
SKINNER ORGAN COMPANY 598
F. R. SMITH 612
SMITH UNIT ORGAN CO. 613
E. A. SPENCER 632
HERMAN STAHL 633
J. W. STEERE & SON ORGAN COMPANY 634
EDWARD STEIN 636
STEVENS ORGAN COMPANY 636
SYMPHONY PLAYER COMPANY 637
TELLERS-KENT ORGAN COMPANY 638
UNITED STATES PIPE ORGAN COMPANY 643
BERNARD VAN WYCK 652
CHAS. VINER & SONS 653
THE VOTTELER-HOLTKAMP-SPARLING ORGAN CO. 655
WANGERIN ORGAN COMPANY 662
WELTE-MIGNON CORPORATION 673
WESTERN SERVICE CO. 693
WICKS PIPE ORGAN CO. 694
C. F. WINDER ORGAN COMPANY 729
THE WIRSCHING ORGAN CO. 731
WM. WOOD PIPE ORGAN CO., INC. 736

PARTS SUPPLIERS TO THE ORGAN INDUSTRY 740
BLOWERS 741
Bayley Manufacturing Co. 741
B. F. Blower Co., Inc. 742
Kinetic Engineering Company 744
Conrad Preschley 748
G. Meidinger & Co. 748
The Spencer Turbine Co. 755
The Zephyr Electric Organ Blower Co. 776

CHAMBER HEATERS 778
Buffalo Gas Radiator Corporation 778
Cramblet Engineering Corporation 779
Prometheus Electric Corp. 780

ELECTRICAL PARTS 781
American Steel & Wire Company 781
Belden Manufacturing Company 781
Electric Vibrato Co. 782
Electric Specialty Company 782
August A. Klann 784
Magnetic Organ Action Co. 786
Emil Meurling 787
Pittsburgh Organ Parts Company 787
The W. H. Reisner Mfg. Co., Inc. 788
Triumph Electric Corporation 792
The Widney Company 792

ELEVATORS 793
Bartola Musical Instrument Co. 793
Warsaw Elevator Co. 793
Curtis Pneumatic Machinery Company 794
Otis Elevator Company 795
Peter Clark, Inc. 797

GENERAL SUPPLIES 798
Durst, Boegle & Co. 798
The A. Gottfried Co. 806
Hausmann & Co. 817
Jarvis Organ Co. 817
Aug. Laukhuff 818
Organ Supply Corporation 821
National Organ Supply Company 821
Herman Stahl 832

KEYBOARDS 833
Comstock, Cheney & Co. 833
The Piano & Organ Supply Company 834
Pratt, Read & Co., Inc. 834
Wood & Brooks Company 837

LEATHER, FELT & CLOTH 837
Geo. W. Braunsdorf, Inc. 837
The Carlton Sales Co. 838
Hand & Company 838
T. L. Lutkins, Inc. 839
L. J. Mutty Co. 839
C. Weilbier 840
White, Son Company 840
Wood & Werner, Inc. 841

MISCELLANEOUS PARTS 841
Bilmer Mfg. Co. 841
E. R. Howard 842
The James P. McGreece Company 842
Standard Rolling Mills 843

PERCUSSIONS 843
J. C. Deagan, Inc. 843
Walter H. Durfee & Co. 865
Excelsior Drum Works 865
The Kohler-Liebich Co. 866
Leedy Mfg. Co., Inc. 882
Ludwig & Ludwig 883
R. H. Mayland & Son 887
Morris Electric Action Company 888

PIPEWORK 888
George W. Badger Co. 888
James H. Bolton 890
Frederick S. Brockbank 890
Dennison Organ Pipe Company 891
Erie Reed Pipe Co. 896
Firma Ernst Doelling 896
Gutfleisch & Schopp 898
Edwin B. Hedges 901
Hirst Organ Specialty Company 902
Illinois Organ Supply Co. 902
Hoyt Metal Co. 903
F. W. Krebs 903
Kaylor & Clark 904
Mansfield Organ Pipe Works 904
Jerome B. Meyer & Sons, Inc. 905
Mid-West Organ Supply Company 910
Oliver Organ Co. 910
Titan Tool Company 911
Frederick I. White 911

PLAYERS & ROLLS 912
Automatic Musical Instrument Company 912
Clark Orchestra Roll Company 914
L. B. Doman Corporation 915
The Moore and Fisher Manufacturing Company 916
Roesler-Hunholz, Inc. 916

STOP KEYS & ENGRAVING 922
Denison Brothers 922
Thomson Engraving Company 923

ADDENDA TO VOLUME I 924
AEOLIAN 924
BARTON 926
GSCHOFF 928
LENOIR 928

OPUS LIST CORRECTIONS & ADDITIONS TO VOLUME I 929
ERRATA FROM VOLUME I 934
FOOTNOTES 934
ILLUSTRATION ACKNOWLEDGMENTS 940
INDEX 942

ACKNOWLEDGMENTS

The author is grateful to the following individuals who responded to pleas for help. Some shared reminiscences; others loaned photographs and other reference materials; all were gracious and willing to contribute:

Elizabeth Abbs, Paul Abernethey, John Apple, Robert Arndt, Kenneth Aultz, Lowell Ayars.

Robert Balfour, Nelson Barden, David Barnett, S. H. Barrington, William Bartlow, Walter Beaupre, Fred Beeks, William Benzeno, Jack Bethards, William Biebel, Lawrence Birdsong, Jr., Clealan Blakely, Walter Blanchard III, Ron Bogda, Terry Borne, Lance Bowling, Harold Bradley, Alfred Branam, Clarence Braun, Jim Breneman, Lawrence Broadmoore, Dorothy Bromage, George Brown, William P. Brown, David Broskowski, Ray Brubacher, Bill Bunch, Robert Bunn, Jr., Floyd Bunt, Hugh Burdick, James Burke, Arthur Dean Burnett, Jerome Butera.

Rodney Cavanaugh, John Chappell, Terry Charles, Paul Chavanne, John Clancy, Robert Clark, Ray Colby, Robert Coleberd, Jr., Peter H. Comstock, David M. Conway, Jim Crawford, Jerry Critser, Ken Crome, E. W. Cunningham.

Fred Dahlinger, Jr., Bruce Davis, Daniel Dawson, Edith DeForest, Michael Detroy, David Dickson, Robert Dilworth, James C. Donald, E. E. Donaldson, Ron Downer, Brant Duddy, Dorothy Dupont.

Irv Eilers, Harvey Elsaesser, Roy Emison.

John Fett, Alan Fisher, Charles Fleck, Robert Foley, David Fortner, David Fox, Rubin Frels, Walter Froelich, John Fuhrmann, David Fuller, David Fultz.

Walter Gelinas, Randy George, R. E. Giesbrecht, Earl Gilbert, Gene Gladson, Bill Glasson, Fred Gollnick, Mike Grandchamp, M. Lee Green, Allen Greene, Bill Greenwood, Richard Groman.

William Hale, Geoffrey Hansen, Richard Harger, William Hatzenbuhler, Tom Hazleton, Harvey Heck, Dennis Hedberg, Elizabeth Heffer, Charles Hendrickson, Barry Henry, Fred Hermes, Douglas Hickling, Esther Higgins, John Hill, Guenther Hille, Robert Hillgreen, Jr., Robert W. Hobbs, George Hockmeyer, Hank Hoevenaar, Clay Holbrook, Henry Hunsicker.

W. Tiny James, George R. Johnson, Lance Johnson, Roland Johnson, Robert C. Jones, Jacques Jonneret, Lawrence Junchen.

John Kadlec, Stan Kann, Steve Kauffman, Charles Kegg, D. Stuart Kennedy, Larry Kerecman, Gordon Kibbee, Richard Kichline, Michael Kinerk, Weldon King, Phil Klann, Terry Kleven, Lloyd Klos, Syl Kohler, Don Kohles, Jim Koller, Dave Krall, Joel Kremer.

Eugene Laplante, Laurence Leonard, Robert Letherer, James Lewis, Sanford Libman, Alan Lightcap, Hugh Lineback, Jack Little, Robert Longfield, Warren Lubich, George Lufkin, Edgar Lustig.

Harold Maerten, Bob Maes, Joe Marsh, Vic Marsilio, Bob Martin, Harvell Mason, Kay McAbee, Douglas McGee, Dean McNichols, Anthony Meloni, Allen Miller, Franklin Mitchell, Ron Mitchell, Edward Mullins, Roger Mumbrue, Don Murphy.

Fred Nagel, Max Nagel, Chris Nagorka, Tim Needler, Russ Nelson, Albert Neutel, John Newall, Buddy Nolan.

Robert Oberlander, Mike Ohman, David Olson, Allan Ontko, Ed Openshaw, Barbara Owen, Tom Owen, Fred Oyster.

Bob Pasalich, Harold Pearrell, Lauren Peckham, John Perschbacher, Stanton Peters, William Pilgermayer, Steve Plaggemeyer.

Paul Quarino.

Don Rand, Maxine Rash, Art Reblitz, Eric Reeve, Gary Rickert, Robert Rickett, E. A. Rider, Robert Ridgeway, George Rice, Scott Rieger, Greg Rister, Albert Robinson, George Robinson, Mel Robinson, Manuel Rosales, Steve Ross, Bill Rosser.

Jed Satchwell, John Schantz, John Schellkopf, Curt Schmitt, Robert F. Schmitt, Richard Schneider, Victor Searle, John Shanahan, Russ Shaner, Garrett Shanklin, George Shaw, Gregory Simanski, Helena Simonton, William Singleton, Richard Sklenar, Leonard Smith, Jim Spohn, John Spohn, Ewell Stanford, Jr., Dick Starr, John Steele, Susan Steer, Charles Stein, Dorothy Steiner, Howard Stocker, Franklin Stolzenburg, Martin Stoner, Arthur Stopes, Don Story.

William Taber, Irv Toner, Jack Townsend.

Dennis Unks, Hollis Upson.

Frank Vanaman, William Van Pelt, Robert Vaughan, Richard Villemin.

John R. Wagner, Randall Wagner, Jack Walden, Paul Wasserman, Ronald Wehmeier, Jeff Weiler, Tim Wheat, Robert Whiting, David Whitmore, Harvey M. Whitney, Martin Wiegand, Albert Wiggins, Jr., Tom Williams, Paul Williamson, Alva Wilson, Bill Wilson, David Winges, Edward Wood, Herb Wottle, George Wright.

Rodney Yarbrough.

The author is especially grateful to the following individuals who made major contributions in the manner indicated: Earl Beilharz shared information about the Page Organ Company. Homer Blanchard and Stephen Pinel opened the Organ Historical Society archive to the author. Dave Bowers shared his collection of Wurlitzer documents. Alfred Buttler and Michael Miller spent hours making corrections and additions to the opus lists of the New York City area. Brother Andrew Corsini and Joseph Duci Bella made available the Theatre Historical Society archive of photographs. Arthur Cox, Jr., gave the author part of Ben Hall's collection of organ memorabilia. Tom DeLay shared his extensive knowledge of California theatre history and loaned several rare catalogs and documents. Malin Dollinger, Alfred Ehrhardt, Grace McGinnis and Ken Rosen proofread the book. Chris Feiereisen and Rosalie Luedtke provided copies of the B. F. Blower Company records. Robert Gilbert, editor of *Theatre Organ,* gave permission to use many photographs from that publication. Irvin R. Glazer provided much information about theatres and organs in the Philadelphia area. The late Henry Gottfried gave the author complete access to the remaining records of the Gottfried firm. W. S. "Stu" Green, editor and publisher of *The Posthorn,* provided a complete set of that publication. Allen Harrah and Steve Adams allowed the author complete access to records of the E. M. Skinner and Aeolian-Skinner companies. Jerry Hickey and Anne Millbrooke provided information about the Otis Elevator Company. Walter Holtkamp, Jr., provided photocopies of every document in the Holtkamp files pertaining to theatre organs, as well as a number of photographs. Bill Lamb made his archive of photographs available for examination and provided copies of over one hundred of them. Robert Lent made available the files of the United States Pipe Organ Company. David McCain gave the author a nearly complete set of *The Diapason* and gave permission to use many photographs from that magazine. Mr. and Mrs. Gordon Meyer made available the archive of Jerome B. Meyer & Sons and loaned a number of rare catalogs and documents for reproduction. Tony Moss provided photographs and much information about British Wurlitzers. Geoffrey Paterson shared his extensive files on the Radio City Music Hall. Harvey Roehl granted permission to reproduce photographs from several Vestal Press publications. Jay Rosenthal edited the manuscript. Bob Schopp made available the Gutfleisch & Schopp factory records and also loaned a number of rare documents and photographs. Henry Tellers allowed the author complete access to records of the Tellers and Felgemaker companies. Donald Traser, publisher of *The Tracker,* granted permission to use a number of photographs from that publication. Martin Wick and John Sperling allowed the author to examine the Wicks factory records and also supplied a number of rare photographs.

The contributions of nine people deserve special recognition. Without their help these volumes would be considerably less complete. The author wishes to convey his extreme gratitude to the following very special people:

★ Steve Adams assisted in more ways than can be enumerated or remembered. His help can only be described as out of this world.

★ Judd Walton loaned his collection of Wurlitzer factory records. Had it not been for his scholarship, foresight and perseverance, these records would not exist today, because most of them were destroyed after Farny Wurlitzer's death in 1972.

★ George Buck made the entire Wurlitzer archive available and entrusted the author with the loan of many one-of-a-kind photographs.

★ The late Jim Suttie, whose personal files document the location of thousands of pipe organs, was of inestimable assistance in the preparation of the opus lists.

★ David Hunt and Lester C. Smith of the Spencer Turbine Company allowed the author complete access to that company's files of over 36,000 Spencer Orgoblos. Without their cooperation many of the opus lists would be only fragmentary.

★ Peter Moller Daniels, former president of M. P. Moller, Inc., opened the enormous archive of the Moller and Kinetic companies for the author's inspection and entrusted the author with the loan of many rare documents and photographs.

★ Tom B'hend, editor of *The Console,* owns what is undoubtedly the world's largest collection of theatre organ memorabilia. He graciously made his entire archive available to the author.

★ Preston J. Kaufmann is responsible for the excellent layout and graphic design of these volumes. He constantly monitored every step of the publishing process to ensure books of the highest possible quality. When the author would say "Oh, that's good enough," Preston would counter, "No, it's not! We're going to do it *right.*"

L. D. MORRIS & CO.

Leonard D. Morris (1863-1945) began his career in the organ business with Steere & Turner in Springfield, Massachusetts, later moving to Chicago where he was superintendent of the Kimball company. Eventually he went into business for himself, specializing in tuning and maintenance services. Initially he did business under the name L. D. Morris & Co.; in 1916 he incorporated as the L. D. Morris Company.[1]

In 1909 Morris purchased a four-horsepower Spencer Orgoblo, #1612, which was shipped to a Strand Theatre in either Oak Park or Chicago (the Spencer records are unclear as to which). Considering the modest wind pressures in use at that time, four horsepower would have powered a fairly large organ for a theatre instrument. Inasmuch as Morris specialized in areas other than new instruments, the organ in the aforementioned Strand Theatre was undoubtedly of another make, although it may have carried a Morris nameplate.

In 1926 Morris retired and sold the business to William Anderson, a man who from the age of sixteen had worked for him.[2]

L. D. MORRIS & CO.

Electric and Pneumatic ORGANS

TUNING, REPAIRING AND REBUILDING

Electric Fan Blowers

64 E. Van Buren St., CHICAGO

This ad appeared in The Diapason *throughout the early teens.*

J. H. & C. S. Odell & Co.

Pipe Organs

18 Belmont Avenue

Yonkers, N. Y.

CALEB H. ODELL
WILLIAM H. ODELL

TELEPHONE

John Henry Odell (1830-1899) and his brother Caleb Sherwood Odell (1827-1892) opened an organ shop in New York in 1859, having learned the organ building trade working in the shop of Davis & Ferris, which became Ferris & Stuart. Richard Montgomery Ferris and Levi and William Stuart were among the best organ builders of the mid-nineteenth century and they influenced the Odell brothers to build instruments of excellent quality.[1]

In 1866 the Odells received a patent for an innovation which has become an integral part of most organs built to this day. These "pneumatic composition knobs" were the forerunner of today's combination pistons. In 1872 the Odells were granted the first patent in America for a tubular pneumatic action.[2] A history of organ building cannot overemphasize the importance of these two inventions.

As the years went by, new generations of the Odell family continued the business. In 1927 the firm moved to Mount Vernon, New York and in 1940 to Yonkers, New York. The company's later years were devoted primarily to tuning and maintenance. In the 1980s, following the retirement of the last of the Odell family, Anthony Meloni & Co., Inc., of New York City acquired the company records and certain assets. Mr. Meloni had been an employee of the firm in its later days.[3]

One Odell organ was installed in a theatre: Opus 510 was built in 1917 for the Steinway (later Astoria) Theatre in Astoria, New York. This 2/15 instrument was voiced on 5" pressure and used Kinetic blower #F75 having a two-horsepower motor and rated at 6" wind.

2/15 ODELL ORGAN, OPUS 510
Steinway Theatre, Astoria, New York

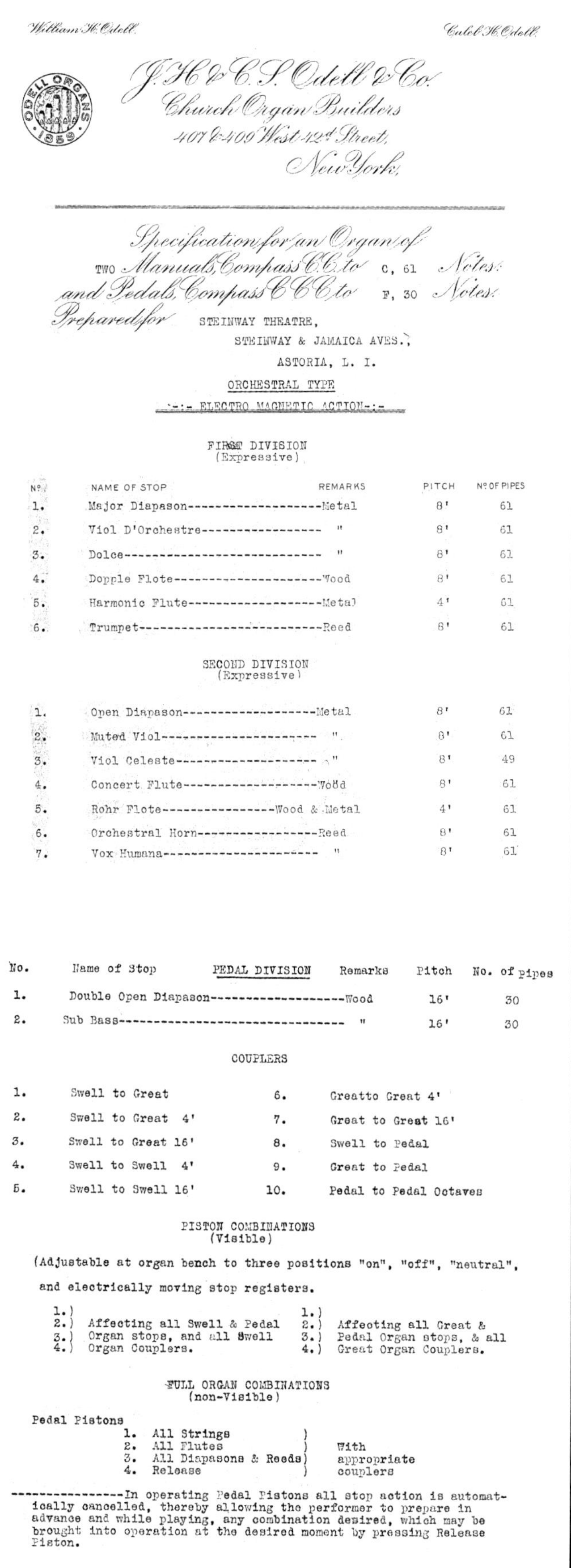

William H. Odell   Caleb H. Odell

ODELL ORGANS 1859

J. H. & C. S. Odell & Co.
Church Organ Builders
407 & 409 West 42nd Street,
New York.

Specification for an Organ of
TWO Manuals, Compass CC to C, 61 Notes
and Pedals, Compass CCC to F, 30 Notes
Prepared for STEINWAY THEATRE,
STEINWAY & JAMAICA AVES.,
ASTORIA, L. I.

ORCHESTRAL TYPE

-:- ELECTRO MAGNETIC ACTION -:-

FIRST DIVISION
(Expressive)

No.	NAME OF STOP	REMARKS	PITCH	No. OF PIPES
1.	Major Diapason	Metal	8'	61
2.	Viol D'Orchestre	"	8'	61
3.	Dolce	"	8'	61
4.	Dopple Flote	Wood	8'	61
5.	Harmonic Flute	Metal	4'	61
6.	Trumpet	Reed	8'	61

SECOND DIVISION
(Expressive)

No.	NAME OF STOP	REMARKS	PITCH	No. OF PIPES
1.	Open Diapason	Metal	8'	61
2.	Muted Viol	"	8'	61
3.	Viol Celeste	"	8'	49
4.	Concert Flute	Wood	8'	61
5.	Rohr Flote	Wood & Metal	4'	61
6.	Orchestral Horn	Reed	8'	61
7.	Vox Humana	"	8'	61

PEDAL DIVISION

No.	Name of Stop	Remarks	Pitch	No. of pipes
1.	Double Open Diapason	Wood	16'	30
2.	Sub Bass	"	16'	30

COUPLERS

1. Swell to Great
2. Swell to Great 4'
3. Swell to Great 16'
4. Swell to Swell 4'
5. Swell to Swell 16'
6. Greatto Great 4'
7. Great to Great 16'
8. Swell to Pedal
9. Great to Pedal
10. Pedal to Pedal Octaves

PISTON COMBINATIONS
(Visible)

(Adjustable at organ bench to three positions "on", "off", "neutral", and electrically moving stop registers.

1.) 2.) 3.) 4.) Affecting all Swell & Pedal Organ stops, and all Swell Organ Couplers.

1.) 2.) 3.) 4.) Affecting all Great & Pedal Organ stops, & all Great Organ Couplers.

FULL ORGAN COMBINATIONS
(non-Visible)

Pedal Pistons
1. All Strings
2. All Flutes
3. All Diapasons & Reeds
4. Release
} With appropriate couplers

----------------In operating Pedal Pistons all stop action is automatically cancelled, thereby allowing the performer to prepare in advance and while playing, any combination desired, which may be brought into operation at the desired moment by pressing Release Piston.

PEDAL MOVEMENTS

1. Crescendo Pedal--(This Pedal to control entire organ, bringing on and off all speaking stops in the order of their power; slowly and gradually, or with great rapidity, at will of organist).
2. Swell Electric Pedal on (Swell Organ) First Div.
3. Swell Electric Pedal on (Great Organ) Second Div.
4. Great to Pedal Reversible

ACCESSORIES

1. (Swell) Tremulant First Div.
2. (Great) Tremulant Second Div.
3. Wind Indicator
4. Crescendo Indicator
5. Electric Action Generator
6.) 7.) 8.) Indicator lights for Pedal Pistons
9. Electric Motor & Fan Blower

DETAILS OF CONSTRUCTION

Design and Materials

1. Suitable chambers to accomodate the instrument are to be provided by the Owners, (and situated back of Picture Screen at the rear of stage.) No Case-work or Display Pipes are to be supplied.

2. The Reservoirs to be of ample size, double leathered throughout, and of sufficient capacity to supply the fullest legitimate demands, and to be equipped with a Rotary Fan Blower and Electric Motor, set up with all automatic work, except the wind trunking, electric wiring, and starting device.

3. The Wind Chests to be those known as the "Odell Improved Chests" with individual valves for each pipe and universal wind supply, and so designed that every pipe receives a full supply of wind, preventing the customary falling off in tone of the smaller pipes when full organ is drawn.

4. The Action to be constructed on the "Odell Electro-Magnetic System" which entirely eliminates all pneumatic and mechanical complications occurring in the electro pneumatic type now in general use. This Action is of the utmost simplicity and reliability, and responsive to a highly perfected degree, and is to be equipped with an electric generator of special design for furnishing the current necessary for its complete operation.

5. The Expressive Divisions to be enclosed to obtain the maximum tonal results, and to be equipped with equilibrium expression shades operated by pneumatic motors, electrically controlled from balanced swell pedal placed in convenient positions over the pedal keys.

6. The Console to be placed in a (central) position (at the front of the stage,) and to be designed in accordance with valuable suggestions obtained from the foremost organists of the world, the arrangement being such as to assure the utmost flexibility and the greatest facility of control for the organist. All interior wood-work of the key-desk, between and including the key frames, shall be constructed of Mahogany. The Manual Keys shall be of the overhanging type, and made of the best Ivory and Ebony. The Pedal Keys to be of the latest and most approved pattern, concave and radiating, and to be made of light and dark hard wood. All speaking stops and couplers to be operated by tilting tablets placed over manual keys. All Condits necessary for containing electric cables between Console and Organ, and Motor, shall be provided by the Owners of the Building. All wind trunking between Fan Blower and Organ is to be provided by the aforesaid Owners.

PIPE-WORK AND VOICING

7. The Wood Pipes to be made of the best seasoned material, glue-sized inside and varnished with shellac outside, except the large pedal pipes which shall be painted with oil paint.

8. The Metal Pipes to be made of pure tin and lead, varied according to the tonal requirements. All Metal Pipes shall be in accordance with this article except the large flue pipes which shall be made of the best zinc.

9. The Scale of each and every pipe in the foregoing specification to be in accordance with the best standards, and such as are only adopted in strictly high grade instruments.

10. The Voicing of the Organ, upon which its value as a musical instrument chiefly depends, to combine the best points of the American and European Schools.

11. The various registers, Metal and Wood, shall be of uniform calibre throughout, and the contrasted varieties of tone shall harmoniously blend into a satisfactory whole without either harshness or undue ponderosity.

ARTICLES OF AGREEMENT

made this 19th day of January, in the year One Thousand Nine Hundred and Seventeen (1917).

BETWEEN J. H. & C. S. ODELL & CO., Organ Builders, of New York, N. Y., Parties of the First Part, and THE STEINWAY AVENUE THEATRE CO., a Corporation organized and existing under and by virtue of the laws of the State of New York, Party of the Second Part.

WITNESSETH, That the Parties of the First Part, in consideration of the Agreement hereinafter contained on the part of the said Party of the Second Part, agree to build for the said Party of the Second Part an instrument in conformity with the annexed scheme and specification, of the best material and in the most thorough manner, and deliver the same set up complete and ready for use in THE STEINWAY THEATRE, STEINWAY & JAMAICA AVES., ASTORIA, L. I., NEW YORK, warranted perfect in every respect, on or before the 29th day of May, 1917. The Party of the Second Part doth agree that upon due performance of this Agreement on the part of the Parties of the First Part, the said Party of the Second Part shall and will pay to the Parties of the First Part, the sum of FOUR THOUSAND DOLLARS ($4000.00) in cash as follows:-
ONE THOUSAND DOLLARS ($1000.00) in cash at the time this Agreement is signed, TWO THOUSAND DOLLARS ($2000.00) in cash when the instrument is set up complete in factory of Parties of the First Part, and the balance ONE THOUSAND DOLLARS ($1000.00) in cash when the instrument is set up complete and ready for use in the aforesaid Theatre.

All risk of damage to the organ or parts thereof by fire or water, shall be incurred by the Party of the Second Part, after the organ or parts thereof have been deposited in the above named Theatre.

IN WITNESS WHEREOF, The Parties of the First and Second Parts have interchangeably executed the same, the day and year above written.

Parties of the First Part J. H. & C. S. Odell & Co. F.S.

Party of the Second Part Chas. [illegible] Secretary

The Sixth Odell Organ

to be built within a period of forty-five years for Trinity Corporation, New York City, is now in process and will be installed about the first of the new year in St. Agnes' Chapel, (Dr. G. Edward Stubbs, organist).

This is a large three-manual with Odell Electro-Magnetic Action, our new system which does away with all the pneumatic and mechanical complexity of the Electro-pneumatic type.

A cordial invitation is extended to organists or others interested to visit our plant while in the Metropolis to see this and other organs being erected.

Correspondence will also receive every attention.

J. H. & C. S. Odell & Co.
407-409 West 42nd Street
New York City

Established 1859

This ad in the November 1914 Diapason *touted the latest Odell invention: a direct electric chest action.*

General Office and Factory
715 North Kedzie Avenue
Phones Kedzie 2357-58

The Operators Piano Company, Inc.

L. M. Severson, President

Manufacturers of

AUTOMATIC MUSICAL INSTRUMENTS

Electric Pianos, Orchestrions, Theatre and Mortuary Organs

CHICAGO

Pipe Organs

The Operators Piano Company was in business in Chicago from around 1904 to 1934 producing Coinola coin-operated pianos and Reproduco (pronounced reproduce-oh) organs. The piano products of the firm were also sold on contract to other dealers who marketed them under such trademarks as Empress Electric, Welte Multitone, Victor and Rockola.[1] With very few exceptions, most of the instruments produced by this firm were roll operated.

Before 1920 the rolls used to operate these instruments were purchased from the QRS Company in Chicago. In 1920 Roy Rodocker was hired by Operators to form a roll-making subsidiary in their building at 22 S. Peoria Street in Chicago. Rodocker, who had been head of the QRS coin-operated roll division, was put in charge of the newly-christened Columbia Music Roll Company. In 1924 Operators and their Columbia roll division moved to a new building at 721 N. Kedzie Avenue and shortly thereafter decided to branch out into the phonograph record business. Columbia was already a well-established trademark of another record company so Operators came up with a new name: the Capitol Roll & Record Company. The records never sold well and are quite rare today. In a few years the records were dropped and the name changed to the Capitol Music Roll Co.

Operators also made 88-note rolls for the home player piano market. Their largest customer was Sears Roebuck who marketed the rolls under the Supertone and Challenge trademarks. Other 88-note rolls were sold under the American, Broadway, Capitol, Cecile, Columbia, Orpheum, Red Seal, Starck, Sterling and Synchronized labels.

Operators' best known products were their Coinolas and Reproducos. A few of the Reproducos found their way into funeral homes and churches but most were sold to smaller theatres. Most Reproducos, having pianos as their tonal foundation, fall into the photoplayer classification and hence are outside the scope of this book. One early model, however, the Reproduco Orchestral Pipe Organ, had no piano and was, indeed, an actual (albeit tiny!) pipe organ with one manual and tubular pneumatic action. It must have been produced in extremely limited quantities inasmuch as no examples are known to survive today.

One other Reproduco model qualifies as a real pipe organ: the Unified Theatre Organ. This 2/4 tubular pneumatic instrument was produced, also in limited quantities, in the mid- and late 1920s. The metal pipes in these instruments were ordered from Jerome B. Meyer in Milwaukee, Wisconsin. The author searched the files of this firm to determine the number of ranks purchased by Operators. Based on this research, the author's estimate of the production of Reproduco Unified Theatre Organs is as follows: 1925, 1; 1926, 3; 1927, 1; and 1928, 6. It is possible, of course, that Operators also purchased pipes from other suppliers, in which case these estimates may be too low. The author can confirm the existence of only three or four of these instruments as of 1986, and only one can be traced to its original home: the Door Theatre in Sturgeon Bay, Wisconsin.

The Operators factory still stands as of 1985.

The New Unified Reproduco Pipe Organ is the last word in the art of organ building---It embodies all the best qualities of a Unified Organ but in addition there-to has many other qualities. Primarly constructed as a pit organ for theatres having seating capacity of 400 to 1600 seats it has all the best qualities that have been embodied in the largest organs made in late years.

The simplicity of construction (tubular pneumatic) that has made the regular Reproduco the most popular organ ever built is maintained in this Unified Organ---The volume is large but not rasping—the unification is the most modern and gives this organ the volume—the flexibility the changes of tone that are so much sought after by modern organ builders and organists.

The two manual semi horse-shoe type console, and the pedal organ give the organist all that he would desire—the two chambers give him the opportunity of fine shadings that give perfect music.

See page four (4) for specifications.

Most wonderfull of all is the Automatic Playing of this instrument—The mechanism is so constructed that it exactly reproduces what the Recording Artist played—It puts on and takes off all stops just as the recording artist did—It reproduces all swell effects, all shadings, all ritards, all tempos in fact an actual and exact reproduction as played by the recording artist. This statement can not be fully appreciated until you have heard this wonderful Reproduco Unified Pipe Organ.

-: Specifications. :-

Instrument controlled by two manuals C C to C 4 and pedal organ C C C to F--- or by the Unified new 135 note automatic hand-played roll and rewind mechanism.

PEDAL ORGAN. C C C to F.

Bourdon to Pedal.	16 Ft.	wood	12 Notes
Stop Flute to "	8 "	"	12 "
" " " "	2 "	Metal and "	30 "
" " " "	4 "	"	30 "
" " " "	8 "	"	18 "
" " " "	16 "	"	6 "
Viola " " "	2 "	Metal	30 "
" " " "	4 "	"	30 "
" " " "	8 "	"	18 "

GREAT (Swell) ORGAN. C C to C 4

Flute Stop	16 Ft.	wood	37 Notes
" "	8 "	"	49 "
" "	4 "	"	61 "
" "	2 "	Metal and "	61 "
Viola	8 "	Metal	49 "
"	4 "	"	61 "
"	2 "	"	61 "

SOLO (Swell) ORGAN. C C to C 4.

Quintadena	4 Ft.	Metal	37 notes
Tibia Clausa	4 "	wood	61 "
" " Tenor C.	16 "	"	37 "
Great to Solo Bourdon	16 "	"	12 "
" " " Stop Flute	8 "	"	12 "
" " " " "	2 "	Metal and "	61 "
" " " " "	4 "	"	61 "
Great to Solo Stop Flute	8 "	wood	49 "
" " " " "	16 "	"	37 "
" " " Viola	8 "	Metal	49 "
" " " "	4 "	"	61 "
" " " "	2 "	"	61 "

SPECIES OF PIPES.

Quintadena	Metal	37 Pipes
Tibia Clausa	Wood	61 "
Viola	Metal	73 "
Bourdon, Stop Diapason and Flute.	Wood and Metal	97 "

COUPLER STOPS.

Flute	16 Ft. and 4 Ft.
"	8 " " 4 "
"	8 " " 2 "
"	4 " " 2 "
Viola	8 Ft. and 4 Ft.
"	8 " " 2 "
"	4 " " 2 "
Tibia Clausa	16 " " 4 "

ACCESSORY STOPS.

To Play.
To Rewind.
Tremolo.
Manual control stops to cut off automatic device.
Distinct and separate swell for the solo as well as the Great Organ.

ACCESSORIES.

Blower and 3-4 H. P. Motor.
Tremolo
Vacuum Pump-and Accessories.

Reproduco Pipe Organ Co.

715 North Kedzie Ave. Chicago, Illinois

By the time the Reproduco Unified Theatre Organ was introduced in this c. 1925 brochure,

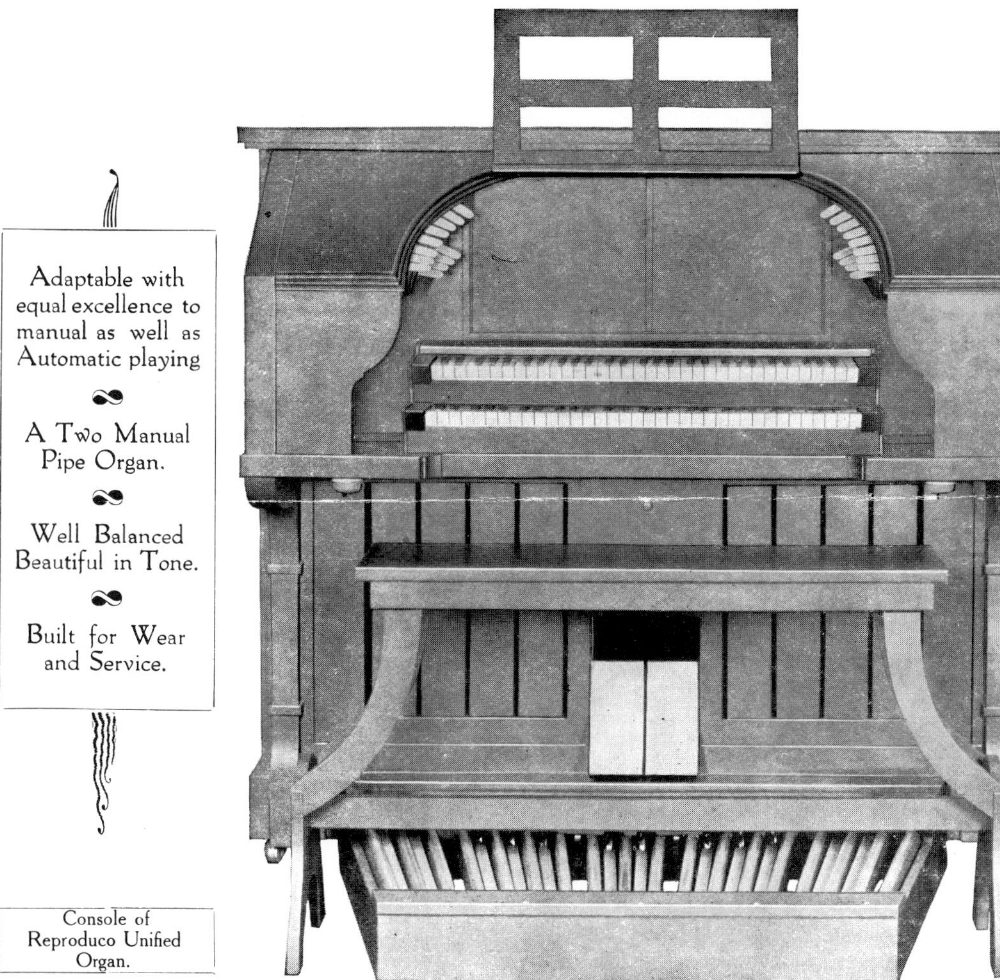

Adaptable with equal excellence to manual as well as Automatic playing
A Two Manual Pipe Organ.
Well Balanced Beautiful in Tone.
Built for Wear and Service.
Two chamber units one, the solo organ the other the great or swell organ, each governed by their respective shutters working independently of each other.

Console of Reproduco Unified Organ.

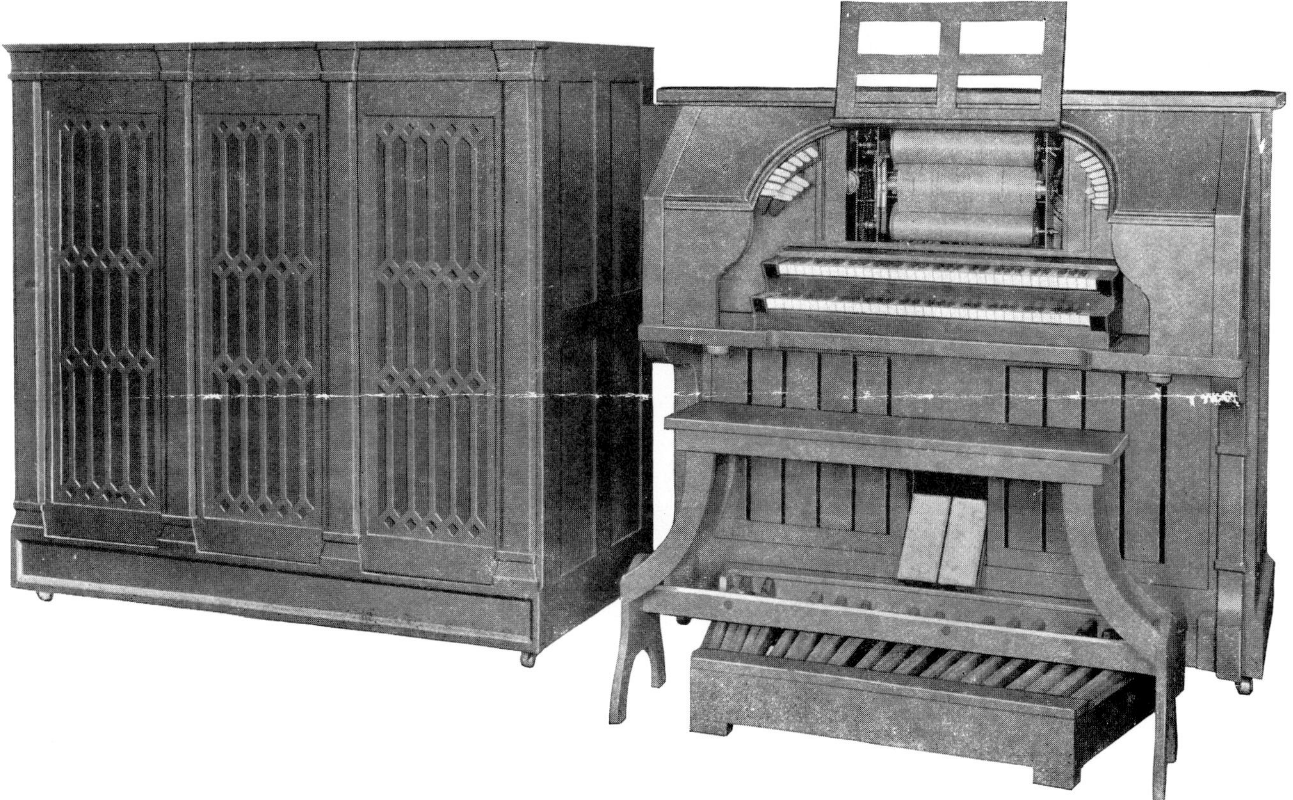

demand for self-playing theatre instruments was waning and few were sold.

Reproduco Pipe Organ and Show Pipes with or without Player Mechanism.
Height, 8 feet; Width, 5 feet 4 inches; Depth, 3 feet 4 inches

On this and the following two pages are reproduced pages from an extremely rare and heretofore unknown Reproduco catalog from the early 1920s. The instrument shown above was the most popular Reproduco model although this particular example is unusual in that it has no roll player. The cabinet of display pipes was not a popular option. Most Reproducos were located in the fronts of smaller theatres where any excessive height would interfere with the movie screen.

THE REPRODUCO ORCHESTRAL PIPE ORGAN

This instrument is exclusively a Pipe Organ. It may be equipped with or without a self-playing device. It is portable in that it can be set up or taken down and removed quickly without injury to the premises and at a small expense.

SPECIFICATIONS

1—Super Oct.	16 ft. Tone	4—Viol D'Orch 8 ft. Tone
2—Super Oct.	4 "	5—Flute Harmonic 4 "
3—Stop Diapason 8 "		6—Vox Humana 8 "

MECHANICAL ACCESSORIES

7—Tremolo
8—Organ Manual—61 notes.
9—Automatic tracker bar and rewind mechanism.
10—Electric motor and Rotary Blower for Organ.
11—Electric motor and pump for wind and rewind self-playing mechanism.
12—Organ Swell and Automatic Organ Action.

OPERATORS PIANO COMPANY, CHICAGO

REPRODUCO PLAYER PIPE ORGAN

The REPRODUCO PLAYER PIPE ORGAN is constructed with an Organ manual immediately above the Piano manual, giving the musician the advantage of playing either the Piano or Pipe Organ without changing his position. The Piano is constructed of the best material and workmanship. The blower operated by an electric motor is installed in a separate "sound-proof" cabinet. The Violin, Flute and Stop Diapason Pipes together with other accessories such as Swell, Tremolo, Mandolin and coupler devices, etc., give the musician ample range to express in music every feeling from the heavy March to the plaintive song of the Flute or sympathetic Violin.

Not alone can the skillful musician operate it, but automatically from the hand-played rolls it will *Reproduce* the music of the great Organ Artists. Hence the name *Reproduco Player Pipe Organ.*

All this may be done electrically; there is no pumping or pushing; no squeaking of bellows, no unusual sounds, but the reproductions of the "masters" who have played the "original rolls."

The REPRODUCO PLAYER PIPE ORGAN is especially adaptable to the Theatre, Church and Lodge Hall.

REPRODUCO PLAYER PIPE ORGAN

SPECIFICATIONS:

1—8 foot Tone Diapason (12).
2—8 foot Tone Flute (49).
3—8 foot Tone Violin (metal, 37).
4—Piano Manual 7⅓ Oct.
5—Organ Manual 61 notes.
Mechanical Registers.
6—Tremolo.
7—Diapason Stop.
8—Flute Stop.
9—Violin Stop.
10—Mandolin Stop Accessories.
11—Coupler.
12—Electric Blower and Motor for Organ.
13—Electric Motor for Vacuum.
14—Complete Coinola rewind mechanism.
15—Mandolin.
16—Blower Chest and Cabinet.

The Unified Reproduco contains a multitude of valve boxes and hundreds of feet of rubber tubing, all of which is necessary for the unification inasmuch as the action is entirely tubular pneumatic. If this were an electric action instrument, all this tubing would be replaced by simple electric wires.

REPRODUCO PIPE ORGAN

Satisfied Reproduco Owners

Partial List of Theatres

Palace, Waycross, Ga.
Strand, Jesup, Ga.
Amusus Theatre, Lincolnton, Ga.
Rivoli Theatre, Rome, Ga.
Colonial, Vidalia, Ga.
Rivoli, LaGrange, Ga.
A. H. McCarty, Barnesville, Ga.
W. P. Riggins, Jesup, Ga.
Lindale Auditorium, Lindale, Ga.
J. E. Simpson, Milien, Ga.
Rex, Hopkinsville, Ky.
Liberty Franklin, Ky.
Dreamland, Guthrie, Ky.
Palace, Bowling Green, Ky
Orpheum, Fulton, Ky.
Bleach, Owensboro, Ky
Dreamland, Bowling Green, Ky.
Houston, Houston, Miss.
City, Philadelphia, Miss.
New Theatre, Emory, Miss.
Liberty, Malden, Mo.
Roth's West Asheville, N. C.
Eagle Theatre, Asheville, N. C.
Royal, Wilmington, N. C.
Ideal, Gastonia, N. C.
Capital, Asheboro, N. C.
Broadway, Reidsville, N. C.
Princess, Henderson, N. C.
Lyric, Rocky Mount, N. C.
Princess, Shelby, N. C.
American, High Point, N. C.
Victory, Wilmington, N. C.
Cameo, Rockmont, N. C.
Broadway, Mt. Airy, N. C.
Taylor, Edenton, N. C
Richard, Ahoskie, N. C.
Iris Belmont, N. C.
Osborn, Hillsboro, N. C.
Princess, Fayetteville, N. C.
C. I. Gresham, Mooresville, N. C.
Sunset Amus Co., Charlotte, N. C.
Charlotte, Charlotte, N. C.
Broadway, Columbia, S. C.
Palace, Charleston, S. C.
Lincoln, Charleston, S. C
Dreamland, Chester, S. C.
Albert Sottile, Charleston, S. C.
S. G. Rogers, Marion, S. C.
Strand, Nashville, Tenn.
Rialto, Nashville, Tenn.
Rialto, Nashville, Tenn.
Tony Sudekum, Nashville, Tenn.
Hillsboro, Nashville, Tenn.
Cameo, Memphis, Tenn.
American, Memphis, Tenn.
Princess, Memphis, Tenn.

Concord Theatre, Concord, Tenn.
Booth's, Sweetwater, Tenn.
Booth's, Greenville, Tenn.
Lillian, Martin, Tenn.
Sudekum's, Harriman, Tenn.
Tom Young's, Dyersburg, Tenn.
Strand, Tallahoma, Tenn.
Howard, Lebanon, Tenn.
Rivola, Winchester, Tenn.
Princess, Columbia, Tenn.
Lillian, Clarksville, Tenn.
Majestic, Clarksville, Tenn.
Dixie, Paris, Tenn.
Dorodele, Copperhill, Tenn.
Dixie, Russellville, Tenn.
Strand, Morristown, Tenn.
Franklin, Franklin, Tenn
Gem, Jackson, Tenn.
Cameo, Etowah, Tenn.
J. P. Sharp, Humboldt, Tenn.
Oldhams McMinnville, Tenn.
Princess, Murfreesboro, Tenn.
Dixie, Lewisburg, Tenn.
Princess, Morristown, Tenn
Best, Pulaski, Tenn.
Victory, Richmond, Va.
Jake Wel's, Richmond, Va.
J. D Wineland, Picher, Okla,
World-In-Motion Theatre
Kansas City, Mo.
Strand Theatre, Hays, Kans.
Mainstreet Theatre, Lexington, Mo.
Wallis Bros. & Johnson, Russell, Kans.
Nusho Theatre, Wetumka, Okla
New Grand Theatre, Pittsburg, Kans.
Royal Theatre, Hoisington, Kans.
Rainbow Theatre, Sulphur, Okla.
Consolidated Amus. Co., Ardmore, Okla.
Mrs. W. T. Brooks, Broken Arrow, Okla.
Empress Theatre, Osawatomie, Kans.
Summit St. Theatre, Kansas City, Mo.
Sam Fillson Opera Co.,
Scott City, Kans.
A. R. Powell, Guthrie, Okla.
Liggett Theatre, Madison, Kans.
Regent Theatre, Kansas City, Mo.
Empress Theatre, Paola, Kans.
Beatrice Amusement Co.,
No. Platte, Nebr.
Rivoli Theatre, St. Joseph, Mo.
Cantwell Theatre, Marceline, Mo.
Anton S'epka, Okemah, Okla.
W. A. Weaver, Hartshorne, Okla.
Hickory Theatre, St. Joseph, Mo.
Cozy Theatre, Wagoner, Okla.
Rialto Theatre, Hobart, Okla.

Loula P. & Wesley Williams,
Tulsa, Okla.
Cosmo Theatre Co., Winner, S. Dak.
Liberty Theatre, Columbus, Kans.
C. E. Allison, Rush Springs, Okla.
Jackson Theatre, Pawhuska, Okla.
Art Theatre, Tulsa, Okla.
Kemp & Hughes, Heavener, Okla.
J. A. Scott, Chandler, Okla.
State Theatre, Elk Point, S. Dak.
Liberty Theatre, Watonga, Okla.
A. J. Kremer, Stanton, Nebr.
Dunkin Theatre, Cushing, Okla.
S. B. Callahan, Broken Bow, Okla
D. V. Terry & L. N. Sewell,
Woodward, Okla.
Lancaster, Wilbern & Spears,
Duncan, Okla.
Sultana Theatre, Williams, Ariz
Alice T. Hamly, Clinton, Okla.
Centro-American Theatre,
Kansas City, Mo.
A. H. Records, Hebron, Nebr.
Lyric Theatre, Tulsa, Okla.
Majestic Theatre, Oakland, Nebr.
E. E. Sprague, Goodland, Nebr.
Mrs. M. R. Johnson, Tulsa, Okla.
Walmur Amus. Co., Bristow, Okla.
Orpheum Theatre, Joplin, Mo.
Strand Theatre, Tulsa, Okla.
C. B. Kelley, Wakeeney, Kans.
Cozy Theatre, Tulsa, Okla.
Cozy Theatre, Hollis Okla.
Strand Theatre, Muskogee, Okla.
H. G. Stettmund, Jr., Chandler, Okla.
Wichita Theatre, Wichita, Kans.
H. B. Duering, Garnett, Kans.
Cozy Theatre, Winfied, Kans.
Sequoyah Theatre, Tahlequah, Okla.
45th St. Theatre, Kansas City, Mo.
Cozy Theatre, Pratt, Kans.
Bays Theatre, Blackwell, Okla.
Gilbert Theatre, Beatrice, Nebr.
Beatrice Amus. Co., Holton, Kans.
Sun Theatre, York, Nebr.
C. W Hermes, Ellinwood, Kans.
Yale Theatre, Henryetta, Okla.
Francis Theatre Braman, Okla.
R. D. Howell Holdenville, Okla.
Fox & Maricle, Grandfield, Okla.
Gust Mestdagh, Kansas City, Mo.
Dixie Theatre, Mt Park, Okla.
Grand Theatre, Collinsville, Okla.
Empire Theatre, Altus, Okla.
L. C Largen, Creighton, Nebr.
Crystal Theatre, Scribner, Nebr.

Elite Theatre, Greenleaf, Kans.
C. G. Miller, Atkinson, Nebr.
Kemp & Hughes, DeQueen, Ark.
Oklahoma Theatre, Norman, Okla.
Walmur Amus. Co., Cushing, Okla.
Acme Theatre, Winslow, Ariz.
Geo. Marlow, Atoka, Okla.
R. Lewis Barton, Stroud, Okla.
Palace Theatre, Syracuse, Nebr.
Community Theatre, David City, Nebr.
Tackett Theatre, Coffeyville, Kans.
Strand Theatre, Lincoln, Nebr.
R. V. Mayes, Erick, Okla.
Geo. Herber, Apache, Okla.
Favorite Theatre, Schuyler, Nebr.
H. F. Kennedy, Broken Bow, Nebr.
Crystal Theatre, Wayne, Nebr.
Weeks Theatre, Dexter, Mo.
F. B. Pickrell, Pawhuska, Okla.
Rialto, Birmingham, Ala.
Norwood, Birmingham, Ala.
Famous, Birmingham, Ala.
Princess, Birmingham, Ala.
N. Birmingham, Ala.
West End Family, Birmingham, Ala.
Camco, Birmingham, Ala.
Five Points, Birmingham, Ala.
Wescon Co., Birmingham, Ala.
Princess, Birmingham, Ala.
Capitol, Birmingham, Ala.
Frolic, Birmingham, Ala.
Dixie, Birmingham, Ala.
Dixie, Birmingham, Ala
Wheeler, Montgomery, Ala.
The Leak Co., Montgomery, Ala.
Cricket, Collinsville, Ala.
Tiger Theatre, Auburn, Ala.
Jaffe's Ensley, Ala.
Belle, Gadsden, Ala.
Lee, Eufaula, Ala.
Rose, Tuskegee, Ala.
Star, Tuscaloosa, Ala.
Diamond, Tuscaloosa, Ala.
Jaffe's Bessemer, Alabama
King's, Tuscaloosa, Alabama
Palace, Molton, Alabama.
Princess, Booneville, Ala.
Wadesonia, Caleria, Ala.
Lightman's, Camden, Ala.
Palace, Piedmont, Ala.
W. D. Patrick, Florala, Ala.
Princess, Florence, Ala.
Lyric, Sheffield, Ala.
Strand, Tuscumbia, Ala.
Gary, Fairfield, Ala.
Franklin, Ensley, Ala.

A Reproduco brochure from the 1920s listed a number of the firm's customers. Only a handful of these represent Unified Theatre Organs or Orchestral Pipe Organs; most were smaller Reproduco models.

REPRODUCO PIPE ORGAN

Don't Take the Word of a Solicitor

Partial List of Theatres

Imp. Benton, Ark.
Queen, Brownwood, Texas
Crystal, Center, Texas
Olympic, Canyon, Texas
Queen, Ft Stockton, Texas
Ideal, Ft Worth, Texas
Star, Goose Creek, Texas
Wright, Gurdon, Ark.
Victory, Henderson, Texas
New, Harlingen, Texas
Gem, Kenedy, Texas
Dixie, Kerrville, Texas
New, Loraine, Texas
Gem, Mineral Wells, Texas
New, McCamey, Texas
Palace, Nacogdoches, Texas
Gem, Norphlet, Ark.
Strand, Paris, Ark.
Pharr, Pharr, Texas
Majestic, Rotan, Texas
Dixie, Rockdale, Texas
Star, Rogers, Texas
Cozy, Strawn, Texas
Sonora, Sonora, Texas
Theatre, Waldron, Ark.
Rialto, Wellington, Texas
Princess, Whitesboro, Texas
Palace, Yorktown, Texas
Queen, Crosbyton, Texas
Shuler Auditorium, Raton, N. M.
Blackstone, Detroit, Mich.
Bijou, Detroit, Mich.
Courtesy, Detroit, Mich.
Cozy, Detroit, Mich.
Dunbar, Detroit, Mich.
Dequindre, Detroit, Mich.
Embassy, Detroit, Mich.
Ferndal, Detroit, Mich.
Norwood, Detroit, Mich.
Picadally, Detroit, Mich.
Republic, Detroit, Mich.
Willis, Detroit, Mich.
Wolverine, Detroit, Mich.
Woodward No. 1, Detroit, Mich.
Woodward No. 2, Detroit, Mich.
Universal, Detroit, Mich.
Campeau, Detroit, Mich.
Eagle, Monroe, Mich.
Strand, Port Huron, Mich.
Park, Highland Park, Mich.
Auditorium, St. Croix Falls, Wis.
Star, Stanley, Wis.
Orpheum, Menominee, Wis.
Cozy, Medford, Wis.
Empire, Two Rivers, Wis.
Door, Sturgeon Bay, Wis.

Comet, Milwaukee, Wis.
Rudalt, Columbus, Wis.
Orpheum, Lancaster, Wis.
Idle Hour, Jefferson, Wis.
Majestic, Lake Mills, Wis.
Pastime, Kiel, Wis.
Cosmo, Winner, S. D.
State, Elk Point, S. D.
Cozy, Tyndall, S. D.
Cozy, Wagner, S. D.
Liberty, Sioux Falls, S. D.
Maryland, Omaha, Neb.
Victoria, Omaha, Neb.
Ideal, Des Moines, Ia.
Strand, Marinoo, Ia.
Muzu, Fonda, Ia.
Strand, Boone, Ia.
Lake View, Lake View, Ia.
Lyric, Rolf, Ia.
Empress, Cherokee, Ia.
King, Ida Grove, Ia.
New, Eidon, Ia.
Star, Sioux City, Ia.
Strand, Sioux City, Ia.
Comfort, Sharpsburg, Pa.
Monarch, Wilson, Pa.
Amherst, Amherstdale, W. Va.
Amherst, Braeholm, W. Va.
Paramount, Latrobe, Pa.
Ritz, Irwin, Pa.
Arcade, Morgantown, W. Va.
Regent, Linesville, Pa.
Blue Bird, Mill Hall, Pa.
Strand, Farrell, Pa.
Orpheum, Clarksburg, W. Va.
Seven Stars, Phillipsburg, Pa.
Lincoln, Hollidays Cove, W. Va.
Wampum, Wampum, Pa.
Nelson, Fairmont, W. Va.
Monaca, Monaca, Pa.
White Eagle, So. Bend, Ind.
Indiana, So. Bend, Ind.
Honeymoon, So. Bend, Ind.
Chas. Wolf, Winnamac, Ind.
Fairy, Napanee, Ind
John Sanders, Kentland, Ind.
H. A. Giles, Garrett, Ind
S. Karticek, Cleveland, Ohio
Michael Hudack, Cleveland, Ohio
Joe Leavitt, Cleveland, Ohio
Dreamland, Akron, Ohio.
K. E. Bradley, Cleveland, Ohio
Geo. Barlow, Powhatan Point, Ohio
Odeon, Canton, Ohio
Regent, Akron, Ohio
Bijou, Toledo, Ohio

Victory, Rule, Texas
Crown, Houston, Texas
Grand, Electra, Texas
Pastime, Warren, Ark.
Sidney M. Nutt, Hot Springs, Ark.
Adams, Decatur, Ind.
Apollo, Grand Rapids, Mich.
Minor, Dayton, Ohio
Bolton & Jones, Santa Barbara, Cal.
Capitol, California, Pa.
Chicago Home Co., Chicago, Ill.
Ideal, Hobart, Ind.
Dixie, Russellville, Ky.
Dreamland, Roodhouse, Ill.
Dreamland, Guthrie, Ky.
Eimore, Pittsburgh, Pa.
Masonic, Hinton, W. Va.
Family, Braddock, Pa.
Fox, Minneapolis, Minn.
Eagle, Monroe, Mich.
Eastwood, Dayton, Ohio
Palace, Richmond, Ind.
The Imp, Pikeville, Ky.
Kaypee, Mt. Gilead, Ohio.
Strand, Kenosha, Wis.
Laurel, London, Ky.
Dixie, Paris, Ill.
Liberty, Franklin, Ky.
Imperial, Gadsden, Ala.
Palace, Athens, Tenn.
Princess, Morristown, Tenn.
Fred L. Freemand, Live Oak, Fla.
Rivoli, LaGrange, Ga.
Liberty, Malden, Mo.
Liberty, Miami, Ariz.
C. A. Lopeman, Tipton, Ia.
J. B. Mills, Dayton, Ohio
M. T. Mitchell, Petersburg, Ind.
Strand Co., Reed City, Utah
Old Mill, Minneapolis, Minn.
Opera House, Tell City, Ind.
Palace, Malta, Mont.
Peoples, Dayton, Ohio.
Playhouse, Justell, Ky.
Poppy, Calipatria, Cal.
Rex, Minneapolis, Minn.
Rivoli, Winchester, Minn.
Wabash, Clinton, Ind.
Strand, Pitcairn, Pa.
Subway, Elkhart, Ind.
Taylor, Big Stone, Va.
Victoria, Chicago, Ill.
Victory, Shippensburg, Pa.
Western States, Miami, Ariz.
Tokyo, Veedersburg, Ind.
Hattie Mizelle, Dothan, Ala.

Marshall County Enterprises, Albertsville, Ala.
A. G. McCarty, Barnsville, Ga.
W. P. Riggins, Jesup, Ga.
S. G. Rogers, Marion, S. C.
Electric, Dardanella, Ark.
Woodies, Apollo, Pa.
Morfield, Detroit, Mich.
Coniff, Detroit, Mich.
The Fun, Detroit, Mich
The Pastime, Detroit, Mich.
White Star, Detroit, Mich.
F. R. Mellinger, Bement, Ill.
Sam Warick, Sheldon, Ill.
C. Armintrout, Pittsfield, Ill.
Columbia Amusement Co., Paducah, Ky.
Iris, Belmont, N. C.
Bell, Tarrent City, Ala.
Star, Arcadia, Fla.
Strand, Alexander City, Ala.
H. B. Duering, Garnett, Kans.
Mrs. W. T. Brooks, Broken Arrow, Okla.
J. H. Thomas, Winfield, Kans.
Bijou, Indianapolis, Ind.
Gem, Hobart, Ind.
Columbia, Hammond, Ind.
Smith, Indiana Harbor, Ind.
Glen Ellyn, Gary, Ind.
Bradley, Buchanan, Mich
Owen, Cassiopolis, Mich.
Reeves, Paw Paw, Mich.
Adams, Chicago, Ill.
Babitz, Chicago, Ill.
Cameo, Chicago, Ill
Cornell Square, Chicago, Ill.
Crystal, Chicago, Ill.
Crystal, Chicago, Ill.
Edwards, Chicago, Ill.
Empire, Chicago, Ill
Garden, Chicago, Ill.
Gem, Chicago, Ill.
Harding, Chicago, Ill.
Harmony, Chicago, Ill.
Home, Chicago, Ill.
Hoyne, Chicago, Ill.
Irving, Chicago, Ill
Cozy, Chicago, Ill.
Lawn, Chicago, Ill
Lawndale, Chicago Ill
Liberty, Chicago, Ill.
Lynn, Chicago, Ill
Marion, Chicago, Ill.
Newberry, Chicago, Ill
Peerless, Chicago, Ill.
State, Chicago Ill
Chas. T. Rock, Watonga, Okla

Walton, Selma, Ala.
Liberty, Roanoke, Ala.
Wells, Anniston, Ala.
Ingram, Ashland, Ala.
First National, Sylacauga, Ala.
Pastime, Leeds, Ala.
Bijou, Mobile, Ala.
Empire, Mobile, Ala.
W. D. Patrick, Dothan, Ala.
Woodlawn, Woodlawn, Ala.
Strand, Alexander City, Ala.
Princess, Albertsville, Ala.
American, Sylacauga, Ala.
Bell, Tarrent City, Ala.
Imperial, Gadsden, Ala.
Hattie Mizelle, Dothan, Ala.
Royal, Opp, Ala.
Lyric Theatre, Townly, Ala.
Opera House, Talladega, Ala.
Grand, Wylam, Ala.
Meade's, Marked Tree, Ark.
Princess, N. Little Rock, Ark.
Highland, Little Rock, Ark.
Best, England, Ark.
J. F. Norman, England, Ark.
Garfield, Hollywood Fla.
Hollywood, Hollywood, Fla.
Flamingo, West Palm Beach, Fla.
Capitol, Miami, Fla.
Dixie, Appalachicola, Fla.
Royal, Tarpon Springs, Fla.
Biggers, Winter Garden, Fla.
Grand, Lake City, Fla
Biltmore, Buena Vista, Fla.
Princess, Lakeland, Florida
Rialto, Orlando, Fla.
Crescent, Dade City Florida
Eustis, Eustis, Fla.
Delray, Delray, Fla.
Star Theatre Co., Arcadia, Fla.
American, Orlando, Fla.
Bender, Largo, Fla.
Seminole, Homestead, Fla.
Fred L. Freeman, Live Oak, Fla.
Larkin, Larkin, Fla.
J. R. Minneham, Okeechobee, Fla.
S. M. Perkins, Jasper, Fla.
Frank C. Thompson, Frostproof, Fla.
Famous, Cocoa, Fla.
Dania, Dania, Fla.
H. Pettman, Clearwater, Fla.
10th St., Atlanta, Ga
Cameo, Atlanta, Ga.
Tudor, Atlanta, Ga.
Ponce de Leon Theatre, Atlanta, Ga.

Paramount, Atlanta, Ga.
Toyland, Atlanta, Ga.
Victory, Atlanta, Ga.
J. A. Rebb, Atlanta, Ga.
Cameo, Atlanta, Ga.
Alamo, Atlanta, Ga.
Palace, Atlanta, Ga
Austin Dillon, Atlanta, Ga.
Eighty-One Atlanta, Ga.
West End, Atlanta, Ga.
Robert's new colored house, Atlanta
T. F. Thompson, Cedartown, Ga.
Palace, Cedartown, Ga.
Star, Savanah, Ga.
J. H. Wheeler's, Decatur, Georgia
Criterion, Macon, Ga.
Strand, Athens, Ga.
Logan, Augusta, Ga.
Palace, Athens, Ga.
Palace, Athens, Ga.
Star, Covington, Ga.
Lyric, Columbus, Ga
American, Columbus, Ga.
Lyric, Columbus, Ga.
Dream, Columbus, Ga.
Lenox, Augusta, Ga.
Wise, Winder, Ga.
Palace, Dawson, Ga.
Lee, Cuthbert, Ga.
New Theatre, Montezuma, Ga.
Fairfax, East Point, Ga
Capitol, Cordele, Ga.
Kidd (Colored), Gainesville, Ga.
Alamo, West Point, Ga.
Randall's, Lavonia, Ga.
Golden, LaGrange, Ga.
Colonial Milledgeville, Ga.
Pastime, Sandersville, Ga.
Franklin Ft. Valley, Ga
Burton, Toccoa, Ga.

Palace	Colorado, Tex.
Best	Colorado, Tex.
Palace	Denton, Tex.
Olympic	Wichita Falls, Tex.
Connellee	Eastland, Tex.
Fair	Amarillo, Tex.
Deandi	Amarillo, Tex.
National	Breckenridge, Tex.
Lamb	Ranger, Tex.
Queen	Tyler, Tex.
Unique	El Paso, Tex.
Queen	Big Springs, Tex.
Broadway	Cisco, Tex.
Aldine	Corpus Christi, Tex.
Amusu	Corpus Christi, Tex.

American	McKinney, Tex.
Gem	Palestine, Tex.
Star	Palestine, Tex.
Adline	Robstown, Tex.
Queen	Sweetwater, Tex.
Odeon	Whitewright, Tex.
Key	Galveston, Tex.
Dixie No. 2	Galveston, Tex.
Dixie No. 3	Galveston, Tex.
Pastime	Canadian, Tex.
Queen	Pecos, Tex.
Crown	Houston, Tex.
Rembert	Longview, Tex.
Elk's	Longview, Tex.
Victoria	Victoria, Tex.
Dreamland	Cuero, Tex.
Queen	Cuero, Tex.
Queen	Winters, Tex.
Alcove	Stamford, Tex.
Dixie	Bryan, Tex.
Palace	Childress, Tex.
Majestic	Chillicothe, Tex.
Mission	Clarksville, Tex.
Queen	Clifton, Tex.
Dixie	Coleman, Tex.
Majestic	Comance, Tex.
Mission	Dalhart, Tex.
Ronile	Dallas, Tex.
Strand	Dallas, Tex.
Liberty	DeLeon, Tex.
Majestic	Del Rio Tex.
Majestic	Dublin, Tex.
Aztec	Eagle Pass, Tex.
Lyric	Gainesville, Tex.
Crescent	Garland, Tex.
Regal	Gatesville, Tex.
Crystal	Gilmer, Tex.
Colonial	Greenville, Tex.
Yale	Groesback, Tex.
Haskell	Haskell, Tex.
Queen	Hearne, Tex.
Pastime	Itasca, Tex.
Opera House	Jacksboro, Tex.
Palace	Kirbyville, Tex.
Majestic	Lamesa, Tex.
Rialto	Midland, Tex.
Long's	Navasota, Tex.
Olympic	Plainview, Tex.
Liberty	Mason City, Ill.
Majestic	Jacksonville, Ill.
Gem	Rosebud, Tex.
Jewell	Rusk, Tex.
Arcade	Weslaco, Tex.
Palace	Wortham, Tex.

Albany	Albany, Tex.
Liberty	Beaumont, Tex.
Beltonian	Belton, Tex.
Simon	Brenham, Tex.
Rialto	Brownsfield, Tex.
Queen	Brownsville, Tex.
Gem	Brownwood, Tex.
Royal	Arkadelphia, Ark.
Dunlap	Clarksville, Ark.
Majestic	Ft. Smith, Ark.
Hobson	Hot Springs, Ark.
Lyric	Harrison, Ark.
Liberty	Nashville, Ark.
Grand	Searcy, Ark.
Palace	Hico, Tex.
New Theatre	Weatherford, Tex
Royal	Hamilton, Tex.
Rialto	Harlingen, Tex.
Star	Humble, Tex.
Peoples	Munday, Tex.
Helton	Port Arthur, Tex.
Majestic	Santa Anna, Tex.
Castle	Havana, Ill.
Coliseum	Marseilles, Ill.
Orpheum	Savanna, Ill.
Colonial	Urbana, Ill.
Princess	Galva, Ill.
Morrows	Decatur, Ill.
Central	Fairbury, Ill.
Royal	Minonk, Ill.
New Palace	Nekomis, Ill.
Odd Fellows	Mount Olive, Ill.
New Grand	Mount Olive, Ill.
Liberty	Delevan, Ill.
Kozy	Eureka, Ill.
Capitol	Springfield, Ill.
Strand	Rockford, Ill.
Columbia	Rockford, Ill.
Victor	Davenport, Ia.
Zenith	Davenport, Ia.
Ashton	New Orleans, La.
Arcade	Brookhaven, Miss.
Amite	Amite, La.
Blackman	St. Joseph, La.
Grand	Baton Rouge, La.
Home	Alexandria, La.
Majestic	McLain, Miss.
Melz	Ferriday, La.
Opera House	Rayne, La.
Princess	Winnsboro, La.
Richelieu	Tallulah, La.
Scout	Minden, La.
Temple	Baton Rouge, La.

THE PAGE ORGAN COMPANY

BUILDERS OF PIPE ORGANS

LIMA, OHIO

Harry Page Maus was a piano dealer in Lima, Ohio who had a questionable reputation as an "operator." Among his business pursuits was a route of coin-operated pianos which were serviced by Dode Meeks Lamson and Ellsworth A. Beilharz, whose wives were sisters. Lamson, a drummer and sax player as well as a piano tuner, built the first Page organ on his back porch around 1922. Some components of these first instruments were purchased from Hillgreen-Lane, another Ohio firm. A factory was soon occupied in Defiance, Ohio, of which Lamson was superintendent. Beilharz was in charge of installations.[1]

A big shot in the arm for the company was the acquisition of Joseph A. Malotte as sales manager early in 1924. Mr. Malotte had been assistant manager of the organ department at Wurlitzer's Cincinnati store and really knew the theatre business.[2] Malotte's and Maus' efforts created a slick and highly successful organization which proceeded to sell a remarkable number of instruments for such a fledgling firm. Business was perhaps a little too good: on August 20, 1924 a fire at the Page factory destroyed four organs, two church instruments and two instruments intended for theatres in Grand Rapids, Michigan and in Winchester, Indiana.[3] Suspicious timing of the fire might be inferred from the fact that the company's bookkeeper spent four days paying bills following the insurance settlement![4] After the fire the factory relocated to Lima, Ohio where business became better than ever. The salesmanship of Maus and Malotte was largely responsible for this success but an equally important factor was the high quality of Page instruments. This is all the more remarkable in light of the fact that Dode Lamson, head of the factory, was not a particularly well educated man.

Mechanically, Page organs were in a constant state of evolution. Designs of trap actions, relays, chests and reservoirs were often changed. Early chests were similar to Gottfried's, having side-mounted pouches operating levers with valves on the other ends. Later chests featured standard pouchboard construction and, on late church instruments, a well-designed pitman action. Page relays were exceptionally compact, featuring a switch design similar to Wicks but operated electropneumatically. Some Page relays had Reisner electric note relays in lieu of electropneumatic action. Because of the limited contact wiping of the Page switch design, they are unreliable today. When new, however, Page relays enjoyed a reputation which resulted in their selection for a composite organ for the St. Louis World's Fair which was made of the best parts of a number of organ companies. Page reservoirs were made in several different styles including inside curtain valve, outside curtain valve and single cone valve designs. A later design employed a small cone and several pallet valves, similar to Wurlitzer, except that Page believed in multiple pallets: one reservoir was actually built with eight pallet valves! Page built many of their own wood pipes but purchased all metal pipes, usually

Page factory as it appeared in 1983.

from Gutfleisch & Schopp or occasionally from Gottfried.[5]

Within two or three years of the company's move to Lima, E. A. Williams succeeded Maus as president. Some of the nameplates thereafter read "Williams Master Organ built by Page Organ Company." As was the case with most companies, times were tough after the 1929 stock market crash. Dode Lamson left the firm in 1930 or 1931 to form the unsuccessful Liturgical Organ Company who installed the first electrically amplified reed organ in a Catholic church in Minster, Ohio. Lamson ended his career in the jukebox, pinball machine and background music business, harking back to his earlier days as a nickelodeon tuner. By 1932 there was only one man in the Page factory: the bookkeeper, Walter W. Scott, who spent most of this time staving off creditors. He was more or less successful at this pursuit until August of 1934 when bankruptcy was finally declared. Mr. Scott listed assets of $143,000 versus liabilities of $272,000 and noted that many churches owed money to the company.[6] [7]

Most theatre organ companies suffered financially because, after the advent of talking pictures, many theatres simply stopped paying for their organs. It is ironic that Page's downfall was exacerbated by the defaults of churches. While many theatre organ firms sought in vain to get a foothold in the church market, Page sold around half their output to churches, according to the widow of Harry Page Maus.[8]

Following the bankruptcy, Ellsworth Beilharz, former chief of installations for Page, purchased many of the company's assets and in 1935 formed the Lima Pipe Organ Company. He was joined by his son Earl Beilharz in 1936 who assumed ownership of the firm in 1972, one year before his father's passing. In 1973 Mr. Beilharz was instrumental in founding the American Institute of Organbuilders. In 1984 he retired and sold the firm to two long-time employees, brothers Tom and Larry Holycross.[9] Organ building remains in Earl's blood, however; not content with retirement, he assumed the position of executive director of the AIO in 1985, a move applauded by many of his friends in the industry.

Model M-X-40 Page console featuring twin 88-note roll players.

(opposite) The best known of all Page organs, the 4/15 in Fort Wayne's Embassy Theatre, is being played by Buddy Nolan, its caretaker for many years. The console has the same number of stops as a 4/20 Wurlitzer, reflecting the fact that Page organs were among the most highly unified ever built.

This novel Page player featured twin 88-note rolls in a cabinet no larger than a small bureau. Page advertising stressed that it could be attached to any modern organ and that prices started at $2,000.

ANOTHER PAGE IN HISTORY

"In every instance they have given PERFECT SATISFACTION"

THE Young and Wolf Corporation, owners of a chain of theatres in Ohio and Indiana, has recently installed its third Page Unit Organ. This organ was installed in the Palace Theatre at Marion, Ohio—a new link in its chain. Thus, Messrs. Young and Wolf have expressed in the only real substantial way, the satisfaction they have had with the first two installations.

Then, too, there is the word of Mr. John Eberson of Eberson & Eberson, well known theatre architects. Mr. Eberson designed the theatre and speaks very highly of the Page Unit Organ installation. He says, "I frankly admit that this is one of the slickest little installations I have seen, hence I shall have no hesitancy to call your product to the attention of my clients."

* * * *

After all is said, nothing can take the place of pipe organ music in the theatre. It has won its way there to remain, due to a certain attractiveness and individuality that it alone can provide. So you need pipe organ music and you owe it to yourself to find out how well Page can serve you.

Exterior of the New Palace Theatre at Marion, Ohio. This theatre is one of a chain in Ohio and Indiana owned by the Young-Wolf Corporation

Interior of the beautiful Palace Theatre at Marion, Ohio, owned by the Young-Wolf Corporation

Mr. V. U. Young of the Young-Wolf Corporation, owners of the Palace Theatre at Marion, Ohio, and several others in Ohio and Indiana. Mr. Young is a well-known Shriner. His temple is Orak located at Hammond, Indiana, and his consistory is Fort Wayne

Mr. Young says in writing to a Page prospect, "I have repeatedly told Mr. Williams that I would be glad to recommend the Page Organ at any time. We have a number of Page Organs in our theatres and in every instance they have given perfect satisfaction. We are especially pleased with the Page Organ that was recently installed in our Palace Theatre, Marion, Ohio."

V. U. Young

Find out what Page can do for you

THE PAGE ORGAN COMPANY
523 N. Jackson St.
Lima, Ohio

PAGE UNIT ORGANS

In the late 1920s Page ran a series of full-page ads in theatrical trade journals. This one appeared in the December 22, 1928 issue of Exhibitors Herald-World. *The campaign was apparently successful: 25% of Page's theatre business came in 1928 and 1929, at a time when theatre organ sales were all but dead for a number of other builders.*

ANOTHER PAGE IN HISTORY

Speeding Planes rushed the plans

AT 2 P. M. Wednesday the telephone rang in the Chicago office. Los Angeles was on the line. "We want complete organ specifications by tomorrow night," they said.

They had in mind a large unit orchestral organ, one of the biggest ever to be built, for a 2,000-seat theatre. This was no small task!

Twenty-eight Hours Later

Chicago 'phoned headquarters at Lima. A special airplane was chartered and late that afternoon, with detailed specifications on board, the plane hopped off for Chicago to connect with the westbound air mail.

At 5:45 Thursday evening the plans were in Los Angeles, twenty-eight hours after the inquiry was received at the factory! A modern epic of business!

For Catalina Island

The organ was built—a de luxe instrument, one of the finest of its kind, similar to the marvelous Page Unit Organ which daily delights radio listeners everywhere from Station WHT, of the Radiophone Broadcasting Corporation, Wrigley Building, Chicago.

This new Page achievement was ordered by the Santa Catalina Island Company for the beautiful theatre at Avalon, Santa Catalina Island, Calif., one of the properties of William Wrigley, Jr.

"Page possibly best"—Wrigley

About the Page Unit Organ, Mr. Wrigley recently wrote:

"It is not necessary for me to hear the Page Organ as there is one in the Wrigley Building which goes out over the radio every day.

"I know the Page Organ is a good organ and have an idea it is possibly the best."

Complete Orchestral Organ

Four manuals, 1,500 pipes and all the tonal varieties of a large orchestra distinguish the Page Unit Organ built for Mr. Wrigley's Catalina Island theatre.

It has such stops as the brass with copper bell saxophone; English post horn of 16-foot range on the pedals; 16-foot French horn of 85 pipes; two tibias of special scale.

In the reeds are included the kinura, trumpet, tuba horn, vox humana, clarinet, oboe, sousaphone and saxophone. A special Page flute stop combines into one stop five families of flute.

Master Achievement

There are also in this huge organ, a master xylophone and large marimba band. Other percussions are the glockenspiel, orchestra bells, harp, chrysoglott and chimes, all of Deagan make.

Truly this organ can be said to be a master achievement. Throughout it reflects the ability of Page to serve every theatre requirement with superb workmanship. Careful attention to details and the use of only the finest materials are unchangeable elements of the Page code of craftsmanship.

Learn today what Page can do for *you*. Learn why Page always means marvelous tonal quality, instant response and dependable performance. Page architects are glad to give their advice without obligation.

Keyboard of huge Page Unit Organ purchased by the Santa Catalina Island Co., for new theatre at Avalon, Catalina Is., Calif. Owner, William Wrigley, Jr.

Consult us about your requirements

THE PAGE ORGAN COMPANY

521 N. Jackson St., Lima, Ohio

PAGE UNIT ORGANS

This ad in the November 3, 1928 issue of* Motion Picture News *trumpeted Page's largest theatre installation. Its console with three complete rows of stops was unique in vintage American theatre organ building.

The three-manual Page above, installed in Fort Wayne radio station WOWO in 1929, featured the same decorative carvings found on most Page theatre instruments.

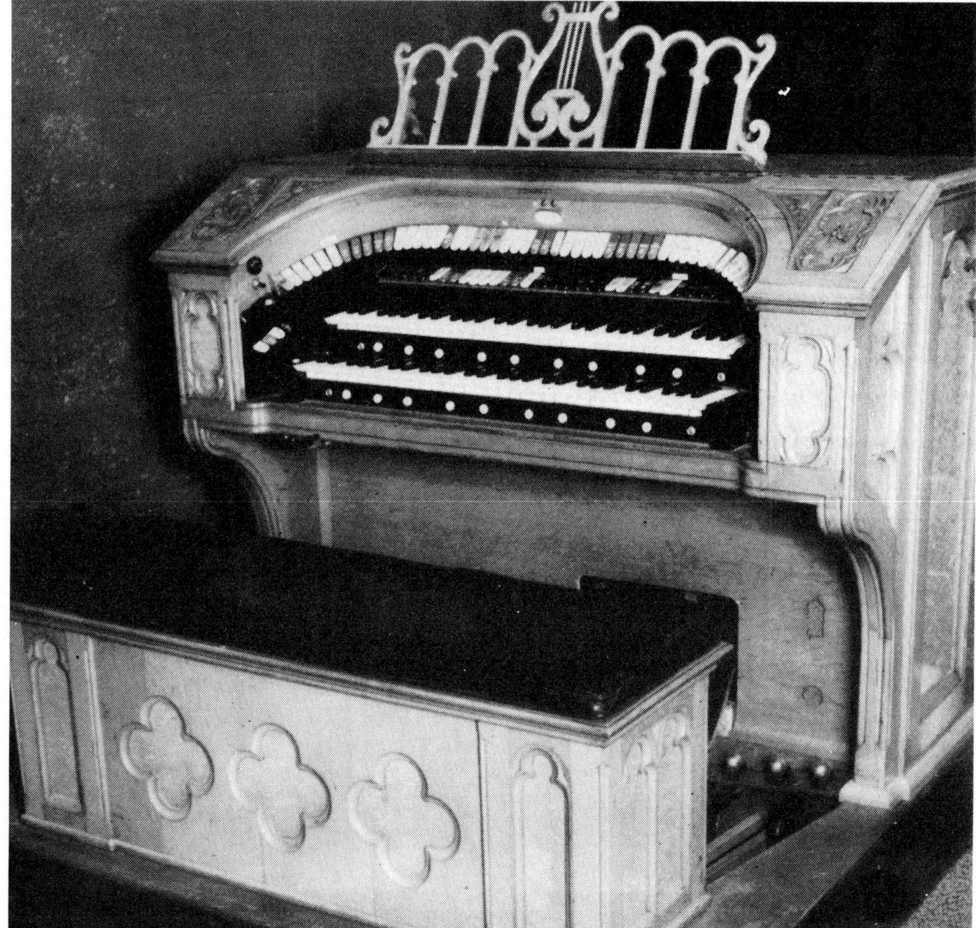

An interesting irony: Many theatre organs have been transplanted to homes. This 2/5 Page, originally installed in the Harold Lipes residence in Fort Wayne, Indiana in 1924, was transplanted to the Hedback Theatre, Indianapolis, Indiana in the 1970s.

Petite and plain Page in the Paramount Theatre, Kokomo, Indiana was a deviation from the company's usually more flamboyant design.

PAGE OPUS LIST

CITY/STATE	LOCATION	SIZE	YR	BLWR	REMARKS
CALIFORNIA					
Avalon	Casino Th.	4/16	1928	21990	
			1928	22012	
FLORIDA					
Tampa	Park (Falk) Th.	3/	1928	22262	With two-manual console on stage.
GEORGIA					
Vidalia	Pal Th.		1928	21469	
ILLINOIS					
Chicago	WGBN Radio	3/			
	WHT Radio	4/15	1927	21042	10 hp, 10″ & 15″ wp; moved in 1929 to Michigan Theatre, Flint, Michigan.
INDIANA					
Anderson	Paramount Th.	3/7	1929	23257	5 hp.
Fort Wayne	Mr. A. Centline		1924	M835B	2 hp, 10″ wind.
	Emboyd (Embassy) Th.	4/15	1927	21119	10 hp, 10″ & 15″ wind.
	Harold Lipes residence	2/5	1924	M339B	¾ hp, 4½″ wind; later moved to Hedback Theatre, Indianapolis, Indiana.
	Robbins School of Music				
	State Th.	3/			
	WOWO Radio	3/	1929	22800	
Gary	Glen Park Th.		1927	21143	
Indianapolis	Roosevelt Th.	2/	1927	20315	
Kokomo	Indiana Th.	2/	1928	21999	
	Isis Th.	2/	1924	M811B	5 hp, 10″ wind and 25″ vacuum.
	Paramount Th.	3/			
Ligonier	Crystal Th.	2/			
Marion	Royal Grand Th.				
Muncie	Strand Th.	2/	1924	M225	5 hp, 10″ wind and 30″ vacuum.
New Castle	Princess Th.	2/	1927	20758	
Portland	Princess Th.		1929	23010	
Union City	Victory Th.	2/			
Winchester	Lyric Th.	3/12	1924		
MARYLAND					
Westminster	State (Star) Th.	2/	1924		
MICHIGAN					
Bay City	Temple Th.		1927	20791	
Detroit	Pasadena Th.		1925	18307	
Grand Haven	East End Th.		1928	22596	
Grand Rapids	Alcazar (Bird's State) Th.				
	Beecher Th.		1924	M358	5 hp, 10″ wind and 25″ vacuum.
	Burton Th.				
	Fulton Th.	2/5	1927	20849	
	Liberty Th.	2/			

CITY/STATE	LOCATION	SIZE	YR	BLWR	REMARKS
Grand Rapids	Lyric Th.		1928	22617	
	Miller & Boshoven, Inc.		1928	22118	
	Our Th.	3/7			Moved in 196? to Sparta Theatre, Sparta, Michigan.
	Rivoli Th.		1924	M433B	2 hp, 10″ wind.
	State Th.				
Monroe	unidentified new theatre		1928	21802	
MINNESOTA					
Fairmont	State Th.		1927	20135	
Jackson	Jackson Th.	2/4			
MISSOURI					
Kansas City	Kansas City Hockey Club (Playmore Rink)		1927	21225	
NEW JERSEY					
Clifton	Acme Th.	2/			
	Capitol Th.	2/			
Glassboro	Roxy Th.	2/6	1928	22328	
Maple Shade	Roxy Th.		1927	19943	
Metuchen	Metuchen (Forum) Th.	2/3	1927	21239	
NEW YORK					
Buffalo	Ellen Terry Th.		1924		With double roll player.
Mount Kisco	Kino Photoplay Corp.		1927	21305	
New York	Bronx Th.				
	Empire Th.		1926	18941	
	Tremont Th.		1927	20907	
OHIO					
Akron	Boyd Th.	3/			
	Rialto (Kenmore) Th.	2/			
	Royale Th.	2/			
Athens	Athena (Majestic) Th.	2/13	1926	18347	
Barberton	Park Th.	2/			
	Rondo Th.	2/	1926	19653	
Bedford	Bedford Th.		1927	20664	
Berea	Pastime Th.	2/6	1928	21494	
Celina	Lake Th.		1928	21612	
Cleveland	Marvel Th.		1928	22143	
Columbus	Ritz Th.		1927	20000	
	Motion Picture Theatre Owners of America, Neil House		1927	20346	
Dayton	A. P. Blum residence	2/	1924	M2288	2 hp, 4½″ wind.
	Federation Th.	2/			
	Nichol & May	2/			
	Riverdale Th.	2/	1927	21135	
	Sigma Th.	2/			
Delaware	Fred Huntsberger		1924	M229B	1½ hp, 4½″ wind.
Delphos	Capitol Th.	2/4	1923	14054	
Dover	Ohio Th.		1925	18166	
Findlay	Victory Th.	2/	1925	M910B	2 hp, 10″ wind.
Fremont	Strand Th.	3/7	1928	22582	
Kenmore	Rialto Th.				
Lima	Lyric Th.	2/	1925	16866	
	Quilna Th.	2/4			
	State Th.	2/7	1926	19521	
			1929	22811	
Marion	Palace Th.	3/7	1928	21942	
Napoleon	New State Th.	2/	1928	22324	
Newark	Gem Th.	2/			
	Grand Th.				
	Strand Th.		1927	20749	
Ravenna	Lee's Th.	2/			
St. Mary's	Regent Th.	2/			
	Strand Th.				
Sandusky	State Th.	3/8	1928	22440	5 hp.
Sidney	Majestic Th.		1927	20614	
Springfield	Liberty Th.	2/			
Wapakoneta	Brown's Opera House	2/			
Washington Court House	Fayette Th.		1928	21475	
Wooster	Lyric Th.	2/	1928	21764	
PENNSYLVANIA					
Allentown	Franklin Th.		1927		
Bangor	Strand Th.		1928	21567	
East Stroudsburg	Mr. Victor Austin		1928	21666	
Girardville	Opera House				
Hanover	Strand Th.		1927	20682	
			1928	21626	

CITY/STATE	LOCATION	SIZE	YR	BLWR	REMARKS
Lebanon	Capitol Th.	3/			
Lehighton	Park Th.	3/8	1927	20702	
Nazareth	Royal Th.		1928	22073	
Philadelphia	Colonial Th.	3/12	1927	20414	Located on Moyamensing Avenue.
Pittston	Roman Th.	2/	1927	20860	
SOUTH DAKOTA					
Huron	State (Huron) Th.	2/4	1928	21472	

EARL PAVETTE

The case of Earl Pavette is a rather sad story. Having helped Sandy Balcom install Kimball theatre organs in the Seattle area,[1] he longed to be an organ builder himself. The only organ he ever built[2] was a 2/8 for the Kent Theatre in Kent, Washington in 1928. It contained Gottfried pipework and other new and used parts.[3]

For a short time Mr. Pavette represented Moller but he wasn't much more successful selling Mollers than he was at selling his own instruments.[4] In the depth of the Depression Sandy Balcom discovered that Pavette was burning organ chests and parts to keep warm, after which Sandy purchased his remaining inventory to help him out. Earl Pavette finally died in the mid 1930s, a victim of tuberculosis.[5]

Earl Pavette displays his handiwork in his backyard workshop at 1022 E. 92 Street in Seattle. He erected the organ here before its installation in the Kent Theatre.

PELOUBET AND COMPANY

CHURCH AND THEATRE
PIPE ORGANS
KINETIC ORGAN BLOWERS

SPECIALLY EQUIPPED FOR PIPE ORGAN TUNING, REPAIRS, MAINTENANCE, AND REBUILDING. PIANO TUNING AND REPAIRS.

STRAND THEATRE BLDG.
(OAKLAND)
SCHENLEY 1135

PITTSBURGH, PA.

Leonard Peloubet received his early training from George Jardine and Son in New York City and went into business for himself in Pittsburgh in 1888. He later represented Moller for the sale of new organs[1] and eventually built organs himself.[2] He maintained a working relationship with Moller, however, and frequently bought parts from them as well as nearly complete organs with chests made to his own peculiar design.[3] Moller employees weren't keen on constructing Peloubet's special chests, particularly when he personally visited the factory to supervise their construction. To evidence his displeasure one Moller chest builder actually defecated into a Peloubet chest as it was being assembled for shipment![4]

In 1918 the financially troubled Wirsching Organ Company of Salem, Ohio entered into an agreement with Peloubet to form the Wirsching-Peloubet Company. Each party was to contribute $12,500 to the total $25,000 capitalization of the new firm. Wirsching's contribution was that company's tools and fixtures. Peloubet's cash contribution was not forthcoming, and Wirsching filed suit. The suit was later dropped,[5] and Peloubet continued in business under the name of Peloubet and Company. The Moller company also found Peloubet's financial dealings to be somewhat less than satisfactory. He had ordered several organs on credit and in acknowledging a further order Moller secretary E. O. Shulenberger informed him tersely that no further orders would be shipped until his overdue accounts were settled.[6] The payments were eventually made, and cordial feelings restored to the extent that Moller hired Peloubet to design and build a twelve-roll automatic changer for one of their player organs.[7] The location of this wondrous device has unfortunately not been disclosed as yet by the Moller files.

WIRSCHING-PELOUBET COMPANY

MAIN OFFICE
3531-3533 FORBES STREET
PITTSBURGH, PA.

FACTORY
SALEM, OHIO

ADDRESS REPLY TO

Elegant letterhead used by the short-lived Wirsching-Peloubet partnership.

PELOUBET OPUS LIST

Following is a list of the known organs installed in theatres under the Peloubet or Wirsching-Peloubet nameplates. None was a unit organ and all were on modest pressures.[8] They probably don't even qualify to be called orchestral instruments. In truth, their tonal design is based on the open diapason-melodia-dulciana-harmonic flute mentality unfortunately so pervasive in church organ designs of the day.

CITY/STATE	LOCATION	SIZE	YR	BLWR	HP	WP	REMARKS
GEORGIA							
Atlanta	Grand Th.	3/	1919				Moller opus 2760.
PENNSYLVANIA							
Braddock	Crystal Th.	3/19	1922	K714	3	5″	Moller opus 3116.
Homestead	Carnegie Music Hall		1911	6810K	4	5″	
Meadville	Park Th.	3/15	1924	M542B	3	5″	Moller opus 4030.
New Kensington	Liberty Th.	3/10	1921	J27	2	3½″	Moller opus 3014.
Pittsburgh	Brushton Th.	3/14	1918	G76	2	3½″	
	Schenley Th.	3/11	1919				Moller opus 2757.
	Strand Th.	3/	1920				Enlargement of existing organ; Moller opus 2978.
	Victory Th.	3/11	1921				Moller opus 3115.
Sharon	Strand Th.	3/10	1921	J12	2	3½″	Moller opus 3015.
Uniontown	Pennsylvania Amusement Co.	3/19	1922	K524	3	6″	Moller opus 3221; with 4-rank echo.
Wilkinsburg	Colonial Th.	2/10	1923	G32	2		Moller opus 3764.

The following seven organs are *probably* Peloubets; the Moller files are unclear on them.

CITY/STATE	LOCATION	SIZE	YR	BLWR	HP	WP	REMARKS
PENNSYLVANIA							
Pittsburgh	Columbia Th.	2/	1919				Moller opus 2712.
	Foster's Cafeteria	2/	1919				Moller opus 2714.
	Hill Top Th.	3/	1919				Moller opus 2758.
	Squirrel Hill Th.	3/	1922	J522	3	8″	Moller opus 3256.
	State Th.	3/	1922	J521	3	8″	Moller opus 3255.
Somerset	Pascal Th.	3/	1919				Moller opus 2759.
SOUTH CAROLINA							
Greenville	unidentified theatre	2/	1920				Moller opus 2715.

R.E. Pilcher W.E. Pilcher

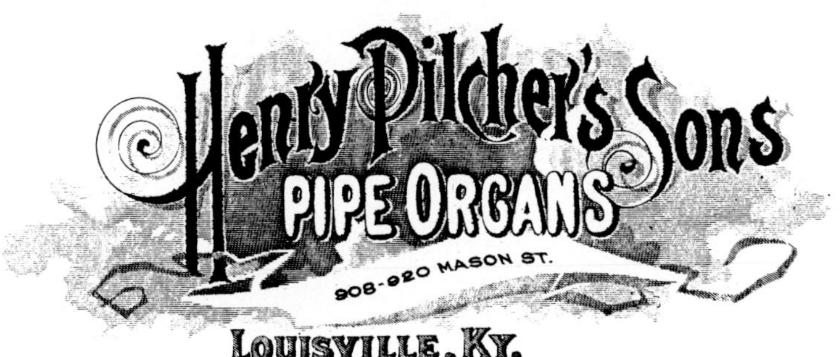

BRANCH OFFICES
ST. LOUIS
KANSAS CITY
DALLAS
ATLANTA

SUPERIORITY IN
VOICING
ACTION
AND
DESIGN

THE PILCHER ORGAN OF TODAY IS KNOWN AS A STANDARD OF PERFECTION BECAUSE OF ITS INHERENT QUALITIES THE RESULT OF AN HEREDITARY KNOWLEDGE OF NEARLY ONE HUNDRED YEARS INTERWOVEN WITH TWENTIETH CENTURY IDEAS AND METHODS.

WE EMPLOY EVERY MODERN IMPROVEMENT OF PRACTICAL VALUE KNOWN IN PIPE ORGAN CONSTRUCTION AND TONE CHARACTER.

"PERFECT IN WORKMANSHIP AND MATERIAL"
"PURITY OF TONE."
"A MASTERPIECE OF THE ORGAN BUILDER'S SKILL AND A GOOD REPRESENTATION OF THE STAGE TO WHICH THE ART HAS PROGRESSED."—
Verdict Jury of Awards, World's Fair, Chicago.

Pilcher was a name highly respected in the organ industry and in fact was one of the oldest names in American organ building, spanning a period of 114 years. In 1813 Henry Pilcher (1798-1880) began a seven-year apprenticeship in organ building in London, England and founded his own organ business in Dover in 1820. In 1832 he moved to the United States and operated an organ business in several locations including New Haven, Connecticut, Newark, New Jersey and New York City. In 1852 he moved to St. Louis, Missouri with his sons William (1830-1912) and Henry, Jr. (1828-1890) and operated his business under the name Henry Pilcher & Sons. Henry Pilcher retired in 1858 and the firm then became known as Pilcher Bros.[1]

In 1863 the Civil War caused the Pilcher brothers to move to Chicago where they formed a partnership with organist W. H. Chant under the name Pilcher & Chant. Their factory was destroyed by the great Chicago fire of 1871 at which time the partnership was dissolved. Henry Pilcher, Jr. continued the business on his own for a few years and then moved to Louisville, Kentucky in 1874, establishing the firm Henry Pilcher & Sons with his sons Robert E. and William E. Pilcher[2] (1859-1946). The latter son invented the unique style of pitman chest later used in most of the firm's organs and, in his obituary in the April 1946 *Diapason*, was referred to as the "dean of American organ builders . . . one of the most highly respected men in the organ industry."[3]

In 1883 Henry Pilcher, Jr. retired and the firm changed names, for the last time, to Henry Pilcher's Sons. The firm incorporated in 1925 with the following officers: R. E. Pilcher, chairman of the board; W. E. Pilcher, president and general manager; Paul B. Pilcher, vice president; William E. Pilcher, Jr., secretary; and Gerard W. Pilcher, treasurer. Gerard and William Pilcher, Jr., sons of William E. Pilcher, represented the fourth generation in this family of organ builders.[4]

Mr. Sylvester Kohler, one of the few key men in the Pilcher organization still alive, shared some personal reminiscences with historian Bob Coleberd in 1974. His observations offer a colorful insight into the history of the Pilcher firm in its later years: "The pay for me was $12 for a 55-hour week. I started on a Saturday morning [at age 16 in October 1923].

". . . My first work that Saturday morning was to lay out a set of wood pipes in their proper order on the workbench and trim the metal from the tip of the metal toes down to where the curved channel started. I was shown this first operation in the Pilcher plant by Mr. Tony Spevere who was one of the pipe voicers. There were two other voicers: Mr. Ira Moser, the master voicer, and Mr. Raymond Price, who in later years would voice pipes for the Schantz Organ Company, as would . . . Mr. Spevere.

"The environment to me seemed excellent . . . As time went by I grew to like my work and the men at the factory. They were most all excellent craftsmen. I spent the early years preparing wood and metal pipes for the voicers.

". . . I . . . asked Mr. Gerard [Pilcher] if I could learn the action of an organ—just preparing and maybe later, when the business improved, voicing pipes. [It] was to me like working in an auto plant where a workman just put a nut or bolt or some other part on a car every day. He agreed with me. So, we had classes on the construction of the organ each evening after working hours if Mr. Gerard [Pilcher] was free to teach us. After a few months I stopped . . . music lessons and enrolled in an electrical engineering course. The reason for taking this course was that, with all the wiring in an organ, one needed to know what was happening when a key was depressed. At least I had it figured that way at the time. Looking back, I have never regretted taking that course.

"In my third year I was taught to voice wood pipes and later a few metal pipes. The following year, 1927, Pilcher decided that they needed a reed voicer. The reeds they were buying just did not come up to the quality they demanded. So, who was elected? Right, I was. Mr. Moser knew reeds, but he was needed more for the strings and diapasons. That was the year I started on reeds and little did I know then that I would voice all (except a very few) that ever came out of the Pilcher factory.

". . . In the late twenties things were going great for me. I was married on Friday, April 13, 1928. My salary was raised quite a bit. The Pilcher factory was producing about one fair-sized organ per week and the largest organ ever built by Pilcher was started in 1928. The organ was placed in the World War I building in Louisville, Kentucky and was completed in May of 1929. It consisted of more than 5,000 pipes, 98 stops. Of this amount I voiced all the reed stops (except the English horn — Dennison) and a number of the flue stops, more than 2,000 pipes in all. This organ contained the only 32′ bombard (wood) built by Pilcher. All the employees attended the first recital on the giant instrument by Mr. Charles Courboin. Later that year, as everyone knows, the crash came. The crash of the stock market did not seem to affect building of organs, especially for the first year, as most churches honored their commitments.

". . . In the fall of 1931 the work week was reduced to four days and all wages reduced to 40 cents per hour. This was not good, but we learned to live with it. The following year I made a trip south. I always liked to make these trips for the company as it meant a larger check for that week.

". . . In the late summer of 1932 the work week was reduced to three days. Things were looking very bad indeed but we managed to have some work through the winter. Sometime early in 1933 the factory discharged all but their key men. This, of course, left me without a job . . . About March of 1934 . . . Mr. William Pilcher, Sr. came by the house and left word that he wanted to see me in his office. I was at the factory the next morning. I sat in Mr. Pilcher's office until he had finished with his mail. He then asked me if I would be interested in taking over the city service department at a salary of $100 per month. I was also to voice the reed stops for which I would be paid 40 cents an hour in addition to the monthly salary. This I accepted without any hesitation whatsoever. This, for me, was no big chore since there were very few new orders coming in — mostly repair and rebuilding during these years.

"In 1937 we had our major flood. Many of the churches suffered damage to their organs. This work and the new orders coming in made things look good again . . . Old employees began returning to the factory . . . Then the war came! 1941. It was not too long after Pearl Harbor (at least it seemed that way) we were notified that no more musical instruments could be manufactured. Existing stock could be used in rebuilding, but after this stock was depleted the Pilcher company began subcontracting government work.

"During these war years I was busy doing service work in the city as well as traveling through the southern states servicing organs. This last took quite a bit of time as the speed limit was 35 miles per hour. On one of the service runs I came to Chattanooga, Tennessee . . . I proceeded to

CONTINUOUSLY engaged in the manufacture of Pipe Organs for more than one hundred years.

INSTRUMENTS unexcelled in purity of tone, reliability of action, artistic design.

SPECIALLY planned for the requirements of churches, auditoriums, theatres, lodge rooms and residences.

HENRY PILCHER'S SONS
LOUISVILLE, KY.

Pilcher ad in the October 1921 Diapason.

check over the organ . . . and found many things wrong with the instrument. The worst was many silent notes, due mostly to the rocker coupler switches being corroded and in need of cleaning. To get the back of the console open was the problem . . . There was an access panel at the rear of the console which was covered with beautiful red carpet . . . I took the liberty of cutting the carpet and thoroughly cleaned all contacts and bussbars. Then I went to work on the pipes. Some were off speech and out of tune. I ended the day very tired from all the trips from the console to the organ pipes. I was happy the organ was in the best shape a lone man could make it, but regretted cutting that beautiful carpet.

"Sometime later, after I had returned to the factory, Bill Pilcher came to the voicing room with a letter in his hand. My heart did a flip. I was so sure I was going to get a good raking over because of the damage I had done to the carpet, and maybe be charged with it. Instead it was a very gracious letter thanking me for all that I did for the organ and that the instrument had not sounded nor worked as well since it was first installed. There was no mention of the carpet. Bill Pilcher was always ready to show the men the good news as well as the bad.

". . . The Pilcher company did all they could to keep their men with them, especially the key men. They even

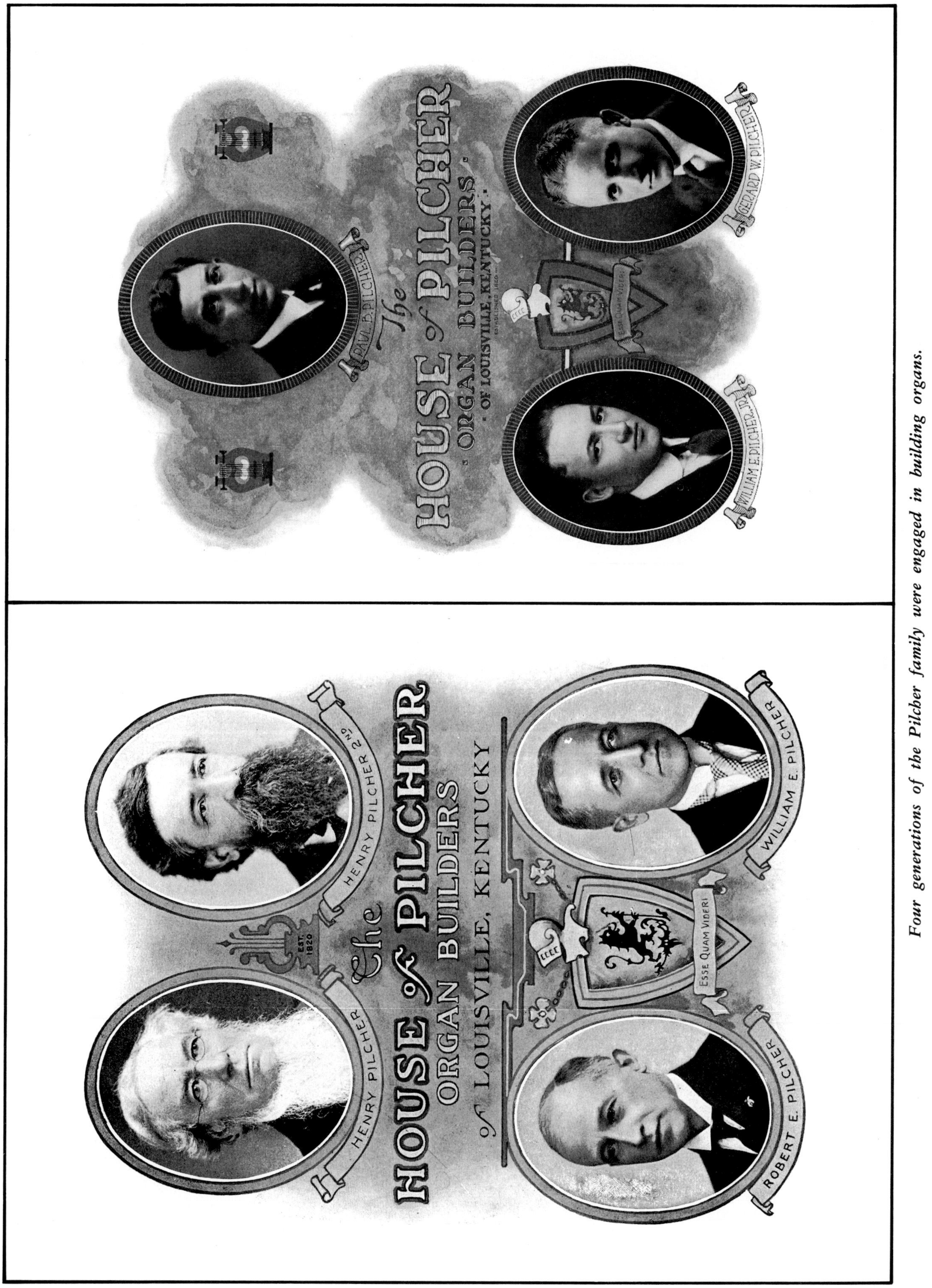

Four generations of the Pilcher family were engaged in building organs.

Pilcher theatre organs were sold primarily in the South. These examples were in Birmingham, Alabama (left) and Atlanta, Georgia.

had us making wooden frames for ice boxes. But do what they could to keep their men was to no avail. Before the war came to a close the Pilcher Organ Company was forced to close its doors on July 1, 1944. A few of the original employees and myself were the last to leave . . . Mr. William Pilcher [Jr.] joined the Moller company [and] the good will and Pilcher stock of supplies were sold to Moller."[5]

The last new Pilcher organ was opus 1944, built in 1941.[6]

The Pilcher factory records disclose that between 1911 and 1921 thirty new organs were built for theatres, all of them with mostly straight specifications. Opus 779 had a 65-note player and some of its ranks were of 65-note compass instead of the usual 61! At least three of these organs had a glockenspiel in addition to the usual harp and chimes, but for the most part the Pilcher organs in theatres were virtually identical with the company's church organs.

During the preparation of this volume the author received an unsolicited letter from Texas organist Harvell Mason. His comments offer an idea of the quality of the Pilcher product from an organist's point of view: "I've always been a sort of Pilcher buff. I'm Presbyterian and Pilcher did much Presbyterian work in the Oklahoma-Arkansas-Louisiana-Texas region so I've played a good many . . . I never had a cipher on a Pilcher, always found them reliable and generally tonally consistent from instrument to instrument. E. M. Skinner organs are about the only other that I found as tonally consistent, on the whole.

"Never could say that about other organs I've played. Some ranks would be scratchy strings, then go to another organ by the same builder and the strings would be smoother. Some diapasons would be powerful here, then on another by the same make might be anemic there. I found I could always depend on Pilcher and when I sat down to play one I'd not played before I could look at that tilt-tab and know what I was going to hear and what would blend with what. That's what I mean by tonally consistent."[7]

In the years 1922-27, the busiest era in theatre organ history, Pilcher didn't sell a single theatre instrument! Finally in 1928 the company signed a contract for their last theatre organ, the only one with a horseshoe console and also the only unified example of their 31 organs in theatres. This organ featured an excellent specification and it is indeed unfortunate that more such organs of high Pilcher quality were not sold to theatres.

2/17 PILCHER ORGAN, OPUS 866

Jefferson Theatre, Philadelphia, Pennsylvania

A typical specification is reproduced here from the original factory ledger books, courtesy of Dr. Homer Blanchard and the Organ Historical Society.

866 (Lease agreement)
Jefferson Theatre – Philadelphia Penn.
Electric Action.

Great Organ.
(Enclosed in separate Expression Chamber)

Open Diapason	8'	Metal	73 Pipes
Concert Flute	8'	wood	73 "
Muted Violin	8'	metal	73 "
Tuba Horn	8'	reed	73 "
Orchestral Clarinet	8'	reed	73 "
Harp Celeste	8'	(from Swell)	37 "
Glockenspiel	4'	(Orchestral Bells)	37 "

Swell to Great — Great Octave
Swell to Great Octave — Great Sub Octave
Swell to Great Sub Octave — Great Unison off
4 Pistons affecting Great + Pedal Organ stops + couplers, moving registers, instantly adjustable at console.

Swell Organ.
(Enclosed in separate Expression Chamber)

Bourdon	16'	Wood	73 Pipes
Horn Diapason	8'	metal	73 "
Stopped Flute	8'	wood	73 "
Violoncello	8'	metal	73 "
Viole Celeste	8'	metal	73 "

Swell Organ (cont'd)

Quintadena	8'	Metal	73 Pipes
Harmonic Flute	4'	"	73 "
Orchestral Oboe	8'	reed	73 "
Harp Celeste	8'	(Orchestral Harp)	37 "
Glockenspiel	4'	(from Great)	37 "

Tremolo
Swell Octave — Swell Sub Octave
Swell Unison off.
4 Pistons affecting Swell + Pedal Organ stops + couplers, moving registers, instantly adjustable at console.

Echo Organ.
(Operated from Swell Manual)
(Enclosed in separate Expression Chamber)

Echo Flute	8'	Wood	61 Pipes.
Vox Humana	8'	reed	61 "

Tremolo
Cathedral Chimes 8' (Tubular Bells) 20
Chimes Forte — Chimes Piano
Chimes Dampers.
Echo Sub Octave — Echo Octave
Echo to Swell "on" + "off" pistons, providing for playing each organ independently, or both together.

Pedal Organ.
(Enclosed in separate Expression Chamber)

Contra Bass	16'	Wood	32 Pipes
String Bass	16'	metal	32 "
Bourdon (from Swell)	16'	wood	32 "
Violoncello (ext. from String Bass)	8'	metal	32 "

Swell to Pedal — Great to Pedal
Pedal Octave.

Accessories.
Great to Pedal Reversible Pedal, moving registers.
Piston cancelling all combinations, moving registers.
3 reversible pistons operating Unison couplers.
Balanced Crescendo + Diminuendo Pedal, affecting all stops + couplers (unison) not moving registers.
Sforzando Pedal (Full Organ) affecting all stops + couplers, reversible.
Balanced Swell + Echo Expression Pedal.

Accessories (cont'd)
Balanced Great Organ Expression Pedal.
Indicator for action current generator.
Indicator for Crescendo Pedal.
Indicator for Sforzando.
Orgoblo (console detached) $6000.00.

2/5 PILCHER ORGAN, OPUS 1396
Capitol Theatre, Louisville, Kentucky

1396. Unit Theatre Organ - Capitol Theatre
"Electric" Louisville, Ky
Console.
circular Type, with stop keys.
Manual keyboards inclined hinged & sliding for convenient access to contacts.
Pedals A.G.O. Pattern, Concave & Radiating.
Pitch
Orchestra A 440 - Wind Pressure 6" to 10"

Accompaniment

16' Tibia (Tenor C)	Wood
16' Contra Flute	Wood
16' Viol d'Orchestra (Tenor C)	Metal
8' Tibia	Wood
8' Concert Flute	Wood
8' Viol	Metal
4' Tibia	Wood
4' Flute	Wood
4' Viol	Metal
2-2/3' Quint	Wood
2' Piccolo	Wood
16' Vox Humana (Tenor C)	Reed
8' Tuba	Reed
8' Vox Humana	Reed
4' Vox Humana	Reed
Chrysoglott	37 Notes

Traps
Snare Drum
Tambourine
Castanets
Chinese Block
Tom-Tom

Accompaniment (2nd Touch)

16' Tuba	Reed
8' Tuba	Reed
Sleigh Bells	37 Tones
Xylophone	37 "
Chimes	20 "

Solo

16' Tibia (Tenor C)	Wood
16' Contra Flute	Wood
16' Contra Viol (Tenor C)	Metal
8' Tibia	Wood
8' Concert Flute	Wood
8' Viol	Metal
4' Tibia	Wood
4' Concert Flute	Wood
4' Viol	Metal
2-2/3' Quint	Wood
2' Piccolo	Wood
2' Fifteenth	Metal
1-3/5' Tierce	Wood
16' Tuba	Reed
16' Vox Humana	Reed
8' Tuba	Reed
8' Vox Humana	Reed
4' Clarion	Reed
Xylophone	37 Tones
Orchestra Bells	37 "
Sleigh Bells	20 "
Chimes	20 "

Pedal

16' Contra Flute	Wood
8' Tibia	Wood
8' Concert Flute	Wood
8' Viol	Metal
4' Tibia	Wood
4' Concert Flute	Wood
4' Viol	Metal
16' Tuba	Reed

Traps.
Bass Drum
Cymbal (Crash)
Cymbal (Stroke)
Tympani
Tambourine
Tom-Tom

On Pedal Buttons.
Fire Gong
Bird Whistle
Boat "
Horses Hoofs
Auto Horn
On Key Check
Telephone Bell

Combinations
Accompaniment Adjustable 1-2-3-4-5-6-7-& Cancel
Nos. 5-6-7-& Cancel also include Pedal
Solo Adjustable 1-2-3-4-5-6-7-& Cancel-
Nos. 5-6-7 & Cancel also include Pedal

Accessories
Tremolo (Main)
Tremolo (Solo)
Tremolo (Vox Humana)
Balanced Solo Expression Pedal
Balanced Accompaniment Expression Pedal
Balanced Crescendo Pedal
Crescendo Indicator
Action Current Indicator
Blower Silencer
Organist's Bench
Electric Blower & Gen — $5000.00

This beautifully engraved nameplate reflects the quality of the instrument behind it.

Pilcher factory at Louisville, Kentucky.

Sylvester E. Kohler voices an oboe in the Pilcher factory in 1929.

A view of the Pilcher erecting room c. 1938. The organ on the floor was destined for the First Presbyterian Church in Staunton, Virginia.

This was the entire Pilcher voicing staff in 1925. From left to right are Ira L. Moser, master voicer, Ray Price, Sylvester Kohler and Tony Spevere.

Pilcher employees pose for a photographer c. 1927. Mr. Gerard Pilcher is at the left of the back row of three men. A number of really young girls were employed in the Pilcher factory.

PILCHER OPUS LIST

Following is a complete list of this firm's theatre-type installations.

OPUS	LOCATION/CITY/STATE	SIZE	YR	PRICE	REMARKS
735	Lyric Th., Macon, GA	2/	1911	$ 2,150	Blower 6806K, ¾ hp, 3½" wind.
759	Bonita Th., Columbus, GA	2/	1913	$ 1,500	Blower 4695.
774	Vaudette Th., Atlanta, GA	2/	1913	$ 3,100	
778	H. M. Newsomey Th., Birmingham, AL	2/	1913	$ 3,500	
779	Hippodrome (Strand) Th., Dallas, TX	2/21	1913	$ 7,000	With 65-note roll player.
788	Odeon Th., Birmingham, AL				Never built.
797	Queen Th., Galveston, TX	2/15	1913	$ 4,800	Blower 6625.
805	Tivoli (People's) Th., Beaumont, TX	2/8	1913	$ 3,050	Tubular pneumatic.
808	Queen Th., Houston, TX	2/23	1913	$ 7,025	
810	Hippodrome (Waco) (Hippodrome) Th., Waco, TX	2/12	1914	$ 4,000	
848	Star Th., Arcadia, FL	2/9	1914	$ 3,065	
853	Queen Th., Dallas, TX	2/23	1915	$ 8,525	Blower 5989; price included allowance of $2,000 on old Hillgreen-Lane from Orpheum Theatre, Dallas, TX.
862	Grand Th., Camden, NJ	2/12	1915	$ 4,750	Blower 6286; with orchestra bells.
866	Jefferson Th., Philadelphia, PA	2/17	1915	$ 6,000	With orchestra bells.
871	Strand Th., Birmingham, AL	2/12	1915	$ 4,500	With orchestra bells and echo.
882	Logan Th., Philadelphia, PA	2/12	1915	$ 5,000	Blower 6626.
951	Empire Th., Montgomery, AL	2/10	1917	$ 3,000	See opus 973.
973	Empire Th., Montgomery, AL	2/15	1918	$ 2,700	Additions: 5 ranks to opus 951.
979	Queen Th., Dallas, TX	2/16	1918	$ 5,800	Blower 8711, price included $1,000 allowance for old parts.
1033	Palace Th., Fort Worth, TX	2/17	1919	$ 6,500	
1046½	Trianon Th., Birmingham, AL		1920	$ 2,100	Additions to existing organ.
1047½	Strand Th., Birmingham, AL		1920	$ 1,400	Additions to existing organ.
1049½	Montgomery Th., Montgomery, AL		1919	$ 1,500	Additions to existing organ; $200 allowed for old console.
1058	Old Mill Th., Dallas, TX	2/18	1920	$ 9,600	
1066	Tivoli (People's) Th., Beaumont, TX	2/9	1920	$ 4,000	
1068	Imperial Th., Gadsden, AL	2/9	1920	$ 4,600	
1072	Strand Th., Asheville, NC	2/9	1921	$ 4,800	Originally built for Griffin, Georgia.
1073	Lyric Th., Jackson, TN	2/9	1920	$ 4,800	
1074	Metropolitan Th., Atlanta, GA	3/25	1921	$ 17,210	Blowers 11953, 11982, 13457.
1075	Modjeska Th., Augusta, GA	2/12	1921	$ 7,125	
1076	Rialto Th., Louisville, KY	3/24	1921	$ 18,000	
1085	Rivoli Th., Columbia, SC	2/9	1921	$ 5,250	
1088	Lucas Th., Savannah, GA	2/19	1921	$ 12,000	
1090	Rialto Th., Birmingham, AL	2/12	1921	$ 6,550	
1110	Rialto Th., Fort Worth, TX	2/13	1921	$ 10,450	Blower 12679.
1343½	Metropolitan Th., Atlanta, GA	3/25	1926		Rebuild of opus 1074.
1396	Capitol Th., Louisville, KY	2/5	1928	$ 5,000	Blowers 20496, 22326.
1518	factory showroom, Louisville, KY	2/4	1930		With roll player; possibly sold to a Chicago radio station.

REBUILDING TUNING REPAIRING

PIPE ORGAN SERVICE COMPANY

PROMPT OBLIGING SATISFACTORY CONSCIENTIOUS

DEALERS IN USED AND MANUFACTURERS OF NEW ORGAN PARTS

BUILDERS OF THE CHAMPION SUCTORIAN

H. T. DEPUE, MANAGER 3318 SPRAGUE STREET **TELEPHONE KENWOOD 2991**

OMAHA

The Pipe Organ Service Company was begun in Omaha, Nebraska in 1923 by former Barton employees Harold T. Depue and Richard W. Dirksen.[1] As the company's name implied, their primary business was service, although they did secure a contract in 1925 for a new two-manual organ to be installed in an Omaha theatre being built by W. H. Creal and Son.[2]

In 1927 Dirksen left to join the Bennett Organ Company and Depue later represented Hillgreen-Lane in Omaha. Depue was quite a recluse who never owned a car nor drove, preferring instead to walk or to take the train or streetcar.[3]

Before forming the Pipe Organ Service Company, Depue played an interesting role in organ history: he installed a two-manual organ in the Apollo Theatre in Princeton, Illinois. Although this organ was assembled from secondhand parts and carried no nameplate, it was the first organ ever played by the late organ virtuoso Virgil Fox.[4]

POWERS

In 1969 organist Edith Steele recalled playing a two-manual drawknob Powers organ installed in the Crystal Stairs Theatre, Joliet, Illinois around 1909. She thought it was built in Chicago[1] but the author has yet to discover a firm by that name operating in Chicago (or anywhere else) during that era. There was a Cincinnati builder named Hiram Powers whose business was founded in 1819[2] and it is possible that the Crystal Stairs organ was a secondhand transplanted example of his work.

The Reuter Organ Company

Reuter Electro-Pneumatic Pipe Organs

Lawrence Kansas

OSKAR L. RASMUSSEN
FACTORY REPRESENTATIVE

SIBLEY G. PEASE
SALES REPRESENTATIVE
RES. 322 SO. MANSFIELD AVE.
PHONE WHITNEY 2814

LOS ANGELES OFFICE
187 SOUTH ALVARADO ST
FITZROY 3375

Adolph C. Reuter was born in Pomeroy, Ohio on December 3, 1880. In June of 1901 he began working for the Barckhoff Organ Company in Pomeroy and in March of 1905 moved to Mason City, Iowa to become associated with William Verney, a Barckhoff representative. From June 1908 to October 1912 Reuter was shop superintendent for Wicks in Highland, Illinois, leaving there to join Casavant in South Haven, Michigan. In January of 1913 he left Casavant and joined Pilcher as shop superintendent.[1]

Meanwhile, back in Highland, a businessman named Earl Schwarz was promoting the idea of organizing a company to build pipe organs. He interested the following people in his enterprise: Henry Jost, a photographer; Cullie Reuger, an insurance agent; and Brink Hamel, a dentist in nearby Trenton, Illinois, and eventually sold $50,000 worth of stock. This group sought the services of A. C. Reuter, whom they had known during the period he was at Wicks, and the Reuter-Schwarz Organ Company was born in April of 1917. Reuter asked his nephew, Albert G. Sabol, Sr., to join the new company. Sabol had worked for his uncle at Wicks and was at Casavant in South Haven when the Reuter-Schwarz company was formed. Reuter also persuaded another Casavant man, Jake Schaeffer, to join the new company as the voicer. The other original employees were: woodworker E. J. "Pat" Netzer, who had worked under Reuter at Wicks; console builder Frank Jost, who was Henry Jost's brother; and pipe maker William Zweifle.[2]

The original factory was a building 30′ x 80′ in Trenton, Illinois. It was heated by exhaust steam from the adjacent power company in exchange for the organ shop's wood shavings![3] When Casavant closed their South Haven plant in 1918, much of the machinery, pipe-making equipment and other materials were acquired by Reuter-Schwarz.[4] By 1919 the company had outgrown its small building in Trenton and needed to move. The university town of Lawrence, Kansas was selected and the company was incorporated in September of 1919, putting a second issue of stock worth $90,000 on the market.[5] The last organ built in Trenton, opus 26, was actually the first Reuter-Schwarz instrument built for a theatre.[6] By March of 1920 the move was completed and organs were being built in the Lawrence facility.[7] During the move Mr. Reuter discovered that Earl Schwarz had not been totally honest in stock manipulations and Schwarz soon left.[8] The company name was changed to the Reuter Organ Company in July of 1920 and at the same time the title of

Reuter executives confer on a new instrument about to be built. Left to right are Henry Jost, A. C. Reuter, John Selig, C. B. Russell and A. G. Sabol, Jr.

The 2/7 Reuter at radio station KMA in Shenandoah, Iowa was one of the few Reuter organs ever equipped with a player mechanism. This example played ordinary 88-note player piano rolls.

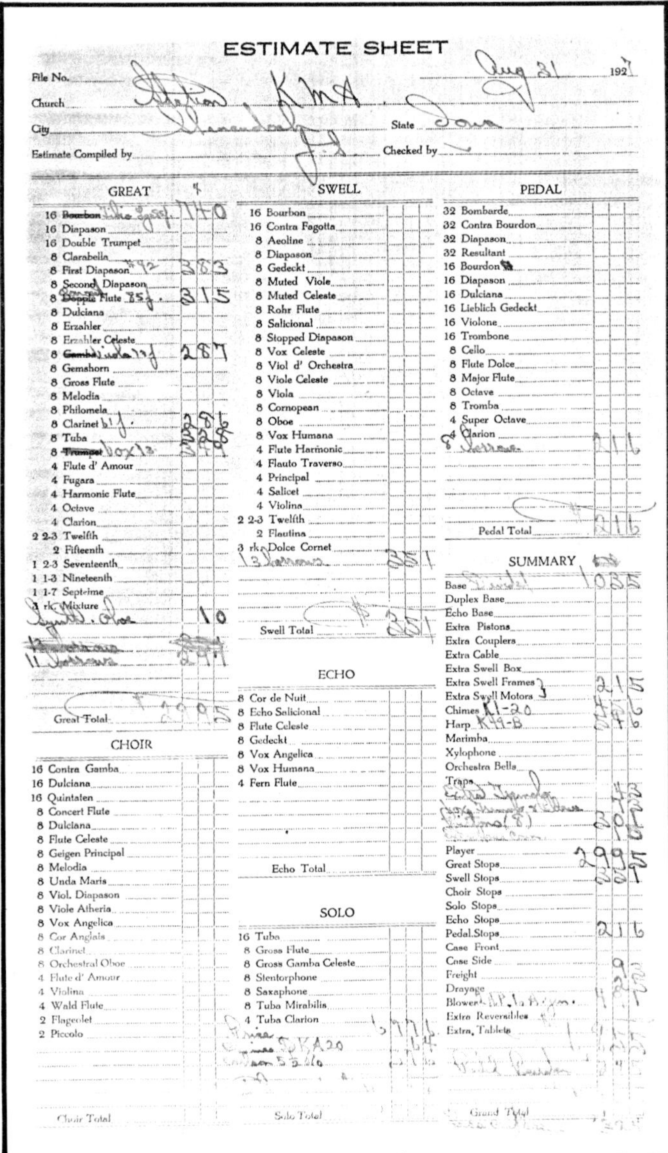

ESTIMATE SHEET

File No. ______ Aug 31 192[7]

Church Station KMA

City Shenandoah State Iowa

Estimate Compiled by ______ Checked by ______

GREAT

16 ~~Bourbon~~	740	
16 Diapason		
16 Double Trumpet		
8 Clarabella		
8 First Diapason	383	
8 Second Diapason		
8 ~~Doppel~~ Flute	315	
8 Dulciana		
8 Erzahler		
8 Erzahler Celeste		
8 ~~Gamba~~	287	
8 Gemshorn		
8 Gross Flute		
8 Melodia		
8 Philomela		
8 Clarinet		
8 Tuba		
8 ~~Trumpet~~		
4 Flute d' Amour		
4 Fugara		
4 Harmonic Flute		
4 Octave		
4 Clarion		
2 2-3 Twelfth		
2 Fifteenth		
1 2-3 Seventeenth		
1 1-3 Nineteenth		
1 1-7 Septeime		
3 rk. Mixture		
	10	
Great Total	2995	

CHOIR

16 Contra Gamba		
16 Dulciana		
16 Quintaten		
8 Concert Flute		
8 Dulciana		
8 Flute Celeste		
8 Geigen Principal		
8 Melodia		
8 Unda Maris		
8 Viol. Diapason		
8 Viole Atheria		
8 Vox Angelica		
8 Cor Anglais		
8 Clarinet		
8 Orchestral Oboe		
4 Flute d' Amour		
4 Violina		
4 Wald Flute		
2 Flageolet		
2 Piccolo		
Choir Total		

SWELL

16 Bourbon		
16 Contra Fagotta		
8 Aeoline		
8 Diapason		
8 Gedeckt		
8 Muted Viole		
8 Muted Celeste		
8 Rohr Flute		
8 Salicional		
8 Stopped Diapason		
8 Vox Celeste		
8 Viol d' Orchestra		
8 Viole Celeste		
8 Viola		
8 Cornopean		
8 Oboe		
8 Vox Humana		
4 Flute Harmonic		
4 Flauto Traverso		
4 Principal		
4 Salicet		
4 Violina		
2 2-3 Twelfth		
2 Flautina		
3 rk. Dolce Cornet		
13	351	
Swell Total	351	

ECHO

8 Cor de Nuit		
8 Echo Salicional		
8 Flute Celeste		
8 Gedeckt		
8 Vox Angelica		
8 Vox Humana		
4 Fern Flute		
Echo Total		

SOLO

16 Tuba		
8 Gross Flute		
8 Gross Gamba Celeste		
8 Stentorphone		
8 Saxaphone		
8 Tuba Mirabilis		
4 Tuba Clarion		
Solo Total		

PEDAL

32 Bombarde		
32 Contra Bourdon		
32 Diapason		
32 Resultant		
16 Bourdon		
16 Diapason		
16 Dulciana		
16 Lieblich Gedeckt		
16 Violone		
16 Trombone		
8 Cello		
8 Flute Dolce		
8 Major Flute		
8 Octave		
8 Tromba		
4 Super Octave		
4 Clarion		
8	216	
Pedal Total	216	

SUMMARY

Base	1035	
Duplex Base		
Echo Base		
Extra Pistons		
Extra Couplers		
Extra Cable		
Extra Swell Box		
Extra Swell Frames	215	
Extra Swell Motors		
Chimes K1-20		
Harp K49-B		
Marimba		
Xylophone		
Orchestra Bells		
Traps		
Player	2995	
Great Stops		
Swell Stops	351	
Choir Stops		
Solo Stops		
Echo Stops		
Pedal Stops	216	
Case Front		
Case Side		
Freight		
Drayage		
Blower		
Extra Reversibles		
Extra Tablets		
Grand Total		

The Reuter factory prepared cost analysis sheets to determine accurately the selling price of each instrument. This example for opus 270 is in John Selig's handwriting. Reuter was apparently not very interested in selling player attachments; their cost of $2,995 for an ordinary 88-note player was outlandish compared to the $1,000 or so charged by other builders for the same equipment.

Reuter theatre organs rarely used relays; most switching was done via the key action in the console. This matrix style of switching was used by several other firms including Moller and Kilgen.

A. C. Reuter, left, advises Edgar Jost, son of Henry Jost, on the voicing of a new trumpet. Edgar Jost became head voicer in the early 1930s when Jake Schaeffer left the company. Schaeffer had been responsible for the excellent quality of Reuter voicing throughout the 1920s.[25]

president was transferred from Mr. Reuter to Henry Jost.[9] Mr. Sabol later assumed the presidency from 1932 to 1934.[10] These title changes were accomplished with no exchange of money or stock so that each of the principal officers could share the honor of the firm's presidency.[11]

Reuter sales increased rapidly in the 1920s. By 1928 sales were four times what they had been in 1920 and a new 10,000 square foot office building was constructed adjacent to the factory.[12] Theatre organs accounted for about 20% of Reuter's business from 1924 to 1929 and the majority of these sales were the work of W. G. Redmond, the Dallas representative. Redmond's specifications rarely called for traps or percussions although all his theatre sales were unit organs. Most of these were voiced on only 5″ wind pressure, the Reuter standard at that time for its church organs. It is interesting to note that most Reuter theatre installations outside Texas did contain traps and percussions and were voiced on pressures up to 10″.[13]

Starting with opus one, Reuter used electropneumatic action consistently. The first four theatre jobs were straight organs with ventil chests; all other theatre work was unit with pouchboard-style chests. Reuter built everything in their organs except blowers, which usually came from Spencer or Zephyr. They even built their own manual keys and chest magnets.[14] The magnets were similar to Reisner latch-cap styles but suffered from troublesome armatures whose coverings would frequently come loose. Virtually all the Reuter theatre organs featured "eliptical" (sic) consoles, as the factory preferred to call them, and most had roll tops. They had mechanical tripper-style combination actions attached to the circular rows of stops via various linkages. Reuter trap actions were designed by chief engineer A. G. Sabol and most were similar to Robert-Morton designs, with hingeless pneumatics and center-pivoted strikers. Others such as the triangle and cymbal had interior power pneumatics pulling linkages through bushed holes, not unlike a Wurlitzer switchstack.[15]

Two Reuter theatre-style organs were equipped with automatic players: opus 444 had an Estey player[16] and opus 270 had a Reuter-made player which used 88-note rolls. The mechanism was simply a Reuter manual key action activated by vacuum pneumatics. Very few Reuter organs were equipped with players, probably because of their outrageous cost and because they used ordinary 88-note rolls instead of special organ rolls.[17] Reuter did purchase a roll perforator and player system designed by Fred Meunier of Denver but never did use it.[18] This perforator was eventually acquired by Durrell Armstrong of Wichita, Kansas.[19]

The last Reuter theatre-style organ was installed in the residence of Dr. John Brinkley in Del Rio, Texas. Brinkley gained notoriety in the 1920s for his claims of being able to rejuvenate men with goat glands and at one time

2/5 REUTER THEATRE ORGAN, OPUS 266

This is a typical example of the most popular model sold by Dallas Reuter representative W. G. Redmond.

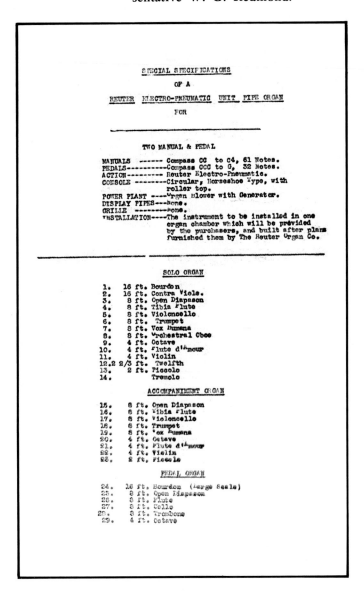

SPECIAL SPECIFICATIONS

OF A

REUTER ELECTRO-PNEUMATIC UNIT PIPE ORGAN

FOR

TWO MANUAL & PEDAL

MANUALS ------ Compass CC to C4, 61 Notes.
PEDALS----------Compass CCC to G, 32 Notes.
ACTION--------- Reuter Electro-Pneumatic.
CONSOLE --------Circular, Horseshoe Type, with roller top.
POWER PLANT ----Organ Blower with Generator.
DISPLAY PIPES---None.
GRILLE ---------None.
INSTALLATION----The instrument to be installed in one organ chamber which will be provided by the purchasers, and built after plans furnished them by The Reuter Organ Co.

SOLO ORGAN

1. 16 ft. Bourdon
2. 16 ft. Contra Viole.
3. 8 ft. Open Diapason
4. 8 ft. Tibia Flute
5. 8 ft. Violoncello
6. 8 ft. Trumpet
7. 8 ft. Vox Humana
8. 8 ft. Orchestral Oboe
9. 4 ft. Octave
10. 4 ft. Flute d'Amour
11. 4 ft. Violin
12. 2 2/3 ft. Twelfth
13. 2 ft. Piccolo
14. Tremolo

ACCOMPANIMENT ORGAN

15. 8 ft. Open Diapason
16. 8 ft. Tibia Flute
17. 8 ft. Violoncello
18. 8 ft. Trumpet
19. 8 ft. Vox Humana
20. 4 ft. Octave
21. 4 ft. Flute d'Amour
22. 4 ft. Violin
23. 2 ft. Piccolo

PEDAL ORGAN

24. 16 ft. Bourdon (Large Scale)
25. 8 ft. Open Diapason
26. 8 ft. Flute
27. 8 ft. Cello
28. 8 ft. Trombone
29. 4 ft. Octave

ACCESSORIES

Balanced Expression Pedal
Balanced Crescendo Pedal, Adjustable.
Crescendo Indicator.
Organist's Bench with Music Compartment.

SUMMARY

Speaking Registers - --- 28
Total Speaking Pipes----- 365
Accessories--------------- 4

ANALYSIS

The following analysis will indicate just what sets of pipes the organ will contain and the pitches at which they will be used on the different manuals and pedal.

	PITCH	PIPES	SOLO	ACCOMP.	PEDAL
BOURDON	16'	97	16-8-4-2 2/3-2	8-4	16-8
VIOLONCELLO	8'	73	16-8-4	8-4	8
OPEN DIAPASON	8	73	8-4	8-4	8-4
TRUMPET	8	61	8	8	8
VOX HUMANA	8	61	8	8	
ORCHESTRAL OBOE	8	Syn.	8		

he was only narrowly defeated in the Kansas gubernatorial election. He operated a radio station in Ciudad Acuna, Mexico, across the border from Del Rio, where he could broadcast his claims without interference from the FCC! The organ was featured on some of these broadcasts.[20] Brinkley also contracted with Reuter to supply carved walnut paneling for the walls and ceilings of his home at a cost of $9,877, over $2,000 more than the organ itself had cost.[21]

The Reuter firm continues in business today with current opus numbers in the 2,000s. They have touched the theatre organ market again in 1983 by supplying replicas of a Wurlitzer brass trumpet, tuba mirabilis and manual keyboards with second touch.[22]

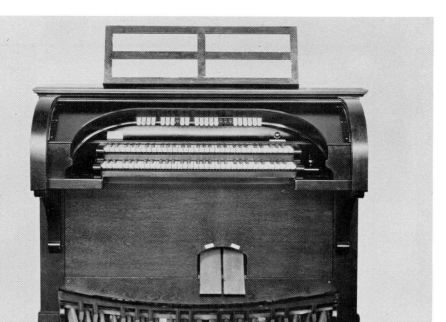

A gallery of Reuter theatre consoles. Most Reuter consoles, including their horseshoe models, had roll tops. An attractive exception (upper left) is the beautiful Moorish design in the Uptown Theatre in Wichita, Kansas.

4/14 REUTER THEATRE ORGAN, OPUS 250
Arcadia Theatre, Dallas, Texas

Memorandum of Agreement entered into this 21st day of May, 1927, by and between THE REUTER ORGAN COMPANY, Lawrence, Kansas, party of the first part, and Louis L. Dent Inc., Dallas, Texas, party of the second part, witnesseth:

1. The party of the first part agrees to build for and erect in the Arcadia Theatre, in the city of Dallas, Texas, a pipe organ in accordance with the annexed specification, complete and ready for use on or about the 15th day of September 1927 subject, however, to delays from fire, water, strikes or causes not within the control of the first party.

2 The party of the first part warrants that said completed organ shall be free from defects in either material or workmanship, and undertakes to replace or repair any such defective parts at its own expense during the term of one year after the completion of said instrument upon written notice thereof. This warranty does not include tuning, regulating or care of said instrument.

3. The party of the second part hereby accepts this contract and requests the party of the first part to proceed with the building of said organ and to construct and erect the same and agrees to accept the completed instrument and pay therefor the sum of Eleven thousand, six hundred, seventyfive ($11,675.30) Dollars in funds as follows:

Upon the signing of this contract the sum of ——— Dollars.

On presentation of bill of lading or other evidence of shipment of the organ or principal parts thereof the sum of ——— Dollars

In the event that the said organ be ready for shipment and the party of the second part is not ready to arrange for the installation of the same as heretofore provided, there shall become due and payable within thirty days after notice has been given to the party of the second part that the said organ is ready for delivery and installation an additional sum which will bring the total payments to seventy-five per cent of the purchase price.

Upon the complete installation of said organ, the balance of said purchase price, to-wit, the sum of ——— Dollars

Upon installation of organ, the sum of $2,075.30. Balance of purchase price to be payable in 24 equal monthly installments, for which notes will be given bearing 6% interest.

4. That immediately upon the complete installation of said organ the said second party will with and in the presence of the representative of the first party examine said organ and if in accord with this contract will then give acceptance of the same.

5. Said second party agrees to provide proper space and a level floor therein for the said organ, also to furnish a suitable room or enclosure for the organ blower, and the necessary airtight galvanized metal piping to convey the organ wind from the blower to the organ and console, constructed and installed in accordance with the directions by the party of the first part. The said second party further agrees to have the blower motor connected with the service wires, to provide the required switches, to furnish and install iron conduits for organ cables and wires, if demanded by local conditions, to supply light, heat and power during the period of the organ installation, if and when needed, and to give the party of the first part exclusive use of said building for the purpose of tuning and regulating said organ .... days prior to its completion. The second party agrees to pay all freight and drayage on the organ, and parts thereof, as well as hoisting charges, if any.

6. The party of the second part agrees to assume all responsibility for said organ and parts thereof, covering loss or damage from the time the said organ or parts thereof have been delivered to the church, and will, until the above-mentioned purchase price is fully satisfied, keep the said organ and parts thereof fully insured against any and all loss or damage, such insurance to protect both parties hereto as their interests may appear and be established.

7. Said second party agrees that it will execute and deliver such other and further papers herein as may be proper or necessary to give full legal force and protection hereto in said state where such instrument is or is to be installed.

8. That said instrument is to be and remain personal property, and the title to and ownership thereof shall continue to vest in said first party until such time as the contract price shall be fully paid in cash or its equivalent.

9. It is mutually agreed that in the event the second party shall fail to comply with the terms of this contract, or any of them that all sums herein paid to said first party shall at its election be considered and treated as liquidated damages for the breach hereof, and this first party shall have the right to remove and take to itself said organ or portion thereof wheresoever the same may be.

10. It is agreed that there are no verbal or other agreements or representations except as contained herein and the same and any changes whatsoever must be in writing and signed by the party of the first part.

11. This contract is subject to the acceptance and approval by an executive officer of the said first party.

Louis L. Dent Inc.,
by [illegible]
President

THE REUTER ORGAN COMPANY
By [illegible]
[illegible]

DETAILS OF CONSTRUCTION

(Forming part of Contract)

CONSOLE to be the very latest pattern, interior of same to be finished in Mahogany. The Reuter improved stop key tablet register system for all speaking stops and couplers, to be used. Console to be placed in position most suitable for same, and approved by the purchaser.

CASE WORK, when such is included in the contract, is to be of native wood, finished and designed in harmony with the architecture of the building.

FRONT PIPES, when such are included in the contract, are to be decorated in Gold Bronze.

BUILDING FRAME supporting bellows, wind chests, pipes and action, shall be of sufficient strength to resist all tendency to settling or derangement.

BELLOWS to be of ample size to supply the fullest legitimate demand, stoutly framed and double-leathered.

WIND-CHESTS to be constructed and arranged with a view to solidity, and of such dimensions as shall afford ample speaking room for every pipe; the valve work being made on the very latest and most approved principles.

KEYBOARD AND REGISTERS to be so arranged as to give the greatest facility to the performer; the manuals to be ivory-faced and projecting. Pedals to be the A.G.O. Pattern, capped with light and dark hard wood. Reuter improved ivory stop and coupler stop key tablets to be used.

ACTION to be the Reuter Electro-Pneumatic Action, the most simple, reliable, and direct attainable, thoroughly bushed to prevent noise.

WOOD PIPES AND WOOD WORK to be of well seasoned clear lumber of various woods best adapted to the several purposes for which it is used. All wood work and wood pipes protected from dampness or moisture by two coats of Nitro-Cellulose lacquer applied with the air brush.

METAL PIPES to be of the best standard materials; spotted and plain metal used thru-out, except in larger pipes where zinc is necessary for proper strength and support. Our compositions of metal always contain as large a proportion of block tin as the character of the tone to be produced will justify.

CRESCENDO PEDAL brings into use all speaking stops and couplers from the softest to the most powerful, inducing in inverse order. Crescendo is adjustable at the Console.

VOICING to be done after the most approved methods to secure characteristic individuality in the various registers, perfect blending in combinations, as well as brilliancy and strength when the entire power of the instrument is in use.

COMBINATION MOVEMENTS to be operated by Pistons under their respective manuals. The combinations are adjustable instantaneous at the Console. They also register.

POWER PLANT to be a Centrifugal Electric Blower, Motor and Generator Outfit, installed complete, exclusive of necessary wiring, wind conduits, floor or wall cutting.

SPECIAL SPECIFICATIONS

OF A

REUTER ELECTRO-PNEUMATIC PIPE ORGAN

FOR

ARCADIA THEATRE, - - - - - - - - - - DALLAS, TEXAS

Four Manual and Pedals, with Echo Organ

MANUALS	Compass CC to C4, 61 notes.
PEDALS	Compass CCC to G, 32 notes.
ACTION	Reuter Electro-Pneumatic, Unit.
STOP ACTION	Controlled by tilting Stop-Keys.
CONSOLE	Four Manual, with roller top.
GRILLE WORK	None.
CASE WORK	None, except Console.
INSTALLATION	The instrument to be installed in three organ chambers which will be provided by the purchasers, and built after plans furnished them by The Reuter Organ Company.
POWER PLANT	Steel Orgoblo, with Generator.
WIND PRESSURE	10".

SOLO ORGAN

1. 16 ft. Tibia Major
2. 8 ft. Open Diapason
3. 8 ft. Viol d'Orchestrie
4. 8 ft. Viol Celeste
5. 8 ft. Tibia Clausa
6. 8 ft. Trumpet
7. 8 ft. Clarinet
8. 8 ft. Kinura
9. 8 ft. Vox Humana
10. 4 ft. Tibia Clausa
11. 2 ft. Piccolo

GREAT ORGAN

12. 16 ft. Tibia Major
13. 16 ft. Bourdon
14. 16 ft. Contra Viole
15. 8 ft. Open Diapason
16. 8 ft. Salicional
17. 8 ft. Viol d'Orchestrie
18. 8 ft. Viol Celeste
19. 8 ft. Clarinet
20. 8 ft. Trumpet
21. 8 ft. Kinura
22. 8 ft. Vox Humana
23. 8 ft. Orchestral Oboe
24. 8 ft. Tibia Clausa
25. 8 ft. Concert Flute
26. 4 ft. Octave

GREAT ORGAN Con.

27. 4 ft. Salicet Amber
28. 4 ft. Violin "
29. 4 ft. Celeste "
30. 4 ft. Clarion Red
31. 4 ft. Vox Humana "
32. 4 ft. Tibia Clausa white
33. 4 ft. Flute d'Amour "
34. 2 2/3 Twelfth "
35. 2 ft. Piccolo "
36. 1 3/5 Tierce "
37. - -- Orchestra Bells Black
38. - -- Harp Celeste "
39. - -- Xylophone "
40. - -- Chimes "
41. - -- Main Tremolo
42. - -- Solo Tremolo
43. - -- Tibia Tremolo
44. - -- Vox Humana Tremolo

ACCOMPANIMENT ORGAN

45. 16 ft. Bourdon white
46. 16 ft. Contra Viole Amber
47. 8 ft. Open Diapason Blue
48. 8 ft. Salicional Amber
49. 8 ft. Viol d'Orchestrie "
50. 8 ft. Viol Celeste "
51. 8 ft. Clarinet Red
52. 8 ft. Trumpet "
53. 8 ft. Kinura "
54. 8 ft. Vox Humana "
55. 8 ft. Tibia Clausa white
56. 8 ft. Concert Flute "
57. 4 ft. Octave Blue
57. 4 ft. Salicet Amber
58. 4 ft. Violin "
59. 4 ft. Celeste "
60. 4 ft. Vox Humana Red
61. 4 ft. Tibia Clausa white
62. 4 ft. Flute d'Amour "
63. 2 2/3 Twelfth "
64. 2 ft. Piccolo "
65. - -- Harp Celeste Black
66. - -- Snare Drum, tap "
67. - -- Snare Drum, roll "
68. - -- Tambourine "
69. - -- Castanet "
70. - -- Tom Tom "
71. - -- Chinese Block "

ECHO ORGAN

72. 8 ft. Tibia Clausa
73. 8 ft. Viole Atheria
74. 8 ft. Melodia
75. 8 ft. Vox Humana
76. 4 ft. Tibia Clausa
77. 4 ft. Viole
78. 4 ft. Forn Flute
79. 2 ft. Piccolo
80. - -- Echo Tremolo

PEDAL ORGAN

81. 16 ft. Tibia Major white
82. 16 ft. Bourdon white
83. 8 ft. Open Diapason Blue
84. 8 ft. Salicional Amber
85. 8 ft. Cello "
86. 8 ft. Clarinet Red
87. 8 ft. Trombone "
88. 8 ft. Kinura "
89. 8 ft. Tibia Clausa white
90. 8 ft. Flute "
91. 4 ft. Octave Blue
92. 4 ft. String Amber
93. - -- Bass Drum Black
94. - -- Cymbal "
95. - -- Tympani "
96. - -- Triangle "

ECHO PEDAL ORGAN

97. 8 ft. Tibia Clausa white
98. 8 ft. Viole Atheria Amber
99. - -- Chimes Black

COMBINATION MOVEMENTS, Operated by Pistons under their respective Manuals. Adjustable at Keyboard and visibly affecting Stop-Keys.

Six, acting on Solo Division.
Six, acting on Great Division.
Six, acting on Accompaniment Division.
Four, acting on Echo Division.
(x)Six Master Pistons, acting on all stops.
Six, acting on Pedal Division

TOE PISTONS

Sforzando Piston.
Six Pedal Combination Pistons marked (x)
Auto Horn
Bird Call
Crash Cymbal

COMBINATION COUPLERS:

Pedal Combinations to Solo.
Pedal Combinations to Great.
Pedal Combinations to Accompaniment.

PEDAL MOVEMENTS:

Three Balanced Expression Pedals.
Balanced Crescendo Pedal.

ACCESSORIES:

Sforzando Indicator.
Crescendo Indicator.
Organist's Bench.

SUMMARY

Speaking Stops	94
Speaking Pipes	~~1010~~ 1022
Tremolos	5
Toe Pistons	9
Accessories	3
Traps	12

ANALYSIS, Main Organ

	Pipes	Pitch	Solo	Great	Acc.	Pedal
TIBIA CLAUSA	85	16'	16-8-4	16-8-4	8-4	16-8
BOURDON	101 97	16'	2	16-8-4-2:2/3-2-1:3/5	16-8-4-2	16-8
SALICIONAL	73	8'		8-4	8-4	8
VIOL D' ORCHESTRIE	73	8'	8	16-8-4	16-8-4	8-4
VIOL CELESTE	61	8'	8	8-4	8-4	
TRUMPET	73	8'	8	8-4	8	8
OPEN DIAPASON	73	8'	8	8-4	8-4	8-4
KINURA	61	8'	8	8	8	8
VOX HUMANA	73	8'	8	8-4	8-4	
CLARINET	61	8'	8	8	8	8
ORCHESTRAL BELLS	37			8		
ORCHESTRAL OBOE	Syn.	8'		8		
XYLOPHONE	37			8		
HARP CELESTE	37			8	8	
BASS DRUM						x
CYMBAL						x
TYMPANI						x
TRIANGLE					x	
SNARE DRUM, TAP					x	
SNARE DRUM ROLL					x	
TAMBOURINE					x	
CASTANET					x	
TOM TOM					x	
CHINESE BLOCK					x	

ANALYSIS, Echo Organ

	Pipes	Pitch	Manual	Pedal
TIBIA CLAUSA	73	8'	8-4	8
VIOLE ATHERIA	73	8'	8-4	8
MELODIA	85	8'	8-4-2	
VOX HUMANA	61	8'	8	
CHIMES	20		8	

Specifications by,

W.G.Redmond,

5531 Vanderbilt Avenue,

Dallas, Texas.

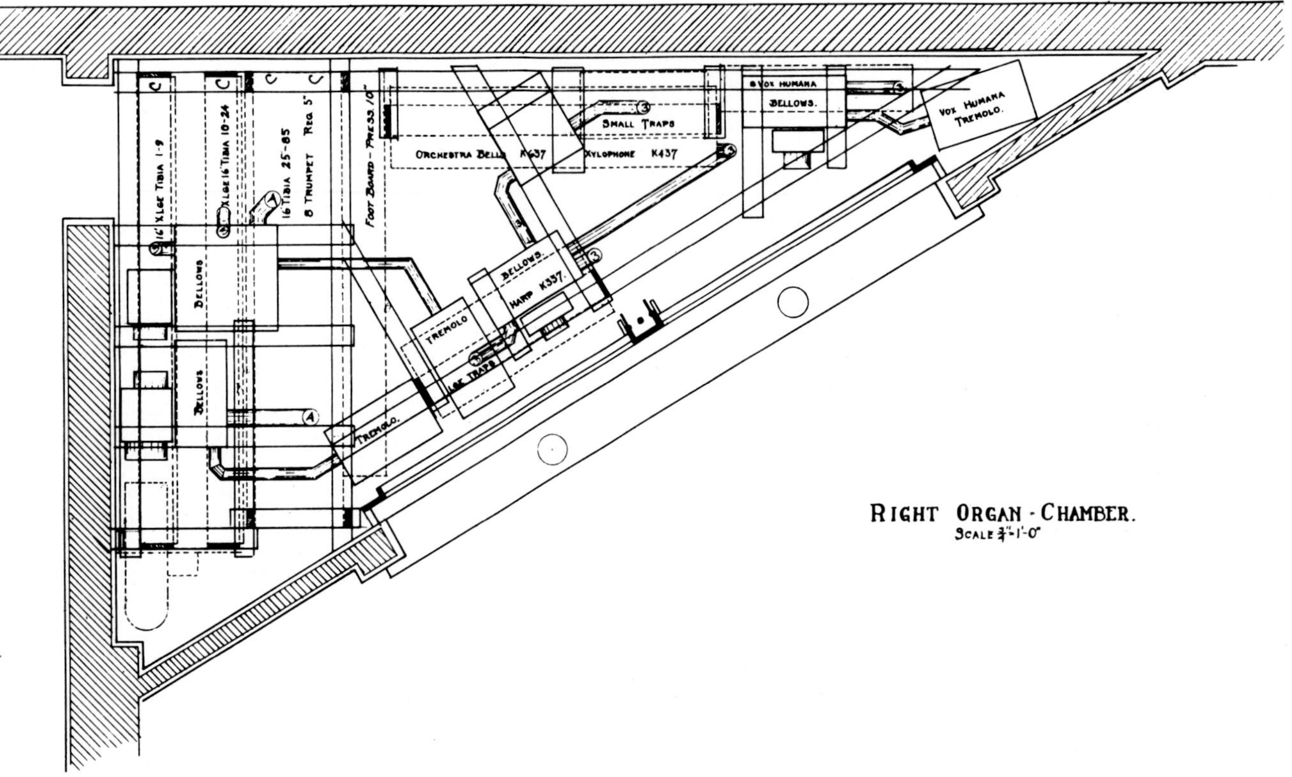

RIGHT ORGAN - CHAMBER.
SCALE ¾"-1'-0"

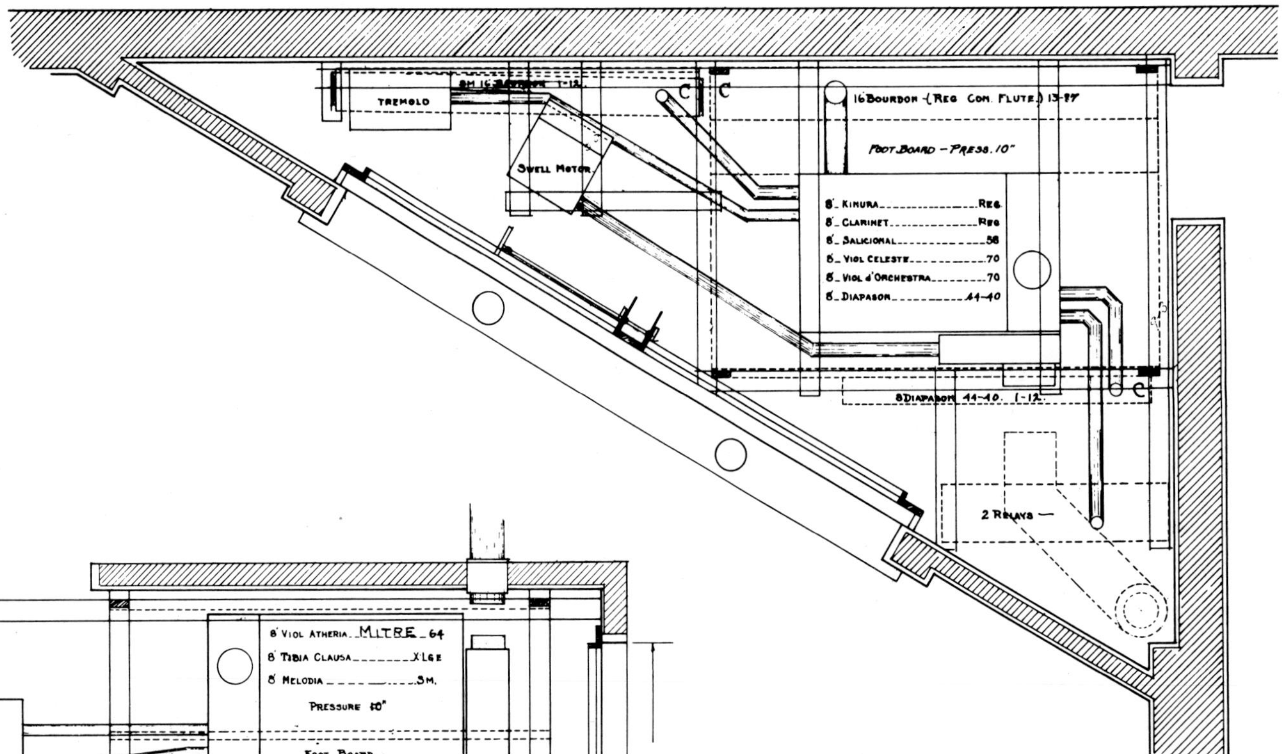

TREMOLO
8H 16 BOURDON 1-12
SWELL MOTOR
16 BOURDON - (REG COM. FLUTE) 13-97
FOOT BOARD - PRESS. 10"
8' KINURA REG
8' CLARINET REG
8' SALICIONAL 58
8' VIOL CELESTE 70
8' VIOL d'ORCHESTRA 70
8' DIAPASON 44-40
8 DIAPASON 44-40. 1-12.
2 RELAYS

8' VIOL ATHERIA MITRE 64
8' TIBIA CLAUSA XLGE
8' MELODIA SM.
PRESSURE 10"
FOOT BOARD.
8' VOX HUMANA REG 61.
X LGE 8' TIBIA CLAUSA. 1-12.
CHIMES K3 20.
6' 0"

FLOOR PLAN ~ LEFT ORGAN.
SCALE ¾"-1'-0"

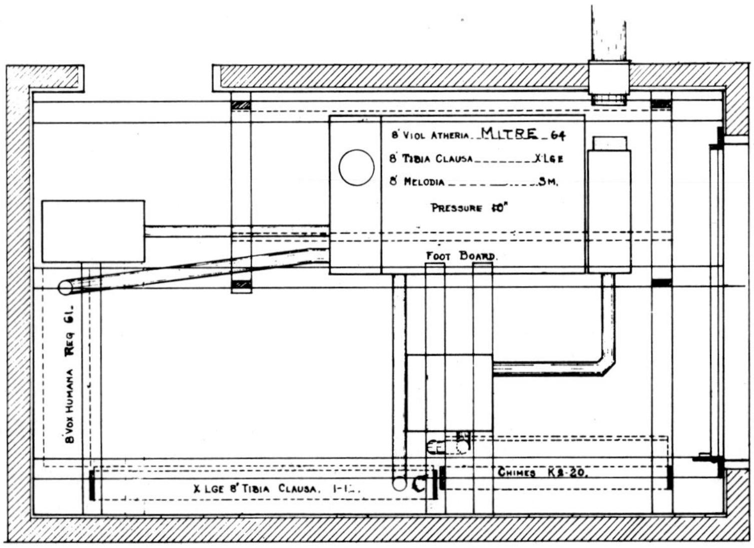

ECHO ORGAN - FLOOR PLAN.
SCALE ¾"-1'-0"

ARCADIA THEATRE ~ DALLAS, TEX.
THE REUTER ORGAN CO - LAWRENCE, KANS.
JULY 18-27 S.S.H. A.C. SABOL.

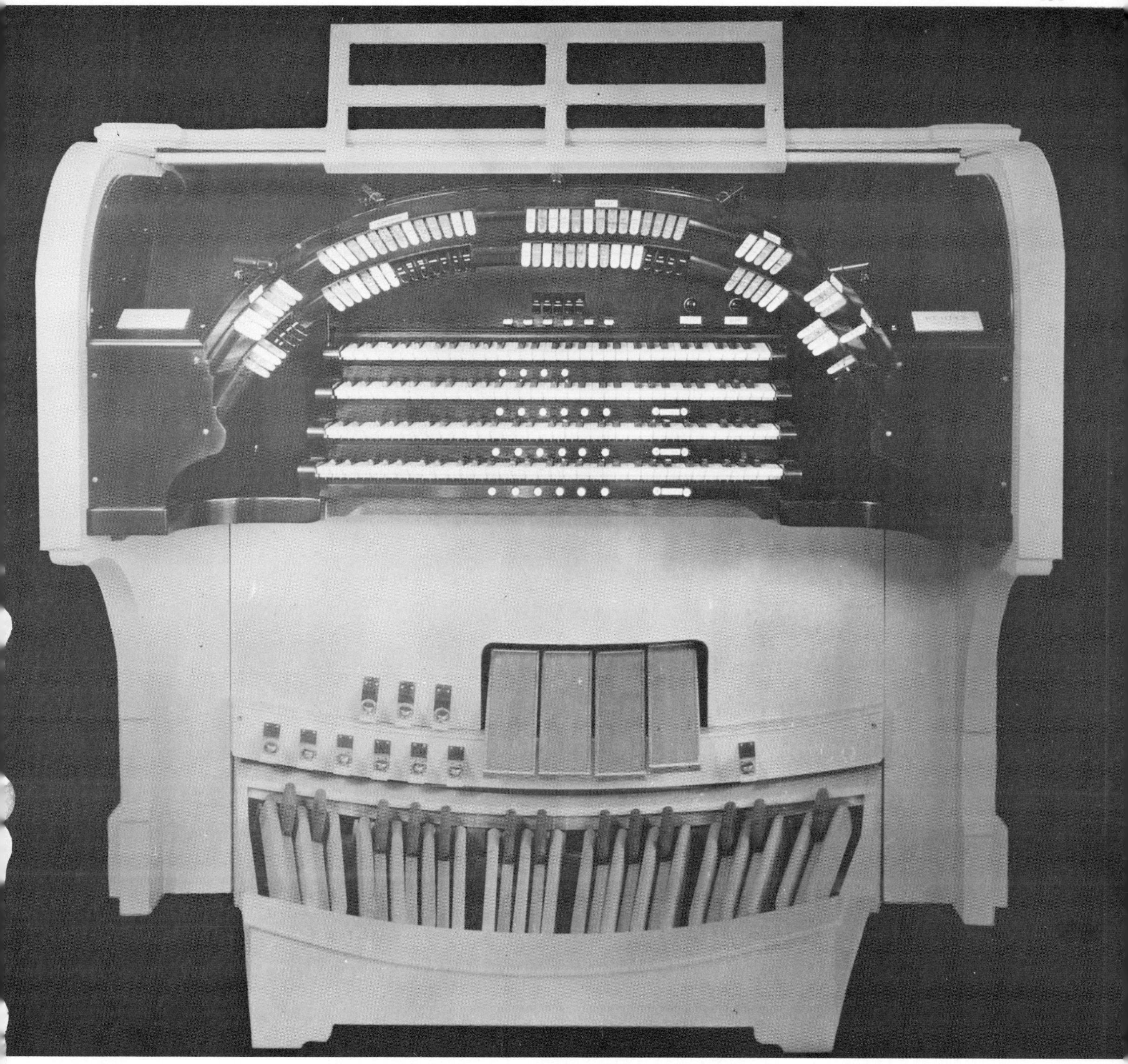

Factory portrait of the Arcadia Theatre's 4/14 Reuter, the largest unified theatre instrument installed by the firm.

The 3/8 Reuter in the Varsity Theatre in Lawrence, Kansas was undoubtedly a company "show" organ. It featured a full complement of traps and percussions and was voiced on 10" wind pressure, the highest ever used by the firm.

UNEQUALED TONE QUALITY
UNEXCELLED MATERIAL
HIGHEST CLASS WORKMANSHIP

All these are found in the
Reuter-Schwarz Organs

REUTER-SCHWARZ ORGAN COMPANY
TRENTON, ILLINOIS
Builders of High Class Pipe Organs

Ad in the April 1917 Diapason *for Reuter-Schwarz, the precursor of the Reuter Organ Company.*

Early Reuter advertisement appearing in the September 1920 Diapason.

REUTER ORGAN COMPANY

BUILDERS OF

The REUTER

ELECTRO-PNEUMATIC PIPE ORGAN

Specifications and Estimates
Cheerfully Submitted Upon Application

612-18 New Hampshire Street
LAWRENCE, KANSAS, U. S. A.

The residence of Dallas representative W. G. Redmond sported a 3/9 Reuter. Mr. Redmond undoubtedly used these surroundings to demonstrate Reuter tone to potential clients and as a result obtained the organ at a substantial discount.

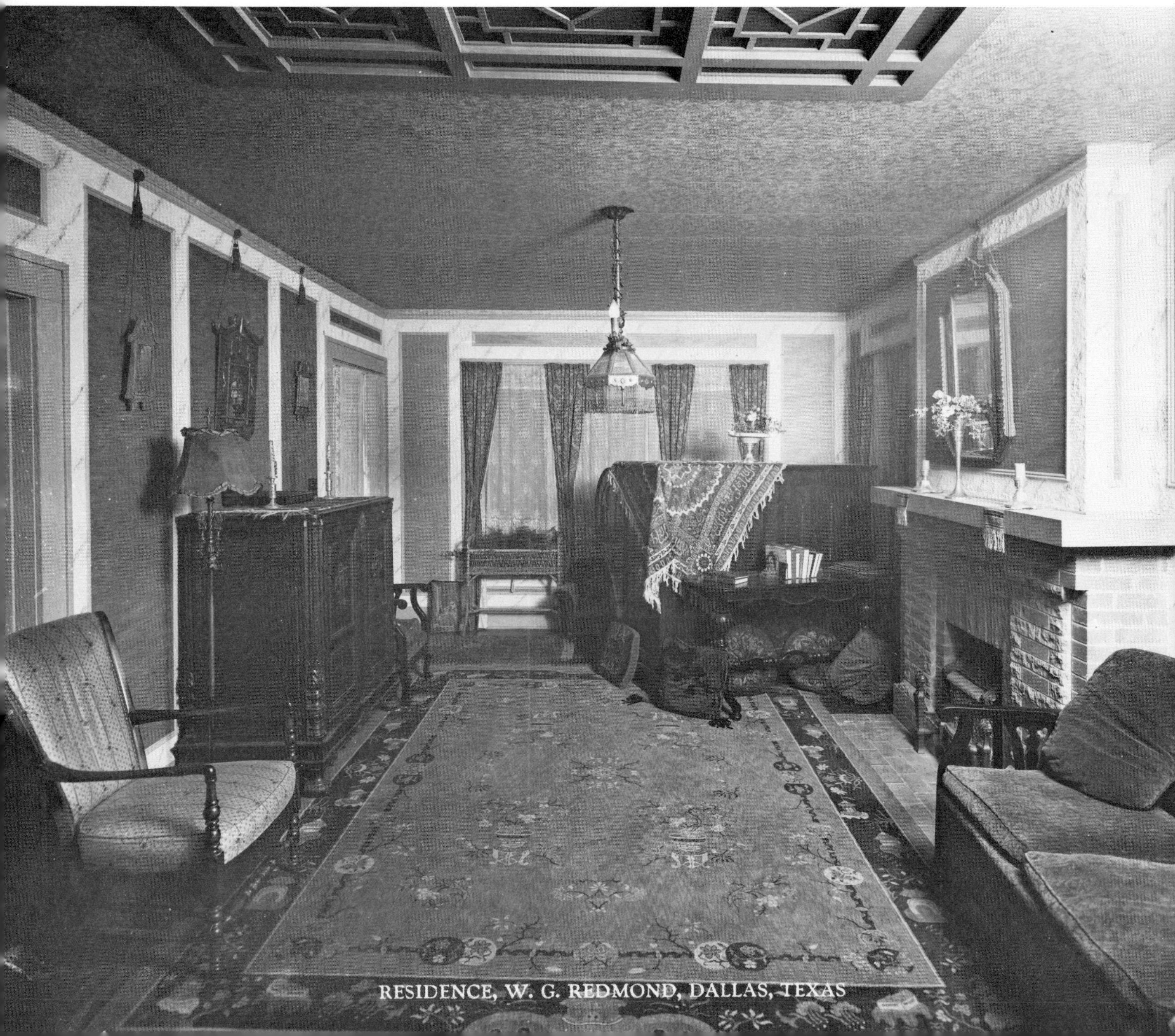
RESIDENCE, W. G. REDMOND, DALLAS, TEXAS

A TRIP THROUGH THE REUTER FACTORY

The Reuter-Schwarz factory in Trenton, Illinois was struck by a tornado in 1917, damaging opus one which was then being erected. The building was soon restored and the damaged parts of the organ remanufactured. As a result, the 2/8 Reuter-Schwarz in Trinity Episcopal Church in Mattoon, Illinois bears opus numbers both one and two.[23]

The office building on the right was added to the Reuter factory in 1928. The building on the left had originally been a shirt factory before Reuter took it over.[24]

(above) Every organ begins its existence in the engineering department where all parts are carefully laid out and drawn to scale. This drafting room occupies the second floor of the 1928 office building.

(below) Leathering department. In the foreground a worker glues gaskets to a chest bottom board while pouch boards are leathered at the rear table.

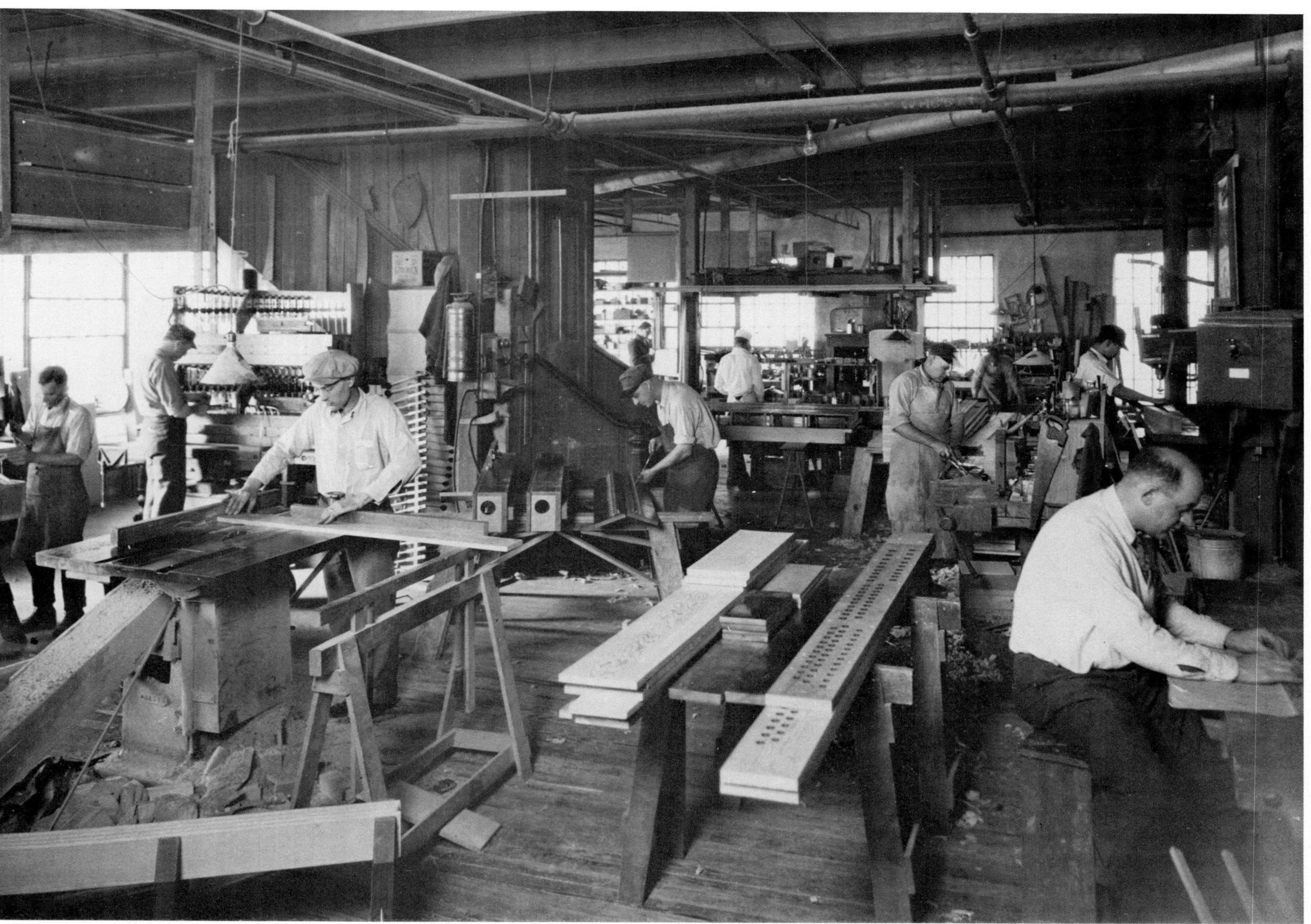

Chests and percussion actions are being built in this section of the woodworking department.

Clockwise from upper left: casting pipe metal into sheets, making zinc bass pipes, glueing wooden pipes, and voicing an 8′ string in the flue pipe department.

(above) One of the four consoles (foreground) being built in the console department is a theatre model, reflecting the fact that from 1924-1929 theatre organs accounted for 20% of Reuter's business.

(below) Chief voicer Jake Schaeffer voices a tuba (left) while a vox humana is being prepared by Willet Wood. The long boots for the vox humana are lying on the table in the foreground.

Each organ is fully assembled before it is shipped. The 30′ x 50′ erecting room was added to the original Wilder Brothers shirt factory building after Reuter purchased it in 1919.[26]

REUTER OPUS LIST

Following is a complete list of this firm's theatre-type installations.

OPUS	LOCATION/CITY/STATE	SIZE	YR	PRICE	BLWR	REMARKS
26	Hippodrome Th., Murphysboro, IL	2/14	1919	$ 4,000.00		Reuter-Schwarz.
33	Royal Th., Little Rock, AR	2/15	1920	$ 4,750.00		Reuter-Schwarz.
113	Strand Th., Wichita Falls, TX	2/9	1924	$ 1,295.00		Additions: 3-rank echo to existing 2/6 Seeburg-Smith; voiced on 4″ wind.
129	Palace Th., El Paso, TX	3/12	1924	$ 8,812.00		Voiced on 4″ and 5″ wind.
130	Queen Th., Bryan, TX	2/4	1924	$ 825.00		Console only.
134	Ideal Th., Corsicana, TX	2/9	1924	$ 950.00		Console only for existing Hillgreen-Lane organ.
135	Palace Th., Corsicana, TX	2/7	1924	$ 1,250.00		New console and tibia for existing Wurlitzer opus 377.
137	Iris Th., Houston, TX	2/5	1925	$ 3,500.00	16708	Voiced on 5″ wind.
140	W. G. Redmond residence, Dallas, TX	2/4	1925	$ 2,175.00		Voiced on 5″ wind.
		3/9	1927	$ 2,800.00		Additions: 5 ranks plus percussions.
140	Parkway Th., Dallas, TX	2/	1927			Console from Redmond residence.
145	Arcadia Th., Tyler, TX	2/5	1925	$ 3,500.00	17231	Voiced on 5″ wind.
149	Auditorium Th., Crockett, TX	2/5	1925	$ 3,500.00	16905	Voiced on 5″ wind.
158	Palace Th., Waco, TX	2/5	1925	$ 3,500.00	17616	¾ hp; order cancelled.
158	Aldine Th., Corpus Christi, TX	2/5	1925		17616	Order cancelled; shipment changed en route to next entry.
158	Broadway Th., Cisco, TX	2/5	1925		17616	
160	Capital Th., New Braunfels, TX	2/6	1925	$ 4,500.00	17457	Voiced on 5″ wind; with xylophone.
172	Queen Th., Abilene, TX	2/6	1925	$ 4,690.00		
176	Strand Th., Wichita Falls, TX	2/10	1926	$ 1,350.00		Additions: new 2-manual console and tibia, 73 pipes, 6″ wind; replace string pipes 13-73.
177	Olympic Th., Wichita Falls, TX	3/7	1926	$ 2,075.00		Additions: 3-manual console and tibia (7″ pressure) for existing 2/6 Wurlitzer, opus 364; center manual for tibia division.
188	Mayflower Th., Florence, KS	2/11	1926	$ 2,830.00	18386	New console and electrify existing Estey organ.
194	Connellee Th., Eastland, TX					Contract changed to next entry.
194	Plaza Th., Paris, TX	2/5	1926	$ 3,850.00		
195	Hotel Orndorff, El Paso, TX	2/6	1926	$ 5,000.00		
199	Orpheum Th., Topeka, KS	2/8	1926			With traps and percussions; unsuccessful; spoke into stage; resold to next entry.
199	Columbia Th., Junction City, KS	2/8	1927	$ 5,000.00	20502	Existing Wurlitzer traded in.

OPUS	LOCATION/CITY/STATE	SIZE	YR	PRICE	BLWR	REMARKS
204	Varsity Th., Lawrence, KS	3/8	1926	$ 12,571.00	19050	Voiced on 10″ wind; with traps & percussions.
204	Dickinson Th., Lawrence, KS	3/8				Installed during 1930s; from Varsity Theatre.
214	Palace Th., Corpus Christi, TX	3/8	1926	$ 7,000.00	19251	Voiced on 7″ wind; with xylophone.
216	unidentified new theatre, Amarillo, TX					Contract changed to next entry.
216	Majestic Th., Wichita Falls, TX	2/7	1926	$ 5,275.00		
218	Mission Th., Amarillo, TX	2/5	1926	$ 3,850.00	19489	¾ hp; voiced on 5″ wind.
224	Booth Th., Independence, KS	2/7	1927	$ 7,716.00	19746	Voiced on 10″ wind; with traps & percussions.
225	Vernon Th., Vernon, TX	2/5	1927	$ 3,850.00		Voiced on 5″ wind.
228	Ellanay Th., El Paso, TX	3/8	1927	$ 7,500.00	19909	3 hp; voiced on 7″ wind; with percussions.
228	Paramount Th., Amarillo, TX	3/8	1931			Moved from Ellanay Th., El Paso, Texas.
236	Florence Th., Los Angeles, CA	2/3	1927	$ 3,500.00		¾ hp; voiced on 5″ wind; located at 7228 South Broadway.
246	Ward Th., Pismo Beach, CA	2/4	1927	$ 3,470.00		Later repossessed.
250	Arcadia Th., Dallas, TX	4/14	1927	$ 11,675.30	20613	5 hp; main on 10″ wind and echo on 7″ wind.
251	Florencita Th., Los Angeles, CA	2/3	1927	$ 2,650.00		¾ hp; voiced on 5″ wind.
256	Colonial Th., Kansas City, MO	2/5	1927	$ 7,032.00	20503	3 hp; voiced on 10″ wind, except vox on 6″ wind; with traps and percussions; later burned.
261	Lyric Th., New Ulm, MN	2/5	1927	$ 6,148.00		Voiced on 10″ wind; with traps.
262	Harlandale Th., San Antonio, TX	2/5	1927	$ 3,325.00		¾ hp; voiced on 5″ wind; later repossessed.
263	Beacon Hill Th., San Antonio, TX	3/9	1927	$ 7,700.00	21009	5 hp; voiced on 10″ wind.
264	Highland Park Th., San Antonio, TX	2/5	1927	$ 3,325.00		¾ hp; voiced on 5″ wind.
265	Alamo Heights Th., San Antonio, TX	2/5	1927	$ 3,325.00		Order cancelled; theatre never built.
266	Main Avenue Th., San Antonio, TX	2/5	1927	$ 3,325.00		Order cancelled; theatre never built.
270	KMA Radio, Shenandoah, IA	2/7	1927	$ 7,686.00	21304	With roll player, harp and chimes; voiced on 7″ wind.
275	Arcadia Th., Harlingen, TX	2/7	1928	$ 5,886.00		3 hp; voiced on 7″ wind, except tibia on 8″.
280	Reuter Studio, Chicago, IL	3/5	1928			Voiced on 6″ wind.
282	Arcadia Th., Ranger, TX	2/6	1928	$ 5,156.00	21604	Voiced on 7″ and 10″ wind.
285	Uptown Th., Wichita, KS	3/5	1928		21657	Voiced on 10″ wind; with traps.
290	Arcadia Th., Temple, TX	2/7	1928	$ 5,379.00	21813	Voiced on 7″ wind.
293	El Morrow Th., Gallup, NM	2/5	1928	$ 5,000.00	21965	3 hp; voiced on 10″ wind; with traps.
310	Uptown Th., Junction City, KS	2/5	1928	$ 3,900.00	22331	Voiced on 8″ wind.
329	Strand Th., Pocatello, ID	2/5	1929	$ 4,000.00		2 hp; voiced on 5″ wind.
444	Dr. John Brinkley residence, Del Rio, TX	2/17	1934	$ 7,725.00	25207	With Estey roll player in separate cabinet.

JAMES N. REYNOLDS

DESIGNER AND BUILDER OF ORGANS

165 FIFTH STREET N. W.

ATLANTA

Reynolds was a builder of "small church and theatre organs" according to a news story in an early 1920s *Diapason*, although the locations of any theatre organs he installed are unknown today. After retiring in 1944 he offered this revealing reminiscence: ". . . Then came, to my mind, the most woeful period of American building—the fluty organ, which led directly to the theatre organ. The real theatre organ was the most terrible thing that ever struck organ building . . ."[1]

Needless to say, not all of us necessarily agree with Mr. Reynolds!

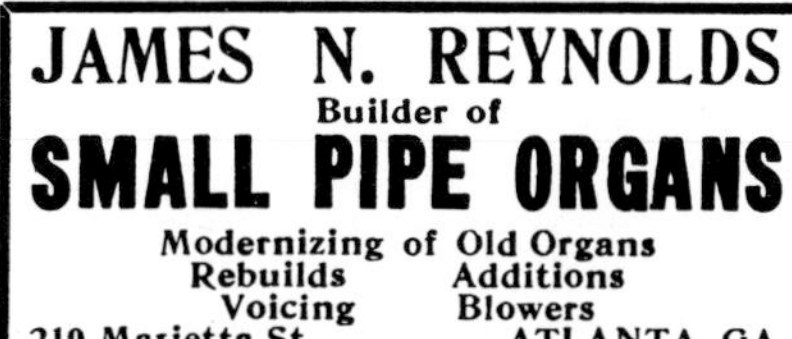

Reynolds advertisement appearing in the June 1921 Diapason.

Builders of
The Robert Morton Organ
The Fotoplayer

FACTORY
VAN NUYS, CALIFORNIA

EXECUTIVE OFFICES
SAN FRANCISCO

Cable Address:"ROMORTON"

SALESROOMS
NEW YORK-CHICAGO
LOS ANGELES

FILM EXCHANGE BLDG.,
1914 SO. VERMONT AVE.,
LOS ANGELES, CALIF.

Before beginning the story of Robert-Morton and its predecessor companies, the author wishes to acknowledge the dedication and scholarship of one man without whose efforts much of the material in this chapter would be lost to history. That man is Tom B'hend, for over twenty years editor of *The Console*. In the early 1960s Tom set about to write a history of the Robert-Morton firm for his magazine. Through diligent research and private detective-like sleuthing Tom located and interviewed virtually every key person alive who had been associated with the firm. This was most opportune for, as of 1986, most of these persons are no longer living. Not only did these individuals share freely of their recollections, but a number of them loaned vintage photographs, with the result that the Robert-Morton factory is photographically the best documented in this book. Tom generously made his entire archive of interviews and photos available, for which the author and the readers of this volume will be eternally grateful.

The Robert-Morton story actually begins in Boston before the turn of the twentieth century. Murray M. Harris (1866-1922) was learning organ building in the factory of George Hutchings, one of the largest organ firms in America at the time. In 1894, at the age of 28, Harris went west to seek his fortune. Landing in Los Angeles, he formed the partnership of Fletcher & Harris with Henry C. Fletcher, a local organist and organ tuner. At first the firm did service work and acted as regional representatives for George Hutchings, for whom they sold a total of four instruments. The building "bug" had bitten the two partners, however, and in 1895 they constructed the first organ ever built in Los Angeles, a 2/12 tracker instrument, in their shop at 325 New High Street. A public recital was held in the organ shop following the organ's completion,[9] [10] a practice which would be repeated often during the later Robert-Morton years because of the local goodwill and publicity thereby generated.

The Fletcher & Harris partnership dissolved in 1897. Fletcher remained in the New High Street shop building organs under his own name before leaving for Phoenix, Arizona in 1898. Harris moved to a building on San Fernando Road and hung out his shingle as the Murray M. Harris Organ Co. He persuaded Edward L. Crome of the Schoenstein firm in San Francisco to move to Los Angeles and superintend the construction of organs in the new shop. Although well-versed in all areas of organ building, Harris chose to concentrate on management, tonal design and voicing.[11] A real entrepreneur, Harris served at one time on sixteen boards of directors of various promotional enterprises and was president of six of them.[12]

The Harris business prospered and moved to a new

Van Nuys Calif. II/18/ 64

Dear Mr. B'hend :

I wish to thank you for the issue of the "Cipher" recently sent me,detailing the history of the Robert Morton Co.

I date my particular interest in this compilation of data to the year I9I2 , when I came out to Los Angeles, having left the W,W.Kimball Co.that year to seek out the organ company I had been told was operating in Los Angeles. I was hired by Mr. E.A.Spencer, in September of that year and remained with the company as draughtsman , and in the late years of their operations as Assist. Superintendant, untill they ceased operations in I929 except for a short period of time in I9I9 when the plant closed, and I returned to the Kimball Co.---and came out again when the company resumed operations.

Your compilation of data brings nostalgic memories to mind, of the years I worked for them. You have certainly gathered together a most interesting and factual chronology of the Robert Morton Organ Co. and its predecessors.Especially interesting to me in this issue are the frontal organ designs which I had so much to do with---which over the years have been forgotten. And your next issues are looked forward to withgreat interest.

The "Big Dance and Barbecue", mentioned on Page 8 featuring a strong land sales campaign and using the new Organ Company Factory as a prime drawing card , was held,NOT on Nov.24/I3 but on April I8/I914 ---- I KNOW, because I had been showing people thru the plant all day, and about 5P.M.I started to leave and go home,and found Mr. Johnson at the door. I said:I'm leaving Mr. Johnson, and he said:Oh No you're not--- see these two Red Heads coming this way? They want to go thru the plant and you're going to show them thru: which I did, then ditched one of them, took the other to the Barbecue and the dance ----AND----4 months later to the day,married her.Just last August I8th.I964, we had our 50th.--- Golden Wedding Anniversary'.

So you see, my early connection with the Rbt.Morton Companybrought me many interesting years working with it and many, many happy married years later.

May I again thank you, and repeat that I think you have done a magnificant work.

Cordially,

Paul S. Carlsted

Robert Morton's chief draftsman and design engineer attests to the scholarly research of Tom B'hend.

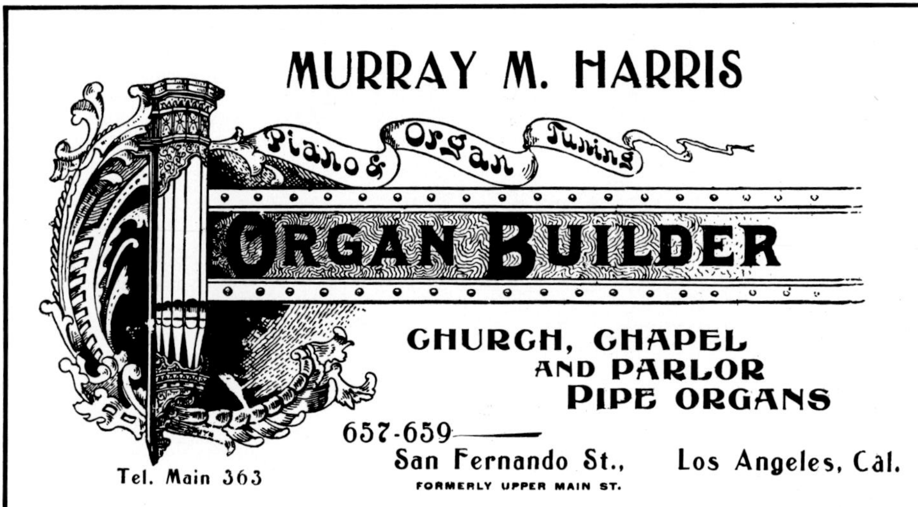

Before business cards came into widespread use, larger size calling cards, often with elaborate engraving, were the norm. This charming example dates from the early teens.

shop at 314½ S. Los Angeles Street in 1900.[13] Additional personnel were sorely needed so Harris began corresponding with William B. Fleming (1849-1940) of the Aeolian Company. In September of 1900[14] Fleming moved to Los Angeles, bringing a group of artisans with him which included electrical expert O. W. Orcutt, console maker Anton Rokus, pipe maker Tommy Ross and voicer F. Bolton. Many of these men had learned their trades in the eastern factories of Roosevelt, Hutchings and Farrand & Votey where craftsmanship was paramount. As a result, few would dispute the claim that Murray M. Harris organs of this period were the "finest in the world."[15]

In 1902 the firm, now numbering over one hundred employees, moved to a large new three-story building at 1515 E. Seventh Street. At about the same time they were awarded the contract for construction of the largest organ in the world, to be displayed at the 1904 Louisiana Purchase Exposition in St. Louis. Harris' finances were inadequate to complete the instrument so other investors assumed control of the firm, renaming it the Los Angeles Art Organ Co. in 1903. Harris' departure left the firm without a tonal director. That void was filled by the arrival of John W. Whitely from England. Whitely was an extremely gifted voicer who had apprenticed with Hope-Jones and, with William Thynne, had developed the imitative strings which would later figure so prominently in theatre organ specifications.[16] [17]

Records disclosed that the factory cost of the St. Louis organ was $105,000![18] Despite enormous financial strain, the company completed several outstanding contracts but a death knell was sounded when the firm was sued by the Aeolian Company for patent infringement of their roll-playing device. Aeolian's patent covered the playing of solo and accompaniment musical parts on one roll. Fleming, who, it will be remembered, came to Harris from the Aeolian Company, devised a mechanism which could play two rolls simultaneously, one containing solo passages and the other the accompaniment. Aeolian's suit proved successful and the Los Angeles Art Organ Co. went out of business in 1905. Fleming and a group of employees purchased the firm's equipment, moved to Hoboken, New Jersey and operated the Electrolian Organ Co. there for

IT seems a peculiarity of Los Angeles that the best and newest inventions and manufactures gravitate toward that city. As a case in point we give an illustration of an organ now nearly completed for the new First Methodist Church, Cor. 6th. and Hill. It is literally a home industry product, manufactured directly from the raw material in the factory of Mr. Murray M. Harris on San Fernando Street. It is of the very best design and workmanship, is twenty five feet wide and thirty five feet high, and contains 2,212 pipes and 46 stops, 2 swell boxes and 11 composition pedals. The smallest pipe is three eighths of an inch long and one eighth of an inch wide, the largest is sixteen feet long and seventeen by twenty inches in diameter. The key desk is so arranged that the organist faces the audience, and the touch is as light as that of a piano. The "Voicing," in which the beauty and sweetness of an organ consists, requires great skill and cultivation. It is in this department that Mr. Harris excels, and, indeed, it is done all by himself, personally.

Mr. MURRAY M. HARRIS, Organ Builder

Electricity furnishes the Motive Power

THE NEW ORGAN NOW IN PROCESS OF CONSTRUCTION FOR THE FIRST METHODIST EPISCOPAL CHURCH OF LOS ANGELES

If——

The Figaro readers will call and inspect this magnificent specimen of the organ builder's art, and the others now in course of construction, they will agree with us that nothing finer could be produced in the world ....

The organ is Romanesque in design, finished in White Oak, and is Exceedingly Beautiful...

Mr. Murray M. Harris
657-659 San Fernando St.
Los Angeles Cal.

Murray M. Harris ad in a local Los Angeles publication, Figaro.

The Los Angeles Art Organ Co.

EBEN SMITH, PRESIDENT AND TREAS.
CHAS. C. LAPHAM, ASS'T TREAS.
C. DUCOMMUN, VICE-PRESIDENT.
W. B. FLEMING, 2ND V.-PRES. AND SUPT.
F. R. COFFIN, SECRETARY.
JOHN G. MOTT, ATTORNEY.

Builders of High-Class
Church, Concert and
Electrolian Chamber Pipe Organs

Largest Organ in the World
THE OFFICIAL CONCERT ORGAN OF THE
LOUISIANA PURCHASE EXPOSITION
Festival Music Hall, St. Louis.

Awarded the Grand Prize and Five Medals.

1515 EAST SEVENTH STREET

Los Angeles, Cal.,

Letterheads of the short-lived third and fourth firms in the lineage of companies which eventually became Robert Morton. "Electrolian" was an attempt to capitalize on the already well-known name of Aeolian.

W. B. FLEMING, Vice-Pres. and Supt.
F. R. COFFIN, Sec. and Treas.

C. C. LAPHAM, Auditor
F. K. HOPKINS, Counselor

Electrolian Organ Co.

SUCCESSORS TO THE LOS ANGELES ART ORGAN CO
Builders of High-Class
Church, Concert and
Electrolian Chamber Pipe Organs

Electrolian Music Salon
353 FIFTH AVENUE, ENTRANCE 34TH ST.
NEW YORK
PHONE 4448 MADISON SQUARE

Largest Organ in the World
THE OFFICIAL CONCERT ORGAN OF THE
LOUISIANA PURCHASE EXPOSITION
Festival Music Hall, St. Louis

Awarded the Grand Prize and Six Medals

Factory
15TH AND ADAMS STS.
PHONE 212 HOBOKEN

Hoboken, N. J.,

one year, during which time only two organs were built.[19 20]

The Electrolian company disbanded in 1906 and many of its men moved back to Los Angeles and sought Murray M. Harris' aid in reorganizing an organ building concern. In September 1906 the Murray M. Harris Organ Co. was again in business, this time with a work force of fifty men in a building at Sichel and Alhambra Streets. Edwin A. Spencer, one of the original Fleming group, was superintendent and Charles McQuigg, a protege of Whitely, was chief voicer. Murray M. Harris, apparently content to leave the voicing in McQuigg's hands, assumed the role of general manager. Because so many previous employees were a part of the new concern, the same high quality of Murray M. Harris organs was maintained. Fleming's chests were supplanted by a new design of E. A. Spencer.[21]

JOHNSTON
ORGAN & PIANO MANUFACTURING CO
VAN NUYS, CAL.
1915

One of the last nameplates used before the firm became the California Organ Co.

The ROBERT-MORTON
a reproduction of the Symphony Orchestra
—more vividly interprets the real action of the Screen story
Organs for Churches, Halls and Theatres
THE AMERICAN PHOTO PLAYER COMPANY
NEW YORK 1600 Broadway
CHICAGO 64 E. Jackson Blvd.
SAN FRANCISCO 109 Golden Gate Ave.

Robert-Morton ad in the August 1921 issue of The Diapason *lists the firm's name as American Photo Player Co. Both firm names were used until 1925, after which the Photo Player name was phased out.*

At this point in the story it is time to introduce a man who was a major influence in the early years of Robert-Morton and its predecessor companies. Stanley Williams (1881-1971) was born in London, England and was apprenticed to Robert Hope-Jones at the age of 18. He recalled that one of the men in the Hope-Jones plant was F. W. Smith who later founded the Smith companies in this country. "Smith was a funny little man who taught me how to sharpen a plane," Williams remembered.[22] "As an apprentice to Hope-Jones I was assigned to work at every phase of organ building. I voiced, I carpentered, I electrified; everything about an organ had to be learned. It was something I later was very grateful for . . . Hope-Jones was not only a genius but a great teacher as well. He was insistent that his apprentices, in fact everyone who worked for him, should always question why a thing was done. He taught all of us to think for ourselves."[23]

Williams emigrated to America in 1906 to become a voicer at the ill-fated Electrolian company. He then spent several years in the employ of Phillip Wirsching of Salem, Ohio. One Wirsching organ he remembered vividly was sold to the Maharajah of Mysore, India, which Williams installed during his honeymoon in 1908. In 1910 he received a telegram from Los Angeles saying that the Murray M. Harris company was broke and that they had lost their voicer, Charles McQuigg, who had left the firm to represent Estey in the west. They needed to finish the organ in St. Paul's Cathedral, and could he help them out? Williams obliged and spent several weeks in Los Angeles before returning east. Not long thereafter another telegram arrived saying that the Harris firm had been refinanced and that the position of head voicer was available. Recalled Williams, "That's how I came to California. I've been here ever since 1911."[24]

The new president of the Harris firm, a retired mining man from Mexico named Huer, soon became despondent over not being able to show a reasonable profit. Murray M. Harris organs continued in their tradition of highest quality and this, coupled with stiff competition from eastern firms for the ripening western market, resulted in a narrow profit margin. Williams recalled that Huer "sold out [in 1913] to a pair of gentlemen, using the word loosely, named Bell and Johnston . . . Bell was smooth and quiet; Johnston was very loud and florid . . . If he demonstrated a piano he put his foot down on the sustaining pedal . . . and pumped some chords out very loudly . . . We used to call him Loud Pedal Johnston." P. Bell had been connected with the Eilers Music Company in San Francisco and E. S. Johnston was manager of Eilers' Los Angeles store. The new firm was called the Johnston Organ & Piano Manufacturing Co. The pianos they sold were known in the trade as "stencil" pianos: they were purchased cheaply from an eastern concern without any manufacturer's labeling and were then "stencilled" with the Johnston name before being sold to an unsuspecting public.[25 26]

At about this same time a real estate development was underway in the San Fernando valley which was attempting to turn orange groves owned by the Van Nuys and Lankershim families into the city of Van Nuys. The guiding light behind this development was W. P. Whitsett[27] after whom, along with Van Nuys and Lankershim, major valley streets were named. Whitsett's enterprise, Suburban Homes Company, sought to sell lots on which settlers could build new homes. Industry was also needed, however, to provide work for these settlers so Suburban Homes entered into an agreement with Johnston for the construction of a new 75,000 square foot factory building at very favorable terms.[28] Stanley Williams recalled more of Bell and Johnston's capers: "These two men were very slick workers . . . the next thing the two decided was that they would go east and raise some money, because it was easier to raise it in the east than here because their reputation hadn't caught up with them! So while they were in the east they made demands on the Suburban Homes Company to help them out with money. The Suburban decided they had had enough and told Bell and Johnston in effect that they were through. They had to take over the organ factory because so many of us had bought land to build our little homes on that something had to be provided to furnish wages to pay for the land. It was like having a bear by the tail: you couldn't let go and had to do *something*."[29]

R. P. "Joe" Matthews

Henry Charles, left, and H. J. Werner watch as Fred Miller signs a contract for the purchase of a new organ for one of his theatres.

That "something" turned out to be the organization of the California Organ Co., whose control rested in the Title Insurance and Trust Company, the legal abstract organization which handled land negotiations in the San Fernando valley.[30] The California Organ Co., its successor, Robert-Morton, and its various predecessors differed from other major organ companies in one important respect: most major firms were family-owned businesses and were operated not just as profit-making enterprises but largely because organ building was "in their blood." In the case of the California Organ Co. and their predecessor and successor companies, however, control usually rested in an amorphous group of businessmen who had no personal interest in organs and who, indeed, were operating the organ business not so much for its profit potential as for the fear of even greater losses if they ceased operations!

Nevertheless, sales of the California Organ Co. were good enough that R. P. Elliot, former president of the Hope-Jones and Kinetic companies, was induced to purchase an interest and thus joined the firm in October 1916 as vice president and general manager.[31] [32] The organs sold to theatres through this period remained straight instruments. This was all to change the following year, however, as we shall soon see.

At this point in the story we move to the northern California city of Berkeley where the American Photo Player factory was located. Fotoplayers had been invented, probably c. 1912, by brothers Harold A. and B. R. Van Valkenburg who, together with Guy Jacobus, were manufacturing and attempting to sell them, albeit in a small way. Their invention was "discovered" by a former salesman for the Eilers Music Company, Fred Ricksecker, who proceeded to share his enthusiasm for it with Harold J. Werner, another Eilers salesman whose territory was then Nevada.[33] It is interesting to note the ubiquity of Eilers salesmen in the Robert-Morton story, from Bell and Johnston earlier on to R. P. Matthews who plays a later role.

At any rate, Ricksecker and Werner started a sales organization to promote Fotoplayers aggressively. Part of their agreement with the Van Valkenburg brothers was that, in the event sales exceeded the factory's production capabilities, the sales organization would take over the manufacturing as well. The Van Valkenburg brothers readily agreed, no doubt thrilled by the idea that production might actually *reach* the capacity of their little factory, let alone exceed it. They had probably never met an operator like Werner, however! This "salesman's salesman" proceeded to set the world on fire and in virtually no time was selling Fotoplayers faster than the factory could produce them. In short order Werner reorganized the company, obtained additional financing, enlarged the factory and became president. Guy Jacobus of the original firm was named secretary and treasurer but the Van Valkenburg brothers didn't enter into management of the new organization.[34] The exact date of this reorganization is not known but it was definitely not before 1913.[35]

Fotoplayer sales continued to skyrocket. One reason was their quality construction, which held up under hard theatre usage better than other brands. Of greater significance was the tremendous sales network established by H. J. Werner which assured excellent nation-wide distribution. Besides Werner there were two other men who were among the "livest wires" in the business: Henry F. "Cocky" Charles and R. P. "Joe" Matthews. Matthews had played piano and slide trombone in theatre orchestras but had to quit after breaking his wrist. He subsequently became a piano salesman for Eilers and, at the time Werner reorganized the American Photo Player Co., was manager of Eilers' Oakland, California store. Matthews prepared most of the trade advertising and both he and "Cocky" Charles figured prominently not only in the Photo Player firm but later on in the Robert-Morton days

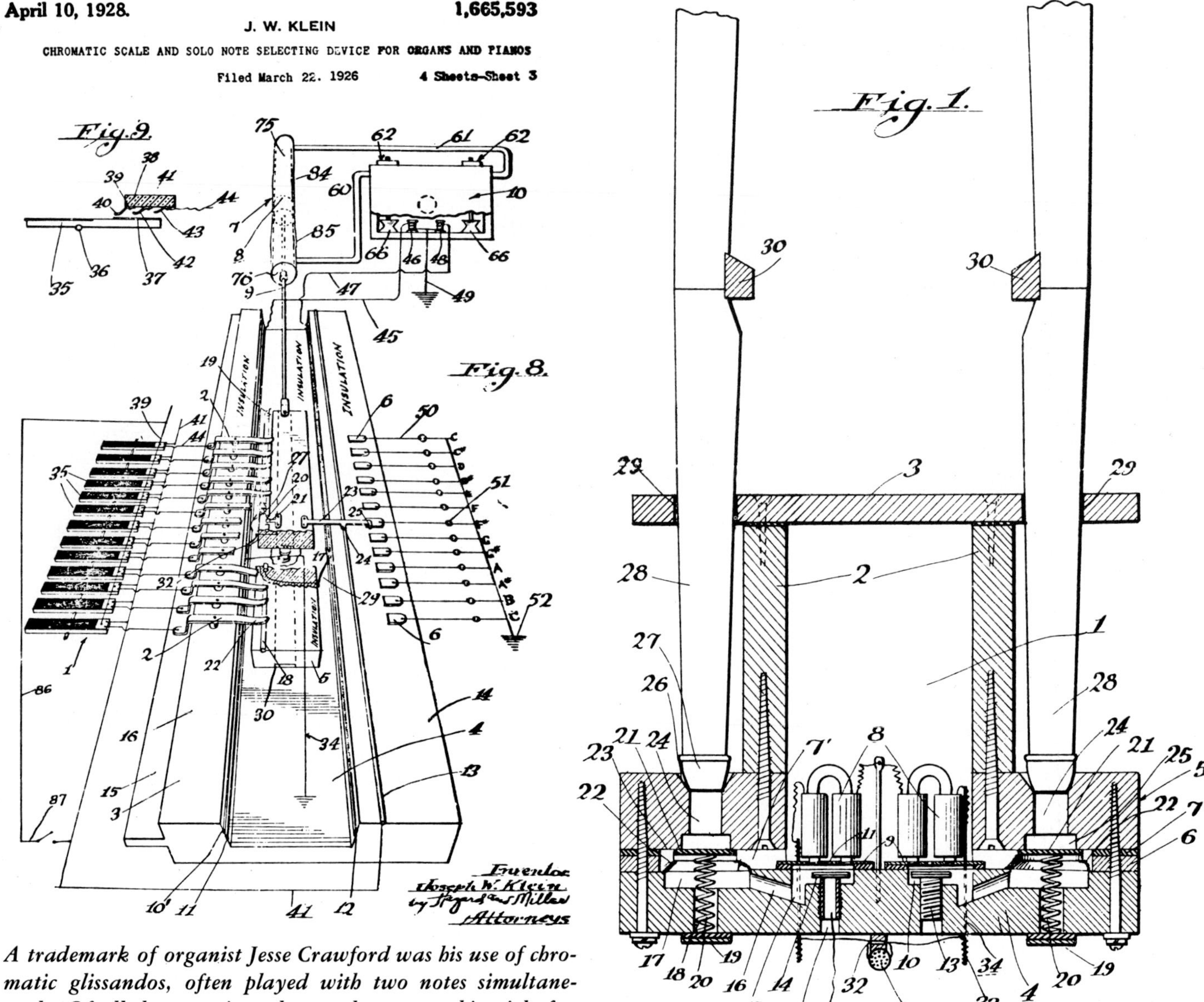

A trademark of organist Jesse Crawford was his use of chromatic glissandos, often played with two notes simultaneously. Of all the organists who sought to copy this trick, few mastered the technique. In an attempt to help organists with lesser skills use this ear-tickling effect, the Robert-Morton company experimented with a mechanical device they called a drawl unit. One of the patent drawings of this complex invention is reproduced here. An organ on the erecting room floor of the Robert-Morton factory was equipped with one of these drawl units but none was ever sold.[80]

Patent drawing of the famous Carlsted chest. Its clever design eliminated several drilling operations, making it quite cost effective to manufacture. The only moving parts were magnet armature 41 and pouch 22, valve 21 and spring 20.

of the company.[36] [37]

Despite tremendous success with Fotoplayer sales, Werner realized that an even greater market lay in unified pipe organs such as the Wurlitzer company was pushing so successfully. He was also astute enough to realize that his Berkeley firm was not in a position to enter this market since they were set up only for the production of small tubular pneumatic pit instruments. Having heard from "Cocky" Charles about the California Organ Co. which was just 400 miles south of Berkeley, Werner went down to investigate. He found a modern, well-equipped organ factory which was not exactly setting the world on fire sales wise owned by men who, except for R. P. Elliot, were not really interested in organ building and were in the business more or less by default. Werner also discovered that one of California's key employees, head voicer Stanley Williams, had been an apprentice of Hope-Jones and was the one man on the west coast capable of designing and building a unit theatre organ.[38]

Of course, the inevitable happened. Werner had found just the ticket for expanding his theatre sales and the owners of the California Organ Co. had found a buyer for the albatross they didn't want anyway. The Robert-Morton Company was duly incorporated on May 2, 1917.[39] Initial capitalization was $500,000 and the officers of Robert-Morton were the same as the American Photo Player Co., with the addition of R. P. Elliot and Sylvain S. Abrams as vice presidents.[40] The name of the firm came about because Werner wanted to use a hyphen. After all,

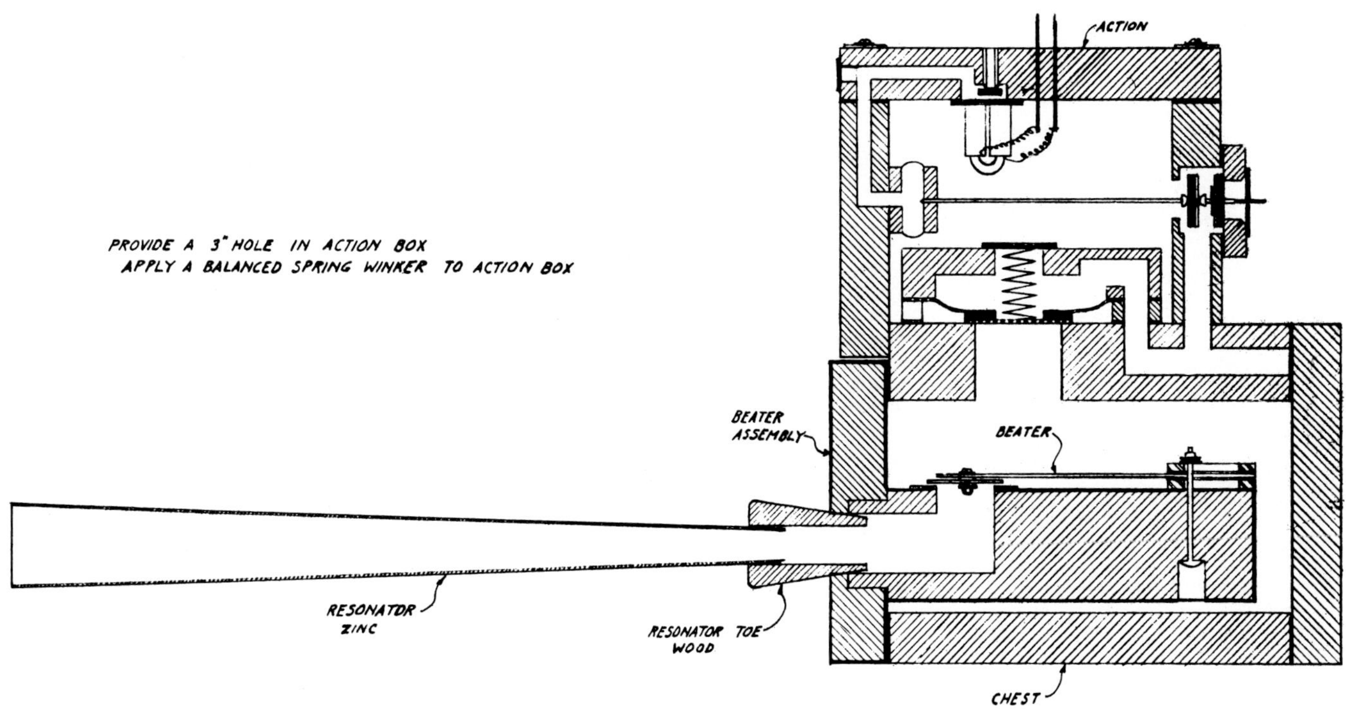

1927 drawing of a Robert Morton aeroplane effect. A very effective fluttering sound is generated by a diaphone beater and amplified by a short resonator.

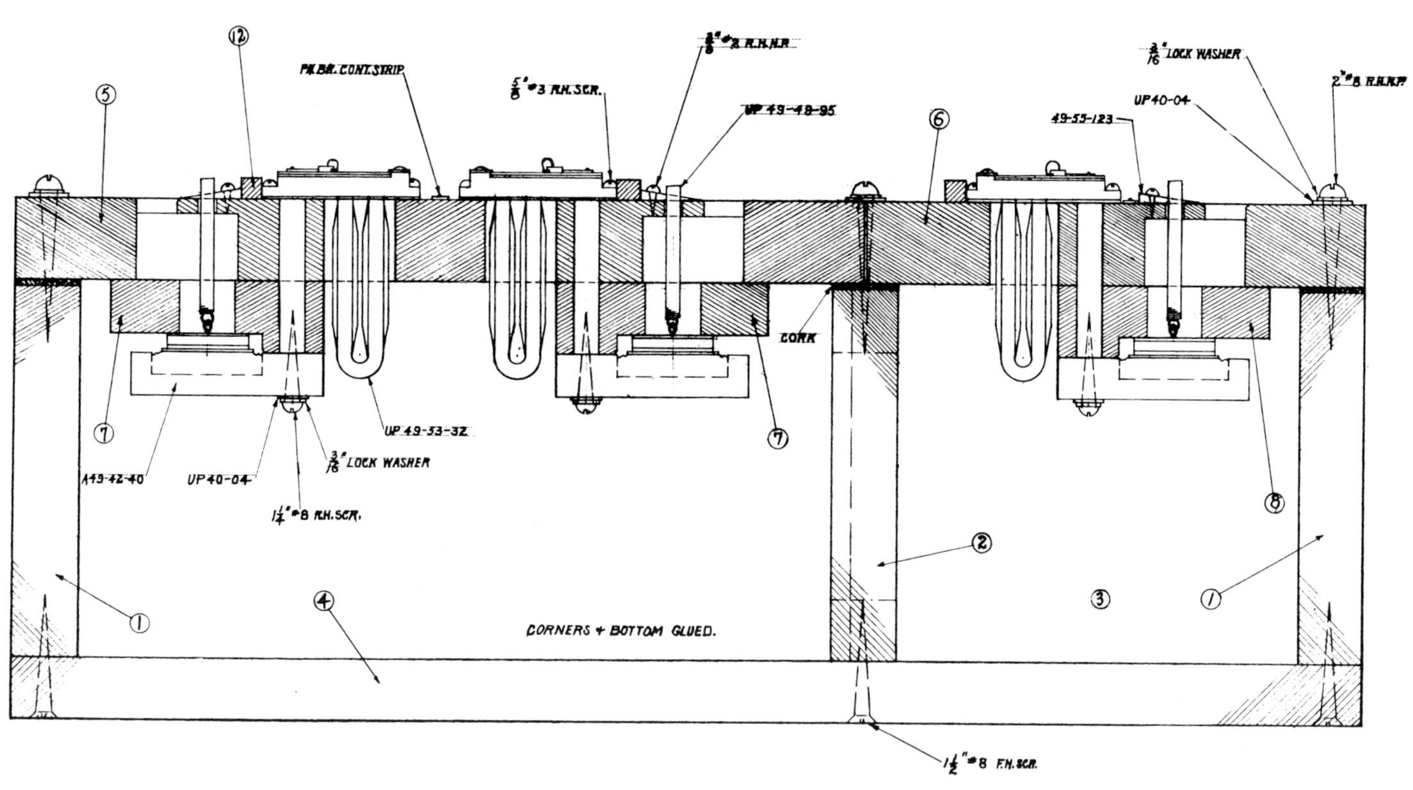

This compact chest design was used in Robert-Morton pit organs. Using top-mounted Reisner C17 chest magnets allowed these chests to be mounted on the floor of the pit organs' pipe cabinets, thus conserving the height required. Note the pouch springs which are cleverly adjustable from the outside of the chest.

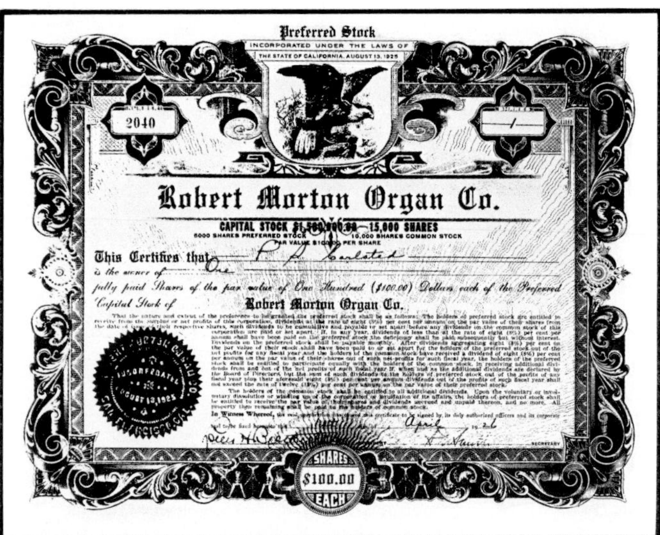
Preferred Stock
INCORPORATED UNDER THE LAWS OF THE STATE OF CALIFORNIA, AUGUST 13, 1925
2040
Robert Morton Organ Co.
CAPITAL STOCK $1,500,000.00 — 15,000 SHARES
5000 SHARES PREFERRED STOCK — 10,000 SHARES COMMON STOCK
PAR VALUE $100.00 PER SHARE
This Certifies that P. S. Carlsted is the owner of One fully paid Shares of the par value of One Hundred ($100.00) Dollars each of the Preferred Capital Stock of Robert Morton Organ Co.
SHARES $100.00 EACH

A share of stock from the last reorganization of the firm. It's a good thing this beautifully engraved document has esthetic value; its monetary value was certainly short-lived.

he wouldn't mind if the public confused Hope-Jones with *his* company! The actual names adjoining the hyphen were those of Werner's two sons, Robert and Morton. It was as simple as that.[41] After the mid 1920s the hyphen was dropped from the firm's logo and advertising.

Having acquired his new factory, Werner wanted to get a unit organ into production right away. He encountered tremendous resistance, however, from superintendent E. A. Spencer, a conservative builder of the "old school" who, recalled Stanley Williams, was "honest [but had no] imagination whatsoever."[42] In fact, initial negotiations between Werner and California had been quite stormy because of Spencer's resistance to building anything but classically voiced organs. The meetings which consummated the sale of the company were ultimately held at night, after Spencer had left for the day.[43]

After the takeover, Spencer was sent east to install a big organ—and to get him out of the factory—and Williams was instructed to build a prototype unit theatre instrument. Recalled Williams, "One night . . . Mr. Werner and the little friends from up north came down to examine my sample organ . . . and I remember so well that I had done it so different from the Spencer system. Used different contacts, different key actions, different chest actions and everything and they approved it . . . Mr. Spencer never forgave me . . . thought I was a snake in the grass. I didn't want the job; I didn't want to go into this but I remember so well that somebody took me to one side, a member of the Photo Player Co., and said, 'Stanley, if you don't do this somebody else will come and take your job and we're going to build the organ according to that model you've designed. You might just as well do it yourself. You are not being disloyal to Mr. Spencer because he is out. He just doesn't understand what we want.' That was how I got into it."[44] This Robert-Morton opus one was later sold to the California Theatre in Santa Barbara.[45]

American Photo Player management recognized the value of E. A. Spencer so rather than firing him they installed him as superintendent of the Berkeley factory. While there he built at least one church organ under the American Organ nameplate.[46] Apparently recanting his opposition to unit instruments, he also built a least two unified pit instruments under the Foto-Orchestra and Fotoplayer nameplates. He finally left the company in 1922 and moved to Pasadena, California[47] where he built church organs until his death in 1947.[48] Upon Spencer's departure from Van Nuys in 1917, Stanley Williams moved into the position of plant superintendent and appointed Bert Kingsley as head voicer to assume his former position.[49]

R. P. Elliot, lacking enthusiasm for the unified theatre organs which were becoming the firm's primary business, left in May of 1918 to become general manager of Kimball's organ division. Stanley Williams succeeded Elliot as vice president and remained until 1922 when he, too, left to join the Kimball company.[50] Assisting superintendent Williams was Louis Maas, a San Francisco organ service man who had joined the company at the request of organist Jesse Crawford. Maas designed new and more responsive trap actions, improved the diaphone and introduced Wurlitzer-style valves into Robert-Morton regulators, supplanting the curtain valves then in use. Maas also left the firm in 1922.[51] After Williams' departure Leo Schoenstein became factory superintendent, remaining until the final days of the firm.[52]

Although Stanley Williams designed the first Robert-Morton organ, another man must be given credit for many of the designs prominent in the firm's products of the 1920s: Paul S. Carlsted. As a youngster Mr. Carlsted had been employed in the drafting department of the Kimball company. Traveling west in 1912, he joined the Murray M. Harris firm and remained with its successor companies until the factory closed in 1929. As chief draftsman he was considered to be in the executive branch of the company although he as well as other executives often went out on the road with installation crews. The Robert-Morton firm was certainly not top heavy at the executive level; furthermore, these executives weren't too proud to roll up their sleeves and pitch in where needed.[53]

The title "chief draftsman" doesn't adequately convey the scope of Carlsted's influence on the Robert-Morton organ. It was he who was responsible for the physical design and appearance of consoles, benches and any number of other parts of the organs. He did the floor plan layouts of each organ and also assisted clients with any special grille requirements, etc., which their own architects had not specified. Carlsted is well known for devising the particularly simple unit chest used by the firm in its later organs, but he should also be recognized as the designer of Robert-Morton's unique console shapes.[54] In later years Carlsted's title was expanded to assistant factory superintendent.

Let's allow the inventor of the famous Carlsted chest to tell the story of its inception in his own words: "The first chests were huge and cumbersome and almost impossible to lift into position without the help of several men. Everything in a chamber was on one big chest. When they got too large, then two chests were put in. But they were still very heavy affairs. Leo Schoenstein, who was superintendent then, wanted to get away from that so he told me what he had in mind . . . Then I told Leo that I had an idea of my own. He was interested and looked over my design.

"Schoenstein said, 'Well, let's build some of mine, try them and then build some of yours and try them . . . ' I applied for patents on my design . . . Schoenstein then directed that my chest design would go into an organ on order for Imperial Valley, [saying] 'It's the hottest place I know of and if it stands up down there, then we'll go into production on it.' The organ went into a theatre in the valley and after no trouble developed within a year we adopted it and went into production. Basically it was designed to eliminate work. I cut down the number of boring operations by about more than half. The patent became the property of the Morton company and I received one dollar for it. I had designed the chest during regular factory hours and therefore, by all legal involvements, the patent was the property of the company."[55]

Under the dynamic leadership of H. J. Werner, sales of Robert-Morton organs eventually surpassed factory capacity, just as Fotoplayer sales had done a few years earlier. He turned for help to the Wicks Organ Company, who were only too happy to sell Wicks organs under the Robert-Morton nameplate. One factor favoring this association was Wicks' location halfway across the country. Shipping an organ to an eastern customer was certainly less expensive from Highland, Illinois than from Van Nuys, California.

The real reason for the Robert-Morton/Wicks alliance, however, was the precarious financial condition of the Van Nuys firm. Despite heavy sales, the company was teetering on the edge of insolvency and, for want of sufficient operating capital, occasionally closed its doors for a few weeks during the years 1919-1924. One such shutdown in 1919 lasted four months, during which time Paul Carlsted returned to work for Kimball, although he rejoined Robert-Morton as soon as they reopened for business.[56] The dynamism and likability of H. J. Werner certainly inspired employee loyalty! Werner's alliance with Wicks allowed sales of Robert-Morton organs to continue even when he had run out of the operating capital which would have allowed him to build the organs himself at a greater profit. This explains the fact that a number of Wicks-built Robert-Mortons were shipped to the west coast. Despite the extra freight costs involved, Werner would rather have sold his customers Wicks-built organs than lose sales because his own nearby factory was idle.

A curious by-product of the Robert-Morton/Wicks affiliation was the Beethoven nameplate. As of 1986 only two such organs are known to the author (see opus list). The Wicks contract for one of them bears a cover page reading "Beethoven Orchestral Organ furnished by American Photo Player Company, Berkeley, distributors of Beethoven organs."[57] The author speculates that the Beethoven nameplate may have been a sales ploy to stimulate Robert-Morton sales through competition of another brand, the idea being that even if the customer bought the "competing" Beethoven organ, the business was actually still coming Werner's way! Similar tactics were employed in the piano industry where, for example, Art Echo reproducing piano mechanisms were made in the same factory as "competing" Ampicos.[58] In another example, Western Electric coin-operated pianos were made surreptitiously by the "competing" Seeburg Piano Company in an effort to stimulate a greater sales effort by Seeburg salesmen.[59] See the Wicks chapter elsewhere in this volume for further details concerning the Wicks/Robert-Morton association.

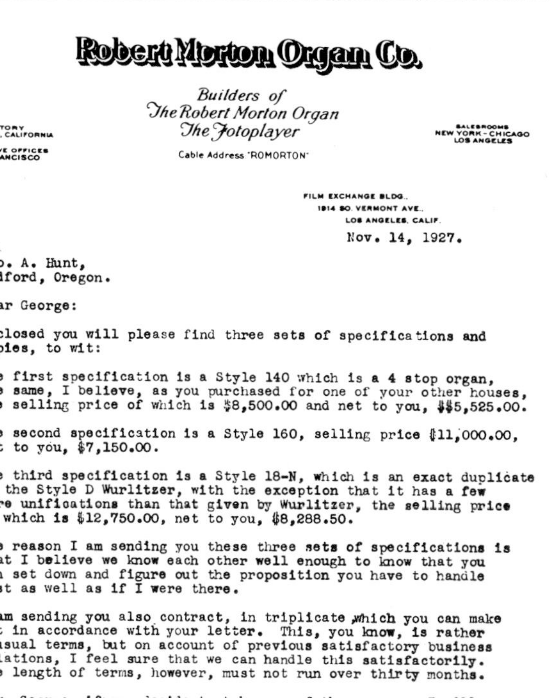

Robert Morton Organ Co.

Builders of
The Robert Morton Organ
The Fotoplayer

FACTORY
VAN NUYS, CALIFORNIA

EXECUTIVE OFFICES
SAN FRANCISCO

Cable Address "ROMORTON"

SALESROOMS
NEW YORK - CHICAGO
LOS ANGELES

FILM EXCHANGE BLDG.,
1914 SO. VERMONT AVE.,
LOS ANGELES, CALIF.

Nov. 14, 1927.

Geo. A. Hunt,
Medford, Oregon.

Dear George:

Enclosed you will please find three sets of specifications and copies, to wit:

The first specification is a Style 140 which is a 4 stop organ, the same, I believe, as you purchased for one of your other houses, the selling price of which is $8,500.00 and net to you, $$5,525.00.

The second specification is a Style 160, selling price $11,000.00, net to you, $7,150.00.

The third specification is a Style 18-N, which is an exact duplicate of the Style D Wurlitzer, with the exception that it has a few more unifications than that given by Wurlitzer, the selling price of which is $12,750.00, net to you, $8,288.50.

The reason I am sending you these three sets of specifications is that I believe we know each other well enough to know that you can set down and figure out the proposition you have to handle just as well as if I were there.

I am sending you also contract, in triplicate which you can make out in accordance with your letter. This, you know, is rather unusual terms, but on account of previous satisfactory business relations, I feel sure that we can handle this satisfactorily. The length of terms, however, must not run over thirty months.

Now, George, if you decide to take one of these organs I will arrange to send Sandy Balcom to Roseburg to go over the organ chambers so that you will have the best possible installation we can give you.

Assuring you of our cooperation and with best personal regards to you and the wild meat-eater, I am

Yours truly,

H. F. Charles

HFC:P

This interesting letter, written by Robert Morton's ace salesman, reveals prices of three popular models of four, five and six ranks, respectively.

Late style brass nameplate used from 1924 until the end of production. Compare with the nameplate used on Wicks-built Robert-Mortons shown on page 696.

ROBERT MORTON STYLE DESIGNATIONS

The company built a variety of stock organs but rarely advertised them by style number. This incomplete list includes those known to the author as of 1986. Among the most popular models were the 39, 49, 75 and 18-N, the last of which was designed to compete with the popular style D Wurlitzer.

MODEL	SIZE	MODEL	SIZE
A		39R	2/4
B	2/4	49	2/3
C		49C	2/4
LS-M	3/	49D	2/
8	2/	49H	2/
14	2/	59	2/
16	2/4	75	2/4
17	2/5	85	2/5
18	2/6	100	
18-N	2/6	140	2/4
19	2/7	160	2/5
20	2/8	176	
21	3/8	177-E	2/7
21-N	3/	179	
22	2/10	183	3/
23	2/11	187	
23-N	3/	188	
24	2/11	200	2/10
25	3/12	200CX	2/12
25-M		250	
27	2/2	290	
39	2/3	300	3/14
39A	2/		

An insightful picture of H. J. Werner, organizer of the Robert-Morton business, was offered by Stanley Williams: "Mr. Werner I was a little scared of because I saw signs of slickness. [He] was a man of short stature, very active and quick on his feet and I don't think he ever went to bed and to sleep because he always seemed to be doing something in the middle of the night . . . [He] had the American Photo Player Company factory in Berkeley, the factory in Van Nuys, an office in St. Louis and an office in New York. And they employed a number of high-speed salesmen. In order to be a good salesman in those days, in the early days of the movie industry, you had to have an enormous capacity for drink and keep more sober than the other man to whom you planned on selling anything . . . I was asked one time to train the salesmen so that they could talk more logically about the workings of an organ. Most of them said, 'Don't tell me about it, Willie . . . it cramps my style because now I don't know when I'm lying!'"[60]

R. P. Matthews added to the picture of Werner's personality: [He] was . . . a dynamic fellow, a terrific guy. He was a wonder! . . . He was not a man of keeping track of small details; he was an organizer . . . [and] wanted to see this a great success and worked toward that goal constantly . . . He was a tremendous optimist. You couldn't get him down for any length of time. He might be gloomy for a day but bounced back. [Unfortunately] he never knew what his expenses were . . . [and] was careless about his details, simply careless, and he would give away anything you wanted."[61]

Werner's inept handling of company finances finally resulted in a group of the firm's creditors forcing the company into receivership in mid-1923. The reorganized firm, called The Photo Player Company, ousted Werner and named James A. G. Schiller as general manager on behalf of the creditors' committee.[62] Schiller, although not an organ man, was a shrewd businessman and an efficiency expert. In the words of Paul Carlsted he "turned the plant upside down [and] surprisingly enough he got everything organized on a plan and it went along much better."[63] Shortly thereafter major financing was found in the person of Mortimer Fleishacker, president of the Anglo-California Trust Company in San Francisco. With Fleishacker's almost unlimited backing, the firm had nothing to hold it back. Forging full-steam ahead, Robert-Morton proceeded to claim a position in theatre organ sales second only to the great house of Wurlitzer.[64]

Early in 1925 The Photo Player Company name was dropped and the final corporate title became the Robert Morton Organ Co.[65] Schiller remained as general manager and R. P. Matthews was elected vice president, remaining in his New York office to oversee the national advertising program as well as the eastern, midwestern and southern sales territories.[66] Under Schiller's management an enormous expansion program was undertaken, nearly doubling the size of the factory before the end of 1925. The peak number of employees remains unknown, although a photograph of the firm's work force before the expansion shows nearly 100 persons. Another clue is that, at the height of production (probably in 1926) twenty people were employed just in the machine shop where chest magnets, reed shallots and other metal parts were fabricated.[67]

Concomitant with the 1925 plant expansion, a further efficiency was effected by closing the Berkeley plant and consolidating all manufacturing at Van Nuys. Executive offices remained in San Francisco, however, home turf of "angel" Fleishacker. In 1927, having successfully completed his mission of restructuring the company, James Schiller stepped down as general manager and was succeeded by R. P. Matthews.[68]

For awhile, sales continued at the same rapid pace as in previous years. The Loew enterprise alone purchased five 4/23 "wonder Mortons" for their deluxe New York area houses. 1927 was also the year, however, when *The Jazz Singer* ushered in the era of talking and singing pictures. Within a few months Robert Morton sales were decimated. Virtually the entire sales impetus of the firm had been directed towards theatre organ sales which, after all, had been keeping the factory operating at capacity. As did many other firms, Robert Morton failed to get a foothold in the church organ market and discovered the mortuary and residence markets too barren to sustain life.

Manufacturing ceased in April 1929[69] and by October 1929 only three people were left in the factory.[70] Because of the financial resources of Mortimer Fleishacker, the firm never declared bankruptcy. He elected instead to liquidate all holdings in order to trim losses most effectively. R. P. Matthews wasn't interested in participating in the dismemberment of the organization he had worked so long and hard to build up, despite a personal request from Fleishacker to do so. Matthews recommended Henry Platt, sales manager of the Los Angeles office, who subsequently oversaw liquidation proceedings until 1933 when C. B. "Happy" Sartwell purchased all remaing assets of the firm—all, that is, except the company name.[71]

Sartwell, who had been Robert Morton's purchasing agent, moved the operation north a few blocks to a building which had been used by the Kimball fruit drying company. Here he hung out a sign which read "C. B. Sartwell, Successor to the Robert Morton Organ Co." He couldn't use the company name directly since it was not purchased with the other assets. New organs were never manufactured; Sartwell's primary business consisted of purchasing unwanted theatre organs and of revamping them for church use. Former Robert Morton employees joining Mr. Sartwell included Arthur C. Pearson and head voicer Bert Kingsley or Kinsley, as he preferred to call himself, dropping the "g" from his legal name.[73] Kinsley had been largely responsible for the sound of the Robert Morton organ as it developed in the 1920s. He developed the beautiful tibias gracing the later organs and was also responsible for the Robert Morton krumet,[74] the first example of which was in the 4/16 instrument installed in the Fox Theatre in Seattle, Washington in 1928.[75] Sartwell continued his business until 1942 when the War Production Board, forbidding the sale of non-essential materials, made continuation impractical.[76]

There is a tragic postscript to the Robert Morton story which, although not officially part of the company's history, is included here in the hope that it will serve as a lesson to fellow researchers. In 1964 Tom B'hend located and interviewed R. P. "Joe" Matthews, one of the founding fathers of the company and ultimately its last general manager. Mr. Matthews shared his recollections extensively but was hesitant to lend factory records in his possession. These consisted of many pages of correspondence, photographs, a salesman's book of specifications and style numbers, and the opus list of the firm, listing the size, cost and destination of each organ that was shipped.[77]

After a few years of persuasion, Mr. Matthews finally agreed to lend these materials to some New York area enthusiasts. They procrastinated only a few weeks, during which time Joe Matthews died. When they contacted Matthews' next of kin, they were informed that those "worthless old papers" had already been burned.[78] Just imagine—the original Robert Morton opus list—denied its rendezvous with history by a scant few weeks! The moral: if you know an "old timer" but have not "gotten around" to visiting him, don't delay! And take your most cheerful attitude, your tape recorder and your camera with you!

The perspicacious reader will note that, in the text and captions of this book, the Robert Morton name is sometimes hyphenated and sometimes not. The author has attempted to follow the firm's own practice by including the hyphen in contexts dealing with the company's earlier years and by omitting the hyphen in post-1925 chronology.

CORPORATE CHRONOLOGY OF THE ROBERT MORTON COMPANIES

1894	Fletcher & Harris
1897	Murray M. Harris Organ Co.
1903	Los Angeles Art Organ Co.
1905	Electrolian Organ Co.
1906	Murray M. Harris Organ Co.
1913	Johnston Organ & Piano Manufacturing Co.
1915	California Organ Co.
1917	Robert-Morton Company
1923	The Photo Player Company
1925	Robert Morton Organ Co.
1933	C. B. Sartwell, Successor to the Robert Morton Organ Co.

The Los Angeles Art Organ Co. had the honor of building what was, at the time (1903), the largest organ in the world, having over 10,000 pipes. Wind was supplied by crankshaft-operated bellows powered by only two ten-horsepower motors. Installed at the Louisiana Purchase Exposition in St. Louis, the organ was featured in recitals by noted French organist and composer Alexandre Guilmant, pictured here at the massive five-manual console. This instrument later became the nucleus of what is currently the world's second largest organ in Wanamaker's department store in Philadelphia. Neither of these instruments appears in opus lists of this book since they were neither installed in theatres nor designed to play popular music.

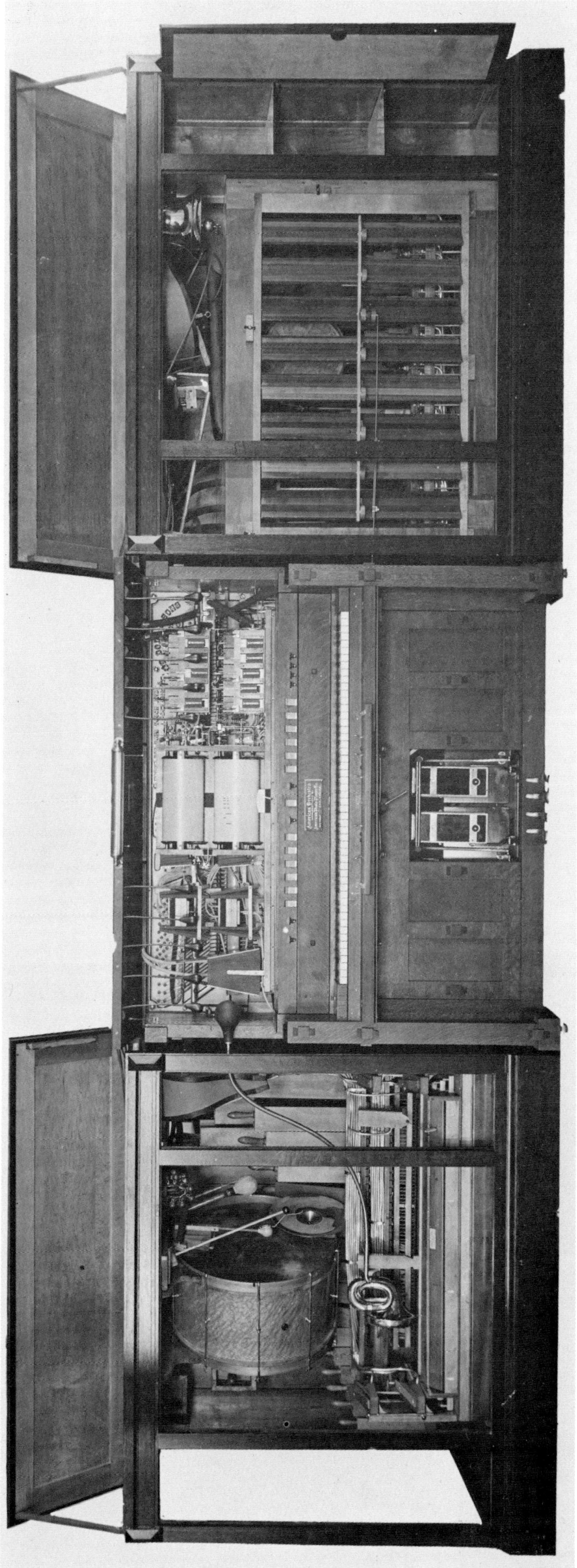

Robert-Morton's parent company, the American Photo Player Company, produced several models of Fotoplayers, their trademark for pit instruments having pianos as their bases. Upper photo shows the interior of a style 40; at right is pictured a style 45.

TALLY'S BROADWAY THEATER--833 S. Bdwy.

MONDAY NIGHT | **Dedication of the Great Pipe Organ** | 7:30 P.M. AND 9:15 P.M.

PLAYED BY CHARLES H. DEMOREST, A. A. G. O.

The World's Greatest Theater Pipe Organ

Special Musical Programme by the Organ, Orchestra, Harry Girard, Vernon Gray, and

"THE BATTLE OF WATERLOO"

A REMARKABLE FIVE-REEL VISUALIZATION OF THE MOST THRILLING EVENT IN HISTORY.

All Seats Reserved for Monday Night

SEATS NOW ON SALE FOR BOTH SHOWS.

Prices 10 and 20 Cents; Loges 30 Cents

Commencing Tuesday, MR. DEMOREST will play daily—11:45 to 1:30, 3 to 5, after 7:30.

The Battle of Waterloo—One Week Only

Ad in the Los Angeles Times *January 18, 1914. Tally's was so proud of their 4/47 Murray M. Harris that even the theatre's exterior proclaimed "World's Finest Theatre Pipe Organ." Note that the ad is for "Tally's Broadway Theatre" while the building's sign reads "Tally's Theatre." This is a good example of the dilemma historians sometimes face when deciding the proper name to call a given theatre.*

Tally's Theatre held the record for largest organ in a small house. The instrument consumed fully one third of each side wall of the theatre. At right is a close-up view of Tally's 4/47 Murray M. Harris console.

California Organ Co. pit organ with a unique three-manual piano console. Destination of this one-of-a-kind instrument is unknown.

3/16 in the St. Francis Theatre, San Francisco. One of the earliest organs to bear the Robert-Morton nameplate, it was installed in 1917.

The California Theatre in Santa Barbara was the home of the first unit organ ever built by the firm. It was installed in 1917 by its designer, plant superintendent Stanley Williams.[5]

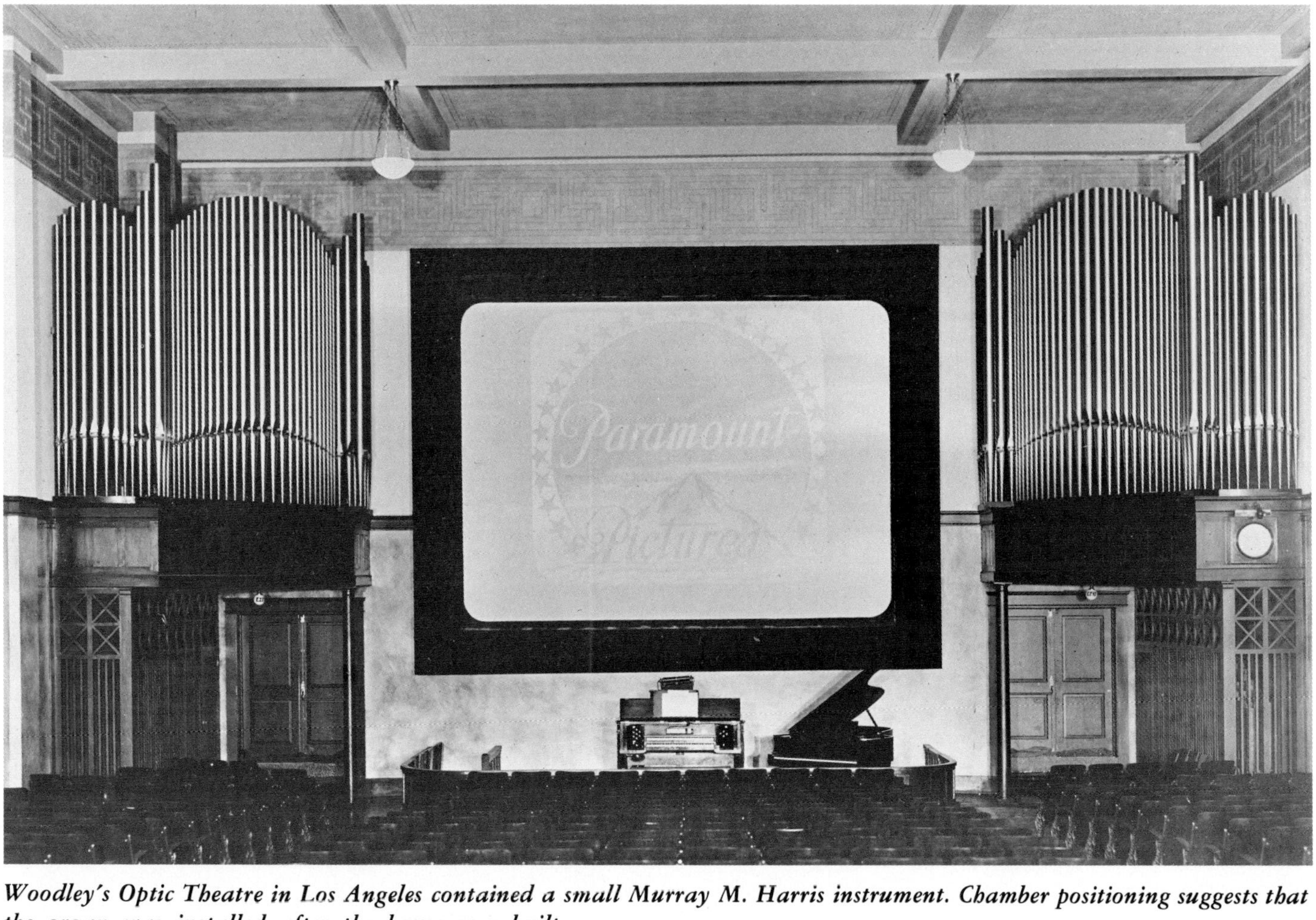

Woodley's Optic Theatre in Los Angeles contained a small Murray M. Harris instrument. Chamber positioning suggests that the organ was installed after the house was built.

These two theatres featured California Organ Co. instruments. Above, the T & D (Appleton) (State) Theatre in Watsonville, California also sported a photoplayer-like device in its orchestra pit. The author has never seen a photoplayer quite like this one and it is possible that it was installed as an adjunct to the organ. Below, the Liberty (Roxy) Theatre in Long Beach, California had a 2/14 with an 88-note player unit, as did many early Murray M. Harris and California Organ Co. instruments.

Jesse Crawford poses at the partially straight organ installed in Miller's California Theatre, Los Angeles. Note that all stops, including couplers, were white.

THE SPIRIT OF THE SCREEN

At Miller's California Theatre
is Musically Interpreted by

THE ROBERT-MORTON ORGAN

A Reproduction of the Symphony Orchestra

Console of The Robert Morton

THE impersonal and Pervading tone of the organ as expressed by the Robert-Morton furnishes a quiet and unobtrusive background of music for any dramatjc action on the screen.

The potent emotional influence of organ music is ultimately realized in the wide range of color and orchestral Expression stimulated and sustained by The Robert-Morton.

Shading its harmonies with the lights of the screen---the symphonic character of The Robert-Morton fits every character, motif and action of dramatic situation.

THE AMERICAN PHOTO PLAYER COMPANY

NEW YORK CHICAGO SAN FRANCISCO LOS ANGELES

Ad from an unidentified publication c. 1918.

One of the few pipe organs to have been built at the Berkeley American Photo Player factory was this 2/15 pit instrument. Bearing the Foto-Orchestra nameplate, it was sold to Miller's Theatre in Los Angeles in 1919 for the relatively large sum of $22,000. It included chimes, harp, a full complement of drums and traps, manual second touch and twin 88-note player rolls.[1]

Close-up view of another pit organ built by superintendent E. A. Spencer at the American Photo Player factory in Berkeley, California. Curiously, this instrument bears Fotoplayer nameplates although it is entirely an electropneumatic pipe organ, unlike Fotoplayers which were basically pianos with a few ranks of pipes operated by tubular pneumatic action.

Earl Abel poses at the Tivoli Theatre in San Francisco. This organ was built under E. A. Spencer's reign at the Berkeley factory in the late teens. Note that the case style and piston spacings are quite different from contemporary practice at Robert-Morton's Van Nuys factory.

On this and the next four pages are reproduced an extremely rare advertising pamphlet issued by Robert-Morton c. 1919. The only one ever seen by the author, it was loaned through the courtesy of Jack Bethards, president of Schoenstein & Co. of San Francisco, whose extensive archive contains many such treasures.

Console of a style 300 3/14 Robert-Morton destined for a Mexico City theatre awaits testing in the factory in 1920.

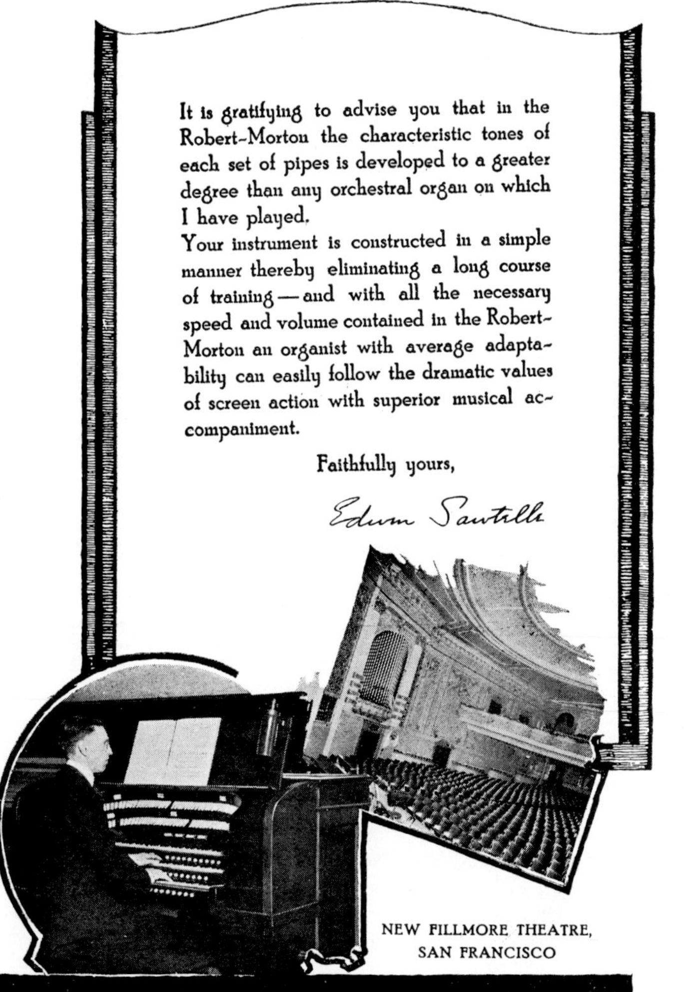

It is gratifying to advise you that in the Robert-Morton the characteristic tones of each set of pipes is developed to a greater degree than any orchestral organ on which I have played.

Your instrument is constructed in a simple manner thereby eliminating a long course of training — and with all the necessary speed and volume contained in the Robert-Morton an organist with average adaptability can easily follow the dramatic values of screen action with superior musical accompaniment.

Faithfully yours,

Edwin Sawtelle

NEW FILLMORE THEATRE,
SAN FRANCISCO

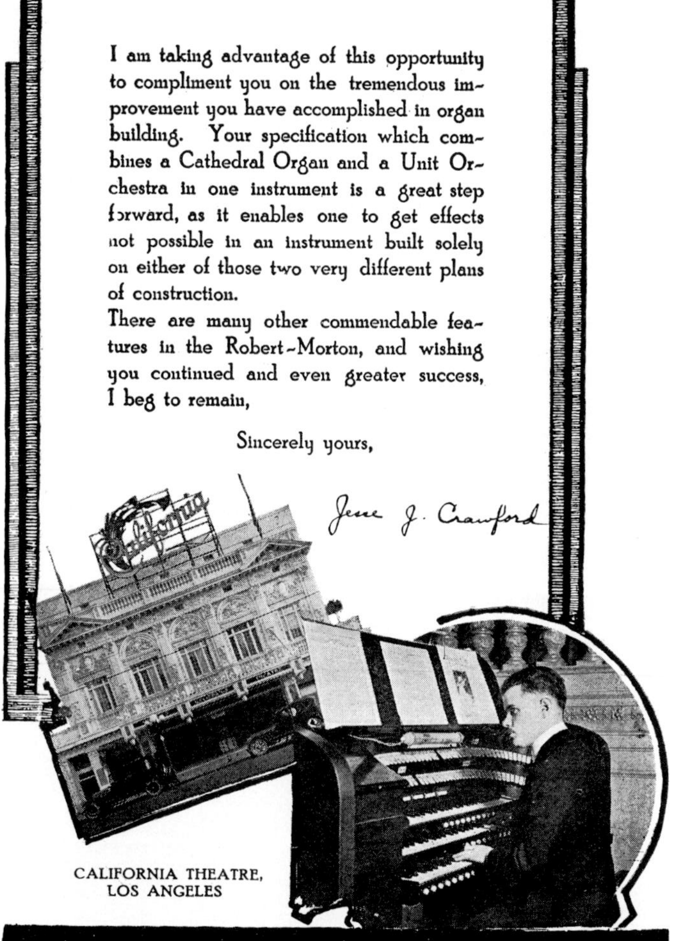

I am taking advantage of this opportunity to compliment you on the tremendous improvement you have accomplished in organ building. Your specification which combines a Cathedral Organ and a Unit Orchestra in one instrument is a great step forward, as it enables one to get effects not possible in an instrument built solely on either of those two very different plans of construction.

There are many other commendable features in the Robert-Morton, and wishing you continued and even greater success, I beg to remain,

Sincerely yours,

Jesse J. Crawford

CALIFORNIA THEATRE,
LOS ANGELES

The first five-manual organ built by Robert-Morton was installed in the Palm Theatre, Philadelphia in 1921. Note the relatively small number of stop keys; the organ may have contained a number of straight ranks, a common feature of early Robert-Mortons.

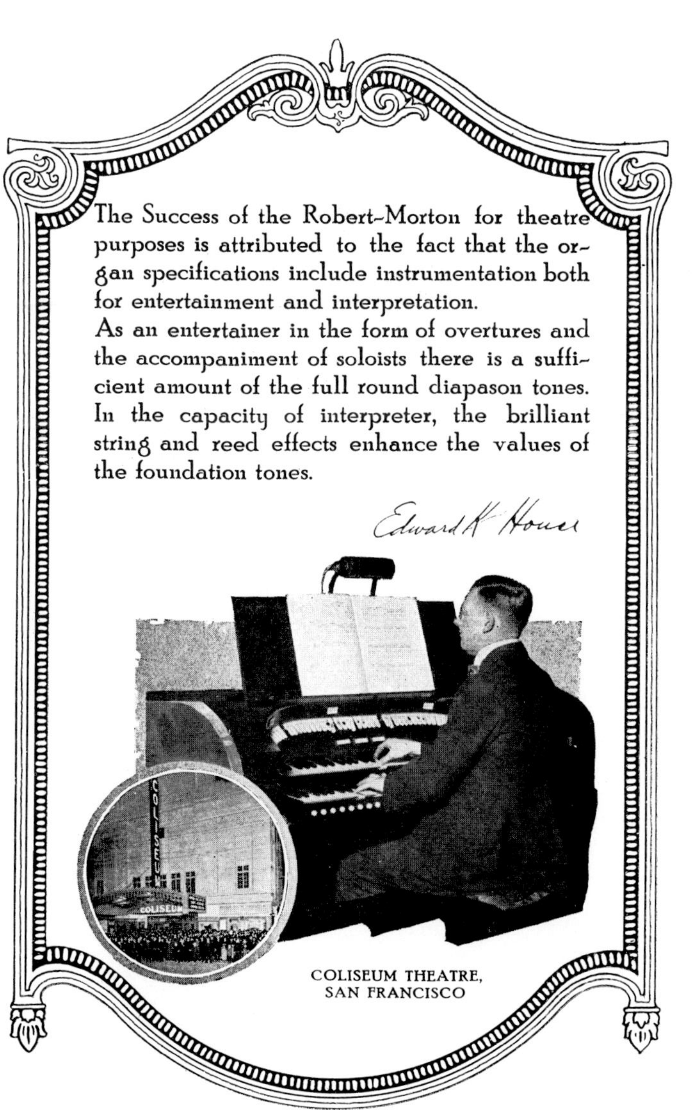

The Success of the Robert-Morton for theatre purposes is attributed to the fact that the organ specifications include instrumentation both for entertainment and interpretation.

As an entertainer in the form of overtures and the accompaniment of soloists there is a sufficient amount of the full round diapason tones. In the capacity of interpreter, the brilliant string and reed effects enhance the values of the foundation tones.

Edward K. House

COLISEUM THEATRE,
SAN FRANCISCO

The Robert-Morton Orchestral organ installed by you in April 1918 has been in use from seven and one half to twelve hours every day and has never been one hour out of commission.

Although several new organs of other manufacturers have lately been installed, it is still the verdict of the general public so far as we can determine, that the music produced by the Robert-Morton at the Rialto Theatre, Des Moines, Iowa, is the finest and best theatrical organ music in the state.

RIALTO THEATRE,
DES MOINES, IOWA

Alice Blue poses at the Hawaii Theatre 4/16 Robert-Morton in Honolulu in the early 1930s. A sister 4/16 was installed in Honolulu's Princess Theatre which also featured sparse unification requiring only one row of stops.

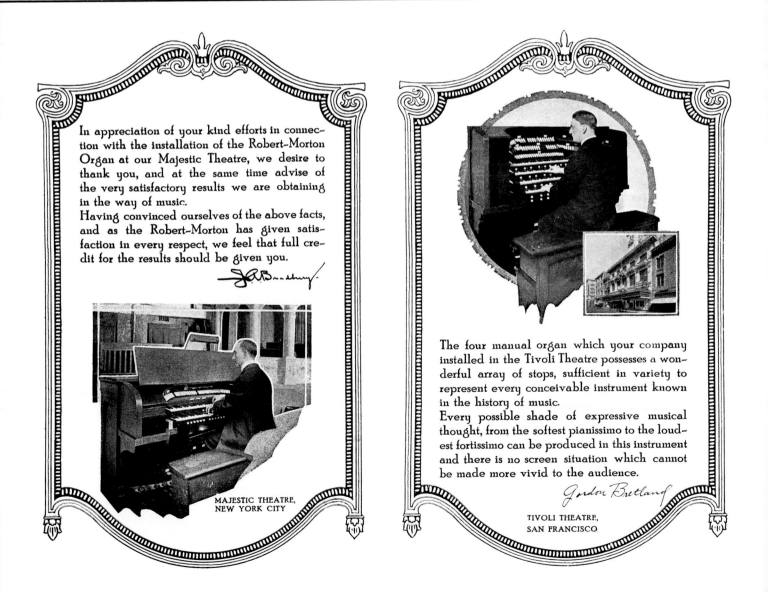

In appreciation of your kind efforts in connection with the installation of the Robert-Morton Organ at our Majestic Theatre, we desire to thank you, and at the same time advise of the very satisfactory results we are obtaining in the way of music.
Having convinced ourselves of the above facts, and as the Robert-Morton has given satisfaction in every respect, we feel that full credit for the results should be given you.

MAJESTIC THEATRE,
NEW YORK CITY

The four manual organ which your company installed in the Tivoli Theatre possesses a wonderful array of stops, sufficient in variety to represent every conceivable instrument known in the history of music.
Every possible shade of expressive musical thought, from the softest pianissimo to the loudest fortissimo can be produced in this instrument and there is no screen situation which cannot be made more vivid to the audience.

Gordon Bretland

TIVOLI THEATRE,
SAN FRANCISCO

5/26 in the Kinema (Criterion) Theatre, Los Angeles. The last of the three Robert-Morton five-manual organs, this was a 1923 enlargement of an earlier three-manual Robert-Morton.

The American Photo Player Co.

NEW YORK CITY
62 W. 45th St. and
John Wanamaker

CHICAGO, ILL.
64 E. Jackson Blvd. and
Lyon & Healy

PHILADELPHIA, PA.
John Wanamaker

BOSTON, MASS.
Geo. L. Parker
120 Boylsten St.

BUTTE, MONT.
Rialto Supply Co.

CHARLOTTE, N. C.
F. H. Andrews

CHATTANOOGA, TEN.
Sterchi Bros.

AUSTRALIA
Pianola Co., Ltd.

ST. PAUL, MINN.
W. J. Dyer & Bro.

KANSAS CITY, MO.
J. W. Jenkins' Sons

SALT LAKE CITY
Beesley Music Co.

DALLAS, TEXAS
J. D. Wheelan
Pipe Organ Co.

SAN FRANCISCO, CAL.
PORTLAND, ORE.
SEATTLE, WASH.
Sherman, Clay & Co.

LOS ANGELES, CAL.
The American
Photo Player Co.

FACTORY BERKELEY, CALIF.

The ROBERT-MORTON
a reproduction of the Symphony Orchestra

—more vividly
interprets the
real action of
the Screen story

Edwin H. Lemare dedicates the 4/72 Robert-Morton in Bovard Auditorium on the University of Southern California campus, Los Angeles, in 1921. Not at all a theatre organ, being mostly straight and containing several mixtures, it was the largest Robert-Morton ever built.

Several notes of the enormous Bovard 32′ bombarde are being tested outside the front door of the factory. The 32′ stops in the Bovard organ are the only ones ever built by Robert-Morton.

Paul Carlsted (left), Bert Kingsley (right) and some of the prettier members of the Robert-Morton staff pose behind low CCCC of the Bovard Auditorium's 32′ double open diapason. In 1987 this very pipe is still rumbling most effectively in another large southern California organ in Garden Grove's Crystal Cathedral.

The Howard Theatre in Atlanta bought a 4/35 Steere in 1919 but the Steere factory burned before the organ could be delivered. Robert-Morton came to the rescue and installed this 3/14 style 300 in 1920. Howard Theatre patrons were rescued from the droning sounds of this early instrument in 1925 when a new 3/15 Wurlitzer replaced it.

On this and the next three pages are reproduced a portion of an extremely rare Robert-Morton advertising brochure issued c. 1920. Although the printing quality is inferior, the testimonials seem sincere. The promotional paragraphs are particularly interesting examples of an advertising department's effort to embroider organ technical matters in a florid manner.

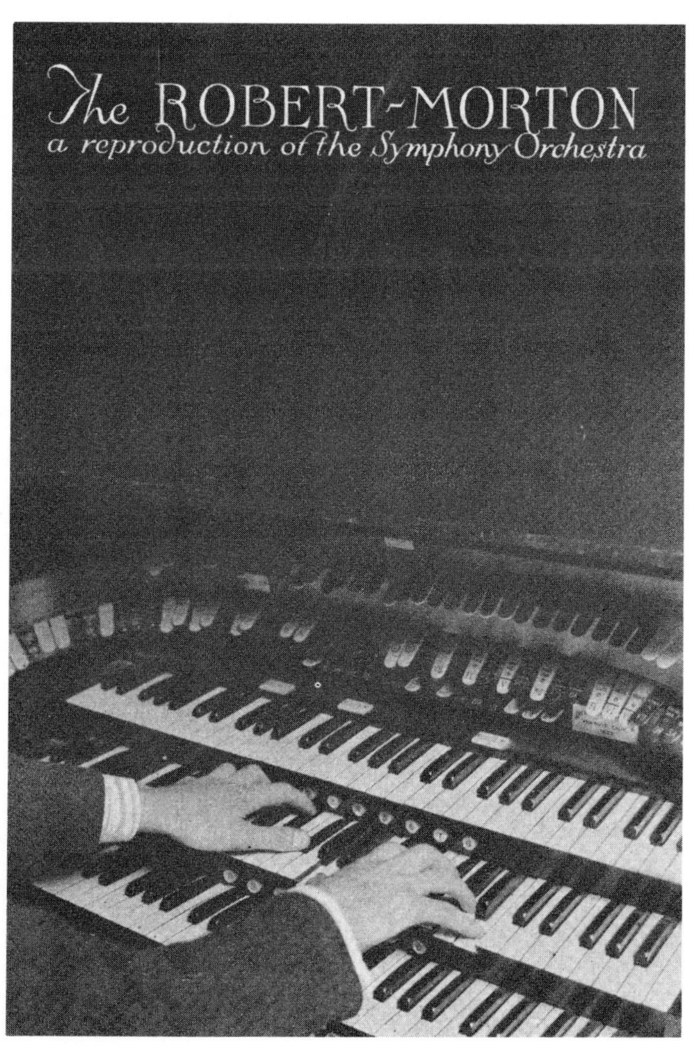

The ROBERT-MORTON
a reproduction of the Symphony Orchestra

TEMPLE THEATRE
MC COOK, NEB.

All divisions of the Robert-Morton are under expression, this being absolutely necessary to get proper orchestral effects. To obtain the best results, expression chambers should be constructed of solid concrete, with only one outlet for tone, the opening filled with shutters operating at the will of the performer.

Each shutter has its own electro-pneumatic engine to operate it and responds instantly to the will of the performer at the console.

PANTAGES THEATRE
SALT LAKE CITY, UTAH

The Robert-Morton Organ installed in this theatre is pleasing our patrons immensely and we can recommend it for tone quality and well adapted for both vaudeville and photoplay presentation.

The fact that we have ordered eleven of these instruments should prove without question of a doubt that we are fully convinced that this organ is the ideal instrument for our purpose.

ALEXANDER PANTAGES.
Per EDW J. FISHER.

OLYMPIA THEATRE
NEW YORK CITY

The Robert-Mortons installed in our Olympia and in our Bunny Theatres have proven entirely satisfactory in every respect.

We also desire to state that we have used the organ at the Olympia with our orchestra with wonderful results, and cannot recommend this combination too highly to the lovers of high-class music, at the same time producing a greater volume, thereby enabling you to use less men with the same results.

BRANDON & BRADBURY.
Per J. A. BRADBURY.

POWERS BROADWAY THEATRE
BOSTON, MASS.

Yours of the 6th inst. at hand. Yes, we are wholly satisfied with our Robert-Morton organ; it has proved all you claimed for it and if we were to build another theatre tomorrow we would install your organ.

You have fulfilled all your promises to us, and we wish you the good luck you deserve.

BROADWAY THEATRE.

CENTURY THEATRE
PHILADELPHIA, PA.

The Robert-Morton electro-pneumatic action is especially designed to meet theatre work. It is wonderfully responsive and is built of material and workmanship to withstand all conditions of use.

The Robert-Morton action is superior to others because there is one less movement between the touch of the key and the speaking of the pipe, thus decreasing the number of working parts and possibility of trouble. This construction increases the speed and efficiency of the action.

IRIS THEATRE
MILES CITY, MONT.

The Robert-Morton relay and switchboard are built in detachable units, any one of which may be disconnected in a few seconds, thus practically eliminating the cost of repairs. Efficient actions are assured by the simplicity of construction and the reliability and perfection of workmanship.

An organ may be perfect musically, but if the action is defective it is of very little use for theatre work.

NEW MISSION THEATRE
SAN FRANCISCO, CAL.

Wind pressure, obtained by the size and speed of the blower and regulated by the bellows in the different divisions of the organ, is responsible for the attack from the keys, promptness of speech and quality of tone of the instrument. The Robert-Morton experts are experienced in determining proper wind pressure, which, in the final analysis, insures a reliable tonal effect.

HOWARD THEATRE
ATLANTA, GA.

It is gratifying to advise you that the Robert-Morton Organ which you have just installed for us in the Howard Theatre, Atlanta, has met in every way with our entire satisfaction.

We selected your organ after careful consideration, as the one most fitted for our theatre which in architectural splendor and design equals, if not surpasses, any other theatre in the United States.

Atlanta Enterprises, Inc.
Troup Howard.

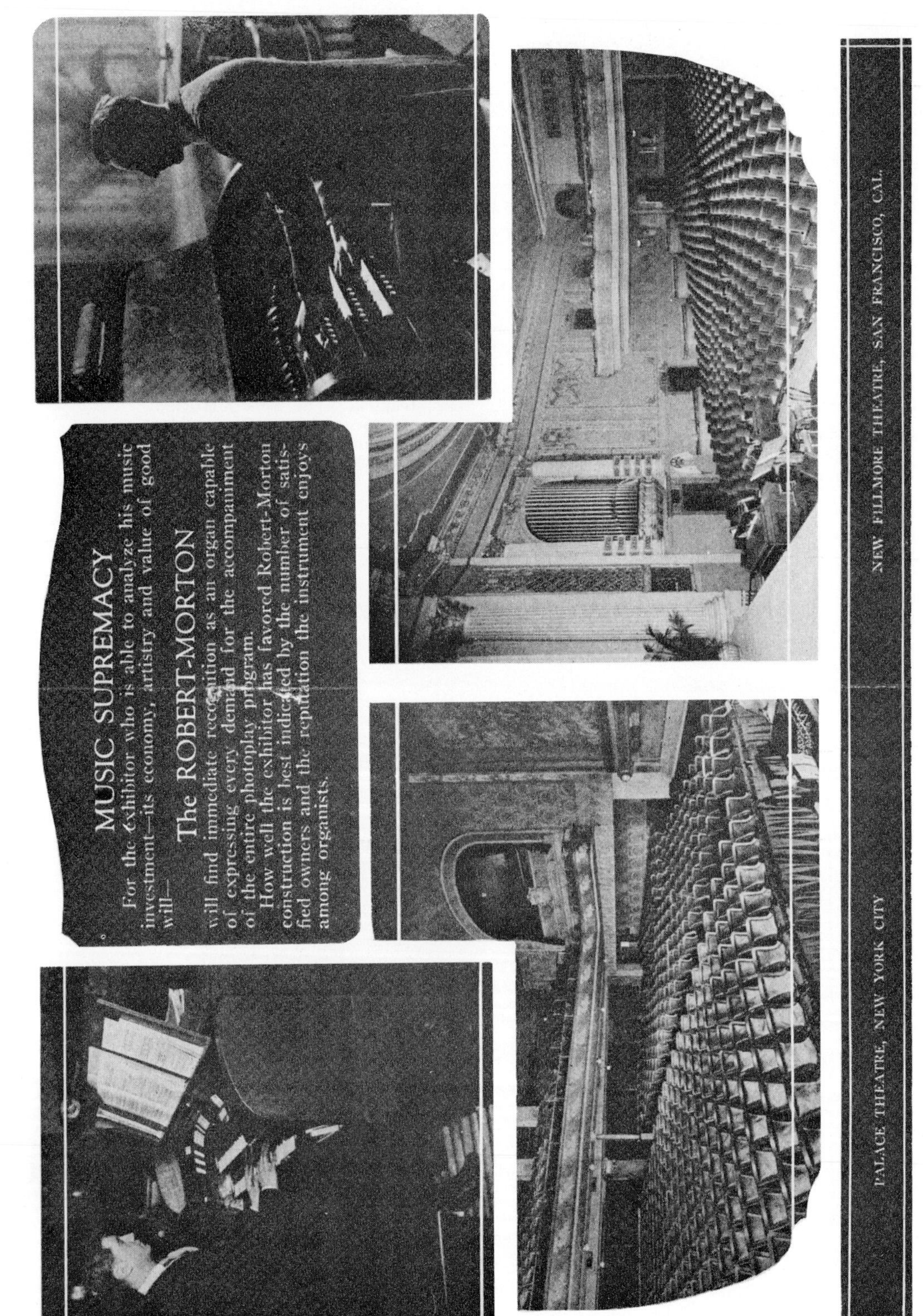

MUSIC SUPREMACY
For the exhibitor who is able to analyze his music investment—its economy, artistry and value of good will—
The ROBERT-MORTON
will find immediate recognition as an organ capable of expressing every demand for the accompaniment of the entire photoplay program.
How well the exhibitor has favored Robert-Morton construction is best indicated by the number of satisfied owners and the reputation the instrument enjoys among organists.
PALACE THEATRE, NEW YORK CITY
NEW FILLMORE THEATRE, SAN FRANCISCO, CAL.

Centerfold of the catalog reproduced on the preceding three pages.

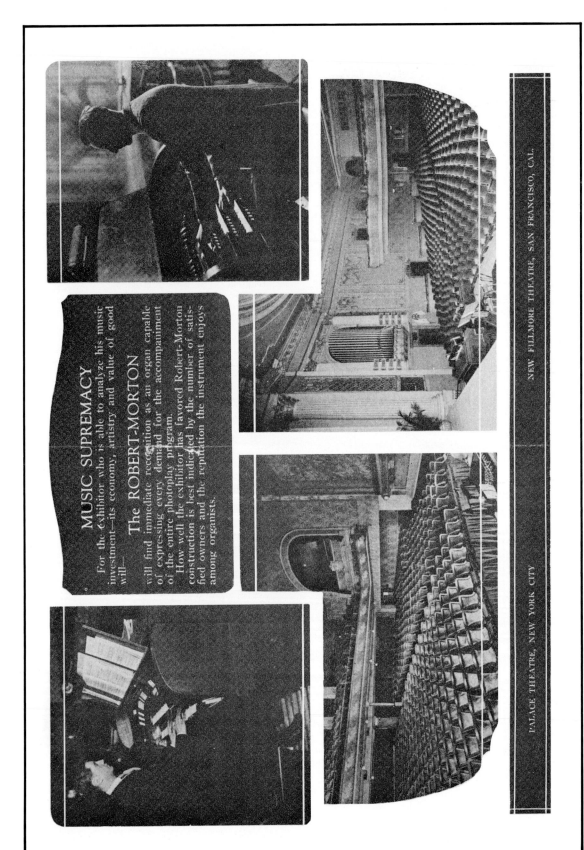

This photo of one of the popular style 75 Robert-Mortons was taken in the factory on October 15, 1920 by head voicer Bert Kingsley. It featured an early style of console with rounded case ends. Its four ranks are, front to back, vox humana, diapason, string and flute. Note that the tremolos are labeled "vibrators."

The second five-manual Robert-Morton was installed in the Kinema Theatre, Fresno, California in 1921. It was reportedly not a large organ, perhaps ten ranks or so, a size consistent with its 7½-horsepower blower.

This ornate little console was installed in the ninth floor apartment of a San Francisco doctor where it controlled a five-rank organ which included a piano. Note twin roll players.

Cecil B. DeMille (right) poses at the portable Robert-Morton in his movie studio. Its music helped actors Jacqueline Logan and Simon De Grasse get in the proper mood for acting in their silent dramas.[7]

At one time proclaimed "the most beautiful motor car showroom in the world," San Francisco's Cadillac dealership on Van Ness Avenue was one of the most unusual locations for a theatre organ. A 2/3 Robert-Morton, one of the earliest pit-style instruments produced by the firm, was installed here in 1922.

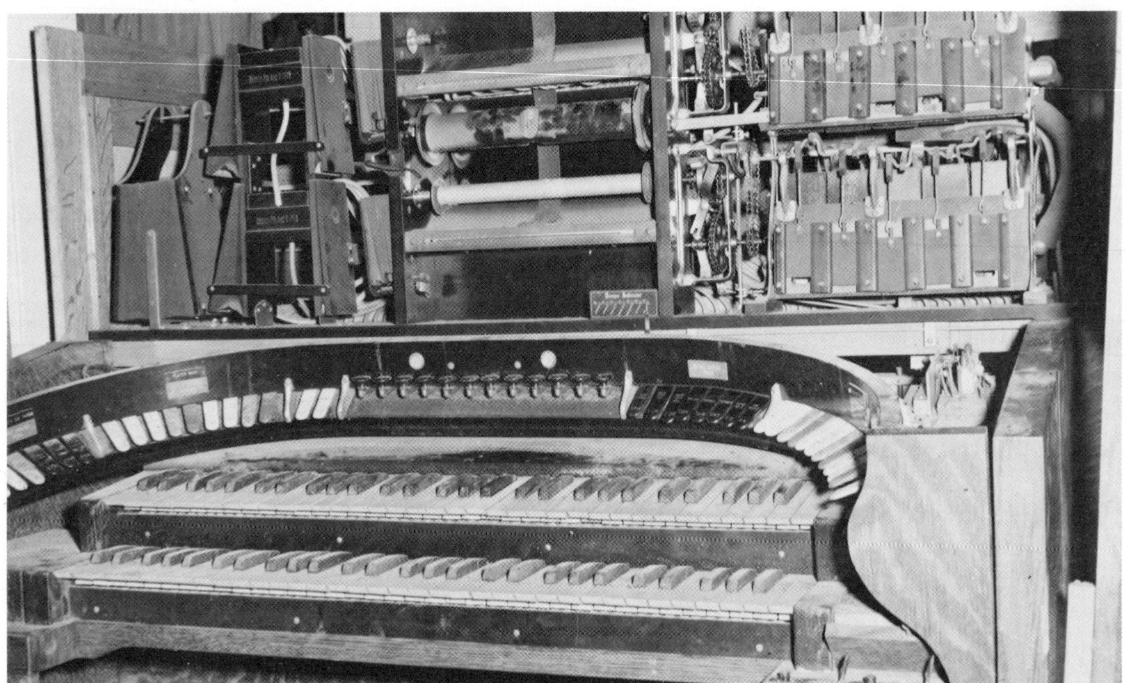

Removing the covers from a Robert-Morton style 49C pit organ console reveals a double roll player mechanism identical to that used in Fotoplayers. The two spool boxes accommodate standard 88-note player piano rolls, allowing an unlimited repertoire of music to be played. Stop keys are especially colorful, featuring white for the tibia, amber for the viol, pink for the diapson, red for the vox humana, black for percussions and blue for tremolos.

Rear of a style 49C pit organ console. In the center is a vacuum relay which plays the organ via one of two 88-note player piano rolls. Above the relay is a brass pneumatic transfer device which switches control of the relay from one roll to the other.

(opposite) Advertisement in the August 1, 1925 Exhibitor's Herald. *The ad's claims were accurate: the Robert Morton pit organs were indeed panaceas for smaller theatres with limited space and/or budgets. The company sold over one hundred of them.*

What hundreds of Exhibitors have been waiting for—

The NEW PIT PIPE ORGAN!

¶ A complete, two-manual-and-pedal Unit Pipe Organ
¶ Can be installed in any theatre — either in the pit or divided — without extra expense
¶ Does not require high priced organist ¶ Can be played by hand or by the genuine original Double Tracker "Fotoplayer" roll device.

A Permanent Music Attraction at a Minimum Cost.

Console of Style 49

Robert Morton Organ Co.

New York
150 W. 46th St.

Chicago
845 So. Wabash

Los Angeles
935 So. Olive

Berkeley
California

ROBERT MORTON ORGAN CO.

Send me without obligation full details of your New Selling Plan

-H-

Name . . . .
Theatre . . . .
Seating Capacity . . . .
City and State . . . .

GENUINE DEAGAN PERCUSSIONS USED

Factory photo of the 4/31 console installed in the Balboa Theatre, San Diego, California and later moved to the San Diego Fox Theatre. A poorly unified organ, it has only one row of stops for all those ranks on all those manuals.

A caravan of trucks transporting the Balboa organ was used to good advertising advantage on the journey between Van Nuys and San Diego.

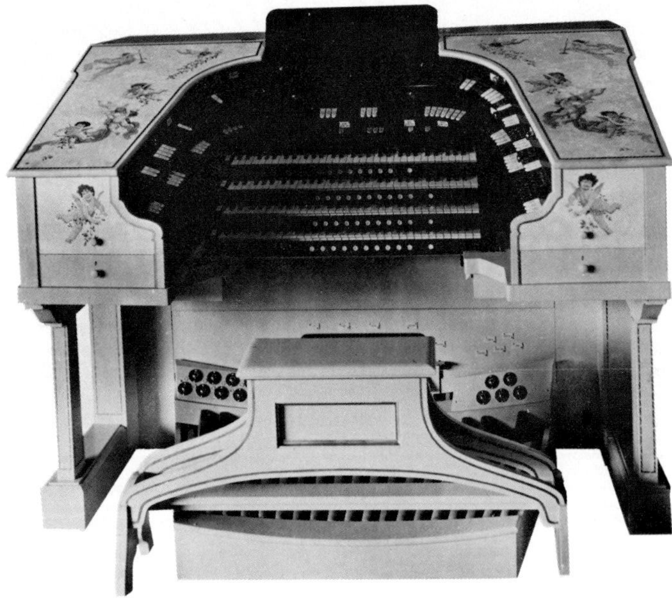

Judiciously applied paintings made this early Robert-Morton case style rather pretty. This design, with columns supporting the key desk, was used as late as 1925. Destination of this console is not known to the author.

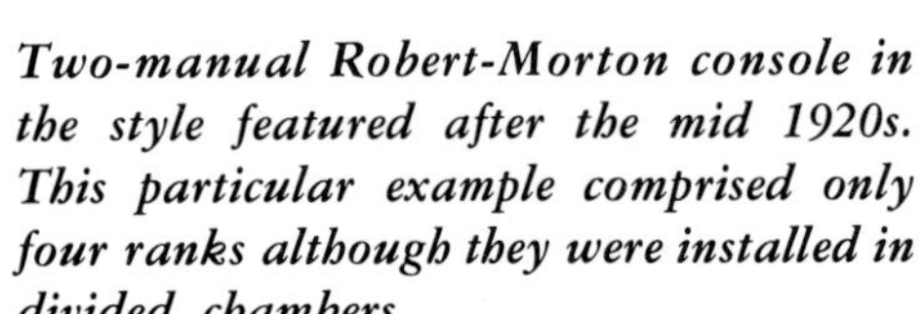

Two-manual Robert-Morton console in the style featured after the mid 1920s. This particular example comprised only four ranks although they were installed in divided chambers.

Two views of the second largest Robert Morton, installed in the Los Angeles Elks Temple in 1926. Note how the console opens for ease of servicing. The main console controls all of the instrument's 61 ranks; a two-manual console in the adjoining lobby (not pictured) plays just the antiphonal organ.

3/10 Robert Morton formerly in the Pantages Theatre, Portland, Oregon. A 1925 instrument, it was among the last to use the early case style with columns supporting the key desk.

4/20 Robert Morton in the Ohio Theare in Columbus sits on a wonderfully decorated lift platform.

The 4/21 Robert-Morton in San Francisco's Pantages (Orpheum) Theatre was unique in American theatre organ history in its panoramic disposition of pipework: Chambers were located on either side of the proscenium, under the stage and near the projection booth at the rear of the house.

(opposite) This 1926 ad features San Francisco installations in the Orpheum (center of page), Castro and St. Francis theatres. Detroit's Riviera is a curious foreigner.

The Robert Morton
UNIT ORGAN
Distinctly different from all other organs, its unapproached value as a Box Office Attraction makes the Robert Morton the choice of progressive Exhibitors everywhere.. Not only the Big Cinema Palaces, but the smaller theatres profitably feature Robert Morton music as a permanent attraction. It is the most powerful single factor any Exhibitor can employ to provide a complete Picture Presentation Program...... No other make of organ approaches Robert Morton in Quality, Volume, Distinctiveness of Tone, Orchestral Resources or Variety of Effects.
Write today for our new
R.M.O.C. PURCHASE PLAN
designed to give the exhibitor the advantage of Convenient Terms of Purchase without the usual High Financing Costs...
Robert Morton Organ Co.
Manufacturers of Pipe Organs Exclusively
New York 1560 Broadway
Chicago 845 So. Wabash
San Francisco 168 Golden Gate
Los Angeles 1914 So. Vermont
PANTAGES CIRCUIT OF VAUDEVILLE THEATRES
ALEXANDER PANTAGES, OWNER AND GENERAL MANAGER
MAIN EXECUTIVE OFFICE LOS ANGELES, PANTAGES THEATRE
ADMINISTRATIVE OFFICES SEATTLE, WASH., PANTAGES THEATRE
OFFICE OF ALEXANDER PANTAGES PANTAGES THEATRE, LOS ANGELES SEVENTH AT HILL
"America's Finest"
PLAYING PANTAGES VAUDEVILLE
BOOKING OFFICES
NEW YORK—FITZGERALD BUILDING
CHICAGO—1106 NORTH AMERICAN BLDG.
SAN FRANCISCO—PANTAGES THEATRE
March 23rd 1926
Mr. J. A. C. Schiller, Gen. Mgr.,
Robert Morton Organ Co.,
168 Golden Gate Avenue,
San Francisco, Calif.
Dear Mr. Schiller:
I want to take this opportunity to congratulate you on the wonderful organ you installed in the New Pantages Theatre here. We have received countless letters of praise on this fine instrument and can truthfully say that in presentation, tone and quality, it is second to none in the United States.
I want you to know that we also appreciate the excellent service you have extended to us on the organ since the opening of the house.
Very truly yours,
PANTAGES THEATRE,
R. Pantages
General Manager
RP
RW
CASTRO
RIVIERA
GENUINE DEAGAN PERCUSSIONS USED

at last!

the incorporation of genuine string tones in a Pipe Organ

¶ VIOLIN — CELLO

all the effects of the string division of an orchestra actually reproduced

VIOLA — BASS VIOL

The Robert Morton

V'OLEON

Robert Morton Organ Co.

New York
1560 Broadway

Chicago
845 So. Wabash

Los Angeles
1914 So. Vermont

San Francisco
168 Golden Gate

write today for complete information

watch for forthcoming announcement

GENUINE DEAGAN PERCUSSIONS USED

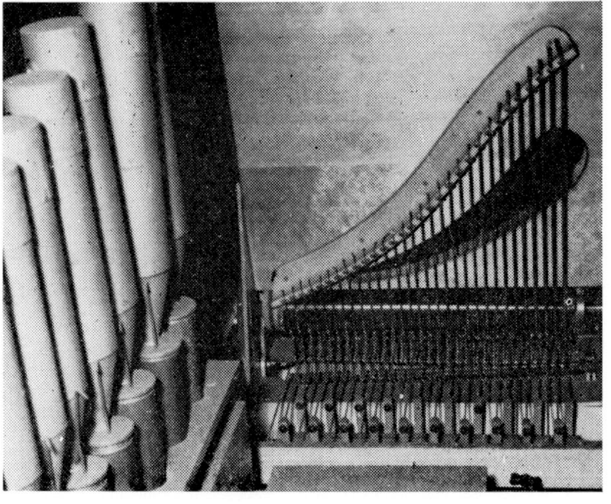

Operation of the V'Oleon was simple and clever. Its strings were coiled and under only light tension, assisting them to remain in tune. Vacuum-operated pneumatics forced the strings in contact with a revolving roller, "bowing" them to produce tones. Any number of strings could be sounded simultaneously, allowing large chords to be played. A tremolo effect was achieved by means of a reciprocating felt-notched bar which gently wiggled the strings back and forth across the revolving roller.

San Francisco, California

Mr. E A Spencer Nov. 7, 1922
19 Chestnut Ave.,
Pasadena, California

Dear Sir:

I am sending you under separate cover photos of my instrument and wish to state that it is a marvel.

I built one and added it to the Tivoli organ and you would have been surprised to have heard the great improvement it made., Every one that heard it claimed it a success and could see where it would make the organ really orchestral, producing not an imitation of the string quality but the real thing, and the tones stand out above any of the pipe sets and played in combination with the pipes adds the real soul quality.

I have completed an instrument and you can see by the photo that it includes the violin, viola, cello and double bass and had it at the Industrial Exhibition and met with good success, and proving that I could produce the string tones that were real, otherwise than by a stringed instrument.

I have arranged for the manufacture of the instruments either for vacuum or pressure, and now I am looking for a market The Photo Player Co. wants the proposition bad bnt on the same terms, similar to those made you, and knowing your results with them, I am not considering them, but trying to handle the situation myself. Now that we are both endeavoring to make a success on our own ability, why not join forces and turn out a wonderful instrument. It is a known fact that your organ construction is the most practical and reliable of any instrument built on this Coast, and with my instrument in one of your organs you would have the world beat.

I am designing the instrument to occupy a space about 48"x48"x24", and will be able to furnish you the instrument at less than $500. According to the specifications, the instrument is going to be wonderful for the church, as it will put the sob into the organ.

Let me have a favorable reply from you and I will ship you an instrument that will put you on the head lines.

Awaiting an early reply, I remain

Yours very truly

2809 Gough Street Harry L Boynton

(opposite) A 1926 ad introduces the V'Oleon. Around this same time the Kilgen company sold organs with Mills Violano attachments. Mills violins exceeded V'Oleons both in volume and in tonal realism but few of either unit were ever installed.

Inventor of the V'Oleon, Harry L. Boynton, offered his device to Pasadena organ builder E. A. Spencer four years before it was adopted by Robert-Morton. Spencer at this time had left the American Photo Player Co. to go into business for himself.

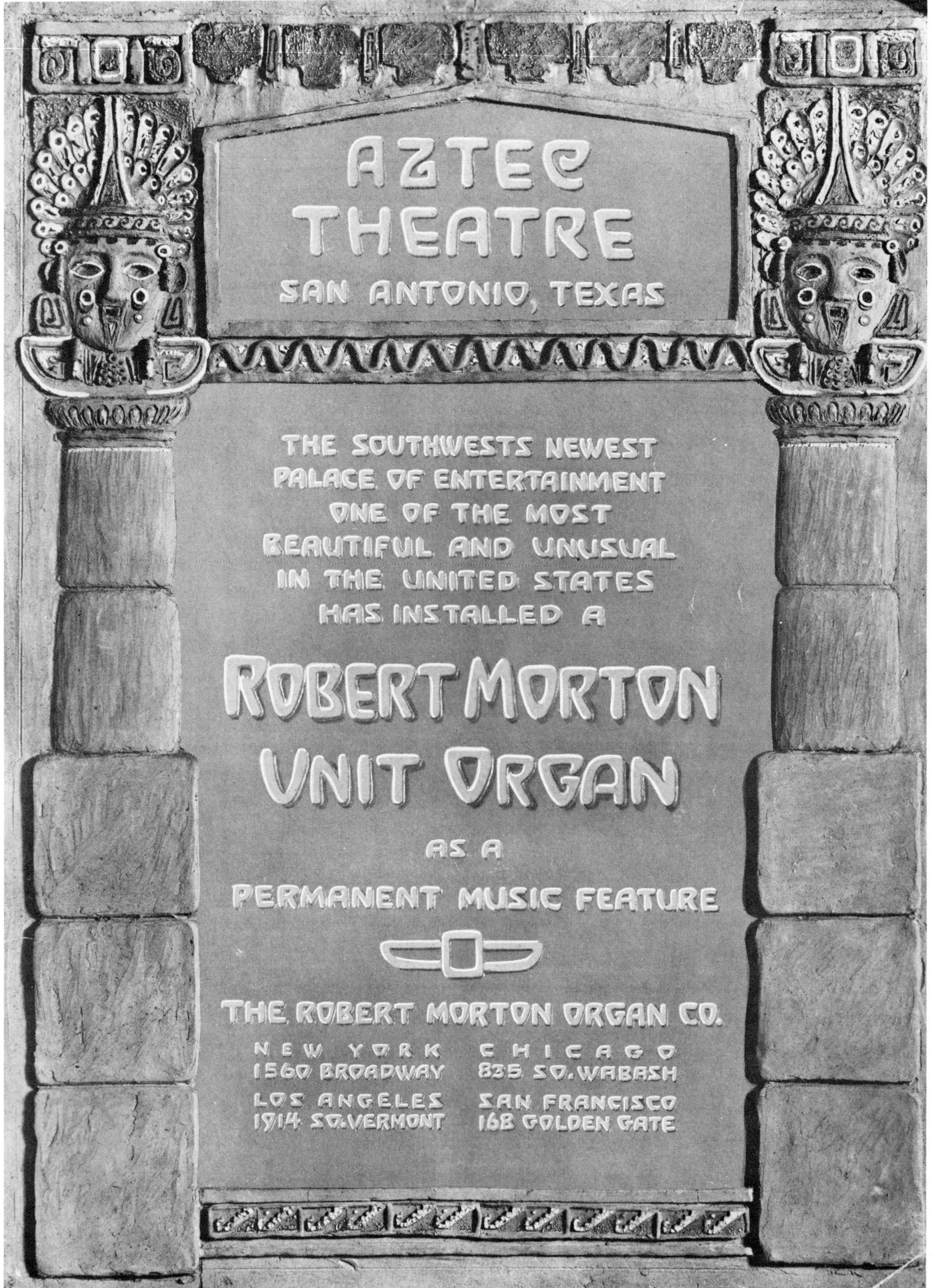
AZTEC
THEATRE
SAN ANTONIO, TEXAS
THE SOUTHWESTS NEWEST
PALACE OF ENTERTAINMENT
ONE OF THE MOST
BEAUTIFUL AND UNUSUAL
IN THE UNITED STATES
HAS INSTALLED A
ROBERT MORTON
UNIT ORGAN
AS A
PERMANENT MUSIC FEATURE
THE ROBERT MORTON ORGAN CO.
NEW YORK
1560 BROADWAY
CHICAGO
835 SO. WABASH
LOS ANGELES
1914 SO. VERMONT
SAN FRANCISCO
168 GOLDEN GATE

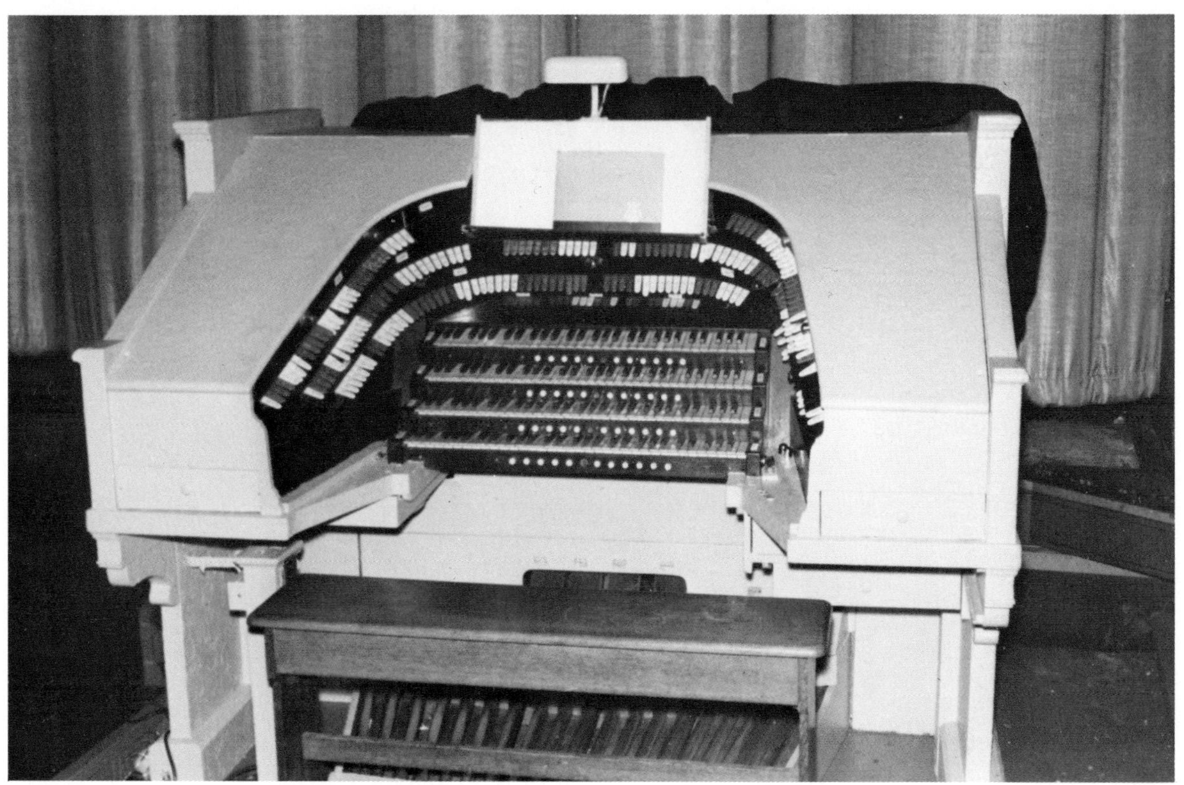

The Saenger Theatre in New Orleans, the flagship of Julian Saenger's southern theatre empire, housed one of Robert Morton's "show" organs, a 4/23 installed in 1927. Shortly thereafter a fife and two more strings were added, bringing the instrument to a total of 26 ranks. The organ originally featured a second console, the only Robert Morton known by the author to be so equipped. The main console is pictured as it appeared in later years with a new paint job and a non-original bench. A particularly unique feature of the Saenger organ is its square *bass drum, shown here in both front and rear views.*

(opposite) R. P. Matthews, Robert Morton's advertising genius and general manager, ran this ad in the June 24, 1927 issue of Motion Picture News. *It is one of the author's favorite ads because its appealing graphics complement the Central American theme of the Aztec Theatre. The Aztec's 3/11 organ was also unusual inasmuch as it contained a piano, a feature uncommon in Robert Morton instruments.*

THE ROBERT MORTON COMPANY
VAN NUYS, CALIFORNIA

PENN-FEDERAL CORP

Organ No. 2314 Built for LOEWS PENN THEATRE Address PITTSBURGH, PA. Date Promised Estimated Cost $ Date Changed Est. Cost $

1927 Style SPECIAL FOUR MANUAL Special 20 STOPS ~~Straight~~ 16 COUPLERS Unified 146 TIMES Divided ~~Undivided~~ Date Started Date Finished Date Shipped JULY 2, 1927 Shipped via SOU. PAC. F. O. B. FACTORY San Francisco Order 2531

REPORTED ON SHIPPING ORDER No. #267 7/30/27

ORGAN SIMILAR TO ORGAN No. SHIPPING ORDER No. Included in #283

BUILT IN SERIES OF

PERCENTAGE OF OVERHEAD

STATE NUMBER OF NOTES ON ALL CHESTS

Shop Order No.		Material	Labor	Overhead	Detail Totals	Grand Totals
	CONSOLE					
7097 6011	Case	6882	14655	10991	32528	
7102	Stop Action 182 KEYS	5134	8772	8383	22289	
7099	Switchboard	1883	4905	3679	10467	
7104	Comb Action Drawers	6949	16883	12602	36434	
7103	Comb Action Box and ~~Piston Action~~ *	6881	6600	4953	18434	
7101	Key Action 4 MANUAL	12061	6209	4654	22924	
	Manual Key Blocks					
	Trap Relays					
5989	Engrave Keys	4435	2698	2024	9157	
	Lamps					
	Transformer					
A18-02 A16-20	Pedal Movements 3 PEDALS 260 CONTACTS	506	1426	1052	2984	
7098	Pedal Keys (Cabinet Work) DOUBLE TOUCH	1535	2898	2172	6605	
	Pedal Keys (Electric Work)					
7096	Assembling	3397	16662	12497	32556	
	Name Plate					
A20-14 5564	Bench	364	1161	870	2395	
	Player Device					
A19-08	4 PISTON ACTION (11 UNIT SETS) *	475	781	582	1858	
7109	WIRE CONSOLE & PEDAL BOARD	3450	8813	6613	18876	
7125 4926	6 SPECIAL PEDAL LEVER ACTIONS	443	1207	905	2555	
	Total Cost	54415	93670	71977		220062
	~~UNIT~~ CHESTS ~~(Main)~~					
A15-03	Number 1 8 VOX HUMANA 73N	1839	1757	1318	4914	
A15-03	Number 2 8 VOX HUMANA 73N	1839	1757	1318	4914	
A15-03	Number 3 8 CLARINET 73N	1839	1757	1318	4914	
A15-03	8' KINURA 73N	1839	1757	1318	4914	
A15-03	4 OBOE HORN 61N	1839	1757	1318	4914	
A15-03	Total Cost 4' ENGLISH HORN & T.O. TUBA 73N	1839	1757	1318	4914	
A15-04	UNIT SEPARATE CHESTS 4' GAMBA 73N	1813	1753	1315	4881	
A15-04	Number 1 4' SALICIONAL 61N	1813	1753	1315	4881	
A15-04	Number 2 4' VIOLIN CELESTE II & T.O. FLUTE 73N	1813	1753	1315	4881	
A15-04	Number 3 4' VIOLIN CELESTE III & T.O. SAX. 73N	1813	1753	1315	4881	
A15-04	Number 4 4 VIOLIN CELESTE & T.O. FRENCH TRUMPET 73N	1813	1753	1315	4881	
A15-04	Number 5 4' CONCERT VIOLIN 61N	1813	1753	1315	4881	
A15-05	Number 6 4' CONCERT FLUTE 61N	1610	1557	1168	4335	
A15-05	2' TIBIA CLAUS 61N	1610	1557	1168	4335	
A15-05	Total Cost 4' HORN DIAPASON 61N	1610	1557	1168	4335	
A15-05	STANDARD ACTION CHESTS 2' TIBIA PLENA 49N	1610	1557	1168	4335	
A15-05	Solo 4' MAJOR DIAPASON 57N	1610	1557	1168	4335	
A15-06	Echo 4' TUBA 49N	1410	1495	1121	4026	
A15-06	Swell 4' FRENCH TRUMPET 49N	1410	1495	1121	4026	
A15-06	Great 4' SAXAPHONE 49N	1410	1495	1121	4026	
A15-07	Choir 8' FLUTE 12N	1056	1303	973	3332	
A15-07	4' TIBIA CLAUSA 12N	1056	1303	973	3332	
A15-07	Total Cost 4' TIBIA PLENA 8N	1056	1303	973	3332	
	STANDARD CHESTS—STOP ACTION					
A15-11	Solo 8' HORN DIAPASON & 8' SAXAPHONE 24N	1447	2065	1548	5060	
A15-11	Echo 16' OBOE HORN & 8' OBOE HORN 24N	1447	2065	1548	5060	
A15-11	Swell 8' TUBA & 8' ENGLISH HORN 24N	1447	2065	1548	5060	
A15-11	Great 8' MAJ. DIAPASON & FRENCH TRUMPET 24N	1447	2065	1548	5060	
	Choir 1568					
	CARRIED FORWARD	15476	42749	32007	90232	
	Total Cost	58624	88248	66119		212991
7693	SWELL FRONTS—State No. TWO 24 BLIND	12715	6107	4580	23402	
	SWELL BOXES—State No. NONE					
A24-01	SWELL ENGINES—State No. FOUR 12 BLIND	5448	7980	5976	19404	
7106	3 MAIN RELAY	17771	29737	22268	69776	
A19-01 A19-17	GAS VALVES—State No. FOUR 3" & THREE 4"	809	937	702	2449	
A19-66 A19-09	BELLOWS—State No. TWO 3'X4', SEVEN 2'X3'	16692	15150	11364	43206	
A19-04	VOX REGULATORS, ETC.—State No. TWO 1'6½"X2'10½"	2057	2376	1781	6214	
A20-01,02,03 & 11	VIBRATORS—State No. SIX 7½"X15" & COVERS, TWO VOX	2692	3785	2824	9301	
	WIRING SEE BELOW					
7696	2 BUILDING FRAMES & 3 FLOOR FRAMES	7583	6312	4737	18632	
7100	3 ORGAN SWITCHBOARD	14210	28468	21353	64031	
	VARNISHING					
A19-02	THREE PRESSURE REGULATORS	292	610	457	1359	
A19-04	ONE 1'6½"X2'10½" REGULATOR FOR 4' TUBA	1029	1188	891	3108	
A22-09	ONE 8"X11½"X15" WIND INTAKE BOX ASSEM. (NO HOLE)	83	72	54	209	
7111	WIRE PERCUSSIONS	1413	1650	1237	4300	
7110	WIRE SWITCHBOARD & RELAY	40518	42203	31664	114385	
7112	WIRE CHESTS & SWELL ENGINES	49267	10271	7703	67241	
	TOTALS FORWARD	172579	156846	117591		447016

*SMALL TRAPS
Consists of Siren, Firegong, Klaxon, Sleighbells, Doorbell, Telephone Bell, Maid's Bell.

Shop Order No.		No.	Pitch	Voicing	Material	Labor	Overhead	Detail Totals	Grand Totals
	FORWARD								
7973	PIPES MITER MISCL. PIPES					1200	360	1560	
5864	TUBA PROFUNDA	85	16'		23327	24668	8498	56493	
6152	OBOE HORN	12	16'		6163	6833	2314	15310	
A27-09 (6152)	OBOE HORN	73	8'		3519	6143	2540	12202	
7119	MAJOR DIAPHONE	12	16'		8393	7633	4792	20818	
7170	MAJOR DIAPASON	73	8'		7207	6499	2414	16120	
6911 (7118)	TIBIA CLAUSA	12	16'		6133	4567	3223	13923	
A25-07 (7115)	TIBIA CLAUSA	85	8'		3064	6865	4240	14169	
A25-01 (7116)	BASS FLUTE	12	16'		4983	3292	2312	10587	
A25-06 (7117)	FLUTE	85	8'		1863	4915	2866	9644	
6154	GAMBA	97	16'		7606	10701	3601	21908	
6910	FRENCH TRUMPET	73	8'		3468	8013	3520	15001	
8049	SAXOPHONE	73	8'		8214	15247	6274	29735	
A27-08	ENGLISH HORN	73	8'		3022	7308	3146	13476	
6932 A26-14	TIBIA PLENA	73	8		4753	8190	5339	18282	
6155	HORN DIAPASON	73	8'		4518	5130	1935	11583	
6156	SALICIONAL	73	8		2446	4914	1629	8989	
6157	VIOLA CELESTE	73	8'		3639	5151	1717	10507	
A26-05 (7063)	CONCERT VIOLIN	73	8'		2629	6432	2174	11235	
A26-14 (7064)	VIOLIN CELESTE II	73	8'		3344	6382	2136	11862	
A26-16 (7065)	VIOLIN CELESTE III	73	8'		3344	6299	2074	11717	
A27-03 (7446)	KINURA	73	8'		1882	5687	2282	9851	
A27-01 (6311)	CLARINET	73	8'		2801	5940	2338	11076	
A27-06 (5907)	VOX HUMANA	73	8'		2371	6484	2570	11425	
A27-24 (6789)	SOLO VOX HUMANA	73	8'		2312	8374	3963	14649	
	Total Cost	1568			121068	182867	78247		382182
7114	ASSEMBLING, GENERAL ERECTING AND TESTING				12004	57683	42993	12004 100676	112680
7115	PACK & SHIP				25386	24407	18303	68096	68096
	TOTAL COST ORGAN				444821	603721	395230		1442972
7113	TRAPS								
	Marimba Harp 49				15000			15000	
	GLOCKENSPIEL ~~Orchestra Bells~~ 37—With ~~or Without~~ Resonators				6075			6075	
	Xylophone 37—~~With or~~ Without Resonators				3272			3272	
	Chrysoglott 49				8546			8546	
	Chimes 20				6152			6152	
	Chimes Direct Electric 20								
A18-01	Bass Drum & ACTION				4412	1516	1134	7062	
A18-02	Snare Drum & ACTION				1446	469	350	2265	
	Tympani								
	Crash Cymbal								
	Cymbal								
	Wood Drum				72			72	
	Castanets				59			59	
	Tambourine				260			260	
	Triangle				71			71	
A18-33	Bird Whistle				104	07	05	116	
	Tomtom				139			139	
A18-09	Piano No. SLEIGH BELL & ACTION				230	329	247	806	
A18-61	Piano Work WIND & WAVE				102	708	531	1341	
A18-69	Suction Bellows SURF ACTION COMP.				333	2034	1525	3892	
	*Small Traps CHINESE GONG 39, DOOR BELL 65, AUTO HORN 214, TELEPHONE BELL 35, FIRE GONG 361, HORSE HOOFS 30				998			998	
7113	TRAP ACTIONS								
A17-05	Marimba Harp				3981	4150	3107	11238	
A17-16	~~Orchestra Bells~~ GLOCKENSPEIL				2356	2558	1890	6804	
A17-02	Xylophone				2180	2779	2063	7022	
A17-04	Chrysoglott				2682	2954	2216	7852	
A17-01	Chimes				1603	1429	1070	4102	
	Chimes Direct Electric								
	Bass Drum								
	Snare Drum								
	Tympani								
	Crash Cymbal								
	Cymbal								
	Wood Drum								
A18-26	Castanets CHINESE GONG ACTION BOX				208	531	397	1136	
A18-44	Tambourine TWO #4 ACTION BOXES				554	612	460	1626	
A18-42	Triangle ONE #2 " "				141	260	195	596	
	Bird Whistle AEROPLANE ACTION				106	733	528	1367	
	Tomtom 1 SET OF 2 CHIMES FOR CHURCH BELL				10638			10638	
7502	Piano 2 NOTE CHIMES ACTION " " "				1221	4280	3210	8711	
7113	Assembling Traps				1264	2743	2056	6063	
	TOTAL COST TRAPS AND ACTIONS				74205	28042	20984		123281
	Blower No. 20433								
	WOODS Motor No. 13872 H.P. 25 A.C. Volt 230 Ph. 3 Cy. 60				87500			87500	
	Generator No. 81812 Amp. 100 Volt 10				8031			8031	
8209	Player Vacuum Blower MOUNT GENERATOR				630	385	289	1304	
	U.S. GEN. ~~Player~~ Motor No. 43066 H.P. 2 A.C. Volt 220 Cy. 60 Ph. 3				5085			5085	101920
	PACKING AND SHIPPING								
	TOTAL COST				619472	632198	416503		1668173

Paul Whiteman (left) grins approval as Dick Leibert plays the 4/20 Robert Morton in Loew's Penn Theatre, Pittsburgh, Pennsylvania.

(opposite) This page, reproduced from one of the remaining Robert Morton cost-accounting ledger books, reveals many fascinating details of one of the company's larger instruments. (below) These items were taped to the ledger sheet reproduced on the preceding page. The organ for Loew's Penn had more chests than could be accommodated by Robert Morton's standard ledger sheet; hence these addenda.

COPIES { FACTORY / DRAFTING / COST / OFFICE / SAN FRANCISCO

5-25-VN NEWS

ROBERT MORTON ORGAN CO.
VAN NUYS, CAL.
MANUFACTURING INSTRUCTIONS

DATE Marc…
This sheet can…
instructions issu…

1 ORGAN NO. 2 3 1 4
2 STYLE ORGAN Special 4 Manual - 20 Stops
3 S. F. ORDER 2 5 3 6 - Sales #5037
4 TO BE DELIVERED TO PENN-FEDERAL CORP., Loews Penn Theatre, Pittsburg, Pa.
5 BILL OF LADING Straight
6 ROUTE Boat
7 PREPAID OR COLLECT f.o.b. installed - prepay freight
8 DATE OF DELIVERY Autumn of 1927 --- Ship about June 25th., to open Labor Day
9 ELECTRIC SPEC. H. P. 25 VOLTAGE 230 PHASE 3 CYCLE 60 AC ORDER NO.
10 GENERATOR VOLTAGE 10 AMPS. 100 DIRECT BELT to sep.2 HP Motor
11 SWELL BOX
12 DIVIDED
13 STANDARD
14 SPECIAL
15 BLUE PRINT To come
16 DATA SHEET
17 SPECIFICATIONS Here
18 PIANO
19 CHIMES
20 TRAPS
TRAPS
21 PERCUSSIONS
PERCUSSIONS
22 REMARKS Stops

20 &

Stops			
15" Tuba Profunda-Low 12 to match 7" at CC		16 - 85	7" at CC
15" Oboe Horn		16 - 85	Capped & Faggoto Bass
15" Diapason 16' Oct. 20" Wind		16 - 85	40 Sc. at 8'
15" Tibia Cl.		16 - 97	#1 Scale
15" Flute		16 - 97	Reg. 9x11½
15" Gamba		16 - 97	9 D
15" French Trumpet		8 - 73	4"
15" Saxophone		8 - 73	Reg.
15" Eng. Horn		8 - 73	Reg. Scale
15" Horn Diap.		8 - 73	44
15" Tibia Plena		8 - 73	Reg.
15" Salicional	(Spotted)	8 - 73	16 D
15" Viola Cel.	(Spotted)	8 - 73	10 D
15" Conc. Violin	(Tin)	8 - 73	3
15" Viol Cel. II	(")	8 - 73	2"
15" " " III	(")	8 - 73	2"
15" Kinura		8 - 73	Reg.
15" Clarinet		8 - 73	Reg.
8" Vox Humana		8 - 73	Reg.
" Solo Vox		8 - 73	Style 2 W or Midwest

Percussions	
✓Mar. Harp	49
✓Chrysoglott	49
✓Xylophone	37 No Res.
✓Glockenspl.	37 Res.
✓Chimes	20

NOTE: Glockenspiel Use (1) instrument & wire action single stroke for Glockenspiel & re-iterating for Orch. Bells

Traps
✓Bass Drum
✓Tympani
✓Cymbal
✓Crash Cymbal
✓Snare Drum
✓Tambourine
✓Castanets
✓Wood Drum
✓Tom Tom
✓Chinese Gong
✓Triangle
✓Bird
✓Klaxon
✓Fire Gong
✓Steamboat
Church Bells
✓Cluster Sl.Bells
✓Surf
✓Wind
✓Door Bell
✓Telephone Bel…
✓Aeroplane
✓Thunder
✓Horse H…

A15-12	16' TUBA PROFUNDA	12N.	14 27	20 51	15 38	50 16
915-13	16' BASS FLUTE 8 8 CON. VIOLIN	24N	16 84	24 45	18 33	59 62
915-14	8' SALICIONAL	12N	5 26	8 60	6 45	20 31
915-24	8' VIOLIN CELESTE II & 8' VIOLIN CEL.	24N	8 67	12 44	9 24	30 35
11525	16' MAJOR DIAPHONE	12N	16 15	31 78	23 78	71 71
7945	8' TIBIA CLAUSA	12N	4 14	23 95	17 96	46 05
7798	SPECIAL CHEST FOR					
	16' TIBIA CLAUSA	12N				
	16' GAMBA	12N				
	8' GAMBA	12N	38 31	94 35	70 78	203 44
	8' MAJOR DIAPASON	4N				
	8' VIOLA CELESTE	12N				
7108	RACK PIPES ON CHESTS		34 53	176 09	131 65	342 27
8252	CUT 4 NOTES FROM TIBIA PLENA CHEST		2 25	6 14	4 61	13 00
7695	8' TIBIA PLENA CHEST	16N	13 68	26 75	20 07	60 50
7991	6 PIPE FEET		66	2 43	1 82	4 91
	FORWARD		154 76	427 49	320 07	902 32

4/14 Robert Morton in the Pantages (Warner) (Warnor) Theatre, Fresno, California. A real "barn burner," this organ, like most Pantages instruments, was installed under the stage. One can only imagine a front-row patron's reaction to the 16′ post horn on 20″ wind pressure. The console lift, just about the fastest in the west, has given unsuspecting organists another variety of thrill.

3/8 Robert Morton installed in the Ritz (Manos) Theatre, Indiana, Pennsylvania in 1928. Even at this late date Robert Mortons were not as well unified as many other brands. Nevertheless, the relatively small number of stops was disposed in a rather large console shell.

Ann Reiling prepares to broadcast a 3/10 Robert Morton over Kansas City station KMBC. The organ was moved to KMBC from the Wade Hamilton studio in Tulsa, Oklahoma where it was originally installed in 1929.

4/16 Robert Morton in the Fox (Seventh Avenue) (Music Hall) Theatre, Seattle, Washington. This organ, recalled Robert Morton vice-president R. P. Matthews, was the first to have a really satisfactory krumet rank.[3]

The Majestic Theatre in San Antonio, Texas had a late model 3/10 Robert Morton installed in 1929. Its jewelled and red leatherette covered console was quite unique, to say the least.

Noted organ and theatre historian Ben Hall expresses glee at the sound of the 4/23 "Wonder Morton" in Peter Schaeble's residence on Long Island. Originally installed in Loew's Valencia Theatre in Jamaica, New York, this organ has a console similar but not quite identical to the other four "Wonder Mortons" installed in New York area Loew houses.

Maurice Cook poses at the 4/20 Robert Morton in Loew's State Theatre, Providence, Rhode Island. Note RM logo in medallion on console's top.

Carl Weiss plays the 3/13 Robert Morton in Loew's Pitkin Theatre, Brooklyn, New York. Console decoration was similar to its big 4/23 brothers in other New York area Loew houses.

4/23 ROBERT MORTON THEATRE ORGAN
Loew's Paradise Theatre, Bronx, New York

PEDAL

red blank stop
32′ Resultant Bass
16′ Tuba Profunda
16′ Oboe Horn
16′ Diaphone
16′ Solo Tibia Clausa
16′ Bourdon
16′ Gamba
8′ Tuba Mirabilis
8′ English Horn
8′ Oboe Horn
8′ Saxophone
8′ Diaphonic Diapason
8′ Horn Diapason
8′ Tibia Plena
8′ Solo Tibia Clausa
8′ Flute
8′ Gamba
8′ Viola Celeste
8′ Violin
8′ Celeste Violin
Bass Drum
Tympani
Cymbal
Snare Drum

PEDAL 2nd TOUCH

Chimes
Bass Drum
Tympani
Cymbal
Crash Cymbal
Snare Drum

ORCHESTRAL

8′ Tuba Mirabilis
8′ English Horn
8′ Oboe Horn
8′ Trumpet
8′ French Horn
8′ Saxophone
8′ Diaphonic Diapason
8′ Horn Diapason
8′ Solo Tibia Clausa
8′ Foundation Tibia Clausa
8′ Flute
8′ Salicional
8′ Concert Violin
8′ Celeste Violin
8′ Kinura
8′ Clarinet
8′ Krumet
4′ Tuba Mirabilis
4′ Solo Tibia Clausa
4′ Foundation Tibia Clausa
4′ Flute
4′ Celeste Violin
2′ Piccolo
2′ Violin
Harp
Chrysoglott
Glockenspiel
Orchestra Bells
Xylophone
Chimes
16′ Orch
4′ Orch
8′ Great

GREAT

red blank stop
16′ Tuba Profunda
16′ Oboe Horn
16′ Saxophone TC
16′ Diaphone
16′ Tibia Plena TC
16′ Solo Tibia Clausa
16′ Bourdon
16′ Gamba
16′ Contra Viol TC
16′ Celeste Violin TC
16′ Foundation Vox Humana TC
8′ Tuba Mirabilis
8′ English Horn
8′ Oboe Horn
8′ Trumpet
8′ French Horn
8′ Saxophone
8′ Diaphonic Diapason
8′ Horn Diapason
8′ Tibia Plena
8′ Solo Tibia Clausa
8′ Foundation Tibia Clausa
8′ Flute
8′ Gamba
8′ Viola Celeste
8′ Salicional
8′ Concert Violin
8′ Celeste Violin
8′ Kinura
8′ Clarinet
8′ Krumet
8′ Foundation Vox Humana
4′ Tuba Mirabilis
4′ Oboe Horn
4′ Diaphonic Diapason
4′ Horn Diapason
4′ Tibia Plena
4′ Solo Tibia Clausa
4′ Foundation Tibia Clausa
4′ Flute
4′ Gamba
4′ Viola Celeste
4′ Concert Violin
4′ Celeste Violin
4′ Foundation Vox Humana
2 2/3′ Twelfth
2′ Piccolo
2′ Fifteenth
1 3/5′ Tierce
Harp
Chrysoglott
Glockenspiel
Orchestra Bells
Xylophone
Chimes
4′ Great

GREAT 2nd TOUCH

red blank stop
16′ Tuba Profunda
16′ Oboe Horn TC
16′ Diaphonic Diapason
16′ Tibia Plena TC
16′ Gamba

ACCOMPANIMENT

16′ Violin TC
16′ Celeste Violin TC
8′ Tuba Mirabilis
8′ English Horn
8′ Oboe Horn
8′ French Horn
8′ Saxophone
8′ Diaphonic Diapason
8′ Horn Diapason
8′ Solo Tibia Clausa
8′ Foundation Tibia Clausa
8′ Flute
8′ Gamba
8′ Viola Celeste
8′ Salicional
8′ Concert Violin
8′ Celeste Violin
8′ Kinura
8′ Clarinet
8′ Foundation Vox Humana
4′ Tuba Mirabilis
4′ Horn Diapason
4′ Solo Tibia Clausa
4′ Flute
4′ Gamba
4′ Viola Celeste
4′ Concert Violin
4′ Celeste Violin
4′ Foundation Vox Humana
2 2/3′ Twelfth
2′ Piccolo
2′ Fifteenth
Harp
Chrysoglott
Xylophone
Snare Drum
Wood Drum
Tomtoms
Tambourines
Castanets
Chinese Gong
16′ Acc
4′ Acc
8′ Great
8′ Solo

ACCOMPANIMENT 2nd TOUCH

8′ Tuba Mirabilis
8′ English Horn
8′ Diaphonic Diapason
8′ Horn Diapason
8′ Solo Tibia Clausa
8′ Foundation Tibia Clausa
4′ Tibia Plena
Chimes
Triangle
Bird

TREMOLOS

Left
Tibia Plena
Foundation Tibia Clausa
Foundation Vox Humana
Right
Right Reeds
Tuba Mirabilis
English Horn
Solo Tibia Clausa
Solo Vox Humana

SOLO

8′ Tuba Mirabilis
8′ English Horn
8′ Oboe Horn
8′ Trumpet
8′ French Horn
8′ Saxophone
8′ Diaphonic Diapason
8′ Horn Diapason
8′ Tibia Plena
8′ Solo Tibia Clausa
8′ Foundation Tibia Clausa
8′ Flute
8′ Gamba
8′ Viola Celeste
8′ Concert Violin
8′ Celeste Violin
8′ Kinura
8′ Clarinet
8′ Krumet
8′ Solo Vox Humana
4′ Tibia Plena
Harp
Chrysoglott
Glockenspiel
Orchestra Bells
Xylophone
Chimes
16′ Solo
4′ Solo
16′ Great
8′ Great
4′ Great

EFFECT BUTTONS

Grand Crash
Cymbal
Triangle
Bird
Sleigh Bells
Telephone
Door Bell
Steamboat
Fire Gong
Bell Low
Bell High

TOE LEVERS

Sforzando 1st touch stops, 2nd touch percussions
Surf
Wind
Thunder
Aeroplane
Horse Hoof

STOP KEY COLORS

Reeds and diapasons: red
Tibias, flutes, strings and couplers: white
Tremolos: black
Traps: amber
Tuned percussions: brown

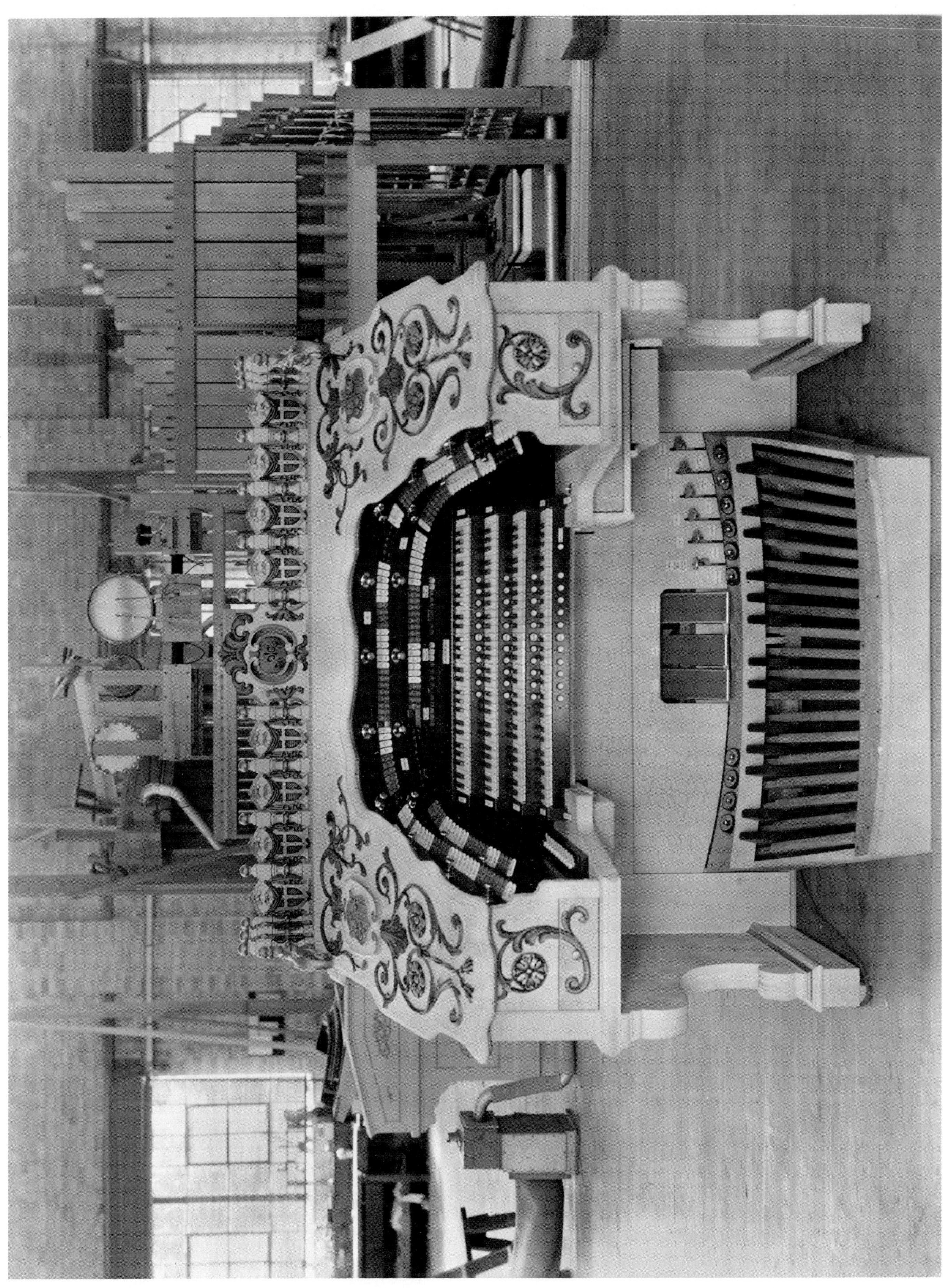

S P E C I F I C A T I O N

OF A
ROBERT MORTON UNIT ORGAN
Style 18-N

Designed for

GEO. HUNT, MEDFORD, OREGON.

PEDAL (Division I)

Bourdon	16'
Diaphone Bass	16'
Trumpet	8'
Violin	8'
Flute	8'
Tibia Clausa	8'
Diapason	8'

Second Touch

Bass Drum
Cymbal
Tympani
Crash Cymbal
Chimes

ACCOMPANIMENT (Division II)

Bourdon	16'
Violincello TC	16'
Diaphonic Diapason	8'
Concert Flute	8'
Trumpet	8'
Violin	8'
Tibia Clausa	8'
Vox Humana	8'
Diapason	4'
Concert Flute	4'
Violin	4'
Vox Humana	4'
Piccolo	2'
Chrysoglott	
Snare Drum	
Tambourine	
Castanets	
Chinese Block	
Tom Tom	

Second Touch

Trumpet	8'
Diaphonic Diapason	8'
Tibia Clausa	8'
Chimes	

Adjustable Combination Pistons

Five Adjustable Combination Pistons affecting
Accompaniment & Pedal.

SOLO (Division III)

Diaphonic Diapason	16'
Bourdon	16'
Vox Humana TC	16'
Diapason	8'
Concert Flute	8'
Trumpet	8'
Violin	8'
Tibia Clausa	8'
Vox Humana	8'
Orchestral Oboe (Syn)	8'
Diapason	4'
Concert Flute	4'
Trumpet	4'
Violin	4'
Vox Humana	4'
Tibia Clausa	4'
Twelfth	2-2/3'
Piccolo	2'
Tierce	1-3/5'
Orchestral Bells	
Xylophone	
Chimes	

Second Touch

Diaphonic Diapason	16'
Tibia Clausa	8'
Trumpet	8'

Adjustable Combination Pistons

Five Adjustable Combination Pistons affecting
Solo & Pedal

PEDAL MOVEMENTS

Balanced Expression affecting entire instrument
Balanced Crescendo

ACCESSORIES

Crescendo Indicator
Stop Key Illumination Switch
Vox Humana Tremolo
Crash Cymbal - Toe Piston
Call Piston to Operator's booth.
General Tremolo

BLOWER EQUIPMENT

Blower Motor Low Voltage Generator

The purchaser to prepare the space for the reception of the Robert Morton Unit Organ and power plant, cut necessary openings through floors, ceilings and partitions, supply and install the electrical connections to the power plant and the starting switch at the console (including "remote control" starter if same is required) and to supply and install conduit for the organ cables if demanded by the local authorities, also necessary galvanized pipe to conduct the wind from the blower to the organ and console - specification to be furnished by the organ company. (The revised rules adopted by the Electrically Operated Organ Committee of the National Board of Fire Underwriters state explicitly: "Conduit may be used but is not required.") The purchaser is also to supply the necessary heat, light, cleanliness and required quiet for erecting, tuning and regulating the instrument. The purchaser is to pay all freight and drayage charges on organ, motor and blower plant, and all appurtenances thereto, from the factories, together with hoisting charges, if any.

One of the company's most popular models was the style 18-N, designed to compete with Wurlitzer's comparably popular style D.

(opposite) The wonderfully ornate 4/23 console for Loew's Jersey Theatre, Jersey City, New Jersey, sits in the Robert Morton erecting room waiting to be connected. Five organs of this size, each with similar but not quite identical ornamentation, were installed in New York area Loew houses. John M. Ferris, who worked in the erecting room, recalled that after a large organ such as this was set up "we would . . . invite in all the local outstanding organists and this is where I first got acquainted with C. Sharpe Minor, Gaylord Carter, Milton Charles and the other fine musicians. I've known many but this little fellow I've mentioned, Gaylord Carter, was always my favorite. He could romp on a pipe organ more than anybody I ever heard and he loved to come out there. There was no shutter control over the organ . . . Carter would sit there and just about blow the roof off. These affairs were held during the evening and the Van Nuys public was invited in and it was quite a gala affair."[2]

ROBERT MORTON ORGANS

for

RESIDENCES, MUSIC ROOMS

ART GALLERIES, CLUBS

and other Public and Private Buildings

ROBERT MORTON ORGAN CO.

Factories and Studios

VAN NUYS, CALIFORNIA

OFFICES

NEW YORK CITY	CHICAGO	LOS ANGELES
1560 BROADWAY	624 SO. MICHIGAN AVE.	1914 SO. VERMONT

THE ROBERT MORTON RESIDENCE ORGAN

THOSE WHO have never considered owning a residence organ because of the expenditure involved, will be surprised to know that anyone who can afford a high grade automobile or a modern reproducing player piano can afford a Robert Morton Residence Organ; and nothing will add so much to your own pleasure and satisfaction, or provide better entertainment for your guests. There are few homes or apartments in which sufficient space for a residence organ cannot be found. The cost for upkeep and maintenance is comparatively nothing and it will last a life-time.

Unless you have kept informed of the tremendous progress made in the art of organ building during the last few years you will have little idea of the achievements actually accomplished in this art and no concern in the world has contributed more to this development than the Robert Morton Organ Co.

What the palette is to the painter the various instruments, or stops, are to the organist. An endless succession of wonderful tone colors is obtained by the blending or combining of the different stops or groups of stops. In the organ as in the orchestra there are the Strings, the Flutes, the Reeds, the Brass Section, and to add beauty and characteristic organ tone the beautiful, rich Diapasons. From these various tone families the instrumentation is selected and arranged so that the proper general tonal effect suitable to a residence is obtained. You have only to sit back and enjoy the music. Organs designed for residences require entirely different tonal treatment than the church organ, or the theatre organ, and we believe we have surpassed all previous efforts in this respect.

The Robert Morton Residence Organ may be played by hand, or may be operated by Robert Morton *Tri-art* records, or by selected ordinary player rolls, and may be purchased either with or without this reproducing equipment.

THE "*Tri-art*" LIBRARY

IF YOU are not able to play by hand, or even have no technical knowledge of music the Robert Morton *Tri-art* Library is available for your pleasure and satisfaction. Hundreds of recordings which include organ classics, fugues, sonatas, orchestral selections, overtures, symphonies, folk songs, and selections of all types of the modern and more popular musical numbers.

A Robert Morton Reproducing Residence Organ, with its complete library of records of the world's finest music, represents the "last and final word" in making the modern home complete. It is equivalent to a fine orchestra in your home, ready to play whenever you desire.

A perfectly balanced instrument for hand playing or operated by means of Robert Morton *Tri-art* records the Robert Morton Residence Organ is a superb example of the very highest type of craftsmanship and musical excellence.

If you are interested in further information please call or write the nearest office of the Robert Morton Organ Co. and we will be pleased to submit to you a specification in keeping with your requirements. Recommendations, advice and technical assistance will be freely given by us without obligation on your part.

On this and the following eight pages are reproduced a Robert Morton residence organ catalog c. 1929, one of the company's last promotional efforts. The author has added explanatory captions to each page. "Tri-Art" rolls were only in the research and development stage and never actually reached production.[8]

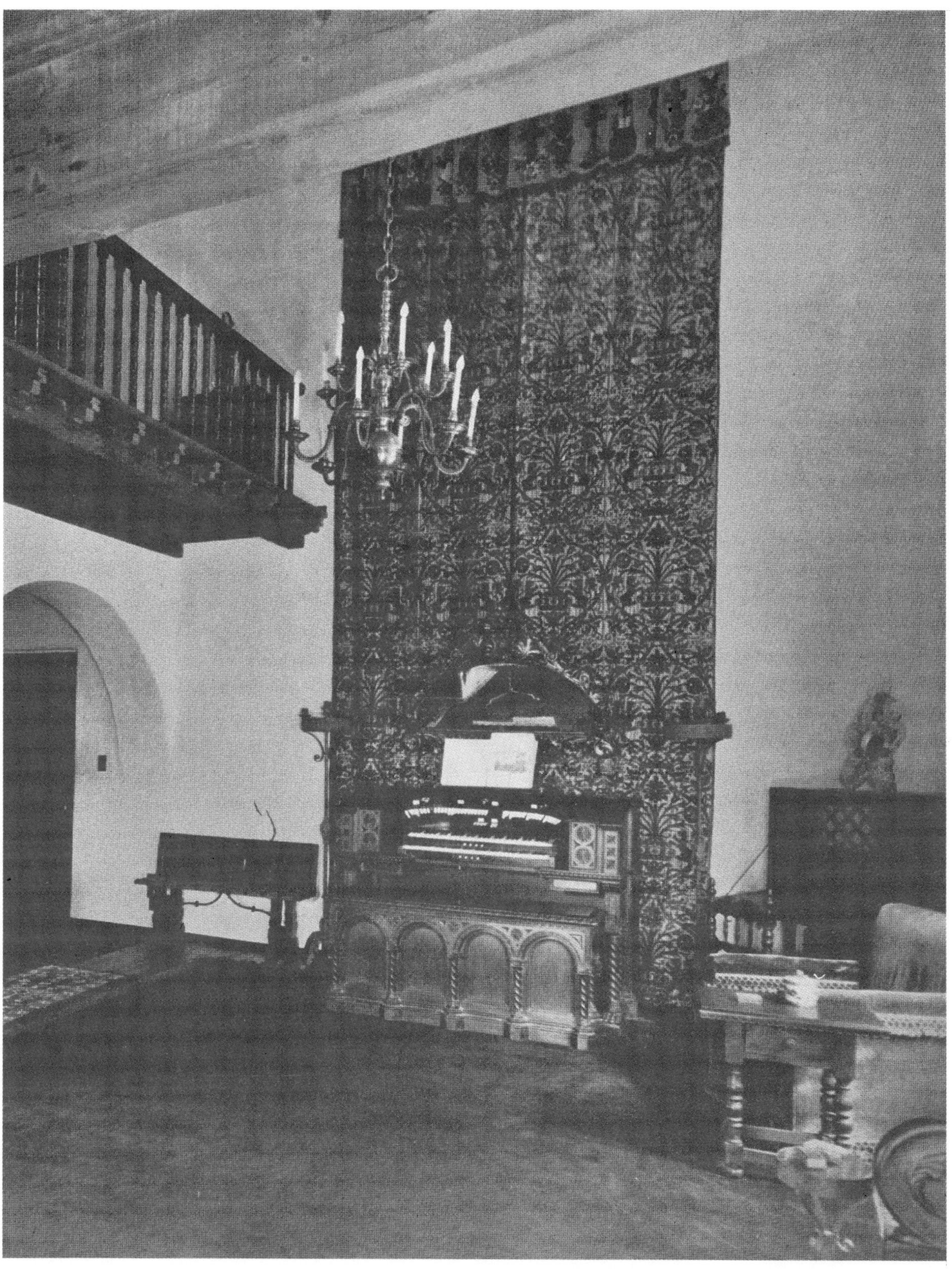

Music Room
Mr. and Mrs. A. B. Zwebell
Ronda Court, Hollywood, California

This 2/4 in a lovely Spanish case with unique matching bench was installed in 1928.

Residence, Mr. and Mrs. L. E. Kauffman
Riviera
Santa Monica, California

This 1927 3/19 featured perhaps the most elaborate carving ever found on a Robert Morton. The Kauffman fortune was made in the sheep and hide business—hence the significance of the rams' heads. Similar carvings could also be found on stairway balustrades elsewhere in the mansion.[6]

Residence, Charles Chaplin
Beverly Hills, California

The tibia from this organ, a really beautiful "wailer," was a featured part of George Wright's Pasadena studio organ in the 1960s and is now (1983) a part of George's new four-manual studio instrument.

Music Room
E. F. Bent Residence
Los Angeles

Residence
Mr. and Mrs. A. B. Zwebell
Ronda Court
1400 Havenhurst Ave.
Hollywood, Calif.

Residence, Mrs. Mel Uhl
1475 Havenhurst Ave.
Andalusia Court
Hollywood, Calif.

*The Bent residence featured another late **Robert Morton** installed in 1928.*

Residence, L. E. Kauffman
Riviera
Santa Monica, Calif.

Music Room
L. E. Kauffman
Los Angeles

Residence, Earnest F. Bent
5108 Ambrose Ave.
Los Angeles

The Kauffman's had two homes, each equipped with a Robert-Morton. The one pictured in the circle was installed in their Los Angeles home in 1922.

Residence
Dr. Mixsell
Pasadena

Robert
Morton
Organ in
C. Sharp
Minor
Broadcasting
Studio
Los Angeles

Residence
Mrs. Mel Uh
Andalusia C
Hollywood

Residence
Mr. Mark Daniels
Los Angeles

Music Room
Mr. Mark Daniels
Los Angeles

Dr. Mixsell's residence contained an early instrument bearing the California Organ Co. nameplate. Mrs. Uhl's organ was a 1925 2/4. C. Sharpe Minor's studio also contained a smaller two-manual Robert Morton although only the larger 3/10 instrument, installed in 1928, is pictured here.

Music Room
J. J. Haggarty
Los Angeles

Console
Mr. Mark
Daniels
Los Angeles

Console and Bench
Mrs. L. E. Kauffman
Los Angeles

Music Room
Mr. and Mrs. A. B. Zwebell
Ronda Court, Hollywood

The Haggarty organ was another California Organ Co. product. The Daniels organ, a 2/8, featured an echo organ of two ranks. It was moved to the Wilshire-Ebell Theatre in Los Angeles in 1940.

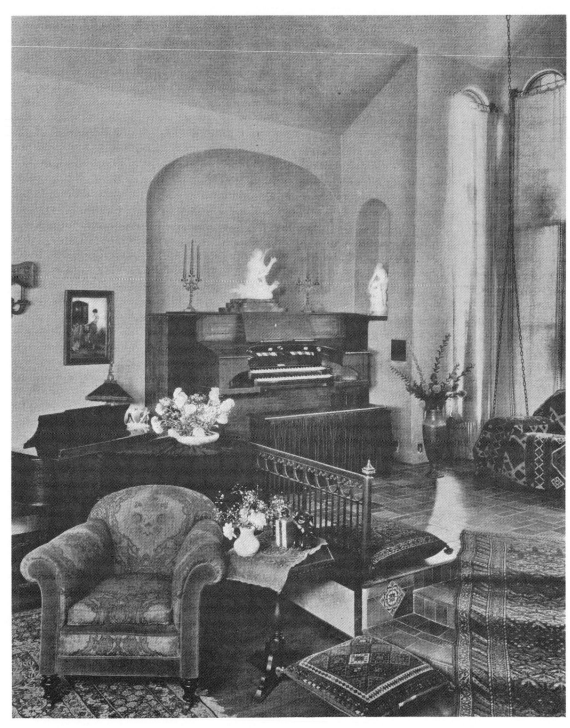

Music Room
Mr. E. Anderson
Los Angeles

Residence
Mr. E. Anderson
Los Angeles

Mr. Anderson's instrument was a 2/8 with an echo organ, installed in 1921. As did several other organs in this catalog, this instrument featured a roll player built into the top of the console case.

FACTORIES OF THE ROBERT-MORTON PREDECESSOR COMPANIES

Above, third home of the Murray M. Harris firm at Seventh and Alameda Streets in Los Angeles. Harris moved here in 1902, shortly after which the business became the Los Angeles Art Organ Co.[4] *Below, a rare photo of the interior of the Los Angeles Art Organ Co. at 1515 East 7th Street. Gentleman on far left is Carl Pearson who later was in charge of the Robert-Morton console department.*

Second home of the Murray M. Harris firm on San Fernando Road in Los Angeles.

Interior of Murray M. Harris' Sichel Street factory c. 1910. Large console on left was destined for the New York City mansion of Senator W. A. Clark. It contained a feature unusual in Murray M. Harris organs: flat-faced drawknobs. Most Harris organs featured bevel-faced knobs similar to those on the console on the right.

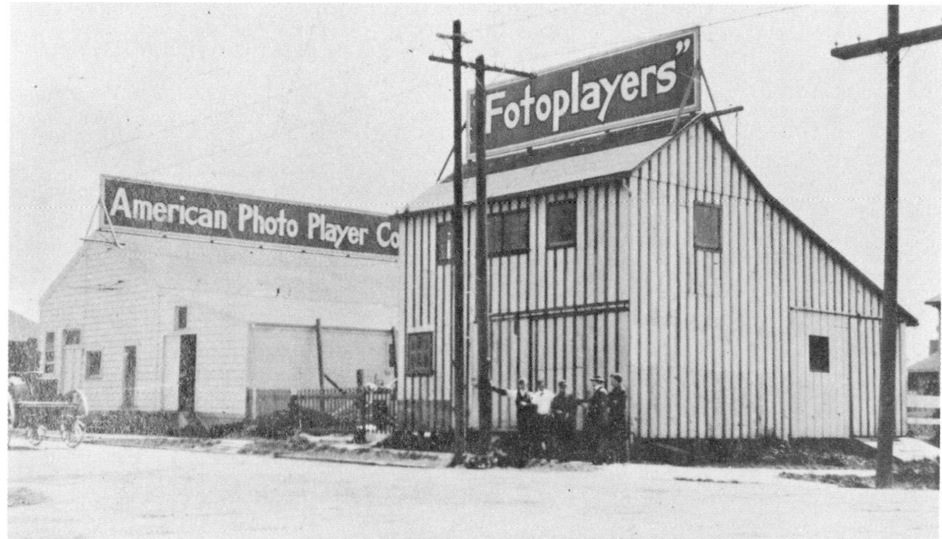

Original American Photo Player factory at Berkeley, California.

Artist's conception of the American Photo Player plant following the major expansion under H. J. Werner's leadership.

Loading dock at the Berkeley factory.

A PHOTOGRAPHIC TOUR OF THE ROBERT MORTON FACTORY
Van Nuys, California

16 pages of rare views behind the scenes of America's second largest theatre organ builder.

Aerial view of the Robert Morton factory. Note the R-M logo on the water tower.

Rear view of the 1925 addition to the plant.

Exterior of Main Factory Building on Sherman Boulevard

Complete, modern and efficient equipment and methods

Erection Room

Competent organ mechanics working under unequaled advantages and conditions

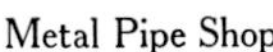

Metal Pipe Shop

Machine Shop

A few of the departments in the factory

of

THE CALIFORNIA ORGAN COMPANY

in

Van Nuys, a suburb of Los Angeles, California

This ad appeared in the March 1917 issue of The Diapason *shortly before the advent of the Robert-Morton name.*

California Organ Company employees pose for a photo November 13, 1915.

This view shows how the work force had expanded by 1924.

General offices.

Bert Kingsley, Stanley Williams and C. B. Sartwell hold a conference in a voicing room on September 19, 1919.

A 1915 conference includes, left to right, two unidentified men, head voicer Stanley Williams and draftsman Paul Carlsted.

Bert Kingsley, who succeeded Stanley Williams as head voicer, visits Paul Carlsted in his drafting room in 1920.

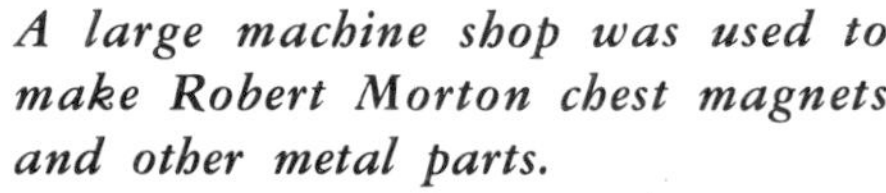

A large machine shop was used to make Robert Morton chest magnets and other metal parts.

Above and below are two scenes in the percussion department.

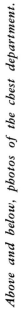

Above and below, photos of the chest department.

Four views of the mill and woodworking departments. All photos except the lower right were taken in the 1925 factory addition. Note large overhead pipes which are part of a vacuum dust collection system.

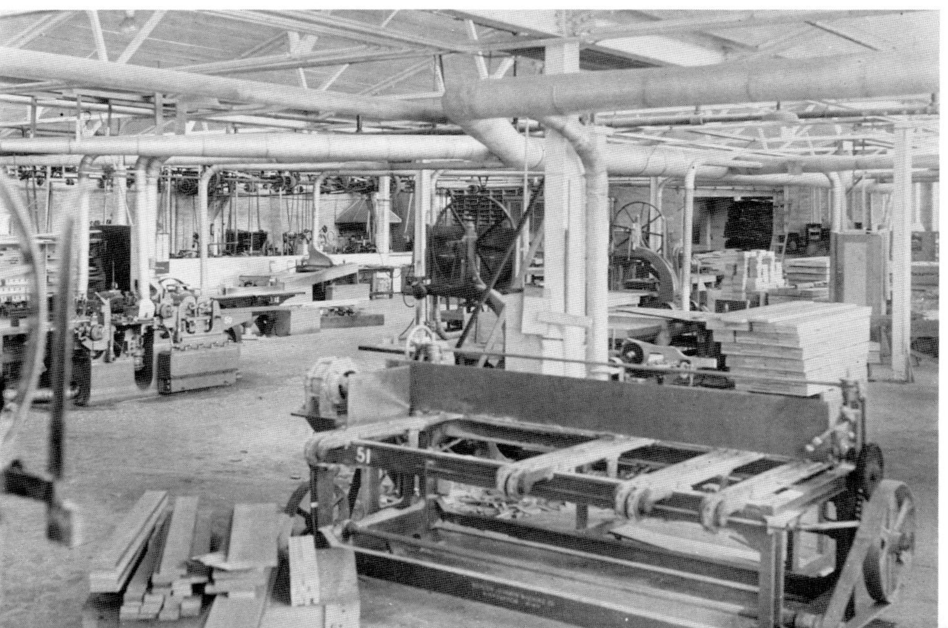

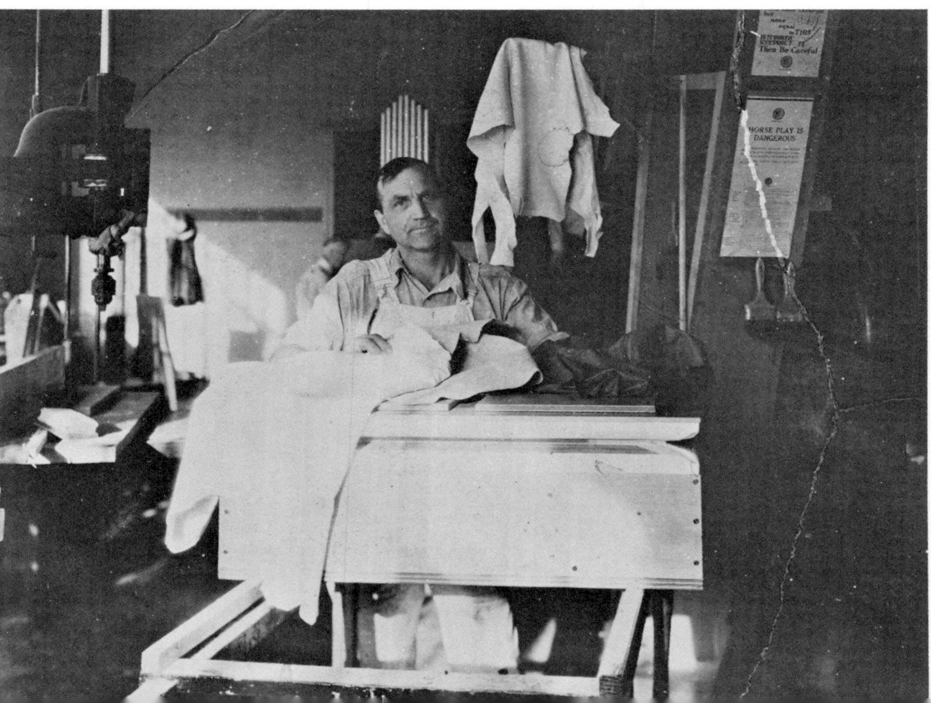

Above, action and console departments c. 1921. Below, Harry Hocker leathers a reservoir in the bellows department.

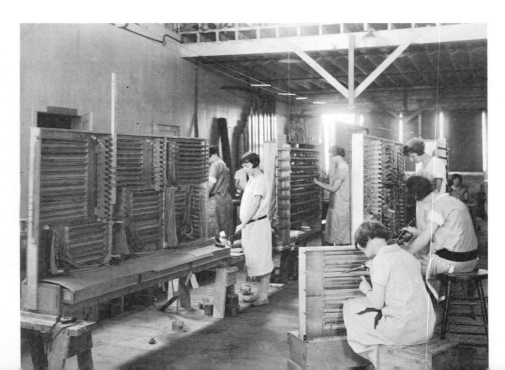

Above, pneumatic department. Below, relay department showing the relay for a fairly large organ being wired.

Chest wiring department.

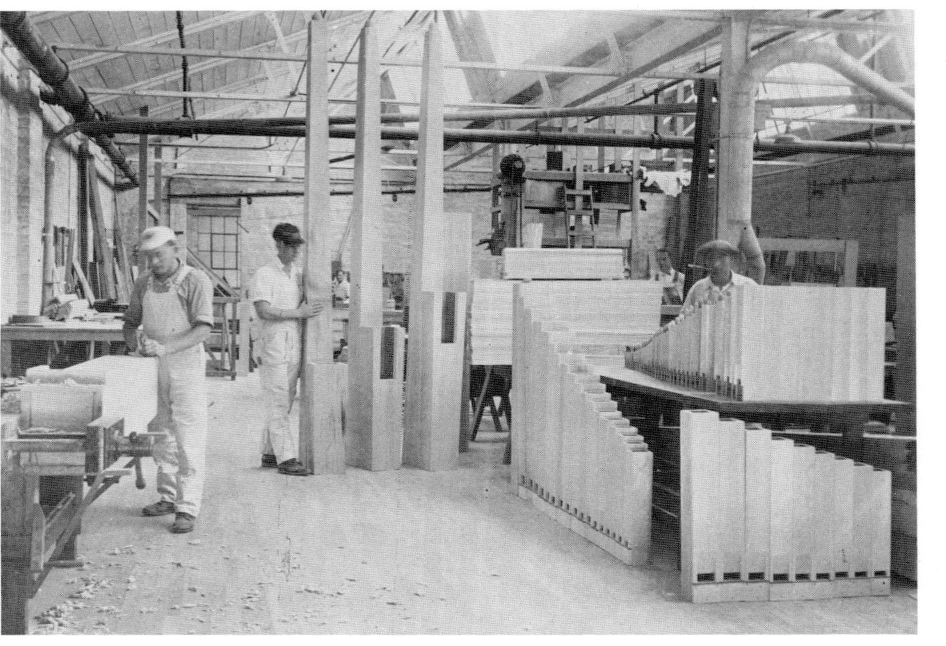

Above and below, two views of the wood pipe department. The upper photo was taken after the 1925 addition to the Morton plant. In the lower photo Bert Kingsley holds low CC of an 8′ flute.

The above photo, taken in 1920, shows head voicer Kingsley being visited by draftsman Paul Carlsted. Below is another voicing room with a clarinet on the voicing machine.

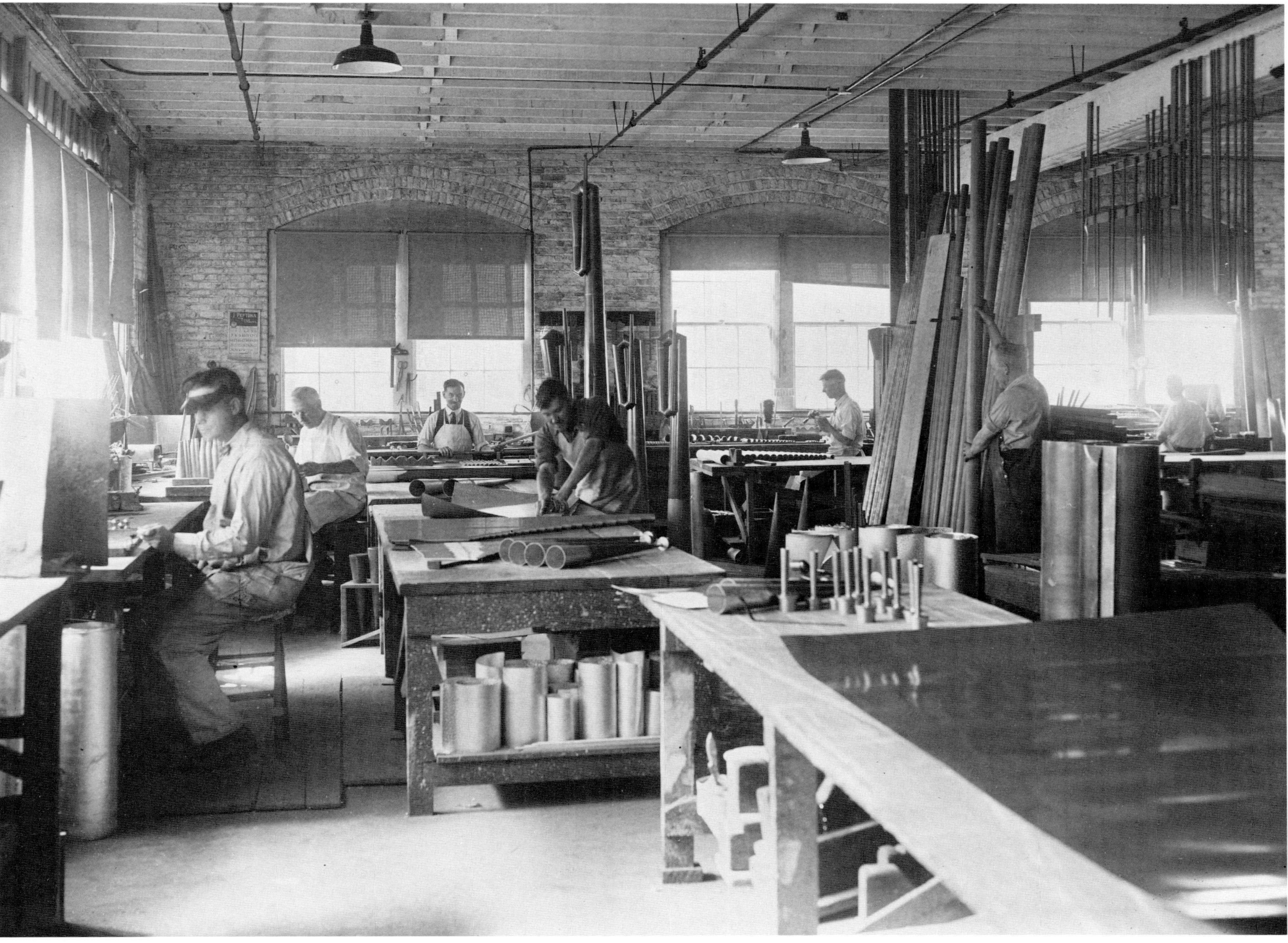

Metal pipe shop c. 1921. Pipe makers, left to right, are Herbert Sutton, Archie March, Sr., Tommy Ross, Archie March, Jr., Ralph Tinker and two unidentified men.

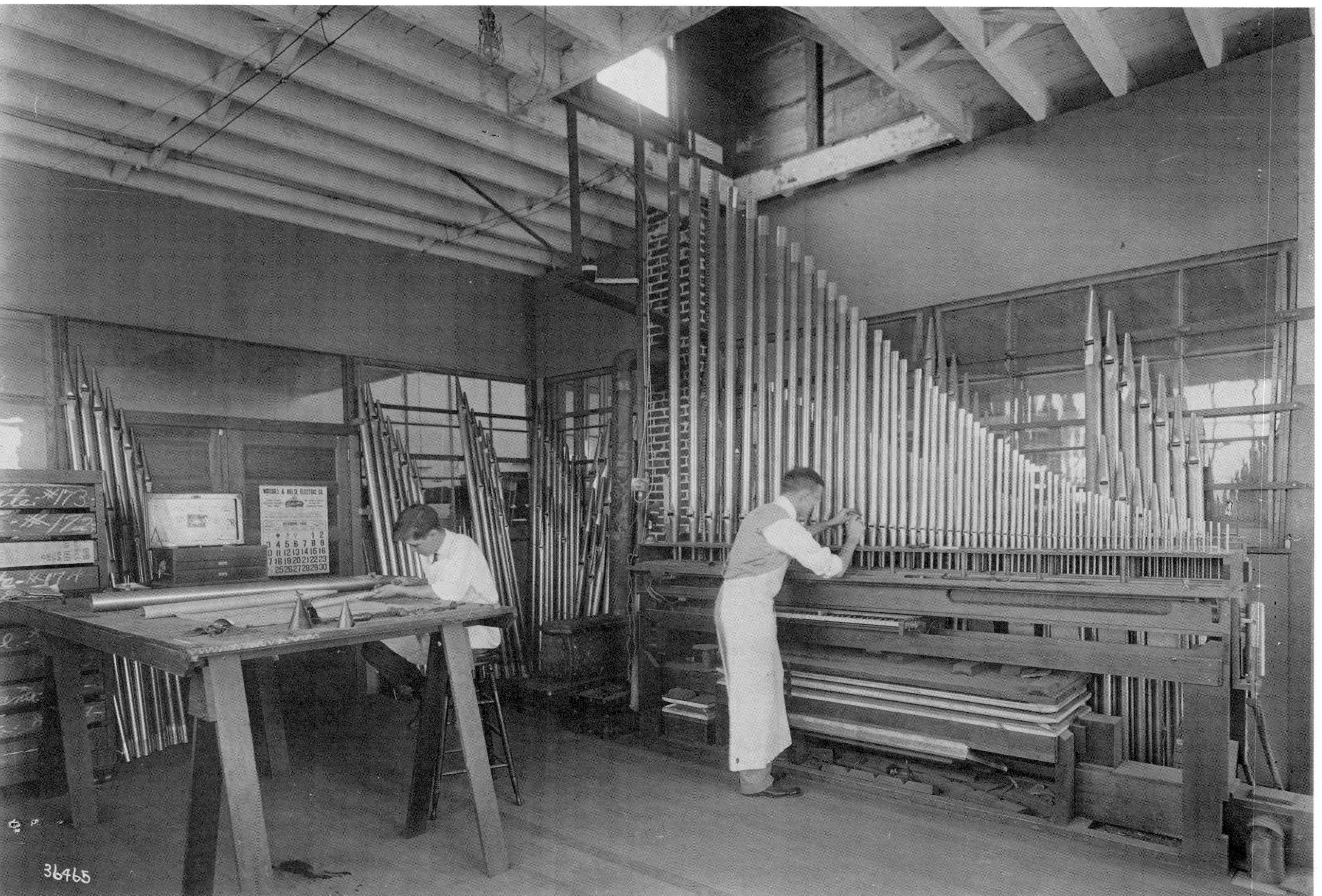

An assistant prepares pipes for voicing by head voicer Stanley Williams (right) at the California Organ Co. Calendar on wall shows the month of October 1915.

Above left, workers prepare to cast a sheet of pipe metal. Above, senior pipe maker Archie D. March plies his trade in the metal pipe department. His wide experience contributed to the excellent quality of Robert-Morton pipework: prior to joining the firm in 1920 he had worked at the Hall, Moller, Wurlitzer, Austin, Hook & Hastings, Gutfleisch & Schopp, Kimball, Hedges, Haskell and Steere companies.[79]

Above, erecting room manager H. P. Seth stands in front of an organ in a rarely encountered self-contained swell box. At left, Clarence Fogg racks a clarinet.

Above, action department and small parts assembly. Below, finishing room.

Above, storage area where parts were held before going to the erecting room. Below, erecting area for the style 39 and 49 pit organs. This was one room where little height was required.

A fair-sized organ is being assembled in the large erecting room. All Robert-Morton organs were completely erected and played before shipment. Even swell shades were erected for testing.

The last vestige of Robert Morton as it appeared c. 1964. From 1933 to 1942 a sign on this building declared "C. B. Sartwell, successor to the Robert Morton Organ Co." It was located just a few blocks north of the Morton factory on Van Nuys Boulevard.

ROBERT-MORTON OPUS LIST

CITY/STATE	LOCATION	SIZE	YR	BLWR	REMARKS
ALABAMA					
Birmingham	Galax Th.	2/	1922	13276	
	Ritz Th.	2/4			
Ensley	Ensley Th.		1927	20599	
Huntsville	Grand Th.	2/	1925	17157	
Mobile	Lyric Th.		1927	21058	
	Saenger Th.	2/10	1927	19145	
Montgomery	Empire Th.	2/4			
Selma	Academy Th.	2/6	1928	21582	
ARIZONA					
Jerome	Liberty Th.	2/			
Phoenix	Columbia Th.	3/10	1920	11382	7½ hp, 15" wp; Style C.
	Strand Th.	2/	1920	11413	3 hp, 10" wp; Style 100; moved in 1925 to Yaeger Theatre, Watts, California.
Yuma	Casino Th.	2/	1925	17540	
ARKANSAS					
Helena	Jewel Th.	2/	1923	14332	
	Saenger Th.	2/	1923	15330	
Hope	Saenger Th.	2/8	1927	20357	
Pine Bluff	Hauber Th.	2/	1922	13608	
			1923	14049	
	Saenger Th.	2/4			
Rogers	Victoria Th.	2/			
Texarkana	Gem Th.	2/			
CALIFORNIA					
Alameda	Neptune Th.	2/4			
Avalon	Riviera Th.	2/6			Moved from unknown location.
Anderson	Anderson Th.	2/4			With roll player.
Bakersfield	California Th.	2/8			
	Fox Th.	2/16	1930		Moved from unknown location.
	Opera House		1924	16362	
Banning	New Banning Th.	2/3	1928	21731	
			1928	21971	
Benecia	unidentified theatre	2/4			
Berkeley	U. C. Th.	2/			
Beverly Hills	Charlie Chaplin residence	2/8	1923	14519	
Brea	Brea Th.	2/4			
Buena Park	Buena Park Th.	2/6	1928	22172	Opus 2437.
Burlingame	Peninsula (Fox) Th.	3/12	1926	18924	10 hp, 15" wp.
			1926	10765TUR	1 hp, 24" vacuum for piano.
Calexico	Fox Capitol Th.	2/			
Carlsbad	Carlsbad Th.	2/4	1927	19679	Opus 2317, style 16.
Carpinteria	Carpinteria Th.	2/	1928	21784	
Chico	National Th.	2/4			
Coronado	Silver Strand Th.	2/10			California Organ Co. nameplate.
Daly City	Daly City Th.	2/6	1928	21963	
Delano	Delano Th.	2/6			
	Strand Th.	2/3			Style 49.
East Los Angeles	Red Mill (Boulevard) Th.		1923	14463	
			1924	15762	

CITY/STATE	LOCATION	SIZE	YR	BLWR	REMARKS
Fresno	Fresno Hotel	2/16	1915		Johnston nameplate.
	Kinema Th.	5/	1921	12403	7½ hp.
	Liberty (Hardy) Th.	3/18			
	Pantages (Warner) (Warnor) Th.	4/14	1928	21897	Opus 2416.
Gilroy	Strand Th.	2/5	1921	12616	
Glendale	California Th.	3/7	1928	22493	Opus 2471; moved in 1938 to KFOX Radio, Long Beach, California.
	Gateway Th.	2/6	1923	14239	
Hawthorne	Hawthorne Th.	2/	1928	22424	
	Plaza Th.	2/6			
Hermosa Beach	Hermosa Th.	2/			
Hollywood	A. B. Zwebell residence	2/4	1928	21385	Located at 1400 Havenhurst; with roll player.
	Hunley (Century) Th.	2/	1921	12191	
	KNX Radio	3/10			Old studio.
	Mrs. Mel Uhl residence	2/4	1925	18154	Located at 1475 Havenhurst; with roll player.
	Mrs. Ruth Anderson residence	2/8	1921	12717	Located at 6787 Whitley Terrace; with two roll players and echo.
			1922	13629	
Kingsburg	American Th.	2/6	1920		Wicks opus 290.
La Jolla	Granada Th.	2/5			
Lodi	Lodi Th.	2/5			
Long Beach	Dreamland Th.	2/8			
	Ebell Th.	2/7			
	Empire Th.	2/	1922	13387	
	Fairyland Th.	2/	1925	16929	
	Imperial Th.	2/12	1926		
	Liberty (Roxy) Th.	2/14	1916		California Organ Co. nameplate; with 88-note roll player.
	Royal Palms Th.	2/	1925	17352	Later moved to Marcal (World) Th., Hollywood, Calif.
	unidentified radio station	2	1929	22987	3 hp, 10″ wp; later moved to KOY Radio, Phoenix, AR.
Los Altos	P. B. Roberts residence		1929	23652	
Los Angeles	Ambassador Th.	2/4			Style 75.
	Arlington (United) (Schwartz) Th.	2/7	1921	12856	Style 85 with 2-rank echo; later moved to Alhambra Theatre, Alhambra, California.
	Arrow Th.	3/	1916		Located in Hamburger Department Store; California Organ Co., with roll player; one set of expression shades for theatre, one set for restaurant.
	Astor Th.	2/			
	Balboa Th.	2/10	1925	17577	10 hp, 15″ wp.
	Banner Th.	2/3			Style 49.
	Broadway (Dalton's Broadway) (Arcade) Th.	2/16			Later moved to Pantages (Orpheum) Th., San Diego, Calif.
	Capitol Th.		1921	12136	
	Carlton Th.	2/10			
	Casino Th.	2/	1924	16131	
			1924	16254	
	Colonial Th.	2/			
	Crescent Th.	2/	1922	13298	7½ hp.
	Crystal Th.	2/	1923	14202	
	C. Sharpe Minor Studio	2/	1928	22320	
		3/10	1928	22379	Two organs in same studio.
	Cecil B. DeMille Studio	2/			
	Elks Temple	4/61	1926	17558	
			1926	17695	With two-manual antiphonal console.
	Ernest F. Bent residence	2/	1928	22322	Located at 5108 Ambrose Avenue; with roll player.
	Florence Th.	2/11			
	Garrick Th.	2/8	1915		California Organ Co. nameplate.
	Globe Th.		1921	12116	
	Jewel Th.	2/			
	Kinema (Criterion) Th.	2/			California Organ Co. nameplate.
		3/	1920		Existing organ enlarged.
		5/26	1923	14471	30 hp, 15″ wp; existing organ enlarged; with 4-rank echo.
	Knoll Th.		1926	19275	
	Larchmont Th.	2/	1921	12895	
			1922	13652	Later moved to Cabrillo Theatre, San Pedro, California.
	Leon Kauffmann residence	2/6	1922	13609	With roll player.
	Mark Daniels residence	2/8	1926	18373	With two-rank echo and roll player; moved in 1940 to Wilshire-Ebell Theatre, Los Angeles, California.
	Mesa Th.	2/12	1925	17973	10 hp; style 200CX; with V'Oleon.
	Miller's California (California) Th.	3/	1917	E706	7½ hp, 5″&10″ wp.
	Miller's (Triangle) Th.	2/15	1919		Foto-Orchestra nameplate; with double roll player; cost $22,000.
	Olympus Th.		1922	12963	
	Omar Th.	2/	1922	13234	
	Pantages (Warner Bros. Downtown) (Warrens) Th.	2/16	1920	10544	
			1920	11323	7½ hp, 15″ wp.
			1921	12686	

CITY/STATE	LOCATION	SIZE	YR	BLWR	REMARKS
Los Angeles	Patine Roller Rink	2/4	1929		With 16′ post horn, 16′ tibia, kinura, diapason, 2 glocks, 2 xylophones and 2 toy counters; moved in 1939 to Roller Center Rink, South Gate, California.
	Pokrowsky Institute Majestic Theatre Organ Studio		1929		
	Quinn's Rialto (Grauman's Rialto) (Rialto) Th.		1917	E745	7½ hp, 5″&10″ wp; California Organ Co. nameplate.
	Regent Th.	2/3			Style 49.
	Ritz Th.		1925	17587	
	Robert-Morton store demo organ		1924	16348	
	Royal Th.	2/	1925	17523	
	Savoy Th.		1923	14549	
	Starland Th.	2/5			Style 85.
	Strand Th.	2/10	1921	12322	7½ hp; style 200.
	Sunset Th.	2/	1920	11334	
	Sunshine Th.	2/4			
	Superba Th.	2/	1916		California Organ Co. nameplate.
		2/4	1921	12654	
	Tally's Broadway Th.	4/47	1913		Murray M. Harris nameplate; located at 833 S. Broadway.
	Trinity Auditorium (Embassy) Th.	4/61	1914	C331	10 hp, 6″ wp; Johnston nameplate.
			1914	C411	¾ hp, 5″ wp.
	Vermont Th.	2/5	1922	13071	Style 85.
	Western Th.	2/10			
	Woodley (Sennett) (Caufield's Riviera) (Victory) (Mission) Th.	2/	1913		Murray M. Harris nameplate.
		3/	1920	11270	7½ hp, 15″ wp; new Robert-Morton organ.
	Woodley's Optic (Optic) Th.	2/			Murray M. Harris nameplate.
North Hollywood	El Portal Th.	2/10			
	Hollywood Th.		1926	19148	
	C. A. Woodmansee's Th.		1924	15640	
Oakland	American (Esquire) Th.				Opened as Reliance Theatre.
	Claremont (Tower) Th.				Opened as L. D. Purdy Theatre.
	Mrs. F. R. Fageol		1929	23498	
	Strand Th.	2/	1921	12231	
Ocean Park	La Petite Th.	2/5	1920	10717	3 hp, 10″ wp; moved in 1930 to Fox Theatre, Visalia, California, by Louis Mass and enlarged to 2/8.
Oceanside	Palomar Th.	2/4	1924	16241	
Ontario	Euclid Th.	2/	1922	13209	
Owensmouth	Scheinberg & Horwitz		1926	19037	3 hp.
Oxnard	Oxnard Th.	2/6	1926	19280	
Palo Alto	unidentified theatre				
Pasadena	Ritz Th.	2/10	1920	10946	7½ hp, 15″ wp.
Pittsburgh	California Th.	3/10	1928	22484	Style 23N; opus 2443.
Piedmont	Piedmont High School	2/12	1923	15160	
Pomona	Belvedere Th.		1921	12137	
Porterville	Monache Th.	2/	1918		
Red Bluff	Orpheum (State) Th.	2/5	192?		With 88-note roll player; moved from unknown location.
Redlands	Liberty Th.	2/4	1924	16357	3 hp.
Redwood City	Sequoia (Fox) Th.	3/13	1928	22203	
Riverside	Golden State Th.	2/6			Opened as Loring Opera House.
Sacramento	Alhambra Th.	3/11	1927	20329	Opus 2297; with V'Oleon.
	Capitol Th.	2/	1914		Johnston nameplate.
		2/	1918		Robert-Morton nameplate.
		2/	1923		Additions.
		2/10	1925		New organ; moved in 1934 to KFBK Radio, Sacramento.
	Liberty Th.	2/	1921	12587	
	Senator Th.	3/11	1924	15770	
	State Th.		1927		Burned August 11, 1927.
San Bernardino	Ritz Th.	2/	192?		With roll player.
	Temple Th.	2/			
San Diego	Balboa Th.	4/31	1923	14568	Moved in 1929 to Fox Theatre, San Diego.
	Broadway Th.	2/4	1920	11114	3 hp, 10″ wp; style 75.
	Cabrillo Th.	2/10			California Organ Co. nameplate.
	California Th.		1923	L253	7½ hp, 12″&30″ vacuum.
	Casino Th.	2/4	1924		
	Elks Lodge	2/	1930	23955	
	Fairmont (Crest) Th.	2/4			
	Mission Th.	2/8	1924		With 2-rank echo.
	Owl (Plaza) Th.	2/4	1920	10718	3 hp, 10″ wp.
	Pickwick Th.	2/	1917	E708	3 hp, 5″ wp; California Organ Co. nameplate.
	Savoy Th.	2/	1912		Murray M. Harris nameplate.
	Strand Th.	2/			
San Francisco	American Photo Player showroom		1917		Located at Jones Street and Golden Gate Avenue.
	Cadillac Motor Car Co.	2/3	1922		
	Castro Th.	2/11	1922	13051	7½ hp.

CITY/STATE	LOCATION	SIZE	YR	BLWR	REMARKS
San Francisco	Coliseum Th.	2/	191?		
	Elks Club	2/6	1924	16638	Located at Post and Mason Streets.
	Empress (Strand) (St. Francis) (Baronet) (St. Francis) Th.	3/16	1917		10 hp.
			1922	13607	Replacement blower.
	Excelsior (Granada) Th.	2/9	1922		
	Garrick Th.	2/			Opened as Orpheum Theatre.
	Don George Studio	2/			Three 2-manual organs; located on Golden Gate Avenue.
		2/			
		2/6			Moved in 1927 to NBC Studios, 111 Sutter Street, 22nd floor.
	Harding Th.	2/7	1926	18363	
	Harrison Th.	2/	1926	19298	
			1926	11065TUR	
	Idle Hour Th.	2/	1915		
	KPO Radio	2/4			Style 59; located in Hale Bros. department store building.
	Marina (Cinema 21) Th.	2/6	1928	21961	5 hp, 10″ wp; opus 2422.
	Marion Davies (Esquire) Th.	2/5			
	Metropolitan (Metro) Th.	2/			
	New Fillmore Th.	3/20	1918		
	New Mission Th.	3/14	1919	10405	
	Orpheum Th.	2/3	1921	12834	Style 49.
	Pantages Th.				10 hp; located at 937 Market Street.
	Pantages (Orpheum) Th.	4/22	1926	18014	With echo; located at 1192 Market Street.
	Portola (Farros) (Paris) Th.	2/	1923	L948	5 hp, 10″ wp and 30″ vacuum.
	Royal Th.	2/	1918		5 hp.
	Section Base Th.	2/6			Located on Treasure Island; moved from unknown theatre in World War II.
	Tivoli Th.	4/	191?		
	West Portal (Empire) Th.	2/6			
San Jose	Liberty Th.	3/20	1922	12675	10 hp.
	T&D (California) (Mission) Th.	2/			Johnston nameplate.
Santa Ana	New Temple Th.	2/7	1915		California Organ Co. nameplate.
Santa Barbara	California Th.	2/	1917		First Robert-Morton nameplate.
	Elks Temple	2/9	1926	19679	Opus 2307.
	Mission Th.	2/11	1923	14302	
Santa Cruz	New Santa Cruz Th.	3/9	1925		Opened as Santa Cruz Theatre.
Santa Monica	Leon Kauffmann residence	3/19	1927	20231	Opus 2313.
	Majestic (Mayfair) Th.	3/7	1929	22851	
Sherman	Sherman Community (Marquis) Th.	2/6	1925	17267	5 hp, 10″ wp; now city of West Hollywood.
South Pasadena	Colonial (Ritz) Th.	3/			
Stockton	Lincoln Th.	2/			
	Rialto Th.	2/	1922		
Universal City	Universal Studios	3/12	1929		
Van Nuys	George W. Borg residence	2/	1920	10469	
	Rivoli (Capri) Th.	2/	1924	15747	
	Strand Th.	2/	1924	16166	
	Van Nuys (Fox) Th.	2/	1924	16136	
Venice	Neptune Th.	2/4	1920	11334	3 hp, 10″ wp; style 75.
	Venice Auditorium	3/	1904		Los Angeles Art Organ Co. nameplate; with roll player.
Watsonville	T&D (Appleton) (State) Th.	2/			California Organ Co. nameplate.
Watts	Yaeger Th.		1922	13703	
	Yost Th.		1924	16388	Later moved to Hoyt's Theatre, Long Beach, California.

COLORADO

CITY/STATE	LOCATION	SIZE	YR	BLWR	REMARKS
Boulder	Curran (Boulder) Th.	2/	1923	14561	
	Fox (State) Th.	3/	1927		
	Isis Th.	2/	1922	13806	
	Rialto Th.		1926	18639	
Delta	Egyptian (Rialto) Th.	2/4	1928	22312	
Denver	Alpine Th.	2/4	1926	19353	3 hp; opus 2312; style 16.
	America Th.	4/17	1922	13297	15 hp; moved in 1978 to Forum Theatre, Binghamton, New York.
	Berkeley Th.	2/	1925	18231	
			1927	20777	
	Colorado (Tabor) Th.	4/17	1922	12578	Opened as Tabor Grand Opera House.
	Folly Th.	2/	1928	21266	
	Highlands Th.	2/3	1928	21823	Opus 2402; 3 hp, 8″ wp.
	KPOF Radio	2/			
	Leroy Rogers		1927	21159	
			1928	21715	
	Lyric Th.	2/4	1920	10926	3 hp, 10″ wp; style 75.
	Oriental Th.	2/6	1928		
	Princess (Victory) Th.	2/	1918	9464	
			1920	10686	Replacement blower.
	Queen Th.	2/4	1920	11003	3 hp, 10″ wp; style 75.
	Robert Morton studio		1928		
	Yates Th.	2/	1928		
Englewood	Gothic Th.	2/	1928	22597	

CITY/STATE	LOCATION	SIZE	YR	BLWR	REMARKS
Florence	Liberty Th.	2/	1922	12931	
Fort Collins	Empress (New America) Th.	2/7	1927	20023	
Greeley	Rex Th.	2/			
Pueblo	Palm Th.	2/	1921	12469	
CONNECTICUT					
Bridgeport	American Th.	2/	1918	F473	7½ hp, 5"&10" wp.
	Bijou Th.	2/	1919	9840	
Danbury	Capitol Th.	3/10	1926	19397	Opus 2293.
Hartford	Strand Th.	3/15	1927	20737	15 hp.
Milford	Capitol Th.	2/4	1921	11782	3 hp, 10" wp; style 75.
	Colonial Th.	2/	1928	21878	
New Britain	Capitol Th.	3/	1922	13340	Moved in 1927 to State Theatre, Newburgh, New York and original blower replaced by #20272.
	Embassy Th.	2/	1929	23754	
	Lyceum Th.	2/	1925	M1043B	5 hp, 10" wp and 30" vacuum.
Norwalk	Regent Th.	2/	1921	12816	
Rockville	Princess Th.	2/	1923	15241	
South Norwalk	Palace Th.		1923	14450	
Wallingford	Strand Th.	2/4	1924		
Waterbury	New Garden Th.	2/	1927	20654	
Winsted	Opera House	2/	1925	M1102B	5 hp, 10" wp and 30" vacuum.
		2/4	1926	O351B	5 hp, 10" wp and 30" vacuum; style 49C; moved in 1928 to Strand Theatre, Winsted, Connecticut.
DELAWARE					
Milford	Plaza Th.	2/	1927	21069	
DISTRICT OF COLUMBIA					
Washington	Broadway Th.		1923	13598	
	Chevy Chase (Avalon) Th.		1922	13733	
	Crandall's Central Th.		1922	12813	10 hp.
	Hippodrome Th.	2/	1927	20833	
	Liberty Th.	2/	1929	22821	
	York Th.	2/	1922	12981	Built by Wicks.
			1923	14193	
FLORIDA					
Bradenton	Palace Th.	2/	1022	20353	
Clearwater	Capitol Th.	2/	1922	13687	Wicks opus 415.
Cocoa	W. T. Bryan	2/	1925	M1154B	5 hp, 10" wp and 30" vacuum.
Daytona Beach	Crystal (Vivian) Th.	2/	1922	13631	
Fort Lauderdale	Sunset Th.		1923	15186	
Fort Meyers	Arcade Th.	2/	1927	20354	
Jacksonville	New Casino Th.	2/4	1920	10929	3 hp, 10" wp; style 75.
Lake Wales	Scenic Th.	2/	1927	21040	
Orlando	Grand Th.	2/	1927	20961	
	unidentified theatre		1917		Wicks opus 218.
Pensacola	Isis Th.	2/	1927	20033	
	Saenger Th.	2/6	1925	16728	
Plant City	Capitol Th.	2/3	1927	O1033B	5 hp, 10" wp and 30" vacuum; style 49.
St. Augustine	Jefferson Th.	2/	1927	20290	
St. Petersburg	Phiel Th.	2/	1918	9377	Wicks opus 264; Beethoven nameplate; double roll player with duplicate stop keys to operate organ from piano via rolls.
Sarasota	Edwards Th.		1927		
	Universal Th.		1925	18156	
Stuart	Lyric Th.	2/3	1925	N346B	5 hp, 10" wp and 30" vacuum; style 49.
Tampa	Victory Th.	2/6			
Vero	Vero Th.	2/	1924	M448B	5 hp, 10" wp and 30" vacuum.
Winterhaven	Williamson Th.	3/	1924	16389	
Winter Park	Baby Grand Th.	2/	1927	21149	
GEORGIA					
Albany	Albany Th.	3/8	1927	19800	Opus 2304.
Atlanta	Capitol Th.	3/15	1927	19819	Opus 2310; with V'Oleon.
	Howard (Paramount) Th.	3/14	1920	11243	15 hp; style 300.
	West End Th.	2/4	1925		
Augusta	Augusta Th.	2/			
Cartersville	Grand Th.	2/4			
Gainesville	State Th.	2/	1924	16282	
Griffin	Imperial Th.	2/4	1927	19899	
Macon	Grand Th.	2/	1925	N241B	5 hp, 10" wp and 30" vacuum.
	Rialto Th.	2/3	1921	12049	
	Ritz Th.	2/4	1927	21070	
McRae	National Th.		1927	20327	
Valdosta	Ritz Th.	2/4	1927	11070	Opus 2305; style 16 special.
HAWAII					
Hilo	New Palace Th.	3/7			Moved in 1940 to Hilo Theatre, Hilo, Hawaii.
Honolulu	Hawaii Th.	4/16	1921		Moved in 1936 to Waikiki Theatre, Honolulu, Hawaii.
	Princess Th.	4/16	1922	13462	Moved in 1969 to Hawaii Theatre, Honolulu, Hawaii.

CITY/STATE	LOCATION	SIZE	YR	BLWR	REMARKS
IDAHO					
Boise	Ada (Egyptian) Th.	2/8	1927	19625	Opus 2298.
Coeur d'Alene	Dream Th.		1925	18149	
	Liberty Th.	2/4	1926	19352	Opus 2302; style 16.
Idaho Falls	American Th.	2/	1929	22802	
	Colonial (Paramount) Th.	2/6	1921	12162	
Moscow	Kenworthy Th.	2/6	1926	19633	Opus 2309.
Pocatello	Strand Th.	2/	1923	14079	
Wallace	Grand Th.	2/6	1924		
ILLINOIS					
Alton	Grand Th.	2/8	1925	18058	
Antioch	Crystal Th.	2/	1923	11991	Built by Wicks.
Berwyn	Auditorium (Roxy) Th.	4/11	1924	16245	
Bloomington	Kirkwood Amusement Co.	2/	1927	O1120B	5 hp, 10″ wp and 30″ vacuum; located at 515 Kirkwood Avenue.
Canton	Capitol Th.	2/3	1926	O557B	5 hp, 10″ wp and 30″ vacuum; style 49.
Carlinville	Paul Bros. Amusement Co.		1922	14003	
Chicago	Adams Th.	2/	1921	11936	
	American Photo Player showroom		1922	13885	Located at 702 South Wabash.
	Claude P. Ball School of Theatre Organ Playing		1928	21977	Located at 645 Buckingham Place.
	Claude P. Ball Studio	3/	1928	21935	Located at 23 East Jackson, suite 1100.
	Clermont Th.	2/3	1924	L1132	5 hp, 10″ wp and 30″ vacuum; style 49.
	Enterprises Theatres, Inc.		1925	17514	
	Harvard Th.		1923	15096	
	H. E. Paley		1924	15567	
	Jessica Clement Studio		1927	20894	
	LaSalle Th.		1929	22829	Located at 110 West Madison.
	Linden Th.	2/4	1923	14342	3 hp, 10″ wp.
	Marquette Th.	2/			
	Milda Th.	2/	1924	M739B	5 hp, 10″ wp and 30″ vacuum.
	Vendome Th.	2/	1925	16995	
Charleston	Lincoln Th.	2/4			Wicks opus 319.
Coal City	Rialto Th.		1927		
Danville	Fischer Th.	2/4			
Elgin	Star Th.	2/	1928		
Moline	Roxy Th.	2/6			
Pekin	Rialto Th.	2/	1927	20371	
Olney	Arcadia Th.	2/4	1926		Style 75; moved from unknown location by Wurlitzer.
Taylorville	Taylorville Theatre Co.	2/	1922	13474	
INDIANA					
Columbus	American Th.	2/3			
	Crump Th.	2/3	1927	20948	
Danville	Royal Th.	2/3	1927	P111B	5 hp, 10″ wp and 30″ vacuum; style 49.
Gary	Family Th.	2/	1928	20510	
	Rex Music Shop		1929	23180	
Indianapolis	Colonial (Empress) (Fox) Th.	2/	1927	20217	
	Garrick (Esquire) Th.	2/	1928	21792	
	Hamilton Th.	2/	1926	O520B	5 hp, 10″ wp and 30″ vacuum.
	Irvington Th.	2/	1923	15222	Later repossessed.
	Rivoli Th.	2/6	1927	20611	
Logansport	Paramount Th.	2/3	1927	20662	
Richmond	Hudson Th.	2/3	1926	O937B	5 hp, 10″ wp and 30″ vacuum; style 49.
IOWA					
Des Moines	Rialto Th.	2/	1918	F600	7½ hp, 5″&10″ wp.
Dubuque	Princess (Avon) Th.	2/4	1928	Q404B	5 hp, 10″ wp and 30″ vacuum.
Fort Dodge	Majestic Th.	2/	1922	13606	
Iowa City	Strand Th.	2/3	1925	N653B	5 hp, 10″ wp and 30″ vacuum; style 49.
Marshalltown	Capitol Th.	3/9	1928	22402	Later moved to KMTR Radio, Los Angeles, California, then to KTLA Radio, Los Angeles.
	Legion Th.	2/3	1925	N6B	5 hp, 10″ wp and 30″ vacuum; style 49.
Mason City	J. M. Heffner		191?		Wicks opus 222.
Newton	Capitol Th.	2/	192?		Wicks opus 317.
KANSAS					
Abilene	Lyric Th.	2/	1927	20245	
Arkansas City	Burford Th.	2/	1927	20615	
Baldwin	Gem Th.	2/5			
Emporia	Strand Th.	2/6	1928	22545	Later moved to Granada Theatre, Emporia, Kansas.
Kansas City	Granada Th.	2/6	1929	23084	
	Kansas Th.	2/6			
Milford	Dr. Brinkley residence and radio station	2/3			
Newton	Regent (Fox) Th.	2/7	1927	20792	
Osawatomie	Dickinson Th.	3/4			
Topeka	Isis Th.	2/	1925	N345B	5 hp, 10″ wp and 30″ vacuum.

CITY/STATE	LOCATION	SIZE	YR	BLWR	REMARKS
Wellington	Wellington Theatre Co.	2/	1928	22121	
Winfield	Regent Th.	2/	1928	22239	
KENTUCKY					
Louisville	Cherokee Amusement Co.	2/	1923	L559	5 hp, 10″ wp and 30″ vacuum.
	Majestic Th.		1922	13284	
	Rex Th.	2/	1926		
LOUISIANA					
Alexandria	Paramount Th.	2/5	1928	22238	
Baton Rouge	Columbia (Paramount) Th.	2/6	1926		Opus 2412
	Louisiana Th.	2/5	1927	20137	
Hammond	Columbia Th.	2/4	1928	21879	
Houma	Grand Th.	2/	1928	21757	
Minden	Saenger Th.	2/3	1926	O301B	5 hp, 10″ wp and 30″ vacuum; style 49.
Monroe	Saenger (Paramount) Th.	2/6	1927	20017	
			1927	20360	
Natchitoches	D. L. Sudduth & Edgar Levy		1928	21973	
New Orleans	Liberty Th.		1922	13197	
	Loew's State Th.	3/13	1926	18354	
	Mecca Th.	2/	1925	N32B	5 hp, 10″ wp and 30″ vacuum.
	Saenger Th.	4/23	1927	19393	25 hp.
		4/26			Additions: fife and 2 strings.
	St. Charles Amusement Co.	2/	1924	M624B	5 hp, 10″ wp and 30″ vacuum.
	Strand Th.	3/8	1928	21759	
	Tivoli Th.	2/			
Shreveport	Majestic Th.	2/5	1927	20837	
	Saenger (Capri) Th.	2/8			
	Strand Th.	2/13	1925	16966	
MAINE					
Bar Harbor	Star Th.	2/	1924	15745	
			1926	18860	
Rockland	Strand Th.	2/	1923	14038	
MARYLAND					
Baltimore	Apollo Th.	2/	1922		
	Broadway Th.	2/4	1920	11335	3 hp, 10″ wp; style 75.
	Highland Amusement Co.	2/	1922	13811	Wicks opus 432.
	Metropolitan Th.	3/	1922	13295	Built by Wicks.
	Regent Th.	2/	1922	13255	
	Waverly Th.	2/	1921	11994	
Crisfield	Arcade (Crisfield) Th.	2/3	1928	22272	Style 39.
Silver Spring	Seco (Roth's Silver) Th.	2/4	1927	P401B	5 hp, 10″ wp and 30″ vacuum.
MASSACHUSETTS					
Arlington	Capitol Th.	3/10	1925	17751	
	Orpheum Th.	2/			
Dorchester	Dorchester Th.		1922	13731	
Framingham	St. George Th.	2/4	1920	10934	3 hp, 10″ wp; style 75.
Haverhill	Palace (Paramount) Th.	2/7	1923	21460	
Lawrence	Broadway Th.	2/	1921	12289	
Leominster	Metropolitan Th.		1929	23028	
	Rialto Th.	3/10	1922	13713	
			1926	18543	
Malden	Orpheum Th.	2/	1921	12067	
Marblehead	Warwick Th.	2/4	1920	10992	3 hp, 10″ wp; style 75.
Medford	Medford Th.	2/	1922	13993	
Salem	New Plaza Th.	2/4	1920	11246	3 hp, 10″ wp; style 75.
Somerville	Ball Square Th.		1923	14110	
			1924	15897	
South Boston	Broadway Th.	2/6	1919	10410	
Taunton	Strand Th.	2/	1924	15872	
Worcester	New Plymouth Th.	2/8	1928	22438	
MICHIGAN					
Detroit	Annex Th.	3/13	1926	19334	10 hp.
			1927	11560TUR	For V'Oleon and piano.
	Conant Th.	2/	1928		
	Crystal Th.	2/3	1923	L15	5 hp, 10″ wp and 30″ vacuum; style 49.
			1926	18855	
	Fine Arts Th.	2/	1919	9858	
		2/5	1927	19853	Opus 2316; style 17.
	Grand Riviera (Riviera) Th.	3/10	1925	17428	
	Irving Th.	2/6	1925	18234	
	LaSalle Garden (Century) Th.	2/	1928		
	Senate Th.		1928		
	Tuxedo Th.	2/	1921	12447	
		3/13	1926	19622	10 hp, 15″ wp; opus 2300; with V'Oleon.
Grand Rapids	Family (Keith's Family) Th.	2/	1924	L314	3 hp, 5″ wp and 25″ vacuum.
	Regent Th.	3/6	1923	14542	
	Wealthy Th.		1924	15763	

CITY/STATE	LOCATION	SIZE	YR	BLWR	REMARKS
Lansing	Plaza Th.	2/3	1928	22216	
Lapeer	Lyric Th.	2/3	1926	N937B	5 hp, 10″ wp and 30″ vacuum; style 49.
Midland	Frolic Th.	2/	1922	13913	Wicks opus 435.
		2/6	1927		Wicks opus 706.
MINNESOTA					
Cambridge	Cozy Th.	2/	1927	21273	
Edina	Edina Th.	2/5			
Minneapolis	Columbia Heights Th.	2/	1928	21306	
	Blue Mouse Th.	3/	1921	12385	10 hp.
	Hitchcock & True		1928	21458	
	Lyric Th.	2/10			
	Pantages Th.	2/	1921		10 hp.
	Princess Th.	2/7	1928		
	University Th.		1928	21332	
Moorhead	Moorhead Th.	2/	1921	12613	
St. Cloud	Capitol Th.	2/	1922	13446	
St. Paul	Capitol Th.	3/	1922	12982	
	KSTP Radio	3/11	1928	21291	
	St. Claire Th.	2/5			
MISSISSIPPI					
Biloxi	Crown Th.	2/	1923	14331	
	Paramount Th.	2/6			
Clarksdale	Clarksdale (Paramount) (Marion) Th.	2/6	1927	20956	
Columbus	Princess Th.	3/8	1927	20005	
Greenville	People's (Paramount) Th.	2/6	1922	13958	
			1927	19868	
Greenwood	Greenwood Th.	2/	1923	13766	
Gulf Port	Strand Th.		1923	14257	
Hattiesburg	Anderson Th.	2/6	1926	18969	
	Strand Th.	2/6	1927	20359	Later moved to Saenger Theatre, Hattiesburg, Mississippi.
Jackson	Century (Royal Music Hall) Th.	2/5	1927	20767	
	Majestic Th.	2/5			
Meridian	Princess Th.	2/	1923	14271	
	Strand Th.	2/	1924	16608	
	Temple Th.	3/8	1928	21761	
Natchez	Baker Grand Th.	2/	1922	13846	
	Saenger Th.	2/4			
Tupelo	Strand Th.		1928	21827	
Vicksburg	Alamo Th.	2/	1923	14136	
	Saenger Th.	2/8	1922	13672	
Yazoo City	Yazoo Th.		1923	14333	
MISSOURI					
Booneville	Lyric Th.	2/4	1926	19412	Later moved to KVOO Radio, Tulsa, Oklahoma.
Chillicothe	Strand Th.	2/3	1923	K1145	5 hp, 10″ wp and 30″ vacuum; style 49.
Clinton	Liberty Th.	2/4	1927	19741	Opus 2315; style 15.
Columbia	Missouri Th.	3/7	1928	21005	5 hp.
Excelsior Springs	Beyer Th.	2/6	1928	22433	
Kansas City	Globe Th.	2/	1922	13395	
	Lindbergh Th.		1928	22685	
	Loew's Midland Th.	4/20	1927	20517	25 hp.
	Pantages (Tower) Th.	2/16	1921	11899	10 hp.
	Rockhill Th.	2/4	1927	19988	
		3/11	1928	22637	New organ.
	Uptown Th.	3/13	1927	21095	Opus 2361.
	Vista Th.	2/4	1928	22452	
	Waldo Th.	2/	1928	22425	
Kirksville	Kennedy Th.	2/6			
Macon	Grand Th.	2/3	1925	N241B	5 hp, 10″ wp and 30″ vacuum; style 49.
Mexico	Liberty Th.	2/4			Built by Wicks.
Moberly	Grand Th.	2/5			
	Moberly Th.	2/5			Located on 4th Street.
Nevada	Star Th.	2/	1925	17512	
St. Joseph	Rivoli Th.	2/	1928	21403	
St. Louis	Aubert Th.	2/6	1923	14070	
Sedalia	Sedalia Th.	2/4	1920	11288	3 hp, 10″ wp; style 75.
Springfield	Jefferson Th.	2/			
	Princess Th.	2/			
Warrensburg	Star Th.	2/7			
MONTANA					
Billings	Babcock Th.	2/6			
	Regent Th.	2/4	1920	10944	3 hp, 10″ wp; style 75.
	Rialto Th.	2/	1920	10977	3 hp, 10″ wp.
Grabel	Grabel Th.	2/4	1921		
Havre	Orpheum Th.	2/4	1923	14576	Wicks opus 455.
Miles City	Iris Th.	2/4	1920	10938	3 hp, 10″ wp; style 75.
Missoula	Fox Th.	3/8	1925	18135	

CITY/STATE	LOCATION	SIZE	YR	BLWR	REMARKS
Missoula	Wilma (Missoula) Th.	2/6	1920	10491	3 hp, 15″ wp.
		3/10			New organ.
	Rialto Th.		1927	20368	
Roundup	Roundup (Orpheum) Th.	2/4	1920	11857	
NEBRASKA					
Alliance	Imperial Th.	2/4	1920	11637	3 hp, 10″ wp; style 75.
Aurora	Mazda Th.	2/4	1928		
McCook	Bison (Temple) Th.	2/	1921	11969	
North Platte	Fox Th.	2/			
NEVADA					
Lovelock	Lovelock Th.	2/3			Style 49B.
Reno	Grand Th.	2/			
	Wigwam (Crest) Th.	2/5			
NEW HAMPSHIRE					
Manchester	Eagle Th.	2/4	1920	11116	3 hp, 10″ wp; style 75.
NEW JERSEY					
Atlantic City	Capitol Th.	3/	1921	12746	
Atlantic Highlands	Atlantic Th.	2/	1923	L302	5 hp, 10″ wp and 30″ vacuum.
Beach Haven	Colonial Th.		1927	20256	
Bergenfield	Palace Th.	2/8	1928	21584	
Brandt Beach	Colony Th.		1928	22208	
Clifton	Park Th.	2/4	1905		Los Angeles Art Organ Co. nameplate.
Dumont	Dumont Th.		1925	17917	
East Orange	Regent Th.	2/	1921	12213	Moved in 1923 to Variety Theatre, New York, NY.
Hillside	Hillside Th.	2/	1926	N1135B	5 hp, 10″ wp and 30″ vacuum.
	Mayfair Th.		1927	20840	
			1928	22072	
Irvington	Grove Th.	2/3	1926	O220B	5 hp, 10″ wp and 30″ vacuum; style 49; moved in 1927 to Capitol Theatre, South River, New Jersey.
			1928	21753	New organ.
Jersey City	Loew's Jersey Th.	4/23	1929	23227	
Keyport	Surf Th.	2/4	1922	13685	Wicks opus 425.
Newark	Center Amusement Co.		1921	12688	
	Colonial Th.	2/3	1926	N1043B	5 hp, 10″ wp and 30″ vacuum; style 49.
			1928	P1116B	5 hp, 10″ wp and 30″ vacuum.
	Congress Th.	2/3	1925	N509B	5 hp, 10″ wp and 25″ vacuum; style 49.
	Grand Th.	2/3	1926	O406B	5 hp, 10″ wp and 30″ vacuum; style 49.
	Grand Palace Th.	2/4	1920	11477	3 hp, 10″ wp; style 75.
	Lincoln Th.	2/	1924	L1152	5 hp, 10″ wp and 30″ vacuum.
	Mayfair Th.		1928	21641	
	Naomi Investment Co.		1921	12479	
North Bergen	New Embassy Th.	3/13	1928	22654	City of North Bergen was originally known as Woodcliffe.
Orange	Colonial Th.		1918	F471	7½ hp, 5″&10″ wp.
	Palace Th.		1918	F472	7½ hp, 5″&10″ wp.
	Washington Th.	2/	1925	17579	
Red Bank	Strand Th.	2/4	1921	11796	3 hp, 10″ wp; style 75.
Salem	Hunt's Th.		1922	13587	
South Amboy	Empire Th.	2/	1925	N7B	5 hp, 10″ wp and 30″ vacuum.
Trenton	Centre Street Th.		1919	9574	
Union City	Strand Th.	2/3	1927	P402B	5 hp, 10″ wp and 30″ vacuum; style 49.
Washington	Washington Th.	2/3	1926	O933B	5 hp, 10″ wp and 30″ vacuum; style 49.
West Hoboken	Colonial Th.	2/4	1920	10978	3 hp, 10″ wp; style 75; city of West Hoboken was later known as Union City.
Westwood	Westwood Th.		1921		
Wildwood	Casino Th.		1923	14397	
NEW MEXICO					
Gallup	Strand Th.	2/3	1925		Style 49.
NEW YORK					
Albany	Clinton Square Th.		1923	14262	
	Leland Th.	2/	1922	13570	
Arverne	Arverne Th.	2/	1922	13341	Wicks opus 405.
Bronx	Boston Road Th.	2/4	1925	N488B	5 hp, 10″ wp and 25″ vacuum; style 49D.
	City Island Th.		1927	20415	
	Loew's Fairmont Th.	3/19	1928	21462	25 hp.
	Loew's Fordham Th.	3/13	1926	19657	Opus 2303.
	Loew's Grand Bronx Th.	3/14	1927		
	Loew's Paradise Th.	4/23	1929	23302	25 hp.
	New Pictorium Th.		1923	14029	
	Plaza Th.	2/4	1920	11199	3 hp, 10″ wp; style 75.
	Webster Th.	2/	1928	Q112B	5 hp, 10″ wp and 30″ vacuum.
Brooklyn	Alba Th.	2/8	1929	23286	
	Belvedere Th.	2/5	1922	13479	Made by Wicks; later moved to Star Th., Malad, Idaho.
	Biltmore Th.		1926	19175	
	Cameo Th.	2/4	1927		
	Chester Th.		1923	14171	
	Court Th.	2/	1923	15582	

CITY/STATE	LOCATION	SIZE	YR	BLWR	REMARKS
Brooklyn	46th Street Th.	2/3	1926	O447B	5 hp, 10" wp and 30" vacuum; style 49.
	Happy Hour Th.	2/	1926	O602B	5 hp, 10" wp and 32" vacuum.
	Loew's Kings Th.	4/23	1929	23106	
	Loew's Oriental Th.	3/13	1927		
	Loew's Pitkin Th.	3/13	1929	23448	
	New Gates Th.	2/3	1926	O709B	5 hp, 10" wp and 30" vacuum; style 49.
		3/7	1927	20593	5 hp.
	Newkirk Th.	2/	1928	21680	
			1928	22725	
	New Plaza Th.		1922	13269	
	Piccadilly (Avalon) Th.	3/13	1927	21282	15 hp.
	Ritz Th.	2/	1926	N1042B	5 hp, 10" wp and 30" vacuum.
	Rugby Th.	2/3	1926	N934B	5 hp, 10" wp and 30" vacuum; style 49.
	Subway Th.	2/3	1926	O223B	5 hp, 10" wp and 30" vacuum; style 49.
	Sunset Th.	2/3	1924	M558B	5 hp, 10" wp and 30" vacuum; style 49.
Canandaigua	Playhouse Th.	2/	1922	13017	
Corona	Palace Th.	2/	1921	11993	7½ hp.
	Granada Th.	2/5	1926	19699	Opus 2306; style 17.
Ellenville	Shadowland Th.		1927	20779	
Flushing	Flushing Th.	3/11	1924		7½ hp; moved in 1930 to 92nd Street Young Men's & Young Women's Hebrew Association, New York, NY.
Glen Falls	Empire Th.	3/	1925		
Hudson Falls	Strand Th.	2/	1922	13987	
Jamaica	Loew's Hillside Th.	3/13	1926	18967	
	Loew's Valencia Th.	4/23	1928	22564	25 hp.
Lake Placid	Adirondack Th.	2/	1926	18780	
Monticello	Rialto Th.	2/	1921	12452	
Newburgh	Cameo Th.	2/3	1927	P461B	5 hp, 10" wp and 30" vacuum; style 49.
	East & West Hudson Th.	2/3	1927	P110B	5 hp, 10" wp and 30" vacuum; style 49.
New York	Acme Th.	2/	1921	12662	
	A. J. Herrlich		1929	23515	Located at 1185 Park Avenue.
	American Photo Player showroom		1923	14268	
	Apollo Th.		1922	13812	
	Astor Th.		1927	19794	
	Bluebird (Ramona) Th.	2/	1928	22307	
	Bunny Th.	2/4	1920	11094	3 hp, 10" wp; style 75.
			1923	L287	3 hp, 10" wp.
	Castro Th.		1927		
	55th Street Playhouse		1927	20058	
	Forest Park Th.				
	Franklin Th.	2/	1924	M741B	5 hp, 10" wp and 30" vacuum.
	Loew's 175th Street Th.	4/23	1930	23778	
	Loew's Victoria Th.	2/			
	Majestic Th.	2/	1919	9502	
	Mount Morris Th.	2/	1920	11831	2 hp, 4" wp.
	Odeon Th.	2/4	1920	11075	3 hp, 10" wp; style 75; moved in 1931 to Julius Hartt School of Music, Hartford, Connnecticut.
	Olympia Th.	2/	1920	10765	
	Palace Th.	2/4	1920	11367	3 hp, 10" wp; style 75.
	Pershing Th.	2/	1927	12486TUR	Located at 1324 Amsterdam Avenue.
	Plaza Music Hall		1917		Wicks opus 220; located on Madison Avenue.
	Rose Th.	2/3	1926	O804B	5 hp, 10" wp and 30" vacuum; style 49.
	Tuxedo Th.	2/	1923	L281	5 hp, 10" wp and 30" vacuum.
	Venice Th.	2/4	1920	11503	2 hp, 7" wp; style 75.
	Verona Th.	2/	1925	N334B	5 hp, 10" wp and 30" vacuum; style 49H.
	Windsor Th.	2/3	1927	P24B	5 hp, 10" wp and 30" vacuum; style 49.
Ossining	Victoria Th.	2/	1922	13241	
Poughkeepsie	Statford Th.	2/4	1920	11414	3 hp, 10" wp; style 75.
Queens	Richmond Hill (Keith's) Th.	3/13	1928	22138	
	Roosevelt Th.	2/	1921	12166	
			1924	18199	3 hp.
	Strand (Spring Valley Community) Th.	2/	1925	N801B	5 hp, 10" wp and 30" vacuum.
Riverhead	Riverhead (Capitol) Th.	2/4	1920	10979	3 hp, 10" wp; style 75.
Saugerties	Orpheum Th.		1928	22168	
Utica	Vincenzo Daniel and Carmine Scala	2/3	1927	O972B	5 hp, 10" wp and 30" vacuum; style 49; located at 725 Varick Street.
Yonkers	Loew's Yonkers Th.	3/13	1927	21224	15 hp.
	New Orpheum Th.		1922		

NORTH CAROLINA

CITY/STATE	LOCATION	SIZE	YR	BLWR	REMARKS
Asheville	Imperial Th.	2/			Built by Wicks.
	Majestic Th.	2/	1927	20926	
Burlington	Carolina Th.	2/	1927	20765	
Chapel Hill	Carolina Th.	2/	1927	20638	
Charlotte	Riggin Th.	2/4	1920	11226	3 hp, 10" wp; style 75.
Durham	Savoy Th.	2/	1922	13416	Wicks opus 411.
Elizabeth City	Carolina Th.	3/8	1929	22914	Opus 2486.

CITY/STATE	LOCATION	SIZE	YR	BLWR	REMARKS
Goldsboro	Acme Th.	2/	1920	11219	3 hp, 10″ wp; style 100.
Greensboro	Bijou Th.	2/6			
		2/6			New organ built by Wicks.
	Carolina Th.	2/6	1927	20649	
	Dyckman Th.	2/	1921		
	Imperial Th.	2/	1923	15364	
			1927	20252	New organ.
	National Th.	2/8	1927	20692	Later moved to Center Theatre, Durham, North Carolina.
Greenville	White's Th.	2/	1924	M418	5 hp, 10″ wp and 30″ vacuum.
Henderson	State Th.	2/	1920		
Kinston	Grand Th.	2/4	1920	11100	3 hp, 10″ wp; style 75.
	Kinston Th.	2/			
Pinehurst	Carolina Th.	2/	1922	13938	
Raleigh	Alamo Th.	2/	1920		
	Capitol Th.	2/4	1920	11070	3 hp, 10″ wp; style 75; traded in or repossessed in 1927.
	Palace Th.	2/	1926	19252	
	State Th.	2/3	1926	O610B	5 hp, 10″ wp and 30″ vacuum; style 49.
Salisbury	Capitol Th.	3/	1924	16650	
Statesville	Crescent Th.	2/	1920		
Wilson	Stallings & Mason Co.		1921	12138	
Winston-Salem	Carolina Th.	2/5			
	Colonial Th.	2/8			
	Liberty Th.		1925	18020	
NORTH DAKOTA					
Devils Lake	Grand Th.	2/	1923	14166	
OHIO					
Brewster	Brewster Th.		1927		
Canton	Loew's Th.	3/11	1926	19506	Opus 2296.
Circleville	Cliftonia Th.	2/	1928	Q542B	5 hp, 10″ wp and 30″ vacuum.
			1928	22458	
			1928	9425TUR	
Cleveland Hights	Cedar-Leo Th.		1925	18162	
Columbus	Champion Th.		1923	13383	
	Empress Th.	3/11	1928	21939	
	Loew's Ohio Th.	4/20	1928	21389	
	Ogden (Lincoln) Th.	3/9	1928	22598	
	WBNS Radio	2/6			
Elyria	Capitol Th.	3/11	1926	18993	
	Rivoli Th.	2/3	1924	M36	5 hp, 10″ wp and 30″ vacuum; style 49.
		2/6	1925	16743	New organ.
Lima	Regent Th.		1922	12953	
Lorain	Ohio (Pantheon) Th.	2/	1922	K176	5 hp, 10″ wp and 25″ vacuum.
	Tendler Amusement Co.	2/	1926	N1038B	5 hp, 10″ wp and 30″ vacuum.
Steubenville	Capitol Th.	3/10	1928	21360	
Uhrichsville	Ohio Th.	2/	1923	K933	5 hp, 10″&15″ wp and 30″ vacuum.
Willoughby	Willoby (Masonic) Th.	2/7	1928	22003	
Youngstown	Gallett-Rulli Th.	2/3	1926	O318B	5 hp, 10″ wp and 30″ vacuum; style 49.
	Youngstown Th.	3/10			
Zanesville	Liberty Th.	3/8	1926	18609	7½ hp.
OKLAHOMA					
Bartlesville	Lyric Th.	2/4	1923	14067	
Durant	Liberty Th.	2/4			
El Reno	Criterion Th.	2/	1929	Q732B	5 hp, 10″ wp and 30″ vacuum.
Henryetta	Blaine Th.	2/4	1926	O302B	5 hp.
Muskogee	Broadway Th.	2/6	1925	18245	
Norman	Sooner Th.	2/4			
	University Th.		1924	16139	
Oklahoma City	KFMJ Radio	2/			
	Ritz Th.	2/8	1928	22695	
	Victoria Th.	3/12	1928	21846	With echo.
Okmulgee	Orpheum Th.	2/			
Pawhuska	Ki-He-Kah Th.	2/4	1926	O939B	5 hp, 10″ wp and 30″ vacuum.
Ponca City	Majestic Th.	2/3	1926	O901B	5 hp, 10″ wp and 30″ vacuum; style 49.
Tulsa	Circle Th.	2/4	1928	22043	
	Main Street Th.	2/4	1928	Q627B	5 hp, 10″ wp and 30″ vacuum; style 39R.
	Majestic Th.	3/16	1923	14107	10 hp.
	Rialto Th.	4/11	1926	18423	
			1926	10195TUR	
	Ritz Th.	4/17	1925	18113	15 hp.
	Wade Hamiliton Organ & Piano Studio	3/10	1929	23450	Later moved to KMBC Radio, Kansas City, Missouri.
Weatherford	Bungalow Th.	2/4	1928	21876	Style 39A Special.
OREGON					
Albany	Globe (Venetian) Th.	2/6	1920	11368	7½ hp, 15″ wp.
Ashland	Vining Th.	2/4	1920	11622	3 hp, 10″ wp; style 75.
Astoria	Blue Mouse Th.	2/4	1922		
	People's Th.	2/6	1923		Moved in 1927 to Olympic Theatre, Seattle, Washington.

CITY/STATE	LOCATION	SIZE	YR	BLWR	REMARKS
Bandon	Bandon Th.	2/4	1922		Built by Wicks.
Baker	Clarick Th.		1929	22731	
Eugene	Eugene Th.	2/	1922		
	Heilig Th.	2/4	1924	15365	
	Mayflower Th.	2/5	1922		
	University Th.	2/	1925	17205	
Grants Pass	Grants Pass Th.	2/	1920		Moved in 1941 to Ice Arena Rink, Medford, Oregon, by Balcom & Vaughan.
	Rivoli Th.	2/3	1924	15561	
Klamath Falls	Empire (Esquire) Th.	2/4			
LaGrande	Liberty (Arcade) Th.	2/6	1927	20571	
McMinnville	Lark Th.	2/6	1927	19829	3 hp; moved in 1936 to Lyon's Music Hall, Seattle, Washington, by Balcom & Vaughan.
Medford	Rialto Th.	2/4	1924	15562	
Pendleton	Alta (United Artists) Th.	2/	1926	19201	
Portland	Bob White Th.	2/6	1924	15200	
	Heilig Amusement Co.		1922		
	H. P. Arnest residence	2/11	1929	23395	
	Moreland Th.	2/6	1925	16799	
	Multnomah Th.	2/	1924	15771	
	Pantages (Orpheum) Th.	3/10	1925	17158	Opened as Empress Theatre.
			1926	18976	Moved in 1954 to Roller Gardens Rink, Federal Way, Washington, by Balcom & Vaughan.
Roseburg	Indian (Antlers) Th.	2/10	1928	21488	
Salem	Maria Th.	2/	1921		
	New Grand Th.	2/4			
Seaside	Seaside (Strand) Th.	2/4	1925		
Silverton	Palace Th.	2/4	1923	14119	
The Dalles	Mission Th.	2/6			Moved in 1929 to Granada Theatre, The Dalles, Oregon.
PENNSYLVANIA					
Aliquippa	Harvey Th.	2/	1928	22089	
Beaver Falls	Granada Th.	3/10			
Bethlehem	Globe Th.	2/	1925	18280	
Bradford	unidentified theatre		1918		Wicks opus 253.
Bridgeville	Granada Th.	2/3	1928	Q507B	5 hp, 10" wp and 30" vacuum; style 49.
	Rankin Th.		1928	22630	
Brownsville	Plaza Th.	2/4	1928	21690	
			1928	21844	
Carlisle	Carlisle Strand Th.	2/	1926	18874	
			1926	19248	
Cresson	Rivoli Th.	2/	1927	20797	
Easton	Israel Krohn	2/3	1927	P5B	5 hp, 10" wp and 30" vacuum; style 49.
Ephrata	Grand Th.	2/	1927	20499	
Greenville	Main Th.		1926	18783	Later moved to Little Theatre, Newark, New Jersey.
	Mercer Square Th.	2/4	1922	13227	Wicks opus 427.
			1926	19300	
Harrisburg	Colonial Th.	3/	1922	13892	
Huntington	Clifton Th.	2/	1926	O102B	5 hp, 10" wp and 30" vacuum.
Indiana	Ritz (Manos) Th.	3/8	1928	21967	
Johnstown	New Park Th.		1923	14163	
Lancaster	Capitol (Krupa) Th.	4/21	1925	17496	
Lebanon	Capitol Th.	3/5	1922		Wicks opus 404.
	Colonial Th.	2/8	1922	13861	Wicks opus 438.
Littletown	Regent Th.	2/	1928	22446	
Lock Haven	Martin Th.		1920	10846	Wicks opus 286.
Marietta	Acri Th.	2/	1926	15234	
Meadville	Academy Th.	3/9	1926	19162	With V'Oleon.
Newcastle	Capitol Th.		1926	18856	
	Dome Th.	2/	1923	K926	5 hp, 10"&15" wp and 30" vacuum.
Norristown	Gloria Th.	2/	1926	O625B	5 hp, 10" wp and 30" vacuum.
			1929	22949	
Old Forge	Louis Pilosi	2/3	1926	O652B	5 hp, 10" wp and 30" vacuum; style 49; located at 117 Foster Street.
Philadelphia	Allen Th.		1925	17204	
	Edgemont Th.	2/3	1927	O931B	5 hp, 10" wp and 30" vacuum; style 49.
	Erie (Century) Th.	2/4	1920	11579	3 hp, 10" wp; style 75; moved in 1928 to Norris Theatre, Philadelphia, by M. P. Moller.
	Liberty Th.	2/4	1920	11292	3 hp, 10" wp; style 75.
	Milgram & Pilch		1925	17906	
	New Ideal Th.	2/4			
	Palm Th.	5/	1921	12063	10 hp.
	Tivoli Th.		1925	18585	
Pittsburgh	Loew's Penn Th.	4/20	1927	20433	25 hp; opus 2314.
	Ritz Th.		1928	21596	
Pottstown	unidentified theatre		1917		Wicks opus 219.
Reading	Hippodrome (State) (Warner) Th.	2/8	1922	13868	
	San Toy Th.	2/4			
Rochester	Oriental Th.	2/6	1930		

CITY/STATE	LOCATION	SIZE	YR	BLWR	REMARKS
Sharon	unidentified theatre	2/4	1923		Wicks opus 459.
South Fork	Rivoli Th.	2/	1927	20711	
Tyrone	Wilson Th.	2/5	1927	19908	Opus 2316; style 17.
York	Jackson Th.	2/			
RHODE ISLAND					
Providence	Loew's State (Ocean State Performing Arts Center) Th.	4/20	1928	22228	
SOUTH CAROLINA					
Florence	O'Dowd Th.	2/	1923	14208	
TENNESSEE					
Memphis	Madison Th.	2/	1925	N356B	5 hp, 10″ wp and 30″ vacuum; style 49H.
	Pantages (Warner) Th.	3/	1921	11833	15 hp, 15″ wp; style C Special.
TEXAS					
Beaumont	Jefferson Th.	3/8	1927	20687	
Dallas	unidentified theatre		1927		Wicks opus 213.
	Old Mill Th.	3/8	1928	21562	Moved in 1985 to Lakewood Theatre, Dallas, Texas.
Fort Worth	Women's Club	2/6			
Houston	Loew's State Th.	3/13	1927	20519	15 hp.
Jacksonville	Palace Th.	2/4	1928	21693	
Ralls	Crystal Th.	2/	1929	Q1104B	5 hp, 10″ wp and 30″ vacuum.
San Antonio	Aztec Th.	3/11	1927	18586	10 hp.
			1927	10654TUR	For piano.
	Empire Th.	3/10	1920	11636	7½ hp; style C; dummy top manual.
	Majestic Th.	3/10	1929	23029	
	Princess Th.	3/10	1922		Dummy top manual.
Texarkana	Saenger (Paramount) Th.	2/6	192?		
UTAH					
Cedar City	Thorley Th.		1928	21778	
Heber City	Andy Murdock		1928	22321	
Ogden	Orpheum Th.	2/4	1922	K403	5 hp, 10″ wp and 25″ vacuum.
	Utah Th.	2/12	1919		Beethoven nameplate.
Provo	Crest (Unitah) Th.	3/10			
Salt Lake City	American Th.		1919	H254	3 hp, 10″ wp.
		4/	1921	12744	
	Pantages Th.	2/16	1920	10774	7½ hp, 15″ wp.
	Star Th.	2/	1928	P1148B	5 hp, 10″ wp and 30″ vacuum.
	Strand Th.		1922	13319	
	Utah Th.	2/10			
VERMONT					
St. Johnsburg	unidentified new theatre	2/3	1926	O423B	5 hp, 10″ wp and 30″ vacuum; style 49; located at 26 Eastern Avenue.
VIRGINIA					
Bristol	Isis Th.	2/	1923	L114	5 hp, 10″ wp and 30″ vacuum.
Charlottesville	Arthur Jordan Piano Co.	2/4	1920	11501	3 hp, 10″ wp; style 75.
Danville	Broadway Th.	2/3	1923	14421	Wicks opus 454.
			1927	21097	
		2/3	1927	O1120B	5 hp, 10″ wp and 30″ vacuum; style 49.
	Rialto Th.	2/7	1927	20178	
	State (Capitol) Th.	2/4	1926	19632	Opus 2308; style 16.
Harrisonburg	Virginia Th.	2/7	1925	18176	
Norfolk	Attuck's Th.	2/3	1925	N435B	5 hp, 10″ wp and 30″ vacuum; style 49.
	Granby (Lee) Th.	2/	1922	13305	7½ hp.
	Newport Th.	2/5	1928	21347	
	Strand Th.	3/	1923	14619	
Portsmouth	Levine Th.	3/	1925	18045	
Richmond	Capitol Th.	2/	1926	19154	
	Colonial Th.	2/	1921	11990	7½ hp; built by Wicks.
	Isis Th.	2/	1922		Wicks opus 402.
	National (Towne) Th.	2/	1923	14231	
	Venus Th.	2/	1924	M726B	5 hp, 10″ wp and 30″ vacuum; moved in 1929 to Bishop Theatre, Hoboken, New Jersey.
			1928	22339	
Roanoke	Park Th.		1921	11891	
Staunton	Strand Th.		1925	18180	
Winchester	Capitol (Empire) Th.	2/6	1928	22330	
	Colonial Th.	2/	1924	M519B	5 hp, 10″ wp and 30″ vacuum; style 49H.
WASHINGTON					
Auburn	Granada (Mission) Th.	2/4	1920		Style 75.
Bellingham	Beck's American Th.	2/9	1919	10219	5 hp.
	Grand Th.	2/3	1927	20757	
Centralia	Grand Th.	2/5	1921		Moved in 1930 to Fox Theatre, Centralia, Washington.
Chehalis	Chehalis Th.	2/8	1923		Built by Wicks.
Edmonds	Edgemont Th.	2/2	1922		Style 27.
Kelso	Vogue Th.	2/			

CITY/STATE	LOCATION	SIZE	YR	BLWR	REMARKS
Longview	Peking Th.	2/4	1921		
Montesano	Gwynn's Th.	2/4	1926	19085	
Omak	Omak Th.	2/4	1923		
	Red Apple Th.		1929	22783	
Pasco	Liberty Th.	2/4	1921	12165	Style 75.
Port Angeles	Mack (Olympian) Th.	2/3	1922	K542	5 hp, 10"&15" wp and 30" vacuum; style 49.
		3/10	1926	18067	New organ.
Pullman	Cordova Th.	2/6	1928		
Renton	Grand Th.	2/4	1924	15450	Wicks opus 494.
Seattle	Danz Th.	2/6			
	Egyptian Th.	2/16			
	Fox (Seventh Avenue) (Music Hall) Th.	4/16	1928	21345	15 hp.
	Heilig Th.	2/			
	Madison Th.	2/4	1922	13159	
	Maiden Th.	2/4	1922		
	Majestic (Ballard) Th.	2/4	1922		
	Music Box (Show Box) Th.	2/5	1928	21986	
	Olympic Th.	2/6			
	Pantages (Palomar) Th.	2/18	1921	12365	10 hp; moved in 1946 to Rollerland Rink, Renton, Washington, by Balcom & Vaughan.
	Queen Anne Th.	2/4	1922		
	Roycroft Th.	2/5	1925	17181	
Spokane	American (Post Street) Th.	2/	1925		
	Hippodrome (Avalon) Th.	2/8	1919	10216	Later moved to Desert Hotel, Spokane, Washington.
	Mr. Newman		1925	16740	
	Pantages (Orpheum) Th.	3/10	1925	17155	
			1925	17746	
	Ritz Th.	2/	1924	13354	
			1925	18308	
Sunnyside	Antler's Th.	2/3			Style 49.
Tacoma	Blue Mouse Th.		1923	14382	
	Heilig Th.	2/4	1927		
	McKinley Park Th.	2/5			
	Pantages (Roxy) Th.	3/	1925	17178	
	Park Th.	2/4	1923	14466	Wicks opus 452; moved in 1931 to KMO Radio, Tacoma, Washington, by Balcom & Vaughan.
	Rhodes Bros. Dept. Store	3/11	1926	19579	Opus 2301.
			1926	11082TUR	For piano.
	Tacoma (Music Box) Th.	3/12			
	Victory Th.		1928	21714	
Toppenish	Lois Th.	2/4	1921		Style 75.
Walla Walla	Arcade Th.	2/5	1922		
Yakima	Pantages Th.	2/			
WEST VIRGINIA					
Fairmont	Virginia Th.	2/	1925	17901	
Parkersburg	Lincoln Th.	2/8			
	Strand Th.	2/	1925	17986	
WISCONSIN					
Milwaukee	Gem Th.	2/	1924	M740B	5 hp, 10" wp and 30" vacuum.
Sheboygan	Masonic Temple	3/	1929		
WYOMING					
Casper	Lyric Th.	2/	1922	12994	
Rawlins	Strand Th.	2/	1923	14447	
Sheridan	Orpheum Th.	2/	1919	10412	
ALBERTA, CANADA					
Calgary	Davidson residence	2/8			
BRITISH COLUMBIA, CANADA					
Nanaimo	Bijou Th.	2/4	1922	13997	3 hp.
Powell River	Powell River Th.	2/4			
Trail	Royal Th.	2/	1927	20784	
Vancouver	Grandview Th.	2/4			
	Pantages (Odeon) Th.	2/14	1925	17154	10 hp.
			1926	18869	10 hp.
	Kitsilano Th.	2/4			
	Maple Leaf Th.	2/3			
Victoria	Plaza (Fox) Th.	2/4			
MANITOBA, CANADA					
Winnipeg	J. J. McLean Ltd.	2/	1923	K934	5 hp, 10" wp and 30" vacuum.
	Parkview Th.	2/	1922	13931	2 hp.
MEXICO					
Mexico City	R. P. Jennings	3/14	1920	11385	15 hp, 15" wp; style 300.
PANAMA					
Panama City	Cecelia Th.	2/10	1927	20105	10 hp; opus 2311.

HILBORNE L. ROOSEVELT

MANUFACTURER OF

Church, Chapel, Concert and Chamber

ORGANS

NEW YORK FACTORY

145, 147 AND 149 WEST EIGHTEENTH STREET

WALTER F. CROSBY, MANAGER

PHILADELPHIA FACTORY

315, 317 & 319 SOUTH TWENTY-SECOND STREET

WM. N. ELBERT, MANAGER

BALTIMORE FACTORY

218 GERMAN STREET

A. STEIN, MANAGER

EVERY MODERN IMPROVEMENT

PNEUMATIC, TUBULAR AND ELECTRIC ACTION

ROOSEVELT ADJUSTABLE COMBINATION ACTION

ROOSEVELT WINDCHESTS

Hilborne Roosevelt (1849-1886) grew up in a prominent New York City family. His younger cousin Theodore, who lived just a few houses away, would one day become President of the United States. One day while in his teens Hilborne saw an organ being serviced in a church near his home. He was so fascinated with the mechanism that he resolved to set up a workshop in his basement and build an organ himself. He apprenticed with the firm of Hall & Labagh in New York but this activity did not set well with his family, most members of which were bankers or attorneys, certainly not common laborers! At the age of 19 he realized his ambition to build an organ. It was exhibited at a local industrial fair where it was awarded a gold medal and a diploma. After this success, young Hilborne's family supported rather than scorned his efforts.[1]

Roosevelt had a keen inventive mind and was particularly fascinated by electricity. The organ he built in 1869 for the industrial fair had an electric action, probably the first in America. It is all the more remarkable that it was devised by a 19-year-old who had never even seen one.[2] [3] Another revolutionary Roosevelt invention, introduced in 1876, was the first combination action which was adjustable by the organist at the console.[4] But that's getting ahead of the story! Following the success of his first organ building venture, young Roosevelt sailed to Europe to visit the Bryceson brothers in London, who had also been experimenting with electric action; Charles Barker, inventor of the Barker pneumatic lever; and noted French organ builder Aristide Cavaille-Coll.[5] This visit apparently had a great influence on the young man since the reeds on later Roosevelt organs tended to be characteristically French, unlike those of many contemporary instruments.

In 1872 after returning from his European trip, Roosevelt leased a building at 40 W. 18th Street in New York and started the Roosevelt Organ Works. His first organ, an ambitious three-manual instrument of 38 stops, was built for the very church in which he had seen his first organ several years earlier. An innovation introduced in this instrument was an electric melody coupler.[6] The Roosevelt business prospered rapidly and branch factories were established in Philadelphia and Baltimore. The firm ultimately became one of the country's premier builders, with a reputation for unexcelled quality. When Hilborne Roosevelt died in 1886 the business was continued by his younger brother Frank, who decided to retire in 1893

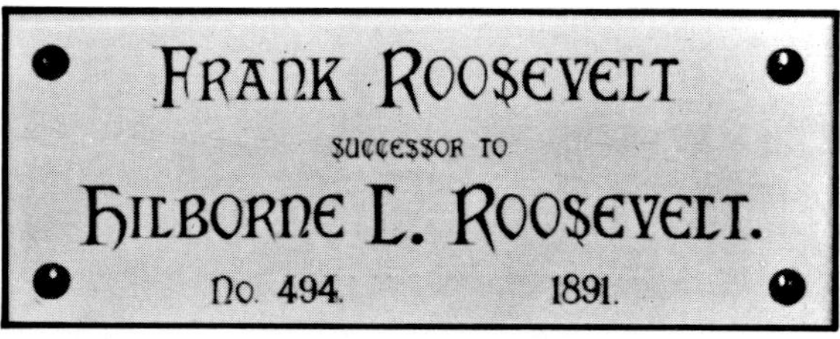

Nameplate of a Roosevelt organ only five opus numbers from the McVickers Theatre instrument. The distinctive typeface was designed by famous organ architect George Ashdown Audsley.[10]

Frank Roosevelt (1861-1894)

Hilborne L. Roosevelt (1849-1886)

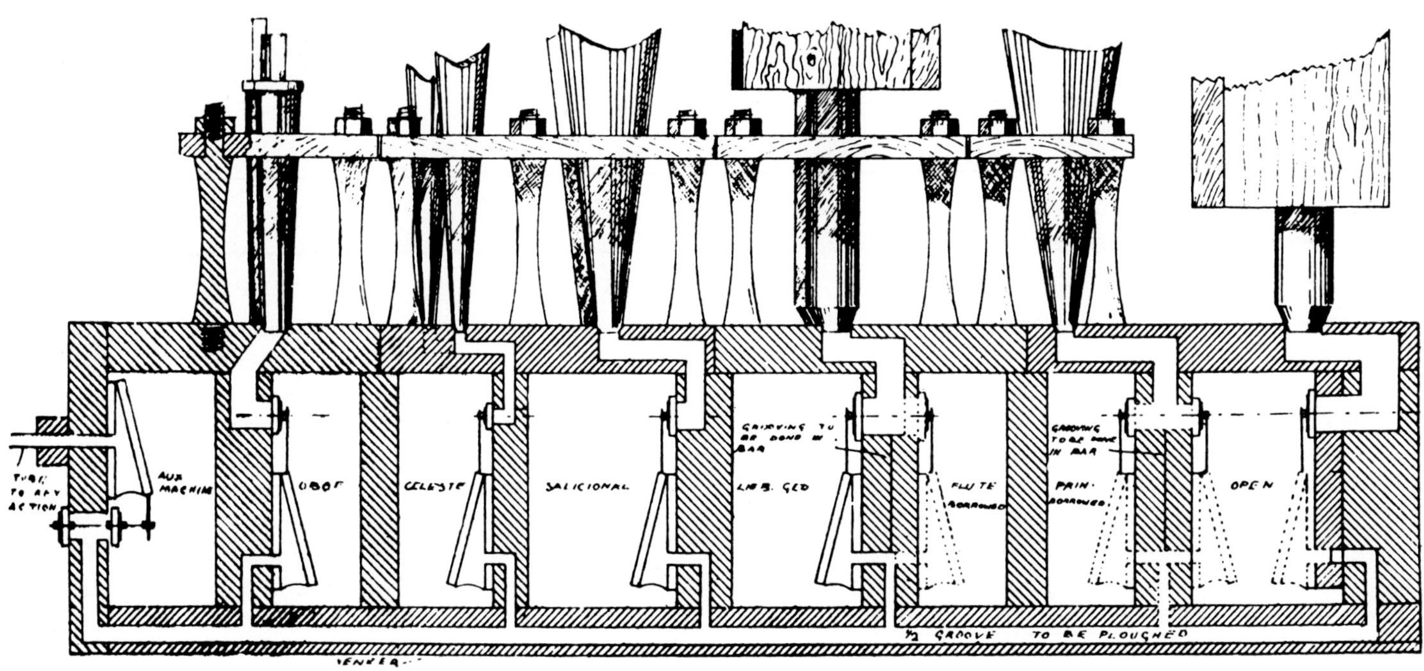

Sectional view of a Roosevelt chest, one of the first to be designed with individual valves for each pipe. This particular example is tubular pneumatic although many Roosevelts had electric action. This style of chest was copied in modified forms by several builders in the 1920s.

after 537 organs bearing the Roosevelt nameplate had been built. The Roosevelt patent rights were sold to Farrand & Votey and several key Roosevelt men moved to Detroit to work for that firm.[7]

In 1883 the Roosevelt company had the honor of building what was at the time the largest organ in the world, a four-manual instrument containing 7,253 pipes, for the Cathedral of the Incarnation in Garden City, New York. The firm also had the distinction of installing the first organ in an American theatre, and they did it with a bang: Opus 400 was installed in the Chicago Auditorium in 1889 as a four-manual instrument of 126 ranks. At the time it was the second largest organ in the country (only the aforementioned Garden City instrument being larger) and the fifth largest in the world.[8] In 1942 the Auditorium organ was purchased by organ architect William H. Barnes whose description of it is most revealing:

"The organ was very badly located for purposes of permitting its vast tonal resources to come out. The entire organ, except the [14-rank] echo, which was over the ceiling of the main body of the theatre, was placed on the left side of the proscenium in a chamber only 25 feet wide and 42 feet deep. The height starting at the back of the chamber was about 30 feet, increasing to 40 feet at the front. The layout was double decked—great . . . back of the lower screen and, immediately above, the swell . . .

Two views of the Roosevelt factory at Park Avenue and 131st Street in New York City, as it appeared in 1950. These premises were occupied from about 1889 until the close of the Roosevelt business in 1893. Two earlier locations of the factory were, first, at 40 West 18th Street and later at 145 West 18th Street.[11]

back of the upper screen, which Dr. Audsley says looked like the portcullis of a medieval castle . . . The solo . . . was behind the great expression box and the choir . . .on top. Each of these latter divisions spoke into the side of the organ chamber and even though the solo wind pressure was eight inches, with the remainder of the organ on four inches, it could scarcely have been effective . . . Behind all of the four enormous expression boxes . . . was the marvelous pedal organ of 19 independent sets. This literally needed a shipping clerk to get the sound out. A quarter of this amount of pedal well placed would have been more effective, I am sure.

". . .The wood pipes are a delight. Seven of the flutes have double mouths . . . In fact, just about everything about the organ was double. There were double the normal number of screws in all the building frames, swell boxes and other parts. All windchests were fifty percent longer than normal, being twelve feet long. Two screws were never used in any place where they could put in five. Lumber one inch thick was never used when they could use lumber two inches thick . . . The diapasons all had wide, low mouths and all were made of . . . about 40 per cent tin . . . while the milder voices . . . were of spotted metal . . . The reeds are the most remarkable stops in the organ, imported from France . . . The strings . . . are the least satisfactory. Roller beards were not used, but the old-fashioned box beards. For the milder, less imitative type of string tone these are satisfactory but such pipes are lacking in character and variety.

". . . The stop action was tubular from the console to an enormous combination machine in the basement and thence to the organ . . . The magnets were enormous solenoids drawing perhaps ten times the current required by a modern magnet. There were only . . . 274 magnets in the entire organ of more than 6,000 pipes. In the heyday of the theatre unit organ these figures were almost exactly reversed. They had usually 6,000 magnets and 274 pipes! . . . The combination machine and crescendo pedal mechanism . . . were something really extraordinary in size and elaborateness. This mechanism required a room 20 feet long by 12 feet wide to house and one of Rube Goldberg's inventions could not have imagined the complications and parts required. The crescendo pedal mechanism . . . [had] a great drum or roller five feet long and two feet in diameter . . . [with] a series of grooves for each stop and coupler . . . so that a great series of levers, cams and shafts could exhaust the stop action mechanism.

" . . . When one looks at this old Roosevelt console mechanism, the last word in modernity in its day, one realizes how much all organists and builders owe to such men as, for example, John T. Austin, for the numerous inventions, simplifications and improvements which gave us the modern organ console. But when one looks at the Roosevelt pipework, it is quite another matter. I will place the pipework in comparison with any that has ever been done by any organ builder at any time."[9]

The Roosevelt firm also built the third organ ever installed in an American theatre, a 2/14 instrument with an all electric action, opus 489, for the McVickers Theatre, Chicago, in 1891.

GLUCK
GOUNOD
VERDI
MOZART
ROSSINI
BERLIOZ

(opposite) The Auditorium in Chicago, the 1889 masterpiece of architect Louis Sullivan, featured the first organ ever installed in an American theatre, a 4/126 Roosevelt. Despite being the second largest organ in the country at the time of its installation, the instrument was disappointing because all those ranks (except the echo) had to vie for tonal egress through one grille on the left side of the house.

Clarence Eddy plays the 4/126 Roosevelt in the Chicago Auditorium. Twenty years before this photograph was taken, Mr. Eddy played the dedicatory recital on this instrument.

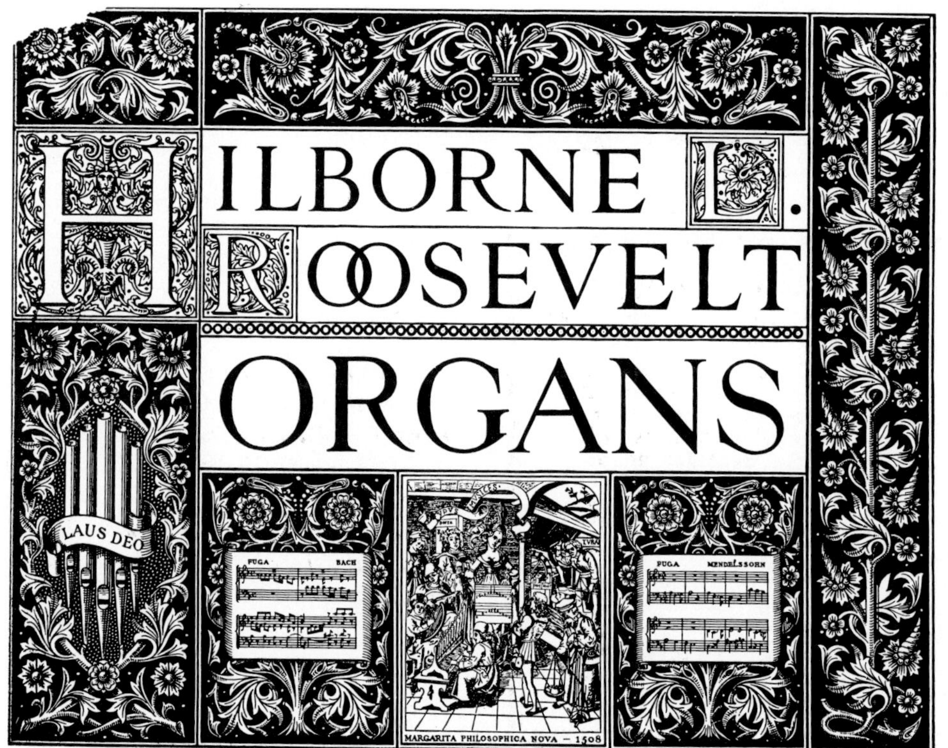

Cover of an 1888 Roosevelt catalog.

SLINGER, WISCONSIN

Bernard S. Schaefer (1845-1921), a native of Bavaria, settled in Milwaukee, Wisconsin in 1873 as a watchmaker. Several months later he moved to Schleisingerville (later known as Slinger), Wisconsin where he built his first organ in 1875. He was quite an entrepreneur and at one time operated match, cigar and pearl button factories in addition to building organs and clocks. He retired from organ building in 1907 but re-entered the business in 1913 with three of his sons, forming the B. Schaefer & Sons Co. Perhaps he should have stayed retired for the following year he suffered a paralytic stroke from which he never recovered.[1] In 1920 his sons incorporated the firm as the Schaefer Organ Co.[2] and in late 1924 entered into partnership with Fred C. and Joseph G. Weickhardt, sons of George Weickhardt of the Wangerin-Weickhardt firm, to form the Weickhardt-Schaefer Organ Company in Milwaukee.[3] This firm lasted only a few months and by January of 1925 the Schaefer Organ Co. was once again operating in Slinger.[4]

The Schaefer firm installed two organs in theatres. The first, a 2/6 unified instrument in the Rainbow Theatre in Milwaukee, was built in 1923 at a cost of $3,320 and had Spencer Orgoblo #14140. The metal pipes were ordered from Jerome B. Meyer of Milwaukee; the wood pipes were made in the Schaefer factory. This organ had no opus number; the Schaefer firm didn't begin assigning numbers until 1924 when they started with #101.[5]

The second Schaefer theatre organ, also a 2/6 unified instrument, was opus 112, built in 1926 for the Opera House in Hartford, Wisconsin. It had a specification not too different from the Rainbow Theatre organ but featured a tibia clausa (playing only at 8′ pitch) instead of the Rainbow's stopped diapason. The flute and bourdon were made in the Schaefer factory; other pipes were ordered from Gottfried. The 49-note harp/xylophone was furnished by Organ Supply, the stop keys by Reisner and the blower by Zephyr.[6]

The last new Schaefer organ was built around 1969. Bernard J. Schaefer, grandson of the company's founder, continues to operate the firm as a tuning and maintenance business as of 1983.[7]

A Quality Organ You Can Afford!

SCHAEFER "Custom Built" organs meet all theatre requirements. Owners of smaller theatres will find in the Schaefer an organ which can be obtained at a cost he can afford and which gives perfectly satisfactory performance.

Investigate our proposition. Write today!

Schaefer Organ Co.

SLINGER, WIS.

Organ Builders Since 1875

This ad pictures the 2/6 Schaefer in the Hartford, Wisconsin Opera House. Bernard J. Schaefer recalls that the firm didn't solicit theatre business too actively because these organs, receiving as much use in a week as most church organs did in a year, were real service headaches.[8]

IN THEATER AT MILWAUKEE.

Schaefer Company Installs Unit Instrument at the Rainbow.

The Schaefer Organ Company of Slinger, Wis., has completed the installation of a twenty-stop unified electro-pneumatic organ in the Rainbow Theater, Milwaukee, one of the leading theaters of the west side. The organ is completely unified, with chimes and xylophone, which can be played from either manual. It has an adjustable combination action with stop-keys. The entire organ is under expression.

The specification is as follows:

GREAT ORGAN.

1. Open Diapason, 8 ft., 85 pipes.
2. Melodia, 8 ft., 85 pipes.
3. Dulciana, 8 ft., 85 pipes.
4. Viola, 8 ft., 61 notes.
5. Wald Flöte, 4 ft., 61 notes.
6. Dulcet, 4 ft., 61 notes.
7. Twelfth, 2⅔ ft., 61 notes.
8. Fifteenth, 2 ft., 61 notes.

Xylophone, 37 tones.
Chimes, 20 tubes.

SWELL ORGAN.

9. Bourdon, 16 ft., 97 pipes.
10. Stopped Diapason, 8 ft., 61 notes.
11. Viol d' Orchestre, 8 ft., 85 pipes.
12. Concert Flute, 8 ft., 61 notes.
13. Orchestral Flute, 4 ft., 61 notes.
14. Violin, 4 ft., 61 notes.
15. Piccolo, 2 ft., 61 notes.
16. Orchestral Oboe, 8 ft., 61 notes.
17. Vox Humana, 8 ft., 61 pipes.

Xylophone, 37 notes.
Chimes, 20 notes.

PEDAL ORGAN.

18. Bourdon, 16 ft., 30 notes.
19. Flute, 8 ft., 30 notes.
20. Viola, 8 ft., 30 notes.

The May 1923 issue of The Diapason *ran this article about Schaefer's first theatre instrument.*

Schaefer factory as it appeared in 1981.

A. J. Schantz, Sons & Co. Orrville, Ohio.

Abraham J. Tschantz was in the third generation of a family who had emigrated from Switzerland to America in 1817. He loved music and had inherited from his father and grandfather a mechanical turn of mind. After serving an apprenticeship in cabinetmaking he made his first reed organ, the Ohio Beauty, in 1873. For the next twenty years he continued making reed organs in his Orrville, Ohio shop. He built his first pipe organ, a two-manual tracker, in 1893. Later he developed tubular and electric actions and was proud that almost all components in a Schantz organ were made in his own factory. He even made his own blowers under the Zephyr trademark and developed a respectable business of supplying them to the trade as well as for his own use.[1]

In 1913, eight years before the death of A. J. Tschantz, the business was taken over by his three sons: E. F., V. A. and O. A. Schantz. Company growth was modest but steady as sales expanded from Ohio to neighboring states.[2] By the 1950s sales were nationwide and in the 1980s a factory force of 100 people is necessary to keep up with the demand. After building over 2,000 pipe organs the company is still family owned and operated. Three grandsons of A. J. Tschantz, Bruce, Paul and John Schantz, and one great grandson, Victor Schantz, control the firm as of 1985.[3]

The company has always been primarily a builder of church organs so it is not surprising that their theatre output consists of but two instruments: a 2/15 straight organ for the Marks Theatre in Cleveland, Ohio, built in 1911, and a 2/4 unit organ built in 1920 for an unidentified new theatre in Ashland, Ohio.[4]

These brothers led the company through its period of greatest expansion. From left to right are E. F. Schantz, O. A. Schantz and V. A. Schantz.

2/4 SCHANTZ PIPE ORGAN
For new theatre, Ashland, Ohio

Schantz console illustration appearing in the contract for the new theatre at Ashland, Ohio.

Memorandum of Agreement

Made the 7th day of September, A. D. 1920

by and between A. J. SCHANTZ, SONS & CO., Organ Builders, of Orrville, Ohio, party of the first part, and

Clark & Edwards Ashland O.

party of the second part, to-wit:

The party of the first part shall build an Organ according to the annexed specifications, of the best material and in the most thorough manner, and deliver it set up in the ~~Church~~ Theatre, in good order, ready for use, on the First day of March A. D., 1921, or as soon thereafter as possible if not delayed by labor troubles or other unavoidable circumstances.

The organ is to be completed in strict accordance with the specifications attached hereto, which are a part of this agreement.

GUARANTEE—A. J. Schantz, Sons & Co., will, at any time within 5 years, remedy at its own expense any defect in construction or material which may develop; natural wear, damage from dampness, heat, fire or water, excepted.

The party of the second part agrees that the said ~~church~~ Theatre shall be in readiness for the erection of said organ 14 days next previous to said time of completion of said organ.

And the party of the second part further agrees that said party, or its representative, shall have undisputed possession of said ~~church~~ Theatre, properly heated and lighted, for the purpose of regulating and tuning said organ, for a period of 7 days next previous to the completion of said organ.

All risk of damage to the organ or parts thereof, either by fire or water, shall be incurred by the party of the second part after the organ, or any part thereof, has been deposited in the ~~church~~ Theatre.

Deferred payments to bear legal interest, and it is agreed the said organ shall remain the property of the party of the first part until it has been paid for in full.

The party of the second part, in full consideration of the above, shall pay to the party of the first part, upon completion of the organ in the ~~church~~ Theatre, the sum of

Four Thousand Dollars

Signed in duplicate this 17th day of September A. D., 1920

In the presence of

A. J. Schantz Sons & Co
Per O. A. Schantz
(Party of the first part)

Clark & Edwards
(Party of the second part)

SPECIFICATION

Of proposed Organ for new Theatre at

Ashland, O.

Clark & Edwards, Proprietors.

Two Manuals and Pedal.
Compass of Manuals – CC to C – 61 notes.
Compass of Pedal – CCC to G – 32 notes.
International Pitch.
Electro Pneumatic Action.
Detached Console. No case or front pipes.
Adjustable combinations.
Concave radiating Pedal Board.
Equipped with Zephyr Electric Organ Blower.
Organ to be placed in recess provided for same, console in center of Orchestra pit.
Unit system of construction with individual valve and magnet for each pipe, to be used throughout.

Great Organ Operated by White Stop Keys placed at the right side above the Swell Manual.

1.	Open Diapason,	8ft.	Derived from two units of 85 pipes each and one unit of 73 pipes and one unit of 61 pipes.
2.	Principal,	4ft.	
3.	Piccolo,	2ft.	
4.	Bourdon,	16ft.	
5.	St. Diapason,	8ft.	
6.	Flute D'Amour,	4ft.	
7.	Viol D'Orchestra,	8ft.	
8.	Gambette,	4ft.	
9.	Vox Humana, (To bring on tremolo)	8ft.	
10.	Blank.		Three Stop Keys to be provided in console for convenient enlargement of Great Organ.
11.	Blank.		
12.	Blank.		
13.	Chime,	20	Tubular Bells

General Release Bar under this group of Stop Keys #1–#13.

Swell Organ Operated by White Stop Keys placed on the left side over the Swell Manual.

14.	Open Diapason	8ft.	Derived from two units of 85 pipes, one unit of 73 pipes and one unit of 61 pipe.
15.	Principal,	4ft.	
16.	Piccolo,	2ft.	
17.	Bourdon,	16ft.	
18.	St. Diapason,	8ft.	
19.	Flute D'Amour,	4ft.	
20.	Viol D'Orchestra,	8ft.	
21.	Gambette,	4ft.	
22.	Vox Humana, (To bring on Tremolo)	8ft.	
23.	Blank		Three Stop Keys to be provided in console for convenient enlargement of Swell Organ.
24.	Blank		
25.	Blank.		

General Release Bar under this group of Stop Keys #14–#25

Details of Construction.

1. Case of console to be of oak neatly paneled with rubbed in oil varnish finish. Lid of console of roll top variety, equipped with lock.

2. Arrangement of stop keys and general design to be like cut attached.
3. The action to be the Schantz Electro Pneumatic from keys to chest.

All contacts to be of sliding type and therefore self-cleaning.

The weight of the touch of the keys to be the standard adopted by the American Guild of Organists.

The action to be capable of the greatest rapidity of repetition, fully equal to a piano.

The magnets used shall be of the improved Vertical Type in which the armature valve is self-cleaning.

Each magnet to be insulated and protected from any climatic changes.

The magnets are to be very closely wound, delivering a maximum efficiency from a minimum current consumption.

All cables to be properly tested. Each wire to have double insulation and to be copper tinned. Each wire to be wound in cable and set in parafine. The gauge of wire to be large enough to prevent any possible friction.

The electric power for the organ shall be produced by a generator attached to organ blower, or a generator set, so constructed as to give constant even power and of sufficient quantity to supply all needs.

The Schantz action is not only to be built durably but to work efficiently.

4. The Swell Box shall be the organ recess if practical and shall be equipped with equilibrium shades acted upon by a balanced swell pedal placed in a convenient position over the pedal keys, with ample room for tuning and regulating the pipes wherever possible.

The Swell shades shall be built up or laminated to prevent warping and shall be of the same thickness as the rest of the Swell Box, double rabbitted and felted to insure an absolutely tight joint. Shades to rest on a steel pivot with adjusting screws to take up the wear.

5. Passage ways to be provided for all regulating purposes.

6. The large metal pipes from Tenor F (8ft. Open Diapason) down, to be made of the finest quality zinc; all of shorter lengths to be made of tin and lead in such proportions as the various stops require, to give the best quality of tone.

Pedal Organ Operated by White Stop Keys placed at the extreme left over the Swell Organ.

26.	Bourdon,	16ft.	Derived from units comprising the Great & Swell Organ.
27.	Violin Cello,	8ft.	
28.	Base Flute,	8ft.	
29.	Diapason,	8ft.	
30.	Principal,	4ft.	
31.	Blank.		Two Stop Keys to be provided for convenient enlargement of Pedal Organ.
32.	Blank.		

General Release Bar under this group of Stop Keys #26–#32.

Combinations Adjustable affecting all stops and tremolo.

Great Organ & Pedal 1, 2, 3.

Swell Organ & Pedal 1, 2, 3.

Pedal Movements

Swell Pedal.

Crescendo Pedal.

Accessories

Tremolo.

Crescendo Indicator.

Circular concave radiating Pedal Board as adopted by the A. G. O.

Seat with music compartment.

Release Bars.

Zephyr Electric Organ Blower.

7. All wood pipes to be made of the best quality of the various woods best suited to the several stops. All pipes to have hard wood caps and mouth pieces and to be thoroughly glue-coated inside and shellaced on the outside. All large open pipes such as 16 ft. Open Diapason, 16 ft. Violone, 8 ft. Violone Cello to be provided with slide for tuning which may easily be secured in place.

8. All stopped pipes to have hand leathered stoppers,

All wood pipes under 4 ft. in length to have patented metal toed feet.

All wood pipes over 4 ft. in length to have a specially designed gate to control the volume.

9. The Scales of all the pipes to be in conformity to the size of the instrument, and in conformity with the very best standards such as are used only in strictly high grade instruments.

10. The Console to be made to conform to the latest approved measurements of the American Guild of Organists.

Natural keys to be covered with best ivory, sharps with ebony.

The keys are to be of the double bevel or curved variety, and made to overhang, giving the best facilities to the organist.

White stop keys to be used for the Speaking Stops and black keus to be used for the Couplers and Unisons.

Combinations to be operated by pistons and to visibly operate the stop keys.

Pedal board to be concave, radiating and circular as approved by the A.G.O. and all measurements to be standard. Naturals to be made of hard light wood and sharps of hard dark wood.

Name board and side terraces to be of mahogany with rubbed in oil finish.

The entire console to be built with a view of giving the maximum convenience to the organist, and to present a harmonious pleasing appearance.

11. A Zephyr Electric Organ Blower of ample size to supply the organ under all conditions of playing to be furnished with the organ.

All electric wiring, switches, etc. to be furnished by the party of the second part; also all air conductor pipe; also any carpenter, mason or tinsmith work necessary to install same.

12. Motor on blower to be furnished for current available. If D.C. give voltage ( ). If A.C. give voltage ( ), phase ( ), cycle ( )

13. The entire organ to be built with a view to supplying an instrument of the highest standard of perfection both from a mechanical as well as a musical standpoint.

2/15 SCHANTZ PIPE ORGAN
Marks Theatre, Cleveland, Ohio

SCHEDULE SPECIFICATIONS

FOR BUILDING THE ORGAN

In ____________________

Prepared by A. J. SCHANTZ, SONS & CO., Organ Builders,

ORRVILLE, OHIO.

Case of Oak or other native woods, varnished and polished, all front pipes richly decorated in gold and colors. Width about . 15 . . feet . 0. 0 . . inches; depth about . . 8 . . . . feet . . 0. 4 . . inches; height about . 16 . . . feet . . 0 . 0 . . inches.

Style of case in harmony with the interior architecture of the church.

Compass of manuals . C, C, . . to C 4 61 (to 73) notes.

Compass of pedals . C,C,C . . to F. 30 . notes.

Registers . . 14 . . . pipes . 974 . .

Article of Agreement

~~Made the~~ 15th . . . . . . day of . . October . . . . . . A. D. 1910, by and between SCHANTZ, SONS & CO., Organ Builders, of Orrville, Ohio, party of the first part, and . . . Wm. H. Mark of Buffalo N.Y. . . . party of the second part, to-wit:

The party of the first part shall build an Organ according to the annexed specifications, of the best material and in the most thorough manner, and deliver it, set up in the ~~Church~~ Theater, in good order, ready for use, on or about the 15th . . . . . day of . . December . . . . . A. D. 1910 . .

The organ is to be completed in strict accordance with the specifications attached hereto, which are a part of this agreement.

The party of the first part further agrees, at his own expense, for the term of one year next after the completion of said Organ, to remedy any and all defects therein, resulting from the use of improper material, or from inferior workmanship.

The party of the second part, in full consideration of the above, shall pay to the party of the first part, upon the completion of the Organ in the ~~Church~~ Theater, the sum of Three Thousand . . . . . . Dollars, as follows, Fifteen Hundred When Installed and Passed by H. J. Sisson . . . Dollars, in cash, and the balance in notes, (same to be satisfactory commercial paper), bearing interest at the rate of 6 per cent. per annum, and payable as follows: One Note Seven Hundred & Fifty Dollars in 30 days
One Note Seven Hundred & Fifty Dollars in 60 days

And the said second party further agrees that the said ~~church~~ Theater shall be in readiness for the erection of said organ . . five (5) Days . . . . . next previous to said time of completion of said organ.

And the party of the second part further agrees that said first party, or his representatives, shall have undisputed possession of said ~~church~~ Theater, for the purpose of regulating and tuning said organ, for a period of . . . (5) five days next previous to the completion of said organ.

Payments to be made in New York draft, payable to the order of the party of the first part.

All risk of damage to the Organ or parts thereof, either by fire or water, shall be incurred by the party of the second part after the Organ, or any part thereof, has been deposited in the ~~Church~~. THEATRE

ELECTRIC CURRENTS.

Direct . . . . Volts . . . .

Alternating . . . . Volts . . . . Phase . . . . Cycle.

Water pressure at Church, lbs. . . . .

Signed in duplicate this . . . 15 Th . . . . . . day of . . October . . . . , A. D. 1910

In the presence of

A. J. Schantz Sons & Co.

Wm. H. Mark per [illegible]

GREAT ORGAN

#	Ft.	Stop		Pipes.
1	8	Open Diapason	Metal	61
2.	8	Doppel Flute	Wood	61
3.	8	Dulciana	Metal	61
4.	4	Flute d'Amour	Wood & metal	61
5.	8	Clarinett	Reeds full scale	61

SWELL ORGAN.

#	Ft.	Stop		Pipes.
6.	16	Bourdon..........	Wood	73
7.	8	Open Diapason	Metal	73
8.	8	Std. Diapason	Wood........	73
9.	8	Vax Celeste.......	Metal.......	134
10.	8	Unda Maris	Metal.......	134
11.	4	Flute Harmonic....	Metal & Wood	73
12.	8r	Orcestral Oboe	Reeds	73

PEDAL ORGAN.

#	Ft.	Stop	Pipes.
13.	16	Double Open Diapason	30
14.	16	Lieblich Gedeckt from #6.......	30

MECHANICAL-REGISTERS.

15. Swell to Pedal
16. Great tp Pedal
17. Swell to Great
18. Swell to Swell Super
19. Swell to Great Super.
20. Great to Great Super.
21. Swoll Tremolo.
22. Motor Starter.

COMBINATION PEDAL.

Great Forte

Great Piano

3. Swell Forte

4. Swell Piano

5. Balanced Sweel Pedal

6. Cresendo Pedal

7. Wind Indicator

8. Crescendo Indicator.

SUMMARY.

Great Organ	5 stops	....	305 pipes.
Swell Organ	7 "	....	609 "
Pedal Organ	2 "	....	60 "
Speaking Stops	14		974 "
Mechanical Stops	8		
Combination Pedal......	6		
Wind Indicator	1		
Crescendo Indicator ...	1		
Motor Starter	1		
	31		

****

Key Action.

Key Action to be Tubular Pneumatic throughout.

Pedal Action.

The Pedal Action to be Tubular Pneumatic throughout.

Stop Action.

The stop action to be tubular pneumatic throughout and to be operated by tilting tablets instead of stop knobs. The stop tablets to be placed above the Swell Manual in a vertical position and the Coupler Tablets to be placed between the Swell and Great, and below the Great Manual, in a horizontal position. The stop action to be prompt and reliable at all times, silencing or actuating the respective stops at the utmost despatch.

Console.

The console to be made to harmonize with the case of the organ. The keyboards to have polished ivory naturals and ebony sharps. The swell and crescendo pedals to be placed between second E and F on the Pedal Keyboard. Middle C of the Great and Middle C of the Pedal board to be in a plumb line running through each. Pedal sharps to be 2 1/2 inches further from the organist than the Great sharps.

The Key board to be concave and radiating, The console to be about 25 feet below the organ

Crescendo Pedal.

The Crescendo pedal to begin at the softest and draw all stops, including reeds and couplers in their regular order of power by a single movement of the foot, and by reversing the movement, stops are to be cancelled in their reverse order, controlling the entire organ in reverse and inverse order of actuation.

Wood Pipes.

The wood pipes to be made of first class kiln-dried lumber, suited to the tonal qualities of the different stops. The lower lips of all the wood pipes to be made of hard wood and all the wood pipes to be glue-coated inside and double coated with shellac or varnish on the outside. The scale of the wood pipes to be mathematically correct.

ORGAN SPECIFICATIONS.

General Detail of Construction.

Case.

The case to be made of quartered oak with panels; the panels to have moulding around the edges of the styles. A heavy moulding to be around the top of the case to support the front pipes. The entire case work to be in harmony with the interior architecture of the church. Blue prints or drawings of the case and the front to be submitted to purchasing committee for approval.

Interior Building Frame.

The interior building frame of the organ to be constructed of faultless heavy timbers, all rails being tenoned into the posts and drawn up to the shoulders with machine bolts and nuts inserted into the rails. This frame work must guarantee ample bearing capacity for the various chests and their respective compliments of pipes, insuring absolute stability in the foundation of the organ.

Bellows.

The Bellows to be the "Schantz Improved Suspension Bellows," on which patents are pending.

Wind Chests.

The wind chests are to be "The Schantz Improved Magazine Wind Chest," having an individual valve for each pipe. The chests to be so constructed that each and every valve shall be easily accessible for adjustment and for the removal of any obstruction under the valve. The wind chests to be made of faultless material with the wind supply so arranged that robbing is absolutely impossible; each and every pipe on the wind chest must have ample speaking room.

Swell Box.

The swell box to be made of heavy lumber; the front of the swell box to be fitted with vertical shades made of strips of wood glued together to prevent warping; the shades to be pivoted and each shade to have an adjusting screw to take up the wear on the pivots. The shades to be brought under control of the organist by a balanced Swell Pedal, between second "E" and "F" of the Pedal Keyboard.

Metal Pipes.

The metal pipes from Tenor F (3 Ft.) up, to be made of spotted metal, containing 40% pure tin and 60% lead. All the metal pipes to be of good weight and to have the thickness of metal suited to the requirements of the tone in the various stops. The voicing to be done by men of long experience and skill, who are prepared to meet the taste and requirements of all in the matter of quality and strength of tone.

Front Pipes.

Front Pipes to be made of heavy zinc having the mouths and lips and tuners made of a composition of 40% tin and 60% lead. Front pipes to be decorated with gold and colors, or in plain gold bronze to harmonize with the decorations of the church.

Passage Ways.

Passage Ways making all divisions of the organ accessible for tuning and regulating are to be provided. Passage ways to have a minimum width of 16 inches wherever possible.

Power.

The power to blow the organ to be furnished by a "Schantz Electric Fan Blower." The blower to be large enough to blow the organ under all conditions of playing. All electric wiring, switches etc., to be furnished by the church; also all tin air conductor pipe, over the usual amount (10 Ft.) and any carpenter or mason work or tinsmithing necessary to install same.

Summary.

The entire organ shall represent the highest attainable perfection from the standpoint of mechanical excellence and durability as well as from the standpoint of artistic tonality of the individual stops and general effect of the ensemble.

Schantz factory as it appeared in the 1970s. Note the considerable expansion over the 1890s building on the right.

Ad in the October 1919 Diapason *offers organs for a variety of uses, although nearly all were sold to churches.*

Schantz Organ Co.
ORRVILLE, OHIO

Established 1873

ORGANS

for

Churches, Halls
Residences and Theaters

THE WM. SCHUELKE ORGAN CO.

Wilhelm Schülke (later Americanized to William Schuelke) was born in West Prussia, an area which is now Poland. He learned organ building in Germany before emigrating to America with his parents in the 1860s. By 1875 he had moved to Milwaukee, Wisconsin where he entered into a partnership with Theodore Steinert, a carpenter from Prussia. The Schuelke and Steinert firm built one tracker organ during the few months of their partnership, after which organ building continued under the Wm. Schuelke name.[1]

Mr. Schuelke patented a unique tubular pneumatic action in 1873 and a new and totally different design in 1895. Many of his organs were trackers, however, perhaps reflecting the lesser reliability of tubular pneumatic action. The author has long marveled at the fact that so few organ builders could actually play the instrument! This was not the case with Mr. Schuelke, however; on at least one occasion he played the dedication recital on one of his new organs.[2]

By the time of Schuelke's death in 1902 he had built 160 organs. At that time the firm was taken over by his son Max Schuelke (1878-1975) who was then only 24 years of age. The company had been building many of their metal pipes, occasionally ordering others from Samuel Pierce in Reading, Massachusetts. Schuelke's death left the firm without a voicer, however, and it was decided to abandon the pipe shop. The pipe metal casting table eventually found its way to the shop of Milwaukee pipe builders Jerome B. Meyer & Sons where it still remains as of 1986.[3]

Max Schuelke was the first of his family to pursue markets unrelated to church music. He built another 100 or so organs after his father's death,[4] around 20% of which were for theatres. A 1913 ad in *The Billboard* announced THEATRE PIPE ORGANS in bold type, and an article in the June 1913 *Diapason* claimed that Schuelke had contracts for 22 organs for Chicago theatres.[5] Apparently only one of these organs was delivered to Chicago, however, before the firm declared bankruptcy in September 1914.[6]

Sometime prior to the bankruptcy, Max Schuelke's younger brother William J. Schuelke (1888-1960) had joined the business. After the firm's demise, each brother established an organ business for himself in Milwaukee. William J. Schuelke built a number of organs and did maintenance work until his death in 1960. Max Schuelke continued to maintain organs and pianos[7] but his "go-getter" spirit remained undaunted as evidenced by these fascinating ads which appeared in *The Billboard*:

> NOVELTY ELECTRIC PIPE ORGAN has two sets of Gabriel Horns with detached keyboard! True electric cable, 22 ft. long. Largest pipe is 6 ft. by 3" thick. Can be used for Circus or stage work. For further information, write to Max Schuelke Organ Co., 270-272 27th St., Milwaukee, Wis.[8]

> AUTOMOBILE ORGAN—Organ consisting of 57 special made Gabriel Horns, with wind chest, bellows, keyboard, and stop action. Can be placed on running board of the car on one side. Very fine tone. Largest pipe is 6 ft. 4 in. Keyboard can be placed inside of the car. Write for further information to Max Schuelke Organ Co., 522-532 16th Ave., Milwaukee, Wis.[9]

William Schuelke (1850?-1902)

A tubular pneumatic organ nears completion in the Schuelke factory. Max Schuelke is on the far right.

THEATRE PIPE ORGANS

All sizes of Pipe Organs for Theatre purposes built to order.

Write for Catalogue and Estimates.

THE WM. SCHUELKE ORGAN CO.,
Milwaukee, Wis.

T. D. HUME, Chicago Representative,
711 Transportation Building, Chicago, Ill.

Facsimile of ad in the April 26, 1913 issue of The Billboard *contains one of the earliest uses of the phrase "theatre pipe organs" known to the author.*

One-manual Schuelke organ in the Lexington Theatre, Milwaukee, featuring display pipes by Jerome B. Meyer.[10] The pipes on the right are dummies installed for symmetry.

THE WM. SCHUELKE ORGAN CO.

Builders of High Grade Pipe Organs, since 1875

"Schuelke's Patented Wind Chests and Tubular Pneumatic Action."

"Schuelke's Patented Stop Action."

"Schuelke's Patented Coupler System."

"Schuelke's Patented Adjustable Combinations."

Write for our Catalogue

The Wm. Schuelke Organ Co.
Incorporated
MAIN OFFICE AND WORKS 2219-2221 WALNUT STREET, MILWAUKEE, WIS.

Schuelke ad in the September 1914 Diapason, *the very month of the firm's bankruptcy.*

WILLIAM SCHUELKE,

BUILDER OF FIRST CLASS

Church and Chapel Organs.

PIPE ORGANS OF EVERY SIZE BUILT TO ORDER, WITH ALL MODERN IMPROVEMENTS.

Highest Degrees of Power, Richness and Singing Quality of Tune, Ease and Elasticity of Touch, Effectiveness of Action, Solidity and Originality, Excellence of Workmanship,

IN THE MOST THOROUGH AND DURABLE MANNER, FROM THE BEST [illegible] ACCORDING TO REQUIREMENTS.

EVERY ORGAN WARRANTED FOR FIVE YEARS.—ORGANS TUNED AND REPAIRED.

2219—2221 WALNUT STREET,

MILWAUKEE, - - WISCONSIN.

A Schuelke calling card from the "gay nineties."

SCHUELKE OPUS LIST

It is reasonable to assume that most, if not all, of the Schuelke organs sold to theatres were tubular pneumatic since the firm never developed an electric action.

CITY/STATE	LOCATION	SIZE	YR	REMARKS
ILLINOIS				
Chicago	Crown Hippodrome Th.	2/		
IOWA				
Des Moines	Garden Th.	3/	1914	
	Star Th.	2/	1912	Tubular pneumatic; with detached console.
	State Th.	2/	1914	
MASSACHUSETTS				
Northampton	Strand Th.	2/		
MISSOURI				
Kansas City	Tenth Street Th.	2/		
St. Joseph	Orpheum Th.	?/18	1911	
MONTANA				
Hamilton	Liberty Th.	2/8		
Helena	Cutler's Antlers Th.	2/10	1914	
WISCONSIN				
La Crosse	Bijou Th.	2/16	1912	Tubular pneumatic; with detached console.
Milwaukee	Alhambra Th.	2/14	1911	
	American Th.	1/	1911	Opus 220; with roll player.
	Butterfly Th.	2/20	1911	Opus 226.
	Lexington (Franklin) Th.	1/	1911	Opus 228; with roll player.
	Parkway (Rock River) Th.	2/		
	Princess Th.	2/	1911	Opus 222; opened as Grand Theatre.
	Whitehouse (Mid City) (Atlantic) Th.	2/		

J. P. SEEBURG PIANO COMPANY

MANUFACTURERS

SEEBURG PIPE ORGANS AND SELF-PLAYING ORCHESTRAS

GENERAL OFFICES AND FACTORY: SEEBURG BUILDING, 419 WEST ERIE STREET
WAREROOMS: 1004-1010 REPUBLIC BUILDING, 209 SOUTH STATE STREET

TELEPHONE HARRISON 6050-1-2

CHICAGO

Justus Percival Sjoberg was born in Gothenburg, Sweden.[1] The Malinjos piano factory adjoined the local high school and Sjoberg spent many happy hours there when he was a school boy. After graduation in the 1880s he emigrated to America where, arriving in Chicago, he immediately sought employment in a piano factory.[2] After working for several piano manufacturers he moved to Rockford, Illinois and organized the Kurtz-Seeburg Action Co. in 1895. After a few years he sold his interest in this business and returned to Chicago where he became interested in the Marquette Piano Co., makers of player pianos and player actions.[3] In 1905 Marquette introduced the Cremona coin-operated piano[4] and around 1907 the J. P. Seeburg Piano Company was organized to sell Cremona instruments. Business was so good that Seeburg decided to start manufacturing instruments himself.[5]

By the 1920s Seeburg was the dominant firm in the coin piano business. They also secured a good share of the photoplayer market, selling around 1,000 of these piano-centered devices.[6] The largest Seeburg photoplayers were fancifully styled "Pipe Organ Orchestras." Despite the imaginative name, they were still basically pianos with other gadgets added and hence are outside the scope of the present volume.

From 1916 to 1921 Seeburg manufactured actual theatre pipe organs in partnership with F. W. Smith, using the Seeburg-Smith nameplate. These instruments are covered in the Smith chapter of this book. In the mid- or late 1920s Seeburg introduced the only instrument to bear the Seeburg name which did *not* include a piano. A four-rank tubular pneumatic pipe organ, it was undoubtedly designed to compete with Operators Piano Company's Reproduco Unified Theatre Organ. Seeburg's device didn't fare any better in the marketplace than did the Operators product; only two such Seeburg organs are known to exist as of 1986. One of them reportedly saw duty in a Calgary, Alberta theatre.[7]

By the late 1920s the market for automatic pianos had dwindled to virtually nothing. Fortunately, Seeburg branched into the coin-operated phonograph industry and became a leader in the field just as they had with coin pianos. By the early 1950s Seeburg employed 1,700 people and controlled 80% of the jukebox market, according to J. P. Seeburg's grandson Noel Seeburg. In 1956 the Seeburg family sold the company and the next two decades saw several subsequent changes of ownership. The firm filed for Chapter 11 bankruptcy in 1979 and closed its plant in 1980.[8]

Several years after parting company with F. W. Smith, Seeburg produced this four-rank self-contained tubular pneumatic organ. Sales were aimed primarily at mortuaries and residences although one was reportedly used in a Calgary, Alberta theatre. Very few of this model were ever sold for any purpose.

Skinner Organ Company

CAPITAL STOCK ISSUED $ 360,000

Organ Architects & Builders for Churches, Auditoriums, Theatres and Residences

Boston, Mass.

ARTHUR HUDSON MARKS · PRES. & TREAS.
ERNEST MARTIN SKINNER · VICE PRES.
WILLIAM EDWARD ZEUCH · VICE PRES.
CHARLES GEORGE PARKER · DIRECTOR.
WALTER GREGORY KEATING · ASST. TREAS.
EDMUND JOHNSON BARNARD · GEN'L. MGR.

· · FACTORIES AT · ·
DORCHESTER · MASS ·
WESTFIELD · · MASS ·

Ernest Martin Skinner (1866-1960), one of the most colorful and influential figures in American organ building, was born in Clarion, Pennsylvania. Even the name of his birthplace heralded his future! His father, a tenor and vocal instructor, often took him to Gilbert and Sullivan operettas, instilling a love of music in him at an early age. Young Ernest also developed an unrequited crush on one of the operatic stars, which only served to strengthen his passion for music.[4] Music seemed to be in his very soul. Throughout his long life most of his friends were musicians[5] but unlike many people moved by the musical muses, E. M. Skinner expressed his creativity not as a performing musician but as a creator of beautiful musical instruments.

Ernest set about to build a barrel organ at age 12. His attempt was a failure; he couldn't make the wooden pipes speak! This anecdote, related by Skinner himself, is particularly amusing since, in his later years, he would achieve renown as one of the finest voicers in America. His first professional contact with the organ industry came in 1886 when, as a young man of twenty, he began working as a shop boy for George H. Ryder of Boston. After four years he moved to the factory of George Hutchings where he worked for eleven years, eventually becoming factory superintendent.[6] Skinner recalled that, when Alexander Graham Bell was developing the telephone, he offered Hutchings a half interest in it for $50 which Hutchings declined![7]

Before he turned his attention to tonal matters, Skinner's fertile mind invented several mechanical devices which proved to be landmarks in the music industry. His famous pitman chest was devised in 1898[8] and in 1900 he invented an accenting device for player pianos which became known as the themodist. He patented this device and licensed it to the Aeolian Company who later developed it into the Duo Art reproducing piano. Royalties from the themodist helped raise enough capital for Skinner to open his own organ factory in South Boston in 1901. His first employee was William I. Hitchcock, foreman of the chest department at Hutchings, who became Skinner's factory superintendent for the next thirteen years. By 1902 the firm was called Ernest M. Skinner & Co. For awhile in 1903 Skinner took on a partner, James Cole, who had 25 years of experience as an organ builder, and the firm's name became Skinner & Cole Organ Co. By 1904 the name was E. M. Skinner & Co. and in 1905 the

Ernest M. Skinner poses with one of his French horn pipes and its orchestral prototype. Of all his tonal inventions, the French horn was the only one he patented.[2] It remains one of the organ's most successful imitations.

firm was incorporated as the Ernest M. Skinner Company.[9]

In 1905 Skinner hired Robert Hope-Jones as a salesman, also making him vice president. His connection with the Skinner firm lasted fifteen months and it is somewhat surprising that it went on that long. A clash between the egos of these two dynamic personalities was, in retrospect, inevitable. There was room in the Skinner organization for only one star—and, of course, that had to be Ernest M. Skinner. Skinner later claimed that Hope-Jones had no mechanical or tonal influence on Skinner organs[10] but the author notes that Skinner used coil springs on reservoirs, round silver wire contacts, unification, high wind pressures, phonon diapasons and tiny-scaled strings, all of which were pioneered by Hope-Jones. Unlike Hope-Jones, however, Skinner confined unification largely to the pedal division, which he called the "augmented pedal." R. P. Elliot used to quip that a more appropriate nomenclature would have been the *diminished* pedal![11]

Ernest M. Skinner was a flamboyant personality who had a penchant for luxury and who had to own the best of everything. He always spent more than he made;[12] he couldn't manage money and couldn't keep track of where it went.[13] He insisted upon maintaining the highest possible quality in his instruments regardless of contract price. Because of this idealism he was a poor businessman—a trait he shared with Robert Hope-Jones![14] In 1917 William E. Zeuch became vice president in charge of sales and business management, allowing Skinner to deal with the artistic side of the business.[15]

Financial problems continued to plague the company, however, despite ever expanding sales. The firm might have folded had it not been smiled upon by dame fortune in the person of Arthur Hudson Marks. Marks, the retired guiding light of the Goodyear Rubber Company, was an organ buff who had organs in both his residence and on his yacht. After buying a Skinner organ for his second residence, Marks' friendship with Skinner flourished. He continued to invest in the firm, purchasing controlling interest in 1919, whereupon it was reorganized as the Skinner Organ Company. Marks became president with Skinner and Zeuch each serving as vice presidents. Under Marks' careful business leadership and Ernest Skinner's tonal and inventive genius the firm became the most prestigious builder in the country. Skinner was elected the first president of the Organ Builders Association of America in 1919.[16]

To help keep up with increasing sales, Arthur Hudson Marks purchased the Steere Organ Company in 1921 and for the next several years Steere's Westfield, Massachusetts factory was kept busy turning out components for Skinner organs.[17] Despite Marks' rein on the budget, however, Ernest Skinner's flamboyance caused considerable financial drains on the company. Skinner was approaching sixty years of age and Marks, looking to the future, began looking for a protege who could succeed him. Skinner himself, having developed the organ to his romantic and orchestral ideals, was looking for someone who could help him improve its classic ensemble. In 1927 a man joined the firm who seemed to meet both of these needs: G. Donald Harrison. Harrison had learned organ

E. M. Skinner plays the organ in the home of Arthur Hudson Marks (standing). Marks' business acumen as president of the company was responsible for its financial success in the 1920s and 1930s.

Traps in a Skinner theatre organ. From left to right are bass drum, tom tom, Chinese block and snare drum.

Skinner's Boston factory studio featured a residence-type organ equipped with the unique Skinner roll player. Because of its ability to play multiple independent musical parts, this player was particularly well adapted for the performance of orchestral transcriptions which were among Ernest Skinner's favorite music.

COMBINING INTERESTS

The Skinner Organ Company and the Organ Division of the Aeolian Company have been merged, and the future Organ activities of these organizations will be conducted by the

AEOLIAN-SKINNER ORGAN COMPANY

Executive Offices and Church Organ Studio

677 Fifth Avenue, New York

Residence Organ Studio

Aeolian Hall, 689 Fifth Avenue, New York

Factory, Boston, Massachusetts

Organists and others interested in any subject relating to Organ problems will always be cordially welcomed at both Studios.

AEOLIAN-SKINNER ORGAN COMPANY

ORGAN ARCHITECTS and BUILDERS

CHURCH RESIDENCE AUDITORIUM UNIVERSITY

This ad, originally running full-page size in the January 1932 Diapason, ***announced the merger of two of America's highest quality organ builders. Although studios on Fifth Avenue in New York were an expensive luxury in the thirties, the company maintained both of them until 1938 when the Aeolian Hall studio was closed. The other studio closed in 1940 when the executive offices were moved to the Boston factory.***

The theatre that chocolate built, the Hershey Community Theatre in Hershey, Pennsylvania, opened with a huge 4/71 Aeolian-Skinner. The organ was actually sold as Aeolian opus 1798 but was built after Aeolian and Skinner merged in 1931. At right, the console sits in concert position atop its Otis turntable lift.

The Skinner Organ in the Cameo Theatre, New York City

The organ you recently placed in the Cameo Theatre here is proving an artistic joy. The voicing of the various orchestral stops, in particular French Horn and Flugel Horn, is an achievement of such exquisite subtlety and delicacy as I have never heard equalled. The beautiful refinement of the strings, so different from the overblown enormities often perpetrated in the name of a string organ, and the rich sonority of the cornopean and diapasons, are equally delightful. As regards the action, in every detail it represents the last word in responsiveness. Withal the balance and blend of the whole organ is wonderful.

By incorporating a grand piano, playable from choir and pedal keyboards, you have discovered limitless possibilities of new tone coloring, and especially welcome from the viewpoint of a theatre player is the realization that the necessary element of gaiety and frivolity can be satisfied by this perfectly legitimate innovation without resorting to the vulgarity of traps.

Sincerely yours,
/s/ JOHN D. M. PRIEST,
Organist, Cameo Theatre

Skinner Organ Company

BOSTON, MASS.

Organ Architects and Builders----Residences, Theatres, Auditoriums, Churches

New York City Studio: 677 Fifth Avenue at 53rd

The Cameo, a theatre of only 539 seats, had quite a large organ for its size: a 3/15 Skinner. This ad appeared in the May 1922 issue of The Diapason.

The 4/32 Skinner in New York's Colony (Broadway) Theatre was one of E. M. Skinner's favorite theatre instruments. He felt that, as played by John Priest, it created the ideal music for film accompaniment.[1]

The first Skinner factory in South Boston served the company from 1901 to 1914.

The building above in Dorchester, Massachusetts served as the Skinner and Aeolian-Skinner factory from 1914 until 1968. In 1956 half of the building was razed to accommodate a new freeway, necessitating a move to a building (below) in South Boston, only a mile or so away, which had been an institute for the blind. Administrative and engineering offices as well as pipe making, voicing and racking departments were moved to the new facility. Both buildings remained in use until the firm moved to a new industial park in Randolph, Massachusetts in 1968.[3]

Two open wood 16′ stops are being erected in the Skinner factory. This spacious erecting room could accommodate 32′ stops with ease, as indeed it often did when a large Skinner was being erected.

building from the great house of Willis in England, a builder for whom Ernest Skinner had the most profound respect.[18 19]

Ernest Skinner would soon regret his support of G. Donald Harrison's joining the Skinner Organ Company. The younger generation of organists was returning to an interest in classic organ literature as opposed to the romantic and orchestral styles then in vogue, and these organists tended to prefer the tonal ideas of Harrison. By 1929 tensions between Skinner and Harrison had reached the point that Skinner wanted to leave the firm, and Skinner started making arrangements to go into the organ business with his son Richmond Skinner. When Marks learned of this plan he told Skinner that if he left, the value of the firm's stock would plummet. To buy some time, Marks persuaded Skinner to sign an agreement in 1931 whereby he would remain with the firm for five years an an annual salary of $5,000. Under the terms of the agreement, Skinner could do whatever he liked and didn't even have to work for the company at all, so long as he didn't lend his name to any competitive firm.[20]

Meanwhile, the Depression was permeating the organ industry. In 1932 Skinner and the organ department of the Aeolian Company merged to form the Aeolian-Skinner Organ Company.[21] For the next four decades Aeolian-Skinner, under the influence of G. Donald Harrison, maintained the same position of prestige which had been enjoyed earlier by the Skinner Organ Company. Aeolian-Skinner actually installed an organ in a theatre in the midst of the Depression, and a large 4/71 at that, in the Hershey Community Theatre in Hershey, Pennsylvania. They also built several theatre-type organs for radio stations: In 1936 Detroit station WWJ purchased a 3/15 Aeolian-Skinner which featured a unified tibia clausa and two consoles with second touch on the choir manuals. A 1941 contract for station WNAC in Boston resulted in a 4/36 orchestral instrument designed by Francis J. Cronin which included second touch, sostenuto on the great, and a full complement of traps and percussions.[22]

In 1933 G. Donald Harrison's influence on the fate of Aeolian-Skinner was recognized by his appointment as technical director and chief of staff.[23] In 1936, at the conclusion of his five-year agreement, Ernest Skinner left to form the Ernest M. Skinner & Son Company in Methuen, Massachusetts.[24] In 1942 Ernest Skinner built the last new organ under his nameplate, his firm going bankrupt that same year. In 1943 his factory burned and he moved to a shop in Reading, Massachusetts where he continued to do rebuilding work until finally retiring in 1949 at the age of 83.[26]

Noted organ historian and author William H. Barnes made these sage observations about Ernest M. Skinner: "It was unfortunate that he lived after organists had lost interest in orchestral voices. They were interested in the classic or baroque organ of the time of Bach to such an extent that Mr. Skinner and his ideas about what constitute a good organ were at a heavy discount.

"It was really pitiful to see him in his later days at a national convention of the Guild. He would just wander around and try to find someone who would talk with him. From being the center of attention in his heyday, he was far from the thinking of many present day organists . . . But he maintained an undaunted and gallant spirit. He knew that every one of his detractors was out of step but himself. He was one of the great organ builders of his time and my admiration for most of what he did is undiminished."[27]

Back at Aeolian-Skinner, business was relatively brisk in the 1930s despite the sorry economic state of the country at the time. This supports the notion that there will always be a market for high quality even under the worst economic conditions. Arthur Hudson Marks died in 1939, leaving the company presidency to G. Donald Harrison[28] who retained it until his death in 1956. At that time the presidency was assumed by Joseph S. Whiteford, a lawyer and majority stockholder. In the late 1960s Whiteford retired and the company moved to new quarters in Randolph, Massachusetts. Head voicer Donald M. Gillett became president. The shortage of operating capital occasioned by the departure of Whiteford and the move to Randolph ultimately led to the company's collapse in 1972.[29]

Ernest M. Skinner had well-defined ideas on many topics and the theatre organ was no exception. He made the following outspoken comments in 1918 following a visit to a theatre equipped with a typical unit organ: "The organist faced a rainbow of many colored devices known by various names; flop keys will do as well as any other. The tones of this organ were voiced as loud as possible. The first that struck my ear was a wood flute of vast proportions and it was subject to a tremolo of terrific effectiveness, accompanied by one of those bean-blower strings on a fifteen-inch wind so stridently voiced that they tasted like copper . . . The effect of the full organ was most original. It put the picture entirely out of business. The whole thing was most carefully designed to create an appetite for vulgarity. I did not hear one single musical note at this performance or the slightest indication of the influence of good taste."[30]

Other Skinner quotations will further illuminate his position on the theatre organ: "For some unknown reason the stops usually present in the theatre unit organ seem to be selected for their antagonism to each other. Perhaps it is because they are so few in number that they are necessarily exaggerated in scale and tone in order to produce a forte.

". . . I hold that of all organs none is more demanding than one suitable for vitalizing pictures. Moving pictures reflect everything of life and are limited in scope only by the imagination of the producer. The organ should be able to reflect every shade of human emotion: love, anger, hate, sorrow, surprise, humor, ugliness, the sinister, and national idioms, to say nothing of dogs, chickens, horses, convulsions of nature, etc., dramatic qualities, fine shades of meaning, the military clang, etc.

"I am unable to convince myself that a colossal flute, an acid string, a vox humana, a biting "kinura," a tuba and a few traps can in any way cover the ground as outlined above . . . The legitimate organ has a pianissimo in variety. The next step up is a variety of soft flutes and strings. Then the larger strings and flutes and a great variety of orchestral reproductions, oboe, English horn, musette, French horn, clarinet, bassoon, harp and so on up to the larger, though *not* thick flutes and big strings, tubas, soft and loud pedal reeds and diapasons . . . all the foregoing voiced to work together or independently and a forte made up of many voices and not of two or three blatant ones, every voice having neighbors in its own scale of dynamics and also in variety.

". . . The organ in the Colony Theatre, New York City, and that in the Capitol Theatre, Boston, are built on the legitimate plan. They are the complete vehicle for anything that ever has to be said in connection with pictures, including first-class traps. Each is a worthy rival of its neighboring orchestra and there is no drop in the effect when the orchestra stops and the organ begins."[31]

A summation of the tonal philosophy of E. M. Skinner was eloquently phrased by organ historian Orpha Ochse: "Although he prided himself on his development of solo stops that imitated orchestral instruments and although his pitch variety was sometimes minimal, Skinner never really tried to force the organ into an orchestral pattern. Paradoxically, in an age that was intoxicated with the sound of the orchestra, Skinner organs were representative of the highest achievement in American organ building not because of their success as orchestral imitations but because they were still fundamentally traditional organs."[32]

3/15 AEOLIAN-SKINNER THEATRE ORGAN, OPUS 942
WWJ Radio Studios, Detroit, Michigan

CONTRACT

1 Articles of Agreement made this 25th day of January 1936, by and between the AEOLIAN-SKINNER ORGAN COMPANY, INC., of BOSTON, MASSACHUSETTS, hereinafter called the Builder and The Evening News Association of Detroit, Michigan. hereinafter called the Purchaser.

2 For, and in Consideration of the sum of $ Eighteen Thousand Seven Hundred Dollars ($18, 700) Dollars, to be paid by the Purchaser to the Builder, the said Builder agrees to build an organ according to the annexed specifications, in a thorough and artistic manner, and install it in WWJ Detroit Michigan complete in every detail and fully warranted, estimated on or about June 1st, 1936.

This date is not a consideration or term of this contract, but is given in good faith and full expectation of prompt delivery, subject, however, to delays from fires, strikes or causes beyond the control of the Builder, and especially subject to delays from freight embargoes or other interferences.

3 It is agreed that the amount of any State or Federal Tax levied on the manufacture or sale of said organ or in any other manner levied on the transaction set forth in this agreement, shall be added to the purchase price hereinabove set forth, and paid by the Purchaser.

4 It is understood and agreed that the materials and labor entering into the organ hereinabove contracted for are to be procured by the Builder in the State of Massachusetts, and that said organ is to be constructed by the Builder in the State of Massachusetts from which State it is to be transported in interstate commerce to the State of Michigan where it is to be installed by the Builder as hereinabove set forth.

5 The Purchaser agrees that when the Builder is ready to proceed with the installation of the organ, the Purchaser will keep the building at a suitable temperature as required by the Builder and provide and allow the use of suitable electric current for tone regulation, tuning, testing and lighting; that he shall provide a condition of quiet within the building for the proper tone regulation of the organ, and that he shall hold the Builder harmless from interference with its workmen during the installation. The Purchaser further agrees to assume all risk of damage to the organ by fire, lightning, water, tornado or otherwise while contained in the said building and to insure the same in good reliable companies for the benefit of the parties hereto as their interests may appear.

6 If the building is not in proper condition for the organ to be erected when the organ is ready for shipment, and it becomes necessary to place the organ in storage, to be held until the building is ready for installation, the Purchaser agrees to pay the cost of such storage, or to arrange for such storage in a proper place at his own expense, provided of course that the organ builder does not complete said organ at the factory before the proper time for shipment, in accordance with contract date of completion.

7 It is mutually agreed that, in view of the fact that the presence of rubbish and dust, especially from plaster, and of noise or disturbance caused by workmen, when an organ is being erected causes not only immediate but future troubles in the functioning of any organ, the building in which the organ herein referred to is to be erected shall not be considered ready for the erection of said organ until the organ chambers and the adjacent parts of the building are entirely free from rubbish and dust. In other words, it is understood that the organ erection shall not be started until any other workmen liable to create rubbish, dust or disturbance shall be out of the way entirely, and furthermore, if after the organ erection men once start their work, they are interrupted by other workmen creating rubbish and dust, or making any disturbance, the losses in time and expense caused by the lack of proper conditions for organ erection and tuning, shall be paid by the Purchaser in addition to the contract price herein mentioned.

8 The Purchaser agrees to inform the Builder as to where the organ and console are to be located, and the dimensions of the spaces to be occupied before the plans or construction of the organ are begun. After these dimensions have been so determined the Purchaser shall not permit any changes to be made in the dimensions of the organ spaces, nor the installation of any obstructions such as pipes, beams, posts, etc., and shall reimburse the Builder for additional cost due to such changes or obstructions.

9 The Purchaser, in consideration of the agreement herein of the Builder, hereby requests the Builder to construct and erect said organ and agrees to purchase the same and to pay therefor the sum of Eighteen Thousand Seven Hundred Dollars ($18, 700)

as follows:—
When the contract is signed, ~~twenty-five (25%) per cent of the total contract price amounting to~~ Five Thousand Dollars ($5000)
~~When the principal portion of said organ is manufactured ready to assemble in the factory of the Builder, twenty-five (25%) per cent. of the total contract price amounting to~~
~~Upon the delivery at the above named building of the principal portion of said organ, twenty-five (25%) per cent. of the total contract price amounting to~~
Upon the erection of said organ complete, in accordance herewith, the Purchaser agreeing to examine said organ immediately in the presence of a representative of the Builder, the balance of said contract price, to wit, the sum of Thirteen Thousand Dollars ($13,700)

provided, however, that when said organ is ready for erection, and completion is held up by the inability for any reason of the Purchaser to have the installation proceed, all payments are due up to ninety (90%) per cent. of the contract price.

10 Final payment is, in any event, immediately due upon use of the organ in service or in other public manner. Interest to be paid at the rate of six (6) per centum per annum from the date of such use upon any balance remaining unpaid upon the expiration of thirty (30) days.

11 Final payment shall not be withheld on account of minor adjustments for which the Builder is liable under its warranty.

12 It is mutually agreed that the title to and ownership of said organ shall be and remain in the Builder until the contract price as heretofore stated and all promissory notes or other evidences of indebtedness and renewals thereof have been fully paid with interest at the current rate upon any amount not paid when due, and that only upon such payment shall said organ become the property of the Purchaser. If the Purchaser shall fail to make the payments as herein provided, or to pay any notes given when due, and such default shall continue for thirty (30) days, the Builder upon written notice to the Purchaser may forthwith take and repossess said organ, and after sale of said organ the Builder shall apply the proceeds of said sale upon the payments due hereunder and shall account to the Purchaser for any balance of said proceeds.

13 It is understood and agreed that the delivery and acceptance of promissory notes or other evidences of indebtedness shall not be considered payment until the full amount of the same and of any renewals thereof shall have been paid in full with interest.

14 All verbal agreements and understandings are merged in this contract and the specifications and details of construction attached hereto which comprise the entire contract, and no change, alteration or modification made verbally or in any other way, will be binding upon the Builder, unless the same be made in writing signed by an executive officer of the said Builder.

15 In witness whereof, the parties hereto have hereunto set their hands and seals this 31st day of January 1936.

AEOLIAN-SKINNER ORGAN COMPANY, INC.

Witness [signature] By [signature] Treas.

THE EVENING NEWS ASSOCIATION (Purchaser)

Witness [signature] By [signature] TREASURER

Skinner Organ Company, Inc.

DETAILS OF CONSTRUCTION

The builder warrants the action and construction in every particular, and agrees to make good any defects in materials and workmanship which may appear within five years.

Action to be electro pneumatic.

Casing of console to be of native oak, or of any other native wood of equal value; of simple design to harmonize with the period of the architecture of the building.

An organist's bench of same material as console casing.

All basses of the larger winded stops on separate chests.

The organ builder is to furnish and install an electric blowing plant, consisting of a motor, blower, remote control self-starter where necessary, and generator for action current, all of ample size to meet any legitimate demand which may be made thereon by the instrument, according to the specifications.

The purchaser shall furnish a suitable foundation for the motor and blower, connect the motor and starting switch with the power current, install wiring from the console to the self-starter and connect same; do all cutting of floors, partitions, etc., and the running of conduits where required and wind conductors from the blower to the console and all organ chambers which may be necessary; and shall prepare the organ chamber in accordance with plans which shall be furnished by the organ builder.

The organ is to be erected in the building, tone regulated, tuned and left ready for use. Freight and cartage to be paid by purchaser.

No organ case or front display pipe work is included.

Æolian-Skinner Organ Company INC.

Organ Architects and Builders

Church Residence Auditorium University

Skinner Organs Æolian Organs

Chicago, Illinois. #12236-C January 22, 1936

SPECIFICATION OF AN ORGAN PREPARED FOR

BROADCASTING STATION W. W. J.,

THE DETROIT NEWS,

DETROIT, MICHIGAN.

SOLO ORGAN (Top Manual)
(Duplexed from Great and Choir)

16' Tibia Clausa	61 notes
[handwritten:] 16 Clarinet	61 "
8' Tibia Clausa	61 "
4' Tibia Clausa	61 "
2' Tibia Clausa	61 "
8' Flute	61 "
4' Flute	61 "
2 2/3' Flute	61 "
2' Flute	61 "
8' Voix Celeste (2 ranks)	61 "
8' Cornopean	61 "
8' French Horn	61 "
8' Clarinet	61 "
8' English Horn	61 "
8' Vox Humana	61 "
8' Flute Celeste (2 ranks)	61 "
8' Soft String Celeste (2 ranks)	61 "
8' Orchestral Flute	61 "
4' Soft String Celeste (2 ranks)	61 "
8' Harp } 4' Celesta }	49 "
Chimes	20 "
Tremolo	

#12236-C - 2 -

GREAT ORGAN (Middle Manual)

8' Diapason	61 pipes
16' Tibia Clausa	12 "
8' Tibia Clausa	61 "
4' Tibia Clausa	12 "
2' Tibia Clausa	12 "
8' Flute	61 "
4' Flute	12 "
2 2/3' Flute	61 notes
2' Flute	12 pipes
8' Voix Celeste (2 ranks)	122 "
8' Cornopean	61 "
8' French Horn	61 "
8' Clarinet	61 "
8' English Horn	61 "
8' Vox Humana	61 "
Chimes	20 tubes
Tremolo	

CHOIR ORGAN (Bottom Manual)

8' Flute Celeste (2 ranks)	122 Pipes
8' Soft String Celeste (2 ranks)	122 "
8' Orchestral Flute	61 "
4' Soft String Celeste (2 ranks)	24 "
8' Harp } 4' Celesta }	49 bars
Chimes	20 notes
Tremolo	

Second Touch

8' Cornopean

8' Tibia Clausa

4' Tibia Clausa

8' Clarinet

8' Diapason

Great to Choir 8' and 4' Couplers.

#12236½C - 3 -

PEDAL ORGAN - Augmented

16' Tibia Clausa	32 notes
16' Waldhorn	12 pipes
16' English Horn	12 pipes
8' French Horn	32 notes
8' Voix Celeste	32 notes
8' Flute Celeste	32 notes
8' Soft String Celeste	32 notes

COUPLERS

Solo to Great }
Solo to Choir } Unison
Choir to Great }

Solo to Solo 4' }
Solo to Solo 16' }
Solo to Great 4' }
Solo to Great 16' }
Solo to Choir 4' } Octave
Solo to Choir 16' }
Choir to Choir 4' }
Choir to Choir 16' }
Choir to Great 4' }
Choir to Great 16' }
Great to Great 4' }
Great to Great 16' }

Solo to Pedal }
Great to Pedal }
Choir to Pedal } Pedal
Solo to Pedal 4' }
Choir to Pedal 4' }

Great Unison Off
Solo Unison Off
Choir Unison Off

COMBINATIONS Adjustable at the console and visibly operating the draw stop knobs.

Great - 1,2,3,4,5,6,7,8
Solo - 1,2,3,4,5,6,7,8
Choir - 1,2,3,4,5,6,7,8
Pedal - 1,2,3,4,5,6

MECHANICALS

Great to Pedal Reversible
Great Expression
Choir Expression
Sforzando
Crescendo Pedal

This proposal provides for two duplicate console - one in the Studio in which the organ will be heard directly, and the other in the large Studio down stairs.

4/41 SKINNER THEATRE ORGAN, OPUS 369
Capitol Theatre, Allston, Massachusetts

CONTRACT.

1. ARTICLES OF AGREEMENT made this twelfth day of June, 1925, by and between the SKINNER ORGAN COMPANY, INC., of BOSTON, MASSACHUSETTS, hereinafter called the Builder and OLYMPIA CONSTRUCTION CO., a Massachusetts corporation, hereinafter called the Purchaser.

2. FOR, AND IN CONSIDERATION of the sum of Fifty Thousand ($50,000.00) Dollars, to be paid by the Purchaser to the Builder, the said Builder agrees to build an organ according to the annexed specifications and details of construction hereto annexed, in a most thorough and artistic manner, and install it in the CAPITOL THEATRE complete in every detail and fully warranted, estimated on or about September 1, 1925. This date is not a consideration or term of this contract, but is given in good faith and full expectation of prompt delivery, subject, however, to delays from fires, strikes or causes beyond the control of the Builder, and especially subject to delays from freight embargoes or other interferences.

3. It is understood and agreed that the materials and labor entering into the organ hereinabove contracted for are to be procured by the Builder in the State of Massachusetts, and that the said organ is to be constructed by the Builder in the State of Massachusetts from which State it is to be transported in interstate commerce to the State of Massachusetts where it is to be installed by the Builder as hereinabove set forth.

4. The Purchaser agrees that when the Builder is ready to proceed with the installation of the organ, the Purchaser will keep the building at a suitable temperature as required by the Builder and provide and allow the use of suitable electric current for tone regulation, tuning, testing and lighting; that he shall provide a condition of quiet within the building for the proper tone regulation of the organ, and that he shall hold the Builder harmless from interference with his workmen during the installation. The Purchaser further agrees to assume all risk of damage to the organ by fire, lightning, water or tornado while contained in the said building and to insure the same in good reliable companies for the benefit of the parties hereto as their interests may appear.

5. If the building is not in proper condition for the organ to be erected when the organ is ready for shipment, and it becomes necessary to place the organ in storage, to be held until the building is ready for installation, the Purchaser agrees to pay the cost of such storage, or to arrange for such storage in a proper place at their own expense, provided of course that the organ builder does not complete said organ at the factory before the proper time for shipment, in accordance with contract date of completion.

6. It is mutually agreed that in view of the fact that the presence of rubbish and dust, especially from plaster, when an organ is being erected causes not only immediate but future troubles in the functioning of any organ, the building in which the organ herein referred to is to be erected shall not be considered ready for the erection of said organ until the organ chambers and the adjacent parts of the building are entirely free from rubbish and dust. In other words, it is understood that the organ erection shall not be started until any other workmen liable to create rubbish and dust shall be out of the way entirely, and furthermore, if after the organ erection men once start their work, they are interrupted by other workmen creating rubbish and dust, or making such noise as to interfere with tuning, the losses in time and expense caused by the lack of proper and reasonable conditions for organ erection and tuning, shall be paid by the Purchaser in addition to the contract price herein mentioned.

7. The Purchaser agrees to inform the Builder as to where the organ and console are to be located, and the dimensions of the spaces to be occupied before the plans or construction of the organ are begun. After these dimensions have been so determined the Purchaser shall not permit any changes to be made in the dimensions of the organ spaces, nor the installation of any obstructions such as pipes, posts, etc., and shall hold the Builder harmless from such changes or obstructions.

8. The Purchaser, in consideration of the agreement herein of the Builder, hereby requests the Builder to construct and erect said organ and agrees to purchase the same and to pay therefor the sum of Fifty Thousand Dollars, ($50,000.00) as follows:

When the contract is signed, ten (10%) per cent. of the total contract price amounting to Five Thousand Dollars, ($5,000.00)

When the principal portion of said organ is manufactured ready to assemble in the factory of the Builder, thirty (30%) per cent. of the total contract price amounting to Ten Thousand ($10,000.00) Dollars in cash, and $5,000. par value of the preferred stock of the Boston Capitol Buildings, Inc..

Upon the ~~delivery of the above named building of the principal portion~~ beginning of the installation of said organ, thirty (30%) per cent. of the total contract price amounting to Ten Thousand Dollars, ($10,000.00) in cash, and $5,000. par value of the preferred stock of the Boston Capitol Buildings, Inc.

Upon the erection of said organ complete, in accordance herewith, the Purchaser agreeing to examine said organ immediately in the presence of a representative of the Builder, and when accepted, the balance of said contract price, to wit, the sum of Five Thousand Dollars, ($5,000.00) in cash and ten thousand dollars, ($10,000.00) (par value) in Preferred stock of the Boston Capitol Buildings, Inc., it being understood that no more than Two Million Five Hundred Thousand Dollars, ($2,500,000.00) par value of this Preferred stock shall be issued, without the consent in writing of 81% of the preferred shares issued and outstanding first having been obtained, or unless at least eighty-one per cent. (81%) of the preferred shares issued and outstanding shall vote at a meeting duly called for the purpose to increase the said preferred stock issue; provided, however, that when said organ is ready for erection and is held up by the inability for any reason of the Purchaser to have the installation proceed, all payments are immediately due up to ninety (90%) per cent. of the contract price.

9. Final payment is immediately due upon use of the organ in service or in other public manner.

10. Final payment shall not be withheld on account of minor adjustments for which the Builder is liable under its warranty.

11. It is understood and agreed that the delivery and

acceptance of promissory notes or other evidences of indebtedness shall not be considered payment until the full amount of the same and of any renewals thereof shall have been paid in full with interest.

12. All verbal agreements and understandings are merged in this contract and the specifications and details of construction attached hereto which comprise the entire contract, and no change, alteration or modification made verbally or in any other way, will be binding upon the Builder, unless the same be made in writing signed by an executive officer of the said Builder.

13. IN WITNESS WHEREOF, the parties hereto have hereunto set their hands and seals this twelfth day of June, 1925.

SKINNER ORGAN COMPANY, INC.
By: Ernest M. Skinner V. Pres.

Witness: G. L. Catlin

Witness: W. E. Holland — Olympia Construction Co. by W. J. Sinnott Pres.

Purchaser.

Rev. 6-23

SKINNER ORGAN COMPANY, INC.

DETAILS OF CONSTRUCTION

The builder warrants the action and construction in every particular, and agrees to make good any defects in materials and workmanship which may appear within five years.

Action to be electro pneumatic.

Casing of console to be of mahogany oak, or of any other wood of equal value; of simple design to harmonize with the period of the architecture of the building.

An organist's bench of same material as console casing.

All basses of the larger winded stops on separate chests.

The organ builder is to furnish and instal an electric blowing plant, consisting of a motor, blower, remote control self-starter and generator for action current, all of ample size to meet any legitimate demand which may be made thereon by the instrument, according to the specifications.

The purchaser shall furnish a suitable foundation for the motor and blower, connect the motor with the power current, instal a No. 14 wire from the console to the self-starter, do all cutting of floors, partitions, etc., and the running of required conduits and wind conductors from the blower which may be necessary; and shall prepare the organ chamber in accordance with plans which shall be furnished by the organ builder.

The organ is to be erected in the building, tone regulated, tuned and left ready for use.

No organ case or front display pipe work is included in this estimate.

The mechanical arrangement of the organ in the chambers shall be made in consultation with the purchaser's architect.

Boston, Mass., June 25, 1925.

RECEIVED
JUN 30 1925
G. L. CATLIN

Olympia Construction Company,
200 Devonshire Street,
Boston, Mass.

Gentlemen:-

Reference is herein made to a contract dated the 12th day of June, 1925, between the SKINNER ORGAN COMPANY, a Massachusetts Corporation, and the OLYMPIA CONTRUCTION COMPANY, a Massachusetts Corporation, under which contract the SKINNER ORGAN COMPANY is to build an organ in the CAPITOL THEATRE, Boston, Mass., for the sum of Fifty Thousand ($50,000.00) Dollars, and it is hereby agreed by both parties to this contract that this letter shall be made a part of said contract.

After the said contract was signed by the SKINNER ORGAN COMPANY, the following clause was attached to the contract:

"It is agreed that all labor to be used on the theatre premises shall be union, if required, and especially such as not to cause strikes by labor employed by other sub-contractors on said job".

It is now agreed by both parties to this contract that the above clause be struck out of the contract, and the following clause be inserted in its place:

"It is agreed, that, if required, the men employed to instal the organ in the said CAPITOL THEATRE, under the contract herein referred to, shall apply for membership in the Organ Builders' Union, in New York City, unless they have already becomemembers of said Union. In other words, as it is understood that there is no Organ Builders' Union at present in Boston, if, for any reason, any labor troubles arise from the fact that the instalation men do not belong to any Union, the SKINNER ORGAN COMPANY will see that these men apply for membership in the New York Union referred to, unless they are already members of said Union".

SKINNER ORGAN COMPANY.

BY G. L. Catlin
Treasurer.

OLYMPIA CONSTRUCTION COMPANY.

BY W. J. Sinnott

SKINNER ORGAN COMPANY, INC.

ORGAN ARCHITECTS AND BUILDERS FOR CHURCHES, AUDITORIUMS, THEATRES AND RESIDENCES

Boston, Mass., March 5, 1925.

SPECIFICATION OF AN ORGAN PREPARED FOR

CAPITOL THEATRE,
Boston, Mass.

GREAT ORGAN	PIPES
16' Bourdon (Extension)	19
8' Diapason	73
8' Major Flute	73
8' Gedeckt	73
8' Violoncello	73
8' Viole Celeste	73
8' Flute Celeste (II Rks.)	134
4' Unda Maris (II Rks.)	122
4' Octave	73
4' Flute Triangulaire	73
2 2/3 Twelfth	61
2' Fifteenth	61
Chorus Mixture (V Rks.)	305
16' Waldhorn	73
8' Harmonic Trumpet	73
4' Clarion	73
8' Vox Humana	61
Celesta } with dampers / Harp }	61 Bars
Tremolo	

SWELL ORGAN	
16' Bourdon	73
8' Diapason	73 Notes
8' Major Flute	73 "
8' Gedeckt	73 "

Shop specification checked with this copy. A. M. 7/21/25

SWELL ORGAN - Cont'd.

	PIPES
8' Violincello	73 Notes
8' Viole Celeste	73 "
8' Flute Celeste	73 "
4' Unda Maris	73 "
4' Octave	73 "
4' Flute Triangulaire	73 "
2 2/3 Twelfth	61 "
2' Fifteenth	61 "
Chorus Mixture (V Rks.)	305 "
16' Waldhorn	73 "
8' Harmonic Trumpet	73 "
4' Clarion	73 "
8' Vox Humana	61 "
Celesta) Harp)	61 Bars

CHOIR ORGAN

8' Doppel Floete	73
8' Concert Flute	73
8' Orchestral Strings (II Rks.)	146
8' Dulciana	73
4' Orchestral Flute	73
4' Gemshorn	73
2 2/3 Nazard	61 Notes
2' Piccolo	61 "
1 3/5 Tierce	61 "
1 1/7 Septieme	61 "
French Cornet (V Rks.)	305
16' Bassoon (Imitative)	73
8' Bassoon "	12
8' French Horn "	61
8' Physharmonica	61

CHOIR ORGAN - Cont'd.

	PIPES
8' Clarinet (Imitative)	61
8' Musette	61
8' Corno d'Amore	61
8' English Horn (Imitative)	61
Celesta) Harp)	61 Bars
Tremolo	

SOLO ORGAN

8' Doppel Floete	73 Notes
8' Concert Flute	73 "
8' Orchestral Strings	73 "
8' Dulciana	73 "
4' Orchestral Flute	73 "
4' Gemshorn	61 "
2 2/3 Nazard	61 "
2' Piccolo	61 "
1 3/5 Tierce	61 "
1 1/7 Septieme	61 "
French Cornet (V Rks.)	305 "
16' Bassoon (Imitative)	73 "
8' Bassoon "	73 "
8' French Horn "	61 "
8' Physharmonica	61 "
8' Clarinet (Imitative)	61 "
8' Musette "	61 "
8' Corno d'Amore	61 "
8' English Horn (Imitative)	61 "
8' Tuba "	73
Celesta) Harp)	61 Bars
Tremolo	

PEDAL ORGAN - Augmented

	PIPES
32' Resultant	32 Notes
16' Diapason	32
16' Violone	32
16' Bourdon	32
16' Echo Lieblich (Swell)	32 Notes
8' Bass Flute	32
8' Gedeckt	12
8' Still Gedeckt (Swell)	32 Notes
8' Violincello	12
4' Fifteenth	32 Notes
3 1/5 Tierce	32 "
2 2/3 Larigot	32 "
2 2/7 Septieme	32 "
32' Bombarde	12
16' Trombone	32
16' Waldhorn (Swell)	32 Notes
16' Bassoon (Orchestral)	32 "
8' Tromba	12
8' Bassoon	32 Notes

C O U P L E R S

Swell to Great)
Choir to Great)
Swell to Choir) Unison
Solo to Great)
Great to Solo)
Solo to Choir)

Swell to Swell 4')
Swell to Swell 16')
Swell to Great 4')
Swell to Great 16')
Swell to Choir 4')
Swell to Choir 16')
Choir to Choir 4') Octave
Choir to Choir 16')
Choir to Great 4')
Choir to Great 16')
Great to Great 4')
Great to Great 16')
Solo to Solo 4')
Solo to Solo 16')
Solo to Great 4')
Solo to Great 16')

C O U P L E R S - Cont'd.

* Swell to Pedal)
** Great to Pedal)
* Choir to Pedal)
Solo to Pedal) Pedal
* Swell to Pedal 4')
* Choir to Pedal 4')
* Solo to Pedal 4')

* Also by reversible pistons
** " " " Piston & Pedal

Swell Unison Off
Great " "
Choir " "
Solo " "

COMBINATIONS - Visible and adjustable

SWELL - 1,2,3,4,5,6,7,8 cancel Pedal to Manual on and off
GREAT - 1,2,3,4,5,6,7,8 cancel " " " " " "
CHOIR - 1,2,3,4,5,6,7,8 cancel " " " " " "
SOLO - 1,2,3,4,5,6,7,8 cancel " " " " " "
PEDAL - 1,2,3,4,5,6,7,8 cancel " " " " " "
GENERAL - 1,2,3,4,5,6,7,8 cancel

* Sforzando mezzo) reversibles
* Sforzando tutti)

* By Pedal & Piston

Swell & Great Expression
Choir & Solo Expression
Crescendo Expression
Traps Expression

Sostenuto - To Great, Swell, Choir & Solo - 49 Notes

TRAPS

Chinese block - repeating action optional
Snare Drum - " " "
Tamborine - " " "
Triangle - single stroke
Castanets - repeating action
Cathedral Chimes - A to E
Xylophone - repeating action
Orchestra Bells " "
Bass Drum - stroke & roll
Tympani
Cymbal
Tom Tom
Bird Song
Auto Horn
Crash Cymbal
Steamboat Whistle
Chinese Gong
Door Bell
Thunder
Rain
Lions Roar

Duplicate Console

SKINNER OPUS LIST

Following is a complete list of this firm's theatre-type instruments.

OPUS	LOCATION/CITY/STATE	SIZE	YR	PRICE	BLWR	REMARKS
216	Elmwood Th., Buffalo, NY	4/	1913	$ 9,000		7½ hp; with 2-rank echo.
217	Alaska (Strand) Th., Seattle, WA	3/23	1914	$ 9,150	5277	5 hp; with 3-rank echo.
324	Victory Th., Holyoke, MA	3/24	1921	$ 13,230	12216	7½ hp; contained some used pipes and parts.
338	Boulevard (American) Th., Baltimore, MD	3/20	1921	$ 16,000	12351	7½ hp.
343	Palace Th., Lawrence, MA	4/20	1921	$ 12,850	12624	Used organ installed and enlarged.
344	Cameo Th., New York, NY	3/15	1921	$ 12,000	12465	
			1922		13583	
354	Lincoln Th., Troy, NY	2/20	1922	$ 11,848	13168	
369	Capitol Th., Allston, MA	4/41	1922	$ 26,150	13582	7½ hp.
444	Ritz Th., Port Richmond, NY	4/24	1923	$ 20,875	15239	7½ hp.
485	Colony (Broadway) Th., New York, NY	4/32	1924		16301	
545	Metropolitan (Music Hall) (Metropolitan Center) (Wang Center For The Performing Arts) Th., Boston, MA	4/51	1925	$ 50,000	17738	Moved in 1930 to Heinz Auditorium, Pittsburgh, Pennsylvania by Wurlitzer.
555	Akron Th., Akron, OH	3/15	1926	$ 14,500	18418	
602	Empire Th., Lawrence, MA	3/30	1926	$ 22,000	19179	
602A	Empire Th., Lawrence, MA	3/31	1926	$ 1,500		Addition: pedal 16′ trombone.
605	Mutual Benefit Life Insurance Co., Newark, NJ	3/35	1926	$ 30,000		With 3-rank echo.
665	John Hancock Hall, Boston, MA	3/32	1928	$ 25,000		
709	Plaza Hotel, San Antonio, TX	3/12	1928	$ 19,500	22057	With roll player.
711	Auditorium Th., Rochester, NY	4/56	1928	$ 35,600		
775	Midland Th., Midland, TX	2/15	1929	$ 15,795		Order cancelled.

AEOLIAN-SKINNER OPUS LIST

OPUS	LOCATION/CITY/STATE	SIZE	YR	PRICE	BLWR	REMARKS
876	Hershey Community Th., Hershey, PA	4/71	1931	$ 39,350	25031	Superseded Aeolian contract #1798.
			1931		25005	
917	WBEN Radio, Buffalo, NY	2/7	1934	$ 7,200	25219	
917A	WBEN Radio, Buffalo, NY	2/9	1936	$ 1,000		Additions: 2 ranks.
923	NBC Studio 3B, New York, NY	3/15	1934		25282	
942	WWJ Radio, Detroit, MI	3/15	1936	$ 18,700	25492	Two consoles.
		3/26				Additions.
1025	WNAC Radio, Boston, MA	4/36	1941	$ 23,275		

F. R. SMITH

Fred R. Smith (1878-1944) was a native of England who moved to Canada at an early age. Later he moved to Marietta, Ohio where he was employed by the Stevens Organ Comany.[1] After the demise of the Stevens factory following a 1913 flood, Mr. Smith reportedly went to work for Gottfried until 1919 or so when he moved back to Marietta and went into business for himself. He was more of an assembler than a builder and his instruments contained mostly Gottfried parts.[2]

Two Kinetic blowers were sold to him for Marietta theatres. The first, #I396, was shipped in 1920 to the C & M Amusement Co. and was rated at one horsepower and 3½″ wind. The second, #K1035, was shipped in 1923 to the Hippodrome Theatre and was rated at two horsepower and 5″ wind. It is unknown whether or not these repre-

Gottfried console of the F. R. Smith organ in the State Theatre, Uhrichsville, Ohio.

sented two different theatres or if the second was a later enlargement of the first. It is known that the Smith organ in one Marietta church had been installed earlier in a local theatre.[3]

Another organ bearing a Smith nameplate was installed in the State Theatre, Uhrichsville, Ohio early in 1928. This three-manual organ utilized Gottfried parts exclusively.

SMITH UNIT ORGAN CO.

Frederick W. Smith was born in England and began his apprenticeship in the organ industry at age 13 with Peter Conacher; later he worked for the Lewis company. In 1892 he entered the employ of Robert Hope-Jones and remained with him through Hope-Jones' many changes of employment during the next 20 years. In 1912 Smith decided to strike out in business for himself, leaving his employment at Wurlitzer and setting up shop in the shadow of the giant at North Tonawanda, New York.[1] Among his first sales was a 4/16 to Shea's Hippodrome Theatre in Buffalo, New York. This prestigious installation gave his firm the shot in the arm it needed to ensure success in those early years.

As has been true of so many organ builders, Smith was apparently a better organ man than businessman. In 1916 he joined forces with the J. P. Seeburg Piano Co. of Chicago, a very successful firm with the financial resources to support such an enterprise. Seeburg also had the advantage of extensive regional sales representation with the result that dozens of organs were sold under the Seeburg-Smith nameplate. The unit organ department was located at 419 W. Erie Street in the same building where Seeburg was assembling coin-operated pianos.

In late 1921 the Seeburg-Smith partnership was dissolved and the Smith Unit Organ Co. was formed with the financial backing of Henry Hogans and his son Walter J. Hogans of Oak Park, Illinois.[2] Manufacturing continued in the building at 419 W. Erie Street until early 1924 when the operation was moved to Geneva, Illinois. From July to December 1924 the firm's ad in *The Diapason* listed the name as Geneva Organ Company, manufacturing both Geneva organs and Smith unit organs. Starting in January 1925 the Geneva ads drop the Smith name altogether, reflecting Smith's departure for California where he again founded his own firm. During the transition period some organs were built with Smith-Geneva nameplates. These instruments show more Geneva influence than Smith and are therefore listed in the Geneva section of Volume I of the *Encyclopedia of the American Theatre Organ.*

The California incarnation of the Smith firm was known as F. W. Smith & Son, located in Alameda. Only about 10% of the organs bearing Mr. Smith's name were built in California and many of them carried the Leathurby-Smith nameplate. George H. Leathurby had been the Wurlitzer representative in San Francisco and in 1918 he launched his own musical instrument business. The Smith firm ceased operations in 1928 although Mr. Smith's son, Charles F. Smith, continued in the organ service business into the 1960s.[3 4]

One other nameplate in the Smith lineage should be accounted for. The Kramer Organ Company of New York City was apparently engaged to install Seeburg-Smith and Smith Unit Organ Co. organs in the New York and New Jersey areas. The records of the Kinetic blower company reveal that some of the blowers for these organs were shipped to Kramer's shop. Curiously, some of these blowers were actually billed to Kramer while others were sold directly to the Seeburg or Smith companies. At least two Smith organs are known to bear Kramer nameplates and others probably do, too.

What were Smith organs like? They had several interesting idiosyncracies, mostly relating to the consoles. The consoles were all of one basic style, similar to the early Wurlitzer paneled model. Stops were arranged in order of pitch by rank, rather than stops of one pitch being grouped together. Some Smith organs featured "amplex" stops which were merely unifications at 5 1/3′ pitch with the imaginative name. Many Smith consoles did not have

Seeburg-Smith
Unified Organ
Patented Dec 4th 1916
Patented June 26th 1917
Chicago Ill.

Smith instruments were sold under this nameplate from 1916 to 1921.

Charles F. Smith poses at the horseshoe console of a Smith church organ, one of the last built before the company ceased operations in 1928. The company built a handful of church instruments in its later years but theatre organs accounted for the bulk of production.

Frederick W. Smith (?-1948) plays one of his unit organs.

At left, the largest Smith organ ever built was this 4/16 in the Forest Hills Theatre in Long Island City, New York. It had several unusual features including a device for operating the swell shades from the manual keys, a sostenuto pedal and a brass cor anglais rank in a four-rank echo division. Below left, 2/5 Leathurby-Smith in the Heathman Hotel, Portland, Oregon. As did most smaller Smith instruments, this console lacks combination pistons.

a combination action. Tonally, Smith usually based his ensemble on the tibia plena, an unfortunate choice inasmuch as it lacked the sweet tone of the tibia clausa, whose sound really endeared the theatre organ to the public. Many of the ranks in Smith organs stop at tenor C, making for a very weak bass and a bottomless ensemble. The author knows of Smith organs as large as six ranks which had only one rank (the flute) extending to the 8′ octave.

A substantial number of Smith organs suffered the ignominious and appropriate fate of being replaced with other brands of unit organs. It was not uncommon for a theatre to replace an outdated *straight* organ with a new unified model, but Smith *unit* organs got replaced by the dozen! One reason might be the tonal shortcomings mentioned above; a more likely reason was the unreliability of the Smith magnets which frequently caused ciphers and dead notes.

4/16 SMITH THEATRE ORGAN
Forest Hill Theatre, Long Island City, New York

The June 1922 issue of *The Diapason* carried an article about what was destined to be the largest Smith organ ever built. It is reproduced here in full. Note the unusual order in which the stops are arranged, a Smith idiosyncrasy.

LARGE SMITH UNIT FOR FOREST HILLS

FOUR-MANUAL TO BE BUILT

Swell Control from Second Touch on Manuals and Tenuto Device Among New Inventions to Be Incorporated.

The Smith Unit Organ Company of Chicago, the youngest, but one of the lustiest, of organ building companies, despite its youth, has won an important contract in the New York district, the order for a four-manual unit organ having been awarded to it a few days ago by the Sheer Amusement Enterprises for the new Forest Hills Theater on Long Island. Forest Hills is one of the most exclusive suburban districts of New York and the new theater is in keeping with the surroundings, and is one of the most palatial houses anywhere in the country. There is only one afternoon and one evening performance and for this all seats in the house are reserved. The organ is to have a beautiful ebony console, designed by F. W. Smith, who before coming to Chicago was associated with the late Robert Hope-Jones for a number of years.

Two features of the organ of special interest to organists are patents of the Smith Company. One is a new arrangement for swell control, by which on using the second touch the swells are opened automatically from the manuals. To control the device a stop-key for each manual is provided. This device enables the player to use both feet on the pedals when necessary and at the same time open and close the swell-boxes. The other invention is the tenuto arrangement. By this the organist, on depressing a foot piston, may sustain any chord he has struck on any manual, leaving both hands free to play on the other manuals.

The specification of the organ, which is to be built immediately at the north side factory of the Smith Unit Company, is as follows:

PEDAL ORGAN.

Diaphone Resultant, 32 ft.
Diaphone, 16 ft.
Bourdon, 16 ft.
String Gamba, 16 ft.
Open Diapason, 8 ft.
Octave, 4 ft.
Tuba, 8 ft.
Clarion, 4 ft.
Flute, 8 ft.
Tibia, 8 ft.
Tibia, 4 ft.
Cello, 8 ft.
Clarinet, 8 ft.
Trumpet, 8 ft.
Oboe Horn, 8 ft.
Chimes, 8 ft.

Second Touch:

Bass Drum.
Cymbal.
Kettle Drum.
Crash Cymbal.
Roll Cymbal, First Touch.
Diaphone Resultant, 32 ft.
String Gamba, 8 ft.
Tuba, 8 ft.
Three adjustable combination pistons.

ACCOMPANIMENT ORGAN.

Bourdon, 16 ft.
String Gamba, 16 ft.
Diaphonic Diapason, 8 ft.
Tuba Horn, 8 ft.
Flute, 8 ft.
Flute, 4 ft.
Twelfth, 2⅔ ft.
Piccolo, 2 ft.
Tibia Clausa, 8 ft.
Tibia, 4 ft.
String Gamba, 8 ft.
Violin, 8 ft.
Viol Celeste, 8 ft.
Clarinet, 8 ft.
Trumpet, 8 ft.
Oboe Horn, 8 ft.
Harp, 8 ft.

Second Touch:

Tuba Horn, 8 ft.
Tibia, 8 ft.
Chimes, 8 ft.
Clarinet, 8 ft.
Xylophone, 8 ft.
Oboe Horn, 8 ft.
Triangle.
Ten adjustable combination pistons.

First Touch:

Snare Drum.
Tambourine.
Castanets.
Chinese Block.
Tom Tom.

GREAT ORGAN.

Sub bass, 16 ft.
String Gamba, 16 ft.
Clarinet T. C., 16 ft.
Diaphone, 16 ft.
Diaphonic Diapason, 8 ft.
Octave, 4 ft.
Tuba, 8 ft.
Clarion, 4 ft.
Concert Flute, 8 ft.
Flute, 4 ft.
Twelfth, 2⅔ ft.
Piccolo, 2 ft.
Tierce, 1 3/5 ft.
Tibia Clausa, 8 ft.
String Gamba, 8 ft.
String Gamba, 4 ft.
First Violin, 8 ft.
First Violin, 4 ft.
Viol, 2 ft.
Viol Celeste, 8 ft.
Celeste, 4 ft.
Clarinet, 8 ft.
Trumpet, 8 ft.
Oboe Horn, 8 ft.
Vox Humana T. C., 16 ft.
Vox Humana, 8 ft.
Vox Humana, 4 ft.
Kinura, 8 ft.
Wood Harp (Marimba) Vibrato, 8 ft.
Orchestral Bells, 8 ft.
Glockenspiel, 8 ft.
Xylophone, 8 ft.
Chrysoglott, 8 ft.
Chimes, 8 ft.

Second Touch:

Tuba.
Tibia.
String Gamba.
Clarinet.
Oboe Horn.
Harp.
Glockenspiel.
Orchestral Bells.
Chimes.
Ten adjustable combination pistons.

SOLO ORGAN.

String Gamba, 16 ft.
Diaphonic Diapason, 8 ft.
Tuba Horn, 8 ft.
Flute, 8 ft.
Flute, 4 ft.
Tibia Clausa, 8 ft.
Tibia, 4 ft.
String Gamba, 8 ft.
First Violin, 8 ft.
Viol Celeste, 8 ft.
Clarinet, 8 ft.
Trumpet, 8 ft.
Oboe Horn, 8 ft.
Vox Humana, 8 ft.
Kinura, 8 ft.
Harp Marimba (Single stroke), 8 ft.
Harp Marimba (Single stroke), 4 ft.
Harp Marimba (Single stroke), 2⅔ ft.
Orchestral Bells, 8 ft.
Glockenspiel (Single stroke), 8 ft.
Xylophone, 8 ft.
Chrysoglott, 8 ft.
Chimes, 8 ft.
Amplex Gamba, 8 ft.
Amplex Violin, 8 ft.
Amplex Clarinet, 8 ft.
Amplex Kinura, 8 ft.

ECHO ORGAN.

Flute, 8 ft.
Flute, 4 ft.
Piccolo, 2 ft.
First Violin, 8 ft.
First Violin, 4 ft.
Cor Anglais (Brass Bells), 8 ft.
Cor Anglais, 4 ft.
Vox Humana, 16 ft.
Vox Humana, 8 ft.
Vox Humana, 4 ft.
Chimes, 8 ft.
Tremulant.

Ten combination pistons. Three expression pedals. One general pedal. Crescendo pedal. Four tremulants. Sforzando pedal bringing on full wind stops. Sforzando pedal bringing on all traps and percussions. Swell pedal for flutes, strings and vox humana, etc. Swell pedal for percussions. Swell pedal for heavy reeds and remainder of organ. Three stop-keys for connecting all three swell pedals to the general swell pedal.

This 2/5 Seeburg-Smith was entirely self-contained within two cabinets in the theatre's orchestra pit. The left cabinet contains a flute, string and clarinet and the right cabinet houses a trumpet, vox humana and some percussions. The console contains two tracker bars playing either MSR rolls on the left or 88-note rolls on the right. As in Seeburg orchestrions, the percussions are vacuum operated. A most inexpensive instrument (not to say cheap!), only the flute goes to 8′ pitch, the other four ranks running out at tenor C.

Smith organs usually featured tibia plena ranks instead of the tibia clausas found on most other makes of theatre instruments. The tibia plena does not "shake" as violently on the tremulant as does the tibia clausa and hence does not impart as sweet a tone to the organ. Some smaller firms purchased metal pipes but made their own wood pipes; Smith purchased even his wood pipes from suppliers such as Gottfried and Pierce.

1926 Smith in the Atascadero, California Playhouse was a real economy model with no combination action. Glen Playman's Orchestra, appearing on the Playhouse stage in 1935, dwarfs the petite 2/3 console.

This cute one-manual Seeburg-Smith console seems to have had a keyboard and pedal clavier more for appearance than utility since it's primarily a player cabinet. The upper two spool boxes play 88-note rolls and the lower one, with its controls located inaccessibly below the operator's knees, plays MSR rolls. The inclusion of a crescendo pedal on an organ this tiny is incredibly pretentious.

(left) Smith chests featured a Roosevelt-style action. Some were built with primary valves and some without; most used a magnet of F. W. Smith's own design which often caused trouble. Just before the end of production the company switched to much more reliable Reisner chest magnets. (following page) The name "Smith" was rarely mentioned in Seeburg advertising in order not to dilute the public's identification with the well-established house of Seeburg. This ad appeared in the July 15, 1916 issue of Moving Picture World.

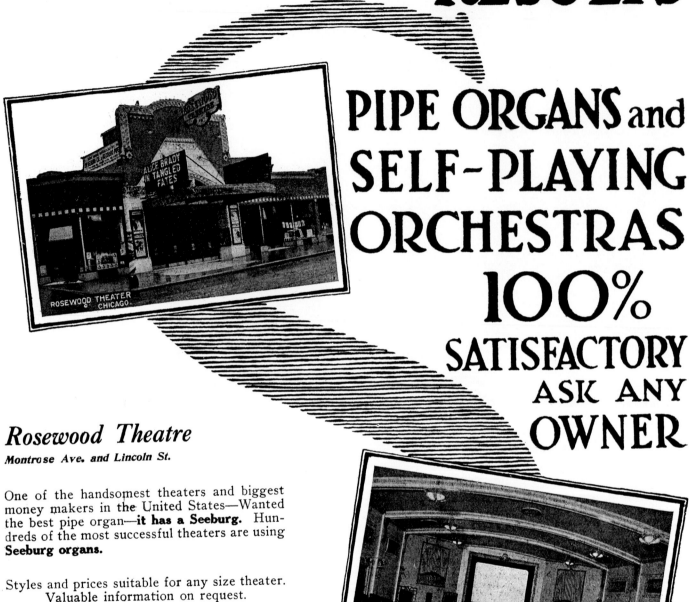

SEEBURG GUARANTEES RESULTS

PIPE ORGANS and SELF-PLAYING ORCHESTRAS

100% SATISFACTORY

ASK ANY OWNER

Rosewood Theatre

Montrose Ave. and Lincoln St.

One of the handsomest theaters and biggest money makers in the United States—Wanted the best pipe organ—**it has a Seeburg.** Hundreds of the most successful theaters are using **Seeburg organs.**

Styles and prices suitable for any size theater.
Valuable information on request.
Address nearest branch.

J. P. SEEBURG PIANO COMPANY

Manufacturers

1004 REPUBLIC BUILDING, CHICAGO

BOSTON **162 Boylston St.**	**NEW YORK** **729 Seventh Ave.**	**PHILADELPHIA** **923 Walnut St.**	**PITTSBURGH** **791 Penn St.**	**ATLANTA** **65 N. Pryor St.**
MINNEAPOLIS **80 So. 8th St.**	**BEAUMONT, TEXAS** **702 Pearl St.**	**FARGO, N. D.** **Stone Bldg.**	**ST. LOUIS** **602 Princess Theatre Bldg.**	**SAN FRANCISCO** **52 Turk St.**

The De Luxe, Detroit's Latest and Finest Theatre Equipped With a Seeburg-Smith Organ

We were convinced that you were the house for us to place our order with. Your system of construction and your many new ideas appealed to us greatly.

De Luxe Theatre Company,
F. A. Schneider, Pres.

Pictures were an experiment in the Mozart, but our business increased daily, all during the summer, and much credit is due your instrument for its share of the wonderful showing.
M. D. Gibson, Mozart Theatre, Elmira, N. Y.

A rare Seeburg-Smith catalog is reproduced on this and the following two pages. The truth is stretched in several instances: the organs in the Hippodrome and Mozart Theatres were Smith, not Seeburg-Smith organs; and only four of the twelve instruments sold to Jake Wells were actually unit organs, the other eight being Seeburg photoplayers. Seeburg advertising fancifully referred to its photoplayers as "pipe organ orchestras."

Atlanta, Ga., Dec. 12, 1916

J. P. Seeburg Piano Co., Chicago, Ill.

Gentlemen:—A feature in our circuit of theatres is the Seeburg Pipe-Organ. We have twelve of these splendid instruments and they have given most satisfactory results.

Through the Seeburg Pipe-Organ we are enabled to secure volume and effect that we could not otherwise afford, owing to a prohibitive cost in the operating of theatres where every attention must be paid and caution exercised as to the overhead expense. The Seeburg Pipe-Organ has done wonders in helping us solve this problem, I am most pleased to say. It is hardly necessary for me to say that with the addition of theatres to the circuit our assets in Seeburg Organs will be accordingly increased. We have experimented with all makes and we use the Seeburg because we know it to be the best. It is the ideal instrument for vaudeville and motion pictures.

Yours truly,

Jake Wells, The Forsyth, Atlanta, Ga.

Lobby, Mezzanine Floor, and Auditorium of Shea Hippodrome

WHAT can be achieved in the development of the motion picture theatre is splendidly illustrated in the case of Shea's Hippodrome theatre, Buffalo, which is under the direction of Harold B. Franklin. This theatre, which recently celebrated its third anniversary, has a seating capacity of over 2200 and cost almost $1,000,000. Equipped with a $25,000 Seeburg-Smith Unified Organ.

SMITH UNIT ORGANS

HE SMITH UNIT ORGANS are of notable general interest because their musical elegance and mechanical perfections are obtainable at prices and dates of delivery which are still well within the realm of reason.

From the largest diaphonic bass pipe to the most minute or concealed part, Smith Unit Organs are mechanically irreproachable. Musically resourceful in tone color—with every part proved—Smith Unit Organs represent Perfection in modern Organ Building—the work of a master organ builder.

In realistic tonal qualities—durable construction—and the ease of playing that appeals to musicians who appreciate the niceties of a modern unit console, the desire for the Smith Unit Organ is self-evident.

At the age of thirteen Frederick W. Smith began his apprenticeship as an organ builder in England, working under Peter Conacher, later working with the world renowned builder, Lewis, of London, England.

Combining their inventive genius in 1892, Mr. Smith and the late Robert Hope-Jones, became associated in the development of the Unit Pipe

In 1912, Mr. Smith established himself in his own organ factory at North Tonawanda, N. Y., and continued in the perfecting of his original ideas of the Unit methods of pipe organ construction and today after thirty-six years of practical organ building Mr. Smith backed by unlimited resources is building in his own plant in Chicago the Greatest Achievement in Pipe Organ Building, The Smith Unit Organ.

Console of a Two Manual Smith Unit Organ

A rare Smith catalog is reproduced above and on the following five pages. One wouldn't expect a sales brochure to be modest and this one is certainly no exception! Mr. Smith's attempts to posture himself as an equal of Hope-Jones and as the inventor of the horseshoe console are certainly interesting, if not credible.

Organ in Birkenhead, England. Their ideas put into practice revolutionized all accepted principles of pipe organ construction and today the successful work of these two great organ builders stands as a monument to that self conviction which is always evident in lives of famous inventors.

Mr. Smith came to America in 1903, and it was while living in Boston in 1905 that Mr. Smith first conceived the idea and designed the first Unit Type of Console with the register keys arranged in semi-circular form above the manual keys.

This design of console immediately won many friends amongst the leading organists of the country, and today Mr. Smith's original idea is being extensively adopted by the leading American organ builders.

During his associations with Mr. Smith at their first American factory established in Elmira, N. Y., in 1907, Mr. Hope-Jones paid the following tribute to his friend and colaborator: "The man at the head of our building department is Mr. F. W. Smith, than whom there is not a more skilled or scientific organ builder in America."

It was at Elmira that the first wonderful Unit Organs were given to the American public, Mr. Smith colaborating in the designing of and personally supervising every detail of construction. Today Mr. Smith has employed in his Chicago factory six of the original and most skilled mechanics who were employed by Mr. Hope-Jones and himself at their Elmira factory, each of these older employees being at the head of various departments employing the best paid and most skilled organ mechanics in America.

DESCRIPTION OF THE SMITH UNIT ORGAN

All Smith Unit Organs built under the personal supervision of Mr. Frederick W. Smith

GENERAL. The Smith Unit Organ successfully combines the advantageous musical features of a Cathedral Pipe Organ with that of a Symphony Orchestra, scientifically constructed, making it possible for a musician of ordinary talents to render music of the highest order.

CONSOLE. The control and playing of these instruments is simplified by the use of the Unit Type Console, designed by Mr. Smith.

The inclined solid ivory keys; the radiating concave pedal keys and the register or stop finger keys, arranged in semi-circular form above the manual keys, affords the musician every comfort and ease of manipulation when rendering difficult musical numbers or playing for continued long periods.

CONSTRUCTION. Every mechanical feature of a Smith Unit Organ is a perfected design resulting from years of successful and scientific organ building. The materials used in each part are those which give the best service for which that particular part is intended.

All main wood parts of the organ chests and wind trunks are made of selected weather seasoned and kiln dried white pine, weather proofed inside and out by several coats of pure shellac.

The best grades of sheep skin and bark tanned leather carefully selected as to weight and quality are used throughout.

The electrical contacts under the console keys, stop keys, in the relay and upon switch boards are of pure silver.

The metals entering into the construction of the organ chests are special alloy metals, or phosphor bronze, wherever a spring action is needed. The metal pipes are made from a special composition of pure tin or zinc, insuring perfect tonal qualities and durability. The wood pipes are constructed of high grade woods which give the best musical results obtainable.

ACTION. F. W. Smith's Patented Electric Pneumatic Action used throughout. An individual magnetic primary and pneumatic secondary valve being placed directly under each pipe, thus insuring

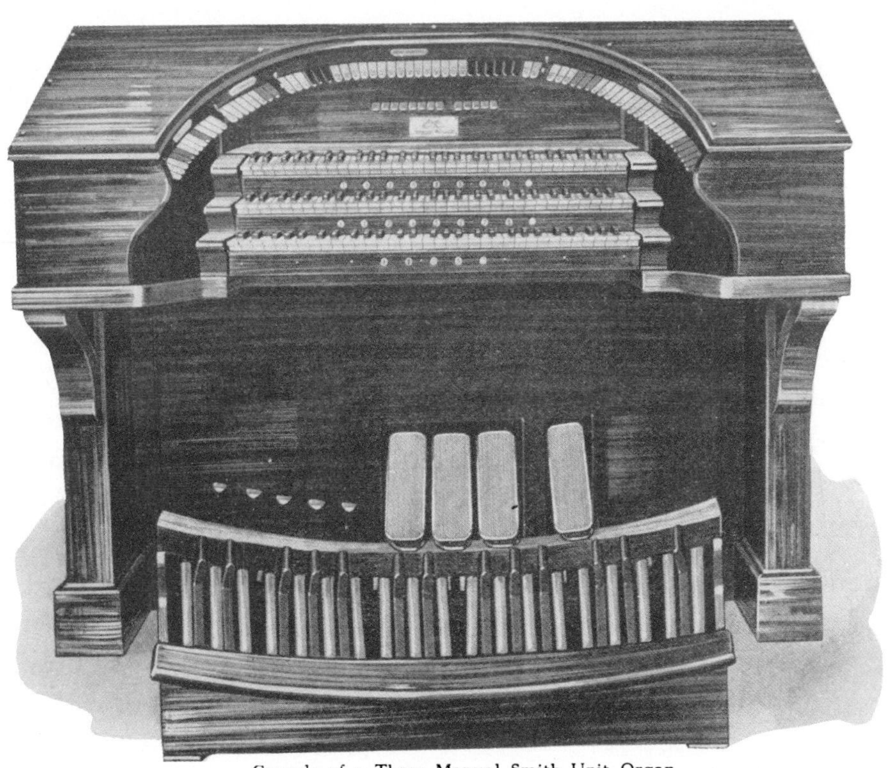

Console of a Three Manual Smith Unit Organ

STOPS AND INSTRUMENTATIONS. Every modern tone quality enters into the specifications of Smith Unit Organs. Such pleasing tones as the diaphones, tibias, violins, horns, cellos, oboes, clarinets, saxophones, tubas, trombones, flutes, harps, marimbas, bells, and xylophones, including the delicate toned celeste and vox humana stops are reproduced in a realistic quality in all Smith Unit Organs.

The trap sets when desired consist of the best quality and generous sized drums, cymbals, and effects obtainable. All being playable from the console and pedal keys and toe pistons, various touches being employed producing the most realistic effects.

Console of Four Manual Smith Unit Organ Installed in Shea's Hippodrome Theatre, Buffalo, N. Y., in 1912.

promptness of speech. The wind at all times surrounding the valve which covers an opening of generous size, leading directly to the foot of the pipe, producing an instantaneous full round musical tone.

EXPRESSION. Thick laminated sound proof wood swell shades with heavy felt edges, serving as non-conductor of sound, cover the entire front openings of each expression chamber containing its individual sets or families of pipes. The graduated control of the shades is simple and instantaneous, thus insuring the greatest flexibility of tonal expression.

In the large size organs double sets of swell shades are installed, which enables the operator to reduce the heaviset fortissimo to the most delicate pianissimo without changing the registration or composition of the pipe stops.

TONE. Every instrumentation is real in its tone qualities. This is made possible by the scientific scales used and the perfected methods which are employed in the making of and voicing of the pipes.

Every Smith Unit Organ is built and voiced especially to harmonize with the acoustic properties of the building in which it is to be installed. The different families or groups of pipes, producing the foundation tones, the wood wind, string and reed tones, as well as the percussion stops such as chimes, orchestral bells, marimbas, harps, drums, xylophones, sleigh bells, etc., are placed in separate sound proof or expression, chambers, all subject to individual expression control, thus enabling the operator to control his instrument just as a conductor would control a large symphony orchestra.

ADDED FEATURES. By means of the Smith Patented Double Touch and Pizzicato Touch Methods, introduced under the console and pedal keys, the greatest range of musical expression is obtainable; by their means the organist can bring out a melody on any special instrument, at the same time using the tones of that particular instrument in combination with other pipes as an accompaniment, this result being obtainable without raising the hands from the ivory keys.

REPRODUCING RECORD DEVICE. In placing this latest Smith Invention upon the market we believe we have filled a long felt want. This device reproduces the hand playing of an artist just as though the artist were present playing upon your Smith Unit Organ Console. Every degree of technique is reproduced in life like realism.

Unlike a piano or other musical instruments the musical expression or tone shading of a pipe organ is not dependent upon the strength or power of touch as applied to the keys. When an organ key is struck an electro-penumatic valve releases the air which causes a pipe or any family or sets of pipes to speak, these pipes being located in expression chambers, the expression of which is controlled by the manipulation of the swell shades which are under the easy control of the organist.

HOW LIFE LIKE REPRODUCTIONS ARE MADE. Mr. Smith has perfected a patented method by which every movement and exact playing of the artist is recorded at the time he is playing upon a specially designed Smith Unit Organ, thus producing a master record from which duplicates are made in the form of perforated player rolls containing a row of 137 perforations. An especially designed cabinet containing electrically driven mechanism which controls the paper record and the electrical contacts, is connected to the main switch board of the organ by a flexible multi-stranded electrical cable. The reproducing device can be attached to any Smith Unit Organ, thus bringing to your theatre or home the actual playing of the world's foremost organists. A large library of records is already available and from time to time additional records are being made, thus preserving for all time the originial playing of the organist, just as the phonograph has recorded for all time the voices of the great singers.

Cabinet Containing the Reproducing Record Device and Controlling Mechanism

"My Smith Unit Organ has never given the least trouble, in fact trouble is unknown. I now know the organ and would not trade it for two of any other make, or would not sell it for twice what I paid for it if I could not secure another Smith Unit Organ." — W. P. Archibald, Owner, Garden Theatre, Burlingame, Calif. Dated January 29, 1920.

"From the very first time I heard the Smith Unit Organ play up to the present time I have been congratulating myself daily for my decision in choosing this instrument, and you doubtless are aware of the hard time I had in arriving at my decision, as I was offered all kinds of propositions and was prevailed upon from all sides, by other organ builders."—S. Gordon, Owner, Orpheus Theatre, San Rafael, Calif. Dated February 10, 1920.

"Upon visiting your plant in Chicago I was so greatly impressed with the character and earnestness of the mechanics employed in your factory that I feel absolutely safe in placing my order with you for a Smith Unit Organ, knowing full well that my instrument will have the same high standard of construction which is so evident in all the Smith Unit Organs I inspected." — Statement by Wm. T. Pierce, Kewanee, Ill., February 27, 1920.

"The Smith Unit Organ has more than fulfilled its purpose. I hear a lot about the music and am convinced that music of this really beautiful character is bringing me a better and more permanent patronage."—Henry Goldman, Owner Grand-Colonial Theatre, Green Bay, Wis. Dated February 15, 1918.

"Early in January of this year we installed one of your organs, and to say that we are pleased is putting it very mild, as we are receiving comments daily from our hundreds of patrons.

"We consider that it is the greatest drawing card we have added to our theatre since we opened it, as there are requests daily from our patrons for special selections, which is positive proof that our patrons are as much pleased as we are with the instrument.

"Any exhibitor who wishes to purchase an instrument should see and hear a SMITH Organ and get your prices before buying, and we will be only too glad to give a demonstration of same and show the workings of same.

"We have a young lady handling our organ, who never played an organ until we installed ours, and from the number of applause she receives, we feel that when she has a few weeks longer time on same that she will be able to handle the largest features better than any orchestra that we might select from the Beaver Valley.

"Trusting that I will be called upon at any time to demonstrate this WONDERFUL SMITH ORGAN."—John M. Strub, Manager, Alhambra Theatre, Beaver Falls, Pa. Dated July 12, 1916.

EXPRESSIONS FROM TESTIMONIAL LETTERS

THE ORIGINALS OF WHICH ARE ON FILE IN OUR OFFICE

"It affords me great pleasure to tell you how highly pleased we are with the magnificent instrument installed by your company in Shea's Hippodrome.

"You are at liberty to use our name at any time as being perfectly satisfied with the purchase of a Smith Unit Organ." —Isador Moses, Manager Shea's Hippodrcme, Buffalo, N. Y. Dated August 30, 1915.

"I find the Smith Unit Organ in a class by itself and prefer it to some instruments costing two or three times the cost of my instrument."—J. E. Smith, Owner, Smith's Theatre, Pittsburgh, Pa. Dated August 7, 1916.

"So far I haven't had a bit of trouble and the instrument is growing more in favor with me and the patrons of the house. So far I haven't seen anything that can beat the Smith Unit Organ for tone and durability."—W. E. Richmond, Exhibitor, Pittsburgh, Pa. Dated August 19, 1917.

"I can only speak in the highest terms of your workmanship on this contract. We use the organ almost continuously from 11 to 12 hours a day, 7 days a week, for the past several years. Would be pleased at any time to go into detail with any one who may wish to purchase an organ."—Herman E. Schultz, Musical Director, Shea's Theatre, Buffalo, N. Y. Dated August 29, 1917.

"Personally I feel that you have given us a good organ; you certainly are to be commended for the prompt manner of installation. The lodge after hearing the organ and inspecting the installation unanimously ratified our action in every particular."—W. A. Russell, Chairman Organ Committee, Highland Lodge F. & A. M., Buffalo, N. Y. Dated September 2, 1916.

"It is with pleasure I can write you telling you how highly pleased we are with the results obtained with your splendid instrument installed in our Mozart Theatre two years ago. Our business increased daily and much credit is due the Smith Unit Organ for a share of the credit of the wonderful showing."—M. D. Gibson, Manager Mozart Theatre, Elmira, N. Y. Dated September 30, 1916.

SMITH
UNIT ORGANS
FOR
Theatre, Church, Residence, Lodge
Musical Elegance *and* Mechanical Perfection

Sales and Demonstration Rooms
339 SOUTH WABASH AVENUE
Smith Unit Organ Co.
Factory-General Offices
419 W. ERIE STREET, CHICAGO, ILL.

This Smith ad ran in The Diapason *through 1924. The console pictured was built in 1913 for Shea's Hippodrome Theatre in Buffalo, New York, one of only two four-manual organs Smith ever built.*

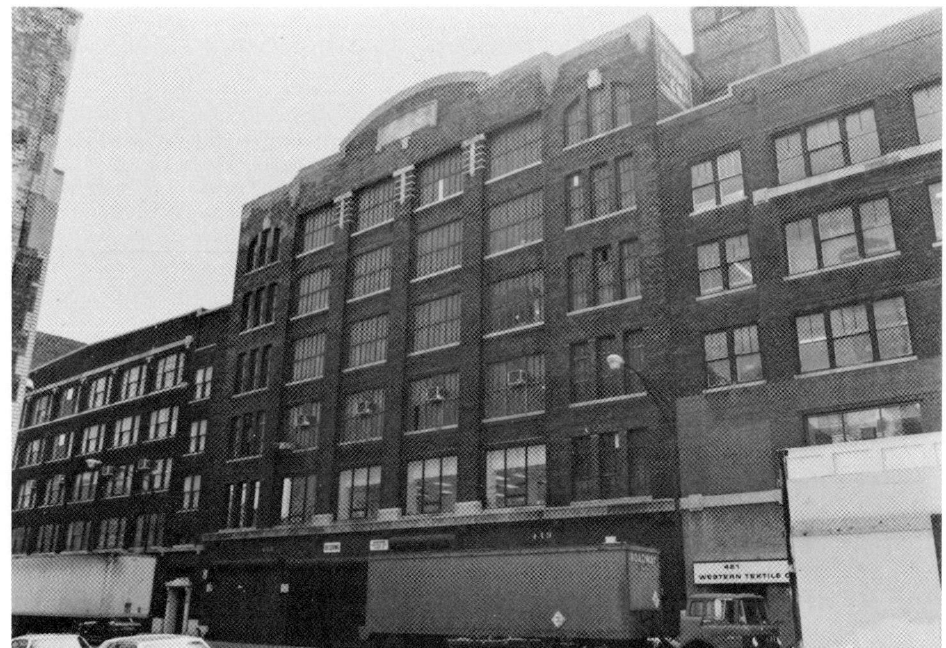

Seeburg-Smith and Smith organs were built in this building at 419 W. Erie Street in Chicago. The building also housed the Seeburg coin-operated piano operation in the teens.

SMITH OPUS LIST

CITY/STATE	LOCATION	SIZE	YR	BLWR	HP	WP	NAMEPLATE/REMARKS
ALASKA							
Ketchikan	Liberty Th.	2/4					Leathurby-Smith; later moved to Alki Natatorium, Seattle, Washington.
CALIFORNIA							
Atascadero	Playhouse Th.	2/3	1926				
Auburn	Auburn Th.	2/4	1925				Leathurby-Smith.
Berkeley	Oaks Th.	2/	1925				Leathurby-Smith.
Burlingame	Garden (Broadway) Th.	2/					
Coronado	Art Gallery Th.						
Covina	Covina Th.		1923	15477			
Fort Bragg	Liberty Th.						
Glendora	Glendora (Mission) Th.	2/7	1923	15129	2	10"	Smith.
Hayward	Hayward Th.	2/					
Hollywood	Page Military Academy	2/7					For auditorium.
	Page Military Academy	2/5					For practice studio.
Long Beach	Egyptian Th.	2/	1924				Smith.
	Home Th.	2/4					
	Mission Th.						
	State Th.	2/4					
Los Angeles	Arcade Th.	2/					
	Palace Th.	2/15					
Marysville	State Th.	2/7					
Napa	Hippodrome (Fox) Th.	2/11	1923				
Oakland	Broadway Th.	2/					
	Golden State (Gateway) Th.	2/7	1926				With roll player.
	Hotel Leamington	3/14					
	KROW Radio	2/6					
	New Fruitvale Th.	2/7	1926				
	Orpheum (Twelfth St.) (Follies) (Twelfth St.) Th.	2/					Located at 568-12th Street.
	Piedmont Th.		1920	I181	2	10"	Seeburg-Smith; opened as Kadie Hilber Theatre.
Oxnard	unidentified theatre	2/3					
Palo Alto	Fox Stanford Th.	3/10	1925	16848	5	10"	Leathurby-Smith.
	Varsity Th.	2/7					Leathurby-Smith.
Pasadena	Pasadena Th.	3/					
Pittsburgh	California Th.	2/9	1924	15874			
Porterville	Monache Th.	2/10					Smith.
San Francisco	Leathurby-Smith store	2/7					Leathurby-Smith.
	Lincoln Th.	2/					
	Regal Th.	2/6	1926				Opened as Pompeii Theatre.
	Strand Th.	2/7					
	Verdi (World) Th.						

CITY/STATE	LOCATION	SIZE	YR	BLWR	HP	WP	NAMEPLATE/REMARKS
San Jose	unidentified theatre	2/5					
San Mateo	Balboa Th.	2/8	1925				Leathurby-Smith.
San Pedro	California Th.		1923	14187			
San Rafael	Orpheum Th.						
Santa Maria	Santa Maria Th.	2/9					Leathurby-Smith.
Stockton	National Th.	2/					
Turlock	Turlock Th.	2/6					Smith.
COLORADO							
Colorado Springs	Odeon Th.		1923	L624	2	10″	Smith.
CONNECTICUT							
Hartford	Grand Th.		1918	9320			Seeburg-Smith.
Stamford	Rialto Th.						
GEORGIA							
Atlanta	Strand Vaudette Co.		1919	G146	1½	10″	Seeburg-Smith.
	Tudor Th.		1918	F449	2	10″	Seeburg-Smith.
ILLINOIS							
Aurora	Fox Th.		1923	14439			Smith.
Chicago	Bell Th.						
	Biltmore Th.	3/	1921	H707	1½	10″	Seeburg-Smith.
	Blaine Th.						
	Brookline Th.						
	Dearborn Th.		1922	13086			Smith.
	Langley Th.		1916	6938			Seeburg-Smith.
			1916	7375			
	New President Th.						
	Rosewood Th.						Seeburg-Smith.
	Seeburg-Smith showroom		1918	9320	5		Seeburg-Smith.
	Smith showroom	3/	1922				Smith; located at 339 South Wabash.
	Wicker Park Th.						
Cicero	Clifford Th.	2/	1923	14559			Smith.
Danville	Fischer Th.						
Elgin	Rialto Th.	3/	1923	14426			Smith.
Kewanee	Peerless Th.	2/10	1921	J132	2	10″	Seeburg-Smith.
Nokomis	New Palace Th.						Seeburg-Smith.
INDIANA							
Anderson	Riviera Th.						
Brazil	Sourwine Th.	2/	1919	G381	2	10″	Seeburg-Smith.
Elkhart	Orpheum Th.	2/	1920	10866	2	10″	Seeburg-Smith.
Goshen	Lincoln Th.						
Indianapolis	Alhambra Th.	3/11	1920	10999	5	10″	Seeburg-Smith.
	Rialto (Family) (Lincoln Square) Th.	2/7					Seeburg-Smith.
Lafayette	Luna Th.		1918	F462	2		Seeburg-Smith.
	Mars Th.		1920	I518	2	10″	Seeburg-Smith.
Michigan City	Tivoli Th.	2/9					Smith.
Peru	Loomis Th.		1921	J380	2	8″	Smith.
			1921	J427		10″	
Richmond	Washington Th.	2/					
South Bend	Castle Th.		1920	H332	1½	10″	Seeburg-Smith.
	LaSalle Th.						
	Linden Th.	2/4					
Warsaw	Centennial Th.		1917	6681			Seeburg-Smith.
IOWA							
Boone	Rialto Th.	2/7					Smith.
Council Bluffs	Broadway Th.	2/8	1922				Smith.
Muscastine	Palace Th.	2/	1918				Seeburg-Smith.
Waterloo	Strand Th.	2/	1920	11079	2	10″	Seeburg-Smith.
KENTUCKY							
Madisonville	Garrick Th.	2/					
LOUISIANA							
Lafayette	Jefferson Th.		1920	H334	1½	10″	Seeburg-Smith.
Lake Charles	Paramount Th.	2/	1920	I183	2	10″	Seeburg-Smith.
MICHIGAN							
Detroit	DeLuxe Th.		1918	F624	5	12″	Seeburg-Smith.
Niles	Riviera Th.						
MONTANA							
Great Falls	Imperial Th.		1924	16099			
NEW JERSEY							
Jersey City	Fulton Th.	2/	1921	J355	1½	10″	Smith.
			1921	J414	3	10″	
New Brunswick	Rivoli Th.		1921	J207	3	10″	Smith.
Nutley	Nutley Th.	2/8					Seeburg-Smith.

CITY/STATE	LOCATION	SIZE	YR	BLWR	HP	WP	NAMEPLATE/REMARKS
Passaic	Capitol Th.	2/	1921	J120	3		Seeburg-Smith organ; Kramer nameplate.
Paterson	Plaza Th.	2/6	1921	J131	2	10″	Seeburg-Smith.
Union Hill	Lincoln Th.		1920	I241	1½	10″	Seeburg-Smith; Union Hill was later known as Union City.
NEW YORK							
Brooklyn	Beverly Th.		1919	G382	1½		Seeburg-Smith.
			1919	H329	1½		
			1919	H627	3	15″	
Buffalo	Shea's Hippodrome (Centre) Th.	4/16	1913	B446	5	12″	Smith.
Elmira	Mozart Th.		1914	C346	1	10″	Smith.
Far Rockaway	Columbia Th.	2/8					
Long Island City	Forest Hill Th.	4/16	1922	11951			Smith; with 4-rank echo.
			1922	13568			
Mt. Vernon	Westchester Th.						
New York	Belmont Th.	2/	1921	I453	2		Seeburg-Smith.
	Cosmo Th.	2/8	1921	J415	3	10″	Smith organ; Kramer nameplate.
	Delancey Street Th.		1921	J169	5	10″	Seeburg-Smith.
	New Douglas		1921	J416	5	10″	Smith.
	New Strand Th.		1916				Located at 78 East Broadway.
	Plaza Music Hall	2/	1919				Seeburg-Smith; located on Madison Avenue.
	Superior Th.						Located at 81st Street and First Avenue.
	34th Street Th.		1920	I134	2	10″	Seeburg-Smith.
Niagara Falls	Cataract Th.		1914	C121	1	10″	Smith.
Utica	Benber Th.		1917	F424	2	10″	Seeburg-Smith.
NORTH CAROLINA							
Charlotte	Imperial Th.	2/	1920	H330	1½	10″	Seeburg-Smith.
	Superior Th.	2/					
Gastonia	Gastonian Th.	2/					
Hendersonville	Queen Th.	2/					
Pinehurst	Carolina Th.	2/	1922				Smith.
OHIO							
East Liverpool	Strand Th.		1916	E565	1	10″	Smith.
Toledo	Alhambra Th.		1913	A757	1	10″	Smith.
OREGON							
Klamath Falls	Pine Tree Th.	2/5					
Portland	Alameda Th.	2/4					Leathurby-Smith.
	Blue Bird Th.	2/4					Leathurby-Smith.
	Granada Th.						
	Heathman Hotel	2/5	1926	18588	3		Leathurby-Smith.
	Laurelhurst (Burnside) Th.	2/5					Leathurby-Smith.
	Roseway Th.	2/5	1926				
Salem	Liberty Th.	2/	1924	15483			
Tillamook	Coliseum Th.	2/5					
PENNSYLVANIA							
Allentown	Regent Th.	2/	1917				Seeburg-Smith.
Beaver Falls	Colonial Th.		1916	E214	1	10″	Smith.
	Regent (Alhambra) Th.	2/	1916	D656	1	10″	Smith.
Bellevue	Bellevue Th.						
Braddock	Braddock Th.						
Brookville	Brown (Columbia) Th.						Seeburg-Smith.
Brooklyn	Brown Th.						
Brownsville	Bison Th.	2/	1915	D559	1	10″	Smith.
Butler	Grand Th.	2/					
	Lyric Th.	2/					
Cannonsville	E. T. Beedle & Sons						
Columbia	Elks Opera House	2/4					Seeburg-Smith.
Connellsville	Paramount-Soisson Th.		1921	12561			Seeburg-Smith.
East Pittsburgh	Frederick Th.	2/					
	Sedler Th.	2/					
Elliott	Elliott (Richmond) Th.		1915	D519	1	6″	Smith.
Franklin	Orpheum Th.	2/					
Greenfield	Smith Th.						
Greensburg	Grand Th.	2/					
	Manos Th.		1916	E224	1	10″	Smith.
	Strand Th.						
Homestead	Stahl (Leona) Th.	2/	1919	G152	2	10″	Seeburg-Smith.
Jeanette	Eagle Th.						
Johnstown	National Th.	2/					Seeburg-Smith.
Kittaning	Wick Th.	2/					
McKeesport	Liberty Th.		1921	J468	2	10″	Smith.
Millvale	Grant Th.	2/					
Mt. Washington	Polk Th.	2/					
Newcastle	William Penn Th.	2/	1920	H636	1½	10″	Seeburg-Smith.
Oil City	Vanango Th.	2/					
Philadelphia	Palm Th.		1918	F447	1½	10″	Seeburg-Smith.

CITY/STATE	LOCATION	SIZE	YR	BLWR	HP	WP	NAMEPLATE/REMARKS
Pittsburgh	Metropolitan Th.						
	Shiloh Th.	2/	1916	E143	1	10″	Smith.
	Smith's Th.						
Point Marion	Barney Th.		1921	12828			Seeburg-Smith.
Republic	Charles Johns						
Rochester	Majestic Th.		1920	H637	1½	10″	Seeburg-Smith.
Sharpsburg	Main Th.						
Somerset	Pasco Th.						
Vandergrift	Iris Th.	2/					
SOUTH CAROLINA							
Greenville	Casino Th.		1918	F451	1½	10″	Seeburg-Smith.
TEXAS							
Beaumont	Liberty Th.	2/					
Houston	Rialto Th.	3/	1922	13104			Smith.
Port Arthur	Strand Th.	2/					
Rosenburg	Liberty Th.		1919				Seeburg-Smith.
Wichita Falls	Strand Th.	2/6	1920	H331	3	10″	Seeburg-Smith.
UTAH							
Logan	Capitol Th.	2/8	1924				
VIRGINIA							
Hampton	Scott Th.		1921	12577			Seeburg-Smith.
Norfolk	American Th.	2/					Seeburg-Smith.
	Granby (Lee) Th.	2/					Seeburg-Smith.
	Wells Th.	2/					Seeburg-Smith.
Portsmouth	Olympic Th.						
Richmond	Bijou (Strand) Th.		1921	J407	2	10″	Smith.
WASHINGTON							
Chehalis	Liberty Th.	2/	1924	15536			
Enumclaw	Liberty (Enumclaw) Th.	2/9	1924	16423			Leathurby-Smith.
Olympia	Capitol Th.	2/9					
Seattle	Gala Th.	2/5	1924				
	Madrona Gardens Th.	2/5	1924				
Tacoma	Victory Th.	2/5	1927				
WEST VIRGINIA							
Wierton	Rex Th.	2/					
WISCONSIN							
Green Bay	Grand Colonial Th.		1917	F317	1	10″	Seeburg-Smith.
Kenosha	Butterfly Th.		1923	L836	1	10″	Smith.
Portage	Home Th.	2/					
Stoughton	Stoughton (Badger) Th.	2/6	1920	I572	2	10″	Seeburg-Smith; with roll player.
WYOMING							
Cheyenne	Lincoln Th.	2/6					
MANITOBA, CANADA							
Bandon	Strand Th.	2/6					
Winnipeg	Lyceum Th.						
ONTARIO, CANADA							
Niagara Falls	Strand (Queen) Th.		1915	D57	2	10″	Smith.

COLO. 6466
RES. COLO. 4203

FACTORY 2948-2954 EAST WALNUT STREET

E. A. Spencer

ORGAN BUILDER

PIPE ORGANS FOR
CHURCHES, HOMES
AND AUDITORIUMS

PASADENA, CAL.

Edwin A. Spencer (1870-1947) was born in Canada[1] and received his early training in organ building there.[2] He was associated with Murray M. Harris as plant superintendent beginning in 1906 and held that position through the reorganizations of the company, first to the Johnston Organ & Piano Manufacturing Co. and later to the California Organ Company in Van Nuys, California. Mr. Spencer was violently opposed to the idea of getting into unit theatre organ business; he preferred straight classic instruments.[4]

In 1917 negotiations were begun which resulted in the merger of the California Organ Company and the American Photo Player Company to form the Robert-Morton Company. The firm's executives wanted to build unit theatre organs at the Van Nuys factory and were forced to transfer Mr. Spencer to the Berkeley, California plant of the American Photo Player Company because of his opposition to the idea.[5] After spending a couple of years as the Berkeley plant superintendent, Spencer appeared to recant his opposition concerning unified theatre organs and designed an instrument called the Foto-Orchestra which was built at the Berkeley facility.[6] He really never found making theatre instruments satisfying, however, so he left Berkeley in 1922 to establish his own firm in Pasadena, California.[7]

Operating his own shop, Mr. Spencer was free to concentrate on building the church organs he loved most, although he did make at least one theatre instrument, no doubt just to keep the wolves away from the door. This organ was a two-manual in the Roosevelt Theatre in Los Angeles.

The Spencer organ that played more popular music and was heard by more people than any other Spencer product started its career, ironically enough, as a church organ. Spencer had an agreement with music retailer Sherman, Clay & Co. to handle sales of his organs, and a three-manual model with 18 or 19 ranks was installed in their San Francisco showroom. Its nameplate read "Sherman, Clay Cathedral Organ." Apparently no cathedrals were interested in the instrument and it was acquired by KFRC Radio in the early 1930s at a very low price in exchange for radio advertising.[8]

The organ had few unified ranks, being mostly straight, and it also sported fan tremulants *a la* Austin. In its original state it must have sounded dreadful performing popular music. Standard bellows tremulants soon replaced the fans and during the tenure of organist George Wright the organ was souped up in other ways as well. One of the changes made by George was to replace five of the straight ranks on the swell manual with tibias playing at 8′, 4′, 2 2/3′, 2′ and 1 3/5′ pitches. Even though these five tibias were straight ranks, the musical effect was that of a unified theatre organ.[9]

Mr. Spencer operated his firm until his death in 1947. He had been joined in 1939 by Leonard Dowling who was formerly with the Artcraft Organ Company. In 1940 Dowling became a partner although the firm did not change names. Following Spencer's death Dowling continued the business under the name Spencer-Dowling.[9]

One aspect of the career of E. A. Spencer has always puzzled the author: The instruments built in his Pasadena shop contained the cheapest materials he could obtain and featured some of the most Rube Goldberg mechanical designs to be found in American organ building. In contrast, the Murray M. Harris organs built while Spencer was plant superintendent were among the finest quality instruments ever built.

Edwin A. Spencer
(1870-1947)

Console of the Spencer organ in the KFRC radio studios in San Francisco.

The Spencer factory in Pasadena is still standing in 1986.

HERMAN STAHL

Herman Stahl conducted a business of supplying organ parts to the trade in the early 1920s. By the mid 1920s his ads no longer appeared in *The Diapason*. Records of the Kinetic Engineering Company reveal that two blowers were sold to him with theatre destinations. A 1½ horsepower unit rated at 5″ wind, #0720B, was shipped to the Strand Theatre, Greenville, Pennsylvania in 1926 and another 1½ horsepower blower rated at 6″ wind, #P341B, was shipped to the Guthrie Theatre in Grove City, Pennsylvania in 1927. It is not known if these were for new organs or were merely replacement blowers for existing instruments.

Organ Consoles?

Actions--Electric, Pneumatic?

Finished Products?

Wood-Pipes?

Generators?

To quote you, is a pleasure

Herman Stahl

209 W. 5th St. - ERIE, PA.

Stahl ad in the December 1920 Diapason. *Only parts are offered; no mention is made of complete organs.*

THE STEERE ORGAN COMPANY

ESTABLISHED 1867

273 ELM STREET

TELEPHONE 1250 **WESTFIELD, MASSACHUSETTS**

John Wesley Steer was employed as a voicer by the William A. Johnson Organ Company of Westfield, Massachusetts when he left that firm in 1866 to build organs on his own. When he was joined one year later by George William Turner, who also worked for Johnson as an action maker, the partnership of Steer and Turner was formed. Following a fire in their Westfield factory the firm moved to Springfield, Massachusetts in 1879 and sometime around 1880 Steer changed the spelling of his name to Steere. The workmanship and tonal qualities of Steere and Turner instruments were among the finest of the day.

J. W. Steere (1824-1900)

G. W. Turner (1829-1908)

WOOLSEY HALL, YALE UNIVERSITY

When you visit Woolsey Hall at Yale University, you will hear *another* beautiful

Steere Organ

"I believe that I have given the contract to the best firm in the country. * * * The voicing throughout seems to me to combine all the fine qualities of the most advanced ideas, without the attending faults. For the first time in this country I have heard some stops sound as I think they should sound. The organ is all that I expected it would be, and that is certainly sufficient.

"The manner in which you carried out the contract exceeded my optimistic expectations. Your firm certainly deserves its prosperity, and its reputation for the highest class of workmanship and integrity in business."

Faithfully, (Sd.) H. B. JEPSON,

Professor of Applied Music and University Organist, Yale University.

The Steere Organ Company

Westfield, Mass.

Organ Architects and Builders

Churches Auditoriums Theatres Residences

This Steere ad appeared in the October 1921 Diapason. ***At this time the company's output was mostly parts for Skinner organs. The organ referred to in this ad, the large four-manual instrument in Woolsey Hall, was the firm's magnum opus. Later rebuilt and enlarged by Skinner, this organ stands today as one of the outstanding examples of American organ building in the romantic style.***

Turner left the partnership around 1890, after which the firm became known as J. W. Steere & Sons. This name lasted until 1901 when it was changed to the J. W. Steere & Son Organ Company. For a brief time after leaving Steere, from 1893 to 1894, George Turner was in partnership with one of Steere's sons using the old Steere & Turner name.[1,2]

The last change of name for the firm occurred in 1919 when it became the Steere Organ Company. The firm's Springfield factory burned early in 1920 after which they moved back to Westfield, purchasing the old Johnson factory building then occupied by the Horsewhip Company. This was coming full circle inasmuch as it was here that the firm's original partners first learned organ building. Early in 1921 the Steere Organ Company was purchased by the Skinner Organ Company. It was a perfect amalgamation: Skinner's sales were exceeding his factory capacity while Steere sales were waning. Steere products were of the same high quality as Skinner's and the Steere factory superintendent, Harry F. Van Wart, had been a Skinner man for some years previously. For another year or so the Steere firm continued to advertise Steere organs although the primary output of the factory was parts for Skinner instruments. By 1922 Steere advertising ceased and by 1924 the Westfield plant was closed.[3,4]

Three organs built by the Steere companies are known to have been installed in theatres. The Mabel Tainter Memorial Theatre in Menomonie, Wisconsin purchased a 2/29 Steere & Turner tracker organ in 1890 at a cost of $4,160. This instrument, the firm's opus 300 and the second organ ever installed in an American theatre, has been restored and is still intact in its original home as of 1984. It is powered by Spencer Orgoblo #1066, installed in 1907. The second known Steere theatre instrument was

The Mabel Tainter Memorial Theatre in Menomonie, Wisconsin is the home of the second organ ever installed in an American theatre, a 2/29 Steere & Turner tracker. Its console sits in the alcove to the left of the stage, the pipes being located behind the grille directly above it.

sold in 1914 to the Bijou Theatre in the firm's home town of Springfield, Massachusetts. A three-manual organ, it was powered by Spencer Orgoblo #5980.

The third known Steere organ in a theatre was sold to the Olympia (Paramount) in New Haven, Connecticut in 1915. This 4/14 fully unified instrument was on high pressure (probably 10″) typical of Steere organs of that period and was powered by a 7½-horsepower Spencer Orgoblo.

There was to have been a fourth Steere organ in a theatre: Late in 1919 a contract was signed for a 4/35 straight organ with a five-rank echo division for the Howard Theatre in Atlanta, Georgia.[5] Alas, the Steere factory burned on February 17, 1920 and the theatre instead purchased a 3/14 Robert-Morton.

4/14 STEERE THEATRE ORGAN
Olympia (Paramount) Theatre, New Haven, Connecticut

These specifications appeared in the November 1915 issue of *The Diapason.*

SWELL SECTION 1.

A. Wood Diapason, 16 ft., 97 pipes.
B. Diapason, 8 ft., 73 pipes.
C. Viole da Gamba, 8 ft., 73 pipes.
D. Vibrant Strings, 8 ft., 73 pipes.
E. Double Flute, 8 ft., 73 pipes.
F. Clarinet, 8 ft., 61 pipes.
G. Trumpet, 8 ft., 73 pipes.

SWELL SECTION 2.

H. Bourdon, 16 ft., 97 pipes.
J. Horn Diapason, 8 ft., 73 pipes.
K. Viole d'Orchestre, 8 ft., 73 pipes.
L. Viole Celeste, 8 ft., 73 pipes.
M. Oboe, 8 ft., 61 pipes.
N. Vox Humana, 8 ft., 61 pipes.
O. Tuba, 16 ft., 97 pipes.

TRAPS.

AA. Chimes.
BB. Harp.
CC. Sleigh Bells.
DD. Swiss Bells.
EE. Triangle.
GG. Snare Drum.
HH. Bass Drum.
JJ. Cymbals.

PEDAL ORGAN.

1. Diapason (from A), 16 ft., 32 notes.
2. Bourdon (from H), 16 ft., 32 notes.
3. Great Flute (from A), 8 ft., 32 notes.
4. Stopped Flute (from H), 8 ft., 32 notes.
5. Octave Flute (from A), 4 ft., 32 notes.
6. Trombone (from O), 16 ft., 32 notes.
7. Tromba (from O), 8 ft., 32 notes.
8. Clarion (from O), 4 ft., 32 notes.
9. Chimes (from AA), 20 notes.
10. Bass Drum (single stroke; from HH), lowest octave.
11. Bass Drum (roll; from HH), lowest octave.
12. Snare Drum (roll; from GG), second octave.
13. Cymbals (from JJ), lowest octave.

FIRST MANUAL—(CHOIR).

14. Viola da Gamba (from C), 8 ft., 73 notes.
15. Vibrant Strings (from D), 8 ft., 73 notes.
16. Double Flute (from E), 8 ft., 73 notes.
17. Flute (from A), 4 ft., 73 notes.
18. Harmonic Piccolo (from A), 2 ft., 61 notes.
19. Clarinet (from F), 8 ft., 61 notes.
20. Celesta (harp; from HH)-BB, 49 notes.
21. Sleigh Bells (from CC), 25 bells.
22. Chimes (from AA), 20 notes.
23. Triangle (from EE), second octave.
24. Snare Drum (from GG), lowest octave.
25. Swiss Bells (from DD), 20 bells.
26. Tremolo (1st and 2nd Manuals).

SECOND MANUAL-(GREAT).

27. Diapason (from B), 8 ft., 73 notes.
28. Great Flute (from A), 8 ft., 73 notes.
29. Double Flute (from E), 8 ft., 73 notes.
30. Viola da Gamba (from C), 8 ft., 73 notes.
31. Vibrant Strings (from D), 8 ft., 73 notes.
32. Flute (from A), 4 ft., 73 notes.
33. Harmonic Piccolo (from A), 2 ft., 73 notes.
34. Trumpet (from G), 8 ft., 73 notes.
35. Clarinet (from F), 8 ft., 73 notes.
36. Triangle (from EE), lowest octave.
37. Snare Drum (from GG), second octave.

THIRD MANUAL—(SWELL)

38. Bourdon (from H), 16 ft., 73 notes.
39. Horn Diapason (from J), 8 ft., 73 notes.
40. Gedeckt (from H), 8 ft., 73 notes.
41. Viole d'Orchestre (from K), 8 ft., 73 notes.
42. Viole Celeste (from L), 8 ft., 73 notes.
43. Flute (from H), 4 ft., 73 notes.
44. Trombone (from O), 16 ft., 73 notes.
45. Tuba (from O), 8 ft., 73 notes.
46. Oboe (from M), 8 ft., 61 notes.
47. Vox Humana (from N), 8 ft., 61 notes.
48. Clarion (from O), 4 ft., 73 notes.
49. Tremolo (third and fourth Manuals).

FOURTH MANUAL—(SOLO).

50. Horn Diapason (from J), 8 ft., 73 notes.
51. Gedeckt (from H), 8 ft., 73 notes.
52. Viole Celeste (from K and L), 8 ft., 73 notes.
53. Flute (from H), 4 ft., 73 notes.
54. Trombone (from O), 16 ft., 73 notes.
55. Tuba (from O), 8 ft., 73 notes.
56. Oboe (from M), 8 ft., 61 notes.
57. Vox Humana (from N), 8 ft., 61 notes.
58. Clarion (from O), 4 ft., 73 notes.
59. Celesta (Harp; from BB), 49 notes.
60. Sleigh Bells (from CC), 25 bells.
61. Swiss Bells (from DD), 20 bells.
62. Chimes (from AA), 20 notes.

EDWARD STEIN

Edward Stein of Baltimore, Maryland, was possibly a member of the family of Adam Stein who had been manager of the Roosevelt factory in Baltimore in the 1880s.[1] Records of the Spencer Turbine Company show that blower #19779 was sold to him in 1927 and shipped to the Ritz Theatre in Baltimore. Whether or not this blower powered an organ with a Stein nameplate is unknown to the author.

STEVENS ORGAN COMPANY

The pipe organ department of the Stevens company was started about 1908 by Allan G. Sparling, who moved to Cleveland in 1911 to join the Votteler-Hettche company. This firm later evolved into the Votteler-Holtkamp-Sparling Company.[1] The Stevens firm was apparently engaged in the building of reed organs and pianos as well, but a disastrous flood in 1913 put the firm out of the pipe organ business.[2] One Stevens theatre installation is known: a 1913 two-manual instrument in the Quimby Theatre, Zanesville, Ohio.

Stevens Organ Company

Manufacturer's of

TUBULAR AND ELECTRIC PNEUMATIC CHURCH ORGANS

Look Into Our Work and Become Convinced of Its Merit

MARIETTA - - OHIO

Stevens ad in the July 1911 Diapason.

The Majestic Theatre in Erie, Pennsylvania opened in 1904 and installed a 2/8 Tellers-Kent in 1918. A new 3/24 was installed in 1921 after the name was changed to the Perry Theatre. This photo was taken after the house was renamed Shea's in 1931.[7]

This relatively petite console operated the 4/32 Tellers-Sommerhof in the Columbia Theatre in Erie, Pennsylvania. A nearly identical console graced the 4/33 Tellers-Kent in the Columbia Theatre in Sharon, Pennsylvania.

These interesting theatres, all unidentified, were the homes of Tellers-Kent organs.

Tellers-Kent Organ Company
ERIE, PA.

Close personal supervision of all parts of our instruments during construction, made possible by over thirty years' experience as practical organ builders, and the use of only the best materials obtainable, insures a product which will pass the most rigid examination upon completion.

Correspondence Solicited. Catalogue on Request.

A typically conservative Tellers-Kent ad from the October 1924 Diapason.

TELLERS - KENT ORGAN CO.
ERIE, PENNA.

Incorporated **Established 1906**

Builders of

Electric and Pneumatic Pipe Organs

for Churches, Halls, Residences & Theaters

CORRESPONDENCE SOLICITED

Tellers-Kent ad from the June 1918 Diapason. *Previous to 1918 a nearly identical ad ran for several years with the Tellers-Sommerhof name.*

2/7 TELLERS-KENT THEATRE ORGAN, OPUS 466
Winthrop Theatre, Winthrop, Massachusetts
This contract typifies the unit organs produced by the firm in the late 1920s.

Memorandum of Agreement

Made this 14th day of September A. D. 1927, by and between the **TELLERS-KENT ORGAN CO.,** Church Organ Builders, of Erie, Pennsylvania, party of the first part, and Charles L. Hatch of Winthrop, Mass.

party of the second part.

Witnesseth. That the party of the first part, for and in consideration of the covenants and agreements hereinafter set forth to be performed by the party of the second part, does hereby agree to build an Organ after and according to the specifications hereto annexed, dated Sept. 13, 1927, (xxxxxxxxxxxxxxx) (special scheme) of the very best materials and in the most thorough and workmanlike manner, and delivered set up in Winthrop Theatre, Winthrop, Mass.

in good order, complete, ready for use, ~~within~~ on or before December 1, 1927 from date, or as soon thereafter as possible if delayed by labor troubles or other unavoidable circumstances.

Said party of the first part further agrees, at their own expense, for the term of 5 years next after the completion and acceptance of said Organ, to remedy any and all defects therein resulting from the use of improper material or from inferior workmanship upon receipt of notice from party of the second part. This does not include tuning, regulating or the care of the instrument.

Party of the second part agrees that the building shall be in readiness for the erection of said Organ, including a suitable location for the electric blower and that the said party of the first part or their representatives shall have undisturbed possession of said building for the purpose of erecting, regulating and tuning said Organ, for a period of days next previous to the completion of said organ.

Party of the second part also agrees to furnish light, heat and power necessary for the proper erection and tuning of the Organ.

Party of the second part further agrees to have the Organ examined immediately upon notice of its completion, and if it fully comes up to specifications they will accept the same.

Should said Organ, upon such examination, not accord with the terms of the agreement and specifications, party of the first part agrees, upon notice in writing of the points in which said Organ does not comply with agreement, to remedy the same.

All risk of damage to the Organ, or parts thereof, by fire, water or debris, shall be incurred by the party of the second part, after the Organ or parts thereof have been deposited in said building; such assumption of risk not to be construed as an acceptance of the said Organ.

Party of the second part also agrees to keep the Organ insured in a sum equal to the amount owing to Party of the first part, for the benefit of said party, without expense to them.

The party of the second part, in full consideration of the above, agrees to pay to party of the first part the sum of six thousand dollars upon the fulfillment of their said agreement.

Terms of payment, cash upon completion of Organ, or as follows: The organ to be tonally and mechanically satisfactory before acceptance

Upon signing of contract

Upon shipment of Organ and bill of lading

Upon completion in church

Collateral Notes

All deferred payments after Organ is completed, either notes or otherwise, to bear legal interest, and it is agreed that the said Organ is and shall remain the property of the party of the first part until paid for in full.

All verbal agreements and understandings are merged in this instrument, which comprises the entire contract as concluded.

Witness our hands and seals the day and year first above written.

TELLERS-KENT ORGAN CO.
Per B. B. Terrell L. S.

In presence of
John H. McAuliffe — C. L. Hatch L. S.

L. S.

L. S.

"SPECIFICATION OF AN ORGAN"
prepared for
Winthrop Theater, of Winthrop, Mass.,
by the
TELLERS-KENT ORGAN COMPANY
September 13, 1927.

* * *

To have Two Manuals and a Pedal
Compass of Manuals from CC to C4, 61 notes
Compass of Pedals from CCC to G, 32 notes

ACTION - ELECTRO-PNEUMATIC

* * *

- ACCOMPANIMENT ORGAN -

1.	8'	Open Diapason	73 notes
2.	8'	Tibia Plena	73 notes
3.	8'	Orchestral Viole	73 notes
4.	4'	Principal	61 notes
5.	4'	Tibia Flute	61 notes
6.	4'	Violina	61 notes
7.	2-2/3'	Nazard	61 notes
8.	2'	Piccolo	61 notes
9.	1-3/5'	Tierce	61 notes
10.	8'	Clarinet	73 notes
11.	8'	Oboe	73 notes
12.		Marimba Harp	49 notes
13.		Chimes	13 notes
14.		Xylophone	37 notes

- SOLO ORGAN -

15.	16'	Bourdon	73 notes
16.	8'	Open Diapason	73 notes
17.	8'	Stopped Diapason	73 notes
18.	8'	Orchestral Viole	73 notes
19.	4'	Flute D'Amour	73 notes
20.	4'	Violin	61 notes
21.	2-2/3'	Nazard	61 notes
22.	2'	Piccolo	61 notes
23.	1-3/5'	Tierce	61 notes
24.	8'	Clarinet	73 notes
25.	8'	Oboe	73 notes
26.	8'	Vox Humana	73 notes
27.	8'	Tuba	73 notes

- PEDAL ORGAN -

28.	16'	Sub Bass	32 notes
29.	16'	Bourdon	32 notes
30.	8'	Flute	32 notes
31.	8'	Cello	32 notes

- COUPLERS -

1. Accompaniment to Pedal
2. Solo to Pedal
3. Solo to Accompaniment
4. Solo to Accompaniment 16'
5. Solo to Accompaniment 4'
6. Solo to Solo 16'
7. Solo to Solo 4'
8. Accompaniment to Accomp. 16'
9. Accompaniment to Accomp. 4'
10. Pedal to Pedal 4'

- PISTON COMBINATIONS -
(Visibly Adjustable)

1. Three Piston Combinations for Accomp. Pedal & Couplers
2. Three Piston Combinations for Solo, Pedal & Couplers

- PEDAL MOVEMENTS -

1. Balanced Solo Pedal
2. Balanced Crescendo & Diminuendo Pedal

- ACCESSORIES -

1. Solo Tremolo
2. Wind Indicator
3. Crescendo Indicator
4. Electric Generator
5. Electric Blower
6. Organist's Bench

- TRAPS -

1. Bass Drum
2. Snare Drum
3. Cymbal
4. Auto Horn
5. Fire Gong
6. Triangle
7. Tympani
8. Castanets omit
9. Wood Drum omit
10. Tom Tom
11. Tambourine omit
12. Bird Whistle
13. Siren omit
14. Glockenspeil omit

* * *

Our latest Improved ELECTRO-PNEUMATIC Action to be applied throughout the entire organ, together with our patented Individual Valve Wind Chests.

One strictly first class Electric Blower to be included, except the necessary wiring and tinsmithing, sufficiently large to supply the fullest legitimate demands of the organ.

Console to be detached and extended.

Organ to be divided.

Two Lattice Work Screens to be furnished.

The Tellers factory building is pictured here sometime between 1911 and 1918. Still serving the organ industry in the 1980s, this building now houses the pipe shop of Organ Supply Industries.

TELLERS-KENT OPUS LIST

Following is a complete list of this firm's theatre installations.

OPUS	LOCATION/CITY/STATE	SIZE	YR	PRICE	BLWR	HP	WP	REMARKS
109	Columbia Th., Erie, PA	4/32	1915	$ 9,000.00				Tellers-Sommerhof.
147	Colonial Th., Erie, PA	2/14	1918	$ 4,500.00				
152	Columbia Th., Erie, PA	4/32	1918	$ 12,000.00				
155	Majestic (Perry) (Shea's) Th., Erie, PA	2/8	1918	$ 3,152.48				See opus 229.
171	Library Th., Warren, PA	3/18	1919	$ 5,374.74	H479		3½″	
180	Happy Hour Th., New Orleans, LA	2/12	1919	$ 4,200.00				
192	Foto's Folly Th., Algiers, LA	2/12	1920	$ 4,600.00	I233	¾	4″	
208	National Th., New Orleans, LA	2/12	1920	$ 5,100.00				
226	Strand Th., Erie, PA	2/8	1921	$ 3,500.00				
229	Perry (Shea's) Th., Erie, PA	3/24	1921	$ 8,750.00	J343	3	6″	Replaced opus 155; opened as Majestic Theatre.
237	Columbia Th., Sharon, PA	4/33	1922	$ 11,700.00	K720	5	6″	
259	United States Th., New Orleans, LA	2/10	1922	$ 3,300.00	14027			
269	Rialto Th., Erie, PA	2/10	1922	$ 4,700.00				
270	State Th., Erie, PA	3/18	1923	$ 8,000.00				
283	Cosmopolitan Th., New Orleans, LA	2/10	1923	$ 4,200.00				
307	Horn Th., Baltimore, MD	2/12	1924	$ 5,610.00	M838B	2	6″	
351	Legionnaire Th., Milton, PA	2/8	1925	$ 5,750.00				
354	Columbia Th., Erie, PA	4/32	1925	$ 14,000.00				
355	Aris Th., Erie, PA	2/8	1925	$ 5,000.00	N480B	2	5″	
374	Mozart Th, Milwaukee, WI	2/5	1926	$ 4,000.00				
376	LaGrande Th., Conneaut, OH	3/10	1926	$ 6,950.00				
403	Hollywood Th., Dormont, PA	3/15	1926	$ 9,000.00				
414	Gross Th., Roseburg, OR	2/4	1926		0902B	2	7″	
415	J. W. Bascome's Th., Mt. Shasta, CA	2/4	1927		01006B	2	7″	
427	Braverman Th., Pittsburgh, PA	2/6	1927	$ 3,350.00	19983			Old organ taken in on trade.
440	Keller Th., North East, PA	2/6	1927	$ 5,350.00	20218			
441	Penn Th., Wesleyville, PA	2/9	1927	$ 5,000.00	P332B	1½	5″	
466	Winthrop Th., Winthrop, MA	2/7	1927	$ 6,000.00	21152			
467	Berwyn Th., Berwyn, IL	2/3	1928	$ 3,500.00	21157			Located at 3308 Oak Park Ave.

OFFICERS

R. L. KETCHAM
President

O. W. KETCHAM
Vice-President

H. E. GOODELL
Secretary and Treasurer

G. H. KLOEHS
General Manager

UNITED STATES PIPE ORGAN COMPANY

MAIN OFFICE AND PLANT

CRUM LYNNE · PENNSYLVANIA

DELAWARE COUNTY

SALES OFFICES

PHILADELPHIA
125 N. 18TH STREET

NEW YORK
130 W. 42ND STREET

WASHINGTON, D. C.
METROPOLITAN BANK BLDG.

The United States Pipe Organ Company was founded around 1920 by Philadelphia organ men A. R. Payne and Gustav Kloehs who were described by former company employee Bob Lent as "a couple of fast-talking operators." The company name was chosen to take advantage of the patriotic spirit that was prevalent in the country following World War I. Although the company later did some church work, it found early success catering to the fast-growing Philadelphia theatre market as evidenced by sales of over thirty organs to Philadelphia theatres alone.[1]

The company was first located in a small space rented from the O. W. Ketcham Terra Cotta Works in Crum Lynne, Pennsylvania. As business picked up, this space proved inadequate causing the firm to move to somewhat larger quarters at 8105 Tinicum Avenue in Philadelphia early in 1921.[2] By 1924 their small factory was definitely overcrowded, employing sixteen people[3] and ultimately necessitating another move. O. W. Ketcham, owner of the building where the company got its start, decided to erect a new 24,000 square-foot building next to his Terra Cotta Works and in June of 1924 the company moved into this new building.[4] Around this same time Payne left the company and Gus Kloehs assumed full command.

For several years business thrived. Company records disclose that 1924 sales numbered fourteen organs worth $103,355, up from 1923 sales of thirteen smaller instruments valued at $84,499. In 1925 the company opened a showroom with a demonstration organ in New York City and also operated an office in Washington, D. C. Organs were leaving the factory nearly as fast as they could be built but some delivery problems resulted from the lead times required by the firm's outside suppliers. Most of the pipes were purchased from the Dennison and National Organ Supply companies; the Kinetic Engineering Company in nearby Lansdowne, Pennsylvania supplied the blowers. Since factory production capacity exceeded the lead times of these suppliers, many consoles, chests and other parts were simply mass produced and stockpiled.[5]

After the advent of talking pictures, however, orders stopped coming in virtually overnight and the company was left holding the bag, so to speak, with many parts in inventory and no customers for them. Furthermore, many organs had been financed through the company and when theatres no longer needed organs they simply stopped making payments. As a result many organs were repossessed, enlarging an already surplus inventory.[6] Apparently thinking "if you can't lick 'em, join 'em," Gus Kloehs tried to sell sound movie equipment for a time but this venture proved unsuccessful and he left the firm late in 1929.[7]

O. W. Ketcham, the primary financier of the United States Pipe Organ Company, obviously didn't want to lose his investment so he encouraged Conrad C. Boyer to make what he could out of the business. Boyer was originally with the Terra Cotta Works and in the mid-1920s had become an accountant for the organ company. Boyer apparently had managerial skills but knew little about organs from a technical standpoint. Until his retirement in 1968 he could still remember theatre managers' phone numbers but barely knew the difference between a tibia and a diapason! Boyer did manage to keep the company alive by specializing in maintenance work and by selling repossessed theatre organs to churches. This practice didn't create a very good reputation for the United States Pipe Organ Company inasmuch as the organs weren't of the greatest quality to begin with and were certainly not well suited for liturgical use.[8]

United States Pipe Organ Company organs had some interesting mechanical features: Relays were rarely used; instead, unit switches copied after Wurlitzer designs were wired to key contacts and were placed right in the consoles. Junction boards were rarely soldered because fumes from soldering gave Gus Kloehs headaches. Pneumatic combination actions were on the drawing board but were never used. In some consoles the stops were moved electrically and in others the combinations were blind. Some wooden flutes and tibias were made at the United States factory but most pipes were purchased from Dennison and National Organ Supply. Some orders for pipework

The cut at left appeared in this position on the company's stationery. Note the two-story erecting room on the right.

Robert F. Lent poses at the Collingswood Theatre, Collingswood, New Jersey in 1929. This 3/18, a rebuild and enlargement of an existing Moller, was the largest instrument to bear the United States Pipe Organ Company nameplate. Robert F. Lent is the father of Robert G. Lent who purchased the United States firm in 1982.

went to Badger and to Erie Reed Pipe Co., and Laukhuff in Germany supplied at least one vox humana.[9] [10]

Perhaps the most unique features of United States organs were the patented "cypherless devices" which were actually ventil cutouts for each rank. If a cipher developed, the organist merely had to touch a stop key to activate the ventil on the affected rank, thereby turning off its wind until the cipher could be corrected after the show. This feature seemed like a good idea and in fact was a good selling point for United States organs, but it also had a liability: Sometimes an organist would activate these stops not realizing what they did, resulting in a service call to fix the "inoperative" organ![11]

The organ specifications were mostly the work of Gus Kloehs.[12] Among several stock styles offered were the style A, a 2/3; styles B and C, 2/4; style D, 2/5; and style E, a 2/6. The style E was the only one of these to offer a tibia. United States Pipe Organ Company's advertising boasted that their organs were unified "just enough" but some of the stops offered were amusing, if not tragic. Styles C, D and E had a 1 3/5′ tierce on only the accompaniment manual with no corresponding 2 2/3′ stop, and the style B had a 16′ vox humana TC in the pedal.[13]

In later years the Terra Cotta Works closed and the organ business, under the direction of J. Fred Ade′ following Boyer's retirement, moved into the area which had been the Terra Cotta office and drafting room. The old organ factory was abandoned and over the years became a target for arsonists. In 1969 a fire reached the office portion of the building where the old files of the firm had been left to rot. One of the newer employees, Robert G. Lent, braved life and limb to enter the burning office and managed to retrieve a four-drawer filing cabinet before the roof caved in. Lent was severely burned and was, in the words of Fred Ade′, nearly fired for "taking such a stupid risk over some dumb old papers that were totally useless."[14] [15] Much of the detail in this article comes from those "useless old papers" which Lent risked his neck to save. Other company records and photographs had been rescued before the fire by employee Alan Lightcap who also lent them for reproduction in this volume.

In 1971 the United States Pipe Organ Company factory was razed to make way for Interstate 95. Stock inventory and a number of chests, consoles and workbenches were bulldozed along with the building. In 1982 Robert G. Lent purchased what was left in the old Terra Cotta Works building and the United States Pipe Organ Company finally came to an end.[16]

The standard two-manual United States Pipe Organ Company console was cheaply made but was aesthetically attractive.

CONSOLE OF THE PAYNE AND KLOEHS ORGAN
IN HULSE'S OPERA HOUSE, MT. HOLLY

**A BETTER ORGAN
AT A LOWER PRICE**

Exhibitors know that an organ company located in Philadelphia, employing no pensive salesmen, is in a position to give better service and lower prices. That the reason for the increasing popularity of the

PAYNE AND KLOEHS

ORCHESTRAL PIPE ORGANS

The Payne & Kloehs Organ is not an experiment. It is built by artisans with ye of experience in the manufacture of superfine pipe organs. Every part of each org is made in our own factory under the personal supervision of Messrs. Payne a Kloehs.

EXPERT REPAIR WORK ON ALL MAKES OF ORGANS

WE ARE ON THE OTHER END OF YOUR PHONE

DELIVERIES IN 90 DAYS

UNITED STATES PIPE ORGAN C(

3105-07-09 TINICUM AVE Bell Phone, Woodland 3505 PHILADELPI

This 1922 United States ad pictured the first new organ built by the firm. It was assigned opus number fifty. Note that the ad stressed repair work in addition to new organs. Prior to 1922, repairs were the only income the fledgling company had.[17]

12

Points of Superiority

Fastest Action on the Market
Super Construction (long life)
Highest Grade Materials
Orchestral Qualifications
Beauty of Tone and Design
Unified *Just Enough*
Cypherless Devices (patented)
Cue Combinations (patented)
Built to Order
Delivery When Promised
Immediate Maintenance Service
Personal Attention

[*In addition our prices are right and our business relations are of the highest caliber*]

Investigate!

UNITED STATES PIPE ORGAN CO.

Main Office and Factory: Crum Lynne, Pa.
Phila. Branch: 125 N. Eighteenth St.
New York Office: 130 W. 42nd St.

One page from a promotional brochure issued in the mid-1920s.

DON'T BUY A UNITED STATES ORGAN

unless you want an instrument
Built by Experts and Unequaled for Sweetness and Variety
of Tone, Fast Repetition, Reliability and Long Life.
CORRESPONDENCE SOLICITED.

UNITED STATES PIPE ORGAN COMPANY

CRUM LYNNE, Delaware Co., Pa.

This is the third of a series of "ads" to appear in this paper.

The firm advertised for business nationwide in this 1924 Diapason *ad, although sales were consummated only in Connecticut, New Jersey, New York and Pennsylvania.*

4/17 UNITED STATES THEATRE ORGAN, OPUS 154

Park Theatre, Philadelphia, Pennsylvania

The letters to the left of the stop numbers are a key to the stop key color: white, red, blue or amber.

JOB # 154

TENOR SOLO Played from Top Manual

W 1 - Violin 16'
W 2 - Tibia 8'
W 3 - Salicional 8'
W 4 - Violin D'Orchestra 8'
W 5 - Stopped Flute (soft) 8'
R 6 - Vox Humana 8'
R 7 - Clarinet 8'
W 8 - Violin 8'
W 9 - Violin 4'
W 10 - Soft Flute 4'
W 11 - Tibia 4'
W 12 - Pfiefe 2'

COUPLERS

13 - Tenor Solo to Solo 8'
14 - Tenor Solo to Orchestra 8'
15 - Tenor Solo to Accompaniment 8'
16 - Tenor Solo to Tenor Solo 16'
17 - Tenor Solo to Tenor Solo 4'
Movable & Adjustable Combination Pistons

SOLO ORGAN Played from 2nd Manual

W 18 - Bass Flute 16'
R 19 - Tuba 16'
W 20 - Open Tibia Plena 16'
W 21 - String Bass 16'
W 22 - Salicional 8'
W 23 - Vox Celeste 8'
W 24 - Violin D'Orchestra 8'
W 25 - Open Diapason 8'
W 26 - Tibia Clausa 8'
W 27 - Stopped Flute 8'
R 28 - French Horn 8'
R 29 - Kinura 8'
R 30 - Trumpet 8'
R 31 - Clarinet 8'
R 32 - Oboe 8'
R 33 - Vox Humana Alto 8'
R 34 - Vox Humana Soprano 8'
R 35 - English Post Horn 8'
W 36 - Flute 8'
R 37 - Tuba 8'
W 38 - Tibia Plena 8'
W 39 - Cello 8'
W 40 - Violin 4'
W 41 - Salicional 4'
W 42 - Flute 4'
W 43 - Tibia Plena 4'
W 44 - Tibia Clausa 4'
W 45 - Piccolo 2'
W 46 - Pfiefe 2'
W 47 - Tierce 1-3/5'
B 48 - Chimes 8' 20 tubes
A 49 - Marimba Harp 8' 49 bars
A 50 - Xylophone 8' 37 bars
A 51 - Orchestral Bells 8' 37 bars
A 52 - Chrysglotte 8' 49 notes

COUPLERS

53 - Solo to Orchestra 8'
54 - Solo to Accompaniment 8'
55 - Solo to Solo 16'
56 - Solo to Solo 4'
Movable & Adjustable Combination Pistons

Sheet # 2

ORCHESTRAL ORGAN

W 57 - Contra Bass 16'
W 58 - Tibia Plena 16'
W 59 - Violin 16'
R 60 - Tuba 16'
W 61 - Viol D'Orchestra 8'
W 62 - Vox Celeste 8'
W 63 - Salicional 8'
W 64 - Open Diapason 8'
W 65 - Tibia Clausa 8'
W 66 - Stopped Diapason 8'
R 67 - French Horn 8'
R 68 - Trumpet 8'
R 69 - Clarinet 8'
R 70 - Oboe 8'
R 71 - Kinura 8'
R 72 - Vox Humana Alto 8'
R 73 - Vox Humana Soprano 8'
R 74 - English Post Horn 8'
W 75 - Concert Flute 8'
R 76 - Tuba 8'
W 77 - Tibia Plena 8'
W 78 - Violin 4'
W 79 - Salicional 4'
W 80 - Vox ~~xxxxxx~~ Celeste 4'
81 - Viole 4'
W 82 - Concert Flute 4'
W 83 - Tibia Clausa 4'
W 84 - Tibia Plena 4'
W 85 - Octave 4'
W 86 - Stopped Flute 4'
W 87 - Flageolet 2'
W 88 - Nazard 2-2/3'
W 89 - Pfiefe 2'
A 90 - Xylophone 8' 37 bars
A 91 - Bells 8' 37 bars
A 92 - Chrysglotte 8' 49 notes
A 93 - Marimba Phone (Syn) 8' 49 notes

COUPLERS

94 - Orchestra to Accompaniment 8'
95 - Orchestra to Orchestra 16'
96 - Orchestra to Orchestra 4'
Movable & Adjustable Combination Pistons

SECOND TOUCH

96a-
1 - Tuba 8'
2 - Kinura 8'
3 - English Post Horn 8'
4 - Tibia 8'

ACCOMPANIMENT ORGAN Played from 4th Manual

W 97 - Bourdon 16'
W 98 - Violin Bass 16
R 99 - Trumpet 8'
W 100 - Open Diapason 8'
W 101 - Flute 8'
W 102 - Violin 8'
W 103 - Salicional 8'
W 104 - Vox Celeste 8'
R 105 - Vox Humana 8'
R 106 - Kinura 8'
R 107 - Clarinet 8'
W 108 - Tibia Clausa 8'
W 109 - Stopped Flute 8'
W 110 - Flute 4'
W 111 - Tibia Clausa 4'

Accompaniment Organ CONT'D

W 112 - Octave 4'
W 113 - Stopped Flute 4'
W 114 - Violin 4'
W 115 - Salicional 4'
W 116 - Celestina 4'
W 117 - Piccolo 2'
A 118 - Marimba Harp 8' 49 bars
A 119 - Snare Drum
A 120 - Castanets
A 121 - Tambourine
A 122 - Tom Tom
A 123 - Wood Block

COUPLERS

124 - Accompaniment to Accompaniment 16'
125 - Accompaniment to Accompaniment 4'
Movable & Adjust. Comb. Pistons

PEDAL ORGAN Compass: 32 Notes

W 126 - Bourdon 16'
R 127 - Tuba 16'
W 128 - String Bass 16'
W 129 - Tibia Plena 16'
W 130 - Open Diapason 8'
R 131 - Trumpet 8'
R 132 - French Horn 8'
W 133 - Flute 8'
R 134 - Tibia Clausa 8'
R 135 - Tibia Plena 8'
W 136 - String Bass 8'
W 137 - Cello 8'
W 138 - Violin 8'
W 139 - Flute 4'
W 140 - Tibia Clausa 4'
A 141 - Bass Drum
A 142 - Cymbal
A 143 - Triangle

COUPLERS

144 - Tenor Solo to Pedal
145 - Solo to Pedal
146 - Orchestra to Pedal
147 - Accompaniment to Pedal
Mov. & Ajust. Comb. Pistons

TOE PISTONS:
148 - Crash Cymbal
149 - Fire Gong
150 - Thunder Sheet
151 - Train Whistle
152 - Rain Sheet
153 - Boat Whistle
154 - Siren
155 - Kettle Drum
156 - Bird Whistle
157 - Cymbal Revl.
158 - Sand Block Shuffle
159 - Auto Horn

159 a- SECOND TOUCH
Snare Drum

ACCESSORIES

160 - Main Tremolo
161 - Tremolo (High Pressure)
162 - Vox Tremolo
163 - General Tremolo
164 - Detached Console
X165 - ~~Roll top for Console~~
166 - Crescendo
167 - Swell Shoe for each Chamber
168 - Electric Motor & Blower
169 - Electric Generator
170 - Music Rack
171 - Organist Bench 172 - Stop Finger

4/17 United States Pipe Organ Company console installed in the Park Theatre. This may have been the only four-manual organ built by the company.

STYLE D UNITED STATES THEATRE ORGAN

This 2/5 stock model was one of the company's most popular.

SOLO ORGAN

Played from Top Manual

1 - Contra Bass	16'	61 notes
2 - Contra Violina TC	16'	49 notes
3 - Orchestral Oboe (Synthetic)	8'	61 notes
4 - Horn	8'	"
5 - Concert Flute	8'	"
6 - Violina Orchestra	8'	"
7 - Vox Humana	8'	"
8 - Kinura	8'	"
9 - Octave	4'	"
10 - Orchestral Flute	4'	"
11 - Violina	4'	"
12 - Vox Humana	4'	"
13 - Flageolet	2'	"
14 - Xylophone	8'	37 notes
15 - Orchestral Bells	8'	"
16 - Cathedral Chimes	8'	20 notes

ACCOMPAINMENT ORGAN

Played from Lower Manual

17 - Bourdon	16'	61 notes
18 - Violina TC	16'	49 notes
19 - Vox Humana TC	16'	"
20 - Baritone Principal	8'	61 notes
21 - Concert Flute	8'	"
22 - Viola	8'	"
23 - Vox Humana	8'	"
24 - Horn Octave	4'	"
25 - Orchestral Flute	4'	"
26 - Violina	4'	"
27 - Vox Humana	4'	"
28 - Piccolo	2'	"
29 - Tierce	2'	"
30 - Xylophone	8'	37 notes
31 - Orchestral Bells	8'	"

32 - Snare Drum
33 - Castanets
34 - Tambourine
35 - Tom Tom
36 - Wood Block

PEDAL ORGAN

Played from Pedal Keyboard

37 - Bass Flute	16'	30 notes
38 - Horn	8'	"
39 - Flute	8'	"
40 - Cello	8'	"
41 - Vox Humana	8'	"
42 - Orchestral Diapason	4'	"

43 - Bass Drum

44 - Cymbal

45 - Triangle

ACCESSORIES

46 - Tremolos

47 - Detached Console

48 - Roll Top for Console

49 - Crescendo

50 - Swell Shoe, -controls entire organ

51 - Electric Motor and Blower

52 - Electric Generator

53 - Organist Bench

54 - Music Rack

55 - Electric lights for finger stops

DETAILS OF CONSTRUCTION

ACTION: - This organ is Electric-pneumatic throughout. Positively no tublar action used in any part of organ. Each pipe, trap and precussion has its individual, outside adjustable magnet and primary also, its own valve and pneumatic. This will insure a full supply of wind at all times as well as a steady tone.

PITCH: - The pitch of this organ is Philharomic 440-A as adopted by the majority of symphony orchestras of the world.

CHESTS: - This organ contains our lates improved "patented" individual valve chests, CONSTRUCTED from the best kiln-dried California Sugar Pine and LEATHERED with the finest grade of packing leather. Each organ will have a separate reservoir which will distribute an even flow of wind to alll parts of organ, thereby obtaining better tonal reuslts. Entire organ to be shellac-sized as a preventive of organ troubles.

PNEUMATIC WORK: - All pneumatics, etc., to be made from the finest material. Positively no paper used.

CONSOLE: - Organ to be operated from a detached console to which it is connected by means of a cable. The console is constructed from Cherry Wood and finished to match the interior wood work or any color desired. It can be placed in any position. Finger stops are placed in elliptical form over and around the keyboard and are used to bring on or cancel the different instruments. The different instruments are operated from a two manual keyboard and pedals.

MANUAL KEYS: - Standard scale, 61 notes C to C. Constructed from the best ivory with ebony sharps and to be of a standard make as adopted by the Americna Guild of Organists.

PEDAL KEYS: - To be radiating and concaved.. Thirty notes C to F. The naturals are capped with White Maple and the sharps with Cherry.

EXPRESSION SHADES: - The different instruments are enclosed in sound proof expression shades which are operated from a shoe underneath the console. This permits the organist to obtain almost unlimited tonal effects. The shades are constructed from selected 1 3/8" stock and painted two coats of black paint to keep dampness out of chambers.

WOOD PIPES: - To be made from selected kiln-dried stock, glue-sized on inside and finished on outside with two coats of the best orange shellac.

METAL PIPES: - To be of scales according to best standards and to contain requisite amount of tin to suit their respective demands.

These three views were taken from a broadside published when the United States Pipe Organ Company was in its Tinicum Avenue home.

MANUFACTURED BY
UNITED STATES PIPE ORGAN CO.
CRUM LYNNE, PA.

These brass nameplates were discovered in the United States factory inventory in the 1960s. Curiously, no United States organ bore such a nameplate to the best of the author's knowledge.

This early United States Pipe Organ Company console, with a roll top, bears the nameplate "Payne and Kloehs Orchestral Pipe Organ."

Principals of the United States Pipe Organ Company pose for a photo c. 1924 in the Crum Lynne erecting room. From left to right are Conrad C. Boyer, accountant; H. E. Goodell, office manager; A. R. Payne and Gus Kloebs, founders of the firm; and Mrs. Conrad Boyer.

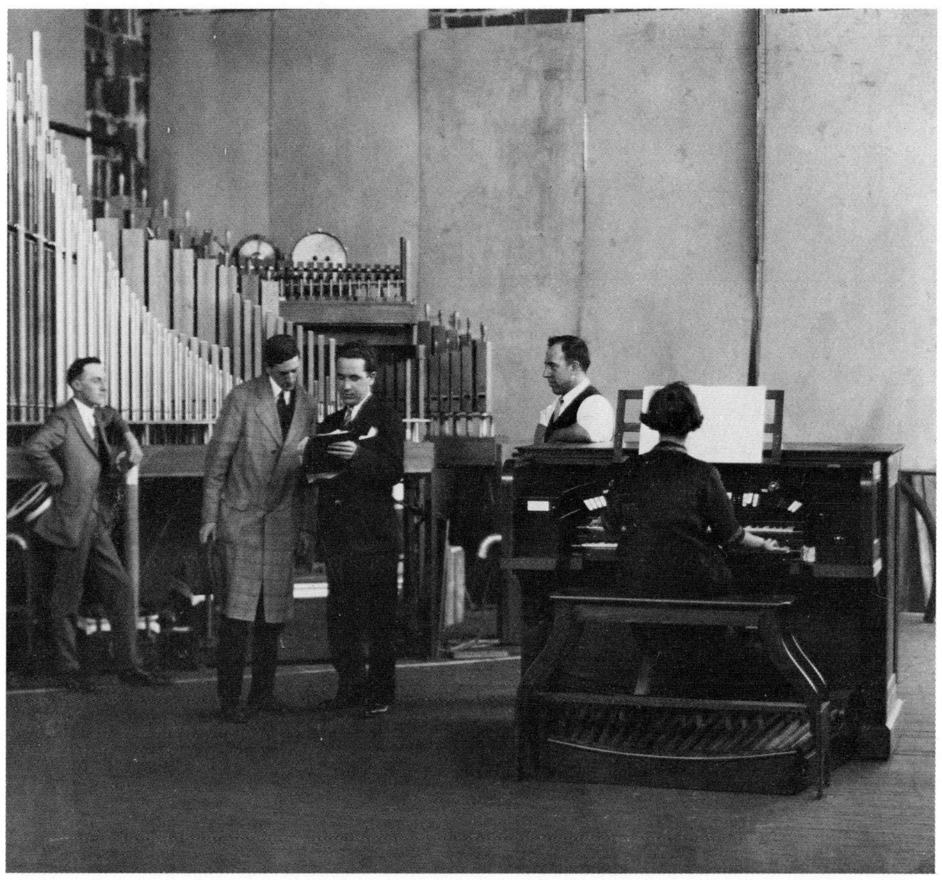

A small organ nears completion in the two-story erecting room of the Crum Lynne factory.

In the small factory at 8105 Tinicum Avenue in Philadelphia, manufacturing, erecting and testing were all done in the same room.

UNITED STATES OPUS LIST

CITY/STATE	LOCATION	SIZE	OPUS	YR	BLWR	HP	WP	REMARKS
CONNECTICUT								
Hartford	Plaza Th.	3/12	209	1928				
New Canaan	Playhouse Th.	2/7	205	1928	Q341B	5	8″	
NEW JERSEY								
Bridgeton	Criterion Th.	2/5	66	1923	L553	3	8″	Style D; cost $8,400.
Caldwell	Park Th.							
Camden	Parkside Th.		91R	1925				
Carteret	Ritz Th.	2/4	153	1928	P1142B	3		
Collingswood	Collingswood Th.	3/18	161	1928	P1101B	7½	6″	Existing Moller opus 3016 unified and tibia added.
Elizabeth	Elmora Th.	2/7	111					
	Embassy Th.			1925	N34B	3		
	State Th.	2/5	162	1928				
Hawthorne	Hawthorne Th.	2/7	159	1928	P613B	5	10″	
Highland Park	Park Th.	2/7		1927	P448B	5	10″	
Merchantville	unidentified theatre			1924	M235B	2	6″	
Mt. Holly	Mt. Holly Opera House	2/	50	1922				
Ocean City	Moorlyn Th.	?/8	120					
Palmyra	Broadway Th.			1922	K816	3	10″	
Sea Isle City	Cini's Amusement Pier			1924				
Sowers Point	Seaside Th.	2/		1924	M514B	2	10″	Cost $5,900.
West Collingswood	Crescent Th.	3/7	155	1927	P653B	5	10″	
West Orange	State Th.	2/8	204	1928	Q340B	5	10″	Rebuild existing Moller opus 3346.
Woodbine	Capitol Th.			1924	M801B	2	10″	
Woodbridge	State Th.	2/7	157	1927	P446B	5	10″	
NEW YORK								
Bellaire	Bellaire Th.	2/5	103	1926				
Bellerose	Bellerose Th.	2/7	163	1928				
Bronx	B-B Th.			1925				
	Burke Th.	2/6	112	1927				
	Mosholu Th.			1926				
Floral Park	Floral Park Th.	3/8	152	1928				
Hicksville	Playhouse Th.	2/7	165	1928	Q26B	5	10″	
Jamaica	unidentified new theatre			1925				
New Hyde Park	New Hyde Park Th.		90A	1925				8′ trumpet, bells and chimes added to existing organ.
New York	Jefferson Th.	3/10	102	1926				
	Regent Th.	3/12	61	1923	L47	7½	10″	
	United States Showroom		99					
South Ozone Park	South Ozone Park Th.	2/5	104	1926				
PENNSYLANVIA								
Ardmore	Ardmore Th.	3/13		1922	K114	7½	15″	
Berwyn	Berwyn Th.							
Chester	Benn Th.	2/4	156	1928				
	Lyric Th.		118					
Conshohocken	Forrest Th.	2/4	160	1927	P611B	2	10″	
Darby	Parker Th.	3/12	208	1928	Q1022B	7½	15″	
Doylestown	Stanley (Strand) Th.			1925	M628B	2	10″	
Freeland	Refowich Th.	2/8	151	1927				
Harrisburg	National Th.	2/5	201	1928	Q11B	3	10″	
Hazleton	Hersker Th.	2/5	107	1928				
Lansdale	Lansdale Th.	3/8	101					
	unidentified theatre	3/9						Moved in 1928 to Hamilton Theatre, Philadelphia, Pennsylvania.
Mifflinburg	Mifflinburg Th.			1926				Used Wurlitzer organ.
Milton	Bijou Th.	2/5	106	1927				
Nesquehoning	Strand Th.		87	1925				Cost $7,000.
Norristown	Colonial Th.	2/		1924				
	Twin Towers Th.	2/9		1925	M1022B	2	10″	
Parksburg	Parksburg Opera House		67	1923				
Pen Argyl	Liberty Th.			1923	L713	3	6″	
Philadelphia	Admiral Th.		202	1928	Q317B	7½	15″	
	Aurora Th.		119	1928				Moved from Garden Theatre in unidentified city.
	Bell Th.		63	1923	L369	3	8″	Located at 2907 North 5th Street.
	Bellevue Th.			1924	M556B	3	12″	
	Broadway (Cameo) Th.		69	1923	3	6″		
	Brunswick Th.		87	1925	M1023B	3	10″	
				1926	O152B	3	10″	
	Cayuga Th.		57	1922	K437	3	10″	
			J	1924				Additions: tibia and percussions.
	D'Annunzio (Italia) Th.		203	1928				

CITY/STATE	LOCATION	SIZE	OPUS	YR	BLWR	HP	WP	REMARKS
Philadelphia	Diamond Th.	2/9	55	1922	K438	5		With 2-rank echo.
		3/11	K	1924				Additions: tibia, post horn, Chinese gong and rooster crow.
	Dreamland Th.			1925	M1025B	3	10″	
	Edgemont Th.			1925				Used Seeburg; cost $1,000.
	Elk Th.		70	1924	L758	2	6″	
	Elrae Th.	2/	206	1928	Q510B	2	10″	
	Grand Th.			1925	N347B	3	9″	
	Great Northern Th.			1923	L3	5	9″	
	Hamilton Th.	3/9	116	1928	Q318B	5	10″	Moved from Lansdale, Pennsylvania.
	Holme Th.	3/12	301	1929	R501B	7½	15″	Cost $13,500.
	Howard Th.			1925	N155B	2		
	Liberty Th.	3/		1922	J596	7½	15″	
	Lindy Th.	3/12	164	1928	P1124B	7½	15″	
	Lyric Th.	2/5	105	1926	O538B	2	7″	Opened as Manheim Theatre.
		2/6	117	1928				Additions: tibia, siren and crash cymbal; cost $450.
	Majestic (Eagle) Th.		100	1924				
	Nelson Th.		109	1927	O620B	2		
	Park Th.		65	1923	L370	5	10″	
		4/17	154	1927	P231B	10		
	Pastime Th.							
	Queen Th.	2/3		1924				Moved in 1926 to Queen Theatre, St. Clair, Pennsylvania.
	Rexy Th.	3/8	207	1928	Q610B	7½	15″	
	Rialto Th.			1923				
	Ritz Th.		114	1928	P1142B	3	10″	
	Spring Garden Th.		64	1923	L371	3	8″	
	Star (State) Th.			1924	M515B	2	10″	Located at 2703 North 5th Street.
	Temple Th.							
	Wayne Palace Th.	2/7	108	1926	O619B	5		With 2-rank echo.
Royersford	Penn Th.		71	1924	L1035	3	8″	
Shickshinny	Peoples Th.	2/5	110	1926		3		
White Haven	Legion Th.		113					

BERNARD VAN WYCK

The author has been able to learn little about Bernard Van Wyck other than the information published in the adjoining article which is reproduced from the March 1, 1923 issue of *The Exhibitor*. The Wurlitzer style K mentioned there was the largest photoplayer in the Wurlitzer line. It consisted of a piano having an extra 61-note organ keyboard plus two side cabinets each larger than the piano itself, all operated by tubular pneumatic action. The Point Breeze Theatre was located in Philadelphia.

Point Breeze Theatre Renovated

Clarence G. Hexter, who was the first to put the Point Breeze Theatre, 1638 Point Breeze Avenue on the map, after many others had tried and failed, has entirely renovated that house and renamed it The Breeze.

Among the many improvements is a new organ built by Bernard Van Wyck around an old Wurlitzer Style K, which has been in use for nearly six years. Mr. Van Wyck enlarged the K to a modern electrified pipe organ which, according to Mr. Hexter, is pleasing the patrons in fine fashion.

Catalog illustration of a Wurlitzer style K. The largest photoplayer in the Wurlitzer line, it retailed for $4,850 with a duplex roll system or $4,500 with a single roll player. Inasmuch as several case variations were produced, the style K in the Point Breeze Theatre may not have had these same grilles on its side cabinets.

CHAS. VINER & SONS

Charles Viner was born in England in 1839. He and his father, an organist and composer, came to the United States in 1858. In 1888 Viner moved to Buffalo, New York and started the firm bearing his name. In 1909 he moved to San Diego, California to install an organ in the Superior Theatre. He remained in San Diego until his death in 1919. At that time he had one surviving son, Charles B. Viner,[1] who apparently continued the business in Buffalo through the 1920s.

2/8 Viner in the LaFayette Theatre, Batavia, New York.

2/6 VINER THEATRE ORGAN, OPUS 217
Aurora Theatre, East Aurora, New York

These specifications are reproduced from the original Viner factory record book.

217. Aurora Theatre East Aurora, N.Y.

Accompaniment
16' Bass Flute
8' Diapason
8' Violin
8' Concert Flute
4' Octave
4' Flauto Traverso
4' Violin
2' Super Octave
2' Piccolo
8' Trumpet
8' Clarinet
8' Vox Humana
4' Clarion
Orchestral Bells
Xylophon
Glockenspiel
16 Solo to Acct
16 Acct " "
8 Solo to "
4' Acct to "
4' Solo to "

Solo.
16' Bass Flute
8' Concert Flute
8' Diapason
8' Violin
8' Trumpet
8' Clarinet
8' Vox Humana
4' Flauto Traverso
4' Octave
4' Violin
4' Clarion
2 2/3 Octave Quint
2' Piccolo
2' Superoctave

Aurora Theatre East Aurora N.Y. continued

1 3/5 Tierce
Orchestral Bells
Chimes
Glockenspiel
16 Solo to Solo
4 " " "

Pedal
16 Double Bass.
16' Bass Flute
8' Octave
8 Flute
8' Cello
4' Clarion
Acct to Pedal
Solo to Pedal

Pedal movements
Balanced Expression
" Crescendo.

Accessories 240 set up switches
3 H.P. Orgoblo
200 Watt Generator
Indicator
Tremolo.

Traps
Tom Tom — Toe Piston
Tympani — Stop Key
Auto Horn — Toe Piston
Crash Cymbal — " "
Fire Gong — " "
Steamboat Whistle — " "
Thunder effect — " "
Siren — " "
Tambourine
Castanets
Chinese Blocks
Telephone Bell
Bird Whistle
Snare Drum
Bass "
Cymbals.

Bdn 97
Diap 85
Violin 85
Tuba 73 TR.
Clarinet 61 " "
Vox Hum 61 " "

$6600.
Electric action

He later sold it to Salem Ch. S. Buffalo

VINER OPUS LIST

CITY/STATE	LOCATION	SIZE	YR	OPUS	BLWR	REMARKS
CALIFORNIA						
San Diego	Superior Th.	3/	1909			
NEW YORK						
Akron	Park Th.	2/5	1923	199		Unified with traps.
Batavia	LaFayette Th.	2/8	1925	216	17183	Unified with tuned percussion.
Clarence	Ryley Th.		1921			
East Aurora	Aurora Th.	2/6	1925	217		Unified with traps and tuned percussion; cost $6,600.
Silver Creek	Geitner Th.		1926		19608	Probably a rebuild of an existing Link organ.

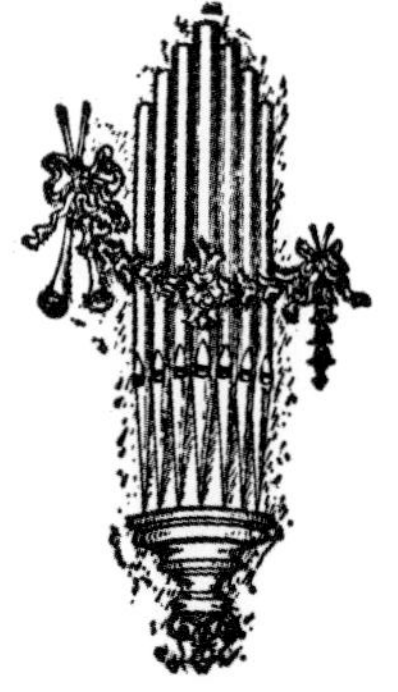

ESTABLISHED 1855

THE VOTTELER-HOLTKAMP-SPARLING ORGAN CO.

Factory, Corner West 14th St. and Abbey Ave.

CLEVELAND, OHIO

PIPE ORGANS

Phones { Bell, Harvard 1931 W
Cuy., Central 8398 L

H. B. VOTTELER, PRESIDENT
A. G. SPARLING, VICE-PRES.
H. H. HOLTKAMP, SECRETARY
M. E. HOLTKAMP, TREASURER

The firm of G. F. Votteler & Co. was formed in Cleveland, Ohio in 1855 by Gottlieb F. Votteler, a German who had immigrated to the United States in 1847. When he died in 1894 control of the firm passed to his son, Henry B. Votteler. The year 1894 was also significant in that it was the birthdate of Walter Holtkamp, Sr.[1] who would eventually become owner of the firm as well as one of the most influential personalities in American organ building. But that's getting ahead of the story!

Votteler was a small regional builder whose products were seldom sold outside Ohio. One of the best Votteler organ salesmen was a man not even on the company payroll: Henry H. Holtkamp operated a retail music store in St. Mary's, Ohio, which sold pianos, reed organs and an occasional Votteler pipe organ. So great were Holtkamp's sales abilities that he was invited to move to Cleveland in 1903 to join the firm as sales manager. Later in 1903 a local brewery owner, John Hettche, became a substantial investor and the firm name was changed to the Votteler-Hettche Organ Co. In 1905 Henry Votteler retired and left the firm in the hands of Henry Holtkamp who, with his daughter, Mary E. Holtkamp, treasurer of the firm, ran the business through the teens and twenties. Shortly after Mr. Votteler's retirement Mr. Hettche lost interest in the firm, whereupon he took his money to Detroit and invested in a hotel.[2] [3]

In 1911 Allan Gordon Sparling joined the firm. He was born in Canada and became an apprentice in the Dougherty (reed) Organ Company of Clinton, Ontario after graduating from high school in 1891. In 1894 he joined the Goderich Organ Company of Goderich, Ontario and in 1899 moved to Toronto to assume the post of factory superintendent of the Compensating Pipe Organ Company. Mr. Sparling remained with the Compensating company through their move to Battle Creek, Michigan in 1901 and their subsequent purchase by Lyon & Healy in 1906. After Lyon & Healy liquidated their pipe organ department in 1908, Mr. Sparling moved to Marietta, Ohio where he started a pipe organ department for the Stevens Organ Company. In 1911 he moved to Cleveland and became a partner in the Votteler-Hettche company, whose name was finally changed in May 1914 to the Votteler-Holtkamp-Sparling Organ Co. to reflect the new ownership.[4] [5] [6] [7]

A. G. Sparling was a mechanical expert who had little interest in tonal design. Henry Holtkamp charted the firm's course in tonal matters and remained the firm's chief salesman and public image figure, a tradition later carried on by his son, Walter Holtkamp, Sr., and *his* son, Walter Holtkamp, Jr. With Henry Holtkamp's salesmanship the small firm's production rose from an average of six organs annually in the years 1903-1909 to an average of 14 organs annually during the period 1910-1919. As the roaring twenties progressed, the firm continued to prosper, reaching an all time high of 23 organs built in the year 1928.[8]

The Votteler firm could never really compete with the giant firms in the industry but nevertheless managed to secure seven contracts for theatre business, all in Ohio, between 1915 and 1927. These organs were not high pressure instruments but they did have electric action and were unified to a certain extent. Votteler's last two theatre instruments even sported horseshoe consoles with colored stop keys,[9] quite a daring move for a conservative little firm.

In 1931 both Henry and Mary Holtkamp died, leaving artistic control of the firm to Walter Holtkamp, Sr., who had begun working for his father's company in 1913 at age 19. And the rest, as they say, is history. Walter Holtkamp, Sr. spearheaded the classical organ reform movement in this country and became one of the industry's most influential personalities. A. G. Sparling retired in 1943 and in 1951 the firm name was changed to Holtkamp Organ Company, having become exclusively a family business.[10] [11] Upon the death of Walter Holtkamp, Sr. in 1962 the business was taken over by his son, Walter "Chick" Holtkamp, Jr. (1929-   ) who today carries on the traditions begun by his father and grandfather. The author is especially indebted to Mr. Holtkamp for his courtesy in making the Holtkamp factory archives available for this book. By no means a theatre organ buff, Mr. Holtkamp is, however, a student of organ history and was of enormous assistance in ensuring the historical accuracy of this chapter.

This unusual console for Votteler's first theatre instrument was installed in the Youngstown, Ohio Hippodrome. It featured a player mechanism built into the top of the case and combination setters on either side of the key cheeks.

This is the nameplate used by the firm during the 1920s.

The only three-manual horseshoe console ever built for a theatre by the Votteler company was installed in the Lincoln Theatre in Lakewood, Ohio in 1926. This 3/10 organ was an enlargement of an earlier 2/7 Votteler installed in 1923.

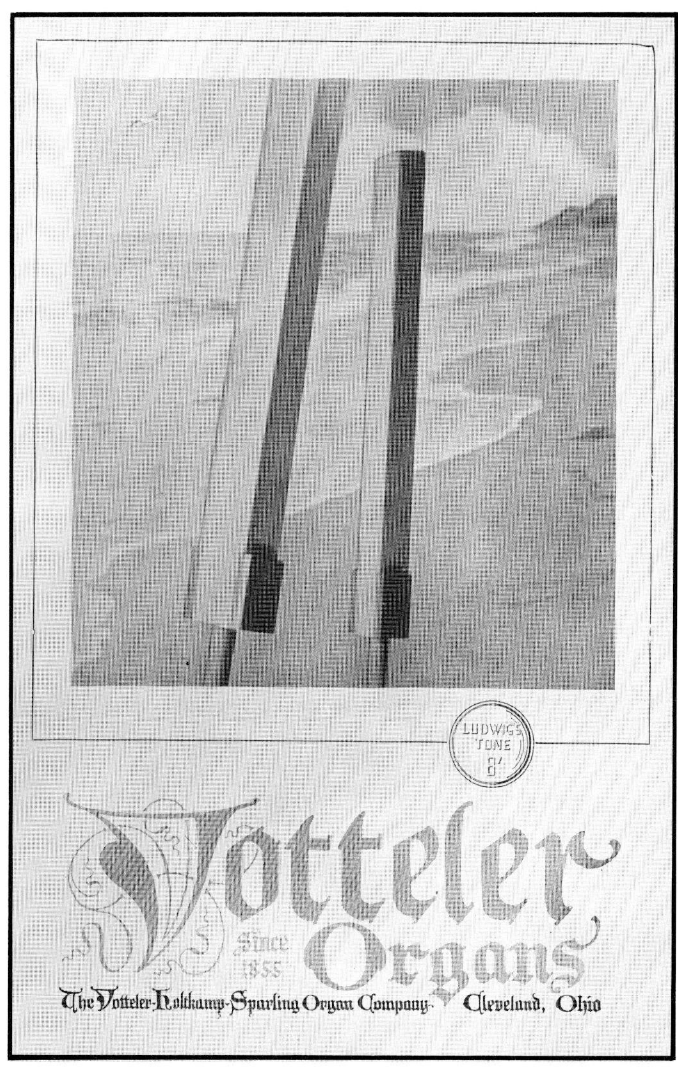

Although the Votteler firm was noted for its conservative tonal philosophy, it did manage to introduce one new voice to the tonal palette of the organ: the Ludwigtone, pictured here in what was originally a full-page ad in the May 1927 issue of The Diapason. *Waves of the sea here form a background for the double-mouth Ludwigtone, which is most appropriate inasmuch as its tone is reminiscent of the unda maris. The Ludwigtone was routinely introduced into even small Votteler church organs but, interestingly enough, none of their theatre instruments was equipped with one.*

TONE VERSUS TABLETS

The
Votteler-Holtkamp-Sparling
Organ Company

ESTABLISHED 1855

CLEVELAND, OHIO

Votteler ads, in keeping with company philosophy, were simple and tasteful. This one appeared in the April 1925 issue of The Diapason.

2/4 VOTTELER-HOLTKAMP-SPARLING THEATRE ORGAN, OPUS 1496
State Theatre, Westerville, Ohio

This is a typical contract for one of the firm's theatre instruments, in this case the last one they ever sold.

THE VOTTELER HOLTKAMP SPARLING ORGAN COMPANY

Cleveland, Ohio 7/20/27

To A. D. Curfman
Of Westerville Ohio

The Votteler Holtkamp Sparling Organ Co., of Cleveland, Ohio, hereby proposes to build for you one pipe organ, including setting up in your Theatre ready for use and in accordance with the attached specifications, marked attached all of which are a part of this proposal, freight and drayage (or express) and any hoisting charges to be paid by you.
All materials and workmanship shall be first-class in every particular.
~~You are to provide us when request with essential plans and information;~~ to prepare suitable space in the above designated building for said organ and its appurtenances, clean and thoroughly dried out before the parts thereof are delivered, and to give us the necessary use of said building for approximately 14 days for setting up and tuning said organ, which with all parts thereof shall be at your risk after delivery to carrier. We agree to have said organ ready for use about October 1st, 1927 months after we receive your acceptance of this proposal and the same is countersigned in our Cleveland office, unless delayed by labor trouble or other causes beyond our control. ~~Due to the uncertain condition of the labor and material market and the shipping situation, the time for completion of the said organ is only approximated.~~

You are to insure said organ against all loss or damage by fire or otherwise in favor of The Votteler Holtkamp Sparling Organ Co., as its interest may appear, and to execute and deliver any further documents which we may require at any time during the life of this contract to give full legal protection to our title or equity hereunder in the state in which the organ is or is to be installed. It is agreed that said organ is and shall remain our property until paid for, and upon failure to pay as agreed we shall have the right at our option to enter your premises and remove said organ, with or without force or process of law, and to apply all payments in liquidation of damages for breach of contract.

Your acceptance of this proposal shall be in your corporate name by duly authorized offi~~cers or agents thereof~~.

You agree to pay us upon fulfilment of said conditions, the sum of Four Thousand and 00/100 Dollars ($4000.00) payable in exchange on New York or Cleveland, at our office in Cleveland, as follows:
One Thousand and 00/100 ($1000.00) dollars upon signing this contract:
($____) dollars upon presentation of bill of lading or other evidence of shipment of the organ or principal parts thereof:
($____) dollars upon completion of the organ in your building; and the remaining Three Thousand and 00/100 ($3000.00) dollar in Fifteen (15) successive payments of 200.00 ($200.00) dollars each, the first of which shall be due first month after said completion, with interest on each of said sums at the rate of Six (6%) per cent per annum from the date of completion. You agree further, in the event that your building be not ready for installation of the said organ as herein provided, to pay us within thirty days after our written notice to you of our readiness to ship the organ or principal parts thereof, the sum above specified to be due upon shipment and upon completion of the organ in your building, and thereafter to make the remaining payments successively at the times above specified.

It is acknowledged that there are no agreements or understandings between the parties except as included herein.

THE VOTTELER HOLTKAMP SPARLING ORGAN CO.
By Walter Holtkamp

THE VOTTELER HOLTKAMP SPARLING ORGAN CO.
Your proposition herein contained is hereby accepted this 20th day of July, 1927.
Signed A. D. Curfman

Countersigned in Cleveland this 21st day of July 1927
THE VOTTELER HOLTKAMP SPARLING ORGAN CO.
By [signature] Sparling

DETAILS OF CONSTRUCTION

1. THE FRAME WORK to be substantial and a firm foundation for the various parts, to be rigidly constructed of well seasoned material every portion firmly put together.

2. THE BELLOWS to be of ample size and best material, framed with removable panels, double leathered, provided with internal safety or regulating valve maintaining an even pressure and sufficient capacity for all legitimate demands.

3. THE WIND TRUNKS which convey the air to the various divisions of the organ, are to be made large size to prevent all possible friction, to be so constructed as to insure air tight connections with flexible joints wherever necessary.

4. THE WIND CHESTS made of thoroughly seasoned and best quality lumber, with inter-augmentations and so arranged that every pipe get a full supply of wind without robbing or tonal interference, giving a freshness of tone thruout the whole instrument, with no falling off of tone when full organ is used. All valves to be covered with appropriate leather, connected by the most direct action attainable, producing the most perfect objective points of a perfect action; an easy and free touch of elastic quality, rapid and accurate REPETITION, silent and reliable OPERATION, SIMPLICITY AND DURABILITY.

5. THE CONSOLE, the only finished exterior, our regular accessible type finished in oil or varnish in harmony with the prevailing woodwork of the surroundings. The manual keyboards to be of an approved standard and so arranged as to give the greatest facility to the organist. Pedal keys to be concave and radiating.

6. THE LOUVERS fitted by us to the framed and grilled openings (the latter supplied by the second party) tobe carefully made, to be so constructed as to insure tight connections and padded, made to serve on pivots by a self-balancing pedal.

7. THE WOOD PIPES to be made of the best stock Pine, Spruce, Poplar or other appropriate wood glue sized on the inside and carefully treated with shellac or paint on the outside: all to be supplied with wooden feet, metal toes used for smaller pipes and gates for the larger.

8. METAL PIPES to be of a composition of tin and lead varied from 40 to 90% of tin according to the requirements of the organ and the utility of same. Bases have zinc where stiffness is required. Display pipes if embodied in design included by us.

9. THE TONAL DIVISIONS to be characteristic and appropriate for the different functions and while each register especially patterned after our own models will be perfect in speech and tone with regular fundamental proportion of unisons, the general effect of all or any portion of the ORCHESTRAL compass to be similar to a well balanced SYMPHONY in artistic effect with correct and pleasing individuality, giving registers their specific timbre of tone, pre-eminently imitative of ORCHESTRAL instruments represented. The DIAPASON to be FULL, MAJESTIC, POWERFUL and SONOROUS. Full organ free from all harshness maintained thruout the organ.

10. A BENCH of graceful design furnished with the organ so constructed as to allow the organist perfect freedom.

11. ALL MATERIAL TO BE OF THE HIGHEST GRADE FOR THEIR RESPECTIVE PARTS, WORKMANSHIP TO BE OF SUPERIOR ORDER AND CONSTRUCTION OF OUR REGULAR STANDARD AND OUR USUAL TYPE OF ENSEMBLE, INSURING DURABILITY AND PERFECT OPERATION OF ALL PARTS.

ESTABLISHED 1855
The Votteler-Holtkamp-Sparling Organ Company
Cleveland Ohio

SPECIFICATION

Of two manual and pedal unit type organ
For A.D.Curfman of Westerville Ohio.

PEDAL - Compass 32 Notes

Bourdon	I6'	
Basso	I6'	
Diapason	8'	
Gedeckt	8'	
Cello	8'	
Flute	4'	
Addition Proviso		
Addition Proviso		
Addition Proviso		

Master Combinations - Visible and adjustable
I - 2 - 3 - 4 - 5 - 6

GREAT - Compass 6I Notes

Bourdon	I6'	
Diapason	8'	
Gedeckt	8'	
Violin	8'	
Octave	4'	
Flute	4'	
Salicet	4'	
Piccolo	2'	
Major Twelfth	2 2/3'	
Cathedral Chimes		
Orchestra Bells		
Celesta		
Addition Proviso		
Addition Proviso		
Addition Proviso		

SWELL - Compass 6I Notes

Contra Viole	I6'	Tenor C
Gedeckt	8'	
Violin	8'	
Vox Humana	8'	Tenor C
Diapson	8'	
Flute	4'	

THE VOTTELER IS ONE OF THE FINEST ORGANS BUILT IN AMERICA TO-DAY

ESTABLISHED 1855
The Votteler-Holtkamp-Sparling Organ Company
Cleveland Ohio

SPECIFICATION

SWELL continued

Salicet	4'
Vox Humana	4'
Piccolo	2'
Twelfth	2 2/3'
Tierce	I 3/5'
Addition Proviso	
Addition Proviso	
Addition Proviso	

GENERAL

Expression Pedal
General Tremulant
Electric Blower
ElectricGenerator
Circular Console

Holtkamp
7/20/27

The Votteler-Holtkamp-Sparling
Organ Company ESTABLISHED 1855

H. B. VOTTELER, PRESIDENT
A. G. SPARLING, VICE-PRESIDENT
H. H. HOLTKAMP, SECRETARY
M. E. HOLTKAMP, TREASURER

3265 WEST 30TH STREET, CORNER MEYER AVENUE
Cleveland, Ohio

DISPOSITION #I496

7/2I/27 A-440 W.P. 8" Theatre, Westerville

PEDAL

No.	Stop	Pitch		
I	Bourdon	I6	Ous #I	97
2	Basso	I6	Pulls #3 and GG of #I	
3	Diapason	8	Dennison #44	73
4	Gedeckt	8	From #I	
5	Cello	8	Dennison #68	85
6	Flute	4	From #I	
7	Extra Contact - but no breaker			
8	Extra Contact - but no breaker			
9	Extra Contact - but no breaker			

GREAT

No.	Stop	Pitch		
I0	Bourdon	I6	From #I	
II	Diapason	8	From #3	
I2	Gedeckt	8	From #I	
I3	Violin	8	From #5	
I4	Octave	4	From #3	
I5	Flute	4	From #I	
I6	Salicet	4	From #5	
~~I7~~	~~Piccolo~~	2	From #I	
I8	Major Twelfth	2 2/3	From #I	
I9	Cathedral Chimes		Deagan #I" G - G	I3
20	Orchestral Bells		Deagan #2230 Hard Hammer	30
2I	Celesta		From #20 Soft Hammer	
22	Extra Roller with contacts but no wiring			
23	" " " " " " "			
24	" " " " " " "			

SWELL

No.	Stop	Pitch		
25	Contra Viole	I6	From #5 Tenor C	
26	Gedeckt	8	From #I	
27	Violin	8	From #5	
28	Vox Humana	8	Dennison #Reg Ten C	49
29	Diapason	8	From #3	
30	Flute	4	From #I	
3I	Salicet	4	From #5	
32	Vox Humana	4	From #28 upper I2 from #I	
33	Piccolo	2	From #I	
34	Twelfth	2 2/3	From #5	
35	Pierce	I 3/5	From #I	
36	Extra Roller with contacts but no wiring			
37	" " " " " " "			
38	" " " " " " "			

One Tremolo overall

Last page of the contract at left.

A. G. Sparling watches a workman rack a rank of diapason pipes in the erecting room of the Votteler factory.

These buildings at 14th and Abbey Streets housed the company through 1922. The significance of the mural is unknown; perhaps it had to do with World War I.

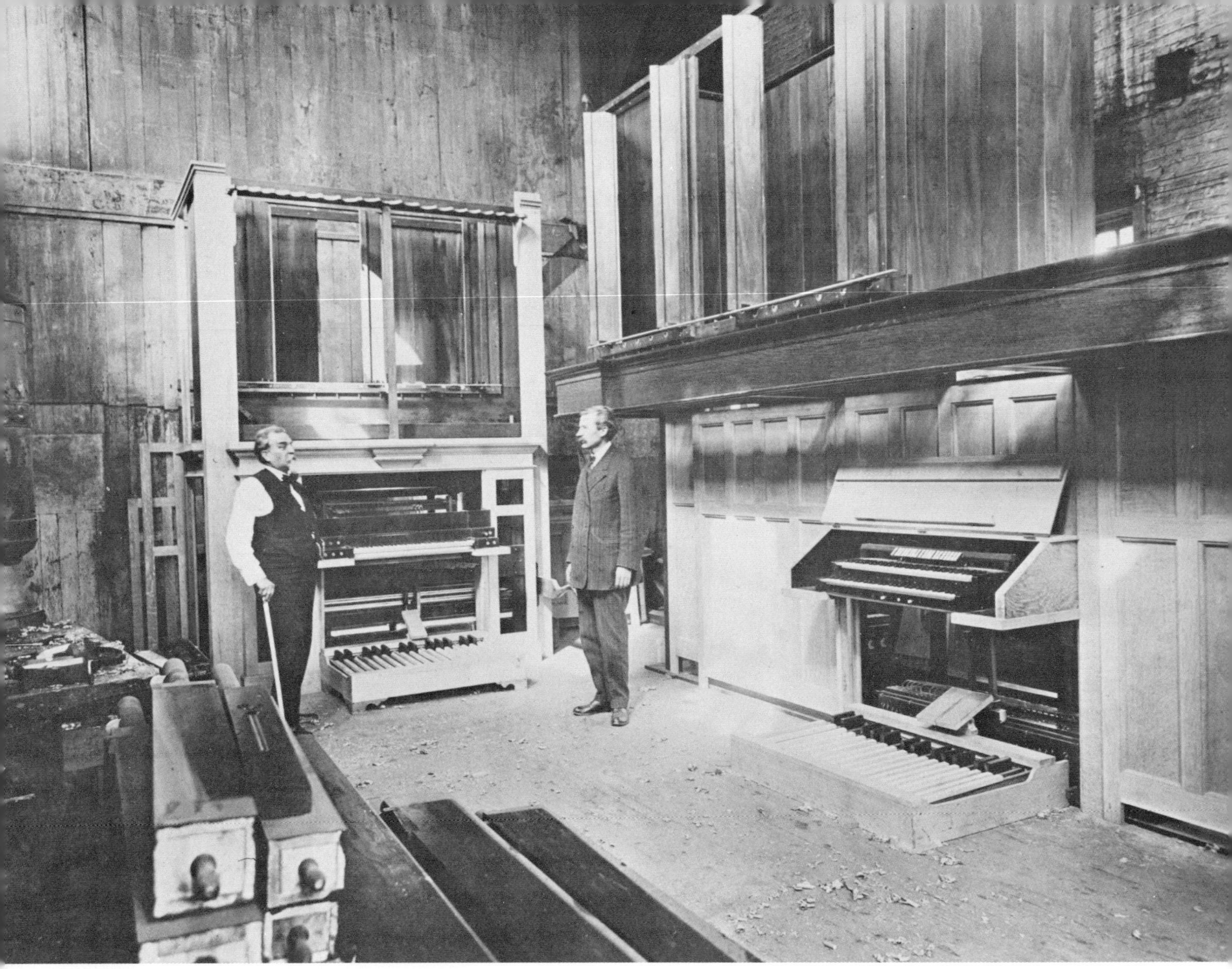

H. B. Votteler (left) and H. H. Holtkamp pose in the erecting room of the Votteler factory at 14th and Abbey Streets. The organ on the right has tubular pneumatic action; the small one-manual organ on the left is a tracker. The conservative Votteler firm built trackers well into the 1920s.

Henry Holtkamp (right) discusses the voicing of a melodia with voicer Louis Toth. Through the 1920s the firm made their own wood pipes but purchased metal pipes from trade suppliers such as Pierce, Gottfried and National Organ Supply.

Holtkamp headquarters from 1923 to the current day. Offices are on the right; erecting room is on the left.

The last two theatre instruments built by the company bore this nameplate.

VOTTELER-HOLTKAMP-SPARLING OPUS LIST

Following is a complete list of this firm's theatre installations.

OPUS	LOCATION/CITY/STATE	SIZE	YR	PRICE	REMARKS
1273	Hippodrome Th., Youngstown, OH	3/24	1915	$ 8,000.00	With roll player, orchestral bells and 4-rank echo.
1273	Southern Th., Columbus, OH	3/24	1920	$ 3,954.18	Organ moved from Hippodrome Theatre, Youngstown, Ohio; player unit removed.
1363	Gardner Th., Toledo, OH	2/7	1920	$ 4,800.00	Piano console; 5″ wind.
1364	LaGrange Th., Toledo, OH	2/7	1921	$ 6,000.00	Piano console; 5″ wind; with harp and chimes.
1408	Lincoln Th., Lakewood, OH	2/7	1923	$ 6,500.00	5″ wind.
1408A	Lincoln Th., Lakewood, OH	3/10	1926	$ 5,610.00	Additions: 3 ranks, harp, xylophone, glockenspiel and horseshoe console.
1496	State Th., Westerville, OH	2/4	1927	$ 4,000.00	Horseshoe console; chimes and orchestra bells with hard and soft hammers; Spencer blower #20810.

WANGERIN ORGAN COMPANY

110-124 BURRELL STREET
MILWAUKEE, WISCONSIN, U.S.A.

The Hann-Wangerin Company was organized in 1895 by Adolph Wangerin and Frederick Hann to build church furniture.[5] Nearby in Milwaukee was another firm whose activities were similar, not only in woodworking but in sales to churches: the Wm. Schuelke Organ Company. The shop foreman of the Schuelke firm was George J. Weickhardt, a native of Bavaria who had learned organ building in Europe before immigrating to America in 1893. His first employment was with Phillip Wirsching in Salem, Ohio where he worked for two years before moving to Milwaukee. Weickhardt's tenure at the Schuelke company didn't last too long, his progressive organ building ideas clashing with those of the conservative William Schuelke. Hann and Wangerin offered to let Weickhardt use their factory to build organs, which he did, coming in at night after the regular work force had gone home.[6 7]

Mr. Weickhardt was eventually persuaded to become a member of the Hann-Wangerin Company. The firm officially entered the organ business in 1903 under the name Hann-Wangerin-Weickhardt Company. The Hann name was dropped in 1912, the firm then being known as the Wangerin-Weickhardt Company, the name it would keep for the next dozen years. Although Wangerin was a part of the company name, ads of the firm referred to their product as "the Weickhardt organ" reflecting the esteem with which Mr. Weickhardt was held in the organ industry. The name of the company was finally changed to the Wangerin Organ Company in 1924, five years after Mr. Weickhardt's death.

George Weickhardt had been vice president and factory superintendent of the Hann-Weickhardt Company. He was succeeded in these positions by Edmond Verlinden (1881-1961), a native of Antwerp, Belgium whose family was known for church sculpture and decoration. It was appropriate that Mr. Verlinden should have entered the employ of an organ firm which was also a builder of church furniture after he immigrated to Milwaukee in 1910. Edmond Verlinden was a clever inventor and an exceptionally skilled craftsman who introduced a number of improvements and refinements to the Wangerin product during his years of employment with the firm.[8]

The company's owner, Adolph Wangerin, was for many years president of the Organ Builders Association of America and shared Mr. Verlinden's interest in high quality. The author has long been keenly impressed with the quality of Wangerin instruments of the 1920s and, in fact, believes that their excellence of construction has never been surpassed by any American builder. Many of their components were crafted with almost a jeweller's precision, featuring niceties of cosmetics which only the organ tuner would ever appreciate. This attention to minute details of quality paid off in incredible longevity and reli-

Adolph Wangerin

George J. Weickhardt
1858-1919

Edmond A. Verlinden (1881-1961) was directly responsible for much of the mechanical excellence of Wangerin organs in the 1920s.

Console of the 1925 Wangerin in the Lake Theatre in Milwaukee.

ability of Wangerin organs. For instance, in 1976 the author played a 3/14 Wangerin-built Barton still in its original 1927 home, the Iowa Theatre in Cedar Rapids. This organ had never seen more than ordinary maintenance over its half century of service but not one dead note could be found and even all 37 notes of the xylophone reiterated perfectly!

Wangerin organs excelled in voicing as well as in excellence of construction. Prior to 1920 Jerome B. Meyer was in charge of Wangerin's pipe shop. After Meyer and Wangerin parted company a new pipe shop was implemented which turned out some of the finest flue pipes of the era. Wangerin string voicing was particularly notable; their theatre organ strings out-"zing" even those of Robert-Morton. Some of the quality of Wangerin voicing was undoubtedly the result of Philipp Wirsching's employment. Following the demise of his own company, he worked for the firm from 1922 until shortly before his death in 1926.[9] Wangerin purchased most, if not all, of their reeds from quality suppliers such as Illinois Organ Supply Co. and Dennison.

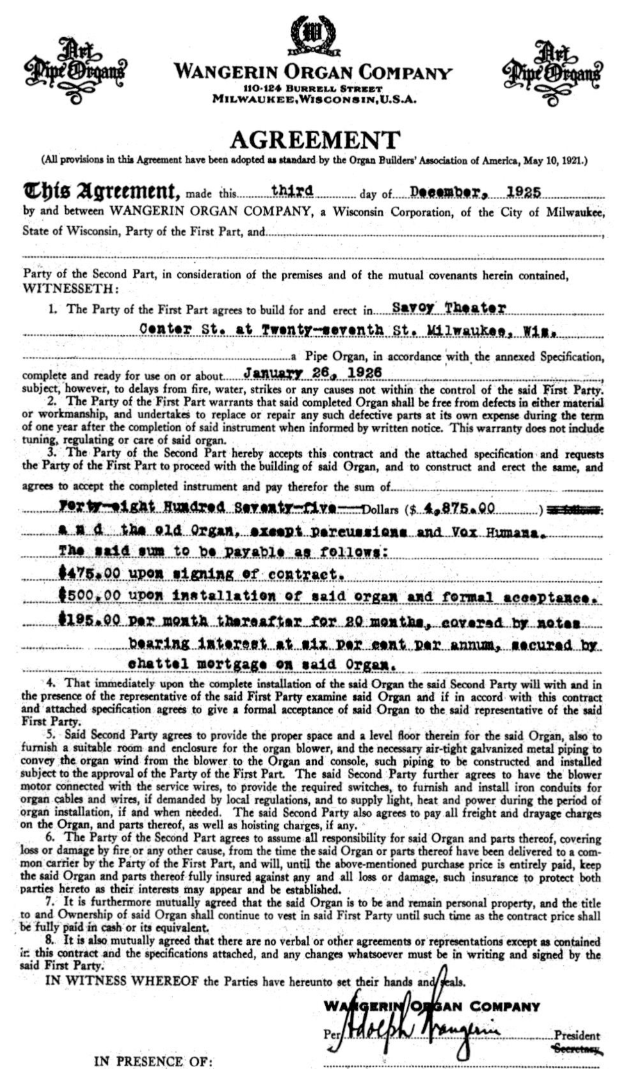

Art Pipe Organs

WANGERIN ORGAN COMPANY
110-124 BURRELL STREET
MILWAUKEE, WISCONSIN, U.S.A.

Art Pipe Organs

AGREEMENT

(All provisions in this Agreement have been adopted as standard by the Organ Builders' Association of America, May 10, 1921.)

This Agreement, made this third day of December, 1925 by and between WANGERIN ORGAN COMPANY, a Wisconsin Corporation, of the City of Milwaukee, State of Wisconsin, Party of the First Part, and ....

Party of the Second Part, in consideration of the premises and of the mutual covenants herein contained, WITNESSETH:

1. The Party of the First Part agrees to build for and erect in Savoy Theater Center St. at Twenty-seventh St. Milwaukee, Wis. a Pipe Organ, in accordance with the annexed Specification, complete and ready for use on or about January 26, 1926, subject, however, to delays from fire, water, strikes or any causes not within the control of the said First Party.

2. The Party of the First Part warrants that said completed Organ shall be free from defects in either material or workmanship, and undertakes to replace or repair any such defective parts at its own expense during the term of one year after the completion of said instrument when informed by written notice. This warranty does not include tuning, regulating or care of said organ.

3. The Party of the Second Part hereby accepts this contract and the attached specification and requests the Party of the First Part to proceed with the building of said Organ, and to construct and erect the same, and agrees to accept the completed instrument and pay therefor the sum of Forty-eight Hundred Seventy-five—Dollars ($ 4,875.00) ~~as follows:~~
and the old Organ, except percussions and Vox Humana.
The said sum to be payable as follows:
$475.00 upon signing of contract.
$500.00 upon installation of said organ and formal acceptance.
$195.00 per month thereafter for 20 months, covered by notes bearing interest at six per cent per annum, secured by chattel mortgage on said Organ.

4. That immediately upon the complete installation of the said Organ the said Second Party will with and in the presence of the representative of the said First Party examine said Organ and if in accord with this contract and attached specification agrees to give a formal acceptance of said Organ to the said representative of the said First Party.

5. Said Second Party agrees to provide the proper space and a level floor therein for the said Organ, also to furnish a suitable room and enclosure for the organ blower, and the necessary air-tight galvanized metal piping to convey the organ wind from the blower to the Organ and console, such piping to be constructed and installed subject to the approval of the Party of the First Part. The said Second Party further agrees to have the blower motor connected with the service wires, to provide the required switches, to furnish and install iron conduits for organ cables and wires, if demanded by local regulations, and to supply light, heat and power during the period of organ installation, if and when needed. The said Second Party also agrees to pay all freight and drayage charges on the Organ, and parts thereof, as well as hoisting charges, if any.

6. The Party of the Second Part agrees to assume all responsibility for said Organ and parts thereof, covering loss or damage by fire or any other cause, from the time the said Organ or parts thereof have been delivered to a common carrier by the Party of the First Part, and will, until the above-mentioned purchase price is entirely paid, keep the said Organ and parts thereof fully insured against any and all loss or damage, such insurance to protect both parties hereto as their interests may appear and be established.

7. It is furthermore mutually agreed that the said Organ is to be and remain personal property, and the title to and Ownership of said Organ shall continue to vest in said First Party until such time as the contract price shall be fully paid in cash or its equivalent.

8. It is also mutually agreed that there are no verbal or other agreements or representations except as contained in this contract and the specifications attached, and any changes whatsoever must be in writing and signed by the said First Party.

IN WITNESS WHEREOF the Parties have hereunto set their hands and seals.

WANGERIN ORGAN COMPANY
Per Adolph Wangerin President ~~Secretary~~

IN PRESENCE OF:

Per ....(SEAL)
Per ....(SEAL)
Per ....(SEAL)

Sample of a Wangerin theatre organ contract, never actually consummated, which was to have replaced an early Wangerin straight organ with an up-to-date 2/7 unit instrument including a "circular type" console.

Wangerin got started in theatre business quite early (1913), selling straight orchestral instruments, as did most builders of that era. A most fortuitous transaction occurred about this same time when Dan Barton visited the factory and asked for a miniature 30-note organ to be built. This little unit was the nucleus of the first Bartola and was the precursor of the Barton organ. Dan Barton was highly satisfied with Wangerin's quality and this simple sale was the first of hundreds between the two firms.

Wangerin manufactured the organ sections of Bartolas by the dozen. After Barton began building complete organs their small factory was often inadequate to keep up with Dan Barton's selling pace. As a result, Barton fre-

On this and the following two pages is reproduced a portion of a rare 1916 Wangerin theatre organ catalog.

THE MOST REFINED TYPE OF

PIPE ORGANS

FOR

THEATERS

Wangerin-Weickhardt Co.
112-124 Burrell Street
MILWAUKEE WISCONSIN, U.S.A.

The Weickhardt Pipe Organ for the Theater

THE intelligent and growing demand for Organ Music in Motion Picture Theaters has led towards a widespread introduction of the Pipe Organ into numerous show-houses throughout the country. This is not to be wondered at since, in the words of Honoré de Balzac, *"the organ is in truth the grandest, the most daring, the most magnificent of all instruments invented by human genius. It is a whole orchestra in itself. It can express anything in response to a skilled touch"*.

That organ music lends itself with singular adaptability to emotional and dramatic film scenes is an established fact, and it is equally certain that the popular musical mind is quick to discriminate between the grandeur and dignity of refined pipe organ tones and the cheap, commonplace drone and blare of the average theater organ.

In but very few cases has the question of quality in the purchase of theater organs received the amount of consideration which is strictly its due. While in some gratifying instances careful attention has been paid to the point of positive excellence in workmanship, tone, action and reliability, surprisingly many contracts have been and are still awarded on the basis of low price and easy terms of payment. Imprudent competition has often misguided theater organ purchasers and caused them to arrive at remarkably erroneous conclusions. To avoid this the various individual claims of organ builders must be carefully investigated, and that is exactly what we urge interested theater owners to do respecting the Weickhardt Pipe Organ.

Ever since the first Weickhardt Organ was installed in a prominent motion picture theater of Chicago it was promptly acknowledged to be an instrument of rare artistic refinement, characteristic of the real and strictly essential orchestral tone quality, and every existing example in use today calls forth the highest expressions of praise and appreciation.

Each organ is constructed under the personal supervision and direction of our Mr. George Weickhardt, widely known as a master of the art of organ building by everyone familiar with his many achievements.

The foremost structural feature of our instruments is the Weickhardt Universal Wind-Chest, patented August 20th, 1907. Anyone conversant with the importance of the wind-chest in an organ will readily admit that our universal wind system is the only method by which perfect tonal results are obtainable.

Every Weickhardt Organ is operated and controlled by our special electro-pneumatic action which yields the highest possible efficiency. Our magnets are made up in the most dependable and advantageous form, wound with the best enamel-insulated copper wire, and an eight-volt current is sufficient to incite them.

It is of the utmost importance that the pipes in an organ be made of absolutely suitable materials, correctly scaled and properly constructed, in order to yield the most refined quality of tone when scientifically voiced. In view of this prerequisite we have ever devoted painstaking care to our fully equipped Metal and Wood Pipe Departments and are therefore enabled to obtain that artistic degree of tonal excellence which is indispensable to denote true quality.

We lay particular stress upon the weight of the metal used in our Diapasons, as we employ the same in an exceedingly heavy form in order to produce that grand, full sonority and strikingly rich fundamental tonal body which has been instrumental in quite a degree towards establishing the renown of the Weickhardt Organ.

However perfect the component parts of an organ may be, its real worth will largely depend upon the skill exercised in the voicing of the pipes. Only an extensive and thorough knowledge of the construction, character and treatment of pipes, combined with a trained ear for perfect tone quality, can give to an organ that one grand mark of eminence and superiority towards which all else is but an auxiliary.

It is also necessary to mention the importance of heavy Swell Boxes in pipe organs. The two most desirable objects to be secured thereby are: Musical Expression and Flexibility of all tonal resources in the Swell Division. A really effective swell box can only be produced by following a plan calling for ample dimensions as well as proper thickness of the walls and shades. We build our swell boxes by strongly framing the sides, backs and tops to a full thickness of two inches, the vertical shades,—built up of narrow strips, glued together, rabetted front and back and heavily padded,—being of the same solid measurement. The result of this treatment is that the gradual opening of the silently moving shades produces a magnificent *crescendo* and by reversed movement a strikingly expressive *diminuendo*. It may not be amiss to mention in this connection that all the many cheap and commercial organs contain a flimsy swell box of no more than seven-eighths of an inch in thickness, yielding practically no expression whatever.

In the Weickhardt Organ everything down to the minutest detail is provided and particularly that portion receives painstaking consideration which is under the immediate control of the organist. A noted poet extols the latter's significant function in the following inspiring stanza:

"His fingers wander over fields of song,
Where winds of harmony blow soft, blow strong;
Now all the sky is bright, then overcast,
With mighty thunder-clouds from far and fast.
He sings a mother's evening lullaby,
And voices nations in their battle cry.
Mountains and seas upon his view arise,
Poets and kings attend his minstrelsies,
And all the master spirits of the past
Rise at the summons of his trumpet-blast."

We build our consoles in the most serviceable and advantageous form and follow out the latest approved methods in providing the utmost convenience to the player for instantaneous manipulation of tonal combinations or specially striking effects.

In conclusion it may be unreservedly asserted that the Weickhardt Organ is the ideal Theater Organ, owing to its magnificent pure organ as well as orchestral tone qualities. Always artistically and modernly built, it offers such exquisitely glorious results of never-ending variety, beauty and interest as to guarantee the richest musical efficiency, and a perpetual source of intellectual enjoyment to every one brought under its influence.

Location of the Organ

HE question respecting the most suitable position and space dimensions for a Pipe Organ should receive very particular attention when planning and building a theater.

First of all the architect should be warned against a freak organ chamber, otherwise it will be left to the Organ Builder to discover too late that an impossible room of an equally impossible shape and size has been provided, or one barely large enough for a commonplace commercial stock organ offering but slightly more space than might be required by a piano, thus totally and effectively debarring the installation of a really artistic Pipe Organ.

An example of this nature may be cited with a view of cautioning architects, as well as those preparing to build a show-house, against irremediable deficiency of organ space conditions. A well-known theater man, controlling several prominent motion picture houses, all equipped with a Weickhardt Organ, had completed arrangements in leasing a new theater just going up and practically instructed our firm to build the organ for it. Upon looking over the architect's plans we found an organ recess provided in a size completely precluding the possibility of installing any high-grade real pipe organ. The owner of the building refused to make any alterations, our client was forced to cancel his order with us, and if he wanted anything like an organ in that theater he found himself compelled against his own will and better judgment to purchase a very common commercial stock instrument of insignificant musical value, simply because the architect had accepted misguiding and deplorably inadequate information.

In all cases where the building of a theater is projected, and the plans are still subject to alterations it is well to know that *any really artistic and high-grade organ of average size can be properly installed only in a space approximately fourteen feet in height, ten to twelve feet in width and eight to ten feet in depth.*

An ample *sound opening* of approximately seven feet width and nine to ten feet height is extremely essential. The top line of this should be carried up as close as possible to the ceiling line so that no sound pocket or hood may be formed over the instrument. In all the most modern theaters the sound opening is fitted out with an ornamental grille, whereas formerly display pipes were used for this purpose.

If an *ECHO ORGAN* is under consideration its chamber must be very thoughtfully provided at a location where it will be possible to maintain a reasonably equable temperature. *A height of no less than ten to twelve feet, a width of nine feet and a depth of seven feet is needed for an Echo Organ of average size. A proportional sound opening must also be prepared.*

Our electric *CONSOLE* (Keyboard Case) for a two-manual theater organ with an Echo Division is five feet in width, four feet six inches in depth, including pedal keyboard and bench, and four feet in height. The available floor space in the orchestra pit should therefore be five feet three inches in width and four feet nine inches in depth.

It is also necessary that a proper space be provided for the *Organ Blower* in a room so situated as to prevent the hum of the motor from reaching the theater auditorium. Due care should also be taken to enable a supply of air to the blower at the same temperature as that in the theater. It is likewise quite important for architects to observe that piping connections between the organ blower and the organ wind regulators can be made conveniently.

On the following pages we offer several Specimen Schemes of organs, such as we recommend for the average requirements. *EACH ORGAN MUST BE BUILT TO ORDER IN CONFORMITY WITH LOCAL CONDITIONS.* Price quotations will be submitted on request.

Style "W-7"

GREAT ORGAN

1. Open Diapason	8′	Metal	61 Pipes	Great Unison Off	8′	Disconnector
2. Muted Viol	8′	Metal	61 Pipes	Swell to Great	4′	Coupler
3. Cathedral Chimes		Tubes	20 Bells	Swell to Great	8′	Coupler
Great to Great	4′		Coupler	Swell to Great	16′	Coupler
Great to Great	16′		Coupler			

SWELL ORGAN

4. Stopped Flute	8′	Wood	73 Pipes	Swell to Swell	4′	Coupler
5. Viol d'Orchestre	8′	Metal	73 Pipes	Swell to Swell	16′	Coupler
6. Vox Humana	8′	Reeds	61 Pipes	Swell Unison Off	8′	Disconnector
Tremulant						

PEDAL ORGAN

7. Sub Bass	16′	Wood	30 Pipes	Swell to Pedal	8′	Coupler
Great to Pedal	8′		Coupler			

PEDAL MOVEMENTS

Balanced Swell Pedal — Balanced Crescendo Pedal
Great to Pedal Reversible

ACCESSORIES

Electric Organ Blower — 8-Volt, 10 Ampere Generator
Regulator — Organ Bench

ACTION

Weickhardt Electro-Pneumatic Action to be used throughout entire organ system in conjunction with the Weickhardt Universal Wind Chest (Patented August 20, 1907)

Style "W-8"

WITH

Echo Organ

GREAT ORGAN

1. Open Diapason	8′	Metal	61 Pipes	Great Unison Off	8′	Disconnector
2. Muted Viol	8′	Metal	61 Pipes	Swell to Great	4′	Coupler
3. Cathedral Chimes		Tubes	20 Bells	Swell to Great	8′	Coupler
Great to Great	4′		Coupler	Swell to Great	16′	Coupler
Great to Great	16′		Coupler	Echo to Great	8′	Coupler

SWELL ORGAN

4. Concert Flute	8′	Wood	73 Pipes	Swell to Swell	16′	Coupler
5. Viol d'Orchestre	8′	Metal	73 Pipes	Swell to Swell	4′	Coupler
Tremulant				Swell Unison Off	8′	Disconnector

ECHO ORGAN

(Controlled from Swell Organ Keyboard)

6. Echo Flute	8′	Wood	73 Pipes	Echo to Echo	4′	Coupler
7. Vox Humana	8′	Reeds	61 Pipes	Echo Unison Off	8′	Disconnector
Echo to Echo	16′		Coupler	Tremulant		

Three Pistons: *Echo Only — Echo and Swell — Swell Only*

PEDAL ORGAN

8. Sub Bass	16′	Wood	30 Pipes	Swell to Pedal	8′	Coupler
Great to Pedal	8′		Coupler	Echo to Pedal	8′	Coupler

PEDAL MOVEMENTS

Balanced Swell Pedal — Balanced Crescendo Pedal
Great to Pedal Reversible

ACCESSORIES

Electric Organ Blower — 8-Volt, 10 Ampere Generator
Regulator — Organ Bench

ACTION

Weickhardt Electro-Pneumatic Action to be used throughout entire organ system in conjunction with the Weickhardt Universal Wind Chest (Patented August 20, 1907)

Style "W-9"

GREAT ORGAN

1. Open Diapason	8′	Metal	61 Pipes	Great to Great	16′	Coupler
2. Concert Flute	8′	Wood	61 Pipes	Great Unison Off	8′	Disconnector
3. Muted Viol	8′	Metal	61 Pipes	Swell to Great	4′	Coupler
4. Cathedral Chimes		Tubes	20 Bells	Swell to Great	8′	Coupler
Great to Great	4′		Coupler	Swell to Great	16′	Coupler

TWO NUMBERED PISTONS, controlling Great and Pedal Organs and Couplers

SWELL ORGAN

5. Stopped Flute	8′	Wood	73 Pipes	Tremulant		
6. Viol d'Orchestre	8′	Metal	73 Pipes	Swell to Swell	4′	Coupler
7. Viol Celeste	8′	Metal	49 Pipes	Swell to Swell	16′	Coupler
8. Vox Humana	8′	Reeds	61 Pipes	Swell Unison Off	8′	Disconnector

TWO NUMBERED PISTONS, controlling Swell and Pedal Organs and Couplers

PEDAL ORGAN

9. Sub Bass	16′	Wood	30 Pipes	Swell to Pedal	8′	Coupler
Great to Pedal	8′		Coupler			

PEDAL MOVEMENTS

Balanced Swell Pedal — Balanced Crescendo Pedal
Great to Pedal Reversible

ACCESSORIES

Electric Organ Blower — 8-Volt, 10 Ampere Generator
Regulator — Organ Bench

ACTION

Weickhardt Electro-Pneumatic Action to be used throughout entire organ system in conjunction with the Weickhardt Universal Wind Chest (Patented August 20, 1907)

Style "W-10"

with

Echo Organ

GREAT ORGAN

1. Open Diapason	8′	Metal	61 Pipes	Great Unison Off	8′	Disconnector
2. Concert Flute	8′	Wood	61 Pipes	Swell to Great	4′	Coupler
3. Muted Viol	8′	Metal	61 Pipes	Swell to Great	8′	Coupler
4. Cathedral Chimes		Tubes	20 Bells	Swell to Great	16′	Coupler
Great to Great	4′		Coupler	Echo to Great	8′	Coupler
Great to Great	16′		Coupler			

SWELL ORGAN

5. Stopped Flute	8′	Wood	73 Pipes	Swell to Swell	4′	Coupler
6. Viol d'Orchestre	8′	Metal	73 Pipes	Swell to Swell	16′	Coupler
7. Harmonic Flute	8′	Metal	73 Pipes	Swell Unison Off	8′	Disconnector
Tremulant						

ECHO ORGAN

(*Controlled from Swell Organ Keyboard*)

8. Echo Violin	8′	Metal	73 Pipes	Echo to Echo	4′	Coupler
9. Vox Humana	8′	Reeds	61 Pipes	Echo to Echo	16′	Coupler
Tremulant				Echo Unison Off	8′	Disconnector

Three Pistons: *Echo Only* *Echo and Swell* *Swell Only*

PEDAL ORGAN

10. Sub Bass	16′	Wood	30 Pipes	Swell to Pedal	8′	Coupler
Great to Pedal	8′		Coupler	Echo to Pedal	8′	Coupler

PEDAL MOVEMENTS

Balanced Swell Pedal
Balanced Crescendo Pedal
Great to Pedal Reversible

ACCESSORIES

Electric Organ Blower
8-Volt, 10 Ampere Generator
Regulator
Organ Bench

ACTION

Weickhardt Electro-Pneumatic Action to be used throughout entire organ system in conjunction with the Weickhardt Universal Wind Chest (Patented August 20, 1907)

Style "W-14"

GREAT ORGAN

1. Open Diapason	8′	Metal	61 Pipes	Great to Great	4′	Coupler
2. Concert Flute	8′	Wood	61 Pipes	Great to Great	16′	Coupler
3. Muted Viol	8′	Metal	61 Pipes	Great Unison Off	8′	Disconnector
4. Orchestra Bells		Bars (*with* *Resonators*)	49 Notes	Swell to Great	4′	Coupler
				Swell to Great	8′	Coupler
5. Cathedral Chimes		Tubes	20 Bells	Swell to Great	16′	Coupler

THREE NUMBERED PISTONS, controlling Great and Pedal Organs and Couplers

SWELL ORGAN

6. Stopped Flute	8′	Wood	73 Pipes	Tremulant		
7. Viol d'Orchestre	8′	Metal	73 Pipes	Swell to Swell	4′	Coupler
8. Viol Celeste	8′	Metal	49 Pipes	Swell to Swell	16′	Coupler
9. Harmonic Flute	4′	Metal	73 Pipes	Swell Unison Off	8′	Disconnector
10. Clarinet	8′	Reeds	73 Pipes			
11. Vox Humana	8′	Reeds	61 Pipes			
12. Concert Harp		Bars (*with Resonators*)	49 Notes			

FOUR NUMBERED PISTONS, controlling Swell and Pedal Organs and Couplers

PEDAL ORGAN

13. Violone	16′	Wood	30 Pipes	Great to Pedal	4′	Coupler
14. Sub Bass (soft)	16′	Wood	30 Pipes	Swell to Pedal	8′	Coupler
Great to Pedal	8′		Coupler	Swell to Pedal	4′	Coupler

PEDAL MOVEMENTS

Balanced Swell Pedal
Balanced Crescendo Pedal
Sforzando Pedal
Great to Pedal Reversible

ACCESSORIES

Electric Organ Blower
8-Volt, 10 Ampere Generator
Regulator
Organ Bench

ACTION

Weickhardt Electro-Pneumatic Action to be used throughout entire organ system in conjunction with the Weickhardt Universal Wind Chest (Patented August 20, 1907)

Style "W-16"

with

Echo Organ

GREAT ORGAN

1. Open Diapason	8′	Metal	61 Pipes	Great to Great	16′	Coupler
2. Concert Flute	8′	Wood	61 Pipes	Great Unison Off	8′	Disconnector
3. Muted Viol	8′	Metal	61 Pipes	Swell to Great	4′	Coupler
4. Orchestra Bells		Bars (*with* *Resonators*)	49 Notes	Swell to Great	8′	Coupler
				Swell to Great	16′	Coupler
5. Cathedral Chimes		Tubes	20 Bells	Echo to Great	8′	Coupler
Great to Great	4′		Coupler			

THREE NUMBERED PISTONS, controlling Great and Pedal Organs and Couplers

SWELL ORGAN

6. Stopped Flute	8′	Wood	73 Pipes	Tremulant		
7. Viol d'Orchestre	8′	Metal	73 Pipes	Swell to Swell	4′	Coupler
8. Viol Celeste	8′	Metal	49 Pipes	Swell to Swell	16′	Coupler
9. Harmonic Flute	4′	Metal	73 Pipes	Swell Unison Off	8′	Disconnector
10. Clarinet	8′	Reeds	73 Pipes			
11. Concert Harp		Bars (*with Resonators*)	49 Notes			

FOUR NUMBERED PISTONS, controlling Swell and Pedal Organs and Couplers

ECHO ORGAN

(*Controlled from Swell Organ Keyboard*)

12. Echo Violin	8′	Metal	73 Pipes	Echo to Echo	16′	Coupler
13. Clarabella	8′	Wood	73 Pipes	Echo Unison Off	8′	Disconnector
14. Vox Humana	8′	Reeds	61 Pipes	Tremulant		
Echo to Echo	4′		Coupler			

Three Pistons: *Echo Only* — *Echo and Swell* — *Swell Only*

PEDAL ORGAN

15. Contra Bass	16′	Wood	30 Pipes	Swell to Pedal	8′	Coupler
16. Bourdon (soft)	16′	Wood	30 Pipes	Swell to Pedal	4′	Coupler
Great to Pedal	8′		Coupler	Echo to Pedal	8′	Coupler
Great to Pedal	4′		Coupler			

PEDAL MOVEMENTS

Balanced Swell Pedal
Balanced Crescendo Pedal
Sforzando Pedal
Great to Pedal Reversible

ACCESSORIES

Electric Organ Blower
8-Volt, 10 Ampere Generator
Regulator
Organ Bench

ACTION

Weickhardt Electro-Pneumatic Action to be used throughout entire organ system in conjunction with the Weickhardt Universal Wind Chest (Patented August 20, 1907)

quently bought components such as consoles, relays, swell shades, reservoirs, etc. from Wangerin and actually bought 40 completely Wangerin-built organs which were sold under the Barton nameplate. Several such Wangerin/Barton consoles are pictured in the Barton chapter of *Encyclopedia of the American Theatre Organ*, Volume I.

In 1931 Edmond Verlinden left to form the Verlinden-Weickhardt-Dornoff firm together with Joseph Weickhardt, son of the founder of the Wangerin organ business, George Weickhardt. After building around 700 organs the Wangerin Organ Company ceased operations in late 1942[10] shortly after the retirement of Adolph Wangerin. After World War II a former Wangerin salesman, W. J. Brockman, formed another organ building concern called the Wangerin Organ Company, at 2213-2223 N. 30th Street in Milwaukee. Mr. Brockman's questionable business practices, according to Gordy Meyer, did nothing to enhance the sterling reputation of the earlier Wangerin organization.[11] This firm went out of business in the late 1940s.[12]

Interior of the richly appointed Wangerin factory studio, opened in 1925. Chambers are behind the grille at the end of the room. Two different consoles controlled the organ using two different styles of rolls: one used ordinary 88-note piano rolls and one featured reproducing organ rolls which automatically controlled all stops and swell shades. The organ contained a variety of ranks allowing church, residence or theatre-style voicing to be demonstrated.[2]

Harvey L. Gustafson plays a 2/8 Wangerin in Grace Lutheran Church, Fargo, North Dakota. Wangerin repossessed this organ from a theatre and sold it to the church in 1938.[3] *Only a few Wangerin theatre instruments featured horseshoe consoles.*

Weickhardt Pipe Organs

are not stock instruments, but built to order according to the ever varying individual requirements. Result: Wonderful musical effects, such as only a real, complete and genuine MASTER PIPE ORGAN can produce.

WRITE FOR THEATRE ORGAN CATALOG

WANGERIN-WEICKHARDT CO.

112-124 BURRELL STREET
MILWAUKEE, WISCONSIN U.S.A.

Above, Wangerin ad in the July 15, 1916 issue of Moving Picture World *pictured an organ installed in the Palm Theatre, Chicago in 1913. The grille on the lower right side of the case bears a remarkable resemblance to that on a Bartola. At right, a truck bearing the Wangerin motto on its door is dispatched with a load of parts for Wangerin's largest customer.*

The

Unit Organ

is the ideal Pipe Organ for theaters. It is a whole orchestra in itself. It can express anything in response to a skilled touch. Organ music lends itself with singular adaptability to an accompaniment of motion pictures, but you, Mr. Exhibitor, must bear in mind that popular musical judgment is quick to discriminate between the grandeur and wonderful effectiveness of refined pipe organ tones and the cheap, commonplace drone and blare of the average theater organ. If you are ready to equip your theater with an organ do not fail to have the WEICKHARDT UNIT ORGAN demonstrated to you. Investigate its merits and your choice will be gratifyingly easy.

CATALOG ON REQUEST

The **UNIT ORGAN**

Wangerin-Weickhardt Co.
112-124 Burrell Street
MILWAUKEE, WISCONSIN, U.S.A.

The **UNIT ORGAN**

EASTERN OFFICE: 729 Seventh Ave., NEW YORK CITY

Wangerin ad from the early 1920s. The company made only a token attempt to secure unit theatre organ business, perhaps out of deference to Barton, their major client who ordered many components and even complete organs. Few unit organs were built under the Wangerin nameplate for theatres; most were straight organs. The Merrill Theatre in Milwaukee, pictured in this ad, didn't even have a unit organ; it had a 2/7 straight Wangerin installed in 1915.

The Biograph Theatre in Chicago installed a two-manual Wangerin in 1914 but replaced it with a 2/7 Wurlitzer in 1924. A similar fate befell several other early Wangerin instruments.

The Milwaukee Savoy Theatre's 2/7 Wangerin was installed in 1915. Most theatres feature canopies at their entrances; the Savoy had them inside the theatre as well!

The Oakland Theatre in Chicago installed a 2/8 Wangerin in 1914. The theatre's owner, remarking on the instrument's quality, noted that "although used daily for many hours, it has never given any trouble; on the contrary it is at all times a pleasure to note the satisfaction its music gives to our patrons."[4]

WANGERIN ORGAN COMPANY

110-124 BURRELL STREET
MILWAUKEE, WISCONSIN, U.S.A.

AN OPEN STATEMENT!

In the March issue of The Diapason the announcement was made that the corporate name of the WANGERIN-WEICKHARDT CO. had formally been changed to WANGERIN ORGAN COMPANY. That this change of name be more clearly understood and correctly interpreted the following absolute facts are brought to the attention of anyone interested:

FIRST: In 1918 Mr. George Weickhardt, whose health at that time was in a precarious condition, sold his entire interests in the then Wangerin-Weickhardt Co., these amounting to ten per cent of the capital stock, to Adolph Wangerin, pioneer organizer and executive head of the establishment ever since its original incorporation.

SECOND: Mr. George Weickhardt died in February, 1919. The firm's name, however, was not changed at that time purely for the sake of tact and courtesy. Frequent misinterpretation of the retention of the Weickhardt name finally resulted in the present corporate name—WANGERIN ORGAN COMPANY.

THIRD: Since Mr. George Weickhardt's death of over five years ago no one by the name of Weickhardt has in any way been financially interested in the former Wangerin-Weickhardt or present Wangerin Organ Company, or connected with either in any capacity, except by regular employment.

FOURTH: In view of the easily proven fact that within the last five years there has been a decided and highly important progress in organ construction and system of building it is a significant point to be observed that the product of our factory during the stated period and at present markedly overshadows and outdistances any achievements of earlier times. Practically every constructive feature today differs from and is conspicuously improved over the type of mechanism used several years back.

FIFTH: Anyone reviving today a terminology, in the nature of a trade-mark, featured by us several years ago, may technically be beyond legal restraint, but on neither moral nor ethical grounds can this be condoned, if the object is clear to arrogate to oneself the reputation which our organization enjoys and will positively retain under all conditions.

NOTE: We invite full inquiries and will present any further proof and facts desired.

WANGERIN ORGAN COMPANY

110-126 BURRELL STREET **MILWAUKEE, WIS.**

This ad appeared in the September 1924 issue of The Diapason *at about the same time as the Weickhardt-Schaefer Organ Co. was founded. The angry tone of the ad came as a result of Weickhardt-Schaefer ads using "The Weickhardt Organ" logo once featured by the Wangerin-Weickhardt firm. In a case of really speedy karmic justice, the Weickhardt-Schaefer company lasted in business only a few months.*

Wangerin player cabinet designed to sit atop a console.

Wangerin buildings are still standing on Burrell Street in Milwaukee in 1984. The building on the right housed the demonstration studio.

Left, the original Wangerin pipe shop, now home of Jerome B. Meyer & Sons. At right are remaining portions of the Wangerin factory. The complex formerly included buildings, now razed, in the center of this site.

Factory portrait of Wangerin opus 510, a 3/14 contracted by Barton for the Iowa (Cedar Rapids Community) Theatre, Cedar Rapids, Iowa. The Barton decals on the front of the console have been air brushed out in this photo. The gaudiness of all those rhinestones has made this one of the author's all-time favorite organs.

WANGERIN OPUS LIST

CITY/STATE	LOCATION	SIZE	YR	BLWR	HP	WP	REMARKS
ARKANSAS							
Jonesboro	Strand Th.		1926				Opus 450.
ILLINOIS							
Chicago	Biograph Th.	2/	1914	5677			
	Colonial Th.		1916	6927	1¼	4″	
	Crawford Th.	2/	1913	5149			With echo.
	Hamlin Th.		1913	4772			
	LaSalle Th.	2/8	1914				
	Lexington Th.		1923	14951	2	5″	
	Madison Square (Byrd) Th.	2/	1917	8353	3	7″	
			1917	8394	¼	3½″	
	Madlin Th.		1916	7506	1½	3½″	
	Oakland Th.	2/8	1914	5482			
	Palm Th.	2/	1913	5077			
	Paramount (Logan) Th.	2/	1915	6569			
			1915	6536			For echo organ.
	Vitagraph Th.	2/	1914	5612			
IOWA							
Estherville	Grand Th.	2/					
MICHIGAN							
Escanaba	Delft Th.		1915	6104			
MINNESOTA							
Minneapolis	Strand Th.	2/26	1914	5580			With echo.
			1914	5585			
Rochester	Empress Th.	2/10	1922				
Winona	Colonial Th.	2/	1916	7356	1½	3½″	
MISSOURI							
Kansas City	New Center Th.		1916	7504	2	3½″	
NEW JERSEY							
Jersey City	Apollo Th.		1917	8140	1	5″	
Passaic	Rialto Th.		1917	7876	2	6″	
NEW YORK							
New York	Costello Th.		1916	7671	2	5″	Later moved to Paul Forster Studio, Syracuse, New York.

CITY/STATE	LOCATION	SIZE	YR	BLWR	HP	WP	REMARKS
New York	Harlem Strand Th.		1917	7773	2	5″	
PENNSYLVANIA							
Scranton	Regent (Palace) Th.		1917	7784	¾	3½″	
Washington	Regent Th.		1917	6358			
WISCONSIN							
Burlington	Crystal Th.	2/4	1924	16466	1½	5″	Opus 412.
			1925	16709	1½	5″	
Green Bay	Saxe's Strand Th.		1921	11709	1	3½″	
LaCrosse	Majestic (Rivoli) Th.	2/22	1919	9928	5	5″	
Milwaukee	Alhambra Th.	2/	1918	8973	5	7″	Later moved to Hipp Theatre, Sioux City, Iowa.
	Downer Th.	2/7	1915	6562			
	Juneau Th.	2/	1922	13499	2	5″	Opus 338.
	Arnold Krueger residence		192?				Opus 347; cost $3,800.
	Lake Th.	2/	1925				Opus 442; cost $6,500.
	Merrill Th.	2/7	1915	6563			With echo.
	Palace Th.	2/	1919	9898	3	5″	
	Rialto Th.						Opus 307.
	Riviera Th.	2/	1919	10166	1	5″	Opus 243.
	Rivoli Th.						Opus 313; opened as Silver City Gem Theatre.
	Savoy Th.	2/7	1915	6292			
	Saxe's Grand Th.		1920	11827	1¼	3½″	
	State Th.	2/					With echo.
	Strand Th.	2/7	1914	5822			
	World (Royal) Th.		1926				Opus 485; cost $8,300; located at 830 S. 6th Street.
Waukesha	Park Th.						Opus 301.

The following Wangerin instruments were sold to the Bartola Musical Instrument Company who then sold them under their Barton nameplate.

OPUS	LOCATION/CITY/STATE	SIZE	YR	PRICE	BLWR	HP	WP	REMARKS
236	unknown		191?					Probably a Bartola.
237	unknown		191?					Probably a Bartola.
238	unknown		191?					Probably a Bartola.
240	unknown		191?					Probably a Bartola.
241	unknown		191?					Probably a Bartola.
242	unknown		191?					Probably a Bartola.
270	Riviera Th., Chicago, IL	2/9	1918		9073	3	7″	
303	Bartola stock organ.							
304	Bartola stock organ.							
305	Bartola stock organ.							
306	Bartola stock organ.							
311	Bartola stock organ.							
312	Bartola stock organ.							
332	Bartola stock organ.							
333	Bartola stock organ.							
334	Bartola stock organ.							
335	Bartola stock organ.							
339	Bartola stock organ		1922					
357	unidentified location, Canton, OH	2/	1922					
358	Classic Th., Watertown, WI	2/	1922		13771	2	12″	
359	Rivoli Th., Two Rivers, WI	2/6	1922		13750	2	12″	
			1922		13813			Replacement blower.
362	Adler Th., Marshfield, WI	2/6	1922		13744	2	12″	
363	unidentified location, Janesville, WI		1922					
364	Family Th, Monroe, MI	2/	1923		13872	2	5″	
368	Grand Th., Gary, IN	2/	1922		13964	2	9″	
369	Eastwood Th., Madison, WI		1923		14055	3	5″&10″	
384	unidentified location, Sterling, IL		1923					
494	unidentified location, Whitewater, WI	2/4	1927	$ 3,470				Style 21.
496	Majestic Th., Cudahy, WI	2/4	1927	$ 4,000	20511	2	12″	Style 21; with duplex roll player.
497	stock organ	2/4	1927	$ 3,395				Style 21.
503	Orpheum Th., Burlington, WI	2/5	1927	$ 4,637	20470	2	12″	Style 22.
504	Ozaukee Th., Port Washington, WI	2/5	1927	$ 4,637	20577	2	12″	Style 22.
506	unidentified location, Chicago, IL		1927	$ 2,583				Pit organ.
507	Bartlett Th., Highwood, IL	2/3	1927	$ 2,750	19850	1	12″	Style 20.
508	Strand Th., Fort Dodge, IA	2/4	1927	$ 3,395	20665	2	12″	Style 21; moved in 1937 to KOY Radio, Phoenix, Arizona.
510	Iowa (Cedar Rapids Community) Th., Cedar Rapids, IA	3/14	1927	$ 13,000	21294	7½	19″	
512	Majestic Th., Muskegon, MI	2/6	1927	$ 5,350	20903	3	13″	Style 23.
513	Regent Th, Muskegon, MI	2/6	1927	$ 5,630	20905	3	13″	Style 23.
516	National Th., Milwaukee, WI	3/10	1927		21192	7½	19″	
517	Rialto Th., Gladstone, MI	2/9	1927	$ 3,395	20991	2	12″	
518	Palace Th., Wisconsin Rapids, WI	2/	1927	$ 3,500	20937	2	12″	
519	Avalon Th., Detroit, MI	3/10	1927		21172	7½	19″	

WELTE-MIGNON CORPORATION

Builders of the World Famous

WELTE PHILHARMONIC REPRODUCING ORGAN

Residence, Church, Concert, Lodge, Hotel & Theatre Organs

Organists' Personally Recorded Music Records

NEW YORK

STUDIO
665 FIFTH AVENUE
NEW YORK
TELEPHONE
PLAZA 8761

FACTORIES
297-307 EAST 133RD ST.
NEW YORK
TELEPHONE
MOTT HAVEN 5200

ADDRESS REPLY TO

The Welte name has been associated with musical instruments since 1832 when Michael Welte (1807-1880) began the manufacture of musical movements for clocks in his home town of Vohrenbach, Germany. By 1849 he had built a large automatic pipe organ which became known as an orchestrion. The success of this device was immediate and Mr. Welte eventually formed the firm of M. Welte & Soehne with his three sons, Berthold, Emil and Michael, Jr. The eldest son, Emil Welte, came to New York City in 1865 and established a showroom for the sale of orchestrions. These innovative instruments sold nearly as fast as they could be imported. [1 2]

In 1901 the Welte firm admitted three other family members: Edwin Welte, son of Berthold Welte; Carl Welte, son of Emil Welte; and Karl Bockisch, who had married Edwin Welte's sister.[3] Bockisch is the man primarily responsible for the invention of the reproducing piano which was introduced as the Mignon in 1904 and later became known as the Welte-Mignon.[4] Following this invention it was only natural that the reproducing pipe organ would be developed and Welte found a ready market for these instruments in homes of the wealthy.

The Welte business in the United States grew so rapidly that a large factory was built in Poughkeepsie, New York. Not all of the Welte organs sold in this country before World War I were built in Poughkeepsie. Some parts were made there while others were imported from Welte's Freiburg, Germany factory. Some pipework was ordered from Gottfried since the Poughkeepsie plant apparently never had a metal pipe shop. Often entire instruments would be ordered from such firms as Moller, Skinner or Hook & Hastings. These organs would be outfitted with Welte-built consoles and, of course, sold under the Welte nameplate. The author has never encountered a Welte residence organ without a player unit and it is a good probability that the few Weltes sold for theatre use before World War I featured player mechanisms also.

During World War I the American assets of German businesses were seized by the United States government, including the majority of stock in M. Welte & Sons, Inc. In 1919 the Alien Property Custodian offered the Welte stock and certain patents at public auction and they were acquired by George W. Gittins for $100,000. In 1917 Gittins had acquired control of the Estey Piano Company in the Bronx, New York, after being associated for many years with the Kohler industries, magnates in the music business. Gittins subsequently sold the Poughkeepsie factory at a profit and in 1922 built a new organ factory at 297 E. 133rd Street in the Bronx, adjacent to the Estey piano factory.[5]

At this time, as had been the case previously, nearly all Welte organs were sold for residential use although a handful made their way into theatres. In a magnanimous gesture, E. M. Skinner, who was not very interested in the residential market at the time, invited George Goll and a few other technicians from the Welte factory to visit the Skinner factory and to copy anything they wished. They introduced an "improved" version of the Skinner chest which gave nothing but trouble. Soon thereafter Max Beyer took over the technical and tonal design of Welte organs. Beyer was remembered by his brother-in-law

The Welte studios at 665 Fifth Avenue in New York City housed this beautifully encased organ on which Welte reproducing rolls were recorded.

The new Welte studios at 695 Fifth Avenue contained an auditorium twenty feet high, lavishly appointed with tapestries and walnut paneling. The room could accommodate 200 persons for an evening musicale. The Early Italian organ case fronted the main organ of 31 ranks and a seven-rank echo division spoke through an ornamental iron grille at the end of the room. The large console pictured at the left controlled the entire 38-rank organ. The console in the organ case was connected to a roll recording machine although by this late period in Welte history few rolls were actually recorded here. However, the organ was heard regularly over NBC station WEAF which offered a virtual Who's Who *of the New York organ world including Gaston Dethier, Clarence Dickinson, Lynnwood Farnam, Gottfried Federlein, T. Tertius Noble, C. A. J. Parmentier and many others.*[32] *These artists' services were often secured through their professional and personal relationships with R. P. Elliot.*

In 1926 the aggressive Welte firm opened a luxurious salon in the Gothic Building on North Michigan Avenue in Chicago. Occupying the entire top floor of the new building, the studio featured a three-manual organ with a player in a separate cabinet. At the opposite end of the room sat an original Welte-built Welte-Mignon reproducing grand piano. The studio was managed by James Topp, a veteran Chicago organ man who for many years had been the Chicago representative of the Spencer Turbine Co.[33]

Welte men gather at the University of Vermont in 1927 where a new Welte organ had just been installed. From left to right are R. P. Elliot, guiding genius of the company; Henry Burkhard, an organist who recorded many Welte organ rolls; Theodore Clark, tonal finisher; Rudolph Glatz, player mechanism expert; and M. E. Burnham, manager of the New York City Welte studios. Mr. Burnham holds a roll before inserting it into the player unit at his left.

Henry Gottfried as "a brilliant man." He married one of Anton Gottfried's daughters and joined the Gottfried firm in the mid-teens, eventually becoming plant manager. At Welte, Beyer discontinued the troublesome Skinner-copied chests and introduced high-quality unit chests of single rank size which were produced in only four styles, allowing great economy of manufacturing. Beyer, who had studied to be a minister, eventually left the Welte firm and went to Texas to run a religious cult.[6] [7]

Welte owner George Gittins decided early in 1925 that he wanted to enter the church and theatre organ marketplace in a serious way. Needing a general manager of exceptional abilities to spearhead such an expansion, Gittins sought advice from leading industry figures as to who would be the most qualified person. The consensus was that R. P. Elliot, manager of the organ department of the W. W. Kimball Company, was the right man for the job. Gittins' proposal shocked Mr. Elliot, who had come to be regarded as a permanent fixture of the Kimball enterprise. Nonetheless, Gittins got his man and Elliot became Welte's general manager and vice president.[8]

Elliot proceeded to put Welte on the map and virtually overnight turned the company into one of America's major organ building firms, both in prestige and in quality of product. To assist in accomplishing this feat, Elliot hired a number of key Kimball men: Carl A. Benson, head of Kimball's electric action and wiring department, became Welte factory superintendent; Frank H. Niemann, Kimball's Philadelphia representative, became assistant superintendent; G. A. Dominique, head of Kimball's chest department, assumed a similar role for Welte; and J. Vern Fridlund, Kimball's service manager, became assistant general manager. Albin W. Johnson, who had been assistant foreman of Skinner's console department, was hired as head of Welte's console department.[9]

A number of original German employees remained with the company after Elliot's takeover including George Goll, who later became plant superintendent; Paul Sowada, Goll's brother; Rudolph Glatz and a Mr. Dittes. The latter two men were experts on the reproducing player mechanisms. Mr. Dittes at one time redesigned the somewhat troublesome Multi-Control ten-roll changer to eliminate its bicycle chains. His design was never put into production, however, perhaps because Welte didn't actually manufacture the roll changers; they were supplied by the Automatic Musical Instrument Company of Grand Rapids, Michigan. Rudolph Glatz may have been the only

INTER-OFFICE CORRESPONDENCE

ORGAN DEPT.

PLEASE REPLY ☐ NO REPLY ☐

W. W. KIMBALL CO.

ESTABLISHED 1857

CHICAGO

TO

FROM FACTORY

COPIES TO

SUBJECT:

FULL LIST OF COPIES TO APPEAR ON ORIGINAL AND ALL COPIES

FORM 61-1500-11-26 E.V.J.

INTER-OFFICE CORRESPONDENCE

WELTE ORGAN COMPANY

TO

FROM PACIFIC COAST DIVISION

COPIES TO

SUBJECT:

FULL LIST OF COPIES TO APPEAR ON ORIGINAL AND ALL COPIES

Mechanical designs weren't the only things which Welte copied from Kimball. Even the typeface and layout of their inter-office memos were similar!

Welte employee to survive the various company reorganizations from the first days at Poughkeepsie to the purchase of the company by Kimball in 1931. At Kimball, Glatz designed a special player for Vassar College which controlled a three-manual organ from a standard 150-hole Welte roll. The standard Welte and Kimball-Welte players were designed for two-manual instruments.[10]

At about the same time that Gittins hired R. P. Elliot he also entered into an agreement with the Hall Organ Company. As a result of this agreement Welte obtained access to Hall's manufacturing capabilities in exchange for Hall's obtaining access to Welte's player device.[11] At one time Gittins also had options to buy Moller and Austin which for some reason he never exercised. The Hall-Welte association resulted in interlocking directorates between the firms although each firm kept its own nameplate. George Gittins knew little about the organ business so C. B. Floyd, Hall's vice president and sales manager, made weekly trips to New York to offer "expert advice" and also to take the choicest of the incoming contracts to be built in the Hall factory. Elliot's arrival put a stop to this practice and a committee was appointed with members from each factory to decide which organ would be built in which plant. Naturally, some resentment developed because Hall was no longer getting all the best contracts.[12]

Further friction developed because the Welte factory had no pipe shop and therefore relied on Hall's pipe facility. Hall's quality standards were considerably below Elliot's. For example, the caps of Hall's wooden pipes were nailed on instead of being fastened with screws. Also, Hall's pipes were made in pairs, with two adjoining notes having identical dimensions, rather than the scale progressing uniformly from note to note. Floyd maintained that this cost-cutting measure could not be detected in the sound of the finished pipes but quality-conscious R. P. Elliot thought otherwise and proceeded to set up his own pipe shop.[13] The Hall-Welte association was eventually dissolved by mutual consent in June 1927.[14]

Elliot hired two old friends from the Hope-Jones days (Elliot having been president of the Hope-Jones Organ Company) to set up Welte's new pipe shop. James H. Nuttall was given the responsibility of drawing pipe scales and of securing the various equipment needed for a first-class pipe shop, and David Arthur was appointed head reed voicer. Both these men had worked at Wurlitzer for many years following the demise of Hope-Jones. A third Wurlitzer man was hired as a pipe maker and Arthur Birkmaier, formerly with the Skinner and Dennison companies, was appointed head flue voicer. David Arthur's nephew, Henry Vincent Willis, was hired on the strength of his name but proved to be such a disappointment that George Gittins had to let him go. One of Willis' blunders was having the antimony removed from the lead alloy used in pipe making, causing many of the larger pipes to be so soft that they buckled under their own weight.[15] [16]

Welte sales were most numerous near the New York factory, as might be expected, although a number of California sales were effected as the result of the Los Angeles Barker Bros. franchise. Barker Bros. had the largest home furnishings store in the west and had several Welte organs installed in it: a four-manual drawknob concert organ in the foyer, a 3/9 horseshoe console unit organ in the auditorium and other smaller residence organs from time to time. Another factor in California Welte sales was the expertise of Lloyd M. Davey, an accomplished technician who never claimed to be able to sell but did so quite well nonetheless. One job he pursued would have been spectacular had it ever been built: a 5/205 for the Los Angeles Coliseum. His proposal specified a military brass trumpet and wind pressures up to 50 inches. Davey relates in his own words the story of a 3/21 prestige job he did sell:

"Thomas L. Warner, the Pasadena auto parts manufacturer and millionaire, wanted an organ with a three-manual and player console low enough for him to see over so that he could watch his guests as they danced to the music of the organ. We knew that this was an impossibility but we hated to lose a $35,000 contract. I suggested to Gittins that we build such an organ, make the console as low as we could, and trust that Warner would be so excited over his acquisition that he would forget about not being able to see his guests dance. I pointed out that if Welte didn't agree to build such an instrument with a low console, Skinner would promise to do so and he wouldn't be able to build it either. Gittins agreed with my logic and we got the contract.

"I happened to be in Mr. Warner's garage when the organ console was uncrated. Warner was really shocked when he saw how wide it was, and I explained to him that the console mechanisms had to be put somewhere and if he wanted the console to be low then it had to be wide. Although it had been built as low as possible, the top being made of veneered quarter-inch plywood, Warner would really have had to strain to see over it."[17]

Dancing was an avant-garde use for a residence organ in

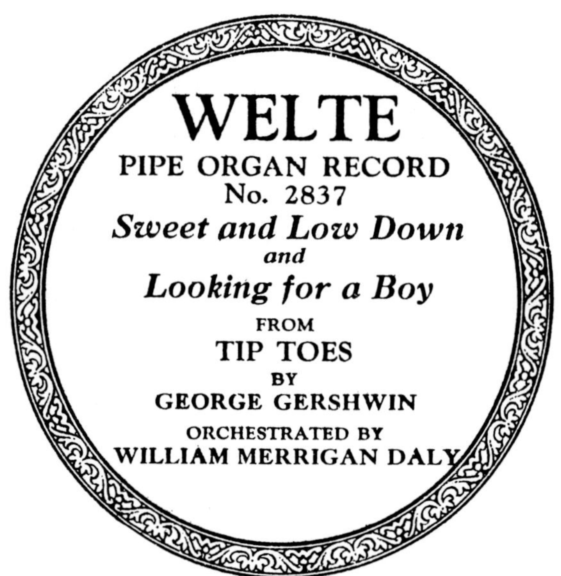

Label of one of the finest popular music rolls ever perforated. Mr. Daly, a close friend of George Gershwin, conducted Gershwin musicals on Broadway and arranged Gershwin songs for concert and radio.[34] Securing his services for Welte was a big coup for R. P. Elliot.

Welte had a beautiful display at the 1927 Exposition of Architecture in New York City. The console controlled a 3/12 being installed in the Wakefield Theatre in the Bronx. To the right of the console can be seen one of the Pathe' phonographs sold in the New York Welte showrooms.

The New York Welte studios also sold Pathe' phonographs and records. In 1916 Welte had installed an organ in the Pathe' recording studios in New York.

WELTE-MIGNON *PATHÉ STUDIO*

AT 669 Fifth Avenue you will find the Welte Pathé Studios where a complete display of this far-famed phonograph and a library of Pathé Records can be seen and heard under the most artistic conditions to be found anywhere.

AN EXAMPLE OF PATHÉ VALUES

1926, but in that year Welte was the first company to issue a catalog of reproducing organ dance rolls.[18] This reflected the progressive policies of R. P. Elliot, who kept his finger on the pulse of what the public wanted. One of the finest rolls of any variety (admittedly a broad statement) ever heard by the author was one of these Welte dance rolls, ***Sweet and Low Down***, arranged by William Merrigan Daly, a close friend of George Gerswhin. This roll, and probably most other Welte rolls of the period, were arranged on a drafting board and did not actually represent the hand playing of an organist. Mr. Davey elaborates: "The bulk of the Welte library of organ recordings consisted of rolls made from masters sent over from Germany prior to World War I . . . While with Welte, I never saw or heard of any organ recording being made from actual performance in this country, although Welte did have a complex recording device which was capable of making such a record . . . I doubt that the organ recorder was ever used . . . from 1925 on.

"Henry Burkhard, a German-born theatre organist, made all of the master recordings I saw made. He would take a pencil and mark the rhythm on a blank roll as it turned in the spool box. This method automatically compensated for the fact that the paper travels over the tracker bar faster as it builds up on the takeup spool. Burkhard later furnished the registrations and an editor marked the playing notes onto the roll from the music following Burkhard's rhythm marks. This marked roll was then punched out by a girl who operated what looked like a large sewing machine equipped with a punch instead of a needle. Some of these recordings were released under Burkhard's own name but most of them bore such pseudonyms as Ormond M. Berrington, Richard Wheeler, Orville Williams, Jacques Gautier, J. A. Beatty, H. A. Lawrence and A. DuBois. Burkhard had quite a drinking problem and the quality of his work is therefore variable. But when he was sober he produced

The Warner residence 3/21 Welte in Pasadena, California featured a console built as low as possible so that owner T. L. Warner could watch his guests dance as he played organ rolls. Although controlled by liturgical-looking tilting tablets, this organ featured a beautiful tibia and a full complement of percussions and traps.

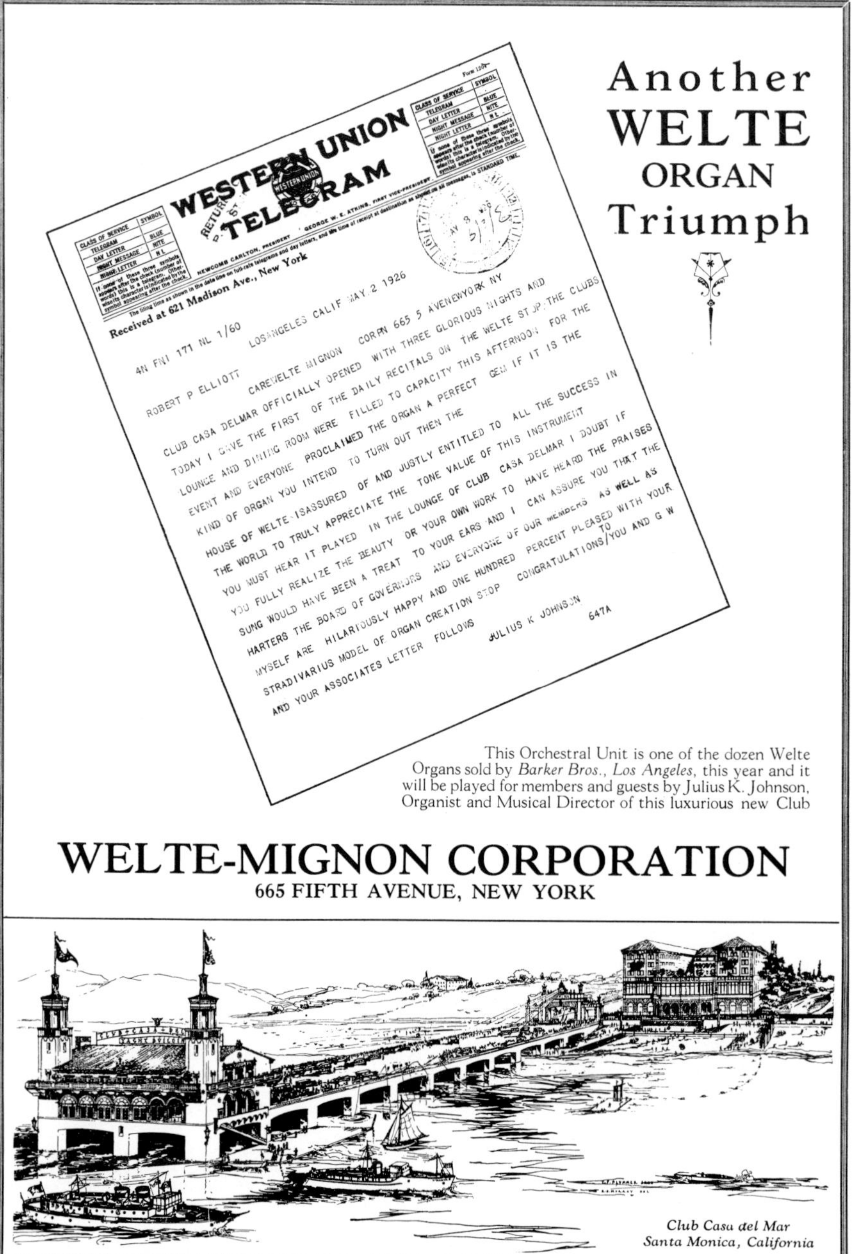

Welte's ad in the June 1926 Diapason *featured a glowing telegram from Julius K. Johnson. It surely ranks among the most enthusiastic endorsements ever written! R. P. Elliot's acquaintance with Mr. Johnson preceded this event by a couple of years since Mr. Johnson had been the organist for the opening night performance at the Forum Theatre in Los Angeles, whose 4/37 Kimball was Elliot's largest unit orchestra.*

some very fine recordings."[19]

Lloyd Davey's recollections continue with a story of Welte's most prestigious installation: "In another job which involved Dr. Preston Pope Satterwhite and his wife, we had some anxious moments. The couple lived in Mrs. Satterwhite's mansion in Great Neck, Long Island, which was named Martin Hall after her first husband, James E. Martin, a former Standard Oil Company executive. Florence Brokaw Satterwhite was enormously weathly and the acknowledged leader of New York society. Their Welte Philharmonic organ, installed at Martin Hall in the early 1920s, was probably the company's most prestigious—and most publicized—instrument. Since residence organs were to a large extent purchased by status-conscious persons, it was extremely important to the company to have a Welte organ in the home of such a prominent social figure.

"The Satterwhites had noted that women standing over the tone grilles in the floor instinctively lifted their skirts when the organ was played, and prior to leaving for Florida late in 1925, they contracted with Welte to rebuild the organ, nearly double its size, and move it out of the basement into new chambers in the attic, the project to be completed prior to their return from Florida in the spring of 1926.

"Upon my return from California I found the factory in a frenzy. The time for the Satterwhites' return was drawing closer and little had been accomplished. It was decided at a management meeting to turn the entire project over to me. I agreed to take the responsibility if they would let me pick my crew without murmur. I selected eleven of the best men in the factory and started out by tearing up the elaborate blueprints which had been drawn up, for the reason that, as designed, the organ would never fit into the attic space as the roof of the mansion was full of dips and valleys. It took many sleepless nights but I finally figured out how to fit everything into the available space, laying the 16′

The beauty of the English console is no longer associated with inconvenience, since modern accessories make it practical, and it has all the dignity of church tradition.

The residence console must be small, practical and refined. Welte consoles are built specially to accord with the furnishings of the most luxurious homes.

The Favorite
Console Types of
N. A. O. Members
Are all Built by

WELTE ORGAN CO.

695 Fifth Avenue
NEW YORK

Each is an Individual Creation,
Practical for its Purpose.

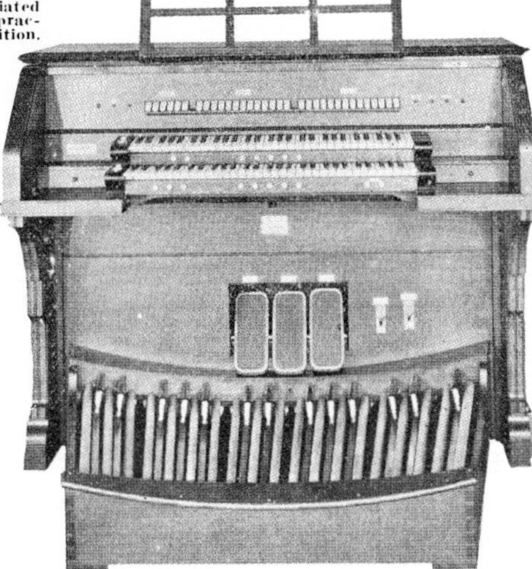

The straight front type is both practical and economical for the small or medium church organ. Many organists prefer it for larger instruments.

The concert type with the low music rack is not only the favorite of the theatre artist, but also of many prominent recitalists.

open diapason rank on the floor and building the rest of the organ over it.

To make matters worse, Dr. Satterwhite came home when we were only half through the work. He met me in the attic the next morning in bathrobe and slippers and, obviously angry over the fact that the work had not been completed, told me that the gates to the place would be closed and locked to Welte's trucks after Friday, it then being Wednesday. I called the factory. They hustled around and got most of the material needed to complete the job delivered in time and I set up shop in the attic with my eleven men where we proceeded to complete the job, Glatz coming in at the end. When we were finally finished, Mrs. Satterwhite, who was really a lovely person, told me that she would miss our noise and bustle.

"I had the greatest thrill in my entire organ career while there. I was playing *Londonderry Air*, the extent of my repertoire, when I heard someone singing to my accompaniment. The voice grew louder until into the great hall came Madame Frances Alda, a reigning soprano at the Metropolitan Opera. She walked over to the console where she finished the song. We had an interesting chat and fortunately she didn't ask me to play anything else!

"On May 22, 1926, the Satterwhites held a dinner party to mark the completion of the organ with Dr. T. Tertius Noble playing the organ and Madame Alda singing. Mrs. Satterwhite's enjoyment of the organ was short-lived as she died the following year. Martin Hall, which was renamed Preston Hall after Dr. Satterwhite bought it from his wife's estate, burned to the ground in 1932 and the organ was completely destroyed.

"George Gittins was a very fine man, a friendly person, and an ethical but clever businessman, and he didn't mind being told the truth. On one occasion a group of us were in his office and he inquired as to what the trouble was with the organ in the New York studio. I spoke up and said, 'You can't make a silk purse from a sow's ear,' and Carl Benson immediately agreed. This instrument was later sold . . . to Jacob Ruppert, the wealthy brewer who owned the New York Yankees.

". . .The New York Welte studios were moved into a new building at 695 Fifth Avenue early in 1927. At that time a large new organ was installed with separate concert and reproducing consoles . . . M. E. Burnham was manager of the New York studio and was a gentleman. Always very properly attired, he never left the studio without his hat and cane. He was also quite formal and no one called him anything but 'Mr. Burnham.' One evening I attended a recital in the organ studio played by a violinist who was accompanied by the recording organ. Burnham put on the roll and closed the spool box doors. At the end of the recording the rewind failed to trip and as the roll came off the tracker bar the entire organ screamed, much wilder than the loudest banshee ever thought of doing. Burnham calmly pressed the rewind control and intoned, 'Gentlemen, it was so good that even the organ applauded!'

"I returned to California in October 1926 to travel the coast for Gittins. I was not doing sales work and I didn't install organs either, although I did install most of the

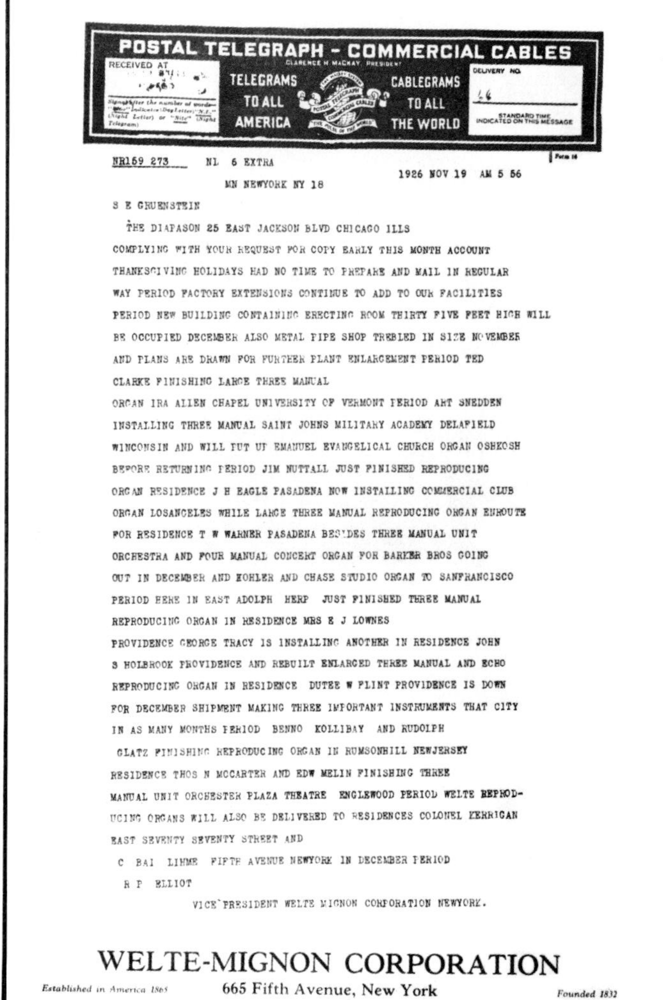

POSTAL TELEGRAPH - COMMERCIAL CABLES
CLARENCE H MACKAY, PRESIDENT
RECEIVED AT
TELEGRAMS TO ALL AMERICA
CABLEGRAMS TO ALL THE WORLD
DELIVERY NO.
STANDARD TIME INDICATED ON THIS MESSAGE

NR159 273 NL 6 EXTRA
1926 NOV 19 AM 5 56
MN NEWYORK NY 18

S E GRUENSTEIN
THE DIAPASON 25 EAST JACKSON BLVD CHICAGO ILLS
COMPLYING WITH YOUR REQUEST FOR COPY EARLY THIS MONTH ACCOUNT THANKSGIVING HOLIDAYS HAD NO TIME TO PREPARE AND MAIL IN REGULAR WAY PERIOD FACTORY EXTENSIONS CONTINUE TO ADD TO OUR FACILITIES PERIOD NEW BUILDING CONTAINING ERECTING ROOM THIRTY FIVE FEET HIGH WILL BE OCCUPIED DECEMBER ALSO METAL PIPE SHOP TREBLED IN SIZE NOVEMBER AND PLANS ARE DRAWN FOR FURTEER PLANT ENLARGEMENT PERIOD TED CLARKE FINISHING LARGE THREE MANUAL
ORGAN IRA ALLEN CHAPEL UNIVERSITY OF VERMONT PERIOD ART SNEDDEN INSTALLING THREE MANUAL SAINT JOHNS MILITARY ACADEMY DELAFIELD WINCONSIN AND WILL PUT UP EMANUEL EVANGELICAL CHURCH ORGAN OSHKOSH BEFORE RETURNING PERIOD JIM NUTTALL JUST FINISHED REPRODUCING ORGAN RESIDENCE J H EAGLE PASADENA NOW INSTALLING COMMERCIAL CLUB ORGAN LOSANGELES WHILE LARGE THREE MANUAL REPRODUCING ORGAN ENROUTE FOR RESIDENCE T W WARNER PASADENA BESIDES THREE MANUAL UNIT ORCHESTRA AND FOUR MANUAL CONCERT ORGAN FOR BARKER BROS GOING OUT IN DECEMBER AND KOHLER AND CHASE STUDIO ORGAN TO SANFRANCISCO PERIOD HERE IN EAST ADOLPH HERP JUST FINISHED THREE MANUAL REPRODUCING ORGAN IN RESIDENCE MRS E J LOWNES
PROVIDENCE GEORGE TRACY IS INSTALLING ANOTHER IN RESIDENCE JOHN S HOLBROOK PROVIDENCE AND REBUILT ENLARGED THREE MANUAL AND ECHO REPRODUCING ORGAN IN RESIDENCE DUTEE W FLINT PROVIDENCE IS DOWN FOR DECEMBER SHIPMENT MAKING THREE IMPORTANT INSTRUMENTS THAT CITY IN AS MANY MONTHS PERIOD BENNO KOLLIBAY AND RUDOLPH GLATZ FINISHING REPRODUCING ORGAN IN RUMSONHILL NEWJERSEY RESIDENCE THOS N MCCARTER AND EDW MELIN FINISHING THREE MANUAL UNIT ORCHESTER PLAZA THEATRE ENGLEWOOD PERIOD WELTE REPRODUCING ORGANS WILL ALSO BE DELIVERED TO RESIDENCES COLONEL KERRIGAN EAST SEVENTY SEVENTY STREET AND
C BAI LIHME FIFTH AVENUE NEWYORK IN DECEMBER PERIOD
R P ELLIOT
VICE PRESIDENT WELTE MIGNON CORPORATION NEWYORK.

WELTE-MIGNON CORPORATION
Established in America 1865 — 665 Fifth Avenue, New York — Founded 1832

The aggressive Welte firm ran full-page ads in The Diapason *throughout the later 1920s but in late 1926 they were so busy building organs that they missed the deadline for the December 1926 issue. As a result, their ad for that month consisted of a telegram sent by Welte's R. P. Elliot to S. E. Gruenstein, editor of* The Diapason. *The telegram's fascinating text reveals the wide scope of the Welte business and also discloses the names of a number of Welte installation men.*

(opposite) R. P. Elliot was closely in tune with the desires of organists of the day and made sure that Welte offered console styles to suit any taste, as advertised here in the September 1927 issue of The Diapason. *The perceptive reader will observe that, with the exception of the swell shoe design, these horseshoe and drawknob consoles are virtual duplicates of Kimball models. The horseshoe console pictured here controlled the 3/9 in the Barker Bros. store auditorium in Los Angeles; the drawknob console controlled a larger organ in the store's seven-story foyer.*

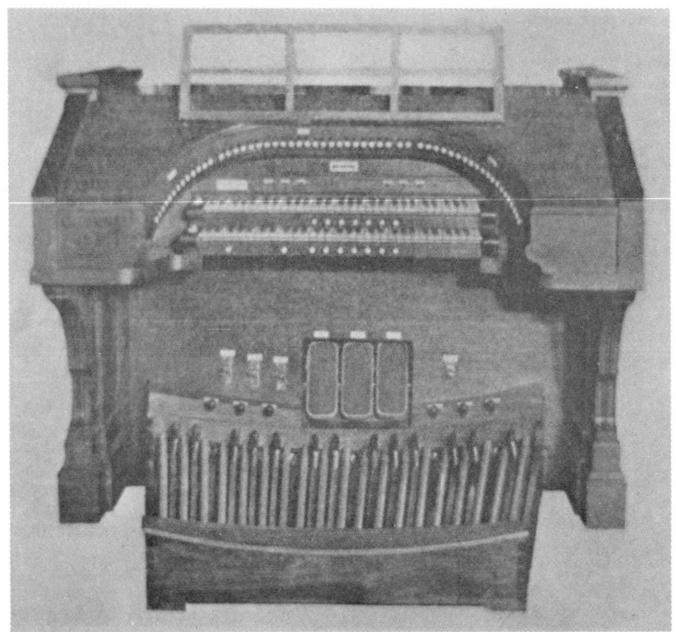

John W. Campbell, president of the Credit Clearing House, luxuriated in a Welte installed in his office in the Grand Central Terminal Building in New York City. Among its special features were a horseshoe console with drawknobs instead of stop keys, a Musicalle ten-roll changer and a grand piano. This unique instrument was designed by Charles M. Courboin.

Lloyd Davey, photographed in 1972 at age 80, examines a Welte Multi-Control roll changer.

Multi-Control roll players. My primary job was to make sure that everything was right. James Nuttall was doing most of the installation and finishing work. Some of his workmen were not too sharp so I would go over their work and correct any mistakes."[20]

One such installation visited by Mr. Davey was the 3/18 in the KPO radio studios in the Hale Bros. department store in San Francisco. This straight organ with a horseshoe console had originally been ordered through Mr. Davey. Uda Waldrop drew the unique specifications which called for the pedal organ to be in a separate expression chamber. Mr. Davey recalls that "I was at the studio when the instrument was being completed. Nuttall had been doing some adjustments on the pedal pipes and was trying them out at the console. Unaccountably, the studio microphone was somehow turned on and the radio audience, which had been listening to a baseball game in progress, heard Nuttall's English-accented voice remarking, 'It has all the beauty of a withered fart!' Several years later this organ was removed, enlarged and installed in the Hollywood NBC studios at Sunset and Vine."[21]

Early in 1927 the organ division of the Welte-Mignon Corporation became a separate entity, the Welte Organ Company. President George Gittins announced to shareholders that sales had grown remarkably in 1926 and that there were enough unfilled orders as the company entered 1927 to ensure capacity operation throughout the year. Before the end of January, however, the shareholders were shocked to see their stock drop in value by over 50%. It turned out that this had nothing to do with the Welte company but was due to the failure of a brokerage house which had pledged unsold Welte stock as collateral for a loan. When the broker's loan was called, the firm was forced to dump all its Welte stock on the market at once, causing the price to plummet. Despite assurances by Gittins that the company was still financially sound, Welte found it impossible to secure credit. The resulting shortage of working capital was a shock from which the company would never recover, despite the fact that a goodly number of sales had been made for future delivery.[22]

About this same time R. P. Elliot had arranged for Richard Whitelegg and G. Donald Harrison to leave England and join the Welte organization. Whitelegg became chief voicer and remained with Welte until their 1931 purchase by Kimball. By the time Harrison arrived, however, it was obvious that Welte was in trouble so Harrison joined the Skinner company instead. Elliot left Welte to work for the Aeolian Company in October, 1927 and took Carl Benson and Lloyd Davey with him, after which Albert E. Whitham became factory superintendent. It was about this time that the famous Belgian organist Charles M. Courboin began his association with Welte. He made some rolls using the pencil-on-moving-paper method earlier described by Lloyd Davey. All of Courboin's Welte rolls were released under pseudonyms since he had an exclusive recording contract with Aeolian.[23] [24]

In mid-1928 Welte lost their new building at 695 Fifth Avenue and moved back to their former quarters at 665 Fifth Avenue.[25] What may have been the company's most unusual sale was consummated there: the organ for Death Valley Scotty's castle. Walter Scott related the story in typically colorful fashion: "Ye know, I sure had a hell of a lot of fun buyin' that organ. I goes up to the big music store back east, Wurlitzer's. Yeah, that's it." (Author's note: !!) "I goes in that store with Johnson right after me. Kinda fallin' back. He likes that. And I walks up to a little shriveled up shill with a flower pinned in his coat and I says,

This ornate and well-unified 2/10 Welte was installed in the John Evans residence in Hollywood, California in 1926. The mansion was later the home of well-known pianist Liberace, who played the Welte to relax.

David Harris inspects the Welte player cabinet in the Liberace residence. Welte offered players in a single-roll format (as pictured) or as ten-roll changers. Single-roll players were often included right in the consoles.

'Mister, can you tell me where to find the man who can sell me an organ?'

"So he says, 'Certainly, sir. I can take care of you.' Hell, I knew he didn't know nothin'. He couldn't even tell me the price. I fooled around with him and trying to explain I wanted it for the castle, and the damn fool didn't even know I had a castle. So I finally got another bum who was a little smarter. Maybe. But he didn't know nothin' either. Can't figure what the hell they had so many dummies around there for.

"Well, I talks 'til I'm sore. Then I starts cussin'. Johnson was over to one side smilin' and sayin' nothin'. Then there was so much commotion goin' on that they sends in a big shot who was a little brighter. He did know that they was selling organs and asks me what size I wanted. I says, 'Hell, mister, I want the biggest size you got.'

"He starts draggin' out the blueprints and we start lookin'. I can't figger out nothin' from these damn things. I jest said, 'Is that big 'nuf for a castle?' and he guarantees it. So I says, 'Hell, all I wants is an organ, right now. That one will do. How much?' So they goes into a huddle and mumble around like a hog waiting for a slop pail. Finally the %#$%¢! says, '$18,000, installed.'

"'Okay,' I says. 'I'm tired of foolin'. It's a deal.' So I pulls out a roll out of my pocket that would choke a stud horse and starts countin'. Those damn shills was jumpin' around like a chicken on a hot stove. I goes on countin' $1,000 bills. I gets up to $10,000 and runs out of $1,000 bills. Then I starts in on the little ones, $500 and like that. I gets up to $16,000 and runs outa them. Well, that was all I had but small $100 and I wasn't goin' to count all day jest for a few extra dollars. So I says, 'There she is, $16,000 for the damn thing. You want it or not? Take it or go to hell!'

"So they grabs it and counts it again and says okay and we gets the bill and that's all there is to it. And now the organ grinder makes a livin' fixin' it. Some racket. Haaa!"[26]

The organ sold to Scott was actually the ten-rank Welte from the Philadelphia Welte studio to which four ranks and a diaphone were added by the factory. The organ was also equipped with a Multi-Control ten-roll changer as well as a single-roll player in an elaborate cabinet. Lloyd Davey, a member of the crew who installed the organ, was called back around 1935 to install one of the rare Wurlitzer six-roll changers which played Wurlitzer style R reproducing organ rolls. Mr. Davey recalls: "To complete the specification for the player I had to have a tuba rank which would play on seven inches wind. I found a high pressure tuba and asked Nuttall if he would revoice it for me to play on the lower pressure. He had me order some brass from Kimball and he cut and curved the new tongues at his home in Glendale. After putting the tongues in the tubas, he didn't have to touch them except to tune them. That's how good Nuttall was!"[27]

In mid-1929 all the assets of the Welte organ division, except real estate, were sold to New York financier Donald F. Tripp for $79,000. The new company was called the Welte-Tripp Organ Corporation and Charles Courboin became general manager and vice president. While touring the Bronx factory one day with Tripp, Courboin suddenly announced that the place was jinxed. It was, actually, a particularly well-equipped and efficient organ factory but Courboin convinced Tripp to move it.[28 29] A fascinating commentary on the situation was contained in a personal letter from R. P. Elliot to Lloyd Davey dated October 10, 1929: "They are moving or have moved to their new factory, the Schick razor factory at Sound Beach, Ct., which they bought—or which the new Angel bought. That is a safe investment as a piece of real

Above, music room of Death Valley Scotty's castle. The 3/15 Welte horseshoe console is hidden behind a removable folding screen on the right. The organ speaks through a large grille, a portion of which is visible on the far left. The photo on the left shows a close-up view of the elaborately carved cabinet for the Welte single-roll player. A Welte Multi-Control ten-roll changer is also included in a remote location. To the right of the single-roll player can be seen a tablet of six push buttons controlling a Wurlitzer six-roll changer which was installed c. 1935 by former Welte man Lloyd Davey.

estate when he gets sickened of the organ business—as he may soon with [Courboin] as general manager. George Goll is superintendent. Their only salvation is the employment of Nils Hillstrom as chief draftsman, to catch Goll's worst mistakes, and Whitelegg, of course, as head voicer."

Welte-Tripp received a number of contracts despite the depressed economic conditions of the time, but not enough to pay a dividend on Tripp's investment. In July 1931 he sold the Welte assets, not including real estate, to the W. W. Kimball Company for $35,000.[30] A full-page Kimball ad in the September 1931 *Diapason* read, in part: "Why Kimball-Welte? The modern Kimball and the modern Welte are scarcely to be distinguished, one from the other. They are alike in system and details of construction and in console appointments, voiced to the same ideals of balanced ensemble and individual beauty of tone. It was eminently fitting that they should be combined—or, let us say, re-combined—in the security of Kimball ownership."

The Welte organs built under R. P. Elliot's leadership were so similar to Kimballs, even in minute construction details, that often experienced organ men have difficulty distinguishing the two makes. Further complicating the situation is the fact that Kimball, after purchasing Welte, installed Kimball nameplates on some earlier Welte instruments![31] From one point of view it could be said that Weltes were "copies" of Kimballs, but it is really more accurate to say that each company was in fact building the Elliot organ. For all their similarities, three noticeable differences come to mind: the shape of the swell shoes, the type of chest magnets used, and the style of voicing.

Welte magnets had a removable maroon-colored bakelite cap, similar to the late Wurlitzer "black cap" style, although Welte's design predated Wurlitzer's black cap by two years. The greatest difference between Welte and Kimball was in voicing. This is not to imply that Welte voicing was inferior; but Kimball did have the voicing genius of George Michel whose strings, for example, set the industry standard of quality. Welte's strings, at best, were quite mediocre. Welte mechanical quality, however, was among the highest ever seen in the organ industry.

An early Welte innovation was the vorsetzer which could be rolled up to nearly any console, turning it into a self-player. Similar vorsetzers for pianos were sold by the thousands but the organ model was apparently more popular in Europe; it is extremely rare in America.

Welte's first American factory was located in Poughkeepsie, New York. A large number of instruments were produced here before the company's assets were seized by the Alien Property Custodian at the outbreak of World War I.

A PICTORIAL TOUR OF THE WELTE-TRIPP FACTORY IN 1930

Overall view of the last factory premises at Sound Beach, Connecticut. Before Welte occupied the building, the Schick company made razor blades here.

In every good organ factory each instrument is first "built" on paper in the drafting department.

Above and below, two views of the erecting area. In the lower left can be seen a reservoir, copied after E. M. Skinner designs, one of the few Welte construction details which weren't Kimball-inspired.

Machine shop.

A 16′ tuba is being fabricated in the pipe shop.

Head voicer Richard O. Whitelegg voices a tuba. To his right are resonators for the 16′ octave; on the workbench behind him are their boots, awaiting his magic touch. After Welte closed in 1931, Mr. Whitelegg's talents were put to excellent use at the M. P. Moller company where he was tonal director until his untimely death in 1944.

A carefully posed view of the console department shows several different styles of consoles produced by Welte.

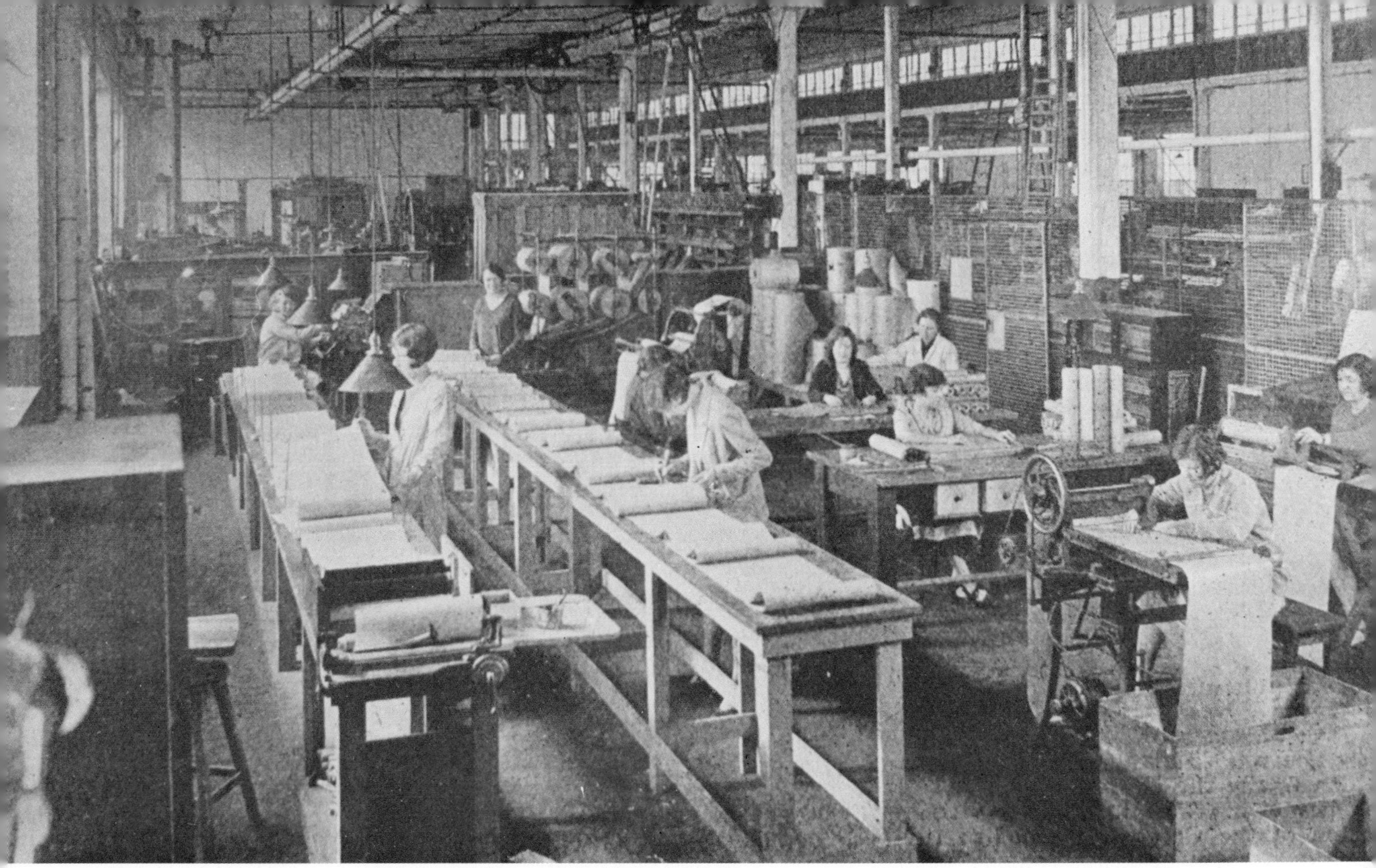

Music roll department. Remarkably, the perforating machine and the library of master rolls still exist in 1987.

WELTE OPUS LIST

CITY/STATE	LOCATION	SIZE	YR	BLWR	HP	WP	REMARKS
CALIFORNIA							
Death Valley	Scotty's Castle	3/14	1928	21747			Originally 10-rank Philadelphia Welte studio organ, plus 4 ranks and new console. Tuba added later by Lloyd Davey as 15th rank.
Downey	Downey Th.	2/					
Hollywood	John A. Evans residence	2/10	1926	18244			
	Hollywood Playhouse Th.	2/10	1927	19836			
	William James Kraft residence		1926	18655			
			1926	10658TUR			
	Walter Q. Patten residence		1925	18079			
Los Angeles	Barker Bros. Auditorium	3/9	1926	19575			
	Commercial Club		1926	19387			
Pasadena	T. L. Warner residence	3/21	1926	19606	10	10"&15"	
Riverside	Bruce Reid residence		1926	18664			Originally on display at Barker Bros. store, Los Angeles, California.
San Francisco	Kohler & Chase Studio	2/11	1927				Located at 111 O'Farrell Street.
	Kohler & Chase Studio	2/	1925	18164			Located at 26 O'Farrell Street; with roll player in drawer under lower manual; later sold to George Campe residence, Burlingame, California and 10-roll player added.
	KPO Radio	3/18	1927	19884			Opus 242; located in Hale Bros. department store; moved in 1944 to NBC studios at Sunset & Vine, Hollywood, California and enlarged.
	KTAB Radio	2/3					
San Pedro	Mrs. Belle Maloy residence						
Santa Monica	Club Casa Del Mar	2/10	1925	17900			
CONNECTICUT							
Roxbury	B. Z. Nutting		1929	22978			
DISTRICT OF COLUMBIA							
Washington	Homer L. Kitt Co.		1924	L1019	3	7"	Located at 1330 "G" Street.
			1924	L1020	1		20" vacuum.

CITY/STATE	LOCATION	SIZE	YR	BLWR	HP	WP	REMARKS
FLORIDA							
Miami	Tuttle residence		1924	M735B	2	6″	
			1924	M736B	1		15″ vacuum.
Palm Beach	Plaza Mignon Studio		1927	19976			
IOWA							
Des Moines	Carl Weeks residence	3/	1927	19541			Top manual for echo.
ILLINOIS							
Chicago	Welte Studio	3/					Located in Story & Clark Bldg., on 7th floor; with echo and roll player.
Wilmette	Village Th.	2/8					
MARYLAND							
Perryville	Miss Eleanor Boteler		1929	23051			Located on Chesapeake View Farm.
MICHIGAN							
Benton Harbor	Liberty Th.		1926	18955			
NEW JERSEY							
Atlantic City	St. Charles Hotel		1926	18711			
			1926	10679TUR			
Bernardsville	Mrs. Francis Lloyd		1924	M561B	3	6″	Also 15″ vacuum.
East Orange	Plaza Th.		1924	M745B	2	10″	
Edgewater	unidentified location		1923	L425	3	10″	
Englewood	Englewood Th.	3/	1926	0101B	5	10″	
Leonia	Palisade Th.		1927	20985			
Palisades Park	Park Lane Th.	3/6	1928				
Paterson	S. W. Carroll		1925	N130B	3	6″	Also 15″ vacuum.
Rahway	Empress (Empire) Th.		1926	0229B	2	10″	
Red Bank	Thos. N. McCarter residence		1926	18988			
	Strand Th.		1928	21888			
NEW YORK							
Bronx	Hughes Th.		1923	L754	2	8″	
	Rosedale Th.	3/	1926	18540			
	U. S. Th.		1923	K931	3	8″	
	Wakefield Th.	3/12	1927	19896			
Bronxville	Bronxville Th.	3/	1926	18541			
			1926	10690TUR			
Brooklyn	Alhambra Th.		1914	5803			
	Berkshire Th.		1925	N550B	2	10″	
	Broadway Th.		1915	6051			
	Century Th.		1915	6570			
	Filmland Th.		1925	N54B	2	10″	
	Lida Th.		1925	M909B	2	10″	
	Mermaid Th.		1923	L468	2	8″	
	New Liberty Th.		1925	N13B	2	10″	
	Mr. Remos YMCA		1927	P514B	3	10″	
Great Neck	Dr. Preston P. Satterwhite		1920	11152	5	8½″	Also 12″ vacuum.
			1923	L555	2	6″	
		4/	1926	18739			Enlarged to 4-manual, with echo; burned November 8, 1932.
Mamaroneck	Dr. R. J. Forhan residence		1931				Welte-Tripp nameplate.
Mt. Vernon	Embassy Th.		1926	N932B	2	10″	
New York	American Movies Th.		1924	M420B	2	10″	
	Astor Th.		1914	5775			
	Benenson Th.		1923	L1154	2	10″	
	Berler residence		1920	11818	5	10″	Also 12″ vacuum; opus 121; located at 809 Riverside Drive.
	Bronx Golden Rule Th.		1923	L14	2	8″	
	John W. Campbell	2/	1929	23846			Office/studio located in Grand Central Terminal building.
	Century Th.		1923	L920	5	10″	
	Congress Th.		1925	M1027B	3	10″	
	Dyckman Th.		1923	L821	2	10″	
			1923	L820	1½	10″	
	Eagle Th.		1927	19870			Located on 3rd Avenue, between 130-140th Streets.
	81st Street Th.		1916				
	Forsythe Th.		1925	N443B	2	10″	
	George Gershwin residence		1929	23059			Located at 316 West 103rd Street.
	Grand Central Palace Th.		1925	N15B	5	6″	
			1925	N14B	¾		15″ vacuum.
	Hamilton Th.		1915	6713			
	Colonel Kerrigan residence		1926	19702			
	Keystone Th.		1926	0450B	2	10″	
	C. Bai Lihme residence		1926	19711	3	7″	Located at 950 Fifth Avenue.

CITY/STATE	LOCATION	SIZE	YR	BLWR	HP	WP	REMARKS
New York	Murray Hill Th.		1914	5512			
	Pathe Freres Phonograph Lab.		1916	7048			
	Photoplay Th.		1923	L286	3	8″	Located at 99th Street & 3rd Avenue.
	Plaza Th.		1916	6564			
	79th Street Th.		1923	K929	3	8″	
	Mrs. James Sheldon residence		1928	22698			
	Temple of Music (Hammerstein) (Ed Sullivan) Th.	3/	1927	20988			
	Mrs. Lucy Cotton Thomas residence		1928	22051			Located in Hotel Pierre.
	Times Th.		1924	M576B	2	10″	
	Valentine Th.		1923	K930	3	8″	
	Van Neste (York) Th.		1924	M330B	2	10″	
	Velazco Studio	3/5	1927	20959			Located at 1658 Broadway.
	Welte Studio	3/	1916	7347			Located at 667-5th Avenue; with echo.
	Welte Studio	3/38	1927				Located at 695-5th Avenue; with 3-manual roll-recording console; with 7-rank echo.
Port Chester	Capitol Th.	3/					
Poughkeepsie	Stratford Th.		1917	8618			
Ramapo	Alfred Clegg residence		1920	11562	2	8½″	Also 12″ vacuum.
Yonkers	Cameo Th.		1925	N454B	2	10″	
	Park Hill Th.		1926	18388			
PENNSYLVANIA							
Norristown	Wm. S. Buckland residence		1927	20267			
Philadelphia	Benjamin Franklin Hotel		1925	N453B	5	6″&12″	
				N452B	1		15″ vacuum.
	Forrest Th.	2/8	1928	21770			
	Stonehurst Hills Th.	3/	1928	22408			
	Welte Studio	?/10					
Pittsburgh	H. J. Heinz Co. Auditorium		1921				With roll player.
Redley Park	Dr. C. A. Ernst residence		1924	L1101B	1	8″	
			1924	L1102B	1		20″ vacuum.
			1924	L1103B	5	10″	
RHODE ISLAND							
Providence	John S. Holbrook residence		1926				
	Mrs. E. J. Lownes residence		1926	18506			
			1926	10674TUR			
TEXAS							
Commerce	Hippodrome Th.		1919				
Greenville	Crystal Th.		1920	10485			
WISCONSIN							
Milwaukee	East Town Restaurant & Hotel		1929	22940			
Stoughton	C. M. Osterheld residence		1931				Welte-Tripp nameplate.
ENGLAND							
London	Craigweil House		1920	11393	5	6″	Also 12″ vacuum.

WESTERN SERVICE CO.

The author has been able to learn very little about Otto Solle, proprietor of the Western Service Company. None of the Chicago "old timers" or anyone else, for that matter, can recall anyone by that name in the organ business. He did install a two-manual organ in the Pastime Theatre, Iowa City, Iowa early in 1926. It had an unusually complete percussion section including a set of tuned sleigh bells. Corners were cut on the console, however, which had a blind combination action and a used Wurlitzer bench. A Simplex blower supplied the wind. According to a local newspaper article, four weeks were required to install the organ by Mr. Solle and two helpers.[1]

The author is tempted to speculate that the owner of the Pastime, a real show-biz promoter and "operator," sought the least expensive organ he could find and as a result had it assembled by someone who wasn't regularly engaged in new organ building.

AT LAST!

"Punch" Dunkel is Going to Dedicate His New $30,000 All American Concert Grand Organ

Saturday at 1 p.m.

Just completed after requiring eight weeks to install and over seven months to build.

Mr. Otto Solle of Chicago and a personal friend of "Punch" specially designed and built for the

It is one of the finest pipe organs west of Chicago. You'll be surprised what a wonderful organ it is.

We are going to give a "Grand Organ Recital" Saturday and Sunday afternoon at 1 o'clock. The recital starts at 1:15 and no one will be seated while the concert is on. So be here in your seat not later than 1:15.

Mrs. Floy Graham Smith, formerly of the School of Music, who has had years of experience playing on some of the biggest organs in the country will preside at the console of the Pastime Organ Grande.

Mr. George Goldkette of Chicago, a very accomplished organist, will render special solos and features during the show. He will be here for one week only so please do not overlook this opportunity to enjoy the added Musical features to our regular program.

OUR FIRST BIG SONG HIT WILL BE IRVING BERLIN'S LATEST,

"REMEMBER"

WITH SLIDES. HE WROTE THIS SONG ESPECIALLY FOR HIS WIFE WHOM HE JUST MARRIED

Don't Fail To Hear It

ALSO SHOWING

Rex Beach's Golden Romance of Alaska With a Wonderful Cast

Anna Q. Nilsson Ben Lyon Viola Dana
Victor McLaglen Hobart Bosworth

in a big 8 reel story of the north

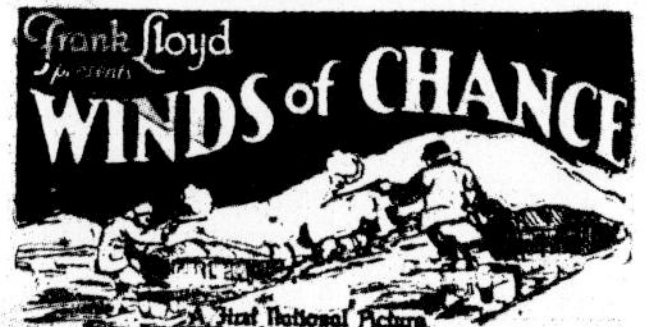

Rex Beach takes you to Alaska again to the stirring days of the gold rush.

—Also Showing—

PATHE NEWS FABLES TOPICS

Continuous All Day Saturday and Sunday

ADMISSION: ADULTS 50c CHILDREN 25c

Advertisement appearing in the Iowa City Press-Citizen, *January 29, 1926.*

The WESTERN SERVICE Co.

O. J. SOLLE, Manager

ORGAN DESIGNERS and BUILDERS

Rebuilding Electric Actions Percussions

Special Theatre Unit and Automatic Organ Service

Old Organs Electrified

Office:
2120 S. MILLARD AVE.
Rockwell 5124
CHICAGO

Shop:
2512 SO. 52d AVE.
Cicero, Ill.

Chicago Factory Representatives:

SIMPLEX ALL STEEL BLOWERS

Mfd. by B. F. BLOWER CO.
Fond du Lac, Wis.

Ad in the November 1926 Diapason.

The tale of the Wick brothers begins in 1906 when John F. Wick (1881-1948), a budding organist, became interested in constructing an organ and read all the books he could find on the subject. An unexpected impetus came when his brother, Adolph Wick, was injured and unable to perform his regular duties as a carpenter and cabinetmaker. John persuaded Adolph to help him construct an organ and also enlisted the services of his other brother, Louis J. Wick (1869-1936), who had been following in his father's footsteps as a watchmaker. The first Wicks organ was built by the trio on the second floor of the Seitz jewelry store in Highland, Illinois, the brothers' home town.[1] [2] After nearly 70 years of faithful service this opus 1 has been repurchased by the Wicks factory and was donated to the museum of Southern Illinois University at Carbondale.[3]

The success of their first instrument prompted the Wick brothers to investigate the possibility of forming a company to build organs and in 1908 the Wicks Pipe Organ Company was duly incorporated. The first instruments featured tracker action; by 1910 the Wick brothers had switched to tubular pneumatic action, following the trend elsewhere in the country. They were never really happy with the tubular action and by 1913 had built a few electro-pneumatic organs. Late in 1913 came an event which would prove the turning point of the fortune of the Wicks company. A graduate engineer of Illinois University, A. J. Katt, visited the Wick brothers and showed them a working model of a direct electric action. Fascinated with the concept, they forged full steam ahead and by 1915 had built the first Wicks direct electric organ.[4]

The years 1915-1919 were a real trial by fire for the Wick brothers not only because the direct electric action was being debugged, but also because they suffered the persecution and ridicule so often visited upon those who are trailblazers. Wicks persevered despite derision from the relatively conservative organ building community and even in the face of financial ruin; ultimately the firm triumphed. The direct electric action was first patented and trademarked in 1922.[5] Although still a registered trademark of the Wicks company, the phrase "direct electric" has received the honor of passing into generic usage as did Cellophane and Victrola, other famous trademarks of the same era.

The Wicks company has been remarkably successful over the years for a variety of reasons. The direct electric action was simpler and therefore less costly to manufacture than almost every other type of action; hence, Wicks organs could be sold at very attractive prices. Wicks decided early on not to confine their sales to the territory in the vicinity of the factory. They developed a nationwide network of sales agents, many of whom were quite aggressive. Some of the agents responsible for theatre organ sales were A. R. Payne in Denver, Edwin Haslam in New Jersey, Walter Evans in Vancouver, British Columbia, W. J. Mullaney in California, the Arthur Jordan Piano Co. in Virginia and the Jenkins Music Co. in Kansas City.

The three most aggressive Wicks agents seemed to be Sherman, Clay, who sold in California, Oregon and Washington; G. L. Parker in Massachusetts; and the Southern Pipe Organ Co. in Dallas, Texas. The last firm was the successor to the J. D. Wheelan company after Mr. Wheelan's death in 1924 and was operated by G. A. Doering, former owner of the Simplex Theatre Supply Company. George Lincoln Parker sold a number of Wicks theatre organs in Massachusetts and even put his own nameplate on at least one of them, opus 680.

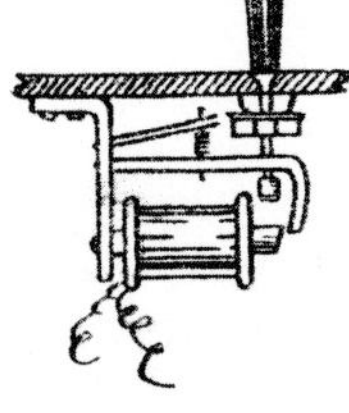

A major factor in the aggressiveness of these agents was a sales technique prevalent in the organ industry in the 1920s. Today, most organ manufacturers have an established price schedule and a fixed sales commission for the agent. Thus any specification will be quoted at the same price by any agent of the company, exclusive of transportation costs. Such was not the case in the 1920s,

WARNING

Since the introduction of the Direct Electric Action and its remarkable success in organ construction it has come to pass that unscrupulous salesmen of competitors have found it necessary to misrepresent, wherever possible, the Direct Electric System and to deliberately spread false reports concerning the Wicks Pipe Organ Company and its product. Evidence is at hand sufficient to prosecute on grounds of these false reports and fair warning is herewith given that unless this practice is discontinued, legal means will be resorted to.

Highland, Ill., Aug. 21st, 1923. WICKS PIPE ORGAN CO.

The direct electric action was a major innovation in organ technology. Many new ideas undergo a period of controversy and ridicule but the Wicks company and the direct electric action seemed to get more than their fair share. Perhaps one of the reasons competitors were upset was that this simple action allowed Wicks organs to be constructed and sold more inexpensively than many others. The above ad in the September 1923 Diapason *represents the somewhat drastic measures the Wicks company pursued to combat their unwarranted persecution.*

Martin M. Wick is the son of John F. Wick, founder of the Wicks firm, and is president of the Wicks Organ Company.

however. The agents were at liberty to sell the organs for as much as they could get and markups of 100% or more were not unusual. Sherman, Clay is the author's favorite practitioner of this technique. Sandy Balcom, a former installation man for Sherman, Clay, recalled that they once sold a 2/4 Wicks to a theatre for $12,000. This same instrument had been invoiced to Sherman, Clay by the Wicks factory for $1,978 including freight![6]

Theatre organ sales were a major factor in the early success of the Wicks company. From 1915 to 1929 theatre organs accounted for fully one third of the Wicks business. Theatre instruments were especially profitable because most of them were stock models, many parts of which could be mass produced at substantial savings.

Ironically enough, Wicks' best customer for theatre organs was not a theatre chain but another organ builder, Robert-Morton. The American Photo Player Company purchased about 75% of the Wicks theatre organs built between 1916 and 1923. These organs bear a nameplate reading "The Robert-Morton Company, factories [in] Highland, Ill. [and] Van Nuys, Calif." No particular attempt was made to make these Wicks-built organs look like Robert-Morton products except in the nameplate design and in the percussions, which used hingeless pneumatics similar to Robert-Morton designs. Otherwise, these instruments contained standard Wicks construction features throughout.

The financial arrangement between the Robert-Morton and Wicks firms remains a mystery today. The November 1917 issue of *The Diapason* ran a brief article noting that "Control of the Wicks Organ Company, whose plant is at Highland, Ill., has been taken over by the American Photo-player (sic) Company, and the Wicks factory is manufacturing organs for the Photo-player company in the central western territory."[7] In the opinion of Martin Wick, current Wicks president, this claim is inaccurate[8] and the author tends to agree. All during this period, 1916 to 1923, Wicks continued to build church organs as well as theatre organs under their own nameplate. A curious fact relating to the Robert-Morton association is that contracts for the church and theatre organs sold to them have been systematically removed from the contract file in the Wicks vault, whereas the contracts for Wicks church organs built during the same years are all intact.

John F. Wick was the founder and first president of the firm until his death in 1948 at which time control passed to his son, Martin M. Wick. As a result, the Wicks firm has been a family-owned business since its inception. Under the leadership of Martin Wick, the Wicks Organ Company has grown to become the second largest pipe organ builder in the country, having built nearly 6,000 organs as of 1984. Because of Mr. Wick's enthusiasm and willingness to try new directions and ideas, the Wicks company built the first new theatre organ in contemporary times for the 1958 Home Show in Chicago and have built a half dozen more since.

This nameplate was used on Wicks organs built for the American Photo Player Company. Robert-Morton organs built at Van Nuys use a similar nameplate except, of course, that Highland, Ill. is not mentioned.

WICKS THEATRE ORGAN STYLES

The following chart lists most of the styles sold for theatre use. Some of the larger models were listed in Wicks catalogs but were never built. The percussion complement is not listed because it was an option on most models and did not affect the style number.

STYLE	SIZE	NOTES	CATALOG PRICE	PRICE WITH PERCUSSIONS
314	2/3	16′ flute, 8′ violin, 8′ diapason	$1,450	$1,895
314E	2/3			
418	2/4	Style 314 plus 8′ oboe	$1,900	$2,345
4192	2/4	16′ stopped diapason, 8′ diapason, 8′ salicional, 8′ oboe		
55	2/4			
65	2/4	Style 314 plus 8′ vox humana	$1,900	$2,570
Special 65	2/4	Same ranks as style 65	$1,900	$2,800
75	2/4	Same ranks as style 65	$2,200	$3,500
Special 75	2/5	Style 75 plus 8′ trumpet	$2,500	$3,800
85	2/5	Same ranks as special 75	$2,700	$3,965
Jackson	2/5	Style 65 plus 8′ tibia clausa		
632	2/6	Special 75 plus viol celeste	$2,940	$4,010
60	2/6	Style 65 plus 8′ tibia clausa and 8′ kinura		
Granada	3/6	16′ flute, 8′ salicional, 8′ diapason, 8′ tibia clausa, 8′ kinura and 8′ vox humana		
70	2/7	16′ flute, 16′ diaphone, 8′ violin, viol celeste, 8′ tibia clausa, 8′ vox humana and 8′ brass trumpet		
743	2/7		$3,745	$5,075
80	3/8	16′ flute, 16′ diaphone, 16′ tibia clausa, 8′ viol d'orchestre, 8′TC viol celeste, 8′ kinura, 8′ tuba and 8′ vox humana		
957	2/9	16′ flute, 16′ diaphone, 8′ violin, 8′ cello, 8′ tibia clausa, 8′ trumpet, 8′ vox humana, 8′ quintadena and 8′ clarinet	$5,000	$6,325
90	3/9	Style 80 plus 8′ saxophone		
1296	3/12		$8,000	$9,325
Wicks Giant	3/12	16′ flute, 16′ diaphone, 16′ tibia clausa, 16′ viol d'orchestre, 8′ celeste sharp, 8′ celeste flat, 8′ tibia plena, 8′ kinura, 8′ brass trumpet, 8′ saxophone, 8′ vox humana and 8′ clarinet		

The clever Wicks balanced valve allows even large pedal pipes to be operated by direct electric action. Since air pressure on both sides of the valves is equal, the magnet has only to overcome a light spring in order to admit a large volume of wind to the pipe.

WICKS PIPE ORGAN COMPANY, Incorporated

DIRECT ELECTRIC ACTION

Factories and General Offices: HIGHLAND, Madison County, ILLINOIS

Builders of Chapel,—Studio,—Theatre,—Concert and Church Organs.

SOLE OWNERS OF "DIRECT ELECTRIC ACTION" PATENTS

THE ORGAN OF THE TWENTIETH CENTURY
SILENT IN OPERATION
RELIABLE UNDER ALL CONDITIONS
RESPONDS INSTANTLY TO THE TOUCH
DURABILITY, LOW MAINTENANCE,
TONE FOR BEAUTY, SINGING, VOICING, PURITY OF ORGAN AND ORCHESTRAL QUALITY UNSURPASSED

DUE TO THE GREATLY INCREASED DEMAND OF **"WICKS DIRECT ELECTRIC PIPE ORGANS"**

We are now MAKING EXTENSIVE ADDITIONS TO OUR ALREADY LARGE PLANT, WHERE WE MAKE EVERY PART OF OUR INSTRUMENTS

We are always pleased to afford every possible convenience to purchasers who desire to make a rigid investigation of our product.

SEE THEM FROM BLOWER UNIT TO CONSOLE, INSIDE and OUT.

CHICAGO, ILLINOIS.
WICKS PIPE ORGAN CO.,
F. W. Wimberley, Mgr.
5227 CORNELL AVE.,
Phone Midway 0763

BUILDERS OF ST. STANISLAUS CHURCH ORGAN

FOR CATALOGUES, LITERATURE and DEMONSTRATION APPOINTMENTS

WICKS PIPE ORGAN COMPANY, Incorporated

FACTORIES AND GENERAL OFFICES

HIGHLAND, Madison County, ILLINOIS

ST. LOUIS, MISSOURI.
WICKS PIPE ORGAN CO.,
3680 LINDELL BLVD.

This ad appeared in a publication local to the Highland, Illinois Wicks factory during the golden age of the theatre organ.

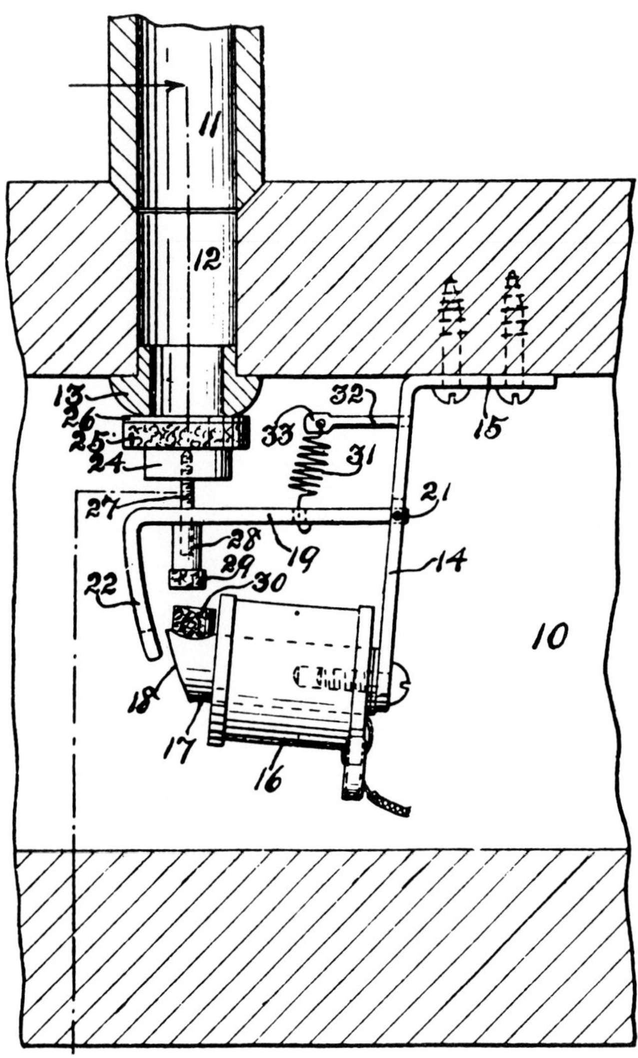

Original patent drawing for the Wicks direct electric chest action, undoubtedly the simplest ever devised, having only one moving part per pipe.

Space

Necessary for the proper installation of an organ often presents serious difficulties.

Recognize the fact that the

DIRECT ELECTRIC ORGAN

due to its simplified and compact construction, requires less room than any other type organ of equal tonal units.

This Service Is Gratis

Church Committees, Theatre Managers, Architects and all others, confronted with particularly difficult problems along these lines, are invited to consult us and to let us work out practical solutions.

Address
Sales Manager

WICKS PIPE ORGAN COMPANY
Highland, Illinois

This Wicks ad appeared in the March 1926 Diapason.

BETTER THAN PROMISED!

When the Artist Organ Builder is planning a new organ, he conceives enthusiastic pictures of its wonders. And then—with some—the actual organ does not always match the visioned pictures.

But here is a different story.

The WICKS "DIRECT ELECTRIC ACTION" PIPE ORGAN—the tonal beauty organ—is so far beyond the most enthusiastic forecast from the factory that the Sales Department has the delight of its life making prospective customers acquainted with the finished product.

THINK of everything you would like to have in a Pipe Organ—artistic design—beautiful tone quality—instant action—durability of construction—excellent workmanship—superior finish—then examine a Wicks Pipe Organ. We'll let you do all the talking.

CHURCH—RESIDENCE—THEATRE.

The "Better Than Promised" Pipe Organ.

WICKS PIPE ORGAN COMPANY
Highland, Illinois.

Direct Electric Action—Direct Electric Tremulant. New Features.

Wicks ad in the December 1920 Diapason. *The direct electric tremulant mentioned in this and other Wicks ads of the period never became popular; most tremulants in Wicks theatre organs were of the standard bellows type used by most other manufacturers.*

On the next three pages is reproduced a portion of an elaborate 1925 Wicks theatre organ catalog. The fascinating text assures potential purchasers that, among other things, Wicks theatre organs will never sound "churchy!" Included are specifications for the two most popular Wicks theatre models, styles 314 and 65. One stop in these specifications is a real howler, the "orchestral diapason." The diapason is the one rank in an organ which is not *imitative of any other instrument but, by golly, in a Wicks theatre organ even the diapason is orchestral!*

WICKS PIPE ORGAN COMPANY

OFFICERS

JOHN F. WICK, President
LOUIS J. WICK, Secretary and Treasurer
EUGENE SCHOTT, Vice-President

BOARD OF DIRECTORS

JOHN F. WICK
LOUIS J. WICK
ADOLPH J. KATT
EUGENE J. BUCHHEIM
EUGENE SCHOTT

HIGHLAND, ILLINOIS, U. S. A.

The Wicks Orchestral Organ

The WICKS PIPE ORGAN COMPANY of Highland, Illinois, is in a unique manner able to present to the trade a pipe organ for theater use which cannot be excelled by any other builder.

Thru long association with a nationally known distributing agency of high grade theater organs, during which time we furnished practically all the instruments used by this organization, we had occasion to meet, study, and overcome all the problems presented to the builder of organs for the theater, and to become familiar with any and all conditions that the theater organ must meet. We have in our organization a practical theater organist who has had long experience in the playing of theater organs, accompanying practically every sort of film entertainment that has yet been devised, and his advice and experience are available in all our work.

In all our theater organs we use our DIRECT ELECTRIC action. This is fully illustrated and described in our separate booklet on this action, to which we refer the reader in search of technical details. It is sufficient to say here that in this type of action we place a magnet directly under each pipe, each magnet operating one pipe only. These magnets are all independent, all standard, and all largely interchangeable. The magnet opens and closes the valve admitting wind into the pipe without the need of any other mechanism. It is absolutely reliable, there is nothing to wear out, nothing to work loose, nothing to need constant adjustment. All magnets are thoroly tested in our factory after being mounted in final position, and when once adjusted and passed by our experts cannot come out of adjustment or cause trouble. There is but one moving part between the key and the pipe-valve, this being a hinged hanger carrying the valve, and rotating on a piece of drill-rod.

Theater work demands rapid speech of pipes, instant response to the pressure, no matter how slight, of the fingers of the performer on the keys. Our DIRECT ELECTRIC action alone meets this demand with absolute reliability. In fact, it more than meets the demand. We have never tested our action to see how many times it will repeat per second, or any other period of time, but we can truthfully say that no organist, no matter how expert, has ever been able to play ahead of it.

ORCHESTRAL TONE

To meet the tonal requirements of the orchestral organ, our voicing department has specialized on producing pipes of the highest grade, and of true orchestral tone, which we use in all of our instruments. Keen strings, softly rounded flutes, a clarinet which is especially imitative of its orchestral prototype, a 'cello with all the singing tone of the best of expert players are but a few of the many orchestral colors available to purchasers of our instruments. We include in all our organs a Vox Humana, that wonderful reproduction of the human singer, so necessary in theater work, and giving an effect entirely different from anything else.

To carry out the orchestral effect, we install in all our organs, at the option of the purchaser, traps as usually found in the orchestra, of the best quality, so mounted and operated by our actions that the effect is equal if not superior to that obtained by the expert drummer.

FLEXIBILITY

After promptness and reliability of action, and faithfulness to orchestral tone, the theater organ must have flexibility. The organist must be able to obtain just the effects he wants, when he wants them, with a minimum of necessity for changing a lot of controls. He must be able, if necessary, in the midst of a great ensemble number, to pick out and play, without even the fraction of a second's delay, even A SINGLE PIPE, returning instantly to his ensemble. He must avoid monotony, must always be interesting. The tone of the organ must be constantly changing by small degrees, as the colors change in the sunset sky. There is only one way to insure the possibility of this effect, and that is by absolute flexibility of control.

This flexibility of control can be obtained efficiently in only one way, by building the organ on the UNIT principle.

Here again we refer the man interested in technical details to our other literature, and explain this principle here briefly, by saying that it is a system where each pipe is used in as many places on the keyboards as desired. In the UNIT organ there are no duplicate pipes, as in other systems of building. We install in the organ as many sets of pipes as called for, but each set is entirely independent and no pipe of any set is exactly like, or nearly like, in BOTH pitch and tone color, any other pipe in the instrument, no matter how large.

According to the size of the instrument, we use the same pipe in three, four, five, six, or more positions on the key-boards, thus insuring far greater efficiency from the individual pipe, far greater flexibility of tone and control than in any other way, and fewer idle pipes at any time than in any other system of building.

By the use of this unit principle, together with the careful regulation of tone qualities incorporated in our organs, we avoid that nightmare of the theater owner, a "churchy" organ. An organ sounds churchy because it has a great mass or volume of tone, absolutely necessary in church work, but unnecessary, and in fact out of place, in the theater organ. This is because the church organ, by its very nature has many pipes, idle most of the time, which are a sort of reserve, a large proportion of them being duplications of one another. Our organs can play loudly or softly, at the discretion of the player, but never with the massive effect that makes an organ sound "churchy."

EASE OF OPERATION

The player of one of our ORCHESTRAL ORGANS has at all times absolute freedom of selection, can change his effects instantly at any time, and with infinite possibility of variety. All this is accomplished with but a minimum of mechanism for him to operate, and while it is always an advantage to have at the key-board an expert player, a player of even very limited experience can produce on our instruments music truly fitted to theater use, for any situation for which the picture he is cueing may call.

DETAILS OF CONSTRUCTION

The Wicks Orchestral Theater Organ is designed to be played from a detached console, placed at the option of the purchaser, on the stage, in the pit, or in any other desired location. This detached console is movable when necessary without any trouble, as there are no wind connections running into it. For this reason the Wicks console is uniquely suited for installation in situations where it is desired to place the console on a rising platform.

The standard console case is of plain oak, dark oak finish. The interior wood-work of the console, key-cheeks, key-slips, stop-key rails, etc., are of genuine mahogany, piano finish. Stop-keys are placed in standard semi-circular arrangement above the top manual. Four colors of stop-keys are used. Flue stops are controlled by white stop-keys: reeds by red: traps and percussions by amber: mechanicals by black. All these stop-keys are distinctly lettered, and when it is desired by the purchaser are illumined by small electric lamps, appropriately mounted, placed above each group.

Wicks Orchestral Theater organs are always tuned to Philharmonic pitch, A-440. This is the pitch adopted by the majority of important orchestras of the world. No difficulty will be experienced by any orchestra player in tuning his instrument, whether of domestic or foreign make, to the pitch of the Wicks organ. This is of great advantage in houses where the musical policy calls for the use of the organ together with the orchestra in ensemble playing.

These organs are all designed to be entirely enclosed in one or more sound-proof expression chambers. At least one side of each of these chambers is a series of shutters, which can be opened and closed at the option of the player, affording utmost flexibility in the intensity or power of tone of the organ at all times. Where there are two or more expression chambers, separate swell controls are provided for each chamber, and in addition, when desired, our new "Multi-Expression" control is also installed. The player can then set the various shutter controls to give just the right balance of tone between the various chambers, and by using the "Multi-Expression" can make the tone coming from all divisions of the organ to increase or diminish without upsetting the previously determined ratio of power of tone from the various individual chambers.

These expression chambers may be constructed entirely of wood, the sides, back, top, and shutter front being furnished by the organ-builder. When possible to do so, it is advisable to build rooms for organ chambers in the building in which the organ is to be installed, one or more sides of these rooms being left open, and the organ builder furnishing the shutter fronts for these open sides. When this is done, the walls, back and top of these rooms should be finished in hard plaster, trowel-smooth, which material and treatment have been found to best preserve and reflect the full intensity and beauty of the tone of the instrument.

ORGANS FOR TEACHING

For Music Schools and Colleges where an instrument is needed for teaching theater organ playing, we recommend the selection of a THREE-FOURTEEN, or a FOUR-EIGHTEEN Orchestral Organ, either just as specified, or with the addition of percussions and traps as usually found in the up-to-date theater organ. When so specified at the time of the original installation, either of these organs can be so built that while traps and percussions are not placed in the organ when first installed, they can be added very quickly at any subsequent time, the necessary supporting construction and the wind and wiring connections having been provided in the original plan.

A WICKS organ presents a teaching medium that is little short of ideal. The fewness and sturdiness of the moving parts of the mechanism absolutely insure that this will stand up under the hard and long-continued use to which a practice and teaching organ is put. The close imitation of orchestral tone yielded by WICKS pipes makes the teaching of effective combinations unusually easy for both pupil and teacher. The WICKS console, even with controls multiplied to a very great number, is still so compact and convenient that the pupil has little difficulty in very quickly grasping the ideas underlying effective performance.

For schools which require an instrument not so especially theatrical in character, but yet built for teaching purposes, we suggest the WICKS STUDIO ORGAN, full details of which can be found in our special literature on this instrument.

ORCHESTRAL THEATER ORGAN SPECIFICATIONS

We offer in the following pages a series of suggestive specifications for Orchestral Theater Organs. Most of these are of instruments built by us, now in use, and successful from every angle. Upon application we will be glad to direct the reader to just where these organs can be heard and tried.

We welcome at all times inquiries as to our instruments and methods of building them. We will quote prices on any of these specifications upon application, or will design and quote on other specifications planned to meet special situations, on receipt of the necessay data.

Prospective purchasers of theater organs, and others interested in knowing of the best and newest developments in the manufacture of such instruments are cordially invited to visit our factory and learn at first hand more about our product.

WICKS PIPE ORGAN COMPANY
HIGHLAND, ILLINOIS

SPECIFICATION

Style Three Fourteen Theatre Organ
DIRECT ELECTRIC ACTION
Two Manuals and Pedal
Manual Compass CC to c4 61 Notes
Pedal Compass CCC to G 32 Notes

DIVISION 1 PEDAL

1	Double Bass	16 ft	32 Notes
2	Horn Diapason	8 ft	32 "
3	Flute	8 ft	32 "
4	Violoncello	8 ft	32 "
5	Orchestral Diapason	4 ft	32 "
6	Bass Drum	CCC to F	18 "
7	Snare Drum	CCC to F	18 "
8	Cymbal	CCC to F	18 "
9	Tympani	CCC to F	18 "

Items 6 to 9 operate from both stop-key and toe piston

DIVISION 2 ACCOMPANIMENT

10	Diapason	8 ft	61 Notes
11	Flute	8 ft	61 "
12	Violin	8 ft	61 "
13	Octave Flute	4 ft	61 "
14	Violina	4 ft	61 "
15	Flageolet	2 ft	61 "
16	Xylophone	c1 to c4	37 "
17	Snare Drum	c1 to c4	37 "
18	Tambourine	c1 to c4	37 "
19	Castenets	c1 to c4	37 "
20	Tom Tom	c1 to c4	37 "
21	Wood Drum	c1 to c4	37 "

Items 18 to 21 operate from both stop-key and toe piston

DIVISION 3 SOLO

22	Horn	8 ft	61 Notes
23	Orchestral Flute	8 ft	61 "
24	First Violin	8 ft	61 "
25	Octave Diapason	4 ft	61 "
26	Concert Flute	4 ft	61 "
27	Piccolo	2 ft	61 "
28	Vibrato		
29	Xylophone	c1 to c4	37 "

ACCESSORIES

Wind Indicator
Crescendo Pedal
Organ Bench with Music Compartment
Blower and Generator
Crescendo Indicator
Swell Pedal
Toe Pistons as shown above

Style 3-14 organ only. $1450.00
Traps. 445.00
Complete organ. . . $1895.00

SPECIFICATION

Style Sixty-Five Orchestral Pipe Organ
DIRECT ELECTRIC ACTION
Two Manuals and Pedal
Manual Compass CC to c4 61 Notes
Pedal Compass CCC to G 32 Notes

DIVISION 1 PEDAL

1	Bass Flute	16 ft	32 Notes
2	Horn	8 ft	32 "
3	Flute	8 ft	32 "
4	Cello	8 ft	32 "
5	Vox Humana	8 ft	32 "
6	Orchestral Diapason	4 ft	32 "
7	Bass Drum	CCC to F	18 "
8	Snare Drum	CCC to F	18 "
9	Cymbal	CCC to F	18 "
10	Tympani	CCC to F	18 "

Items 7 to 10 operate from both stop-key and toe piston

DIVISION 2 ACCOMPANIMENT

11	Horn Diapason	8 ft	61 Notes
12	Concert Flute	8 ft	61 "
13	Viola	8 ft	61 "
14	Vox Humana	8 ft	61 "
15	Horn Principal	4 ft	61 "
16	Orchestral Flute	4 ft	61 "
17	Violina	4 ft	61 "
18	Flageolet	2 ft	61 "
19	Vibrato		
20	Xylophone	c1 to c4	37 "
21	Orchestral Bells	c1 to c4	37 "
22	Snare Drum	c1 to c4	37 "
23	Tambourine	c1 to c4	37 "
24	Castenets	c1 to c4	37 "
25	Tom Tom	c1 to c4	37 "
26	Wood Drum	c1 to c4	37 "

Items 23 to 26 operate from both stop-key and toe piston

DIVISION 3 SOLO

27	Bourdon	16 ft	61 Notes
28	Horn Principal	8 ft	61 "
29	Concert Flute	8 ft	61 "
30	Violin	8 ft	61 "
31	Vox Humana	8 ft	61 "
32	Orchestral Flute	4 ft	61 "
33	Violina	4 ft	61 "
34	Vox Humana	4 ft	61 "
35	Nasard	2 2/3 ft	61 "
36	Piccolo	2 ft	61 "
37	Vibrato		
38	Xylophone	c1 to c4	37 "
39	Orchestra Bells	c1 to c4	37 "

ACCESSORIES

Wind Indicator
Crescendo Pedal
Special Tremolo for Vox Humana
Organ Bench with Music Compartment
Crescendo Indicator
Swell Pedal
Toe Pistons as shown above
Blower and Generator

PAGE TWELVE

Style Sixty-five. $1900.00
Traps. 670.00
Complete organ . . $2570.00

WHOLESALE PRICES ON TRAPS

Harp Celeste	$300.00
Harp Marimba	400.00
Xylophone	225.00
Orchestra Bells	225.00
Chimes Deagan M	200.00
Drum Unit complete (Bass Drum, Snare Drum, Cymbal, Tympani)	160.00
Crash Cymbal	40.00
Door Bell	5.00
Castanets	15.00
Triangle	15.00
Wood Drum	15.00
Tom Tom	15.00
Tambourine	15.00
Bird Whistle	15.00

SPACE REQUIREMENTS FOR STANDARD ORGANS

	Wide	Deep	High for Traps	High without Traps
Style 3-14	9'3"	4'5"	11'6"	10'6"
Style 4-18	9'3"	5'	11'6"	10'6"
Style Sixty-five	9'3"	5'10"	11'6"	10'6"
Style Sixty-fiveSpecial	9'3"	5'10"	11'6"	10'6"
Style Seventy-five	9'3"	5'10"	11'6"	10'6"
Style Seventy-five Special	9'3"	6'8"	11'6"	10'6"
Style Eighty-five	9'3"	6'8"	11'6"	10'6"

Roll tops were standard features of many Wicks theatre consoles in both two- and three-manual models. These photos are reproduced from a 1925 Wicks theatre organ catalog. Aside from the horseshoe stoprails, these consoles aren't too different from many church consoles of the day.

The following three pages are reproduced from an elaborate 1928 Wicks theatre organ catalog. The beautiful color cover, shown here in black and white, pictured the interior of the Ambassador Theatre in St. Louis, Missouri, only an hour's drive from the Wicks factory in Highland. The console of the Ambassador's 4/23 Wurlitzer does not appear in this photo!

The
Wicks
Orchestral
Organ

City Opera House
Frederick, Md.

Effingham Theatre
Effingham, Ill.

A FEW WICKS

These photographs of interiors and exteriors of theatres indicate that the Wicks Orchestral Pipe Organ is used to advantage in both the large and small theatre.

Hippodrome
Murphysboro, Ill.

Illinois
Jacksonville, Ill.

Warner's Metropolitan
Baltimore, Md.

Aladdin Theatre
Denver, Colo.

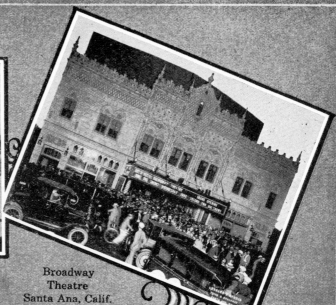

Broadway
Theatre
Santa Ana, Calif.

STALLATIONS

Individual and careful attention is given every instrument, whether it be large or small, and, that marvelous Wicks Tone Quality is an outstanding feature.

Barth
Carbondale, Ill.

Grand Opera House
St. Louis, Mo.

Jewel
Denver, Colo.

3/13 WICKS THEATRE ORGAN OPUS 649

Aladdin Theatre, Denver, Colorado

Reproduced on this and the next page is the contract for the largest Wicks organ ever installed in a theatre. The contract was executed by Wicks' Denver agent, A. R. Payne, who had been one of the founders of the United States Pipe Organ Co. several years earlier. Notice the atrocious typing in the specification—it's a good thing Mr. Payne didn't choose to be a secretary! He was apparently a good salesman, however; the Aladdin was one of four instruments he sold to Denver theatres.

AGREEMENT

THIS AGREEMENT made and entered into by and between the WICKS PIPE ORGAN CO. of Highland, Madison County, Illinois, hereinafter called the party of the first part,
and Aladdin Theatre Corporation and MM. H.E.Huffman.
of Denver. Colo.
hereinafter called the party of the second part.

The party of the first part, for and in consideration of the sum of Eleven Thousand Dollars. ($11,000) Dollars, agrees to furnish and install for the party of the second part, an organ in accordance with the attached plans and specifications and which are a part of this agreement in the building known as the Aladdin Theatre Colfax and Race. St. in Denver, Colo.
said organ to be ready for use on or before sept Ist 1926 possible.

The party of the first part further agrees to guarantee the above organ to be free from imperfections in material and workmanship and will make good at any time, any such imperfections not caused by mis-use or neglect. It is understood that this guarantee does not cover tuning, cleaning or repairs made necessary by the natural wear and tear on the instrument.

The party of the second part also agrees to assume all risks of damage to said organ or parts thereof, after said organ has been deposited in said Theatre

The party of the second part agrees to give the party of the first part free and undisturbed access to the above building for a period of 10 days before the organ is to be ready for use, with adequate light, heat and storage room necessary for the proper installation of the organ

The party of the second part also agrees to furnish, at their own cost, a suitable foundation in the above building, on which the above organ is to be erected, and to make at their own expense any changes in the building which are necessary for the proper installation of the organ.

The party of the second part further agrees to install, under the supervision of the party of the first part, the galvanized iron pipe (furnace pipe) from the blower to the organ proper: also install all wiring connecting the motor and the lights in the organ and console to the power service line, the control line to the console, and the generator line to the organ and console terminals.

The party of the second part further agrees to carry both fire and tornado insurance in the name of the party of the first part, for a sum equal to the amount of indebtedness of the party of the second part to party of the first part, said insurance to be issued and placed in the possession of the party of the first part immediately after the acceptance of the organ by the party of the second part. It is also agreed that the said organ is and shall remain the property of the party of the first part until paid for in full.
By indebtedness, in all cases, is meant any and all deferred payments, whether covered by notes or otherwise.

The party of the second part further agrees to inspect and examine said organ immediately when notified by the party of the first part, or their representative, that such inspection or examination is desired, and, if said organ has been properly installed in accordance with this agreement, and every part thereof, the party of the second part will immediately make payment in the manner prescribed herein, to the authorized representative of the party of the first part

The party of the second part agrees to pay to the order of the Wicks Pipe Organ Co. in the following prescribed manner:
Five Hundred Dollars ($50000) upon the signing of this agreement.
Five Hundred dollars in 90 days. $1000.00 On deliver of organ in Denver.colo. $1000.00 On completion or acceptance pf organ complet installation.and balance in 104 weeklt payments at 6% signed Motes by H.E. Huffman and Aleddin theatre Corporation of Denver Colo.

All deferred payments to be covered by notes, bearing (6%) interest

It is further agreed by and between the parties hereto that this contract is contingent upon strikes, accidents and other delays unavoidable or beyond the control of the party of the first part.

Witness our hand and seal, Denver, Colo. April 30th day of 1926.

Free service for one year from date of installation

WICKS PIPE ORGAN CO.
By A R Payne

Aladdin Theatre Corporation. By H E Huffman Pres.
COMMITTEE
H E Huffman

Note. All changes or additions not covered by this agreement should be incorporated before agreement is signed. Be sure that everything as agreed upon is placed in the contract to prevent possible misunderstandings.

DETAILS OF CONSTRUCTION

THE CASE

The Case to be neat and tasteful in design and in keeping with the architectural features of the building and the place where the organ is to stand. To be built of .... and finished to match the furnishings of the building.

FRONT PIPES

The Front Pipes to be artistically grouped and richly decorated in ....

THE CONSOLE

The Console shall be built in accordance with standard specifications and of modern style and design. The casing and finish to harmonize with the case of the organ proper or the furnishings of the building.

The interior trimmings of the keydesk to be of fine mahogany, piano finish.

All fittings such as stop keys, pistons, indicators, etc., to be of standard type and pattern.

The Console shall be ....
(state whether attached or detached.)

KEYBOARDS

The Manual Keyboards to be of the overhanging type, constructed after standard scales and pattern, laid out true and most carefully made. To be well bushed at the front and center pins so as to work noiselessly and with a free and easy motion.

The Pedal Keyboards to be of the standard A. G. O., concave radiating patterns, carefully laid out and made to the standard scales. The naturals to be capped with white maple and the sharps in black walnut.

ACTION

The Action of this organ shall be electric throughout. There shall be a separate and individual valve directly under each speaking pipe. This valve shall be of an electro magnetic type, and in an individual direct electric circuit with the contact of the corresponding key in the console. In the operation of this mechanism there are but two movements, that of the key and the valve, thereby effecting an instaneous response and repetition.

A valve seat of special construction assures an absolute air tight contact on every stroke and there is no possible chance of a cypher caused by particles of dirt or dust between the valve and the seat.

The valves themselves are made up of three layers, one each of reinforced backing, felt and leather, each of the best quality obtainable.

The electric operating mechanism shall be built of the best possible materials. Magnet cores are of Norway Iron, brackets of mild steel and magnet wire of the very best grade of enameled copper. The design and construction of the magnets is such that will give maximum efficiency with minimum current consumption.

CONTROLS

The Stop and Coupler Controls shall be operated by the standard form of stop keys, placed in a convenient position over the upper manual. The stops of the different divisions of the organ, together with their respective couplers are arranged in groups.

All Controls are operated electrically and bring on or off the respective stop or coupler by making or breaking circuit from the associated stop key.

COMBINATIONS

The Combinations, either of the fixed or adjustable type, are operated by pistons placed under the respective manuals. For the adjustable type the set buttons are placed in drawer below the key bed. These set buttons are grouped and labeled to correspond with the stop keys.

CRESCENDO

The Crescendo Mechanism operates electrically and affects all speaking stops and couplers. Provisions are made that the individual units can be adjusted thus allowing any desired rotation. Control of the crescendo mechanism is effected by the usual form of pedal and a revolving indicator registers automatically the movement of this pedal.

CHESTS

The Chests are of the universal wind type. The materials are of the best selection and thoroughly seasoned. The frames of the chests are tongued and grooved and reinforced by open rib work which forms the supports for the top and bottom boards. The top boards carry the pipes on the upper side and mounted directly underneath is the individual valve mechanism. Thus the wind in the chest, when released by the valve, has a minimum distance to travel to reach the pipe, also by mounting the valve mechanism on the same board that carries the pipes all chances of cyphers through leaks in joints are eliminated, making an absolute perfect and reliable chest action.

The bottom boards, through which access is provided to the valves, are made in sections and held in place by screws fitted with expansion springs that take up any variation in the lumber due to climatic changes. All dry joints are faced with a special heavy insulating packing, forming absolutely air tight joints.

WIND TRUNKS

The Wind Trunks, which convey the air from the blower and thence to the various parts of the organ, are to be made of sufficient size to prevent any loss by friction. These trunks are constructed with loose flanges and hose joints where necessary to insure absolute air tight connections.

RESERVOIRS AND BELLOWS

All Reservoirs or Bellows are made ample in size for all legitimate demands. The materials are carefully selected to withstand the very uncertain conditions of temperature found in basements and organ lofts. Each bellow will be leathered throughout and will have reinforced joints at the corners. All joints will be well packed and united with screws to secure air tight connections. The wind pressure is secured by the use of springs arranged to produce a steady pressure at all times.

SWELL BOXES

In the construction of the Swell Boxes only the very best of extra heavy well seasoned lumber is used. The different sections are built [illegible] joints fitted up perfectly and drawn up tight making a practically sound proof chamber Ample speaking room is provided for all pipes as well as passageway for tuning and regulating purposes.

Expression is effected by a series of vertical equilibrium shades swinging on ball bearings and operated by the usual balanced Swell Pedal, placed in the standard prescribed position over the pedal keyboard.

The shades are of a laminated construction, insuring against warping and twisting. The edges are beveled, fitted perfectly upon each other and faced with heavy cushion felt.

INTERIOR CONSTRUCTION

The Framework of the entire organ is to be of such generons proportions to carry safely the weight of the various parts resting thereon without settling or springing. To be constructed of well seasoned lumber finished with several coats of high grade gloss varnish.

All other parts of the organ such as chest, wind trunks, reservoirs and wood pipes are to be treated in a like manner to protect the wood against effects from dampness and other atmospheric conditions.

The organ throughout will be provided with passage boards and ladders, where necessary to render the various parts easy of access in case of any required adjustments and for tuning.

PIPES

All Pipes, regardless of their class, are constructed in the same careful and skilled manner. The Metal Pipes of more than 4 ft. speaking length (below Tenor C) will be made of the best quality of heavy annealed zinc and will have tuners, lips, lanquids and toes of pipe metal' The metal pipes of shorter length, from Tenor C upwards will be made of an alloy of pure block tin and lead, varying in proportion as the various stops require from 40 to 95 per cent of pure tin.

In the construction of the wood pipes only the best grades of thoroughly seasoned California Spruce, Sugar Pine, Michigan White Pine and Walnut are used, being considered the best materials for tonal effects. All wood pipes are made with perfect glue joints, avoiding the use of screws and nails in the body of the pipe. All caps are screwed on, not glued, so as to be easily removed. The stoppers of the bass pipes are glued at right angles, carefully fitted, felted and leathered to insure a perfect fit and are provided with strong handles, well fastened.

Our reed pipes are the best that artistic skill can produce. The tongues or reeds are made of the best quality of spring brass, highly tempered and polished so as to be pure and clear in tone. The stems of these pipes are made of the same high grade annealed zinc that is used in the construction of the flue pipes and the top part or bells of the pipes is a 45 per cent alloy of pure block tin and lead. All component parts of these reed pipes are made according to standard scales and patterns.

SUPERVISION

Each Instument is planned by our Superintendent, who has designed and perfected the system embodied in our organs. All measurements and data furnished by the prospective purchaser are carefully figured and studied and a general draft of the organ is made. After a reconsideration of this by the Superintendent personally the drawings are placed into the hands of the foremen of the various departments who in turn have at their command a force of expert workmen and electric specialists to whom they entrust the construction of the variaus parts. When these parts are then all assembled we have an instrument, lacking in none of its details and the whole standing as a model of the organ builders art.

PROPOSITION

Our proposition includes delivery and the organ completely set up in the building, ready for use and a guarantee, embodied in the terms of the contract, to make good at any time any defects resulting from the use of improper materials or inferior workmanship.

We do not consider any alterations in the building or the preparation for the organ chamber nor any fees or permits required by local authorities. Our proposition is also exclusive of electric wiring connecting the motor to the service line and the necessary wind duct connecting the blower to the organ proper. These are items out of our line and must be made by local workmen. Purchaser is also required to furnish the necessary light, heat and power during the period of the installation.

Specifications,

For
H.E.Hoffman, #649.

THREE MANUALS. and Pedals,

Manuall CompassCC to C4
Pedal Compass CCCto G
Direct electric action Unitx Type.

Pedals,

1	Resultant Bass	32	32 Notes
2	Diaphone	16	32 Notes
3	Bourdon	16	32 Notes
4	Tibia Clauses	16	32 Notes
5	Violin D Orchestra,	16	32 Notes
6	Flute	8	32 Notes
7	Viola D Gamba	8	32 Notes
8	Tibia Plena,	8	32 Notes
9	Diapason, Horn	8	32 Notes
10	Tuba	8	32 Notes
11	Quint	10 2/3	32 Notes
12	Octave,	-- 4	32 Notes
13	Traps first touch,		

1	Second touch First Div, Pedals,		
14	Chimes,	CCCto FF	17 Notes
15	Bass Drum	CCC to FF	18 Notes
16	Snare Drum	CCC to FF	18 Notes
17	Crash Symbal	CCC to FF	18 Notes
18	Triangle	CCC to FF	18 Notes
19	Cymbal	CCC to FF	18 Notes
20	Tympani	CCC to FF	18 Notes

The above traps and chime play on first touch when no-13 stop down.

Divison TWO Accompaniment.

21	Bourdon		16	61 Notes
22	Gamba Bass T.C.		16	61 Notes
23	Violin Bass		16	61 Notes
24	Tibia Profunda		16	61 Notes
25	Violin D Orchestra		8	61 Notes
26	Viola D Gamba		8	61 Notes
27	Violin Celeste	11 Ranks	8	61 Notes
28	Concert Flute		8	61 Notes
29	Diapason Phonon		8	61 Notes
30	Tuba Sonora	15 Inch wind	8	61 Notes
31	Clairnet		8	61 Notes
32	Tibia Plena		8	61 Notes
33	Orchestra Flute		4	61 Notes
34	Violin		4	61 Notes
35	Octave		4	61 Notes
36	Cornet		4	61 Notes
37	Piccolo		2	61 Notes
38	Acc to Acc 4			
39	Acc to Acc 16,			

40	Snare Drum	C1 to C4	37 Notes
41	Tambourine	C1 to C4	37 Notes
42	Castnets	C1 To C4	37 Notes
43	M rimba Harp	CC to C4	49 Notes
44	Xylophone	C1 to C4	37 Notes
45	Wood drum	C1 to C4	37 Notes
46	Tom Tom	C1 TO C4	37 Notes

Dividon Three Orchestral, Second ManualM

47	Bourdon	16		61 Notes
48	Violin Bass	16		61 Notes
49	Viola D Gamba, T.C.	16		61 Notes
50	Diaphone	16		61 Notes
51	Tibia Profunda	16		61 Notes
52	Violin D Orchestra,	8		85 Pipes
53	Violin D Gamba	8		73 Pipes
54	Violin Celeste	8	Two Ranks	146 Pipes
55	Tibia Clauses	8		85 Pipes
56	Concert Flute	8		97 Pipes
57	Diapson Phonon	8		73 Pipes
56	Tuba Sonora 15 in wind	8		85 Pipes
57	Vox Humana,	8		73 Pipes
58	Clairnet	8		73 Pipes
59	French Horn	8		73 Pipes
60	Kinura	8		73 Pipes
61	Tibia Plena	8		73 Pipes
62	Orchestral Oboe SYN	8		61 Notes
63	Violin	4		61 Notes
64	Gamba	4		61 Notes
65:	Tibia Clauses	4		61 Notes
66	Orchestral Flute	4		61 Notes
67	Octave	4		61 Notes
68	Cornet	4		61 Notes
69	Zart Flute	4		61 Notes
70	French Horn	4		61 Notes
71	Violin Twelfth	2 2/3		61 Notes
72	Nazard	2 2/3		62 Notes
73	Viol	2		61 Notes
74	Flagelot	2		61 Notes
75	Tierce	1 3/5		61 Notes
76	Larigot	1 1/3		61 Notes
77	Orchestral Bells			
78	Chimes			
79	Harp Marimba			
80	Xylophone			
81	Tremelo, Main Organ,			
82	Tremelo Kunora,			
83	Tremelo Vox Humana,			
84	Tremelo Tuba Snora.			
85	Orch to orch 4 Couplers,			
86	Orch to orch 16			

ARPayne

87	Bourdon	16	61 Note
88	Violin Bass	16	61 Notes
89	Viola D Gamba	8	61 Notes
90	Violin D Orchestral	8	61 Notes
91	Violin Celeste	8	61 Notes
92	Concert Flute	8	61 Notes
93	Diapason	8	61 Notes
94	Tuba Bonora	8	61 Notes
95	Vox Humana	8	61 Notes
96	Clairnet	8	61 Notes
97	Kinura	8	61 Notes
98	Tibia Plena	8	61 Notes
99	Octave Viol	4	61 Notes
100	Gamba	4	61 Notes
101	Flute	4	61 Notes
102	Horn Principal	4	61 Notes
103	Viol Twelfth	2 2/3	61 Notes
104	Flute Twelfth	2 2/3	61 Notes
105	Viol	2	61 Notes
106	Piccolo	2	61 Notes
107	Solo To Solo 4		
108	Solo to Solo 16.		

Adjustable combinations Pistons
1.2.3.4.5.Affecting stop key on Div 4 and Div 1
1.2.3.4.5. " " " " " 3 and Div 1
1.2.3.4.5. Affectingstop key on Div 2 and Div 1
1.2.3. Affectin Div 1.

Toe Pistons

Reversible Sfrozando Pedal, — Sleigh Bells
Single touch for crash Cymbal — Auto Horn
Tringle — Steam boat whistle
Snare drum — Door Bell
Bass Drum — Windstorm
Bird Whistle, — Thundersheet

Accessories

Master on and off switch connecting pistons on Div 2 and div 4 to Corresponding Pistons div 3

Master switch connecting Piston div 1 to corresponding pistons Div 2.3.4.

Stop Board and pedal Illumations,
Crescendo Indicator Light
Swell pedal for Main Organ
Swell p edal for Solo Organ
Swell pedal for Vox Humana,
Multi Swell controllin all expressions Indicator Light.
Wind indicator light
Crescendo Pedal,
Organ Bench
Blower and Motor
Generator.

Pipe ON 10 Inch Wind pressure,

	Violin D Orchestra,	16 FT	85 Pipes
	Viola D Gamba,	8	73 Pipes
TWO RANKS	Violin Celesta	8	146 Pipes
	Tibia Clauses	16	85 Pipes
	Concert Flute	16	97 Pipes
Leather Lip	Diapason Phonon	8	73 Pipes
	Clairnet	8	73 Pipes
	French Horn	8	73 Pipes
	Kinura	8	73 Pipes
	Tibia Plena	8	73 Pipes

Pipe on 6 inch Wind pressure

Vox Humana, 8 73 Pipes

Pipe on 15 Inch Wind Pressure,

TUBA SNORA. 16 85 Pipes
Last octave on set to be Diaphones, 12 Pipes,

Tremelos

Main Organ
Solo Organ
Vox Humana,
Kunora,
Tuba Snora,

Chimes, 20 Tubes
Xylophones 37,
Orch Bells 37
Marimaba Harp 49,

Total pipes,

ARPayne

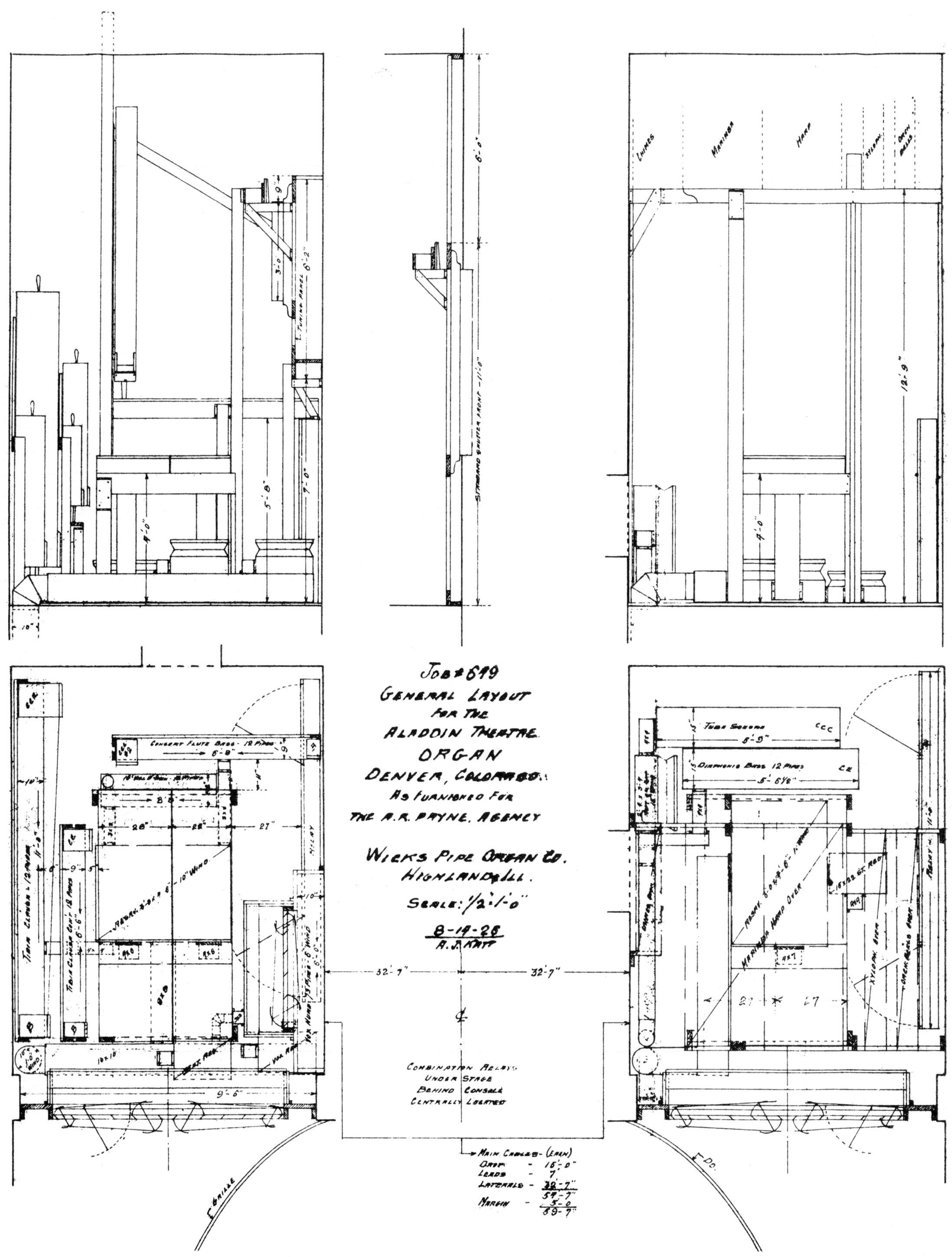

The Aladdin's chambers were located over the theatre's proscenium arch. This chamber location was relatively uncommon in American theatres.

This 3/7 Wicks, now in the residence of Phil and Laura Judkins of Tulsa, Oklahoma, was originally installed in the Best Theatre in Parsons, Kansas.

A Wicks two-manual theatre console of conventional design without a roll top.

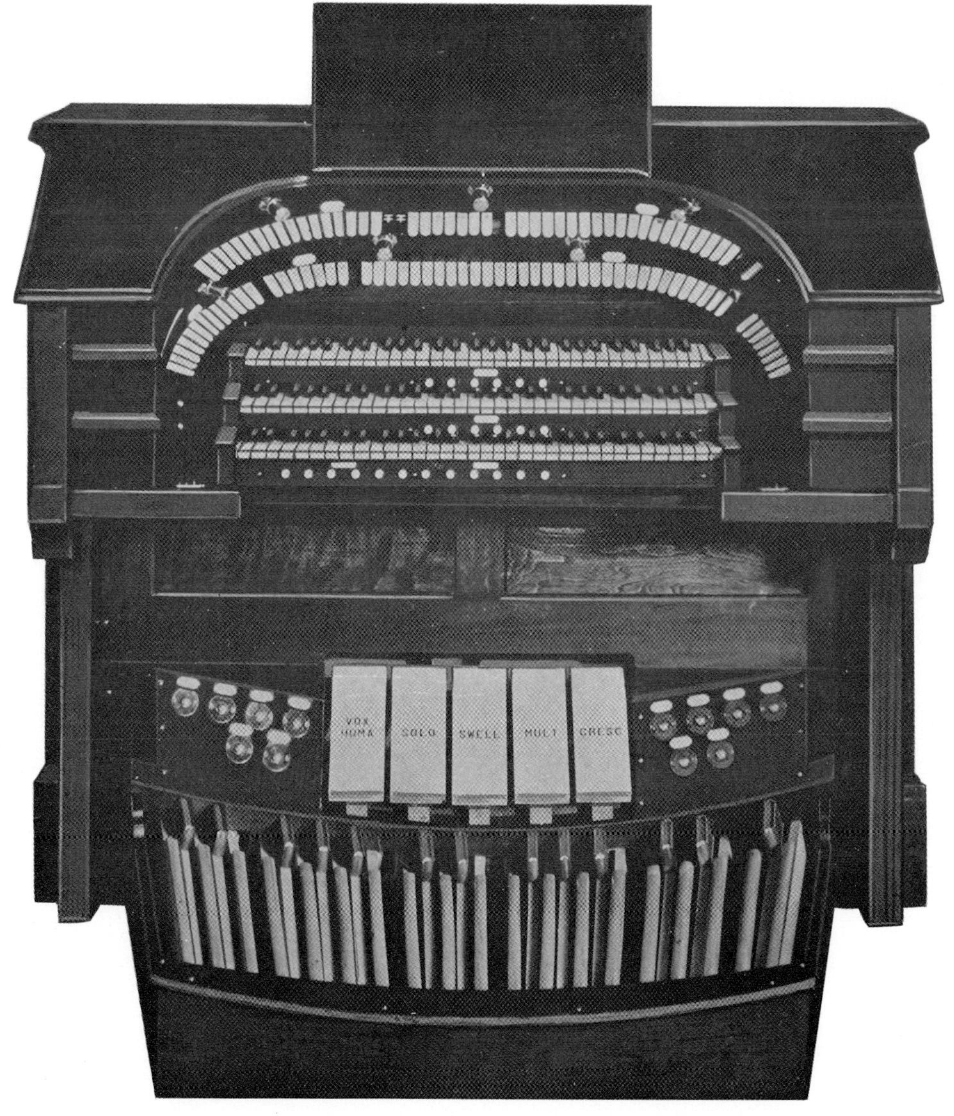

Factory portrait of the 3/13 Wicks console for the Aladdin Theatre, Denver, Colorado.

The last Wicks installation in a theatre was opus 879, built in 1929 for the Orange Theatre, Orange, California.

The solo chamber of the Orange Theatre contained, left to right, a vox humana, tibia clausa and diapason. To the right of the diapason was a trumpet, not shown here.

Ron Mitchell demonstrates the Orange Theatre's 2/8 Wicks.

The most elaborately decorated Wicks theatre console was this three-manual example in the Garrick Theatre in Winnipeg, Manitoba which played 12 ranks of pipes.

This console of space-age design controls the new 3/14 Wicks in the Harvey Kuhlman residence in Menomonee Falls, Wisconsin. The organ was installed in 1970 as a 2/7, opus 5158, and was enlarged to its present size in 1971.

3/10 Wicks console in the Capitol Theatre, Davenport, Iowa. This was not a new Wicks organ but a 1928 rebuild of a 4/23 Moller originally installed in the Capitol in 1920.

Interior view of a Wicks theatre organ as shown in their 1928 theatre catalog.

This lovely console probably graced an opulent home in the 1920s although it certainly wouldn't have been out of place in a theatre. Note how well the 88-note roll player is integrated into its case; similar designs of some other manufacturers weren't nearly so beautifully proportioned.

An "eye line" style console controlled the 3/16 Wicks installed in 1959 in Oral Roberts' Abundant Life Building in Tulsa, Oklahoma. As of 1987 this is the largest Wicks theatre organ ever built.

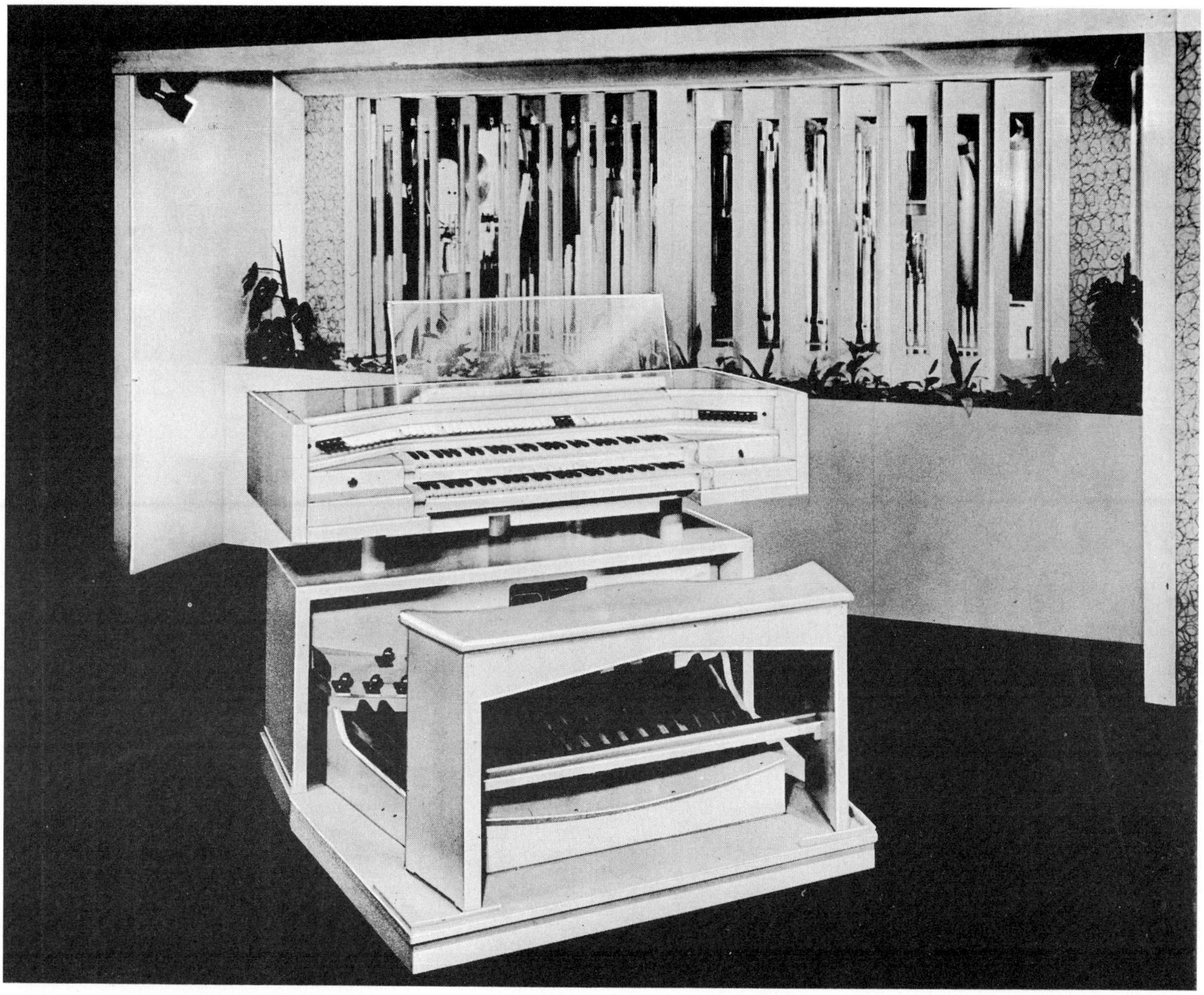

A real pipe organ...
designed for home installation

Only a real pipe organ can produce the full rich tones, the instant response, the fine blending of voices to satisfy the discriminating tastes of theater organ enthusiasts.

Wicks has incorporated all these features into a residential pipe organ, compactly designed for limited space, custom built to suit the tastes of each individual buyer, priced to compete with other types of home organs.

Write Wicks Organ Company, Highland, Illinois, or address your inquiry to Mr. Judd Walton, 227 Texas Street, Vallejo, California.

PIPE ORGANS

THE HOUSE OF WICKS • WICKS ORGAN COMPANY • HIGHLAND, ILLINOIS

This ad in the Summer 1960 issue of Theatre Organ *magazine featured the first new theatre organ built since the "good old days." Wicks opus 3908, a 2/8 fully unified instrument with a beautiful tibia and full percussions, was unveiled at the 1958 Home Show in Chicago and was also shown at several subsequent expositions. In 1964 it was sold to Martinetti's Restaurant in Crystal Lake, Illinois where it entertained patrons for 15 years.*

Wicks opus 5330, a 2/8 theatre organ built in 1972, is shown in the factory erecting room before being shipped to the Red Vest Pizza House in Monterey, California.

Alan Draper (left) and Ben Alarcon of Wicks' engineering staff are the men responsible for the many stunning and innovative visual concepts which have made Wicks a leader in contemporary designs.

(opposite) Two decades after building the first new theatre organ in contemporary history, Wicks built another 2/8 portable display organ, depicted in this ad in the June 1980 Theatre Organ *magazine. Opus 5770, reflecting current technology, features a solid state relay and a digital tape player. After being shown at several conventions the instrument was sold to Albert Bilgen of Lake Forest, Illinois and was installed in his residence in 1982.*

A PICTORIAL TOUR OF THE WICKS FACTORY C. 1915

The balcony of the erecting room was known as the action department. Here is where coils were wound and magnets, relays and other small parts were assembled. The ladies in the upper photo are, left to right, Kathryn Lodes, Rose Mettler, Mae Greeley, Florence Winter, Mayme Lynch and Eleanore Wick. The men in the lower photo are, left to right, Otto Storf, Arnie Kantnor, Joseph Westhoff, Max Runge, Edmund Wick, who is operating a coil winding machine, and Joseph Lodes.

METAL PIPE DEPT.

(above, left to right) Walter Zimmerman, Bill Zweifel, Elmer Winter and an unidentified man are making metal pipes. (below, left to right) Edmund Wick, an unidentified man, Hugo Grimmer and John Brown are pictured in the voicing room.

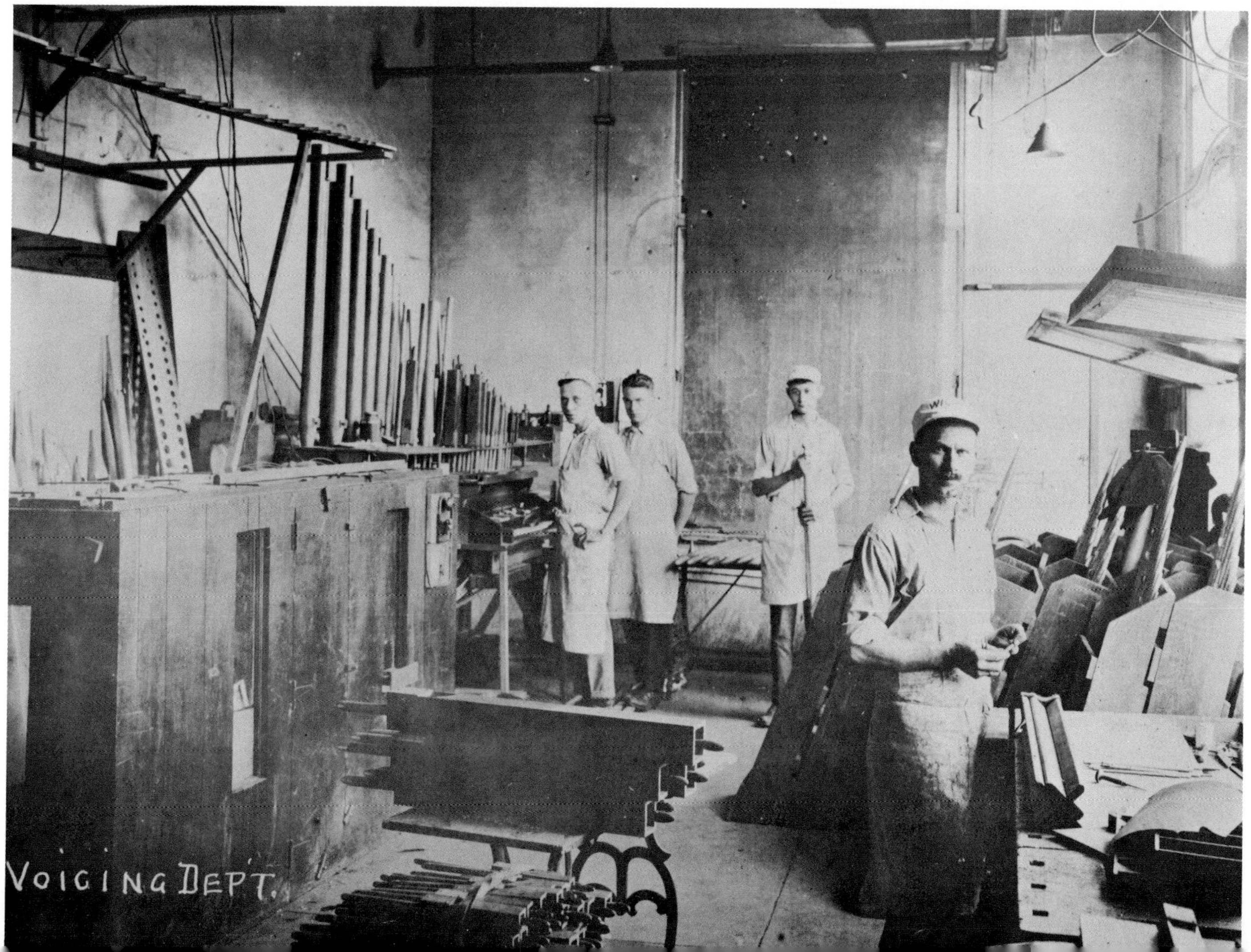

VOICING DEPT.

CONSOLE DEPT.

In the above photo, left to right, Victor Wick, A. J. Katt, John Buchheim, Edgar Wick, Leo Seifried and Adolph Wick are pictured in the console department. In the lower photo, left to right, Pat Netzer, Carl Huber, Otto Kast, Dana Maerz and Ed Friedrich are at work in the mill room.

MILL ROOM

In the upper photo, left to right, William Seifried, Ed Begueline and Henry Redoehl are assembling chests. Below, left to right, Leo Seifried, Adolph Wick, Ed Begueline, John Buchheim, Victor Wick, Edgar Wick and Eugene Buchheim work in the action assembling department making tremolos and wiring keyboards and relays.

Aerial view of the country's second largest pipe organ factory. The building on the right is the oldest, dating from the early teens. As the Wicks business prospered, a number of buildings were added to the complex. The contemporary structure in the upper left houses the executive offices and studio with a 59-rank demonstration organ. Since this photograph was taken another large erecting room has been added to the facility.

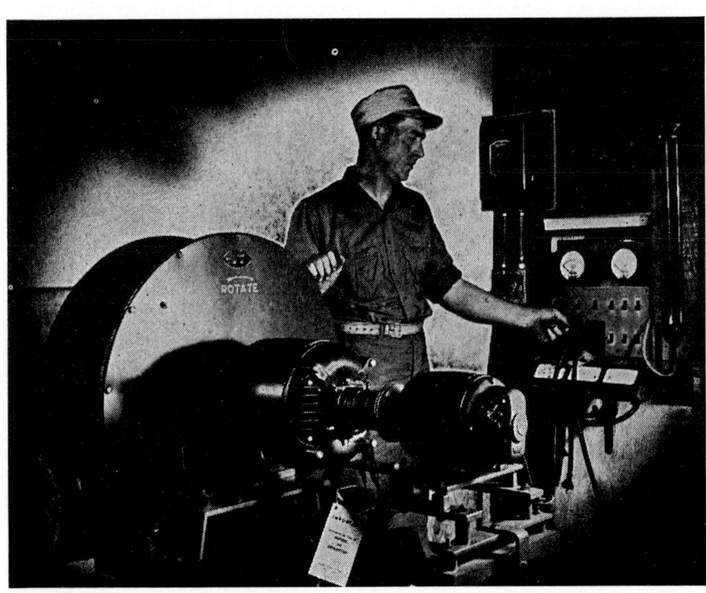

Wicks had a policy of building as many parts of their organs as possible, even blowers. Only a few Wicks organs used blowers built by other firms.

In the 1980s Wicks continues their policy of building all parts of their organs in their own factory. Here a solid state relay is being wired on a wiring jig.

WICKS OPUS LIST

Following is a complete list of Wicks theatre-type organs. An alphabetical index appears first, enabling one to locate an instrument on a city/state/installation site basis, with a corresponding opus number shown adjoining. This number may be used to find the organ in the accompanying chronological list. Statistics for each organ are shown only in the latter list. Inasmuch as Wicks records are incomplete, the alphabetical index does not include all the theatre instruments, about 45% of whose ultimate destinations are not known.

The chronological list does include all the theatre-type organs although it is possible that some of its entries are not theatre instruments. For example, at least one Wicks-built church organ has been discovered with a Robert-Morton nameplate. The chronological list, therefore, may include some non-theatre instruments among the organs whose destinations are not known.

CITY/STATE	LOCATION	OPUS
ARIZONA (AZ)		
Globe	Martin (Alden) Th.	676
ARKANSAS (AR)		
Conway	Conway Amusement Co.	485
Helena	Saenger Amusement Co.	338
Springdale	Concord Th.	713
CALIFORNIA (CA)		
Alhambra	Granada (Coronet) Th.	596
Brawley	Belvedere (Brawley) Th.	591
Calexico	Rialto Th.	590
Glendale	Cosmo Th.	560
Huntington Park	Lyric Th.	816
Los Angeles	Balk & Sobelmann	526
	Blanco Th.	573
	Herbold Th.	589
	Patton Th.	537
Menlo Park	Mike Prideaux-Brune residence	4461
Monrovia	Colonial Th.	644
Monterey	Red Vest Restaurant	5330
Montrose	Montrose Th.	515
Orange	Orange Th.	879
Pasadena	Park Th.	854
Pleasant Hill	Pizza Machine Restaurant	5349
Pomona	Sun Kissed Th.	446
Salinas	Francis Aebi residence	5381
Santa Ana	Broadway Th.	637
	Yost Th.	658
Santa Barbara	Kaplan Louis	595
	Rose Th.	523
COLORADO (CO)		
Denver	Aladdin Th.	649
	Jewell Th.	625
	Milton Park Hill Th.	738
	Ogden Th.	228
	Princess (Victory) Th.	232
	Queens Th.	241
	Strand (State) Th.	565
HAWAII (HI)		
Honolulu	Kalihi (Star) Th.	719
IDAHO (ID)		
St. Maries	St. Maries Th.	458
ILLINOIS (IL)		
Alton	Princess Th.	781
Bunker Hill	Lincoln Th.	870
Cairo	Gem Th.	869
Carbondale	Barth Th.	763
Centralia	Grand Opera House	338
Chicago	Englewood Th.	791
	Maywood Th.	204
	Newberry Th.	175
	Randolph Th.	478
Crystal Lake	Martinetti's Restaurant	3908
Edwardsville	Wildy Th.	630
Effingham	Effingham Th.	753
Gillespie	Colonial Th.	703
Herrin	Grand Opera House	240
	Hippodrome Th.	762
Highland	Palace Th.	203
Hillsboro	Orpheum Th.	733
Jacksonville	Grand Th.	749

CITY/STATE	LOCATION	OPUS
Lake Forest	Albert Bilgen residence	5770
Lawrenceville	Avalon Th.	800
	Lawrenceville Th.	496
Litchfield	Capital Th.	759
Mt. Vernon	Plaza Th.	825
Murphysboro	Hippodrome Th.	757
Nokomis	New Palace Th.	732
Olney	Arcadia Th.	824
Pana	Palace (Rose) Th.	716
Quincy	Belasco Th.	166
Robinson	Strand Th.	750
Royalton	Royalton Th.	558
Springfield	Fox Lincoln (Lincoln) Th.	793
	Princess Th.	866
West Frankfort	Strand Th.	338
INDIANA (IN)		
Bedford	Indiana Th.	793
Greencastle	Granada Th.	777
Indianapolis	American Central Life Insurance Co. Auditorium	832
Mishawaka	Mishawaka Th.	818
Shelbyville	Strand Th.	178
Spencer	Tivoli Th.	869
IOWA (IA)		
Davenport	Capitol Th.	794
KANSAS (KS)		
Coffeyville	New Tackett Th.	826
Kansas City	Home Th.	863
	Tenth Street Th.	856
Parsons	Best (Parsons) (Dickerson) Th.	809
Topeka	Novelty Th.	833
LOUISIANA (LA)		
Baton Rouge	Western Th.	314
Bogalusa	Majestic City Th.	686
Gretna	Hollywood Th.	662
New Orleans	Lyric Th.	433
Ponchatoila	Ideal Th.	838
Ruston	New Astor Th.	836
MARYLAND (MD)		
Baltimore	Highland Amusement Co.	432
	Ideal Th.	689
Cumberland	Belvidere Th.	575
MASSACHUSETTS (MA)		
Boston	National Th.	723
Cambridge	Porter Square	768
Chelsea	Strand Th.	516
Dorchester	Franklin Park Th.	735
Everett	Strand Th.	814
Fall River	Premier Th.	518
Lawrence	Strand Th.	679
Lexington	Lexington Th.	512
Medford	Fellsway Th.	477
Melrose	Melrose Th.	489
Milford	Milford Opera House	843
Needham	Needham Th.	597
Norwood	Norwood Th.	709
Reading	Reading Th.	480
Roxbury	Humboldt Th.	724
	Niagara Th.	613
	Warren Th.	701
Somerville	Broadway Th.	741
Waltham	Waltham Th.	505
Watertown	Coolidge Th.	555
West Lynn	Standard Th.	501
Wollaston	Wollaston Th.	680
MICHIGAN (MI)		
Jackson	Picture Show (Rex) Th.	184
Midland	Frolic Th.	435
MINNESOTA (MN)		
International Falls	Minnesota Grand Th.	223
Minneapolis	Mandarin Cafe	248
St. Paul	Oxford-Grand Th.	257
MISSISSIPPI (MS)		
Picayune	New Ideal Th.	837

CITY/STATE	LOCATION	OPUS
MISSOURI (MO)		
Carrolton	Royal Th.	810
St. Louis	Grand Opera House	779
	WIL Radio	818
MONTANA (MT)		
Anaconda	Margarite Th.	543
NEBRASKA (NE)		
Norfolk	Auditorium Th.	339
	New Grand Th.	342
NEW MEXICO (NM)		
Las Vegas	Coronado Th.	697
NEW YORK (NY)		
Buffalo	WEBR Radio	1083
Flushing	Flushing Th.	315
New York	Gordon Th.	305
Syracuse	Avon Th.	306
NORTH DAKOTA (ND)		
Bismarck	Eltinge Th.	307
OHIO (OH)		
Cadiz	Community Th.	488
Sidney	Majestic Th.	343
OKLAHOMA (OK)		
Durant	Majestic (R&R) (Liberty) Th.	683
Shawnee	Savoy Th.	861
Tulsa	Art Th.	773
	Oral Roberts University	3954
	Smith Th.	242
OREGON (OR)		
LaGrande	Liberty (Arcade) Th.	476
PENNSYLVANIA (PA)		
Clifton Forge	Masonic Th.	453
RHODE ISLAND (RI)		
Centredale	G. L. Parker	815
Pawtucket	Capitol Th.	598
TEXAS (TX)		
Ballinger	Maeroy Th.	684
Big Spring	Ritz Th.	604
Dallas	Rosewin Th.	765
	M. S. White Th.	685
El Paso	Alhambra Th.	239
Lubbock	Lindsay Th.	740
Midland	W. H. Williams	860
Odessa	J. W. Rice Co.	783
San Angelo	Palace Th.	693
	R&R (Ritz) Th.	729
San Antonio	Ft. Sam Houston Th.	656
San Marcos	Palace Th.	661
Vernon	Pictorium Th.	664
Victoria	Victoria Th.	654
VIRGINIA (VA)		
Lee Hall	Ft. Eustic Th.	707
Norfolk	Strand Th.	517
Portsmouth	Tivoli Th.	439
Roanoke	Strand Th.	519
WASHINGTON (WA)		
Renton	Grand Th.	494
Seattle	Grey Goose Th.	539
	Royal Th.	659
Tacoma	Park Th.	452
WEST VIRGINIA (WV)		
Martinsburg	Central Th.	612
WISCONSIN (WI)		
Menomonee Falls	Harvey Kuhlman residence	5158
Wausau	Wausau Th.	246
MANITOBA, CANADA		
Winnipeg	Garrick Th.	823
ONTARIO, CANADA		
Kenora	McClean Co.	534

OPUS	LOCATION/CITY/STATE	SIZE	YR	BLWR	STYLE	REMARKS
166	Belasco Th., Quincy, IL	2/9	1915	6668		Cost $1,500.
175	Newberry Th., Chicago, IL	2/	1916	7076		Cost $1,000.
176	American Photo Player Co.		1916			
177	American Photo Player Co.		1916			
178	Strand Th., Shelbyville, IN	2/12	1916	6900		Cost $2,750; with 3-rank echo.
184	Picture Show (Rex) Th., Jackson, MI	2/12	1916	7352		Cost $2,500.
188	American Photo Player Co.		1916			
189	American Photo Player Co.		1916			
190	American Photo Player Co.		1916			
191	American Photo Player Co.		1916			
192	American Photo Player Co.		1916			
193	American Photo Player Co.		1916			
201	American Photo Player Co.		1916			
202	American Photo Player Co.		1916			
203	Palace Th., Highland, IL		1916	7410		Later burned.
204	Maywood Th., Chicago, IL		1916	7625		
205	American Photo Player Co. Showroom, New York, NY					
206	American Photo Player Co. Showroom, Chicago, IL					
207	American Photo Player Co. Showroom, Philadelphia, PA					
208	American Photo Player Co.					
209	American Photo Player Co., San Francisco, CA		1917			
210	American Photo Player Co., San Francisco, CA		1917			
211	American Photo Player Co., San Francisco, CA		1917			
212	American Photo Player Co., New York, NY		1917			
213	American Photo Player Co., Dallas, TX		1917			
218	American Photo Player Co., Orlando, FL		1917			
219	American Photo Player Co., Pottstown, PA		1917			
220	Plaza Music Hall, New York, NY		1917			For American Photo Player Co.; located on Madison Avenue.
222	J. M. Heffner, Mason City, IA					For American Photo Player Co.
223	Minnesota Grand Th., International Falls, MN		1918	9306		
228	Ogden Th., Denver, CO		1917	8276		
231	purchaser unknown, Kansas City, MO					
232	Princess (Victory) Th., Denver, CO		1917	8402		
239	Alhambra Th., El Paso, TX		1917	8659		
240	Grand Opera House, Herrin, IL					
241	Queens Th., Denver, CO					
242	Smith Th., Tulsa, OK	2/	1918	8828		
246	Wausau Th., Wausau, WI		1918			
248	Mandarin Cafe, Minneapolis, MN		1918			
253	American Photo Player Co., Bradford, PA		1918			
254	American Photo Player Co.		1918			
255	American Photo Player Co.		1918			
257	Oxford-Grand Th., St. Paul, MN			9299		
258	American Photo Player Co.		1918			
259	American Photo Player Co.		1918			
264	Pheil Th., St. Petersburg, FL	2/	1918	9377		Beethoven nameplate; with double roll player piano with duplicate stop keys to operate organ from piano via rolls.
266	American Photo Player Co., New Orleans, LA		1919			
269	American Photo Player Co.		1919			
272	purchaser unknown, Superior, WI		1919			
277	purchaser unknown, Fresno, CA		1919			
279	purchaser unknown, Brooklyn, NY		1919			
283	purchaser unknown, Bakersfield, CA		1919			
286	Martin Th., Lock Haven, PA		1920	10846		For American Photo Player Co.
287	Saenger Amusement Co., Shreveport, LA		1919			
288	Sherman, Clay & Co., San Francisco, CA		1920			
289	purchaser unknown, Palo Alto, CA		1920			
290	American Th., Kingsburg, CA	2/6	1920			For American Photo Player Co.
293	purchaser unknown, Tacoma, WA		1920			
294	Saenger Amusement Co., New Orleans, LA		1920			
305	Gordon Th., New York, NY		1920			
306	Avon Th., Syracuse, NY	2/3	1920	11646		Moved in 1926 to Elmwood Theatre, Syracuse, New York.
307	Eltinge Th., Bismark, ND		1920			
310	purchaser unknown, Lodi, CA		1920			
311	purchaser unknown, Merced, CA		1920			
313	purchaser unknown, Olympia, WA		1920			
314	Western Th., Baton Rouge, LA	2/4	1920		65	
315	Flushing Th., Flushing, NY		1920	11140		
316	purchaser unknown, Streator, IL		1920			
317	Capitol Th., Newton, IA	2/				For American Photo Player Co.
318	purchaser unknown					
319	Lincoln Th., Charleston, IL	2/4				For American Photo Player Co.
320	American Photo Player Co.					
321	American Photo Player Co.					
322	American Photo Player Co.					
323	American Photo Player Co.					
324	American Photo Player Co.					

OPUS	LOCATION/CITY/STATE	SIZE	YR	BLWR	STYLE	REMARKS
325	American Photo Player Co.					
326	American Photo Player Co.					
327	American Photo Player Co.					
328	American Photo Player Co.					
329	American Photo Player Co.					
330	American Photo Player Co.					
331	American Photo Player Co.					
332	American Photo Player Co.					
333	American Photo Player Co.					
334	American Photo Player Co.					
335	American Photo Player Co.					
336	American Photo Player Co.					
337	Walter Evans, Vancouver, BC					
338	Saenger Amusement Co., Helena, AR	2/4				Later moved; see next entry.
338	Grand Opera House, Centralia, IL	2/4				Later moved; see next entry.
338	Strand Th., West Frankfort, IL	2/4	1927			Cost $2,911; rebuilt; harp, xylophone and traps added.
339	Auditorium Th., Norfolk, NE					
340	American Photo Player Co. Showroom, Los Angeles, CA					
341	American Photo Player Co. Showroom, Los Angeles, CA					
342	New Grand Th., Norfolk, NE					
343	Majestic Th, Sidney, OH					
344	purchaser unknown, Greybull, MT					
345	purchaser unknown, Greeley, CO					
346	purchaser unknown, Portland, ME					
347	purchaser unknown		1921			
348	Jenkins Music Co., Kansas City, MO					
349	American Photo Player Co. Showroom, New York, NY		1921			
355	purchaser unknown		1921			
356	purchaser unknown		1921			
357	purchaser unknown		1921			
358	purchaser unknown		1921			
359	American Photo Player Co. Showroom, New York, NY		1921			
360	purchaser unknown		1921			
365	American Photo Player Co.		1921			
366	American Photo Player Co.					
367	American Photo Player Co.					
368	American Photo Player Co.					
369	American Photo Player Co.					
370	American Photo Player Co.					
371	purchaser unknown, Jenkintown, PA	2/4				Style 65 Robert-Morton without relay.
375	purchaser unknown					
376	purchaser unknown					
377	purchaser unknown					
378	American Photo Player office, New York, NY					
379	purchaser unknown					
380	purchaser unknown					
384	purchaser unknown, Glendale, CA					
385	purchaser unknown					
386	purchaser unknown, Los Angeles, CA	2/4	1922		75	
387	purchaser unknown		1922			
388	purchaser unknown, New York, NY	2/4	1922		65	
389	purchaser unknown		1922			
390	purchaser unknown		1922			
391	purchaser unknown, Berea, CA		1922			
393	purchaser unknown, Grass Valley, CA	2/4	1922		55	
395	purchaser unknown		1922			
396	purchaser unknown		1922			
397	Sherman, Clay & Co., Sacramento, CA	2/4	1922		75	
398	purchaser unknown		1922			
399	purchaser unknown		1922			
401	American Photo Player Co.	2/4	1922		55	
402	Isis Th., Richmond, VA	2/	1922			For American Photo Player Co.
404	Capitol Th., Lebanon, PA	3/5	1922		75 Sp.	For American Photo Player Co.
405	Arverne Th, Arverne, NY		1922	13341	Special	For American Photo Player Co.
406	purchaser unknown, Salt Lake City, UT	2/4	1922		55	
407	purchaser unknown, Baltimore, MD	3/5	1922		75 Sp.	
411	Savoy Th., Durham, NC	2/	1922			Style Peerless 55; for American Photo Player Co.
412	purchaser unknown, Whitehall, ?	2/	1922			Style Peerless 55.
413	purchaser unknown, Stratford, ?	2/	1922			Style Peerless 55.
414	purchaser unknown, Calgary, Alberta	2/	1922			Style Peerless 55.
415	Capitol Th., Clearwater, FL	2/	1922			Style Peerless 55; for American Photo Player Co.
416	purchaser unknown, Los Angeles, CA	2/	1922			Style Peerless 55.
417	purchaser unknown, Kalamazoo, MI	2/	1922		314 Sp.	
425	Surf Th, Keyport, NJ	2/4	1922	13685	75	For American Photo Player Co.
426	purchaser unknown	2/4	1922		75	
427	Mercer Square Th, Greenville, PA	2/4	1922		75	For American Photo Player Co.
428	purchaser unknown, Rutherford, NJ	2/4	1922		75	

OPUS	LOCATION/CITY/STATE	SIZE	YR	BLWR	STYLE	REMARKS
429	purchaser unknown, Claremont, NY	2/4	1922		75	
430	purchaser unknown	2/4	1922		75	
432	Highland Amusement Co., Baltimore, MD	2/	1922	13811	314 Sp.	For American Photo Player Co.
433	Lyric Th., New Orleans, LA		1922			
435	Frolic Th., Midland, MI	2/	1922		314 Sp.	For American Photo Player Co.; see also opus 706.
437	purchaser unknown, Fort Dodge, ?	2/4	1922		65 Sp.	
438	Colonial Th., Lebanon, PA	2/8	1922	13861		For American Photo Player Co.
439	Tivoli Th., Portsmouth, VA	2/5				Cost $2,510; no traps or percussions.
442	purchaser unknown, Winnipeg, Manitoba					
443	Homer L. Kitt Co., Washington, D.C.	2/4	1923		55	
444	purchaser unknown, Chicago, IL	2/4	1923		55	
446	Sun Kissed Th., Pomona, CA					
447	purchaser unknown, Chicago, IL	2/4	1923		55	
452	Park Th., Tacoma, WA	2/4	1923		55	For American Photo Player Co.; moved in 1931 to KMO Radio, Tacoma, Washington by Balcom & Vaughan.
453	Masonic Th., Clifton Forge, PA	2/3	1923		314	
454	Broadway Th., Danville, VA	2/3	1923		314	
455	Orpheum Th., Havre, MT	2/4	1923	14576	75	For American Photo Player Co.
457	purchaser unknown, New York, NY	2/	1923		315	
458	St. Maries Th., St. Maries, ID	2/4	1923		55	
459	purchaser unknown, Sharon, PA	2/4	1923		65	
462	Sherman, Clay & Co., Stockton, CA	2/4	1923		55	
465	G. L. Parker, Boston, MA		1923			
475	American Photo Player Co., Sharon, PA	2/4	1923		65	
476	Liberty (Arcade) Th., LaGrande, OR	2/4	1923		75	Moved in 1925 to Granada Theatre, LaGrande, Oregon.
477	Fellsway Th., Medford, MA	2/4	1923		65	
478	Randolph Th., Chicago, IL	2/4	1923		65	
479	American Photo Player Co., Winston-Salem, NC	2/4	1923		65	
480	Reading Th., Reading, MA	2/4	1923		65	
485	Conway Amusement Co., Conway, AR	2/11	1923		Special	Cost $5,000; possibly shipped to Little Rock, Arkansas.
488	Community Th., Cadiz, OH	2/4			75	
489	Melrose Th., Melrose, MA	2/4	1924	15700	65	
494	Grand Th., Renton, WA	2/4	1924	15450	55	For American Photo Player Co.
496	Lawrenceville Th., Lawrenceville, IL	2/5	1924			Cost $6,600 less allowance of $2,500 on Cremona style M3 photoplayer traded in.
497	Sherman, Clay & Co., Multnomah, WA	2/4	1924		55	
501	Standard Th., West Lynn, MA	2/4	1924	15703	65	
504	J. D. Wheelan, Dallas, TX	2/4	1924		65	
505	Waltham Th., Waltham, MA	2/4	1924		65	
508	purchaser unknown, Denver, CO		1924			
509	G. L. Parker, Everett, MA	2/4			65	
510	Sherman, Clay & Co., West Seattle, WA					
512	Lexington Th, Lexington, MA	2/4			65	
515	Montrose Th., Montrose, CA	2/3			314	
516	Strand Th., Chelsea, MA	2/				
517	Strand Th., Norfolk, VA	2/4			75	
518	Premier Th., Fall River, MA	2/4			65	
519	Strand Th., Roanoke, VA	2/4			75	
520	J. D. Wheelan Studio, Dallas, TX	2/4			65	
523	Rose Th., Santa Barbara, CA	2/3			314	
524	Sherman, Clay & Co., Seattle, WA					
526	Balk & Sobelmann, Los Angeles, CA	2/				
534	McClean Co., Kenora, Ontario	2/4			55	
537	Patton Th., Los Angeles, CA		1925			
539	Grey Goose Th., Seattle, WA		1925			
543	Margarite Th., Anaconda, MT	2/	1925			Replaced earlier Wicks of 1918.
555	Coolidge Th., Watertown, MA	2/4			65	
558	Royalton Th., Royalton, IL		1925			
560	Cosmo Th., Glendale, CA	2/3	1925		314E	
561	purchaser unknown, Huntington Beach, CA	2/3	1925		314E	
562	G. L. Parker, Taunton, MA	2/4	1925		75	
565	Strand (State) Th., Denver, CO	2/7	1925		Special	Cost $6,925.
573	Blanco Th., Los Angeles, CA		1925			
575	Belvidere Th., Cumberland, MD	2/4	1925		65	
579	J. D. Wheelan, Dallas, TX	2/4	1925		65	
585	J. D. Wheelan, Dallas, TX	2/4	1925		65	
589	Herbold Th., Los Angeles, CA		1925			
590	Rialto Th., Calexico, CA	2/6				See also opus 873.
591	Belvidere Th., Brawley, CA	2/4				
592	Arthur Jordan Piano Co., Cherrydale, VA	2/3			314E	
593	J. D. Wheelan, Robstown, TX	2/4			65	
595	Kaplan Louis, Santa Barbara, CA					"Orch. Add."
596	Granada (Coronet) Th., Alhambra, CA					Opened as Alhambra Theatre.
597	Needham Th., Needham, MA					
598	Capitol Th., Pawtucket, RI	2/4			65	
599	J. D. Wheelan, Dallas, TX	2/4			65	

OPUS	LOCATION/CITY/STATE	SIZE	YR	BLWR	STYLE	REMARKS
604	Ritz Th., Big Spring, TX	2/4	1926		65	
612	Central Th., Martinsburg, WV	2/4	1926		65	
613	Niagara Th., Roxbury, MA	2/4	1926		65	
614	G. L. Parker, Wollington, MA	2/4	1926		65	
616	J. D. Wheelan Studio, Dallas, TX		1926			
617	J. D. Wheelan, Dallas, TX	2/3	1926		314	
619	J. D. Wheelan, Brownsville, TX	2/4	1926		65	
620	J. D. Wheelan, San Benito, TX	2/4	1926		65	
625	Jewell Th., Denver, CO	2/4	1926			Cost $2,500.
630	Wildy Th., Edwardsville, IL	2/4	1926		65	
637	Broadway Th., Santa Ana, CA	2/7	1926		Special	Cost $4,725.
644	Colonial Th., Monrovia, CA	2/8	1926		Special	Cost $4,850.
647	purchaser unknown, Weehawken, NJ		1926			
649	Aladdin Th., Denver, CO	3/13	1926			Cost $11,000.
651	Southern Pipe Organ Co., Dallas, TX	2/3	1926		314	
652	Southern Pipe Organ Co., Olney, TX	2/3	1926		314	
654	Victoria Th., Victoria, TX	2/3	1926		314	
655	Southern Pipe Organ Co., Dallas, TX	2/3	1926		314	
656	Ft. Sam Houston Th., San Antonio, TX	2/3	1926		314	
657	Southern Pipe Organ Co., Quanah, TX	2/3	1926		314	
658	Yost Th., Santa Ana, CA	2/5	1926		Special	
659	Royal Th., Seattle, WA	2/4	1926		65	
661	Palace Th., San Marcos, TX		1926			
662	Hollywood Th., Gretna, LA	2/3			314	
663	Southern Pipe Organ Co., Colorado, TX	2/3			314	
664	Pictorium Th., Vernon, TX	2/3			314	
666	Southern Pipe Organ Co.				Special	
676	Martin (Alden) Th., Globe, AZ	3/8			Special	
679	Strand Th., Lawrence, MA	2/4			65	
680	Wollaston Th., Wollaston, MA	2/4	1927		65	George Lincoln Parker nameplate.
683	Majestic (R&R) (Liberty) Th., Durant, OK	2/3	1927		314	
684	Maeroy Th., Ballinger, TX	2/3	1927		314	
685	M. S. White Th., Dallas, TX	2/3	1927		314	
686	Majestic City Th., Bogalusa, LA	2/3	1927		314	
687	Southern Pipe Organ Co., New Orleans, LA	2/3	1927		314	
689	Ideal Th., Baltimore, MD	2/4	1927		65	
693	Palace Th., San Angelo, TX	2/4	1927		65	
697	Coronado Th., Las Vegas, NM	2/4	1927		75	Cost $2,550; rebuilt, with roll player supplied by purchaser.
701	Warren Th., Roxbury, MA	2/5	1927		75 Sp.	
703	Colonial Th., Gillespie, IL	2/7	1927			"Add. rebuilt 75"
706	Frolic Th., Midland, MI	2/6	1927			Additions to opus 435 for Robert Morton company.
707	Ft. Eustis Th., Lee Hall, VA	2/4	1927		65	
709	Norwood Th., Norwood, MA	2/4	1927		75	
713	Concord Th., Springdale, AR	2/4	1927		75	
716	Palace (Rose) Th., Pana, IL	2/4	1927		65	Cost $4,000.
no #	Dixie Th., Vandalia, IL		1927			Cost $500; install and repair Seeburg from Palace Theatre, Pana, Illinois.
717	Capital Th., Litchfield, IL	2/3	1927		314	See also opus 759.
718	Jenkins Music Co., Kansas City, MO	2/3	1927		314	
719	Kalihi (Star) Th., Honolulu, HI	2/4	1927		75	
723	National Th., Boston, MA	2/4	1927		75	
724	Humboldt Th., Roxbury, MA	2/4	1927		65	
729	R&R (Ritz) Th., San Angelo, TX	3/8	1927		Special	
732	New Palace Th., Nokomis, IL	2/4	1927			Cost $2,300; rebuild Seeburg-Smith with new console and chests; $800 allowed for reproducer (sic) player piano traded in.
733	Orpheum Th., Hillsboro, IL	2/7	1927		Special	Cost $7,000.
735	Franklin Park Th., Dorchester, MA	2/4	1927		75 Sp.	
738	Milton Park Hill Th., Denver, CO	3/12			Special	Cost $12,000.
740	Lindsay Th., Lubbock, TX	2/4			4192	
741	Broadway Th., Somerville, MA	2/4			65	
749	Grand Th., Jacksonville, IL	2/5			Special	Cost $5,480.
750	Strand Th., Robinson, IL	2/7			Special	With Gottfried French horn.
752	purchaser unknown, Wood River, IL	2/5			75 Sp.	
753	Effingham Th., Effingham, IL	2/5			532 Sp.	Cost $5,480.
757	Hippodrome Th., Murphysboro, IL	2/10			Special	Cost $5,000; Rebuild of existing Reuter-Schwartz organ, with new console, chests and kinura.
			1928			Cost $650; replace existing vox with new vox; exchange oboe for brass trumpet.
759	Capital Th., Litchfield, IL	2/4			65	Replaced opus 717.
762	Hippodrome Th., Herrin, IL	2/9	1927			Cost $5,000; rebuilt, with new console and five ranks.
763	Barth Th., Carbondale, IL	2/6	1927			Cost $2,500; rebuild Wurlitzer with new console and chests.
765	Rosewin Th., Dallas, TX	2/8			Special	
768	Porter Square Th., Cambridge, MA	2/4	1928		65	
769	Southern Pipe Organ Co., New Orleans, LA	2/4			4-19-2	With chimes.

OPUS	LOCATION/CITY/STATE	SIZE	YR	BLWR	STYLE	REMARKS
770	Southern Pipe Organ Co., New Orleans, LA	2/4			65	
773	Art Th., Tulsa, OK	2/3			314	With single roll player.
774	Jenkins Music Co., Kansas City, MO	2/3			A	With double roll player.
777	Granada Th., Greencastle, IN	3/6			Special	Cost $5,704.
779	Grand Opera House, St. Louis, MO	2/				Cost $3,000; rebuild existing organ; everything new except pipes
781	Princess Th., Alton, IL	2/4			Special	Gratian nameplate.
783	J. W. Rice Co., Odessa, TX	2/3			314	
791	Englewood Th., Chicago, IL	2/4			Special	Cost $2,150.
793	Indiana Th., Bedford, IN	3/6				Cost $5,704.80; later repossessed.
793	Fox Lincoln (Lincoln) Th., Springfield, IL	3/7			Special	Cost $6,110; with brass trumpet.
794	Capitol Th., Davenport, IA	3/10	1928			Cost $6,375; rebuild existing Moller opus 2939, using old pipes only.
795	Robert Morton Co., New York, NY	2/5	1928			Rebuild special 75 from Mercer Square Th., Greenville, PA and ship to another theatre.
796	Southern Pipe Organ Co. Studio, New Orleans, LA	2/4	1928		65	
800	Avalon Th., Lawrenceville, IL		1928		Special	
802	Southern Pipe Organ Co. demonstrator, Dallas, TX	2/6	1928		Special	
803	Southern Pipe Organ Co. demonstrator, New Orleans, LA	2/6	1928		Special	
807	Sherman, Clay & Co. studio, San Francisco, CA	2/4	1928		5 Sp.	
809	Best (Parsons) (Dickerson) Th., Parsons, KS	3/7	1928		Special	
810	Royal Th., Carrolton, MO	2/3			314	
814	Strand Th., Everett, MA	2/4			65	
815	G. L. Parker, Centredale, RI	2/4			65	
816	Lyric Th., Huntington Park, CA	2/4			65	Cost $6,000 less $ 2,800 allowance for Wurlitzer style YO traded in.
818	Mishawaka Th., Mishawaka, IN	2/6				Cost $5,885; with double roll 88-note player in separate cabinet; order cancelled.
818	WIL Radio, St. Louis, MO	2/7	1929			Cost $5,500; with reveille tubes and sostenuto pedal; $2,000 credit from WIL for Wicks radio advertising for one year.
823	Garrick Th., Winnipeg, Manitoba	3/12				"Wicks Giant"; with brass trumpet.
824	Arcadia Th., Olney, IL	2/7			Special	Cost $7,836; $3,736 allowed for style 75 Robert-Morton traded in.
825	Plaza Th., Mt. Vernon, IL	2/4				Cost $3,750; used style 75 with new organ guarantee.
826	New Tackett Th., Coffeyville, KS	2/5			Special	
832	American Central Life Insurance Company Auditorium, Indianapolis, IN	2/6				Cost $3,000; with full percussions.
833	Novelty Th., Topeka, KS	2/5			Special	
836	New Astor Th., Ruston, LA	2/4			65	
837	New Ideal Th., Picayune, MS	2/4			65	
838	Ideal Th., Ponchatoila, LA	2/5			Special	
842	J. W. Jenkins demonstrator, Kansas City, MO	2/6			Special	
843	Milford Opera House, Milford, MA	2/4			65	
845	J. W. Jenkins studio, Kansas City, MO	3/4			Special	With piano.
854	Park Th., Pasadena, CA	2/5			85	Cost $8,750.
856	Tenth Street Th., Kansas City, KS	2/3			314	
860	Yucca Th., Midland, TX	2/6				
861	Savoy Th., Shawnee, OK	2/4	1929		Special	With tibia.
863	Home Th., Kansas City, KS	2/3			314	
866	Princess Th., Springfield, IL	3/6			Special	Cost $7,000; with piano.
869	Tivoli Th., Spencer, IN	3/4	1928		Special	Cost $3,500; with piano.
869	Gem Th., Cairo, IL	3/4	1929		Special	Cost $3,500; with piano.
870	Lincoln Th., Bunker Hill, IL	2/4				Cost $2,500; rebuild of existing organ, make unknown.
873	Rialto Th., Calexico, CA	2/6				Cost $2,500 for parts only: console, relay and 3 tremolos; see also opus 590.
879	Orange Th., Orange, CA	2/8	1929			Cost $17,500 less allowance of $10,075 for used organ traded in.
1083	WEBR Radio, Buffalo, NY	2/4	1931			Cost $1,925; Rhapsody model.
3908	1958 Home Show, Chicago, IL	2/8	1958			
3908	Martinetti's Restaurant, Crystal Lake, IL	2/8	1964			Cost $15,168; sold as used organ, without installation.
3954	Oral Roberts University, Tulsa, OK	3/16	1959			Cost $37,799.
4461	Mike Prideaux-Brune residence, Menlo Park, CA	2/4	1964			
5158	Harvey Kuhlman residence, Menomonee Falls, WI	2/7	1970			
		3/14	1971			Enlarged.
5330	Red Vest Restaurant, Monterey, CA	2/8	1972			
5349	Pizza Machine Restaurant, Pleasant Hill, CA	2/6	1974			
5381	Francis Aebi residence, Salinas, CA	3/	1973			Parts only: console, relay and two 16′ strings, 12 pipes each.
		3/7	1974			Parts: 6 ranks and chests.
5770	Portable display organ	2/8	1979			
5770	Albert Bilgen residence, Lake Forest, IL	2/8	1982			

The opus numbers of the following Wicks theatre installations are unknown. All are represented in the numerical list above as unknown locations.

CITY/STATE	LOCATION	SIZE	YR	BLWR	REMARKS
CALIFORNIA					
East Los Angeles	Link Th.	2/			Nee Belvedere Gardens.
Los Angeles	Rampart Th.	2/7			
	Star Th.	2/			
DELAWARE					
Middletown	Everett Th.	2/4			
DISTRICT OF COLUMBIA					
Washington	York Th.	2/			For American Photo Player Co.
ILLINOIS					
Antioch	Crystal Th.	2/	1923	11991	For American Photo Player Co.
Benld	Grand Th.				
Carbondale	Hippodrome Th.				
Chicago	Kim Th.	2/			Located at 6219 S. Halsted.
Collinsville	Miners Th.				
Dwight	Blackstone Th.				
Jacksonville	Illinois Th.				
Maywood	Maywood Th.				
MAINE					
Portland	Portland Th.	2/4			
MARYLAND					
Baltimore	Metropolitan Th.	3/			For American Photo Player Co.
MASSACHUSETTS					
Danvers	Rialto Th.	2/			
Lynn	Capitol Th.	2/			
	Waldorf Th.		1917	8631	
Quincy	Manco Th.	2/6			
Taunton	Casino Th.	2/			
	Grand Th.	2/			
MISSISSIPPI					
Laurel	Arabian Th.	2/5			
MISSOURI					
Lees Summit	Douglass Th.	2/3			
Mexico	Liberty Th.	2/4			For American Photo Player Co.
MONTANA					
Anaconda	Margaret Th.	2/	1918	8981	
NEW JERSEY					
Jersey City	Monticello Th.		1917	8386	
NEW YORK					
Brooklyn	Belvedere Th.	2/5	1922	13479	For American Photo Player Co.; later moved to Star Theatre, Malad, Idaho.
	Morey Amusement Co.		1919		
	Oxford Th.		1918	8760	
New York	Majestic Th.		1917	8376	Not necessarily the same Majestic Theatre on the Robert-Morton opus list.
NORTH CAROLINA					
Asheville	Imperial Th.	2/			For American Photo Player Co.
Greensboro	Bijou Th.	2/6			For American Photo Player Co.
OREGON					
Bandon	Bandon Th.	2/4			For American Photo Player Co.
Portland	Clinton Th.	2/4			
TEXAS					
Cuero	Normana Th.	2/	192?		
Dallas	Oak Lawn Th.	2/			
	Palace Th.	2/			Located at 2407 Elm Street.
Ennis	Lyric Th.	2/4			
Greenville	King Opera House	2/5	1922		Moved in 1928 to Rialto Theatre, Greenville, Texas.
Houston	Iris Th.		1920		
Temple	Gem Th.	2/4			
UTAH					
Lehi	Lehi Th.	2/7			
Provo	Strand Th.	2/5			

CITY/STATE	LOCATION	SIZE	YR	BLWR	REMARKS
WASHINGTON					
Chehalis	Chehalis Th.	2/8	1923		For American Photo Player Co.
Seattle	Beacon Th.	2/6			
	Hollywood Th.	2/4			
	Portola (Admiral) Th.	2/6			

C. F. WINDER ORGAN COMPANY

In 1913 Charles F. Winder (?-1939) founded the company which bore his name. He learned organ building from his father who operated an organ factory at Newcastle upon Tyne, England and later worked for Roosevelt and Hutchings in this country.[1] [2] Winder built chests which were noisy and crude and consoles which were worse; he wisely purchased supply house pipes.[3] Late in 1914 James H. Nuttall, a Hope-Jones protege, purchased an interest in the Winder firm[4] although his influence came too late; the firm produced only about a half dozen organs[5] before going out of business late in 1915.[6] Eventually Winder wound up in southern California, joining C. E. Haldeman in the Artcraft Organ Company.[7] This company didn't have a very good reputation for quality, either, their products being referred to by local builders as "artcrap"![8]

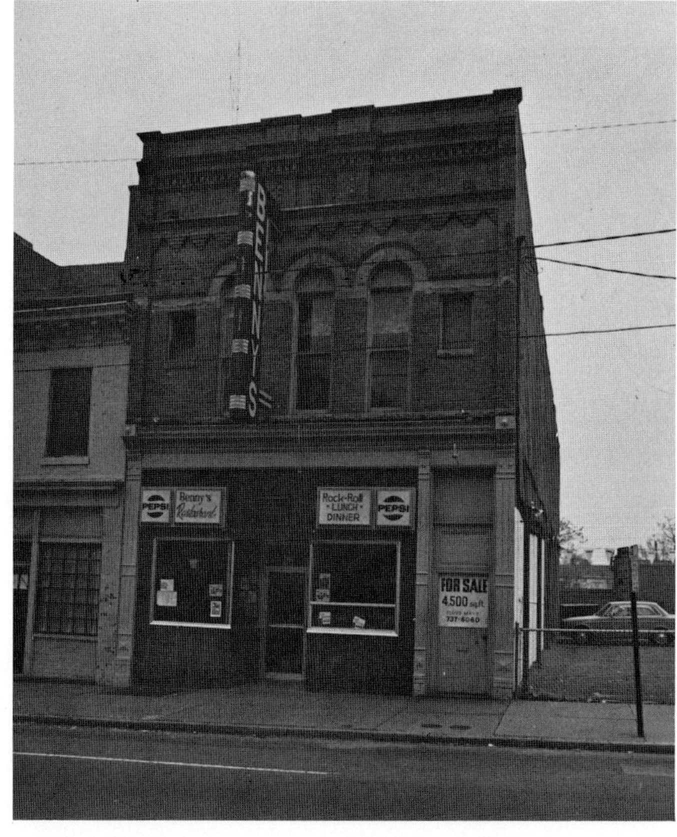

Final location of the Winder factory at 611 W. Main Street, photographed in 1982. The firm had two previous Richmond addresses in the years 1913-14.[9]

CONTRACT GOES TO WINDER

Will Build Two-Manual for Richmond Theater—No Competition.

The C. F. Winder Company's latest contract has just been awarded without competition. It is for a two-manual in the Superior Theater at Richmond, Va. The organ is to be voiced on ten-inch pressure and all the pipes will be in an eight-inch swell box. A detached console and tubular-pneumatic action are provided. The specification follows:

GREAT ORGAN.
1. Open Diapason, 8 feet.
2. Dulciana, 8 feet.
3. Rohr Flute, 8 feet.
4. Violin, 8 feet.
5. Flute D'Amour, 4 feet.
6. Octave, 4 feet.

ORCHESTRAL ORGAN.
7. Lieblich Gedacht, 16 feet.
8. Open Diapason, 8 feet (from No. 1).
9. Orchestral Violin, 8 feet (from No. 4).
10. Rohr Flute, 8 feet (from No. 3).
11. Viole d'Orchestre, 8 feet.
12. Orchestral Celeste, 8 feet.
13. Dulciana, 8 feet (from No. 2).
14. Flute d'Amour, 4 feet (from No. 5).
15. Tuba, 8 feet.
16. Tremulant.

PEDAL ORGAN.
17. Resultant, 32 feet (from Nos. 18 and 19).
18. Sub Bass, 16 feet.
19. Lieblich Gedacht, 16 feet (from No. 7).
20. Violoncello, 8 feet (from No 11).

COUPLERS—21. Swell to swell, 16 feet. 22. Swell to swell, 4 feet. 23. Swell to great, 16 feet. 24. Swell to great, 4 feet. 25. Swell to great. 26. Swell to pedal. 27. Great to pedal.

COMPOSITION PEDALS—28. Piano to great. 29. Mezzo to great. 30. Forte to great. 31. Piano to swell. 32. Mezzo to swell. 33. Forte to swell. 34. Balanced crescendo pedal. 35. Balanced swell pedal (inside). 36. Lock swell pedal (outside).

Specifications of the two Winder theatre organs are reproduced as published in The Diapason, *left, November 1913 and right, September 1914.*

C. F. WINDER BUILDS ORGAN FOR THEATER

UNIQUE SCHEME IS ADOPTED

Three-Manual on Heavy Wind Pressure Has Great and Orchestral Departments, Both Enclosed in Swell Boxes.

The C. F. Winder Organ Company of Richmond, Va., is building a three-manual organ for the Eastern Theater of Columbus, Ohio, which has a unique specification. The scheme follows:

PEDAL ORGAN.
Resultant, 32 ft.
Major Bourdon, 16 ft.
Flute (Open), 8 ft.
Violoncello, 8 ft.

GREAT ORGAN.
Diapason Phonon, 8 ft.
Dulciana, 8 ft.
Flute D'Amour, 4 ft.
Clarionet, 8 ft.
Tuba (harmonic), 8 ft.
Enclosed in heavy swell box.

ORCHESTRAL ORGAN.
Horn Diapason, 8 ft.
Tibia Clausa, 8 ft.
First String, 8 ft.
Second String (Celeste), 8 ft.
Third String, 8 ft.
Fourth String, 8 ft.
Vox Humana, 8 ft.
Enclosed in heavy swell box.

COUPLERS—Orchestral to great, 16 ft. Orchestral to great, 4 ft. Orchestral to great. Orchestral to pedal. Great to pedal. Three composition pistons to great organ. Three composition pistons to orchestral organ. Balanced crescendo pedal.

An electro-pneumatic action is provided and heavy wind pressure is used.

C. F. Winder Organ Co.
INCORPORATED
611-W. Main St., Richmond Va.
C. F. Winder, Pres. J. H. Nuttall, Vice-Pres.
W. J. Tucker, Sec'y-Treas.

HIGHEST GRADE
Pipe Organs

Electro-Pneumatic Actions
Our Specialty

Winder advertisement in the December 1914 Diapason.

WINDER OPUS LIST

CITY/STATE	LOCATION	SIZE	YR	BLWR	HP	WP	REMARKS
OHIO							
Columbus	Eastern Th.	2/15	1914	C497	2	10″	Electric, straight.
VIRGINIA							
Richmond	Superior (Dixie) Th.	2/11	1914	C11	2	10″	Tubular, duplexed.

New York Office
F. W. Haubner, Treas.
~~Steinway Hall~~
107-109 E. 14th St.

Salem, Ohio
W. L. Deming, President
Philipp Wirsching,
Secretary and Manager

Philipp Wirsching was a perfect example of an organ builder who put his heart and soul into his work. Craftsmanship was paramount; financial considerations were quite secondary and as a result, his work shone in quality in an era where mass production was the norm. Unfortunately, his efforts were never successful financially.

Wirsching was born in Bensheim, Germany in 1858, the son of a tanner. At the age of twelve he became organist in the local Catholic church. After graduating from the University of Wurzburg he decided to pursue organ building as a career and apprenticed with the firm of August Laukhuff in Weikersheim for several years. In 1886 he joined the tidal wave of German immigrants to the United States and went directly to Salem, Ohio at the request of organ builder Carl Barckhoff. The following year he married a local Salem girl and established his own firm which was more or less successful until the Panic of 1893 wiped out both Wirsching and Barckhoff. For two years beginning in 1894 he worked for Farrand & Votey as a traveling representative. In 1896 he joined Kimball in Chicago but by 1898 he was back in business for himself in Salem in the former Barckhoff factory building.[1]

In 1904 another calamity befell Wirsching: his factory was destroyed by fire. With the backing of local businessmen, however, the firm was reorganized and incorporated the following year. At the same time a five-year contract was negotiated to build instruments for the Art Organ Company of New York City. This firm was the brainchild of George Ashdown Audsley, famous organ author, and J. Burr Tiffany, of the family of New York jewelers. A salon with a demonstration instrument featuring an "Organola" player was set up in Steinway Hall in New York. Among the customers was the Maharajah of Mysore, India whose organ was installed by Stanley Williams, a Wirsching employee who later became factory superintendent of Robert-Morton. Unfortunately, few other customers materialized for the Art Organ Company and the firm terminated its association with Wirsching in 1909.[2]

Quoting organ historian Robert Coleberd, Jr., "During

MODERN MUSIC RENDERED BY THE WIRSCHING SELF-PLAYER

FEW there are who do not appreciate good music; and many have sought in vain the Royal Road to the art of producing it. We think, therefore, it is our duty to tell you that we have discovered this Royal Road, and have made it possible for you to render such music as could until recently be performed only by the skilled musician. This is accomplished by our Organs when furnished with The WIRSCHING SELF-PLAYER, by the aid of which Orchestral Music can be perfectly rendered.

¶ The pneumatic fingers of a self-player are far more competent to take the place of the organist than they are of the pianist. But the WIRSCHING PLAYER does not merely do this, it plays as does the organist on two manuals at once; *a solo upon one clavier and accompaniment on the other*. A subtle theme may be dwelt upon and given just such emphasis as the composer intended or a bolder melody may be given exactly the prominence it deserves. In a word, it gives the amateur performer the same possibilities that are at the command of the skilled organist.

¶ Hitherto special music rolls had to be provided at great expense to accomplish these results, but now the WIRSCHING PLAYER will enable you to pick out and follow the intricate movements of a dignified Fugue or the melody of a popular composition from an ordinary roll of perforated music of standard scale. This reduces the cost of a music library and puts a practically unlimited selection of all classes of compositions at your disposal.

¶ It must not be thought that the WIRSCHING PLAYER renders organ music only, and in a set style at that. On the contrary, it enables the operator to impart his own individuality to whatever style of music he feels in the mood to render.

Organ Console with Wirsching Player

¶ The tempo, power and color of the tone, and the light and shade that the performer feels to be necessary for his interpretation of the composer's thoughts, are instantly obtainable by the lightest touch upon the mechanism.

¶ We feel sure you will be convinced that these claims can be proven after a demonstration of the WIRSCHING PLAYER.

THE WIRSCHING ORGAN COMPANY,
Salem, Ohio

SEND FOR BROCHURE, "THE ORGAN IN ART"

Early Wirsching ad c. 1907. The name of the firm was changed to Wirsching & Company in a subsequent reorganization.

this period subtle yet far-reaching changes were taking place in the structure of the pipe organ industry which in the end would make it increasingly difficult for the smaller builder to survive. Wirsching had steadfastly adhered to the ideal of organ building as the craft of a skilled artisan designing and building the instrument. He had insisted upon personally superintending every phase of construction and [of] doing the bulk of the voicing himself. But elsewhere the industry had come of age, and [mass] production was the road to profit.

" . . . As a perfectionist at heart who manifested an uncommon devotion to his craft, Wirsching found unthinkable the notion of expansion with its resulting loss of his direct commitment to every phase of organ building. And so he faced the disheartening development of a price-conscious market and severe builder competition in which seemingly only the production-oriented firms could keep going. But he persevered in his faith that somehow the high standards he typified would be recognized and would enable him to survive. Against what must have been repeated discouragement, this faith sustained him for yet another decade during which he built some notable instruments. They were among the few true works of art in an era of organ building conspicuously lacking in high artistic achievement."[3]

After exhausting its working capital, the Wirsching

business finally collapsed in 1917. In December of that year the firm was given one last reprieve when Wirsching's son, Clarence Eddy Wirsching, and long-time employee Eugene M. Bender purchased the insolvent firm's assets and hired the elder Wirsching to manage the business. After limping along for another year, the company sought additional financing from Pittsburgh organ man Leonard Peloubet. (See the Peloubet chapter elsewhere in this volume for further details about this colorful individual.) According to their agreement, Wirsching and Peloubet were to contribute equally to the $25,000 capitalization of a new firm called the Wirsching-Peloubet Company. Wirsching's contribution was his company's tools and fixtures. In February of 1919, however, Wirsching brought suit against Peloubet, alleging that he had failed to subscribe his $12,500 share of the capital as agreed. The suit was later dropped, but the death knell had sounded for Wirsching's firm.[4]

Philipp Wirsching, although in semi-retirement, built two more organs before accepting an offer from the Wangerin-Weickhardt Company to move to Milwaukee. From 1922 to 1926 he designed organ specifications and was chief voicer for the Wangerin firm, where he finally achieved a measure of financial security doing what he loved most. Wangerin and Wirsching were an excellent match inasmuch as each pursued highest standards of quality. After his health began to fail, however, Philipp Wirsching moved back to his Salem, Ohio home where he died of tubercular peritonitis in 1926.[5]

At least one organ bearing a Wirsching nameplate is known to have been installed in a theatre: a two-manual instrument in the Queen Theatre in Chicago, Illinois, probably with tubular pneumatic action. Several Wirsching-Peloubet organs were installed in theatres but since these were the work of Leonard Peloubet they are listed in the Peloubet section of this volume.

Philipp Wirsching (1858-1926)

Wirsching factory employees. Philipp Wirsching, wearing a dark sweater and cap, is at the right of the front row.

Wirsching factory at Salem, Ohio as it appeared on May 27, 1907.

Above, a tubular pneumatic residence organ nears completion in the Wirsching erecting room. The console is designed to jut forth from the organ case and hence has no rear cabinetry. Since a few chests are open there is no wind in the organ; but the reservoirs have been propped up for the photographer. At left, interior of the Wirsching console installed in 1915 in St. John's Lutheran Church, St. Paul, Minnesota. Curiously, the lower manual has rounded fronts while the upper two have single-beveled fronts.

Above, gorgeous photo of the mill room in the Wirsching factory. Voicing room is pictured on the right.

WM. WOOD PIPE ORGAN CO., INC.

The early history of "Billy" Wood is perhaps best told in his own words: "I have been told that I was born at Bradford, Vermont, August 1, 1861, my father being Granville Wood and my mother Electa Dustin Eastman. When I was about one year old we moved to Boston, where my father was employed by H. D. and H. W. Smith as their tuner of reed organs. A year later the family again moved, this time to Toronto, Ontario, where my father was employed by the R. S. Williams Company as reed organ tuner. Two years later we moved to Detroit, my father then being employed by A. A. Simmons as tuner for his organs. Later Mr. Simmons took into partnership James E. Clough and the firm name now became Simmons, Clough & Company. Later Mr. Simmons and his son Fred retired and the Warren brothers joined Mr. Clough, the name being changed to Clough & Warren.

". . . [In 1870] my father bought a building lot at Bush and Bronson streets, 100′ front and 95′ in depth. There was a building on the southeast corner which had been built for a barn but which was never used as such. This was where my father started the building of [tracker] organs. I left school after having completed the ninth grade and in September joined my father in the making of pipe organs. We were successful and moved into a large room over the piano store of the Leicester Piano Company and then into a large factory at State and Park Place owned by Augustus Day . . . We continued to build organs in this factory until 1884, when a company was organized at Northville, Michigan, a good factory building was erected, and a steam engine installed. Things looked very rosy so I decided to get married and selected Miss Hattie Francke of Saginaw.

"We continued building organs in Northville for six years but did not meet with great success financially, so we sold out to Farrand & Votey of Detroit, who were just branching out in the organ field. We moved to Detroit and I became assistant to Mr. Votey. Soon after this we acquired the business and patents of the Frank Roosevelt Company of New York with several of their best workmen, and we built many important organs with the Roosevelt system just as we had acquired it. Then Mr. and Mrs. Votey made a trip to Europe and when they returned Mr. Votey brought complete data concerning tubular pneumatic actions as manufactured by Walcker & Son of Ludwigsburg, Germany. We built a few organs using this form of action but were not satisfied with it because it was too slow.

"Fortunately about this time Robert Hope-Jones, an Englishman, invented a new form of electric action. The special feature of this action was the low voltage hairpin-shaped magnet and very small thin discs of soft iron, which were faced with thin leather, forming perfect pneumatic valves. The valve seats were bored in the top board of a wind box and the magnets were screwed on over the hole and seat. But to make a more nearly perfect seat and fitting for the magnet and its armature I invented a metal base consisting of a three-quarter-inch round brass plug. Milled out to receive the armature and magnet was a brass ferrule screwed into the plug to hold the magnet in place. There were holes drilled through the plug for supply and exhaust and also to feed the intervening pneumatic to the pipe pneumatic and valve. We built several large organs using our style of unit magnets."[1]

In 1923 Billy Wood joined Robert-Morton in the capacity of technical adviser and director of church organ sales.[2] This association lasted only about a year, after which Billy moved to Hillsboro, Oregon, establishing the Wm. Wood Pipe Organ Co., specializing in tuning and

William D. "Billy" Wood (1861-1945)

WM. WOOD PIPE ORGAN CO., Inc.
PIPE ORGAN BUILDERS
ORGANS REBUILT, ELECTRIFIED, MODERNIZED
REPAIRS, TUNING and MAINTENANCE
A SPECIALTY

Northwest Agents
for
MARR & COLTON CO., INC.
America's Finest
Concert Organ

Factory:
HILLSBORO, OREGON
Portland Office:
331 Railway Exch. Bldg.
PORTLAND, OREGON

Wood ad in the December 1924 Diapason.

maintenance.[3] Business apparently flourished for by the end of 1924 the company had incorporated with a capital stock of $25,000, had five employees[4] and had assumed the northwest dealership for Marr & Colton.[5] This liaison was short-lived, however, since Wood soon began manufacturing his own organs. Continued success prompted two changes of location for the company: in 1925 to 101 13th Street in Portland and in 1926 to 1475 E. 27th Street North.[6] Around 1929 Wood moved to Los Angeles. He retired from the organ business in 1933.[7]

Wood, as did many smaller builders, built his own consoles, some wooden pipes, chests and other actions but purchased metal pipes from Gottfried.[8] He was well qualified to craft wooden pipework having built, for example, a 32′ open wood diapason right in a church (St. Ignatius, San Francisco, 1897) during his employ with Farrand & Votey.[9] Wood's chests were similar in design to Marr & Colton's except for the use of Reisner chest magnets[10] which Wood conceded were an improvement over his original "barrel" magnet design.[11] Wood organs had another characteristic in common with Marr & Colton: cheapness! The pipework was of excellent quality but the organs were frequently found wanting in specifications and in mechanical details. Few if any Wood consoles had a combination action; pedals were weak with just a lone 16′ bourdon on organs as large as eight ranks; and many electrical connections were never soldered.[12] At least two of the rink organs (Rollerdrome[13] and Imperial) were installed without swell shades, and the Imperial organ was voiced on only 8″ wind pressure.[14] On the other hand, several of the theatre organs included a piano in the solo chamber,[15] a luxury rarely found on instruments of this size in other makes.

A typical Wood theatre organ was laid out as follows:[16]

SOLO CHAMBER	MAIN CHAMBER
Tuba 8′-4′	Flute 16′-1 3/5′
Tibia Clausa 8′-4′	Open Diapason 8′-4′
Vox Humana 8′-4′	Viole d'Orchestre 8′-2′
Percussions	Viole Celeste 8′-4′
	Clarinet 8′-4′

Band shell at Rollerdrome Skating Rink, Culver City, California. Shell and console were painted by Wood employee Ray Smith.[17]

Close-up view of the Rollerdrome console.

Get Our Prices on Organ Building,
Repairing, Installing, etc.
We Go Anywhere, Any Time
WM. WOOD PIPE ORGAN CO.
Hillsboro, Oregon

Wood's first advertisement in The Diapason, *September 1924.*

Dennis Hedberg stands among Gottfried "friends" at the Imperial Roller Rink in Portland, Oregon. From left to right are the 16′ clarinet, kinura, post horn, and 8′ clarinet.

Bill Blunk at the 4/13 Wm. Wood console originally installed at the Oaks roller rink.

2/6 Wm. Wood organ built originally for the Clark Theatre, Vacaville, California, shown here as later installed in a Vacaville church.

WM. WOOD OPUS LIST

CITY/STATE	LOCATION	SIZE	YR	REMARKS
CALIFORNIA				
Culver City	Rollerdrome Rink	3/6	1929	With tuba mirabilis, flute, kinura, post horn, diapason and tibia.
Los Angeles	Shrine Rink	2/8	1929	
Vacaville	Clark Th.	2/6	1926	Blower 0240B, 5 hp, 10″ wind and 25″ vacuum.
IDAHO				
Lewiston	Temple Th.	2/5		Later moved to Lotus Isle Amusement Park, Portland, Oregon.
OREGON				
Dallas	Majestic Th.	2/8		
Hillsboro	Hillsboro Th.	2/8	1925	
Portland	Alberta Th.	2/6		
	Gellers (Aladdin) Th.	3/9		
	Hippodrome Th.	2/7		
	Imperial Roller Rink	2/5		
		2/8		Additions.
	Jefferson Th.	2/6		
	KEX Radio	2/		
	Nob Hill Th.	2/6		
	Oaks Roller Rink	2/5		
		4/13		Additions.
	Oregon Th.	2/9		Later moved to KXL Radio, Portland, Oregon.
	Sellwood Th.	2/8		
	State (Esquire) (Cinema 21) Th.	2/8		
	Walnut Park Th.	2/		
Silverton	Adams Th.	2/7	1926	
The Dalles	The Dalles Th.	2/8	1926	
WASHINGTON				
Camas	Liberty Th.	2/8		
Kelso	Vogue Th.	2/12		
Seattle	Columbia Th.	2/5	1926	Blower 0323B, 3hp, 10″ wind; later moved to Lakeside Theatre, Seattle, Washington.

PARTS SUPPLIERS TO THE ORGAN INDUSTRY

The many firms which supplied products to the organ industry are indeed unsung heroes. They rarely received the prestige and recognition afforded the organ builder whose nameplate was on the console, yet without them most organ builders couldn't have survived. Virtually no organ builders built absolutely everything in their instruments; all relied to one extent or another on outside suppliers. Even industry giants such as Wurlitzer, Robert Morton, Kimball and Moller, who were large enough to build almost every part of their instruments, ordered percussions and blowers from other firms.

At the opposite end of the sprectrum were builders who built almost no parts of their instruments. Organs bearing the LeNoir, Kohl or F. R. Smith nameplates, for example, were often built entirely in the Organ Supply, Durst or Gottfried factories, respectively. Very few builders built their own blowers. The few who did were (then) smaller firms such as Alnett, Cozatt, Operators Piano Co., Schantz and Wicks. In the 1980s this situation is quite different: America's largest blower manufacturer, Spencer Turbine Company, has discontinued making organ blowers, and several of the country's largest builders (Moller, Wicks and Schantz) now make their own blowers.

Many theatre organ builders were primarily woodworkers who made most of their own wooden parts but sought other sources for metal items such as magnets and pipes. Because so many builders ordered pipework from common suppliers, it was not unusual for organs of different makes to share similar tonal qualities. A kinura made by Dennison, for instance, has an unmistakably distinctive squawk. With a Dennison kinura in the ensemble, a Barton or a Marr & Colton or a Kilgen organ would sound basically alike to most listeners. On the other hand, organs bearing the same nameplate (but with pipework from different suppliers) can sound quite different from each other. This explains why one Barton can sound so dissimilar to another Barton: It depended upon whether the pipes were ordered from Gottfried, Dennison or National Organ Supply.

The organization of the parts suppliers in this section is somewhat different from the rest of this *Encyclopedia*. Only the major suppliers are covered in depth and they are not alphabetized but rather divided into classifications such as percussions, pipework, general supplies, etc. Firms are listed in the areas of their greatest impact on the industry. For example, Gottfried was a major supplier of pipework yet was of even greater significance as America's largest supplier of general organ supplies; hence Gottfried is listed in the "general supplies" section. In another example, Pratt Read supplied roll player mechanisms but was much more important as a keyboard manufacturer. Sometimes an organ building firm would become a "parts supplier" to another builder under special circumstances even though that was not their primary business. For example, Moller supplied a toy counter to Midmer-Losh for their organ in Atlantic City's Convention Hall.

The author now invites you on a behind-the-scenes tour of some of the unsung heroes of the organ industry and hopes they will receive much overdue recognition thereby.

BAYLEY MANUFACTURING CO.

The Bayley company, a manufacturer of ventilating equipment, dabbled in organ blowers just before World War I but discontinued that line in order to complete government contracts. Late in 1919 Bayley decided to re-enter the organ field and hired J. K. Fagan, who had been an organ man for twenty years, to manage their organ blower department.[1] With heavy competition from Spencer, Kinetic and Zephyr, few sales materialized for the Bayley company and they ceased advertising in 1921. This particular ad appeared in the September 1920 Diapason.

All Metal

Bayley Peerless Organ Blower

Try it; you will adopt it

This Blower unit merits the most rigid investigation of all organ builders.

A trial order will prove to your complete satisfaction all claims that we make. If you have not received our literature write us and we will forward it.

Organ repairmen, write for catalog and prices

Bayley Manufacturing Co.

732-744 Greenbush St. **Milwaukee, Wisconsin**

Simplex Organ Blowers

MANUFACTURED BY THE

B. F. BLOWER CO., *Inc.*

45-47 Third Street
Telephone 2219
FOND DU LAC, WISCONSIN

ALL METAL BLOWER

For a brief period during 1917, half-page ads for Obeco blowers made by the Organ Blowing Engineering Co. of Fond du Lac, Wisconsin appeared in *The Diapason*. Apparently the firm got little response and discontinued the ads after a couple of months. Furthermore, the author, who has examined quite a number of organs, has never seen an Obeco blower.

After four years of relative inactivity by the firm, an announcement in the June 1921 issue of *The Diapason* revealed that Fond du Lac businessman Jacob Brenner and organ man J. K. Fagan had formed the B. F. Blower Co. Earlier, Mr. Fagan had been associated with the Bayley Manufacturing Co. of Milwaukee, just 70 miles south of Fond du Lac, in an ill-fated attempt to get the Bayley firm, a manufacturer of ventilating machinery, into the organ blower business.[1] According to the *Diapason* announcement, the B. F. company planned "to cater largely to the theater organ trade."[2]

In the days following the B. F. firm's inception, sample blowers were sold to Kimball, Robert-Morton, Wicks, Symphony and Wurlitzer, although no further orders were received from these firms. Several blowers were sold to the Barton and Seeburg-Smith companies, and the Marquette Piano Company purchased a few for their Cremona photoplayers. The largest customer of B. F. was Kilgen, who purchased about half of the company's output, and quite a few Kilgen theatre organs had Simplex blowers. Most of the 1300 or so blowers built by B. F., however, went to churches.[3]

Simplex blowers were made on the second floor of the Brenner Tin Shop in Fond du Lac until the outbreak of World War II when production was curtailed because of the War Production Board's ban on the sale of new electric motors. The company had diversified into products other than organ blowers, however, and today, known as Brenner Tank, Inc., it is a leading manufacturer of tanker trucks for transporting chemicals and dairy products.[4]

Marr & Colton was one of the theatre organ firms who purchased Simplex blowers occasionally. The blower on this invoice was for a lodge organ.

INVOICE

B. F. BLOWER CO., *Inc.*

MANUFACTURERS OF

Simplex Organ Blowers

45-47 Third Street
Telephone 3160
FOND DU LAC, WIS.,

Sold to Marr & Colton Co., Inc
Warsaw - N.Y.

Shipped to Marr & Colton Co. Inc.
Three Links Temple, Chicago, Ill.

Via C M & St P. R R

Invoice No. 242
Our Order No. 1171
Your Order No. 225
Terms: usual.
Shipped Feb. 1-25.

All claims must be made within ten days. We can not be responsible for damage to blower through improper installation, or through attempts to operate motor in excess of its rated capacity intentional or otherwise.

Quantity	H. P.	Number Motor	R. P. M.	Volts	Cycles	Phase	Pressure	Valve	Pulley	Generator	Each	TOTAL
1	1½	Century #798375	1750	220	60	3	6½	12"	3"	—	Net.	169.70
												8.47

169.70
8.485

THE OBECO ORGAN BLOWER

EFFICIENCY RELIABILITY QUIETNESS

A HIGH POWER UNIT IN EVERY DETAIL

One-fourth to twenty horse power

Compound suction and blowing machines

Write for descriptive literature and price lists

A maximum supply of wind at all times, a minimum of noise in operation, the highest quality of material and workmanship in its construction, manufactured by a company that devotes its entire efforts to the production of an efficient and perfect Organ Blower are the features embodied in the OBECO.

Our specially constructed wind ways and blast wheels allow of no backing up of wind. Every cubic inch of air taken into the blast chambers, becomes a unit of power. The intake at top of blower insures clean, dry air and freedom from dust being blown through Organ.

Organ Blowing Engineering Co. FOND DU LAC WIS.

This half-page ad ran in The Diapason *during mid-1917.*

Write us for Booklet and Price Lists

AGENTS WANTED

The SIMPLEX ORGAN BLOWER

Simplicity, Rigidity, Quietness and Efficiency

YOUR BUSINESS SOLICITED

The B-F Blower Co., Fond du Lac, Wis.

Early Simplex ad which ran in The Diapason *after the firm's founding in 1921.*

Kinetic Engineering Company

QUIET ORGAN & SPECIAL BLOWERS

MAIN OFFICE AND WORKS
UNION AND STEWART AVENUES

Lansdowne, Pa.,

The idea of using multiple rotary fans in series to blow an organ was pioneered by two brothers, R. A. and L. B. Cousans who, with their father, operated a firm known as J. R. Cousans, Sons and Co. of Lincoln, England. This firm advertised in 1892 that they were "builders of electric tubular, lever-pneumatic and mechanical tracker organs and licensees for the Hope-Jones patent electric action."[1] To many of us in the 1980s, the idea of the rotary fan blower seems to have been around forever but until the turn of the twentieth century most organs were blown by hand or by reciprocating bellows.

Early in 1903 the Cousans brothers were issued a British patent for their blower which they called the Kinetic.[2] In this same year, Robert P. Elliot obtained the rights to manufacture this blower in America[3] and the Kinetic Engineering Company was formed in New York City by Mr. Elliot and Herbert Brown. The first American Kinetic blowers were manufactured there in 1904[4] and the factory was soon moved to Lansdowne, Pennsylvania where control was assumed by J. G. and H. A. Bierck. In 1919 the firm underwent a massive reorganization and change of ownership and S. H. Ebert became general manager. He had been Kinetic's New York district manager for ten years and had been associated with Reuben Midmer & Son for 12 years before that.[5]

Kinetic blowers achieved wide acceptance and ran a close second in sales to industry leader Spencer Turbine Company. During the 1920s Kinetic sales averaged a thousand blowers per year compared to an average of 1300 per year for Spencer. As of 1984, Kinetic sales have totaled around 23,000 blowers; Spencer has sold around 37,000. Kinetic received the honor of being awarded the contract of supplying blowers for the largest organ in the world in the Atlantic City Convention Hall. This installation has *seven* Kinetics ranging in size from 30 to 60 horsepower. The factory test report for one of these is reproduced in *Encyclopedia of the American Theatre Organ*, Volume I, page 18. This one 60-horsepower blower cost $1430 in 1930 dollars.[6] [7]

Kinetic's all-time largest customer was M. P. Moller, Inc., who used Kinetics on virtually all of their instruments. Mathias Moller purchased stock in the Kinetic Engineering Company and became one of its directors[8] as indeed he should have since Moller was purchasing half the Kinetic company's output! Moller eventually purchased the company and in 1939 moved it to their Hagerstown, Maryland factory where, in the 1980s, Kinetic blowers are still being manufactured for new Moller organs as well as for the trade.

This enormous blower of 30 horsepower was built for the 5/27 Reginald Foort traveling Moller in 1938, but was never shipped with the organ to England. In the 1930s Kinetic changed their design from the green wooden box to the more conventional steel drum although they maintained the practice of mounting the entire machine on steel I-beams.

Robert Pier Elliot (1871-1941) founded the Kinetic Engineering Company in this country in 1903. He was later associated with the Hope-Jones, Kimball and Welte companies, among others. For a synopsis of the colorful career of Mr. Elliot, see Encyclopedia of the American Theatre Organ, *Volume I, page 208.*

KINETIC ORGAN BLOWERS

With a Kinetic Electric Organ Blower to supply the wind to your Organ, you can be certain that you have the **most quiet,** the **most efficient,** the **most durable** and the **most satisfactory** Electric Organ Blower ever produced.

Kinetics are the most extensively used blowers, on organs both large and small, and are the accepted standard for **Organ Blowing Equipment** in all parts of the world.

Two small special models of Kinetics for Reed Organs.

Awarded the Gold Medal, Panama Pacific Exposition. Also the Grand Prize, Alaska Yukon Exposition.

KINETIC ENGINEERING CO.

Baltimore Ave. and 60th St., Philadelphia, Pa.

Chicago	**New York**	**Boston**
217 W. Illinois St.	**41 Park Row**	**15 Exchange St.**

This ad appeared in the March 1923 issue of The Diapason.

Not all blowers were powered by electricity in the early days. This English-built Kinetic was operated by a gas engine.

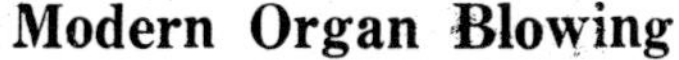

Modern Organ Blowing

KINETIC

The Perfect Organ Blower!

Patented June 4, 1907, March 16, 1915, May 7, 1928.

Gold Medal Award. Panama-Pacific Exposition, 1915

Kinetic Engineering Co.

Main Office and Plant
Union & Stewart Avenue
Lansdowne, Penna.

New York Office, 41 Park Row

The Most Quiet

The Most Efficient

The Most Durable

Over 30,000 in Daily Use

APPROXIMATE DIMENSIONS

Style	H. P.	Length 1 Phase or D.C.	Length 2 or 3 Phase	Width	Height	Size Wind Trunk	Largest Section Will Pass Through	Approx. Shipping Weights
2-S-16	¼	2' 0"		1' 8"	1'10"	4"		190
2 E.V.	¼	3' 9"		1'11"	2' 6"	6"	18"x20"	300
2 E.W.	1-3	3'10"		1'11"	2' 6"	6"	18"x20"	315
2 F.W.	½	3'11"	3'10"	2' 1"	3' 2"	8"	18"x20"	415
2 A.W.	¾	4' 0"	3'10"	2' 1"	3' 2"	8"	18"x20"	425
2 F.X.	1	4' 3"	4' 1"	2' 1"	3' 2"	10"	18"x22"	480
3 F.W.	¼	4' 1"		2' 1"	3' 2"	6"	19"x20"	550
3 A.W.	1-3	4' 2"	4' 0"	2' 1"	3' 2"	6"	19"x20"	560
2 D.X.	½	4' 3"	4' 1"	2' 6"	3' 6"	8"	18"x2[illegible]	600
3 A.X.	¾	4' 9"	4' 6"	2' [illegible]	3' 2"	8"	21"x23"	650
3 D.X.	1	5' 1"	4' 8"	2' 6"	3' 6"	10"	21"x23"	750
3 H.X.	1½	5' 4"	4' 9"	2' 6"	3' 6"	10"	21"x23"	800
3 H.Y.	2	5' 6"	5' 2"	2'11"	3'10"	12"	24"x27"	1100
3 C.Y.	3	6' 1"	5' 5"	2'1[illegible]	3'10"	12"	24"x27"	1150
3 J.Y.	5	6' 4"	5' 9"	3' 2"	4' 1"	14"	24"x27"	1300
3 K.Z.	7½	7'11"	7' 7"	3' 6"	4'10"	14"	20"x38"	1650
3 L.Z.	10	8' 2"	7' 8"	3' 6"	4'10"	16"	20"x38"	2000

Special 15, " 20, " 25 — Dimensions of special blowers furnished to suit Organ specifications.

To the length of the Blower add the following for Direct Connected Generator:

Watts	
100 Watts	1' 1"
150 "	1' 2"
200 "	1' 3"
250 "	1' 7"
300 "	1' 7"
450 "	1' 8"

Above and on the following page is reproduced a Kinetic catalog from the late 1920s.

This automatic starter for DC blower motors was an English Kinetic innovation. As the blower speed increased, a pneumatic moved the rheostat lever, gradually bringing the motor to full speed.

Net Prices f.o.b. Lansdowne, Pa.
Price List U

Style	H. P.	Speed	Single Phase	2 or 3 Phase	Direct Current
2 S. 16	¼	1750	$100.00		$108.00
Designed for Reed Organs. See description below.					
2 E. V.	¼	1750	$145.00		$154.00
2 E. W.	1-3	1750	172.00		186 00
2 F. W.	½	1750	184.00	$178.00	205.00
2 A. W.	¾	1750	204 00	200.00	224 00
2 F. X.	1	1750	230.00	216.00	254.00
3 F. W.	¼	1165	170.00		180.00
3 A. W.	1-3	1165	190.00		200.00
2 D. X.	½	1100	215.00	200.00	225 00
3 A. X.	¾	1165	250.00	240.00	262.00
3 D. X.	1	1165	288.00	262.00	300 00
3 H. X.	1½	1165	324.00	284.00	334.00
3 H. Y.	2	1165	368.00	312.00	380.00
3 C. Y.	3	1165	452.00	378.00	432.00
3 J. Y.	5	1165	560.00	460.00	584.00
3 K. Z.	7½	1165	650.00	532.00	676 00
3 L. Z.	10	1165	850.00	670.00	860.00
Special	15	1165	1075 00	848.00	1100.00
"	20	1165	1320.00	1050.00	1400.00
"	25	1165	1500.00	1212.00	1600.00

Prices for blowers other than those listed above, or blowers for two or more pressures, furnished upon application.

You will note that all slow speed blowers, except Style 2 DX, are three stage blowers.

The above prices include Automatic Regulating Wind Control Valve with counterweights, chain and pulleys, Flexible Joint of Rubber Cloth, with clamps, Insulating Pads on which to set the Kinetic, and a can of high grade oil.

The above prices do not include starters, except that hand rheostats are supplied with Direct Current Motors, if specified on order. Organ motors are usually started by Automatic Starters (Remote Control), and Automatic Starters of any required type can be furnished at prevailing prices.

All prices are based on motors of standard currents such as 60 cycle, 110/220 volt, single phase, and 60 cycle, 220/440 volt, two and three phase, and Direct Current 115 or 230 volt. Motors for odd voltages or alternating current motors for other than sixty cycles will be furnished at corresponding prices.

Quotations will be given on blowers for special purposes, and assistance given to determine an equipment best suited for any purpose.

Capacity in Cubic Feet of Air per minute at various pressures in inches of water

3"	3½"	4"	5"	6"	8"	10"	12"	Style
220	200	180	150					2-S-16
275	230	150						2 E. V.
450	400	350	275					2 E. W.
650	540	475	375	300				2 F. W.
	875	670	500	400				2 A. W.
	1100	1000	650	500				2 F. X.
275	240	150						3 F. W.
350	275	200	75					3 A. W.
650	550	500						2 D. X.
	875	675	500	400				3 A. X.
	1100	1000	650	550				3 D. X.
	1500	1300	950	800				3 H. X.
	1900	1800	1400	1100	800			3 H. Y.
		2100	1800	1500	1000			3 C. Y.
		3400	2900	2500	1750	1500	960	3 J. Y.
			3900	3500	3000	2400	1600	3 K. Z.
			5500	4800	3500	3000	2500	3 L. Z.

Blowers with motors 15 H. P. and over are designed to suit wind pressure and capacity of organ specifications.

Kinetic Style 2 S 16. A slow speed Blower of all metal construction. Exceptionally quiet in operation.

It can be used on any Reed Organ on suction wind (a different model will be furnished for pressure), either of the single manual type without pedals, or two manual and pedal type, as used in small churches, or for student organs of this type in the studio or home.

It is light and easily handled, requires very little space, can be placed near the organ, gives a smooth and steady flow of air, is simple, efficient and durable, and will withstand the most critical examination. THE FANS ARE CARRIED BY INDIVIDUAL BEARINGS AND NOT BY THE MOTOR BEARINGS.

Controlling valve to suit the type of organ furnished with the blower.

The smallest of the blowers at Atlantic City Convention Hall, this 30-horsepower Kinetic delivers wind at 15" and 30" pressures. The square box to the right of the motor is the actual blower, housing the multiple fans necessary to raise atmospheric air to those pressures. The wooden box atop the blower is a filter designed by Seibert Losh. Mounted in the blower's output, it also helps reduce noise and rumble from being transmitted through the windline. If this photograph were in color, the reader would notice the familiar green with which all wooden Kinetics were painted.

CONRAD PRESCHLEY

One of Conrad Preschley's first ads appeared in the July 1916 Diapason. *Despite the fact that he continued to advertise through the late 1930s, his sales were insignificant compared to the major blower manufacturers. Theatre organ builder William Wood claimed that the second blower ever installed on an American organ was in the 1895 4/43 Farrand & Votey in the Pabst Theatre, Milwaukee, Wisconsin, installed by a Mr. Preschley.*[1] *If this were actually Conrad Preschley, he is indeed an unsung pioneer in the annals of organ building.*

G. MEIDINGER & CO.

An organist in his spare time, G. Meidinger began manufacturing electric motors in 1900. He soon got an idea for applying one of his motors to power an organ, the name Meidinger eventually becoming known worldwide as a manufacturer of one of the quietest organ blowers available. According to U. P. Meidinger, grandson of the firm's founder, 200,000 Meidinger organ blowers have been built, a truly astonishing figure.[1]

The firm continues today as a family-owned company. U. P. Meidinger and his brother manage the main plant in Allschwil, Switzerland, a suburb of Basle, and an auxiliary plant in Saint-Louis, France is managed by their brother-in-law. Eighty people are employed in the Swiss plant and twenty more work at the French facility. Current products of the firm are specialty electric motors and a wide variety of air-handling machinery. Organ blowers account for around 10% of current production.[2]

On the next six pages is reproduced an extremely rare Meidinger catalog which sought American business in the early decades of this century. Meidinger sales in the United States were insignificant, however, until the 1950s.

Electrical Organ Blowing Equipments

Manufacturers

G. MEIDINGER & Co.

BASLE

(Switzerland)

Organ Blowers

General.

This pamphlet serves to give full particulars of our Electrically Driven Organ Blowers which are manufactured by us as a speciality.

It is now 15 years since we started this special line on a large scale, at a time when the blowers on the market were of simple construction, blowers which were arranged to provide the wind pressure for the organs through electrical motor drive, hydraulic or mechanical drive. We have carefully studied the construction of special blowers for Organ Work and have made an exhaustive series of tests and patterns enabling us to bring on to the market a Motor Driven Blower not only of excellent mechanical and electrical construction, but also one which is to all intents and purposes silent in operation.

Having manufactured all classes of blowers for many years, and being also laid out for the construction of all types of electrical machinery (up to the end of 1920 we have supplied machines to the number of 40,000 and in sizes up to 400 h. p.) we have the great advantage of being able to supply the combined sets made throughout in our own works.

We are in a position to provide our clients with the set actually needed for every particular requirement and have a great advantage over our competitors, who have to obtain motors from motor manufacturers (motors which are made without due regard to their special requirements as regards silent running etc.) whereas in our case both blower and motor are made at our works, a perfect combination in every way.

Blowers made by our competitors although equipped with mechanically and technically sound industrial motors, will soon prove unsatisfactory as these standard motors do not possess the necessary silent running properties for organ blowing equipments.

The noises which are inherent in standard industrial motors are transmitted to the blowers, the blower case forming a sound box. This will be noted particularly in rooms with good acoustic properties such as Concert Halls, Churches etc., and eventually the noise will become so pronounced that it will be unbearable.

We possess in our works not only every facility and modern device for the construction of technically up-to-date electric motors, but also the very modern and latest plants to produce the most efficient and best blowers.

Amongst this plant we mention specially our balancing test equipments enabling us to test every motor and blower individually as well as the combined sets; this method alone ensuring perfect balance and a silent running combination.

Advantages of Electric Organ Blowers.

The chief advantages of electrically driven Organ Blowers compared with the old methods of mechanical or hand driven equipments are the following:

1) *The Electrical Equipment is always ready for use.* The organist is able to play his organ without other assistance, a fact of special importance when the organ has to be played in the evenings for practice when often no help is available.
2) *Minimum space required and silent operation.* The high speed blower producing a constant and even wind pressure requires a much smaller space for equal output than the slow speed mechanical blower. The silent running of "Meidinger" Blowers has already been mentioned.
3) *Low cost of upkeep.* Our motors and blowers have been designed with a view to obtaining the highest possible efficiency so that running costs are reduced to an absolute minimum, and comparative tests with blowers of other makes will show a considerable advantage in our favour. Once the Set is installed the only attention it will require is an occasional filling of the bearings with oil.

Model design.

The perfection which we have obtained in the construction of these Electrically Driven Organ Blowers is proved by the fact that several of our competitors have since copied our designs and have used them as their own standard.

Guarantee as to output, power consumption etc.

All the outputs etc., mentioned in our offers or lists are based in accordance with the regulations of the various Engineering Associations and are guaranteed figures.

It is well known, however, that with different Organ Builders employing varying systems in the construction of their Instruments, the quantity of wind required for two Organs having the same number of stops etc., may differ, so that it is advisable for the Organ Builder to specify in each case the amount of wind required for his own Instrument. In any case we would recommend that a blower of ample capacity should always be chosen so as to ensure a sufficient supply of wind for "Full Organ", should the building get overheated or during prolonged periods of dry weather.

In order to determine the total number of stops on an organ it is only necessary to include octave couplers and not the ordinary Manual and Pedal couplers.

Those stops which are provided with Super- and Sub-octave couplers, have approximately double the wind consumption and must therefore be counted twice.

Standard types.

Our standard Blowers are arranged for pressures of 120, 140 and 160 m/m water gauge (i. e. $4^3/_4$", $5^1/_2$" and $6^1/_4$" W. G.), these pressures being measured at the fan outlets.

The standard speeds of our Blowers are 2850, 1430 and 930 r. p. m. corresponding to the usual speeds of 1, 2 or 3-phase alternating current motors on 50 period circuits, and the equipment for direct current circuits are normally arranged for the same speeds.

All standard types mentioned in our list are usually in course of construction and ready for quick delivery. Special Blowers can be made up to suit customers own requirements and will be quoted for on application.

Single and multi-stage blowers.

Our standard equipments for pressures of 120—160 m/m water gauge are built as single stage blowers, but for special cases such as for organs having a number of heavy stops, we also build double blowers such as shown in the adjoining illustration. With such a set, the larger blower provides the normal quantity of wind at 120, 140 or 160 m/m pressure, whilst the smaller blower furnishes the necessary additional wind at the requisite higher pressure for the heavy stops.

Although the efficiency of our blowers is very high, yet the use of a single stage, high pressure blower for organs with heavy stops would involve a waste of energy. In such cases double stage blowers would be more economical.

Electric motors.

All the motors which we manufacture are built in accordance with the regulations of the various Engineering Associations, and comply with the standard rules of the Supply Companies.

Our Direct Current Motors are designed with fixed brush positions between no load and full load and sparkless running is ensured at varying loads.

Our Single, Two or Three-phase A. C. Motors are free from magnetic hum. With Single-phase Motors only, we occasionally get a very slight hum, but in such cases we can reduce the hum to an absolute minimum by special arrangements on the motor and blower.

Starting apparatus.

We have taken special care in the design and manufacture of the necessary starting and control gear for our organ blowers. The control gear is of three different types:

1) *Hand Operated Starters.* With these starters the motors are started up by slowly moving a small handle. Amongst these starters are the ordinary starting resistances for Direct Current Motors, or similar starters with slow motion device; the latter enforcing slow starting of the motor.
2) *Push Button Control.* This consists of a starter which is operated from a push button box fitted on the console. To start up the blower the organist has only to press a button, a second press sufficing to stop the equipment.
3) *Automatic Starters.* These consist of starting resistance operated by bellows. With this apparatus the organist operates a switch fixed near the console and all other operations are made automatically with the starter.

The same type of control is used for the blowers fitted with Single, Two or Three-phase Alternating Current Motors.

The method of control of this type of apparatus is so simple that it is impossible to make mistakes even if the starting is left to unskilled hands such as pupils in Colleges, Churches, Schools etc.

Enquiry Forms.

For the guidance and service of our clients, and to ensure that the enquiries and orders for Organ Blowers are given with all the desired information as regards electrical and technical details, we have prepared special forms for the equipments (see page 13—15). We have stated below the important questions relating to an order or enquiry, and if these points are answered we shall in almost all cases be in a position to offer you our extensive experience and to put forward suitable equipments for every individual requirement.

We would therefore ask all our clients or interested firms to answer all these questions, whether for enquiries or orders, as it is obvious that no blower can be taken in hand until all details have been settled.

Notice as to order Forms.

General.

For every order the following information is required:

1) The wind volume in cubic metres or cubic feet required per minute; if this is not obtainable the number of speaking stops and whether the organ has "Pneumatic" or "Tracker" action.
2) The wind pressure required at the blower outlet in m/m or inches water gauge. Information should also be given as to whether the blower will be fixed near the bellows or some distance away from same, and in the latter case

the approximate length of the trunking with the number of bends etc. This would enable us to calculate approximately the loss of pressure in the trunking and to decide the wind pressure required from the blower.

3) The type of housing and position of blower outlet. As will be seen from the silhouettes on page 14 we have 8 standard patterns and it will suffice if the pattern number is stated.

4) The voltage of the electric supply available and whether Direct Current or 1, 2 or 3 phase Alternating Current and if Alternating Current the periodicity of the supply.

a) Direct Current Supplies.

Direct Current Supplies are usually distributed by neans of the 3-wire system where between the two outer wires the double voltage, and between one outer and one middle wire the lower voltage is obtained e. g. 440 volts and 220 volts.

According to general practice motors over 1 H. P. are connected on to the higher voltage whilst smaller motors are connected on to the lower voltage. For safety and other reasons it is advisable to connect the motors wherever possible on to the lower voltage.

For Organ Blowers equipped with Direct Current motors we can supply hand operated starters or automatic starters.

In the case of the hand operated starter, the organist has to switch on the motor by pushing the handle from stop to stop until the motor reaches full speed.

With the automatic starter the organist closes a D. P. switch or presses a push button switch which operates the starter fixed on the bellows, and to stop the D. P. switch is opened or the "stop" push-button switch is pressed.

b) Single, Two & Three-phase A. C. Supplies.

Single, Two and Three-phase Alternating Current Motors are chiefly made in two types i. e. motors with squirrel cage rotors and motors with slipring rotors.

The motors with squirrel cage rotors are the more simple and cheaper type but have the disadvantage that with them it is impossible to have speed regulation, and when starting these motors a current rush is caused which at times might be objectionable, especially where such motors are connected on the same circuit as the lights.

A. C. Motors with squirrel cage rotors are therefore only used up to certain sizes and this size depends on the conditions of the Supply Company concerned. For larger motors and where speed regulation is required slipring motors are used. Different methods are employed in the starting of squirrel cage or slipring motors.

For example to start a three-phase squirrel cage A. C. motor if is sufficient to close a 3-pole switch whilst to start a 3-phase slipring motor one has to close a 3-pole switch for the stator circuits and in addition operate a rotor starting resistance step by step until the motor reaches full speed.

Blowers with three-phase A. C. squirrel cage motors.

In addition to the particulars mentioned under 1—4 the following details should be stated:

May the motor be started by means of a 3-pole switch or has the motor to be started by a "Star-delta" starter, and if the latter case has this starter to be with automatic no-volt release as required by some Supply Companies.

In the case of the 3-pole starting switch there are two types in use viz:

One type with quick break action and
One type with slow break action.

The quick break switch is specially suitable for higher voltages say 400/500 volts, as through quick action on the break, the arcing caused by switching off is reduced to a minimum. This switch has however the disadvantage that when switched off it produces an objectionable noise which may be specially objectionable in Churches where even the smallest noise is undesirable.

Blowers with three-phase A. C. slipring motors.

In addition to the particulars mentioned under 1—4 the following details should be stated:

Whether an ordinary 3-pole switch can be used to control the motor.

A resistance will be required in addition to start the motor and it should be stated whether this must be:

An ordinary plain rotor starter, or
A starter with speed regulation, or
A starter with automatic control.

Certain Supply Companies also demand the use of rotor starters with automatic no-volts and over-load releases. If this applies notice must be given with enquiry or order.

Two-phase A. C. Motors.

For Blowers fitted with two-phase motors the same conditions apply as mentioned for the three-phase motors.

When ordering such equipments it must however be stated whether the two-phase supply available is on the 3-wire or 4-wire system; this information can be obtained from the Supply Company.

Single-phase A. C. supplies.

Organ Blowers with single-phase motors are chiefly supplied with squirrel cage motors. In some cases such as where the Supply Companies make special conditions as to the starting current etc., we are prepared to submit special quotations according to the individual requirements.

Single-phase Motors are started by two operations, the first operation bringing the motor up to its speed and the second operation placing the starting apparatus into the running position.

This starting by two operations is not always desirable for the organist, and we have therefore designed in addition to the ordinary hand operated starters an automatic type of starter operated by the action of the bellows. All that is necessary to start the motor is to close a D. P. switch when the blower will be set in operation, and when the switch is opened the motor stops.

In addition to the general details mentioned under 1—4 the following particulars should be stated:

Is a hand-operated starter required or is the automatic type (as described above) preferred?

Certain Supply Companies make special conditions as to the starting apparatus for single-phase motors such as limiting the amount of starting current per stop and conditions as to automatic features (no-volts and over-load releases) on the starters. For such cases we are prepared to quote specially on receipt off full information.

Silencers.

In some cases, depending on the position of the blower, it may be found necessary to instal a silencer.

It is not possible to produce a high pressure Blower which is perfectly silent in the widest sense of the word, for the boss of the fan revolves in the free air on the inlet side and this together with the high velocity of the blades through the air sets up a certain amount of whirring noise. This will be more pronounced and therefore the most objectionable when no tune is being played, for whilst the organ is being played even the softest notes will suffice to drown the slight noise of the blower.

To overcome this small difficulty we have designed a silencer, in a case, which can be fitted to the blower inlet, and which is provided with a very ingenious system of shutters, shutting off the outside air and so arranged that it only opens to such an extent as the actual wind consumption from the blower demands.

Dynamos for automatic action.

Recent experience has clearly proved the numerous advantages of electric automatic action and in addition to our Organ Blowers we also supply the special dynamos required for this work.

In order that the necessary current for the action may always be available when required, we can supply on our Electric Blowers, a small dynamo direct coupled to the main motor. These small dynamos are particularly essential where only Alternating Current — either 1, 2 or 3 phase — is available for operating the blower, since the current required for operating the action must always be low voltage, direct current.

We have developed a type of dynamo for this work, which by reason of its special windings, will generate its current at a constant voltage, irrespective of the amount of current being consumed (limited of course to the output of the machine) thus ensuring perfect operation of the action.

It is not advisable to instal blower sets which are fitted with such a dynamo in the organ chamber itself as seeing that such a set would have two electrical machines instead of one as on our standard sets, it is impossible for us to definitely guarantee perfect silence in these cases.

In view of the many different sizes of dynamos required, it will be readily appreciated that to produce a price list of our complete range of electric blowers combined with the complete range of action dynamos would be practically impossible, but we are prepared to submit special quotations for these sets on receipt of particulars.

In addition to such equipments comprising blower, main motor and action dynamo, we also build standard converter sets which in the case of Direct Current Supplies consist of a single machine Rotary Converter (vide illustration page 11), transforming the higher line voltage to the lower voltage for the action, and in the case of Alternating Current Supplies they consist of a two machine motor generator set (vide illustration page 10) with 1, 2 or 3 phase motor direct coupled to a small low voltage dynamo.

Regulating, throttle and non-return valves.

In order to prevent the accumulated wind in the bellows from returning through the trunking and blower to the open air when the blower is stopped, we can supply our organ blowers with non-return valves, which can serve at the same time as Regulating or Throttle Valves.

In general, however, we recommend the Electric Automatic Control of the Blower, as this method is not only simpler in operation but it is more economical than the control with hand-operated starters and throttle valves.

Nevertheless, we have prepared a list of standard sized valves and leather coupling sleeves which should be used for connecting the blower to the trunk system, the leather couplers being so designed as to prevent the transmission to the instrument of any vibration which might arise from the blower.

Conclusion.

If you are interested in our Organ Blowers and will fill up the enquiry form enclosed we will send you immediately our detailed offer for the most suitable equipment.

Extract of Reference List of Cathedrals, Churches and other Institutions where our Electrical Blowing Equipments are installed:

Worcester	Stanbrook Abbey
Rome	Sua Santita Papa Pio X
″	Collegio di San Anselmo, Monte Aventino
Firenze	San Firenze
Azpeitia	Colegio de P. P. Jesuitas de Loyola
Barcelona	Iglesia parroquial de San Pedra de las Puellas
Bilbao	″ ″ de San Nicolas
San Sebastian	″ de los Rdos. Padres Carmelitas
Valladolid	Catedral
Aix (Bouches du Rhône)	St. Jean de Malte
Aix en Province	La Madeleine
Arras	Cathédrale
″	Grand Séminaire d'Arras
Besançon	Cathédrale de Besançon
″	Cathédrale Ste. Madeleine
Bordeaux	Ste. Geneviève
Bourg	Cathédrale
Cannes	Dame d'Espérance
Clermont	Cathédrale
Le Hâvre	St. François
″	Notre-Dame
Lyons	Cathédrale St. Jean
″	St. Nizier
Marseilles	Notre-Dame du Mont Carmel
″	St. Vincent
″	St. Pierre, St. Paul
Montbéliard	Cathédrale
Nice	Notre-Dame
″	St. Joseph
Paris	St. Jean d'Evangéliste
″	Ste. Elisabeth
Perpignan	Cathédrale
Rouen	Sacré-Cœur
Soissons (Aisne)	Cathédrale
Strasbourg	″
Toulon	″
Toulouse	Notre-Dame de Tours
Antwerp	Cathédrale
Brussels	Synagogue
″	Notre-Dame de l'Annonciation
Ghent	Cathédrale
Laeken	Eglise Royale de Notre-Dame
Liège	St. Vincent
″	Ste. Marie
Louvain	Collège des Jésuites St. Jean Berchmans
Malines	Cathédrale
Maredsous (Namur)	Couvent de St. Benoît
Namur	Notre-Dame
Amsterdam	H. Rozenkranskerk
″	Konservatorium
Arnhem	Luthersche Kerk
Gouda	Groote of St. Janskerk
s'Gravenhage	Duinoordkerk
s'Hertogenbosch	Kathedraal St. Jan
Maastricht	Eerwarde Zusters v. d. H. Carolus Borromeus, Onder de Bogen 14
Nijmegen	R. K. Kerle van den H. Augustinus
″	St. Josephkerk
Utrecht	Engelsche Kerk

IRA H. SPENCER, PRESIDENT. S. E. PHILLIPS, SECRETARY. H. H. RICHARDSON, TREASURER.

THE SPENCER TURBINE CO.

TURBINE BLOWERS AND EXHAUSTERS

ORGAN POWER APPARATUS "ORGOBLO" VACUUM CLEANING APPARATUS

HARTFORD, CONN., U.S.A.,

Ira Spencer didn't invent the organ blower but he might as well have! The company he founded became the dominant force in the industry, selling 50% more blowers than their nearest competitor, Kinetic. It all began in 1892 when Ira Spencer, a lad of 18, was employed as a clerk by a Hartford grocer. He augmented his income by pumping the organ at a local church. Having an inventive mind, he decided to try rigging up a water-powered hydraulic piston to do the work for him. So successful was his experiment that the church fired him! Soon he established a business of supplying these water motors to churches free of charge, the churches merely giving him half of what they saved in labor costs.[1 2]

In 1895 Mr. Spencer officially organized the Spencer Motor Company whose name was later changed to the Organ Power Company. In addition to water motors for pumping organs, he experimented with differential duplex rotary motors and with piston blowers. These were rapidly superseded by the idea of the multiple fan blower. Mr. Spencer's first blower was developed in 1904 and had a wooden case with laminated wooden blades. Next came the steel cased blower with wooden blades and finally the all steel Orgoblo, the most reliable blower ever built.[3 4]

An outgrowth of the organ blower was the idea for a central vacuum cleaning system which Mr. Spencer developed in 1905. In 1907 he organized the Spencer Turbine Cleaner Company and it flourished as did the Organ Power Company. These two companies were merged in 1918 to become the Spencer Turbine Company. The firm continues to flourish in the 1980s with nearly 300 employees. 37,000 organ blowers bearing the Spencer nameplate have been built to date although organ equipment now represents only a fraction of one percent of the firm's current business.[5]

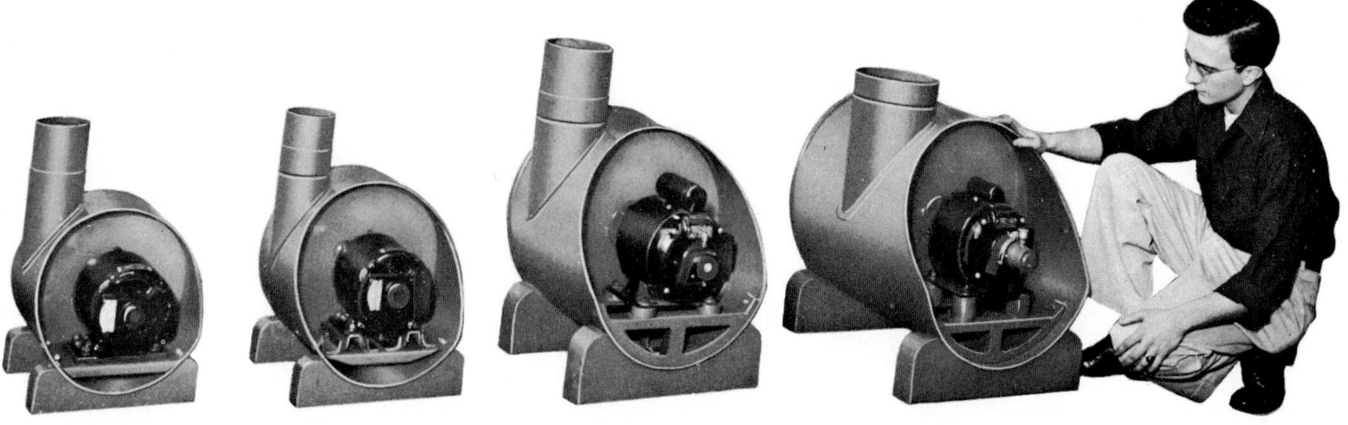

Orgoblo Juniors are built in a number of sizes to handle reed organs and small pipe organs. The Estey company purchased them by the hundreds for their reed organs.

The Steel "Orgoblo"

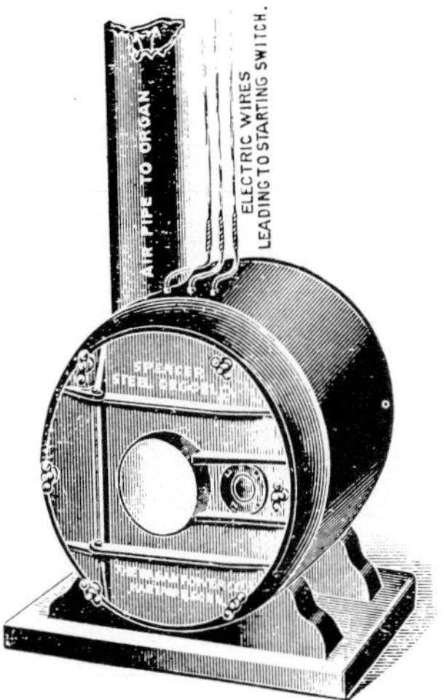

is in a class by itself in that it is the only metal-constructed, highly-efficient, silent, turbine organ blower on the market. Made by a concern of over seventeen years' experience in the organ-blowing specialty. Over 2,000 sold in the past five years, operating instruments from the smallest reed organs to the largest, high-pressure pipe organs in the world.

The Organ Power Company
HARTFORD, CONN.

This ad in the February 1911 Diapason *depicts an early style of Orgoblo in which the motor was entirely enclosed by the outside steel casing.*

Ira Hobart Spencer (1873-1928)

What appears to be a tiny Orgoblo is actually a Spencer portable vacuum cleaner in use in the Indiana Theatre, Indianapolis, Indiana.

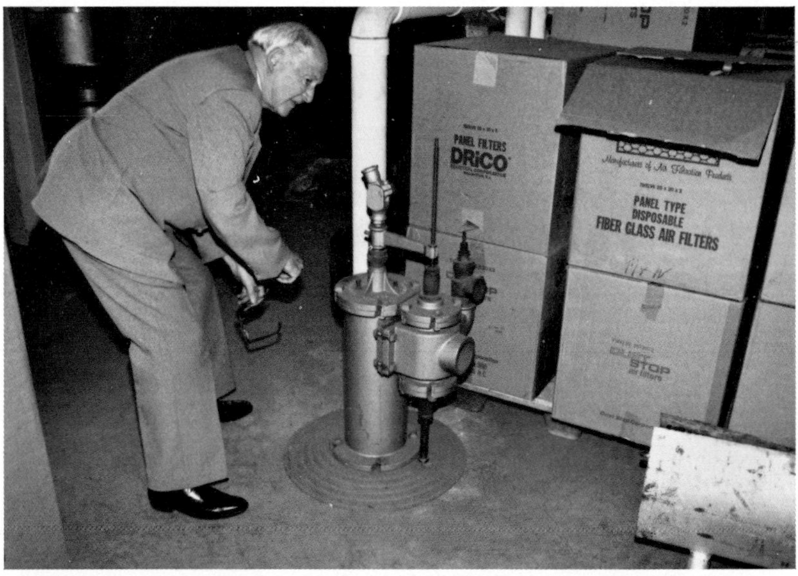

Lester C. Smith examines an original Spencer water motor in a storage area in the Spencer factory. Mr. Smith joined the company in 1925 and quickly became a protege of Ira Spencer. He served as president from 1957 to 1971, having previously been vice president in charge of engineering.

Spencer built the largest organ blower in the world in 1929 to power the 6/51 Barton in the Chicago Stadium. It is 5′ in diameter and over 12′ long. Seven stages each having a 45″ diameter fan culminate in a 28″ diameter wind outlet supplying 25″ pressure; two additional stages with 48″ diameter fans deliver 35″ pressure to the 10″ diameter high pressure outlet. The slow speed of 900 RPM is maintained by a General Electric synchronous motor whose field is powered by a direct-connected DC exciter. This behemoth has a nominal rating of 9300 cubic feet per minute but it delivered 13,600 cubic feet when actually tested.

In the early 1930s Spencer introduced their "air flow regulators," shown here in use on a two-pressure Orgoblo. These regulators perform essentially the same functions as conventional static reservoirs but are less expensive and much easier to install.

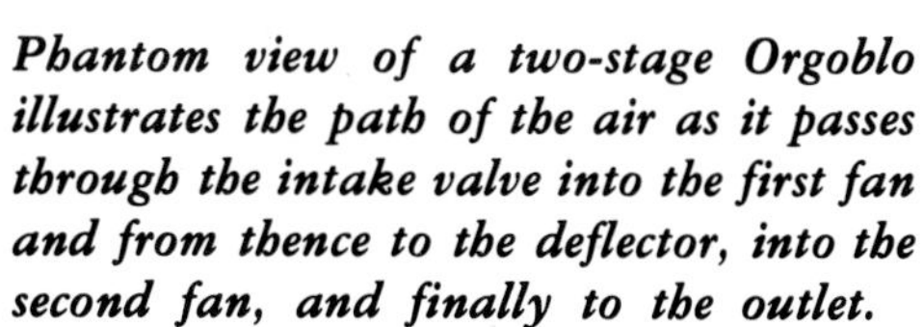

Phantom view of a two-stage Orgoblo illustrates the path of the air as it passes through the intake valve into the first fan and from thence to the deflector, into the second fan, and finally to the outlet.

A fascinating Spencer catalog c. 1922 is reproduced on this and the following seven pages. The hearts of all Flash Gordon fans will be delighted by the wonderful photographs of the Spencer testing department! The list of Orgoblos then in use and the testimonials read like a Who's Who *of the organ industry. Especially interesting are testimonials from M. P. Moller and Robert Hope-Jones, whose respective companies purchased most of their blowers from the rival Kinetic Engineering Company.*

Organ Power

The Spencer Steel Orgoblo

The Spencer Turbine Co.
Hartford, Conn.

The Spencer Turbine Company

Manufacture Three Specialties

The Spencer Turbine Vacuum Cleaning Systems
The Spencer Turbo Compressor
The Spencer Steel "Orgoblo"

each of which is the acknowledged leader in its own field.

For each equipment we have tried to produce not the cheapest, but the *best* for its purpose.

With what success, ASK THE USERS, from whom we have received thousands of repeat orders.

From a glance at the history of the "ORGOBLO," it will be seen that in the past thirty years the Spencer organ blowing apparatus has been through many stages of development, including rotary and reciprocating water motors, electric blowers with: first, wood box construction; second, wood and metal box construction and third, cylindrical metal construction, marking the highest development yet reached in organ blowing apparatus in the present open type, built-in-motor, cylindrical steel "ORGOBLO," the subject of this catalogue.

There can be only one reason for selling more organ blowing apparatus than all the rest of the concerns in this specialty put together, i.e., *merit*, backed by a broad, generous guarantee.

The STEEL ORGOBLO is in a class by itself in that it is the only organ blower on the market in which the air has a correctly designed continuous passage throughout the machine, thereby avoiding the losses incident to stopping and starting the air between stages and also the only organ blower in which the loss by fan side leakage has been entirely overcome.

The above characteristics make the "ORGOBLO" nearer noiseless under the same conditions than any other organ blower made, as well as raising the efficiency so as to make them more economical to operate than others, the "ORGOBLO" requiring less current as the organ is played lighter.

We are such large purchasers of motors

(to the value of over $250,000.00 per year) that the electric motor manufacturers take great pains to produce for us motors with characteristics specially suited to organ blowing, the value of which cannot be over-estimated.

If there is any class of apparatus that needs to be reduced to the highest degree of simplicity, it is organ blowing machinery. Our Standard, built-in-motor, one, two and three stage "ORGOBLOS" are as simple as a desk fan, but worked out and manufactured with great care.

We have a very complete equipment of electrical and pneumatic instruments (see pages 18 19 and 20) by which every "ORGOBLO" is given a careful test, and this test is recorded and approved before machine is passed for shipment. Errors of one or two thousandths of an inch in some parts of the "ORGOBLO" are sufficient cause for rejection by the tester.

SPECIAL "ORGOBLOS"

Years of experience have shown that our line of Standard Compound "ORGOBLOS" meet nine-tenths of the organ blowing requirements better than any other type, and at a moderate cost.

Requirements not covered by our Standard Compound type we have had a very wide experience in handling with our special outfits, which are without exception the quietest organ blowers in the world.

When investigating organ blowers, glittering generalities as to excellence should be reduced to the training and experience in pneumatic engineering back of the design and sound facts of actual mechanical construction.

The Scientific design of the "ORGOBLO" makes it more compact for the same duty than any other organ blower.

PATENTS

We have a large number of patents, the result of over thirty years of careful study and experiment in the organ blowing specialty. We shall be obliged to prosecute any one who persists in infringing.

Partial List of "Orgoblos", 7½ H. P. and Larger, Representing Over Ninety Per Cent. of the Largest and Finest American Organs.

	H.P.
Church of the Advent, Birmingham, Ala.	15
First Baptist Church, Birmingham, Ala.	15
Strand Theatre, Montgomery, Ala.	10
G. A. Mauk, Phoenix, Arizona	7½
First Baptist Church, Jonesboro, Arkansas	10
Kinema Theatre, Fresno, California	7½
Auditorium, Los Angeles, California	15
Misson Theatre, Los Angeles, California	7½
Pantages Theatre, Los Angeles, California	7½
Strand Theatre, Los Angeles, California	7½
Pantages Theatre, Los Angeles, California	10
Crescent Theatre, Los Angeles, California	7½
First M. E. Church, Los Angeles, California	15
Kinema Theatre, Los Angeles, California	30
Chaffey Union High School, Ontario, California	10
Orange Union High School, Orange California	7½
First Presbyterian Church, Pasadena California	7½
Jensen Theatre, Pasadena, California	7½
Unitarian Church, San Francisco, California	7½
New California Theatre, San Francisco, California	30
Bohemian Grove, San Francisco, California	7½
City Auditorium, San Francisco, California	20
City Auditorium, San Francisco, California	20
Pantages Theatre, San Francisco, California	10
New Castro Theatre, San Francisco, California	7½
Strand Theatre, San Francisco, California	10
Liberty Theatre, San Jose, California	10
Dodson Theatre, San Pedro, California	7½
Univ. of Southern California, Van Nuys, California	25
Robert-Morton Company, Van Nuys, California	7½
Macky Auditorium, Boulder, Colorado	20
Auditorium, Denver, Colorado	35
Colorado Theatre Company, Denver, Colorado	15
American Theatre, Denver, Colorado	15
Memorial Hall, Pueblo, Colorado	30
Poli's Theatre, Bridgeport, Conn.	7½
Trinity Church, Hartford, Conn.	7½
Center Cong. Church, Hartford, Conn.	10
Asylum Hill Cong. Church, Hartford, Conn.	10
Wesleyan College Chapel, Middletown, Conn.	7½
South Cong. Church, New Britain, Conn.	15
Yale University, New Haven, Conn.	15
Gordon's Film De Luxe Theatre, New Haven, Conn.	7½
Woolsey Hall, New Haven, Conn.	20
St. James Church, New London, Conn.	10
St. John's Church, Stamford, Conn.	7½

	H.P.
Palace Theatre, Waterbury, Conn.	7½
Church of the Epiphany, Washington, D. C.	7½
First Cong. Church, Washington, D. C.	15
Central Theatre, Washington, D. C.	10
All Soul's Church, Washington, D. C.	10
Joseph Riter, Palm Beach, Florida	7½
Atlanta Auditorium, Atlanta, Ga.	20
Baptist Tabernacle, Atlanta, Ga.	15
First Presbyterian Church, Atlanta, Ga.	7½
St. Luke's P. E. Church, Atlanta, Ga.	7½
Howard Theatre, Atlanta, Ga.	15
Lutheran Church of the Ascension, Savannah, Ga.	7½
Independent Presbyterian Church, Savannah, Ga.	7½
First Baptist Church, Savannah, Ga.	7½
St. John's Church, Savannah, Ga.	7½
St. Peter's Church, Belleville, Illinois	7½
Holy Family R. C. Church, Chicago, Illinois	10
First Presbyterian Church, Chicago, Illinois	15
Tivoli Theatre, Chicago, Illinois	10
Capitol Theatre, Chicago, Illinois	7½
St. Mary of the Angel's Church, Chicago, Illinois	15
St. Hyacinth's R. C. Church, Chicago, Illinois	10
Roosevelt Theatre, Chicago, Illinois	15
Tenth Church of Christ Scientist, Chicago, Illinois	7½
Francis Neilson, Chicago, Illinois	7½
Tivoli Theatre, Chicago, Illinois	7½
Fifth Church of Christ Scientist, Chicago, Illinois	7½
Ninth Church of Christ Scientist, Chicago, Illinois	7½
Eleventh Church of Christ Scientist, Chicago, Illinois	7½
New Kimball Recital Hall, Chicago, Illinois	15
Woodlawn Theatre, Chicago, Illinois	7½
Medinah Temple, Chicago, Illinois	20
Medinah Temple, Chicago, Illinois	7½
St. James' Church, Chicago, Illinois	10
St. Paul's P. E. Church, Chicago, Illinois	7½
Kenwood Evan. Church, Chicago, Illinois	7½
Fourth Presbyterian Church, Chicago, Illinois	15
Hyde Park Baptist Church, Chicago, Illinois	7½
St. Patrick's Church, Chicago, Illinois	7½
Rev. A. L. Bergeron, Chicago, Illinois	7½
St. Luke's Episcopal Church, Evanston, Illinois	20
First Cong. Church, Oak Park, Illinois	7½
First Cong. Church, Oak Park, Illinois	15
First Baptist Church, Oak Park, Illinois	10
University of Illinois, Urbana, Illinois	15
First Presbyterian Church, Franklin, Indiana	7½
Robert's Park Methodist Church, Indianapolis, Ind.	7½
Blackstone Theatre, South Bend, Indiana	7½
Palace Theatre, South Bend, Indiana	7½
Liberty Theatre, Council Bluffs, Iowa	7½
University Church, Des Moines, Iowa	7½
Des Moines Theatre, Des Moines, Iowa	7½
Sacred Heart R. C. Church, Dubuque, Iowa	7½

	H.P.
First Baptist Church, Sioux City, Iowa	7½
First Methodist Church, Topeka, Kansas	7½
Liberty Theatre, Covington, Kentucky	7½
St. Alphonsus Church, New Orleans, La.	7½
St. Mark's Episcopal Church, Shreveport, La.	10
City Hall Auditorium, Portland, Me.	30
Rivoli Theatre, Baltimore, Md.	7½
St. Paul's P. E. Church, Baltimore, Md.	7½
Boulevard Theatre, Baltimore, Md.	7½
Ware Theatre, Beverly, Mass.	7½
New England Conservatory of Music, Boston, Mass.	15
Edwin Farnham Green, Boston, Mass.	7½
Gordon Olympia Theatre, Boston, Mass.	7½
Phineas W. Sprague, Boston, Mass.	7½
Arlington St. Church, Boston, Mass.	7½
King's Chapel, Boston, Mass.	7½
Cathedral of Holy Cross, Boston, Mass.	7½
Harvard Club, Boston, Mass.	15
Modern Theatre, Boston, Mass.	7½
South Cong. Church, Boston, Mass.	7½
Beacon Theatre, Boston, Mass.	7½
Shawmut Theatre, Boston, Mass.	7½
Church of All Nations, Boston, Mass.	7½
Mr. E. B. Dane, Brookline, Mass.	7½
Mrs. R. W. Sears, Brookline, Mass.	7½
Appleton Chapel Harvard Univ., Boston, Mass.	15
First Cong. Church, Fall River, Mass.	7½
First Cong. Church, Great Barrington, Mass.	7½
St. James' P. E. Church, Great Barrington, Mass.	7½
Second Cong. Church, Holyoke, Mass.	7½
Victory Theatre, Holyoke, Mass.	7½
Mt. Holyoke College, Holyoke, Mass.	7½
First Cong. Church, Holyoke, Mass.	7½
Strand Theatre, Lowell, Mass.	10
All Soul's Unitarian Church, Lowell, Mass.	7½
Lowell Memorial Auditorium, Lowell, Mass.	10
First U. B. Church, Lynn, Mass.	7½
Gordon's Olympia Theatre, Lynn, Mass.	7½
First M. E. Church, Lynn, Mass.	7½
Soldiers and Sailors Mem. Bldg., Melrose, Mass.	20
St. Anthony's Church, New Bedford, Mass.	7½
Gordon Theatre, New Bedford, Mass.	7½
Smith College, Northampton, Mass.	15
First Cong. Church, Pittsfield, Mass.	15
Federal Theatre, Salem, Mass.	7½
St. Mark's School, Southborough, Mass.	7½
Notre Dame Church, Southbridge, Mass.	7½
Trinity M. E. Church, Springfield, Mass.	10
Christ Church, Springfield, Mass.	10
First Church, Springfield, Mass.	10
Bijou Theatre, Springfield, Mass.	7½
Municipal Building, Springfield, Mass.	25
Houghton Mem.Chapel,Wellesley Col., Wellesley,Mass.	7½

	H.P.
Second Cong. Church, West Newton, Mass.	7½
Williams College, Williamstown, Mass.	15
Plymouth Cong. Church, Worcester, Mass.	10
Piedmont Cong. Church, Worcester, Mass.	10
Mechanics Hall, Worcester, Mass.	7½
First Cong. Church, Ann Arbor, Mich.	7½
Henry Ford's Residence, Dearborn, Mich.	7½
Majestic Theatre, Detroit, Mich.	7½
Wesley M. E. Church, Detroit, Mich.	7½
St. Paul's Cathedral, Detroit, Mich.	10
Capitol Theatre, Detroit, Mich.	15
Third Church of Christ Scientist, Detroit, Mich.	7½
Fort St. Presbyterian Church, Detroit, Mich.	7½
Regent Theatre, Detroit, Mich.	10
Central Methodist Church, Detroit, Mich.	15
First Universalist Church, Detroit, Mich.	10
First Church of Christ Scientist, Detroit, Mich.	7½
Madison Theatre, Detroit, Mich.	10
St. Mark's Church, Grand Rapids, Mich.	7½
St. Andrew's Cathedral, Grand Rapids, Mich.	7½
Auditorium, Saginaw, Mich.	10
Rex Theatre, Duluth, Minnesota	7½
Plymouth Cong. Church, Duluth, Minnesota	7½
First Pres. Church, Duluth, Minnesota	7½
Plymouth Church, Minneapolis, Minnesota	7½
Hannepin Avenue M. E. Church, Minneapolis, Minn.	15
State Theatre, Minneapolis, Minn.	10
Blue Mouse Theatre, Minneapolis, Minn.	10
Pantages Theatre, Minneapolis, Minn.	10
Carleton College, Northfield, Minn.	10
House of Hope, Saint Paul, Minn.	10
Capitol Theatre, Saint Paul, Minn.	7½
Municipal Auditorium, Saint Paul, Minn.	25
Church of St. John the Evangelist, Saint Paul, Minn.	7½
Hibbing High School, Hibbing, Minn.	10
Central M. E. Church, Winona, Minn.	7½
Linwood Pres. Church, Kansas City, Missouri	7½
Grand Avenue M. E. Church, Kansas City, Mo.	15
Independence Ave. M. E. Church, Kansas City, Mo.	15
Temple Be Nai Juhudah, Kansas City, Mo.	7½
Liberty Theatre, Kansas City, Mo.	7½
Newman Theatre, Kansas City, Mo.	15
First Church of Christ Scientist, Kansas City, Mo.	7½
Pantages Theatre, Kansas City, Mo.	10
Westminister Pres. Church, St. Louis, Mo.	7½
Christ Church Cathedral, St. Louis, Mo.	15
St. Peter's Church, St. Louis, Mo.	7½
Temple Shaer Emeth, St. Louis, Mo.	7½
Third Baptist Church, St. Louis, Mo.	15
First Baptist Church, Omaha, Nebraska	7½
First Presbyterian Church, Omaha, Nebraska	7½
Sun Theatre, Omaha, Nebraska	7½
First Cong. Church, Omaha, Nebraska	7½

	H.P.
John Ringling, Alpine, N. J.	7½
First M. E. Church, Asbury Park, N. J.	7½
St. John's P. E. Church, Jersey City, N. J.	7½
Church of the Divine Paternity, Jersey City, N. J.	7½
Lawrenceville School, Edith Memorial Chapel, Lawrenceville, N. J.	7½
First Cong. Church, Montclair, N. J.	15
Church of the Immaculate Conception, Montclair, N. J.	7½
Central Presbyterian Church, Montclair, N. J.	7½
St. Peter's Church, Morristown, N. J.	7½
Church of the Redeemer, Morristown, N. J.	7½
Peddie Memorial Church, Newark, N. J.	7½
Temple B' Nai Jeshurun, Newark, N. J.	7½
Parks' Presbyterian Church, Newark, N. J.	7½
Naomi Investment Co.'s Theatre, Newark, N. J.	7½
Center Amusement Co., Newark, N. J.	7½
First Presbyterian Church, Newark, N. J.	7½
Grace P. E. Church, Orange, N. J.	20
Grace P. E. Church, Orange, N. J.	20
Church of the Redeemer, Paterson, N. J.	10
Princeton University, Princeton, N. J.	7½
Trinity Church, Princeton, N. J.	7½
Christian Cong. Church, Upper Montclair, N. J.	7½
Dartmouth College, Hanover, N. H.	7½
St. Peter's Church, Albany, N. Y.	15
First Presbyterian Church, Auburn, N. Y.	7½
Strand Theatre, Brooklyn, N. Y.	7½
Strand Theatre, Brooklyn, N. Y.	7½
St. Agnes' Church, Brooklyn, N. Y.	7½
Church of the Messiah, Brooklyn, N. Y.	7½
Plymouth Church, Brooklyn, N. Y.	10
Tompkins Avenue Cong. Church, Brooklyn, N. Y.	13
Central Cong. Church, Brooklyn, N. Y.	15
St. John's Chapel, Brooklyn, N. Y.	7½
Central Presbyterian Church, Brooklyn, N. Y.	7½
Westminster Presbyterian Church, Buffalo, N. Y.	10
Central M. E. Church, Buffalo, N. Y.	15
Hotel Statler, Buffalo, N. Y.	20
Hotel Statler, Buffalo, N. Y., Dining Room	7½
Hotel Statler, Buffalo, N. Y., Ball Room	7½
First Presbyterian Church, Buffalo, N. Y.	7½
Trinity P. E. Church, Buffalo, N. Y.	7½
St. Joseph's Church, Buffalo, N. Y.	7½
Chautauqua Institute, Chatauqua, N. Y.	10
Central Rural School, Chazy, N. Y.	7½
Palace Theatre, Corona, N. Y.	7½
Park Church, Elmira, N. Y.	7½
St. George's Episcopal Church, Flushing, N. Y.	7½
Forest Theatre, Forest Hills, L. I., N. Y.	7½
Colgate University, Hamilton, N. Y.	7½
Cornell University, Ithaca, N. Y.	20
Cornell University, Ithaca, N. Y.	7½
First M. E. Church, Mt. Vernon, N. Y.	7½

	H.P.
Third Church of Christ Scientist, New York City	15
Tivoli Theatre, New York City	7½
Fifth Church of Christ Scientist, New York City	15
Pennsylvania Hotel, New York City	10
Rialto Theatre, New York City	10
Congregational Temple Israel, New York City	7½
Elks Lodge, New York City	12½
Capitol Theatre, New York City	15
Capitol Theatre, New York City	15
All Angels' Church, New York City	10
John Wanamaker, New York City	25
John Wanamaker, New York City	40
First Presbyterian Church, New York City	20
Carnegie Hall, New York City	7½
Strand Theatre, New York City	15
Second Church of Christ Scientist, New York City	10
Rivoli Theatre, New York City	15
Rivoli Theatre, New York City	15
Brick Presbyterian Church, New York City	30
Grace Chapel, New York City	10
St. Bartholomew's Church, New York City	10
Central Presbyterian Church, New York City	7½
Church of the Epiphany, New York City	7½
Lennox Avenue Universal Church, New York City	7½
Society for Ethical Culture, New York City	10
Union Theological Seminary, New York City	7½
St. Luke's Church, New York City	10
St. John The Divine Cathedral, New York City	15
New Amsterdam Theatre, New York City	7½
Church of the Messiah, New York City	7½
Church of the Ascension, New York City	7½
Grace Church, New York City	15
Broadway Presbyterian Church, New York City	7½
Marvin Theatre, New York City	7½
Fifth Ave. Presbyterian Church, New York City	20
St. John the Divine, Synod Hall, New York City	7½
St. Thomas Church, New York City	20
Chapel of the Intercession, New York City	10
Holy Trinity Church, New York City	7½
Hotel Astor, New York City	20
St. James' Church, New York City	13
St. Patrick's Cathedral, New York City	10
College of the City of New York, New York City	20
Columbia Univ. St. Paul's Chapel, New York City	10
Broadway Tabernacle, New York City	15
John Wanamaker Hall, New York City	15
John Wanamaker Hall, New York City, Egyptian Hall	10
First Presbyterian Church, New York City	7½
State Normal and Training School, Pottsdam, N. Y.	7½
Vassar College, Poughkeepsie, N. Y.	7½
Church of the Messiah, Rhinebeck Station, N. Y.	7½
First Church of Christ Scientist, Rochester, N. Y.	7½

	H.P.
Central Presbyterian Church, Rochester, N. Y.	10
Eastman School of Music, Rochester, N. Y.	30
Eastman School of Music, Rochester, N. Y.	40
Eastman School of Music, Rochester, N. Y.	40
Randall Memorial Chapel, Sailors Snug Harbor, N.Y.	7½
First M. E. Church, Saratoga Springs, N. Y.	7½
Bethesda Church, Saratoga Springs, N. Y.	15
St. Paul's P. E. Church, Syracuse, N. Y.	7½
First M. E. Church, Syracuse, N. Y.	7½
Syracuse University, Syracuse, N. Y.	7½
First Baptist Church, Syracuse, N. Y.	7½
Park Central Presbyterian Church, Syracuse, N. Y.	7½
First Presbyterian Church, Troy, N. Y.	10
St. Paul's Church, Troy, N. Y.	10
First Presbyterian Church, Watertown, N. Y.	7½
Grove Park Inn, Asheville, N. C.	15
First Presbyterian Church, Wilmington, N. C.	7½
Baldwin-Wallace College, Berea, Ohio	10
St. Peter's Church, Canton, Ohio	7½
St. Paul's Church, Canton, Ohio	7½
Geo. B. Wilson's Residence, Cincinnati, Ohio	7½
Cincinnati Music Hall, Cincinnati, Ohio	25
Seventh Presbyterian Church, Cincinnati, Ohio	7½
First Church of Christ Scientist, Cincinnati, Ohio	7½
Presbyterian Church of the Covenant, Cincinnati, O.	7½
St. Mary's R. C. Church, Cincinnati, Ohio	7½
East Side High School, Cincinnati, Ohio	10
Allen Theatre, Cleveland, Ohio	7½
Cleveland Museum of Art, Cleveland, Ohio	10
Cleveland Auditorium, Cleveland, Ohio	25
Cleveland Auditorium, Cleveland, Ohio	25
Florence Harkness Mem. Church, Cleveland, Ohio	7½
Plymouth Church (Shaker Hgts.) Cleveland,, Ohio	7½
Calvary Presbyterian Church, Cleveland, Ohio	10
Trinity Cathedral, Cleveland, Ohio	15
Brotherhood of Loco. Eng. Bldg., Cleveland, Ohio	7½
Stillman Theatre, Cleveland, Ohio	10
Emmanuel P. E. Church, Cleveland, Ohio	7½
Masonic Temple, Cleveland, Ohio	15
Fourth Church of Christ, Cleveland, Ohio	7½
Euclid Ave. Cong. Church, Cleveland, Ohio	10
Keith's Theatre, Cleveland, Ohio	7½
Masonic Hall, Columbus, Ohio	7½
St. Joseph's Cathedral, Columbus, Ohio	20
St. Mary's R. C. Church, Dayton, Ohio	7½
National Cash Register Co., Dayton, Ohio	20
D. S. Blossom, Residence, Euclid, Ohio	7½
Finney Chapel, Oberlin College, Oberlin, Ohio	20
Christ Church, Springfield, Ohio	10
Trinity Church, Toledo, Ohio	7½
First Cong. Church, Toledo, Ohio	10
St. Mark's Episcopal Church, Toledo, Ohio	7½
First Presbyterian Church, Warren, Ohio.	7½

	H.P.
Mrs. E. R. Sterns, Wyoming, Ohio	7½
Trinity M. E. Church, Youngstown, Ohio	7½
St. John's Episcopal Church, Youngstown, Ohio	10
First Presbyterian Church, Oklahoma City, Okla.	15
Criterion Theatre, Oklahoma City, Okla.	10
First Christian Church, Oklahoma City, Okla.	7½
First Church of Christ Scientist, Oklahoma City, Okla.	7½
Convention Hall, Tulsa, Okla.	10
First Christian Church, Tulsa, Okla.	7½
Majestic Theatre, Tulsa, Okla.	10
Globe Theatre, Albany, Oregon	7½
Portland Auditorium, Portland, Ore.	20
Liberty Theatre, Portland, Ore.	35
St. Vincent's Abbey, Beatty, Pa.	10
St. Peter's Cathedral, Erie, Pa.	7½
First Presbyterian Church, Greensburg, Pa.	10
St. Mark's Lutheran Church, Hanover, Pa.	7½
Grace M. E. Church, Harrisburg, Pa.	15
Regent Theatre, Harrisburg, Pa.	7½
First Lutheran Church, Johnstown, Pa.	15
Zion Evangelical Lutheran Church, Lancaster, Pa.	7½
Zion Reformed Church, Lehighton, Pa.	7½
Benn Theatre, Philadelphia, Pa.	10
New Stanley Theatre, Philadelphia, Pa.	25
Sts. Peter and Paul R. C. Church, Philadelphia, Pa.	20
Rodeph Shalom Syn., Philadelphia, Pa.	7½
Palm Theatre, Philadelphia, Pa.	10
Killegarry Theatre, Philadelphia, Pa.	10
Kugler Theatre, Philadelphia, Pa.	10
Tioga Presbyterian Church, Philadelphia, Pa.	7½
Girard College, Philadelphia, Pa.	7½
John Wanamaker, Philadelphia, Pa.	75
First Presbyterian Church, Philadelphia, Pa.	7½
Church of the Gesu, Philadelphia, Pa.	7½
Colonial Theatre, Philadelphia, Pa.	7½
Palace Theatre, Philadelphia, Pa.	15
Second Presbyterian Church, Philadelphia, Pa.	10
John Wanamaker's Store, Philadelphia, Pa.	7½
Baptist Temple, Philadelphia, Pa.	30
Baptist Temple, Philadelphia, Pa.	25
John Wanamaker, Philadelphia, Pa.	7½
John Wanamaker, Philadelphia, Pa.	30
John Wanamaker, Philadelphia, Pa.	20
Stanley Theatre, Philadelphia, Pa.	10
Carnegie Music Hall, Pittsburgh, Pa.	30
East Liberty Presbyterian Church, Pittsburgh, Pa.	15
First Presbyterian Church, Pittsburgh, Pa.	15
Calvary P. E. Church, Pittsburgh, Pa.	7½
United Presbyterian Church, Pittsburgh, Pa.	10
Carnegie Institute, Pittsburgh, Pa.	15
Third Presbyterian Church, Pittsburgh, Pa.	7½
St. Andrew's P. E. Church, Pittsburgh, Pa.	10
East Liberty Theatre, Pittsburgh, Pa.	10

	H.P.
Trinity Church, Pottsville, Pa.	7½
Colonial Theatre, Reading, Pa.	15
St. John's German Luth. Church, Reading, Pa.	7½
Rajah Temple, Reading, Pa.	10
Second Presbyterian Church, Scranton, Pa.	10
Asbury M. E. Church, Scranton, Pa	7½
Presbyterian Church, Sewickley, Pa.	7½
St. Stephen's Episcopal Church, Sewickley, Pa.	7½
First M. E. Church, Uniontown, Pa.	7½
St. Stephen's P. E. Church, Wilkes Barre, Pa.	7½
First Presbyterian Church, Wilkes Barre, Pa.	7½
Trinity P. E. Church, Williamsport, Pa.	10
First Presbyterian Church, York, Pa.	7½
Brown University, Providence, R. I.	10
Majestic Theatre, Providence, R. I.	7½
Victory Theatre, Providence, R. I.	7½
St. Stephen's P. E. Church, Providence, R. I.	7½
All Saint's Memorial Church, Providence, R. I	7½
Washington St. M. E. Church, Columbia, S. C.	7½
Pantages Theatre, Memphis, Tenn.	10
St. John's M. E. Church, Memphis, Tenn.	7½
First Presbyterian Church, Nashville, Tenn.	7½
City Temple, Dallas, Texas	7½
St. Matthew's Cathedral, Dallas, Texas	7½
M. E. Church, Fort Worth, Texas	7½
Universal Theatre, Salt Lake City, Utah	7½
Mormon Tabernacle, Salt Lake City, Utah	15
Mormon Tabernacle, Salt Lake City, Utah	15
Pantages Theatre, Salt Lake City, Utah	7½
Hampton Institute, Hampton, Va.	7½
First Baptist Church, Norfolk, Va.	7½
Granby St. Theatre, Norfolk, Va.	7½
St. James' Church, Richmond, Va.	7½
Colonial Theatre, Richmond, Va.	7½
First Presbyterian Church, Seattle, Wash.	15
Plymouth Church, Seattle, Wash.	10
Coliseum Theatre, Seattle, Wash.	30
Pantages Theatre, Seattle, Wash.	10
Neptune Theatre, Seattle, Wash.	10
Scottish Rite Temple, Tacoma, Wash.	10
Kearse Theater, Charleston, W. Va.	7½
Lawrence College, Appleton, Wisconsin	10
First Congregational Church, Eau Claire, Wis.	10
St. John's Cathedral, Milwaukee, Wis.	10
Temple Emmanuel, Milwaukee, Wis.	7½
First Church of Christ Scientist, Milwaukee, Wis.	7½
Second Church of Christ Scientist, Milwaukee, Wis.	7½
Holy Name R. C. Church, Sheboygan, Wis.	15
Mt. Pleasant M. E. Church, Vancouver, B. C., Can.	7½
St. James' Meth. Church, Montreal, Que., Canada	7½

Mexico

R. P. Jennings, Mexico City, Mexico	15

Showing an "Orgoblo" attached to large Cathedral organ with various and high wind pressures

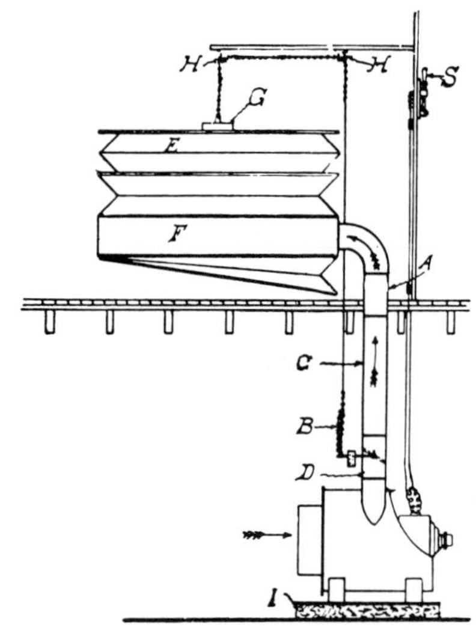

"ORGOBLO" ATTACHED TO PIPE ORGAN WITH PRESSURE TUBE

A - RIGID AIR TUBE
B - CONTROLLING CHAIN
C - CANVAS RUBBER AIR TUBE
D - BALANCED CONTROLLING WIND VALVE (SHOULD BE PLACED NEXT "ORGOBLO")
E - RESERVOIR BELLOWS
F - WELL
G - BELLOWS WEIGHT
H - PULLEYS
I - HAIR FELT
S - STARTING SWITCH

NOTE - SEE INSTRUCTION SHEET PACKED WITH EACH "ORGOBLO"

SPECIAL ORGOBLO EQUIPMENT FOR REED ORGANS

#1547

7"

WALL

J - VALVE DISC SUPPORT.
A - GALV. IRON AIR PIPE.
K - SUCTION BELLOWS.
L - VALVE SEAT (ON FLANGE 'T')
M - ADJUSTMENT HOLES.
N - COTTER PIN.
O - VALVE DISC.
P - SAFETY SPRING.
R - METAL BAND.
S - STEEL REENFORCED HOSE.
T - METAL FLANGE.
V - FELT.

ORGOBLO JUNIOR

HAIR FELT

THE ORGAN POWER CO.

The above cuts show some of our many Testing-Boards

We are equipped to test electrically on more than fifteen different kinds of current; also with air meters, pressure and vacuum gauges, tachometers, etc.

Every "ORGOBLO" is given a thorough running test in the factory and the following data recorded.

(a) Pressure Output at 0, ¼, ½, ¾ and full load.

(b) Volume Output at ¼, ½, ¾ and full load.

(c) Voltage Input at 0, ¼, ½, ¾ and full load.

(d) Ampere Input at 0, ¼, ½, ¾ and full load.

(e) Speed at no load.

(f) Speed at full load.

(g) Test to insure freedom from noise and vibration.

You are cordially invited to visit our works, which we believe are the most up-to-date in the world, devoted exclusively to the manufacture of turbine blowing apparatus.

Testimonials

LINK PIANO COMPANY, INC.

Binghamton, N. Y.

Gentlemen — We are pleased to advise you that the ORGOBLOS we purchase from you from time to time are giving excellent service and both our customers and ourselves are thoroughly satisfied with them. We wish to especially compliment you on the service you have given us in connection with these blowers. You have always been more than fair in making any necessary adjustments.

Yours very truly,
LINK PIANO COMPANY, INC.
G. R. Thayer.

BARTOLA MUSICAL INSTRUMENT COMPANY

Oshkosh, Wis.

Gentlemen — We have used the ORGOBLO on our Bartola organ and on the Barton organ over a period of fifteen years. The ORGOBLO has always done the work satisfactorily, and we have had very prompt and courteous service whenever the same was necessary.

The Bartola installations are made in theatres, many of which are of the older type, where the blower is placed in damp basements, dirty places, and in several occasions in coal holes; and even with all of these adverse conditions, they have performed with 100% satisfaction.

Yours very truly,
BARTOLA MUSICAL INSTRUMENT COMPANY.
Dan Barton, *General Manager.*

THE ROBERT MORTON COMPANY

Van Nuys, Calif.

Gentlemen — We are very glad to recommend the ORGOBLO as being a very efficient apparatus for organ installations. We have found them to be capable to the fullest degree and make a compact and satisfactory unit where space is a factor.

We especially feel grateful for the hearty co-operation we received from yourselves in aiding in every way to see that the ORGOBLO does render the service for which it was built.

We have used them in all types of organs with greatest of success.

Yours very truly,
THE ROBERT MORTON COMPANY.
H. P. Platt, *Factory Mgr.*

THE AEOLIAN COMPANY

Gentlemen — We are pleased to say that our experience with the ORGOBLO, dating from its inception, has been most satisfactory; this, after making many installations in all sections of this country, which have been subjected to long and severe tests, demonstrates that the ORGOBLO is a most simple, efficient and substantial form of organ blowing.

We also wish to express our appreciation of your uniformly courteous and prompt attention to our needs.

Yours very truly,
THE AEOLIAN COMPANY,
A. W. Flegel,
Supt., Pipe Organ Department.

AUSTIN ORGAN COMPANY

Gentlemen — We have used a great number of your organ blowing equipments, and are very pleased to state that they are giving us the best of satisfaction. We believe that you have developed the ORGOBLO to a very high state of perfection, and that it is a very reliable and economical machine for blowing any organs — from a small organ on low pressure to the largest instrument requiring wind in large quantities and at various pressures.

We believe that your liberal guarantee on all machines, and the courteous treatment in all our dealings, are matters that should also be mentioned by us.

Yours very truly,
AUSTIN ORGAN COMPANY,
B. G. Austin, *General Manager.*

KARN-MORRIS PIANO AND ORGAN CO.

Gentlemen — We are pleased to add our testimony to the efficiency of the ORGOBLO. Having installed a good many machines varying in capacity from ½ to 10 H. P., we can cheerfully recommend them to Committees requiring some satisfactory system of wind supply for Church Organs.

Yours very truly,
KARN-MORRIS PIANO AND ORGAN CO., LTD.,
E. C. Thornton, *General Manager.*

THE M. STEINERT & SONS COMPANY

Gentlemen — Replying to your favor of the 23rd inst., we are pleased to say that our experience during the past three years with the ORGOBLO has been very satisfactory, the machines doing all that you claim for them.

Wishing you continued success, we remain,

Very truly yours,
THE M. STEINERT & SONS COMPANY,
M. P. Currier.

M. P. MOLLER, MANUFACTURER AND BUILDER OF PIPE ORGANS

Gentlemen — I have used the ORGOBLO from time to time in the operation of our organs and consider the outfit a first-class and satisfactory blowing apparatus.

Yours very truly,
M. P. MOLLER.

HILLGREEN, LANE & CO.

Gentlemen — We are finding the utmost satisfaction in the use of your admirable blowing device, the ORGOBLO. It furnishes ideal service, and our patrons everywhere are grateful to us for having commended it to them. Wherever electricity is available, the ORGOBLO should be employed.

A word ought to be said as to your honorable business methods. In several instances Power Companies have changed the character of the electrical currents that were being furnished to Churches. These changes involved the installing of new motors. Letters on file from the Church authorities refer to your dealings with them as unexpectedly generous and sympathetic.

You really have provided something the world wanted.

Very respectfully yours,
HILLGREEN, LANE & CO.

MASON & HAMLIN CO.

Gentlemen — We have, as you know, used a large number of your ORGOBLOS, and have found them most satisfactory; in fact, we consider them the best organ blowers yet manufactured.

Very truly yours,
MASON & HAMLIN CO.,
Wm. P. Marsh, *Asst. Sec'y.*

GEO. KILGEN & SON

Gentlemen — Replying to your favor will say that we have used quite a number of ORGOBLOS from the smallest to the largest sizes and find them to give good satisfaction and in all cases fully up to the requirements of our specifications both in pressure and volume of air required and can recommend them to anyone wanting a good organ blower.

Yours very truly,
GEO. KILGEN & SON.

HOPE-JONES ORGAN CO.

Gentlemen — We are in receipt of your favor of the 12th, and in reply wish to say that we have been well satisfied with the machines you have supplied to us.

We are,

Yours very truly,
ROBERT HOPE-JONES.

(The above Company has installed a number of large and high pressure ORGOBLOS.)

THE WARREN CHURCH ORGAN CO.

Gentlemen — Our experience with the ORGOBLO has been very satisfactory and we take pleasure in continuing the use of same.

Yours truly,
WARREN CHURCH ORGAN CO.,
James Hay.

WANGERIN-WEICKHARDT CO.

Gentlemen — We have been using your ORGOBLO in connection with numerous organs built and installed by us in recent years and find it to give universal satisfaction. Its compactness, construction and general arrangement is such that, wherever the necessary motive power is available, it develops the highest degree of serviceableness, meeting even the severest requirements in an admirable manner. We shall continue to use and recommend your ORGOBLO and believe its excellence will be indeed appreciated by all users.

Yours very truly,
WANGERIN-WEICKHARDT CO.,
A. Wangerin, *Secretary.*

THE TELLERS ORGAN COMPANY

Gentlemen — In response to your favor of the 11th inst., we wish to state that we are constant users of the ORGOBLO manufactured by your Company and would say that so far they have given the very best satisfaction.

We also wish to credit your Company for the ready, prompt attention you give to any of your machines, whenever you are called upon to do so.

Yours very truly,
THE TELLERS ORGAN COMPANY.

C. E. MOREY

Gentlemen — During the past five years, I have used a number of ORGOBLOS and they have given excellent satisfaction. The advantages of these blowers are many and I am pleased to recommend them.

Yours very truly,
C. E. MOREY

L. C. HARRISON & COMPANY

Gentlemen — The ORGOBLO is all, if not more than you claim for it.

Very truly yours,
L. C. HARRISON & CO.

HINNERS ORGAN COMPANY

Gentlemen — We have installed upwards of 100 ORGOBLO outfits, with pipe organs of all sizes, and take pleasure in stating that they are giving perfectly satisfactory results. The ORGOBLO supplies an abundant and steady volume of wind, and is practically noiseless. The cost of maintenance is also very small. We consider it the ideal method of organ blowing, and are delighted with the results we have achieved with the ORGOBLO. We, therefore take great pleasure in giving it our unqualified endorsement, and extend our best wishes for your continued success.

Yours very truly,
HINNERS ORGAN CO.,
A. W. Hinners, *Secretary.*

THE HALL ORGAN CO.

Gentlemen — We are advocating the use of the ORGOBLO wherever electric power is available. We do so because we know from experience that it is simple, quiet, economical and durable, and above all, efficient to a degree beyond that of any other method. In fact, your machine is indispensable to the modern organ.

The only fault we have to find with it is that it keeps a lot of old organs in commission, that would otherwise be replaced with new instruments.

Yours very truly,
THE HALL ORGAN CO.,
Geo. A. North, *Manager.*

J. W. STEERE & SON ORGAN CO.

Gentlemen — We are pleased to advise you that we have been using the ORGOBLO for a number of years in connection with our instruments and that they have been uniformly satisfactory, and we heartily recommend them to all prospective purchasers, and that our business relations have been of the most cordial nature, and we wish you continued success.

Yours very truly,
J. W. STEERE & SON ORGAN CO.

HENRY PILCHER'S SONS

Gentlemen — Answering your inquiry, would say that we have as you know been using your blowing outfits for several years and have found them very satisfactory from every standpoint.

Yours truly,
HENRY PILCHER'S SONS.

WM. B. GOODWIN

Gentlemen — I wonder if you can recall that during a long past conversation on water motors, you made the assertion that a quiet fan blower would beat all known blowing apparatus "out of sight," and further, that such a plant would cause an organ to sound in much evener tune and voice. Your youthful prophesy was brought to mind by a little incident. I had just (the Saturday night before) installed one of your fine "extra silent" ORGOBLOS and going to inspect the result Sunday noon was complimented by the chairman of the music committee on the fine, smooth "tuning" which the organ had been given. Now there had been no time for pipe work, and that tuning was done seven years ago. The magic of your blower had renewed its youth as you had predicted. You can certainly count me among those who insist on the ORGOBLO and its proper installation in any organ of pretensions to modern voicing. You certainly have made as notable a series of successes in electricity as you did in water motors.

Yours,
WM. B. GOODWIN,
Organ Expert.

FRED M. TAYLOR, JR.

Gentlemen — In conclusion, I wish to say that in fifteen years' experience with all kinds of appliances for blowing organs, I have never seen an appliance that was so thoroughly satisfactory in every respect, as the ORGOBLO. We have not had one minute's trouble with it since installation.

FRED M. TAYLOR, JR.

J. B. WIARD

Gentlemen — I do not hesitate in recommending the ORGOBLO made by the Organ Power Company of Hartford. It is by far the most efficient organ blower which I have had occasion to investigate. Their claim that the machine operates quietly is fully met in those installations which I have seen.

J. B. WIARD,
Mechanical and Electrical Engineer.

W. W. KIMBALL CO.

Gentlemen — Replying to your favor of September 25th, will say that we have used quite a number of ORGOBLOS from the smallest sizes to the largest and find them to give good satisfaction and in all cases fully up to the requirements of our specifications both in pressure and volume of air required and can recommend them to anyone wanting a good organ blower.

Yours very truly,
W. W. KIMBALL COMPANY,
By O. J. Hagstrom,
OJH-GH *Supt. Pipe Organ Department.*

WILL A. WATKINS CO.

Dear Sirs — After many years' experience with various organ blowing devices, we can state that the ORGOBLO is superior in results obtained to any other device we have used.
Wishing you continued success, we are,

Yours very truly,
WILL A. WATKINS COMPANY.

RNW-B

O. A. MARSHALL

Gentlemen — I am one of the oldest organ builders now living and have installed large numbers of your ORGOBLOS from ½ to 10 H. P. and have yet to have a single complaint. Neither do I know of a cent being expended for repairs on any blowers that I or my sons have installed.

Yours very truly,
O. A. MARSHALL.

THE ESTEY ORGAN COMPANY

Gentlemen — We take this opportunity to express to you the satisfaction we are experiencing in using the ORGOBLO as it is now constructed. We find it is more efficient and more satisfactory in every way than anything we have ever used, and we congratulate you on the successful outfit which you are producing.

Yours very truly,
THE ESTEY ORGAN COMPANY,
By J. G. Estey.

VINER AND SON

Buffalo, N. Y.

Gentlemen — After 15 years' experience with the ORGOBLO we have only praise to offer.
The ORGOBLO has proven satisfactory, wherever we have come in contact with it.
We have found them to be more efficient than you have represented them to be, and we take pleasure in recommending them.
Thanking you for your uniform courtesy, and with best wishes for your future success, we remain,

Very truly yours,
VINER & SON.

REUBEN MIDMER AND SON, INC.

Brooklyn, N. Y.

Gentlemen — The ORGOBLOS we have used in connection with the Midmer Organs, we have found to be efficient and satisfactory in every manner.
We thank you for your prompt and courteous attention to us, and wish you continued success.

Yours very truly,
REUBEN MIDMER & SON, INC.,
Per J. G. Light, *Sec.*

RUDOLPH WURLITZER MFG. CO.

North Tonawanda, N. Y.

Gentlemen — In reply to your letter of the 24th of September, we are very pleased to say that we are satisfied with your blowers and have always found you willing to assist and co-operate with us on every occasion.

Yours very truly,
THE RUDOLPH WURLITZER MFG. CO.,
W. Meakin Jones.

LEONARD DOWNEY

London, Canada

Gentlemen — Previous correspondence in your office will show that I have many times had occasion to commend you on the excellent service given by the ORGOBLO, and I am pleased to report that the remarkable success continues.
Installing ORGOBLOS has made many friends for me amongst those particularly interested in church organs.

Yours respectfully,
LEONARD DOWNEY.

SKINNER ORGAN CO.

Boston, Mass.

Gentlemen — In regard to my experience with the ORGOBLO, I have to say that I have found it competent and efficient. More than all this, I have noted your disposition to give immediate consideration to any questions of insufficiency as to capacity or variation from ratings that have been claimed without quibbling over it, and to go to any length to establish the facts in question one way or other.
I may say further that in every instance where a claim has been made, the fault has been found to be in insufficient potential in the electric service or an expectation in delivery of pressures above what was asked.
Also, I have noted over many years, your persistent and untiring effort to improve the design and efficiency of the ORGOBLO in every possible way.

Very truly yours,
ERNEST M. SKINNER.

One day's production of Orgoblos leaves the factory in the mid-teens. Note that the blowers are not crated; they were shipped as "skid mounted blowing apparatus," a tariff which is still in use today.

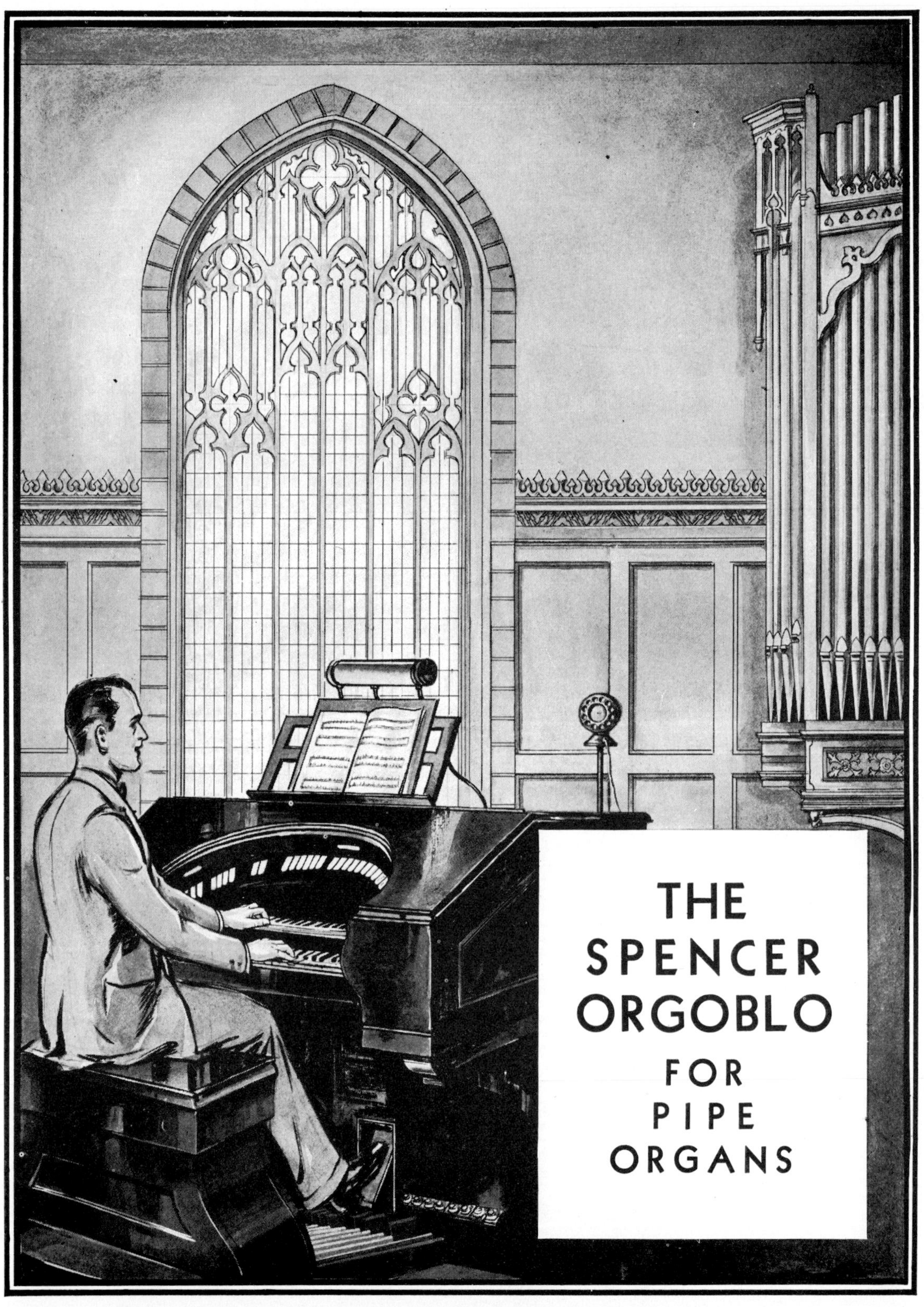

This cover illustration from a 1932 Spencer catalog really covered all the bases so far as Spencer's clients were concerned: it pictures a Wurlitzer theatre organ console in a church with a radio microphone in the background! It was certainly appropriate that a Wurlitzer console was chosen as the artist's model; Wurlitzer was Spencer's all-time largest Orgoblo customer.

THE SPENCER TURBINE CO.

Manufacturers of Central Vacuum Cleaning Systems, Organ Blowers

488 NEW PARK AVENUE :: :: :: :: HARTFORD, CONN.

SPENCER CENTRAL VACUUM CLEANING SYSTEM

OPERATION.—The Spencer system, which is in daily operation in over 10,000 theatres, office buildings, hotels and schools throughout the country, consists of a multi-stage turbine vacuum producer in the basement, and a system of pipes carrying the vacuum to inlet valves conveniently located throughout the building.

The powerful suction is carried to interchangeable cleaning tools by means of light weight flexible hose connected to the nearest inlet valve.

Thus only the cleaning tool and hose are handled by the operator.

Dust and dirt are sucked from rug, leaving the fibres soft and erect with no grit left to cut the fibres

Cleans all types of floors

The Spencer Central Cleaning System removes all dirt from the heaviest carpets as well as from bare floors. Tile, cement, marble, mastic and wood floors are left in immaculate order.

Under the seats

The Spencer System makes cleaning under theatre seats easy, thorough and swift. No dirt can collect in corners or crevices which are ordinarily so inaccessible.

Economical

In the long run, a Central Cleaning System is less expensive than any other method.

As a labor saver it operates two ways: directly and indirectly.

Directly it greatly reduces the time required for cleaning. One or more operators can thoroughly clean the entire theatre where a larger crew otherwise would be required.

Indirectly, by keeping the room free from dust and dirt, it reduces the labor of scrubbing, washing the woodwork, redecorating, etc.

Rugs last longer—stay new longer

It is, of course, well known that dirt and grit imbedded in carpets and rugs cut the fibre. Less modern cleaning methods permit imbedded dirt to remain in the rug fibres. The Spencer Central Cleaning System removes all dirt from the rugs, permitting none to accumulate beneath the surface.

Rugs not only last longer—they retain their freshness of color. In a rug cleaned regularly with the Spencer System the fibres remain erect and soft, instead of matting.

Saves redecorating costs

Not only does the Spencer System eliminate the raising of dust in daily cleaning; occasional use of the Spencer System on walls, hangings, grill-work and decorations quickly removes all dust that has come in from the street.

SIZES. There is a standard size and capacity to fit any theatre from small community theatres to the largest houses.

TOOLS. Spencer interchangeable cleaning tools for the various requirements are light in weight and shaped for fast and effective work. The tools are equipped with the Spencer universal swivel which enables the operator to clean under seats and other furniture, and in corners, and to remove dirt beyond the reach of the rigid tool. This feature is in itself a great time saver. All wearing surfaces are renewable.

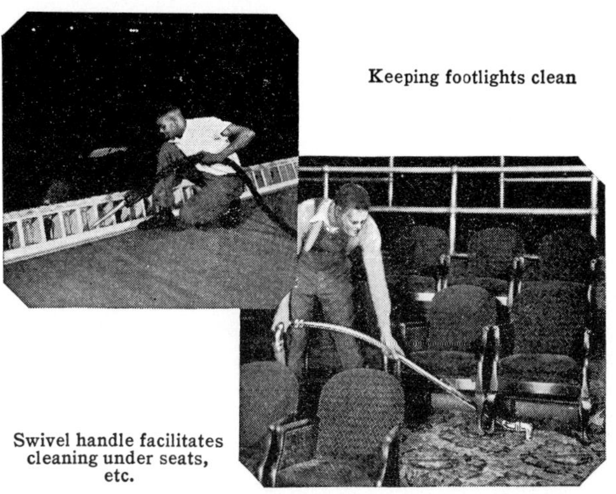

Keeping footlights clean

Swivel handle facilitates cleaning under seats, etc.

THE SPENCER ORGOBLO

OPERATION.—The quiet, dependable operation of the Spencer Orgoblo is the result of 30 years of constant development.

The Orgoblo is designed along the lines of a thoroughly scientific centrifugal turbine. The air follows a smooth and continuous path in passing through the machine. Design of the fans and machine give the Orgoblo a splendid overload capacity.

Motors are built in extra large frames with oversize bearings and heavy shafts to insure quiet operation and a lifetime of trouble-free service. The same policy is carried out in construction of the fans, deflectors and all parts of the machine.

Motors themselves are of special design to eliminate noise and to insure cool operation; each motor is tested individually for noise and vibration.

SIZES.—There is an Orgoblo of proper size for every organ made. They range from small 1/6 H.P. units suitable for student Reed Organs to mammoth 75 and 100 H. P. multi-stage, multi-pressure units such as found in the largest theatres in the country.

SPECIAL ORGOBLOS.—Where unusual conditions can not be met by our standard line, our experience in pneumatic engineering work proves exceptionally valuable in designing special equipment to meet those special needs.

USERS.—The majority of the country's foremost theatres—both large and small—are Orgoblo users. Wherever you are, there is an Orgoblo near you giving noiseless, trouble-free service. A list of users in your locality will be sent on request.

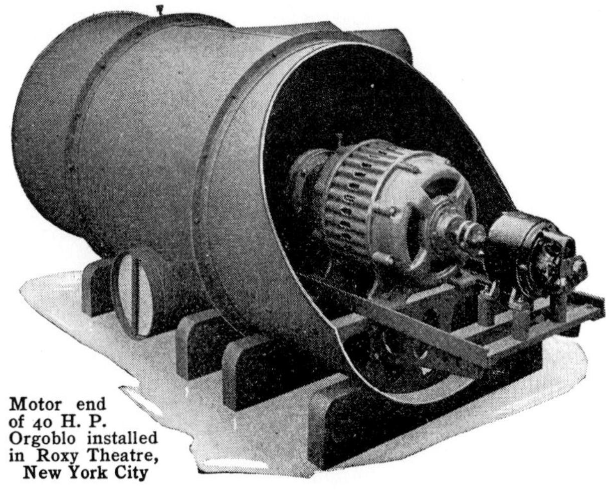

Motor end of 40 H. P. Orgoblo installed in Roxy Theatre, New York City

This Spencer notice appeared in Mancall's Theatre Building and Equipment *catalog c. 1931.*

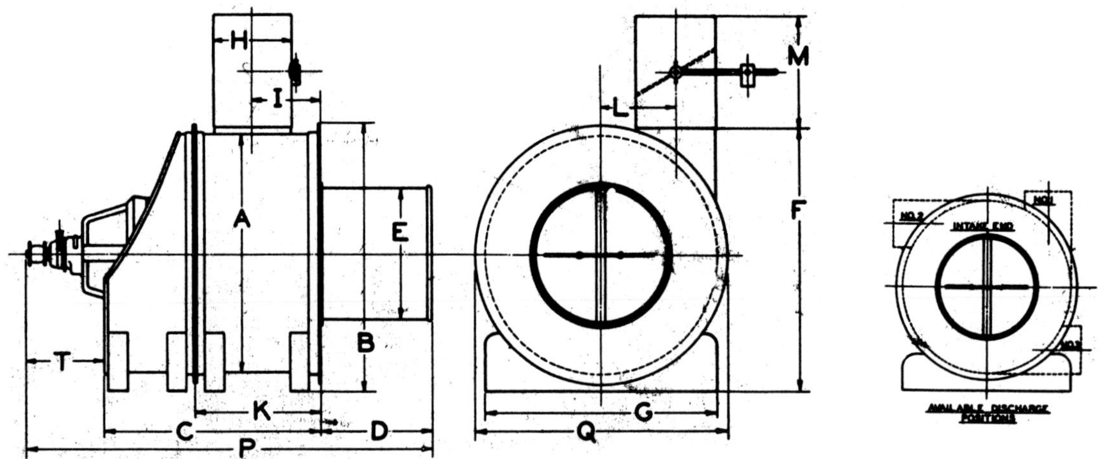

Dimensions of Three Stage, Single Pressure Orgoblos

																With Single Phase Motor			With Poly-Phase Motor			With D.C. Motor		
Speed	H.P.	Catalog No.	App. Ship. Wt.	A	B	D	E	F	G	H	I	K	L	M	Q	C	P	T	C	P	T	C	P	T
FULL 1750 R.P.M.	1/3	8001	310	18	20	8½	10	22	18	6	10½		6	8	18¾	19½	29	1	19½	29	1	20	32½	4
	½	8006	390	24	28	10½	10	30	24	8	9¼		8	13	27	20½	32¼	1¼	20½	32¼	1¼	21	35½	4
	¾	8011-8013	475	24	28	10½	10	30	24	8	9¼		8	13	27	21	35¾	4¼	21	35¾	4¼	21½	38½	6½
	1	8022, 8023	525	24	28	10½	10	30	24	8	9¼		8	13	27	21½	36¼	4¼	21½	36¼	4¼	23	40¾	7¼
	1	8024	525	30	34¾	14½	15	36	30	10	9		10	15	33½	22	40¾	4¼	22	40¾	4¼	23½	45½	7½
	1½	8033	645	24	28	10½	10	30	24	8	9¼		8	13	27	22½	37¼	4¼	22½	37¼	4¼	24	42¼	7¾
	1½	8034	645	30	34¾	14½	15	36	30	10	9		10	15	33½	23½	41¾	3¾	23½	41¾	3¾	24½	46¾	7¾
	2	8045, 8046	750	30	34¾	14½	15	36	30	10	9		10	15	33½	24	42¾	4¼	24	42¾	4¼	25½	48¼	8¼
	3	8056	935	36	41	14½	15	41	36	10	9¾		13	15	39¾	25	43¾	4¼	25	43¾	4¼	26	49	8½
FULL 1150 R.P.M.	¾	8501	550	30	34¾	14½	15	37	30	12	13½		9	17	33½	26½	47¾	6¾	25½	44¼	4¼	28	49¼	6¾
	¾	8502	550	30	34¾	14½	15	36	30	10	9		10	15	33½	23	44¼	6¾	21½	39¾	3¾	23½	46	8
	1	8511	665	30	34¾	14½	15	37	30	12	13½		9	17	33½	27	48¾	7¼	26½	45¼	4¼	28	50¼	7¾
	1	8512-8514	665	36	41	14½	15	41	36	10	9¾		13	15	39¾	24	45½	7	23	42	4½	24½	47	8
	1½	8521, 8522	775	36	41	14½	15	42	36	12	13		12	17	39¾	29	50¼	6¾	28	47	4½	29½	52¼	8¼
	1½	8523, 8524	775	36	41	14½	15	41	36	10	9¾		13	15	39¾	25	46¼	6¾	24	43	4½	25½	48¼	8¼
	2	8532, 8533	935	36	41	14½	15	42	36	12	13		12	17	39¾	30½	52¼	7¼	29	47¾	4¼	31	53	7½
	2	8534	935	36	41	14½	15	41	36	10	9¾		13	15	39¾	26½	48¼	7¼	25	43¾	4¼	26	49	8½
	2	8535, 8536	1100	42	47	17½	20	47½	42	12	8¾		15	17	46	28	52½	7	26	47¾	4¼	27½	53¼	8¼
	3	8542-8544	1150	36	41	14½	15	42	36	12	11½		12	17	39¾	32½	54¼	7¼	30½	49½	4½	32½	56¼	9¼
	3	8545	1265	42	47	17½	20	48½	42	15	12¾		13½	21	46	32	57¼	7¾	30½	52½	4½	32½	59	9
	3	8546	1265	42	47	17½	20	47½	42	12	8¾		15	17	46	30	54¾	7¼	27½	50	5	30	56½	9
	5	8555, 8556	1430	42	47	17½	20	48½	42	15	12¾	22½	13½	21	46	36	61	7½	32	54¾	5¼	34½	61½	9½
	7½	8565	1620	42	47	17½	20	48½	42	15	15½	25¼	13½	21	46	REFER TO FACTORY			38	60¼	4¾	40	67	9½
	7½	8566	1620	50	55½	17½	20	55½	50	15	10¾	21¼	17½	21	55				35	57½	5	37	64¼	9¾
	10	8575	1870	42	47	17½	20	48½	42	15	15½	25¼	13½	21	46				39	61¾	5¼	41	68½	10
	10	8576	1870	50	55½	17½	20	55½	50	15	15	25	17½	21	55				40	62¾	5¼	42	69½	10
	15	8585	2150	50	55½	17½	20	57	50	20	18½	31	15	22	55				43	65¾	5¼	48½	77½	11½
	15	8586	2170	50	55½	17½	20	55½	50	15	15	25	17½	21	55				40	63	5½	45½	74¾	11¾
	20	8595, 8596	2300	50	55½	17½	20	57	50	20	18½	31	15	22	55				44	66¾	5¼	49½	78¾	11¾
	25	8605	2500	50	55½	24	28	57	50	20	22	34¾	15	22	55				48	77½	5½	54	90	12
	25	8606	2500	50	55½	24	28	57	50	20	18½	31	15	22	55				45	74¾	5¾	51½	87¼	11¾
	30	8615, 8616	2700	50	55½	24	28	57	50	20	22	34¾	15	22	55				49½	79	5½	54	90	12

Orgoblo casings in outline are shown in two sections.

Standard practice is to build any casing whose dimension "C" exceeds 35″ in two sections. Any casing under 35″ is built in one section.

This is done so machines may be readily taken through a standard 36″ doorway. Do not be misled if you find a dimension under the heading "K". Even though these figures are given, these casings will not be made in two sections unless "C" is 35″ or more.

Standard accessories furnished with each Orgoblo include:
Check valve and intake valve.
27 inch length flexible tubing with clamps.
Controlling wind valve with counterweight, chain and pulleys.
Flanged collar for organ reservoir.
Hair felt pads.
Motor lubricant.
No allowance made for pulleys on motors of less than ½ H.P.
Discharge position must be given to factory when order is placed.
Dimensions are for reference purposes only.

THE SPENCER TURBINE CO. - HARTFORD, CONN.

ORGAN POWER DIVISION

Chart showing dimensions of all standard Orgoblos available during the theatre organ's golden age.

THE ORGAN POWER CO.
HARTFORD, CONN.

11637
BILLED

Date October 25, 1920. Fill Notify R-Morton before shipping Dec. 1st
Charge to:- Robert-Morton Company, Van Nuys, Cal
Ship to:- Imperial Theatre,
Alliance, Nebr.
Order #1630 Blanket #1165.
Via Freight. ask office
3 H. P. 220 Volts 60 Cycles 3 Phase 1800 Speed WESTINGHOUSE. ~~Watson.~~ Type
Casing No. 30-3 Length 29 1/2"
3 Fans 21" Diameter 1 3/4" Blades 1 1/8" Shaft SET SCREW HUBS.
Nov 30
3" Pul.Ext. shaft for generator 1750 3"
Fennoyer Car, Car Initial D.T. & I. Car. #10093
Triplicate Invoices
PUT CAR NUMBER & ROUTING ON INVOICE.
Drawing #1397. $267.00 net
1 Extra P.D.B.
DRAWING NUMBER OF THRUST BEARING ACTUALLY USED ON THIS ORGOBLO IS 1425.5 1 X 6" long
Fixtures:- 5 ft. tube, B. V. FC. ETC.
Wind Pressure and Volume 10" Style 75
Machine No. 11637 Motor No. 275225
Shipping Clerk:- Date Shipped:- 12/16/20
F 4138

SHOP VOICING MACHINE

The Spencer Turbine Company
Hartford, Conn.

MACHINE #6577

Customer's Order No.	Date of Order	Date Entered	Date Wanted
Letter	8/13/70	8/24/70	9/14/70
Organ Power		Mark on Package: Cat. J-2215	

ACKNOWLEDGMENT OF YOUR ORDER

We thank you for your order. This is an exact copy as has been entered by us. If it does not agree with your understanding, please advise at once.

All correspondence regarding this order should show the above Machine No.

Ship To: David L. Junchen, Junchen Pipe Organ Service, 401 First Street, Sherrard, Illinois 61281

Sold To: Above - Advance Payment Received

Terms: Net 30 Days

PREPAID	We expect to ship	VIA	R.R.	Exp.	Truck	P.P.
	9/14/70 SURE					
COLLECT: XX	F.O.B. / Ship. Pt. / Dest'n	ROUTING: B/W Collect				

QUANTITY ORDERED	DESCRIPTION	UNIT PRICE
	Spencer Orgoblo Jr., Catalogue J-2215	

ORGOBLO		MOTOR				STARTER	
CAT. No.	J-2215	MAKE	Gen. Elec.	SHAFT DIA. & SIZE	1/2"x5-1/2"	MAKE	OMIT
DWG. No.	B-7686-1	H.P.	1/2	FRONT BRG.	Sleeve	BULLETIN	
CASING	18"x15"	VOLTS	115/230	REAR BRG.	Bearings	TYPE	
LINE DIV. HEAD W/FELT		PHASE	1	TYPE	KC	SIZE	
OUTLET	#1-4"	CYCLE	60	FRAME	48	P.O. No.	
		R.P.M.	3500	MODEL No.		HEATER COIL	
DEFL. INT.	4"	No.	KED-10	P.O. No.	288006	PUSH BUTTON	
END HEAD	4"	OTHER INF.	CONNECT FOR 115 VOLTS				
HT. BASE	S.M.	FIXTURES					
VOLUME	100 cfm.	2-1/4' lg. 4" tubing; 2-4" clamp collars;					
PRESSURE	15" press.	1-4" flanged collar. Hair felt pads.					
VALVES		Lubricant for motor if necessary.					
CHECK	1-4" per Dwg. #3209						
INTAKE	Drum type per Dwg. A-16848						
BUTTERFLY	OMIT						
LEV. & WGT.	OMIT	REPLACEMENT AND REPAIRS					
PUL. & CHAIN	OMIT						
COIL WIRE	OMIT						
AIR FLO.	OMIT						

CUSTOMERS ACKNOWLEDGMENT RF8/24/70 ORG

Spencer records spanning fifty years. Only about 10% of these records still remain in the Spencer files, the rest having been lost in the move to their new factory in 1975. What a tragedy, inasmuch as these records were amazingly detailed and often disclosed the size of the instrument. For example, the record on the left shows that blower #11637 powered a style 75 (2/5) Robert-Morton.

ORGAN POWER

Net Selling Prices

Standard Two Stage Single Pressure Orgoblos

1750 R. P. M.

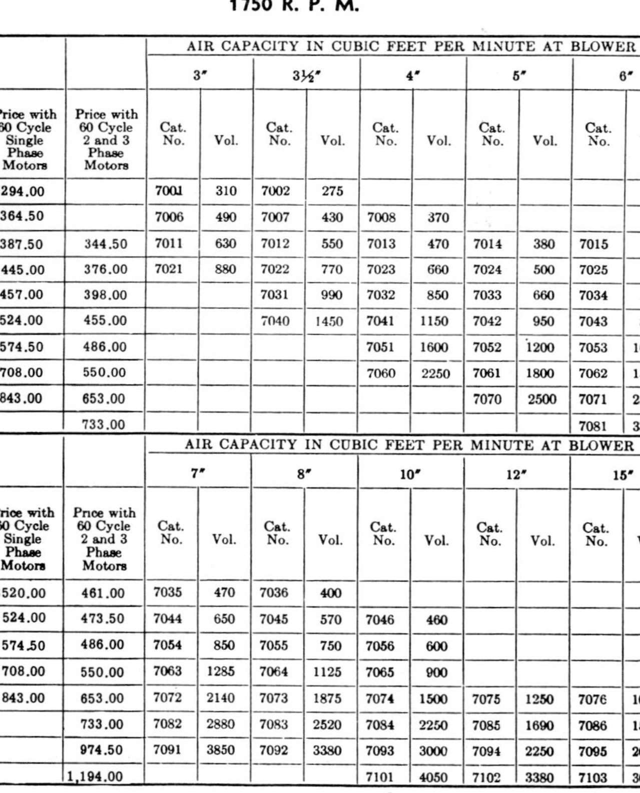

Full 1750 R. P. M.

			AIR CAPACITY IN CUBIC FEET PER MINUTE AT BLOWER									
			3"		3½"		4"		5"		6"	
H.P.	Price with 60 Cycle Single Phase Motors	Price with 60 Cycle 2 and 3 Phase Motors	Cat. No.	Vol.	Cat. No.	Vol.	Cat. No.	Vol.	Cat. No.	Vol.	Cat. No.	Vol.
¼	$294.00		7001	310	7002	275						
⅓	364.50		7006	490	7007	430	7008	370				
½	387.50	344.50	7011	630	7012	550	7013	470	7014	380	7015	315
¾	445.00	376.00	7021	880	7022	770	7023	660	7024	500	7025	415
1	457.00	398.00			7031	990	7032	850	7033	660	7034	550
1½	524.00	455.00			7040	1450	7041	1150	7042	950	7043	800
2	574.50	486.00					7051	1600	7052	1200	7053	1000
3	708.00	550.00					7060	2250	7061	1800	7062	1500
5	843.00	653.00							7070	2500	7071	2500
7½		733.00									7081	3380

Full 1750 R. P. M.

			AIR CAPACITY IN CUBIC FEET PER MINUTE AT BLOWER									
			7"		8"		10"		12"		15"	
H.P.	Price with 60 Cycle Single Phase Motors	Price with 60 Cycle 2 and 3 Phase Motors	Cat. No.	Vol.	Cat. No.	Vol.	Cat. No.	Vol.	Cat. No.	Vol.	Cat. No.	Vol.
1	$520.00	461.00	7035	470	7036	400						
1½	524.00	473.50	7044	650	7045	570	7046	460				
2	574.50	486.00	7054	850	7055	750	7056	600				
3	708.00	550.00	7063	1285	7064	1125	7065	900				
5	843.00	653.00	7072	2140	7073	1875	7074	1500	7075	1250	7076	1000
7½		733.00	7082	2880	7083	2520	7084	2250	7085	1690	7086	1500
10		974.50	7091	3850	7092	3380	7093	3000	7094	2250	7095	2000
15		1,194.00					7101	4050	7102	3380	7103	3000

THE SPENCER TURBINE COMPANY • HARTFORD 6, CONNECTICUT

SPENCER HARTFORD

ORGAN POWER

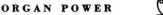

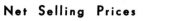

Net Selling Prices

Standard Two Stage Single Pressure Orgoblos

1150 R. P. M.

Full 1150 R. P. M.

			AIR CAPACITY IN CUBIC FEET PER MINUTE AT BLOWER									
			3"		3½"		4"		5"		6"	
H.P.	Price with 60 Cycle Single Phase Motors	Price with 60 Cycle 2 and 3 Phase Motors	Cat. No.	Vol.	Cat. No.	Vol.	Cat. No.	Vol.	Cat. No.	Vol.	Cat. No.	Vol.
¾	517.00	449.50	7501	880	7502	770	7503	660	7504	500		
1	574.50	480.00	7506	1150	7507	990	7508	850	7509	660		
1½	652.00	531.50			7511	1450	7512	1150	7513	950	7514	800
2	733.00	574.50			7521	1875	7522	1600	7523	1200	7524	1000
3	901.00	703.50					7531	2250	7532	1800	7533	1500
5	1,123.50	858.00					7541	3500	7542	3000	7543	2500
7½		975.50							7551	4050	7552	3380
10		1,222.00							7560	5400	7561	4500
15		1,550.00									7571	6750

Full 1150 R. P. M.

			AIR CAPACITY IN CUBIC FEET PER MINUTE AT BLOWER									
			7"		8"		10"		12"		15"	
H.P.	Price with 60 Cycle Single Phase Motors	Price with 60 Cycle 2 and 3 Phase Motors	Cat. No.	Vol.	Cat. No.	Vol.	Cat. No.	Vol.	Cat. No.	Vol.	Cat. No.	Vol.
2	733.00	574.50	7525	850								
3	1,013.50	773.00	7534	1285	7535	1125						
5	1,123.50	858.00	7544	2140	7545	1875	7546	1500				
7½	1,292.50	975.50	7553	2880	7554	2520	7555	2250				
10		1,222.00	7562	3850	7563	3380	7564	3000	7565	2250		
15		1,550.00	7572	5760	7573	5060	7574	4050	7575	3380		
20		1,934.00	7581	7700	7582	6750	7583	5400	7584	4500		
25		2,225.00					7591	6750	7592	5630		

THE SPENCER TURBINE COMPANY • HARTFORD 6, CONNECTICUT

SPENCER HARTFORD

ORGAN POWER

Net Selling Prices

Standard Three Stage Single Pressure Orgoblos

1750 R. P. M.

Full 1750 R. P. M.

H.P.	Price with 60 Cycle Single Phase Motors	Price with 60 Cycle 2 and 3 Phase Motors	AIR CAPACITY IN CUBIC FEET PER MINUTE AT BLOWER													
			5″		6″		7″		8″		10″		12″		15″	
			Cat. No.	Vol.	Cat. No.	Vol.	Cat. No.	Vol.	Cat. No.	Vol.	Cat. No.	Vol.	Cat. No.	Vol.	Cat. No.	Vol.
¼	$383.50		8001	290												
½	443.00	386.50			8006	315										
¾	490.50	418.00			8011	415	8012	350	8013	300						
1	533.50	454.00					8022	470	8023	400	8024	326				
1½	581.00	510.50							8033	570	8034	460				
2	637.50	546.00											8045	500	8046	400
3	790.00	628.00													8056	600
5	1,046.00	824.50														

All of the above prices are given for blowers equipped with motors of standard currents. Odd voltage direct current motors and 25, 30, 40 and 50 cycle alternating current motors cost more than the standard machines. Consequently, application should be made to the factory for prices on blowers requiring any of these features. Also, machines supplying pressures higher than those given in the preceding tables require more stages, and are, therefore, not covered by the above price list. Inquiries for quotations on special equipment will be given our prompt attention.

The above prices include the Orgoblo complete with motor, intake and outlet check valves, balanced controlling wind valve, counterweight, chain and pulleys for operating this valve, one length of flexible double canvas rubber wind tubing, two clamp collars, flange collar, thick pads to be placed under the Orgoblo feet, and lubricant for the motor.

For all direct current outfits, the above prices include a hand rheostat for starting. Prices on alternating current machines do not include compensators of any type, as for organ blowing, some sort of automatic remote control starter is usually required instead of the ordinary hand compensator.

LINESTART motors may be furnished on all polyphase equipment up to 30 H.P. at no extra cost, provided such a motor is so specified when ordering.

All Prices F. O. B. Hartford, Conn.

SPENCER THE SPENCER TURBINE CO. - HARTFORD, CONN.

ORGAN POWER DIVISION Printed in U.S.A.

Form 1202B-1M-10-1-57 Supersedes 1202B-1M-10-1-56

ORGAN POWER

Net Selling Prices

Standard Three Stage Single Pressure Orgoblos

1150 R. P. M.

Full 1150 R. P. M.

H.P.	Price with 60 Cycle Single Phase Motors	Price with 60 Cycle 2 and 3 Phase Motors	AIR CAPACITY IN CUBIC FEET PER MINUTE AT BLOWER													
			5″		6″		7″		8″		10″		12″		15″	
			Cat. No.	Vol.	Cat. No.	Vol.	Cat. No.	Vol.	Cat. No.	Vol.	Cat. No.	Vol.	Cat. No.	Vol.	Cat. No.	Vol.
¾	$576.50	505.00	8501	500	8502	415										
1	631.00	562.00	8511	660	8512	550	8513	470	8514	400						
1½	734.00	613.00			8521	800	8522	650	8523	570	8524	460				
2	823.00	685.00					8532	850	8533	750	8534	600	8535	500	8536	400
3	1,022.00	814.00					8542	1285	8543	1125	8544	900	8545	750	8546	600
5	1,253.00	974.50											8555	1250	8556	1000
7½	1,422.00	1,095.00											8565	1690	8566	1500
10		1,347.00											8575	2250	8576	2000
15		1,726.00											8585	3380	8586	3000
20		2,113.00											8595	4500	8596	4000
25		2,398.00											8605	5630	8606	5000

All of the above prices are given for blowers equipped with motors of standard currents. Odd voltage direct current motors and 25, 30, 40 and 50 cycle alternating current motors cost more than the standard machines. Consequently, application should be made to the factory for prices on blowers requiring any of these features. Also, machines supplying pressures higher than those given in the preceding tables require more stages, and are, therefore, not covered by the above price list. Inquiries for quotations on special equipment will be given our prompt attention.

The above prices include the Orgoblo complete with motor, intake and outlet check valves, balanced controlling wind valve, counterweight, chain and pulleys for operating this valve, one length of flexible double canvas rubber wind tubing, two clamp collars, flange collar, thick pads to be placed under the Orgoblo feet, and lubricant for the motor.

For all direct current outfits, the above prices include a hand rheostat for starting. Prices on alternating current machines do not include compensators of any type, as for organ blowing, some sort of automatic remote control starter is usually required instead of the ordinary hand compensator.

LINESTART motors may be furnished on all polyphase equipment up to 30 H.P. at no extra cost, provided such a motor is so specified when ordering.

All Prices F. O. B. Hartford, Conn.

SPENCER THE SPENCER TURBINE CO. - HARTFORD, CONN

ORGAN POWER DIVISION Printed in U.S.A.

Form 1202C-1M-10-1-57 Supersedes 1202C-1M-10-1-56

Spencer's 1957 catalog listed substantially the same blowers which were available to theatre organ builders in the 1920s although the prices had doubled.

Where The

Spencer Steel Orgoblo

Is Made.

The Orgoblo has won the Highest Award in every Exposition entered

Special "Orgoblo Junior" for Reed and Student Organs

The Spencer Turbine Company

HARTFORD, CONN.

Organ Power Dept.

New York Office:
101 Park Ave.

Chicago Office
64 East Van Buren St.

Spencer advertisement appearing in the March 1923 issue of The Diapason.

Forty-horsepower Orgoblo which powered the 5/34 Kimball in the Roxy Theatre in New York. There are three wind outlets for 10", 15" and 25" pressures. A Woods motor, the make most commonly used by Spencer in the later 1920s, powers both the blower and a direct-coupled DC generator which provides current for the organ's action. The blower's shaft has too many fans to be supported by the two motor bearings alone so a third bearing is employed at the far end of the shaft. This bearing's grease cup is visible near the wind inlet at the top rear of the machine.

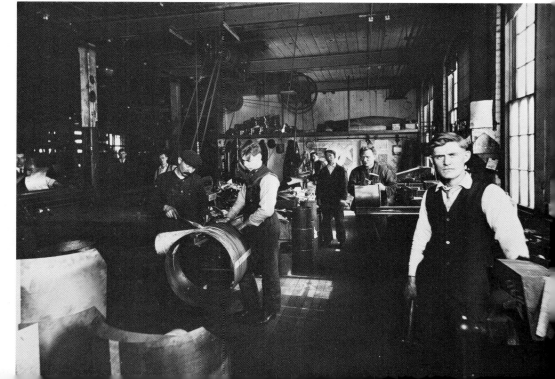

These photographs were taken in the teens in the old Spencer factory on Capitol Avenue in Hartford.

These photos were taken in Spencer's West Hartford factory in the early 1930s. The company moved to this factory in 1919. In the photo on the right, three industrial turbines are being tested in the testing department. These special purpose turbines look little different from their organ blowing brothers but are designed for unique applications such as high temperatures or corrosive or explosive gases.

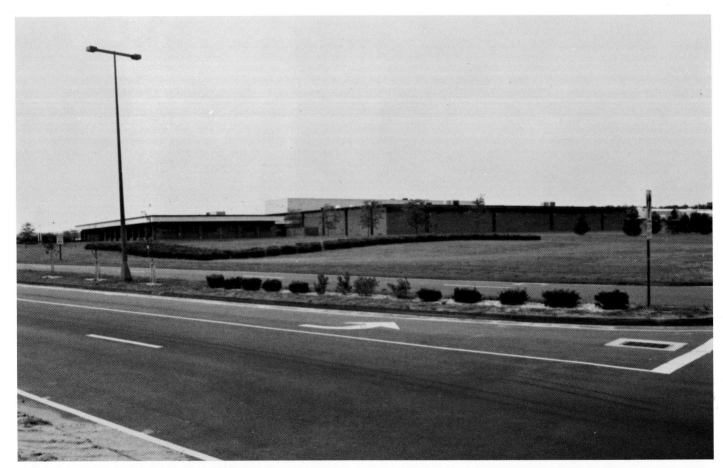

Spencer moved to this beautiful new facility in Windsor, Connecticut in 1975. The wing on the left houses the executive offices and engineering departments. The entire complex, including all manufacturing areas, is air conditioned for maximum comfort of the more than 200 employees.

The new Spencer factory in Windsor, Connecticut is worlds apart from the 1920s. Gone are the overhead belt drives; overhead lighting has supplanted sunlight through the windows; central air conditioning creates optimal working conditions year 'round; and contemporary technology is everywhere, such as the electronic balancing machine (lower right).

The Zephyr Electric Organ Blower Company

MANUFACTURERS OF

ELECTRIC BLOWERS

FOR EVERY KIND OF ORGAN FROM THE SMALL REED ORGAN TO THE LARGEST CATHEDRAL ORGAN

BRANCH OFFICES:

311 ELYSIAN AVE., PITTSBURG, PA.
64 E. VAN BUREN ST., CHICAGO, ILL.
1218 FARNAM STREET, OMAHA, NEB.
1060 PINEWOOD AVE., TOLEDO, OHIO
THE ZEPHYR ORGAN BLOWER SALES CO.,
409 W. 42ND ST., NEW YORK CITY

HOME OFFICE

Orrville, Ohio, U. S. A.

Zephyr blowers were, and still are, manufactured by the Schantz Organ Company of Orrville, Ohio. They are used in all Schantz organs, of course, and are also offered to the trade. After Spencer and Kinetic, Zephyr was the third largest builder of organ blowers in America. See the chapter on Schantz organs in this volume for a detailed history of this firm.

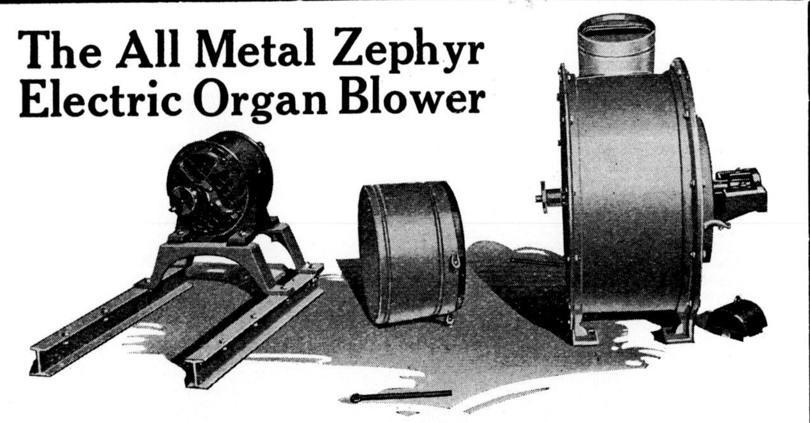

A Zephyr ad in the April 1922 Diapason *noted that over 7,000 had been manufactured at that time.*

Reed Organ Exhaust Blower

H. P.	LENGTH	WIDTH	HEIGHT
¼	1 foot 11 inches	1 foot 10 inches	1 foot 10 inches
1/6	13 inches	13 inches	13 inches

Approximate Capacity in Cubic Feet per Minute of Air

H.P.	3 in.	3½ in.	4 in.	4½ in.	5 in.	6 in.	7 in.	8 in.	10 in.
¼	315	274	240	----	----	----	----	----	----
⅓	485	430	375	----	----	----	----	----	----
½	627	550	472	----	----	----	----	----	----
¾	884	772	664	583	503	----	----	----	----
1	1133	990	852	749	652	----	----	----	----
2	1810	1705	1525	1353	1198	850	730	630	----
3	----	2310	2000	1860	1710	1215	1080	940	755
5	----	3500	3150	2700	2550	2050	1900	1575	1200
7½	----	---	----	4100	3650	3200	2700	2200	1850
10	----	----	----	5550	4950	4010	3650	3050	2600

Shipping Weight

1/6 H. P. Zephyrette Reed Organ Blower	120 lbs.
¼ " Exhaust Reed Organ Blower	190 lbs.
¼ " Pipe Organ Blower	280 lbs.
⅓ " " "	295 lbs.
½ " " "	415 lbs.
¾ " " "	460 lbs.
1 " " "	610 lbs.
1½ " " "	650 lbs.
2 " " "	795 lbs.
3 " " "	925 lbs.
5 " " "	1450 lbs.

Diameter of the Outlet and of Pipe Required for the Various Zephyr Standard Blowers

1/6 and ¼ H. P. Reed Organ Exhauster Blower	5 inch
¼ H.P. Pipe Organ Blower	7 inch
⅓ " " "	7 inch
½ " " "	8 inch
¾ " " "	8 inch
1 " " "	10 inch
1½ " " "	10 inch
2 " " "	12 inch
3 " " "	12 inch
5 " " "	15 inch
7½ " " "	15 inch
10 " " "	18 inch

The Zephyr Versus Water Motors

The use of a Zephyr Organ Blower is a decided improvement over the water motor for the following reasons:

1. It cannot freeze.
2. It gives a constant, even volume of air.
3. It requires no packing.
4. Seldom needs oiling.
5. Cost of operating in most cases less.
6. It does not jerk, squeak, groan, pound or knock.
7. The organ can be tuned much more perfectly, and will stay in tune twice as long.

The Zephyr Versus Other Centrifugal Blowers

The Zephyr has many advantages over other Centrifugal Blowers, among these are:

1. The Zephyr is the only three-bearing machine. One prominent make has only two bearings, thus putting all the weight of the fans on the two motor bearings. Another make has four bearings. The Zephyr having three bearings is the *ideal blower* for long service and economy in operation.

Long life is assured because the weight of the fan is largely carried by the large third bearing, leaving to the motor bearings only the normal load for which they are designed. The economy of operation of the Zephyr is due to the elimination of the useless friction of a fourth bearing, together with scientifically designed fans of light weight.

2. Not affected by heat, cold, or dampness.
3. Special oiling devices.
4. Easy access to all parts.
5. So simple that any mechanic can install.
6. Few parts. Never out of order.
7. Quiet in operation.
8. Fans are one-half lighter than any other, consequently taking less current to deliver the same amount of wind.

Approximate Dimensions

H. P.	LENGTH	WIDTH	HEIGHT
¼	2 feet 11 inches	2 feet	2 feet 4 inches
⅓	2 feet 12 inches	2 feet	2 feet 4 inches
½	3 feet 7 inches	2 feet	2 feet 11 inches
¾	3 feet 8 inches	2 feet	2 feet 11 inches
1	4 f et 1 inch	2 feet 4 inches	3 feet 3 inches
1½	4 feet 3 inches	2 feet 4 inches	3 feet 3 inches
2	4 feet 10 inches	3 feet 1 inch	3 feet 8 inches
3	5 feet 1 inch	3 feet 1 inch	3 feet 8 inches
5	5 feet 2 inches	3 feet 10 inches	3 feet 10 inches
7½	5 feet 6 inches	3 feet 10 inches	3 feet 10 inches
10	5 feet 10 inches	3 feet 10 inches	3 feet 10 inches

Above are two pages from an early Zephyr catalog. Judging from the reference to water motors, it must date from c. 1910 or earlier. Note the references to competing blowers: Spencer Orgoblos had two bearings and Kinetics were four-bearing machines.

CHAMBER HEATERS

BUFFALO GAS RADIATOR CORPORATION

This firm made a brief attempt to capture some business from the organ industry by advertising in The Diapason. *This ad appeared in the June 1927 issue.*

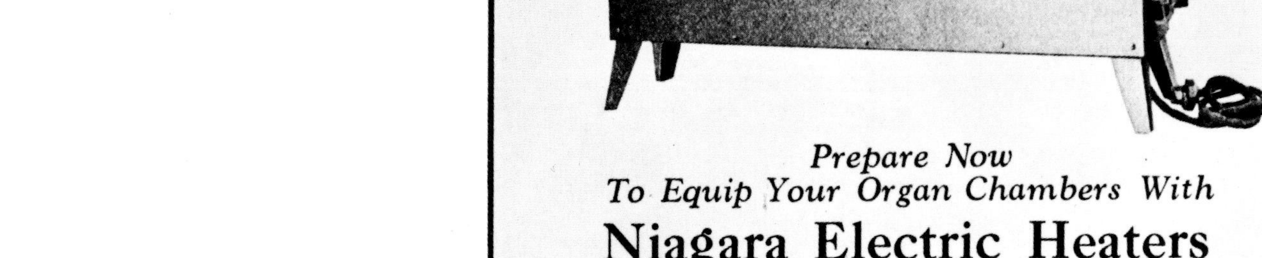

Prepare Now
To Equip Your Organ Chambers With

Niagara Electric Heaters

The best constructed organ will not produce the best results under widely varying temperatures or dampness. During winter and seasons of changeable weather when the heating plant is not operating our Electric Heaters will maintain a uniform temperature, so necessary to avoid "off-pitch" troubles and frequent repair bills.

ELECTRIC HEAT IS IDEAL

Niagara Electric Heaters are particularly adapted to the heating of organ chambers. Our thermostatic control makes their operation automatic and current is used only when the temperature is below the desired point.

Made in three sizes. Easily portable. Require small space. Reasonably priced.

Ask for Our Bulletin No. 32-D

Buffalo Gas Radiator Corporation

NORTH TONAWANDA, N. Y.

Also Manufacturers of Gas and Electric Steam Radiators, Radiator Shields and Enclosures.

Please send, without obligation, your Bulletin No. 32 entitled, "Organ Chamber Heating."

....

....

....

EVENHEETERS
FOR PIPE ORGAN CHAMBERS
THERMOSTATS
ELECTRIC HEATERS
MERCURY CONTACTS

Cramblet Engineering Corp.

ELECTRICAL AND MECHANICAL MANUFACTURING

286-288 MILWAUKEE STREET
Milwaukee, Wis.
PHONE BROADWAY 7942

HOTCHKISS
SIGN FLASHERS
ON AND OFF TYPES
BORDER CHASERS
SPECIAL EFFECTS
MOTOR DRIVEN AND MOTORLESS

Evenheeters and Good Organ Music

ENERGY ALL USED TO CREATE WARM AIR CIRCULATION

NO RADIANT HEAT

OUTSIDE OF HEATER IS COOL TO TOUCH

PROPER pitch and harmonies cannot be rendered by an organ that has chilled pipes, air chests that are affected by weather changes and organ mechanisms that have deteriorated due to climatic conditions. Each organ part must function perfectly if the organ results are to be correct. Every organist knows the humiliation he has suffered when different stops of his console have stuck, or when his whole organ selection has been ruined due to lack of pitch and tone in the organ.

A heated organ chamber, one free from cold and dampness, is a necessity for better organ music, and necessary for proper organ pitch and tone and longer organ life. EVENHEETERS are organ chamber heaters, built to heat your organ chamber with a smooth, even heat. No weather conditions can affect your organ when EVENHEETERS are on the job. Clip the coupon for our descriptive EVENHEETER booklet today.

EVENHEETERS
CRAMBLET ENG. CORP.
286 Milwaukee St. Milwaukee

Cramblet Engineering Corp.,
286 Milwaukee St., Milwaukee, Wis.

Please send me the latest booklet on Evenheeters.

Name ....

Address ....

This Evenheeter ad in the January 1929 Diapason *featured the solo chamber of a Barton theatre organ, probably installed in Cramblet's home town of Milwaukee. Many Barton installations included Evenheeters. Later in 1929 Cramblet was absorbed by the Time-O-Stat Controls Company of Elkhart, Indiana which continued to manufacture Evenheeters into the 1930s.*

PROMETHEUS ELECTRIC CORP.

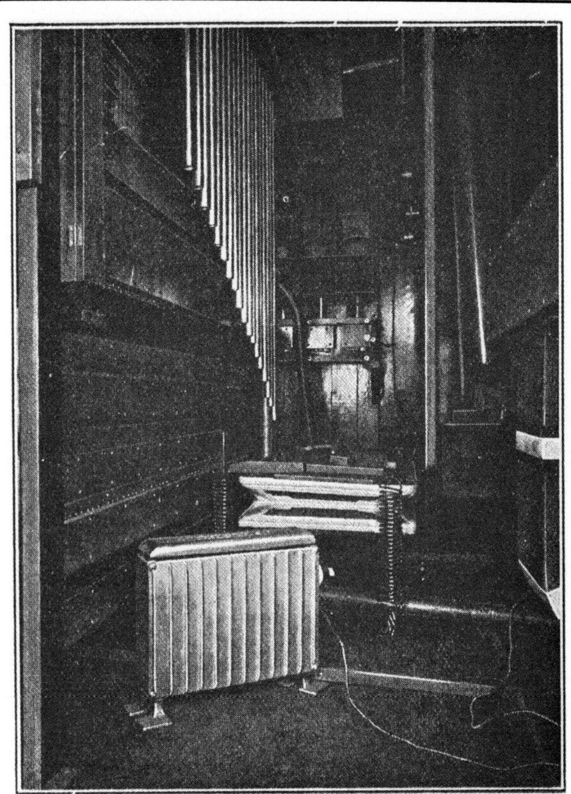

You Don't Buy an Organ Every Day

And, because of that, many of the best known installations in the country are being protected against cold and deterioration by the Prometheus Electric Radiator. The Rialto and Rivoli Theatres in New York are two of the major installations so protected.

The Prometheus Radiator is especially designed to maintain even temperature in organ chambers. Its automatic thermostat will maintain any pre-determined degree of heat, and requires absolutely no attention.

Of special interest to organ owners is the fact that no part of The Prometheus Radiator ever gets red hot. This prevents the air within the chamber being dried out, and insures against the opening of glued seams in nearby woodwork. This feature also permits the radiator to be set directly on the floor, and eliminates all fire hazard.

The radiator is made of cast iron throughout, in aluminum finish, and occupies only 14¼x4 inches of floor space. It is a necessary protection to every organ. ***Write your name on the margin of this advertisement and mail it now for further details.***

PROMETHEUS ELECTRIC CORP.

360 West 13th Street New York City

This ad in the March 1927 Diapason *illustrates a Prometheus heater in use in the chamber of a Wurlitzer theatre organ.*

ELECTRICAL PARTS

AMERICAN STEEL & WIRE COMPANY

This ad appeared in the October 1919 Diapason. *The firm was so solicitous of pipe organ business that they even advertised "reinforcement for concrete swell boxes"!*

AWARDED
PANAMA PACIFIC
GRAND PRIZE
INTERNATIONAL EXPOSITION
Supreme Award of Merit

American Steel & Wire Company

Chicago New York Cleveland Pittsburgh Denver

Maker of

Perfected and Crown Piano Wire

Wire for the Pipe Organ as Follows:

Flat Wire.
Round Wire in various tempers.
Springs.
Wire Rope.
Reinforcement for concrete swell boxes.
Electrical wires, rubber covered; Magnet wire, silk insulated; Pipe Organ wire, paraffined, cotton covered; Console cables, multi-conductors

Highest Standard of Acoustic Excellence

Send for American Piano Wire and Pipe Organ News; sent free for the asking.

BELDEN MANUFACTURING COMPANY

HAIR PIN MAGNETS

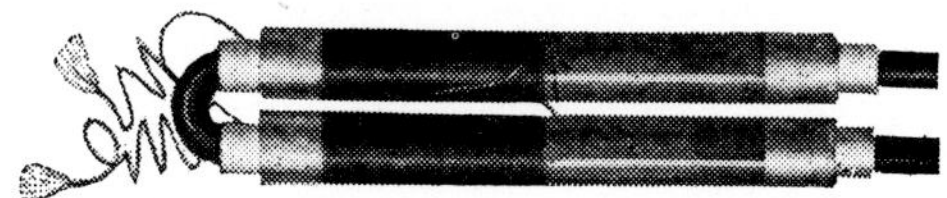

Small magnets for electric organs are made by us at a great saving to organ manufacturers. We have developed standard magnets for this work, prices for which will be sent on application.

Electric control cables designed especially for organ work are not carried in stock; these and other special cables may be manufactured on short notice.

Belden Manufacturing Company
Twenty-Third St. and Western Ave., Chicago

BELDEN

ELECTRIC ORGAN CABLE

Is made up of No. 24 B&S Gauge double cotton covered paraffined copper wire. Conductors stranded with a colored tracer in groups of twelve conductors each (octaves). These groups are cabled together around a group of seven wires, which are used in case of accidents to the octave wire or for extra notes over full octaves. Over all conductors is placed a heavy cotton outside braid, well paraffined.

BELDEN MANUFACTURING COMPANY
2300 S. Western Avenue, Chicago
Eastern Office and Warehouse:
Metuchen, N. J.

In the 1980s Belden is still a major manufacturer of wire and cables. In the 1920s they sought pipe organ business by advertising in The Diapason *as these representative ads in the January 1920 and September 1921 issues indicate.*

ELECTRIC VIBRATO CO.

ALL-ELECTRIC
Seven Tremolos in One
Operates from Console
STAYS PUT
WHERE YOU PUT IT
Trouble Proof
Has Seven Speeds
SPEED CHANGES
INSTANTLY
NO END OF MUSICAL
POSSIBILITIES

THIS ALL-ELECTRIC TREMOLO REVOLUTIONIZES THE PIPE ORGAN

Works Perfectly at Any Wind Pressure and Does Not Drop the Pitch

CONTROL IT AS YOU DESIRE

PATENT PENDING

MANUFACTURED AND SOLD EXCLUSIVELY BY

THE ELECTRIC VIBRATO CO., 114 Howell Ave. **Milwaukee, Wis.**

This firm advertised briefly in 1928 as shown in this ad in the February 1928 Diapason. *The author has never encountered one of these novel tremolos in an organ.*

LONG DISTANCE PHONE 2042

WESTERN UNION CODE
CABLE ADDRESS "ESCO"

ELECTRIC SPECIALTY COMPANY

MANUFACTURERS OF

DIRECT AND ALTERNATING CURRENT MOTORS AND GENERATORS
MOTOR-GENERATORS AND DYNAMOTORS

STAMFORD, CONN., U. S. A.

Electric Specialty supplied the vast majority of generators used in the golden age of the American theatre organ. Generators were often supplied along with organ blowers. Spencer, the country's largest blower manufacturer, was located in nearby Hartford, Connecticut, and this proximity may partially explain the ubiquity of Electric Specialty generators. Their extremely high quality, however, may also account for their widespread use. They were rated quite conservatively and would deliver far more current than their nameplate ratings without strain. As an experiment, the author once untwisted a wire coat hanger, bared its ends and connected them directly across an Electric Specialty generator rated at fifteen amperes. The generator proceeded to pump over 100 amperes into the coat hanger, causing it to glow cherry red—but the generator never even got warm!

A number of other firms built generators for organ use including General Electric, Reliance, Robbins & Myers, and Holtzer-Cabot, to name a few. These firms combined probably accounted for less than 10% of all the organ generators sold in the 1920s and '30s.

"ESCO"

MOTORS AND GENERATORS

TYPE "R" DIRECT CURRENT

(Interchangeable with Type "B" A. C. Motors)

WICK OILED RING OILED

ALSO SUPPLIED WITH BALL BEARINGS

⅛ TO ¾ HORSEPOWER

ELECTRIC SPECIALTY COMPANY

Manufacturers

STAMFORD, CONN., U. S. A.

Bulletin (215A)
Nov., 1923

DIMENSIONS OF MOTORS OR GENERATORS

	Type	A	B	C	D	E	F	G	H	J	K	Pulley Dia.	Pulley Face	Weight Net
Wick Oiled	R1	3⅜	6 5/16	2½	5⅝	3 3/16	4 13/16	3⅜	7	3 11/16	7 3/16	1½	*	24
	R2	4⅛	6 5/16	3¼	5⅝	3 15/16	5 5/16	3¾	7	3 11/16	7 3/16	2	*	30
	R3	4¾	6 5/16	3⅞	5⅝	4 9/16	5⅝	4 1/16	7	3 11/16	7 3/16	2½	2	37
	R4	5¼	6½	4¼	5⅝	5¼	5 13/16	4⅜	7⅛	3 13/16	7⅜	3	2	45
Ring Oiled	R1	3⅜	6 5/16	2½	5⅝	3 3/16	6 1/16	4 3/16	7	3 11/16	7 3/16	2½	2	30
	R2	4⅛	6 5/16	3¼	5⅝	3 15/16	6 7/16	4 9/16	7	3 11/16	7 3/16	2½	2	35
	R3	4¾	6 5/16	3⅞	5⅝	4 9/16	6¾	4⅞	7	3 11/16	7 3/16	2½	2	41
	R4	5¼	6½	4¼	5⅝	5¼	7⅛	5¼	7⅛	3 13/16	7⅜	3	2	49

Shaft diameter of Type R1 wick oiled is ½", all others ⅝" as indicated.
Machines with ball bearings, Dimensions F, ½", and G, ⅝" shorter than for ring oiled types.
*Grooved.

PRICES OF WICK OILED AND RING OILED BEARING MOTORS AND GENERATORS INCLUDING PULLEY

Type	R.P.M.	Motor H.P.	Generator *Watts	5-50 V Wick	5-50 V Ring	115-V Wick	115-V Ring	230-V Wick	230-V Ring	Rating and Price for 500-Volts H.P.	Watts	Wick	Ring
R-1	1150	⅛	80	$31	$35	$28	$32	$30	$34				
	1750	¼	120										
	3500	⅓	160										
R-2	1150	⅙	100	$34	$38	$32	$36	$34	$38				
	1750	⅓	160							¼	150	$42	$46
	3500	4/10	250							¼-⅓	250		
R-3	1150	¼	160	$40	$44	$38	$41	$39	$43	⅕	150	$49	$53
	1750	4/10	240							⅓	200		
	3500	½	320							4/10	300		
R-4	1150	⅓	200		$50	$42	$46	$44	$48	¼	180	$54	$58
	1750	½	300							4/10	250		
	3500	¾	400							½	350		

PULLEYS AND SLIDE BASES: Pulleys are included, for omission deduct $1.00. Slide Bases are not included—if required, add $2.00.

STARTING BOXES are not included with above motor prices. They may be supplied with ½ H. P., 110, 220 and 500 volt motors for $6.00; ¾ H. P., $7.00; 32 volt starters, $9.00.

FIELD RHEOSTATS: For above generators, furnished with 8 contacts for $3.00, or with 21 contacts for $5.00, for voltage of 50 and less. For higher voltages, quoted on application.

*RATINGS: Above generators are all of single commutator type. Wick oiled types have maximum brush capacity for 20 amperes, 1 hour or 18 amperes continuous. Ring oiled or ball bearing types, 40 amperes, 1 hour, or 30 amperes continuous. Wick oiled type has single brush, and ring oiled or ball bearing double brush construction. Type R-4 can be furnished with two commutators for 60 amperes, 1 hour, or 50 amperes continuous and 5 volts—ring oiled $65.00.

OPEN OR CLOSED MACHINES: Ratings are for open construction. For totally enclosed machines allow 70% of ratings given. For such add $1.00 for wick oiled and $2.00 for ring oiled or ball bearing types.

WINDINGS: For shunt or series windings—$1.00 less for first two and $1.50 for last two sizes.

BEARINGS: Ball bearings $6.00 more than ring oiled type. Ball bearing motors can be arranged to run in vertical position without additional expense, when so ordered.

A 1923 Electric Specialty price sheet.

AUGUST A. KLANN

—— MANUFACTURER OF ——

ALL KINDS OF ELECTRO-MAGNETS FOR ORGANS, ETC.

KEY COUPLERS, RELAY COUPLERS, COUPLER SWITCHES

AND ALL OTHER ELECTRICAL PARTS

(PARK STATION)
Waynesboro, Virginia

August Klann was born in Germany in 1872. He emigrated to America in 1898, arriving in San Francisco where he obtained employment with an organ builder. He lost his left hand there while using a power saw. A witness to the accident reported that, to stop the bleeding, Klann thrust his wrist into a pot of hot glue! After the San Francisco earthquake and fire Klann moved to St. Louis where he was employed by Kilgen.[1,2] In 1916 he moved to Alliance, Ohio and began a business of making organ magnets. In 1918 he moved to Basic (now Waynesboro), Virginia where his business expanded to include a variety of organ supplies.[3] Among Klann's clients was Midmer-Losh, who used Klann chest magnets, key actions and remote combination actions in the construction of the world's largest organ, the 7/452 behemoth in Atlantic City's Convention Hall.

August Klann operated the business until his death in 1952 at the age of 80[4] at which time his son Paul Klann took over. In 1988 the firm is still in the organ supply business although plastic injection molding is now a major part of the company's operations. In 1986 Robert G. Lent, the last owner of the United States Pipe Organ Company and a real theatre organ buff, became manager of the pipe organ products division of Klann, Inc., as the firm is now known.

August Klann
(1872-1952)

AUG. A. KLANN
Manufacturer of All Kinds of
Magnets for Organs
Special Magnets for Unit Organ
49 E. Oxford St., Alliance, Ohio

One of Klann's first ads in the September 1917 Diapason *shows his Alliance, Ohio address. Hillgreen-Lane, also located in Alliance, purchased Klann magnets for many years.*

Klann factory as it appeared following a two-story addition in 1928. The original building on the right was built in 1925.[5]

Paul Klann
(1922-)

AUGUST A. KLANN

Manufacturers of

All Kinds of Electro-Magnets for Organs, Etc.

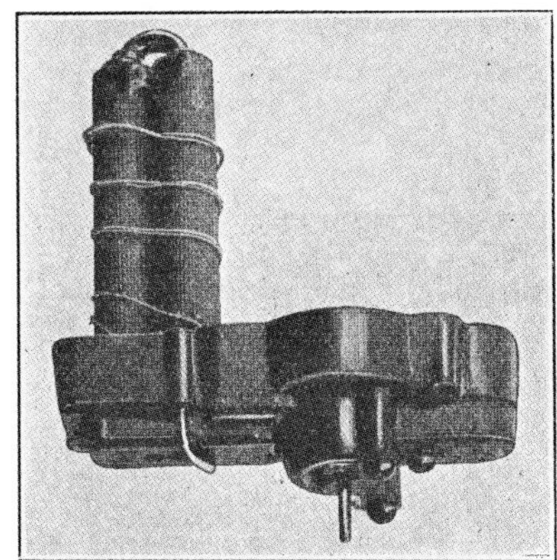

Magnet No. 3/8 for quick action and high pressure.

KEY COUPLERS
RELAY COUPLERS
COUPLER SWITCHES
AND ALL OTHER
ELECTRICAL PARTS

(Park Station) WAYNESBORO, VIRGINIA

Klann's ad in the April 1929 Diapason *featured the type of magnet assembly used for the high wind pressures in the Atlantic City Convention Hall organ. In addition to the magnet itself, the unit included a small pouch and primary valve.*

AUGUST A. KLANN

Manufacturers of

All Kinds of Electro-Magnets for Organs, Etc.

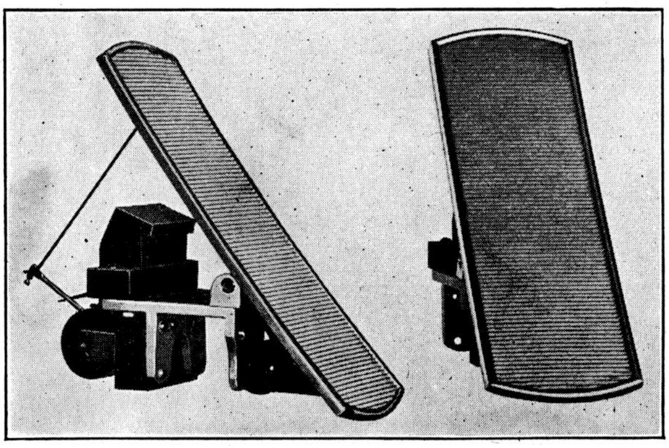

The New Swell Shoe in one unit. The Swell Shoe action. Write for circular.

KEY
COUPLERS
RELAY
COUPLERS
COUPLER
SWITCHES
AND ALL
OTHER
ELEC-
TRICAL
PARTS

(Park Station) WAYNESBORO, VIRGINIA

This swell shoe style was introduced in a* Diapason *ad in July 1930. It is still standard with some builders in the 1980s.

MAGNETIC ORGAN ACTION CO.

NEW ORGAN ACTION ATTRACTS ATTENTION

GREAT SAVING IS CLAIMED

Electric System Designed by St. Louis Concern Eliminates Pneumatics, Etc.—Low Operating Cost as One Feature.

Attention has been directed in the organ trade to a new electric action made by the Magnetic Organ Action Company at St. Louis. It is claimed for the new invention that it will bring about the elimination of pneumatics and that it can be operated on a very low consumption of current.

The Magnetic action is a device, as the name implies, which operates the valves of pipe organs. The unit is so designed and constructed that it moves straight up and down, thus opening and closing the valve. The stroke of the valve is sufficient to allow all the air to pass that can go through the hole in the topboard. The valves are made in sizes up to a one-inch opening in the top-board where ten-inch pressure is used and the voltage is twelve. When the pressure is lower the valves can be scaled to take larger holes.

"For the sake of description we will take the pressure as constant at ten inches and the voltage at twelve," says a letter to The Diapason in response to a request for a description of the invention. "The large valve unit and the one that takes the most current then would be the one-inch topboard hole size. This magnet is wound at sixty ohms resistance. Consequently it would consume two-tenths of an ampere at twelve volts. The current consumption is very small when it is considered that the valve stroke is approximately three-eighths of an inch.

The sparking is practically eliminated; this is necessary because the contacts in organs are very fine and small and must stand up for years.

"The Magnetic organ action units are made in five sizes as follows: 60, 80, 120, 160 and 240 ohms resistance. The sixty and eighty ohms resistance units have a special winding to eliminate the spark; the other units have a regular winding. The units under test should not heat even though left in a closed circuit for hours.

"Unifying becomes very simple when these actions are used; also it appears as though for use in straight organ work there is a possible saving, as the laying out and building of chests is not confined to channeling or pouch sizes.

"The outstanding feature of the action is that it uses no larger generator for the same size organ than is generally used today in unified work, because there are only a few sixty and eighty-ohm magnets used on the low side and the remainder of the units consume little current. At the present time some pedal or bass valves will require pneumatics or pouches. The units can handle such a large volume of wind that there are many places in which they can be used other than for the valves under the pipes; also they can be used to operate stopkeys and switches, and here the efficiency of the action shows itself, for stopkeys can be operated on one-tenth of an ampere at twelve volts. The common solenoid magnet to do the same work would require four to eight times the amount of current and the common magnet eight to ten times the amount."

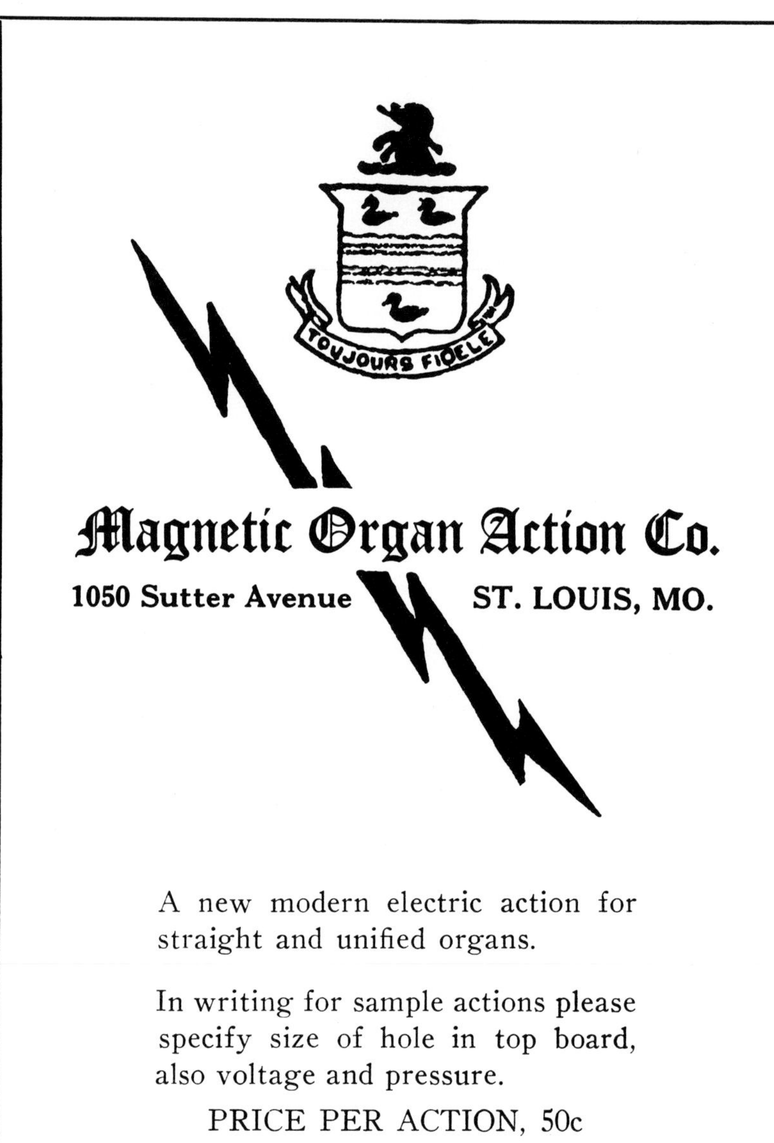

TOUJOURS FIDELE
Magnetic Organ Action Co.
1050 Sutter Avenue
ST. LOUIS, MO.
A new modern electric action for straight and unified organs.
In writing for sample actions please specify size of hole in top board, also voltage and pressure.
PRICE PER ACTION, 50c

The above ad and article appeared in the May 1928 Diapason. *This may have been the first direct electric chest action offered to the trade. The firm was short-lived; perhaps their magnet infringed on the Wicks patents. In 1928 Wicks was the only firm using direct electric action which they had patented c. 1914.*

EMIL MEURLING

EMIL MEURLING ∴ ∴ Reynolds, Ill.

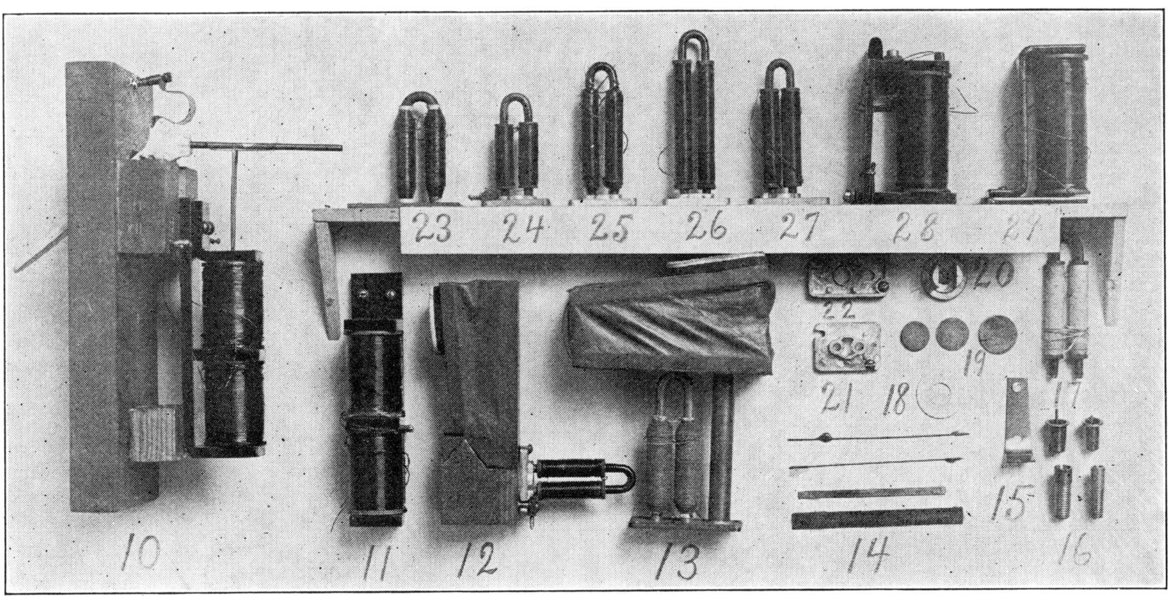

The above cut shows a part of the line manufactured by us. Added floor space and increased working force allows prompt shipments. Circulars and prices on request. Consult us fully regarding your electrical difficulties.

The above ad appeared in the August 1922 Diapason. *Mr. Meurling died in 1929.*

PITTSBURGH ORGAN PARTS COMPANY

The refillable contact block would have been a good idea for organs receiving heavy silent movie usage. Unfortunately, it was first advertised in the July 1929 Diapason *when silent movies were approaching extinction.*

New Refillable Double Contact Block

They Last the Life of the Organ

One Hundred Per Cent Better

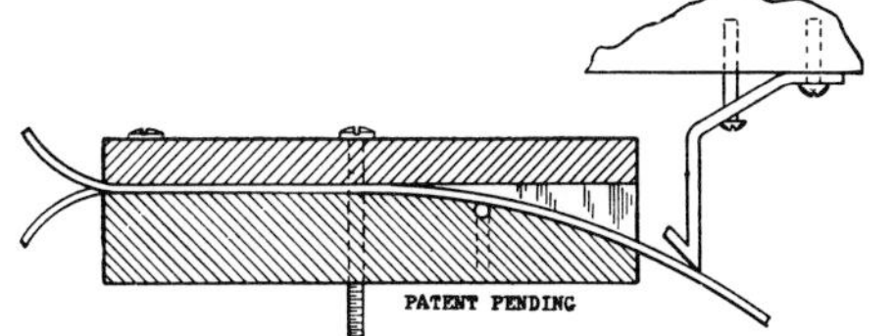

They Cost No More

Contact Block After Key Is Depressed, Showing the Double Contact and Wire With Bend Distributed Over Entire Length

THE PITTSBURGH ORGAN PARTS COMPANY
1012 Forbes Street
Pittsburgh, Pennsylvania

SEND FOR SAMPLES

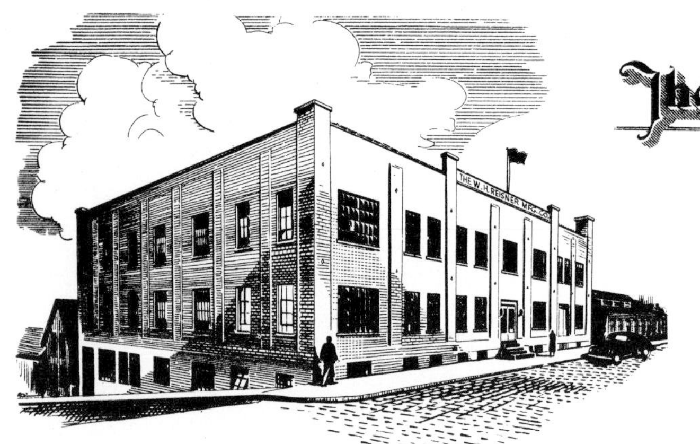

The W. H. Reisner Mfg. Co., Inc.

Coil Winding, Relays and Electrical Specialties
Pipe Organ Magnets and Supplies

Hagerstown, Md.

As a lad of fifteen, W. H. Reisner (pronounced reesener) began his apprenticeship as a watchmaker and engraver. At age 22 he went into business for himself as a manufacturing jeweler. After being in the jewelry business for fifteen years he decided in 1902 to devote his entire efforts to the manufacture of precision optical devices (such as retinoscopes) and precision measuring devices (such as Starrett dial gages).[1] Fishing tackle was also offered by his firm, reflecting Mr. Reisner's lifelong interest in that sport. With the backing of Hagerstown businessman M. P. Moller, Reisner incorporated his firm in 1904; Moller became the company's president. By 1906 Reisner was making springs for the Beckwith Organ Co., a reed organ manufacturer, and by 1907 the firm's logo included the phrase "pipe organ hardware." By 1909[2] magnets were being manufactured for Moller[3] and pipe organ products were becoming a significant portion of Reisner's sales.

In 1920 the optical and precision instrument part of the business was sold and Mr. Reisner became president of the organ supply business. Sales escalated rapidly and in 1924 a new factory with 21,000 square feet of floor space was built just a short walk down Prospect Street from the Moller factory.[4] This building, pictured above in the firm's logo, still houses the company in 1988.

Following Mr. Reisner's death in 1951 his son Bill Reisner, Jr. took over the business. In 1969 it was purchased by the Wright family of Warren, Massachusetts and became known as Reisner, Inc. In 1984 Reisner president Peter Wright negotiated an agreement whereby products of the British organ supply firm Kimber-Allen would be sold under the name Reisner Kimber Allen.[5] This association was disbanded late in 1986.[6]

Although Reisner has produced a variety of organ components for the trade, including complete consoles, the firm is best remembered for their chest magnets. Reisner designs set standards for the industry and were the most widely used of all manufacturers. Some builders, including Page and Aeolian-Skinner, purchased Reisner magnets with their own logos embossed in them. Millions of Reisner magnets have been sold since 1909.

William Harry Reisner (1865-1951)

View in the Reisner machine shop c. 1946.

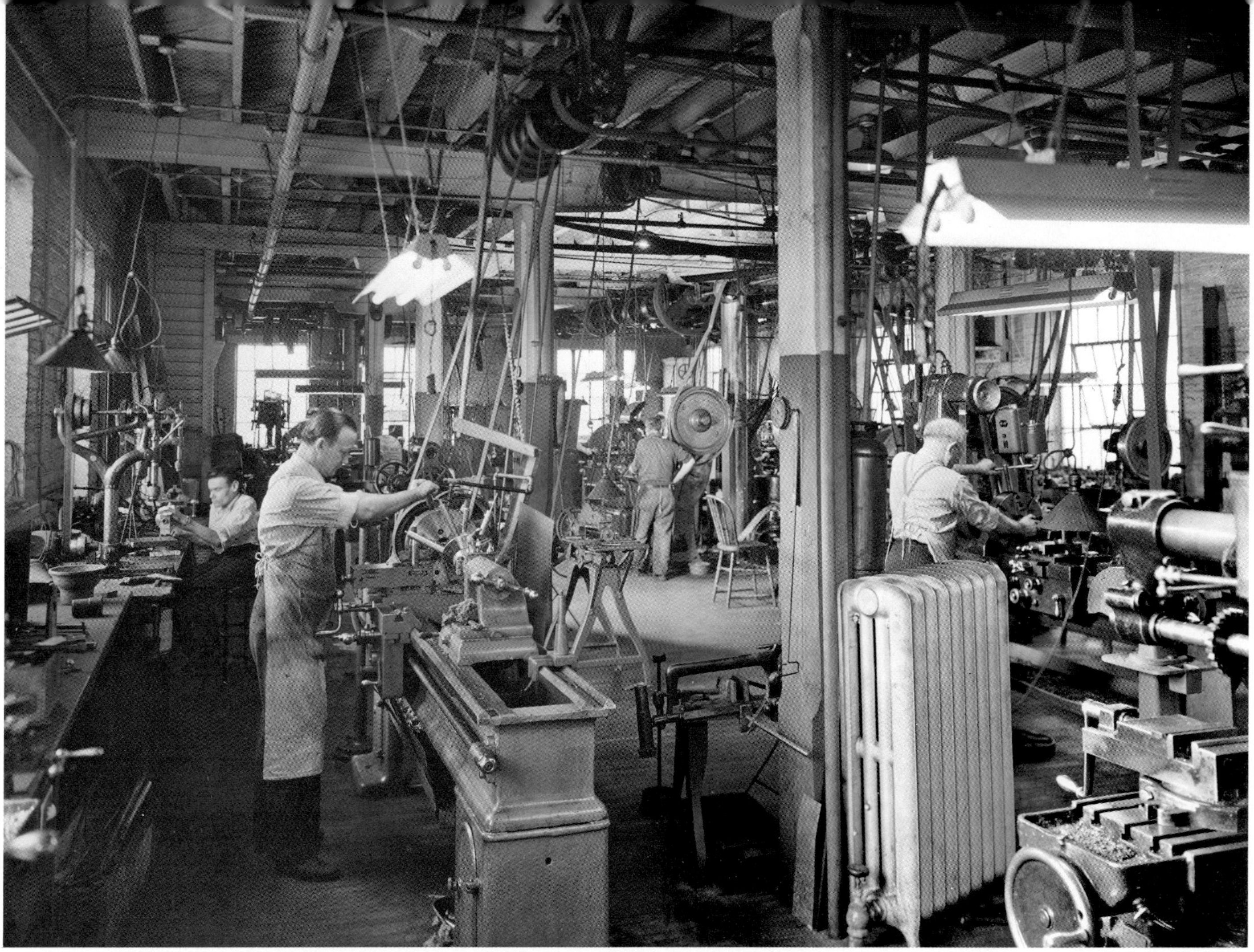

Additional views in the Reisner machine shop c. 1946.

DEPENDABILITY

has been built into

The World's Largest Pipe Organ

in the world's largest auditorium at Atlantic City, New Jersey.

This dependability is confirmed by Roscoe C. Evans, who has serviced this giant since it played its first note in 1929.

ORGANIST'S VIEW OF MAIN CONSOLE gives you some idea of the huge size of this organ. The greatest volume of music ever heard from a single instrument can be produced by its seven manuals and 1250 stops.

The stop action magnets controlling these stops were manufactured by Reisner, and have been giving dependable service for twenty years.

You can depend on parts by Reisner.

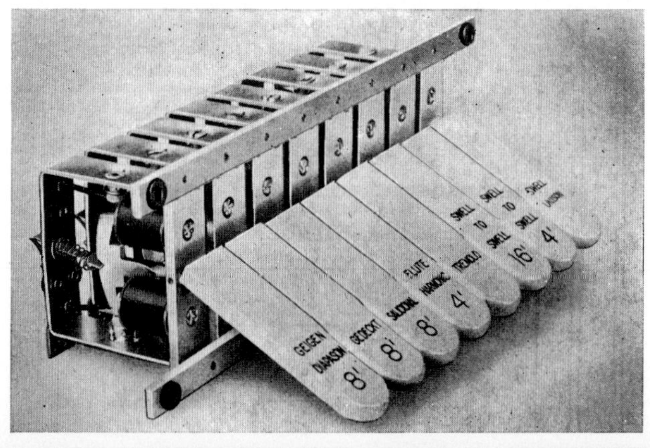

THE W. H. REISNER *Manufacturing* COMPANY, INCORPORATED ◈ HAGERSTOWN, MD., U.S.A.

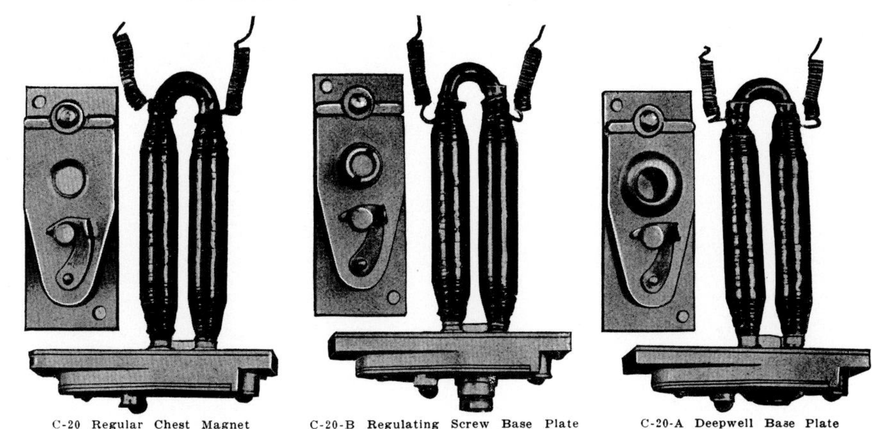

C-20 Regular Chest Magnet   C-20-B Regulating Screw Base Plate   C-20-A Deepwell Base Plate

Magnets for Maximum Service on 4 to 8″ Wind Pressure

Each type is wound for 90 ohms resistance, at 6 to 10 volts. They are absolutely dependable and the greatest care is taken to have every magnet 100% good.

Our C-20 Regular is a good all-around magnet for average pressure. Our C-20-A is a veritable dirt catcher and has much to recommend it. Our C-20-B has a regulating tube screw, which is especially valuable in adjusting for air volume. We are now past the experimental stage on these types, which can be furnished with or without our patented copper bound armature. These armatures are particularly desirable where atmsopheric conditions are such that paper or glue would be affected.

If you have never used our magnets, we are sure if you give them a trial they will please you.

In addition to magnets, we make a complete line of supplies for the pipe organ. Write for information and samples.

THE W. H. REISNER MFG. CO., Hagerstown, Md., U. S. A.

Ad in the January 1927 Diapason *illustrates several of the C series of Reisner chest magnets. These were used by Barton, Bennett, Geneva, Gottfried, Hinners, Howell, Link, Louisville, Page, Wangerin and many other builders.*

Reisner's December 1929 Diapason *ad depicts two additional varieties of their C series magnets. The style on the right was used by Barton in the Chicago Stadium organ to actuate 25″ and 35″ pressure chests.*

C-17 Type Chest Magnets

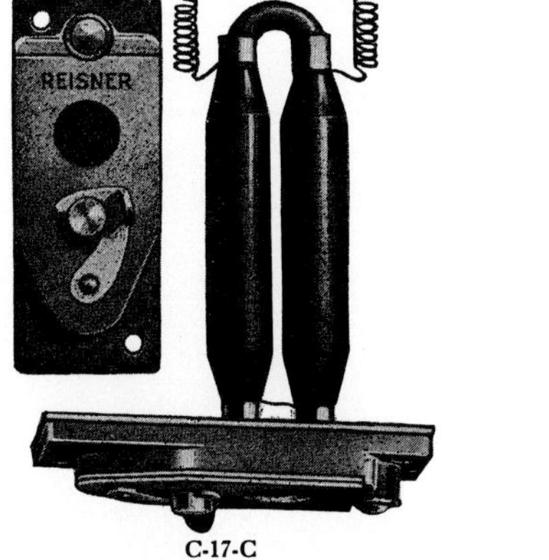

C-17-C

C-17-1M

We make this type in the same style and variety as our C-20 Chest Magnets, the difference being a greater and more evenly divided air accommodation. For low wind pressure they give the maximum quantity of air. Any of our different style base plates can be used as conditions demand.

The C-17-C has 90 ohms resistance, for low wind pressure, with coils uncovered. The C-17-1M has 140 ohms resistance, for high wind pressure, and has a one-piece cover over both coils, giving added protection in their handling and installation.

We shall be pleased to send samples of any of our various type chest magnets.

THE W. H. REISNER MFG. CO.
HAGERSTOWN, MARYLAND U. S. A.
European Representative, Aug. Laukhuff, Weikersheim, Wurttemberg, Germany

(opposite) This ad in the July 1949 Diapason *touts the reliability of another well-known Reisner product, their all-electric stop action magnet. All 1240 stop keys in the Atlantic City console were also supplied and engraved by Reisner.*[6]

TRIUMPH ELECTRIC CORPORATION

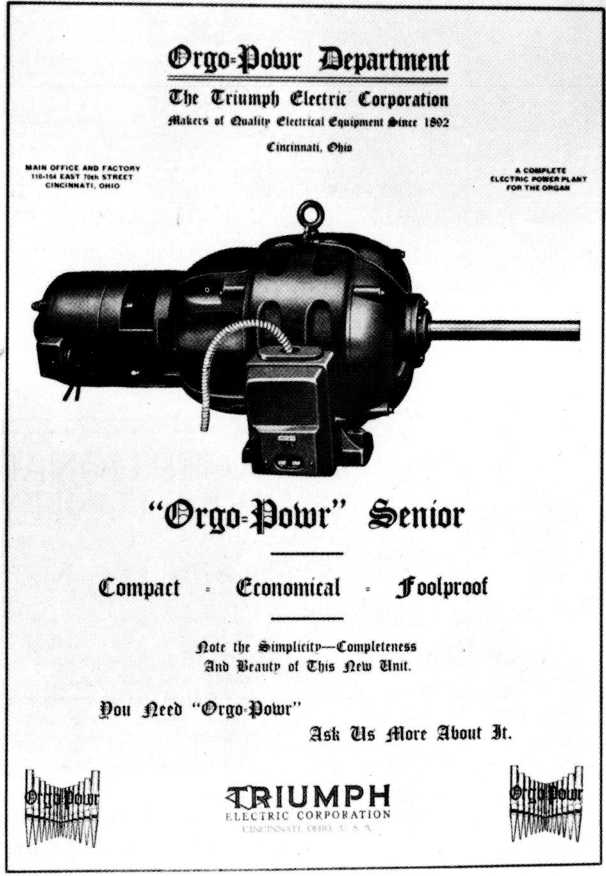

This clever combination of a blower motor and DC generator was introduced in an ad in the September 1928 Diapason. *The novel idea apparently didn't catch on because few were ever sold.*

THE WIDNEY COMPANY

Widney's activity in the organ industry was primarily in the teens. This ad appeared in the March 1917 Diapason.

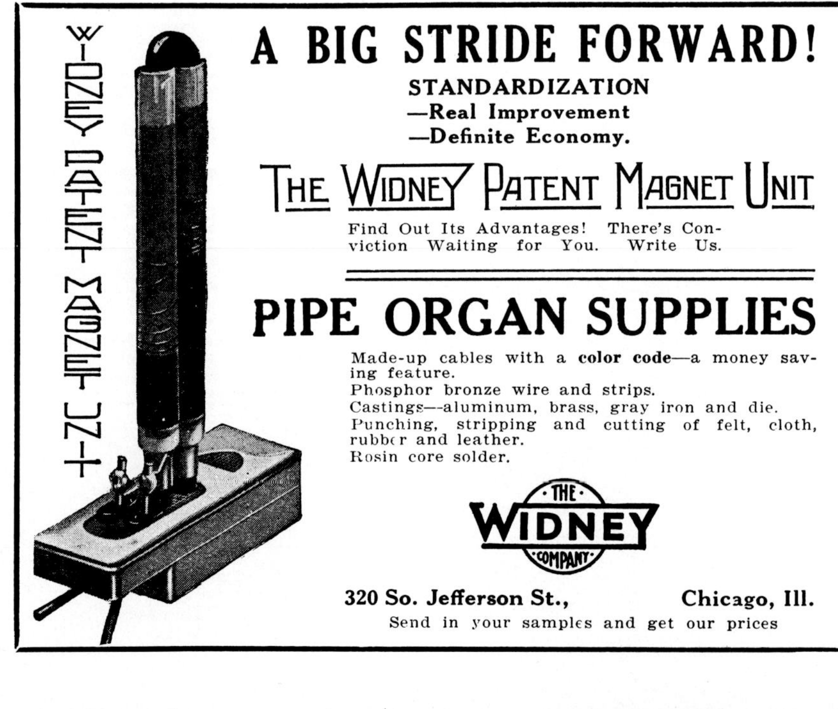

BARTOLA MUSICAL INSTRUMENT CO.

Barton secured a sizable percentage of the console elevator business in the midwest. As might be expected, many Barton consoles rode atop Barton lifts. However, a surprising number of Wurlitzers, Marr & Coltons, Kimballs and other makes of theatre organs were elevated by Barton equipment in midwestern theatres. Barton lifts were made primarily in one style, differing from each other only in platform dimensions. Two Barton turntable lifts are known to the author, both on Barton organs in Chicago: the Regal Theatre's 3/14 and the Chicago Stadium's 6/51.

For a history of the Bartola company and a number of photographs of Barton lift installations, see the Barton chapter in Volume I of *Encyclopedia of the American Theatre Organ.*

WARSAW ELEVATOR CO.

The Warsaw Elevator Co. was located adjacent to the Marr & Colton factory in Warsaw, New York. It evolved from a foundry which made pumps and farm implements. The company's first hand-rope elevator was made in 1889 and by 1920 electric elevators were added to the line.[1] With a theatre organ factory next door, it was inevitable that the Warsaw Elevator Co. would enter the theatre business. They got in on the ground floor, as it were, and their products were sold all over the country for use with Marr & Colton and with other makes of theatre organs. The author once owned a Warsaw turntable lift which raised, as well as revolved, the 3/11 Hinners organ in the Madison Theatre in Peoria, Illinois.

Warsaw was in business until 1962 when it was purchased by the Turnbull Co., elevator manufacturers of Toronto, Canada.[2] For a picture of a typical Warsaw console elevator installation, see the photo on page 292 of *Encyclopedia of the American Theatre Organ,* Volume I.

CURTIS PNEUMATIC MACHINERY COMPANY

The market for console lifts had nearly evaporated when this ad appeared. The installation featured was the 3/8 Wurlitzer in the Plaza Theatre, Kansas City, Missouri, installed late in 1928.

OTIS ELEVATOR COMPANY

Elisha Graves Otis founded the elevator industry in 1853. The year before, in his capacity as master mechanic for the Bedstead Manufacturing Company of Yonkers, New York, he created the world's first safe elevator which would not fall if the hoisting rope broke. The Bedstead company went bankrupt, however, and Otis was making plans to join the California gold rush when he received an unsolicited order for two of his "safety hoisters." The order came from a furniture manufacturer who had an old hoist on which the rope had snapped, sending two employees to their deaths.[1] And the rest, as they say, is history. The name Otis became synonymous with elevators in the public mind in an elite hierarchy of trademarks including Victrola, cellophane—and Wurlitzer! Otis has also had the honor of having one of their trademarks pass into generic usage: the escalator.

Otis became the dominant firm in the elevator industry. In 1898 Otis Brothers & Co. merged with fourteen other elevator firms to form the Otis Elevator Company.[2] Since 1889 every "tallest" building in the world has been equipped with Otis elevators. Preoccupied with prestige installations such as the Woolworth, Chrysler and Empire State buildings, Otis spent little effort soliciting small jobs such as organ console lifts, with the result that most of this business went to other firms. An interesting exception is the Hershey Community Theatre in Hershey, Pennsylvania, which purchased not only an Otis turntable lift for its 4/71 Aeolian-Skinner but also an Otis orchestra lift and seven Otis stage lifts. A photograph of this organ lift appears on page 601 of this volume.

Still the world leader in elevator technology, Otis Elevator Company became a wholly owned subsidiary of United Technologies Corporation in 1976.[3]

Elisha Graves Otis gave a daring demonstration of his safety hoist at the 1854 Crystal Palace Exposition in New York City. After ordering the rope cut, he announced to an astonished crowd, "All safe gentlemen, all safe."[4]

The author has long been fascinated by elevators. In 1957 he was given a thorough education by William Bruns, Otis' chief research engineer, as his mother watched in the background.

AN OTIS CONSOLE ELEVATOR *installed in* SOUTH AFRICA

Organ Console Installed on Elevator Platform

METRO-GOLDWYN-MAYER THEATRE
Johannesburg, South Africa

Architects
Thos. W. Lamb, Inc.,
New York, N.Y.

Supervising Architects
Cowin, Powers & Ellis,
Johannesburg, South Africa.

THIS VERTICAL-SCREW CONSOLE ELEVATOR may be raised, lowered, or turned about, at the touch of a'button. Its operation and construction have met with unqualified approval.

Our Johannesburg office writes: "Mr. Archie Parkhouse, the organist, who was previously engaged with Metro, London, and has also been on an extensive circuit for the Metro-Goldwyn concern, is highly pleased with the installation, and has remarked on more than one occasion that it is the best Organ Console Elevator with which he has come in contact."

The Building

It is interesting, too, to note that the contract for this elevator was placed by the New York office of Metro-Goldwyn-Mayer with the New York office of Otis Elevator Company.

OTIS ELEVATOR COMPANY, NEW YORK

An Otis bulletin issued July 15, 1933 features a 3/13 Wurlitzer.

PETER CLARK, INC.

Peter Clark supplied the majority of console lifts installed in American theatres. Most featured a center screw which required a hole in the pit equal to the rise of the lift platform. A later design incorporated a rear screw which required no extra pit excavation.

A number of other manufacturers made hydraulic, screw and even cable-operated console lifts. Most supplied limited regional markets, leaving the large national business to Peter Clark. Clark's nearest competitor sales-wise was probably Barton, whose famous four-poster screw lifts, requiring no pit excavation at all, were found under many Genevas, Kilgens, Kimballs, Marr & Coltons and Wurlitzers, as well as Bartons. At least two other firms sold a limited number of console lifts on a national basis: the Warsaw Elevator Company, whose factory was adjacent to Marr & Colton's; and the Otis Elevator Company. It is curious that Otis, the world's largest elevator manufacturer, never entered the theatre market in a serious way.

LOEW'S and UNITED ARTISTS PENN THEATRE

Pittsburgh

Rapp & Rapp, Architects

are equipped with our

Revolving Organ Console Orchestra Lift, Piano Lift and Full Stage Equipment

including counterweight system and fire curtain

OTHER IMPORTANT INSTALLATIONS INCLUDE

Roxy Theatre, New York
Paramount Theatre, New York
Colony Theatre, New York
Rivoli Theatre, New York
Ziegfeld Theatre, New York
Strand Theatre, New York
West Farms Theatre, Bronx, N. Y.
Beacon Theatre, Brooklyn
Metropolitan Theatre, Boston
Capitol Theatre, Boston
Uptown Theatre, Chicago
Oriental Theatre, Chicago
Tivoli Theatre, Chicago
Howard Theatre, Chicago
Tower Theatre, Chicago
Marbro Theatre, Chicago
Harding Theatre, Chicago
Belmont Theatre, Chicago
Diversey Theatre, Chicago
North Center Theatre, Chicago
Royal Theatre, Joliet
Missouri Theatre, St. Louis
St. Louis Theatre, St. Louis
State Theatre, Detroit
Orchestra Hall, Detroit
Michigan Theatre, Detroit
Shea's Theatre, Buffalo
Saengers Theatre, New Orleans
Eastman Theatre, Rochester
Kilborn Hall, Rochester
United Artists Theatre, Los Angeles

PETER CLARK, INC.

534-546 West 30th St. NEW YORK CITY

Several of the theatres mentioned in this ad from the October 1, 1927 Exhibitor's Herald *are pictured elsewhere in this volume. See pages 533, 535 and 603.*

A PETER CLARK CONSOLE LIFT as installed in the Southtown Theatre, Chicago, where complete stage equipment by Peter Clark is used.

BOX OFFICE HELPS

CONSIDER the theatre-goer. WHERE to go is his problem. In many communities he has the choice of several theatres where he can see the same picture in the course of time. Why should he patronize YOUR theatre?

A Peter Clark ORGAN CONSOLE LIFT puts the stamp of modernity on YOUR THEATRE. A draw curtain with projection booth control, a better screen—with automatic maskings—by Peter Clark, all help box office receipts. Popularize your theatre by MODERNIZING it. An investment that pays sure dividends.

Correspondence Invited

PETER CLARK, INC.

"Stage Equipment with a Reputation"

542 WEST 30TH STREET, NEW YORK, N. Y.

This ad in Motion Picture Herald *featured Chicago's Southtown Theatre and its 4/20 Wurlitzer. The organ had been moved from its original location in the Congress (Mexico) Theatre in Chicago.*

GENERAL SUPPLIES

DURST & COMPANY, INC.

PIPE ORGANS

AND SUPPLIES

32nd Street Hazel to Poplar

ERIE, PA.

The firm of Durst, Boegle & Co. was formed in 1926 by Val Durst and Ignatz Boegle (pronounced beg-lee), who had been employees of the A. Gottfried Company, and W. C. Kibler. Before joining Gottfried, Val Durst (1888-1965) had been with the Hinners Organ Company in Pekin, Illinois from 1912 to 1917. His brother, Fred Durst, had been superintendent of Hinners and in 1917 moved to Erie to assume a similar position with Gottfried. In 1924 Fred Durst left Gottfried to form the Organ Supply Corporation.[1,2,3] The founding of Durst, Boegle & Co. in 1926 only furthered the rivalry between the Durst brothers.

Durst, Boegle & Co. found a ready market for organ supplies of lower cost (and lower quality) than the competing Gottfried and Organ Supply firms. Within three years they outgrew their first building at 20th and Peach Streets, which had been the Erie Burial Case Company, and in 1929 they purchased the Cambridge trolley car barn at 32nd and Hazel Streets.[4] By 1931 the firm name had become Durst & Company, Inc. In 1944 Val Durst's son, Roland E. Durst, assumed management of the company and in 1971 sold the business to Fred Gluck. In 1972 Mr. Gluck also purchased Organ Supply Corporation. The two factories were consolidated at the Durst building and the firm name was changed to Durst Organ Supply Co., Inc. In 1978 the name was changed to Organ Supply Industries, Inc.[5] and many organ builders who take pride in their work, including the author, were delighted that the name of the company was once again associative of the old Organ Supply Corporation, long the industry standard for the highest quality products.

In 1929 an old trolley car barn became the home of Durst, Boegle & Co. Considerably expanded, the same building today houses Organ Supply Industries, Inc.

This ad in the May 1928 Diapason *featured a console built for organ builder Arthur Kohl who installed it in the Monroe Theatre in Rochester, New York.*

QUALITY SERVICE PRICE

CONSOLES

PIPES
CHESTS
ACTIONS
PERCUSSIONS
RESERVOIRS
TREMOLOS

Durst, Boegle & Co.

MANUFACTURER

ORGAN SUPPLIES

1917 PEACH STREET
ERIE, PA.

An early scene in the Durst factory.

This two-manual Durst console was probably built for Rochester, New York organ builder Arthur Kohl.

Ignatz Boegle, far left, and Val Durst, far right, are pictured in the Gottfried factory in 1925, shortly before they formed Durst, Boegle & Co. This particular console, the only five manual ever built by Gottfried, was constructed for organ builder S. H. Barrington who installed it in the Ardmore Theatre in Ardmore, Pennsylvania.

On the next five pages are reproduced extracts from an early Durst catalog. Wouldn't it be fun to place an order at these prices today!

	Name of Pipe	Compass	Inside Scale	Scale No.	Outside Scale	Unvoiced	Voiced
16′	Pedal Open Violone	CCC 32	6 x 6		7¾ x 7¾	325.00	380.00
16′	Pedal Lieblich Gedeckt	CCC 32	4½ x 5¾		6 x 7¼	105.00	135.00
8′	Pedal Flute (Stopped)	CCC 32	4½ x 5¾		5¾ x 7	65.00	95.00
8′	Pedal Flute (Open)	CCC 32	4½ x 6		6 x 7½	105.00	140.00
16′	Manual Bourdon	CC 61	5½ x 7	Ex.	7 x 8½	125.00	168.00
16′	Manual Bourdon	C 49	3⅜ x 4½		4½ x 5½	45.00	70.00
16′	Manual Bourdon	CC 61	5 x 6½	1	6½ x 8	115.00	160.00
16′	Manual Bourdon	C 49	3 x 4	1	4¼ x 5¼	40.00	65.00
16′	Manual Bourdon	CC 61	4½ x 5¾	2	6 x 7¼	115.00	158.00
16′	Manual Bourdon	C 49	2¾ x 3¾	2	3⅞ x 4⅞	40.00	65.00
16′	Manual Bourdon	CC 61	4 x 5	3	5½ x 6½	105.00	145.00
16′	Manual Bourdon	C 49	2½ x 3½	3	3½ x 4½	38.00	63.00
16′	Tibia Plena	CCC 73	10 x 12	1	12 x 14	360.00	450.00
16′	Tibia Plena	CC 61	6 x 7	1	7½ x 8½	123.00	160.00
16′	Tibia Plena Lower 6 Stpd	CCC 73	10 x 12	1	12 x 14	305.00	375.00
16′	Tibia Plena Lower 12 Stpd	CCC 73	10 x 12	1	12 x 14	280.00	355.00
16′	Tibia Plena	CCC 73	8 x 9½	2	10 x 11½	225.00	310.00
16′	Tibia Plena	CC 61	5 x 6	2	6^1 x 7¼	90.00	130.00
16′	Tibia Plena Lower 6 Stpd	CCC 73	8 x 9½	2	10 x 11½	185.00	270.00
16′	Tibia Plena Lower 12 Stpd	CC 61	8 x 9½	2	10 x 11½	175.00	250.00
16′	Tibia Clausia	CCC 73	10 x 12	1	12 x 14	275.00	335.00
16′	Tibia Clausia	CCC 12	10 x 12	1	12 x 14	163.00	187.00
16′	Tibia Clausia	CCC 73	8 x 9½	2	10 x 11½	180.00	235.00
16′	Tibia Clausia	CCC 12	8 x 9½	2	10 x 11½	95.00	118.00
16′	Tibia Clausia	CCC 73	7 x 8½	3	8⅝ x 10⅛	155.00	200.00
16′	Tibia Clausia	CCC 12	7 x 8½	3	8⅝ x 10⅛	85.00	105.00
16′	Bass Flute	CCC 97	8 x 9½	1	10 x 11½	175.00	245.00
16′	Bass Flute	CCC 97	7 x 8½	2	8⅝ x 10⅛	150.00	218.00
8′	Tibia Clausia	CC 61	6 x 7	1	7½ x 8½	102.00	145.00
8′	Tibia Clausia	C 49	3⅝ x 4⅜	1	4¾ x 5½	62.00	85.00
8′	Tibia Clausia	CC 61	5 x 6	2	6¼ x 7¼	78.00	115.00

	Name of Pipe	Compass	Inside Scale	Scale No.	Outside Scale	Unvoiced	Voiced
8′	Tibia Clausia	C 49	2⅞ x 3⅝	2	3⅞ x 4⅝	49.00	72.00
8′	Tibia Clausia	CC 61	4 x 5	3	5¼ x 6¼	58.00	98.00
8′	Tibia Clausia	C 49	2½ x 3½	3	3½ x 4½	34.00	54.00
8′	Night Horn	CC 61	6 x 7	1	7½ x 8½	103.00	133.00
8′	Night Horn	C 49	3⅝ x 4⅜	1	4¾ x 5½	62.00	80.00
8′	Night Horn	CC 61	5 x 6	2	6¼ x 7¼	79.00	107.00
8′	Night Horn	C 49	2⅞ x 3⅝	2	3⅞ x 4⅝	47.00	64.00
8′	Night Horn	CC 61	4 x 5	3	5¼ x 6¼	60.00	91.00
8′	Night Horn	C 49	2½ x 3½	3	3½ x 4½	34.00	53.00
8′	Doppel Flute (upper Oct. Meta.)	CC 61	4 x 5	1	5¼ x 6¼	79.00	123.00
8′	Doppel Flute (upper Oct. Meta.)	C 49	2¼ x 3¼	1	3⅜ x 4⅜	50.00	87.00
8′	Gross Flute (Stpd Bass)	CC 61	6 x 7	1	7½ x 8½	110.00	140.00
8′	Gross Flute	C 49	3⅝ x 4⅜	1	4¾ x 5½	72.00	92.00
8′	Gross Flute (Stpd Bass)	CC 61	5 x 6	2	6¼ x 7¼	75.00	105.00
8′	Gross Flute	C 49	3⅛ x 4⅜	2	4⅛ x 5⅜	43.00	62.00
8′	Clarabella (Stpd Bass)	CC 61	3¾ x 4¾	1	4⅞ x 5⅞	51.00	80.00
8′	Clarabella	C 49	2⅜ x 3	1	3¼ x 3⅞	32.00	52.00
8′	Concert Flute (Stpd Bass)	CC 61	3⅜ x 4½	1	4⅜ x 5⅝	55.00	85.00
8′	Concert Flute	C 49	2 3/16 x 3	1	3 x 3⅞	34.00	57.00
8′	Concert Flute (Stpd Bass)	CC 61	2¾ x 3¾	2	3⅞ x 4⅞	50.00	80.00
8′	Concert Flute	C 49	1 15/16 x 2⅝	2	2¾ x 3¼	28.00	48.00
8′	Gedeckt	CC 61	3⅜ x 4½	1	4½ x 5⅝	47.00	75.00
8″	Gedeckt	C 49	2 3/16 x 3	1	3 x 3⅞	27.00	47.00
8′	Gedeckt	CC 61	3 x 4	2	4¼ x 5¼	45.00	73.00
8″	Gedeckt	C 49	1¾ x 2½	2	2⅝ x 3⅜	25.00	45.00
8′	Stopped Diapason	CC 61	4 x 5	Ex.	5¼ x 6¼	58.00	89.00
8′	Stopped Diapason	C 49	2½ x 3½	Ex.	3½ x 4½	32.00	53.00
8′	Stopped Diapason	CC 61	3⅜ x 4½	1	4⅜ x 5½	48.00	76.00
8′	Stopped Diapason	C 49	2 3/16 x 3	1	3 x 3⅞	27.00	47.00
8′	Stopped Diapason	CC 61	3 x 4	2	4¼ x 5¼	45.00	73.00
8′	Stopped Diapason	C 49	1¾ x 2½	2	2⅝ x 3⅜	26.00	46.00

Name	Compass	Scale	Voiced
8′ Tuba, Harmonic	C 49	5½″	103.00
8′ Tuba, Harmonic	CC 61	5″	145.00
8′ Tuba, Harmonic	C 49	5″	102.00
8′ Cornopean	CC 61	6½″	158.00
8′ Cornopean	CC 61	6″	154.00
8′ Cornopean	CC 61	5½″	150.00
8′ Cornopean	CC 61	5″	145.00
8′ Trumpet	CC 61	5½″	148.00
8′ Trumpet	CC 61	5″	140.00
8′ Trumpet	CC 61	4½″	141.00
8′ Trumpet	CC 61	4″	132.00
8′ Fagotto	CC 61	Spec.	116.00
8′ Fagotto	C 49	Spec.	82.00
8′ Oboe and Bassoon	CC 61	Reg.	108.00
8′ Oboe	C 49	Reg.	75.00
8′ Oboe, Capped	CC 61	Reg.	114.00
8′ Oboe, Capped	C 49	Reg.	78.00
8′ Orchestral Oboe	CC 61	Reg.	115.00
8′ Orchestral Oboe	C 49	Reg.	76.00
8′ Clarinet, with sliding tops	CC 61	Reg.	108.00
8′ Clarinet, with sliding tops	C 49	Reg.	74.00
8′ Bell Clarinet	CC 61	Reg.	125.00
8′ Bell Clarinet	C 49	Reg.	85.00
8′ Vox Humana	CC 61	Reg.	103.00
8′ Vox Humana	C 49	Reg.	71.00
8′ Saxophone	CC 61	Reg.	128.00
8′ French Horn	CC 61	Reg.	135.00
8′ French Horn	CC 61	Spec.	165.00
8′ French Trumpet	CC 61	Reg.	156.00
8′ English Post Horn	CC 61	Spec.	138.00
8′ English Horn	CC 61	Reg.	147.00
8′ Cor Anglais	CC 61	Reg.	162.00

Name	Compass	Scale	Voiced
8′ Brass Trumpet, all brass resonators	CC 61	Spec.	348.00
8′ Brass Saxophone, all brass resonators	CC 61	Spec.	335.00
8′ Kinura	CC 61	Reg.	92.00
8′ Krummit	CC 61	Reg.	127.00
8′ Mussette	CC 61	Reg.	103.00
4′ Clarion	CC 61	Reg.	105.00

All flue pipe extension octaves of reed stops are equipped with sliding tuners.

STOPPED BASSES

Name of Pipe	Compass	Inside Scale	Outside Scale	Unvoiced	Voiced
8′ Stopped Bass for Dulc	CC 12	2½ x 3½	3½ x 4½	18.50	26.00

DIAPHONE AND CHEST

Name of Pipe	Compass	Inside Scale	Outside Scale	Voiced
16′ Diaphone and Chest	CCC 12	11½ x 11½	14 x 14	445.00
16′ Diaphone and Chest	CCC 18	11½ x 11½	14 x 14	560.00
16′ Diaphone and Chest	CCC 12	9½ x 9½	12 x 12	373.00
16′ Diaphone and Chest	CCC 18	9½ x 9½	12 x 12	470.00
16′ Diaphone and Chest	CCC 12	7½ x 7½	9¾ x 9¾	320.00
16′ Diaphone and Chest	CCC 18	7½ x 7½	9¾ x 9¾	405.00

METALACE GRILLE

Metalace Grille, as per pattern, per sq. ft. $ 1.00 to $ 1.60

These prices include framing, finished to match sample and with grille bronzed.

HARP ACTION

Electro-Pneumatic
With Primary and Secondary Valve

Single Stroke,	37 Notes	$ 185.00
Single Stroke,	49 Notes	240.00
Single Stroke,	61 Notes	300.00

Liberty Temple Electro Pneumatic
With Primary and Secondary Valve

Single Stroke,	49 Notes	$ 250.00
Single Stroke,	61 Notes	310.00

Charge for mounting action to instrument, $25.00
Dampers on Harp Action, if required, per note, 50c

JUNCTION BOARDS AND PLATES

73 Notes	each	$ 2.00
61 Notes	each	1.85
49 Notes	each	1.70
37 Notes	each	1.55
32 Notes	each	1.50
10 Point Brass Plates with 10 Screws, each		.20

KEYS

Genuine Ivory
Mounted with Cheeks and Key Strip

1 Manual	61 notes	$ 42.50
2 Manual	61 notes	82.50
3 Manual	61 notes	125.00

Imitation Ivory
Mounted with Cheeks and Key Strip

1 Manual	61 notes	35.00
2 Manual	61 notes	67.50
2 Manual	61 notes	100.00

Genuine Ivory
Mounted with Key Cheek, Key Strip, Tension Springs Stop, Complete ready for Contact Bar

1 Manual	61 notes	62.50
2 Manual	61 notes	120.00
3 Manual	61 notes	182.50

Second Touch $10.00 per Manual extra.

Imitation Ivory
Mounted with Key Cheek, Key Strip, Tension Springs Stop, Complete ready for Contact Bar.

1 Manual	61 notes	55.00
2 Manual	61 notes	105.00
3 Manual	61 notes	160.00

Second Touch $10.00 per Manual extra.

Rebuilding Manual Keyboards

Rebuilding two Manual Keyboard, attaching Contact Plates and Contact Bars, using old springs	$ 60.00
Rebuilding three Manual Keyboard, attaching Contact Plates and Contact Bars, using old springs	$ 90.00

Recovering Manual Keys

36 Organ Keys recovered with Ivorine	$ 12.00
25 Sharps Replaced	3.00
36 Keys, new fronts, square or straight bevel	1.75
36 Keys, new fronts, Ogee Shape	4.00 to 5.00

Above prices on fronts apply when keys are recovered

61 Keys bushed front and Center	3.50
61 Keys bushed front or Center	1.75
36 Keys relaid with No. 1 Ivory	28.00
Ivory heads furnished and laid, each	.75
Ivory tails furnished and laid, each	.50

Stop Keyboard and Accessories

Straight Stop Keyboard, finished	$ 12.50
2 Side Pieces, finished	15.00
No. 4 Stop Keys Mounted on Board, each	1.70
Telephone Lights—Mounted, each	1.20

Stop Key Blocks

Stop Key blocks for mounting No. 4 stop keys, complete with Contacts but without stop keys each 35c

Manual Keyboard and Accessories

61 Note Manual Keyboard, Genuine Ivory naturals and Ebony Sharps	$ 32.50
61 Note Manual Keyboard, Imitation Ivory Keys	26.00
4 Wire Manual Contact Bar, with either Nickel Silver or Phosphor Bronze Wire	10.00
6 Wire Manual Contact Bar, with either Nickel Silver or Phosphor Bronze Wire	12.00
8 Wire Manual Contact Bar, with either Nickel Silver or Phosphor Bronze Wire	14.00

Above prices do not include contact plates or attaching contact bar to the keys.

4 Wire Manual Contact Block, with either Nickel Silver or Phosphor Bronze Wire each

Item	Unit	Price
6 Wire Manual Contact Block, with either Nickel Silver or Phosphor Bronze Wire	each	.13
8 Wire Manual Contact Block, with either Nickel Silver or Phosphor Bronze Wire	each	.15
Manual Key Contact Plates, Phosphor Bronze	per 100	2.00
Manual Key Contact Plates, Phosphor Bronze with 80% Silver tips	per 100	6.50

Add $6.00 per set, if Contact Bars and Contact Plates are to be attached

Pedal Keyboard and Accessories

Item	Unit	Price
Concave and Radiating Pedal Keyboard, Quartered Oak or Birch Frames	30 Notes	$ 50.00
Concave and Radiating Pedal Keyboard, Quartered Oak or Birch Frames	32 Notes	52.50
Concave and Radiating Pedal Keyboard, Walnut, Cherry or Mahogany Frames	30 Notes	52.50
Concave and Radiating Pedal Keyboard, Walnut, Cherry or Mahogany Frames	32 Notes	55.00
Pedal Contact Plates, Phosphor Bronze	per 100	3.00
Pedal Contact Plates, Phosphor Bronze with 80% Silver Tips	per 100	11.00
12" Foot Levers, Plated	ea.	.40
Toe Studs with two contacts, nickel plated	ea.	1.00
Balanced Crescendo or Expression Pedal, mounted on hinge	ea.	2.50
4 Wire Pedal Contact Block, with Phosphor Bronze or Nickel Silver Wire	ea.	.13
6 Wire Pedal Contact Block, with Phosphor Bronze or Nickel Silver Wire	ea.	.15
8 Wire Pedal Contact Block, with Phosphor Bronze or Nickel Silver Wire	ea.	.17
10 Wire Pedal Contact Block, with Phosphor Bronze or Nickel Silver Wire	ea.	.19
Straight type Pedal Con act Bar (reinforced with angle iron)		2.00
Curved type Pedal Contact Bar		3.50

Straight type Pedal Contact Bar with Positive wire, cable strip and cover with Contact blocks fastened on.

	30 Notes	32 Notes
4 Wire, Nickel Silver or Phosphor Bronze	$ 14.25	$ 14.50
6 Wire, Nickel Silver or Phosphor Bronze	14.90	15.20
8 Wire, Nickel Silver or Phosphor Bronze	15.50	15.95
10 Wire, Nickel Silver or Phosphor Bronze	16.10	16.50
For Curved Bar, add		1.50
For 12′ (Total Length) Cable attached to bar, add		2.00

Item	Unit	Price
Pedal Sharps, Ebonized	each	40c
Pedal Naturals, White Maple	each	40c

LEATHER

Pneumatic Leather,

Extra Light	.006 to .008 thick	$33.00	$18.00	$ 3.25
Light	.009 to .010 thick	33.00	18.00	3.25
Medium	.011 to .014 thick	33.00	18.00	3.25
Heavy	.015 to .020 thick	33.00	18.00	3.25

Item	Unit	Price
Pressure Pneumatic Leather		3.40
Skiver Valve Leather		3.40
Packing Leather	per sq. ft.	.20
R. B. Valve Leather		3.00
Alum Pallet Leather		3.70
Alum Bellows Leather		3.70
Alum Gusset Leather		3.70
German Membrane Leather DOO (Heavy)		.65
German Membrane Leather SOO (Medium)		.52
Leather and Felt glued together for valves	per sq. ft.	1.25

Leather Nuts

3-16" Round	per M	$ 1.05
¼" - Round	per M	1.10
5-16" Round	per M	1.15
⅜" - Round	per M	1.20
7-16" Round	per M	1.35
½" - Round	per M	1.50
½" - Flat	per M	1.50
⅝" - Flat	per M	1.75
¾" - Flat	per M	2.00

LIGHTS

Item	Unit	Price
Pilot Light with Bulb, 10-12 Volt	each	$ .60
Indicator Light, Complete	each	.95
Indicator Light, Socket only	each	.35
Indicator Light, Lamp only	each	.45
Indicator Light, Cap only, red or white	each	.15

MAGNETS AND PARTS

Item	Unit	Price
Chest Magnets	each	$ .26
High or Low Pressure Base Plates	each	.06
Armatures for Magnets	each	.02½
10 Wire Relay Magnets (with rear feed)	each	.70
15 Wire Relay Magnets (with rear feed)	each	.90
Stop Key Magnet, with Stop Key engraved	each	2.25

NAME PLATES

Item	Unit	Price
Name Plates	each	30c
Circular Name Plates for 9-16" Pistons, engraved, General Cancel	each	50c
Organ Name Plates engraved with Builders name 1½" x 3"	each	$ 2.00

PISTONS

9/16" Diameter x 1" long

Item	Unit	Price
Engraved	each	25c
Blank Pistons	each	20c

TILTING TABLETS

Item	Unit	Price
Tilting Tablets, Engraved	each	55c
No. 4 Stop Keys, Engraved	each	75c

Resevoir

10 lb. Coil Resevoir Springs	each	$ .45
15 lb. Coil Resevoir Springs	each	.45
25 lb. Coil Resevoir Springs	each	.50
35 lb. Coil Resevoir Springs	each	.55
50 lb. Coil Resevoir Springs	each	.60
12"—20 lb. Compass Springs	each	.45
12"—30 lb. Compass Springs	each	.50
12"—40 lb. Compass Springs	each	.55

Pedal Keyboard

Pedal Key Tension Springs—wire type	per 100	$ 6.00
Pedal Key Tension Springs—flat wire	per 100	3.00
Pedal Key Tension Springs—flat bent type	per 100	6.00
Pedal Key Second Touch Springs	per 100	12.00

Manual Keys

Manual Key Tension Springs .026 wire	per 100	$ 1.00
Manual Key Tension Springs .030 wire	per 100	1.00
Second Touch Springs for Manual	per 100	1.00

INSULATED STAPLES

No. 1	½" Narrow	per 100	$ .20
No. 3	¾" Narrow	per 100	.20
No. 5	⅝" Wide	per 100	.30
No. 6	¾" Wide	per 100	.30

STOPPER HANDLES

No. 1	each	$ .12	No. 10	each	$ .04
No. 2	each	.11	No. 11	each	.04
No. 3	each	.09	No. 12	each	.04
No. 4	each	.07	No. 13	each	.03
No. 5	each	.06	No. 14	each	.03
No. 6	each	.05½	No. 15	each	.03
No. 7	each	.05	No. 16	each	.02
No. 8	each	.05	No. 17	each	.02
No. 9	each	.04			

SWITCHES AND WIRING

	1 or 2 Switches		3 or More Switches in one Stack	
73 Note Switch	each	$ 11.50	each	$ 8.00
61 Note Switch	each	10.00	each	8.00
49 Note Switch	each	9.00	each	8.00
32 Note Switch	each	8.00	each	8.00
25 Note Switch	each	7.50		
12 Note Switch	each	7.00		

Wiring (Including Cable) 12' Total Length for Manual, Pedal or Relay

61 Notes	Both Ends	$ 5.00	One End	$ 3.00
49 Notes	Both Ends	4.25	One End	2.50
30 or 32 Notes	Both Ends	3.00	One End	2.00
20 or 25 Notes	Both Ends	2.25	One End	1.50

Special Metal Stops

		Scale	
32' Bombard	CCCC—12 pipes	12½" x 12½	$ 840.00
16' Double Open	CCC—12 pipes	No. 28	290.00
16' Double Open	CCC—12 pipes	No. 30	270.00
16' Double Open	CCC—12 pipes	No. 32	250.00
16' Open Diapason	CCC—12 pipes	No. 38	210.00
16' Contra Violone	CCC—12 pipes	No. 42	155.00
16' Dulciana	CCC—12 pipes	No. 44	150.00
16' Salicional	CCC—12 pipes	No. 46	140.00
16' V.D. Orchestra	CCC—12 pipes	No. 48	135.00

Racking Pipes

61 Notes of a 4' or 8' Stop	Wood	$ 4.00
61 Notes of a 4' or 8' Stop	Metal	3.50
61 Notes of Reeds		3.00

Revoicing Metal Pipes

	Approx.
8' Open	$ 23.00
8' String	18.00
4' Stops	14.00
3' Ranks Mixture	28.00
Reeds	$35.00 to $50.00

Revoicing Wood Pipes

	Approx.
16' Double Open, 30 Notes	$ 35.00
16' Bourdon	25.00
8' Flues	18.50
4' Flues	15.00

Display Pipes

		Approx.
Display Pipes	per sq. ft.	$ 1.85
Hooks and Loops	each	.16

Slide Tunners

40 to 44 Scale 8' CC	12 Slides	$ 3.00
Flue Pipes, 40 to 44 Scale, T.C.	61 Slides	4.50
45 to 50 Scale 8' CC	12 Slides	2.75
Flue Pipes, 45 to 50 Scale, T.C.	61 Slides	3.50
Octave and Flute d'Amour, 4' CC	61 Slides	3.50
String Pipes, 54 to 57 Scale, 8' CC	12 Slides	2.10
String Pipes, 58 Scale and smaller 8' CC	12 Slides	1.65
String Pipes, 4' C	61 Slides	2.35

6" Metal Toe Pipe Feet

1"	each	$ .15
⅞"	each	.14¼
¾"	each	.13½
⅝"	each	.12
½"	each	.11½
[illegible]"	each	.11¼
⅜"	each	.10¾
[illegible]"	each	.10½
¼"	each	.10¼
[illegible]"	each	.10

SUPPLIES OF EVERY DESCRIPTION UP TO AND INCLUDING THE COMPLETE ORGAN
SUPERB VOICING A SPECIALTY

METAL AND WOOD PIPES
FLUES AND REEDS
CONSOLES, CHESTS, ACTIONS
WIRES, LEATHER, ETC.

ERIE, PENNA., U. S. A.

The A. Gottfried Co. was for many years the country's largest organ supply house, furnishing all parts up to and including complete organs. See *Encyclopedia of the American Theatre Organ*, Volume I, for a detailed history of the Gottfried firm.

The name Gottfried is best remembered today for the pipes supplied to other builders who were too small or too busy to make their own. Most American builders bought pipes from Gottfried at one time or another. Even large builders who had their own pipe shops ordered ranks from Gottfried when their production fell behind schedule or when they needed special reeds their own pipe shops were unable to produce. The world's largest organ builder, M. P. Moller, ordered hundreds of reed stops from Gottfried through 1930. The world's largest theatre organ builder, Wurlitzer, ordered scale 42 diapasons from Gottfried when their own production lagged.[1] The second largest builder of theatre organs, Robert Morton, also bought Gottfried diapasons and reeds on occasion and at considerably more expense than had they been manufactured in-house.[2]

Although it was reed ranks for which the Gottfried name became most famous, Anton Gottfried began his business in 1890 by manufacturing flue pipes and didn't start producing reeds until 1907.[3] At first he imported most of the reed parts and sometimes entire reed ranks from Carl Giesecke & Sohn in Germany. By the early teens, however, he was making entire reeds in his Erie factory.[4]

The brass trumpet was among the most touted of all the Gottfried reeds. Gottfried brass trumpets can be found in several famous organs all over the world, including the five-manual Willis in St. Paul's Cathedral in London, the five-manual Casavant in the Royal York Hotel in Toronto and the seven-manual Midmer-Losh in Atlantic City Convention Hall. Another famous five-manual organ, the Reginald Foort Moller, *almost* got a Gottfried brass trumpet. The following letter about the latter is most interesting inasmuch as the perceptive reader can get a glimpse of Anton Gottfried's strong Germanic personality:

SUPPLIES OF EVERY DESCRIPTION UP TO AND INCLUDING THE COMPLETE ORGAN
SUPERB VOICING A SPECIALTY

METAL AND WOOD PIPES
FLUES AND REEDS
CONSOLES, CHESTS, ACTIONS
WIRES, LEATHER, ETC.

ERIE, PENNA., U. S. A.
July 18, 1938

M. P. Moller
Hagerstown, Maryland
Attn. Mr. E. O. Shulenberger
Vice President and Sales Manager

Gentlemen:

We wish to acknowledge your inquiry of July 14 in regards to the two sets of Brass Resonators for Reed Pipes with Spun Bells.

Several years ago I designed and worked out the scale for the Brass Trumpet which met with great favor wherever installed. To accomplish this; we have invested approximately $1500.00 in my time for designing and experimenting together with the cost of making special iron mandrels for spinning these Brass Pipes.

We have sold quite a number of Brass Trumpets to various Organ Builders in this Country, Canada and Europe. These Stops were voiced on wind pressures varying from 10" to 25". We have never received a complaint from any of these Organ Builders who rank among the outstanding builders in this Country and in Europe.

On all occasions, we have furnished these builders the complete stop voiced to their requirements. We have felt that in as much as we have expended a good sum to create this Stop to the usual high Gottfried Standard that to absorb this cost we can only offer the Brass Trumpet completely voiced.

Our regular price for one set of 8' Brass Trumpet CC to C, 61 Pipes is $365.00. In as much as you have need of two sets, we can make some saving which we are pleased to pass on to you and therefore quote a special price of $350.00 per set.

In the event that the Stops are to be extended to 73 Pipes, please add $6.00 per set.

We can make delivery from 5 to 6 weeks after receipt of the order, as it takes quite a while for the making of the resonators alone.

We are sure that you will readily realize our position in this matter, since it is only through the sale of the complete Stop voiced, that will enable us, over a period of many years, to be reimbursed for what we expended to produce this Stop.

Since we have had the pleasure of satisfying other builders, in their exact requirements for the Brass Trumpet which as we all know is a most outstanding Reed, we are certain that we can in the same manner satisfy the House of Moller.

We hope that we will have the pleasure of receiving your order which will receive my personal attention.

With kindest personal regards from the writer to you and Mr. Moller, Jr., I remain,

Yours very truly,

THE A. GOTTFRIED COMPANY

A. Gottfried

AG*C Pres.

The brass resonators were not actually made at the Gottfried factory but were produced by the H. N. White Company, who made band instruments in Cleveland, Ohio.[5]

Another special reed rank developed by Anton Gottfried was the English post horn, a very loud and fiery rank which used goosebill shallots. The following correspondence from the Gottfried files should prove quite nostalgic to theatre organ buffs. The first letter was from a 25-year-old organist who would eventually become a living legend. The response, from a firm which was itself a legend in its own time, represented the close of a very colorful chapter in the history of American organ building:

319 West 48th Street
New York 19, New York
December 14, 1945

The A. Gottfried Co.
19th and Myrtle Streets
Erie, Pennsylvania

Attention Mr. A. Gottfried:

Dear Mr. Gottfried:

A few years back you made some pipes for me when I was organist at the Grant Union High School in North Sacramento, California. Among these sets of pipes was an English Post Horn—very fiery and brilliant—an exact duplicate of that you made for the CBS organ in Hollywood.

I would like to know if it would be possible to play an English Post Horn like this on 7 (seven) inch wind pressure and still retain the sharp, fiery quality.

If so, please send me your price for it:

8' English Post Horn—73 pipes

Thanking you in advance I am,

Sincerely yours
George Wright

March 27, 1946

Mr. George Wright
319 West 48th Street
New York 19, New York

Dear Mr. Wright:

We wish to acknowledge your letter of December 14th, 1945 and trust that you will pardon the delay in answering same, but Mr. A. Gottfried and the writer have been away for almost three months.

Yes, I remember the pipes that we made for you and we were surprised to see that you have moved from the west to the east.

Due to government restrictions we are not yet manufacturing new pipes. It may be some months before developing the business as we do not care to get back into the manufacture of new pipes until all materials are available. We believe it would be possible to produce the English Post Horn on 7" wind with as much fire and brilliancy as we made for you in California.

We are sorry that we can't furnish you with this at the present time. As for giving you a price, it will not be possible untill we are again manufacturing new pipes. If you are still in need of this set of pipes later on, please keep us in mind as we would be very happy to again have the opportunity of making another set for you.

With kindest personal regards, I remain,

Very truly yours,
THE A. GOTTFRIED COMPANY

Henry A. Gottfried
Treasurer

HAG:eb

At the time this letter was written, the organ industry was just getting back on its feet again, having been shut down by the War Production Board, and Anton Gottfried, patriarch of the firm, was 84 years old. Furthermore, according to a Dun & Bradstreet report, Gottfried's finances were in trouble due largely to their status as the major supplier to theatre organ builders. When these firms failed after the advent of talking pictures, Gottfried was left holding the bag for thousands of dollars in unpaid accounts.[6] The Gottfried business was dissolved in 1950 and Anton Gottfried died in 1954 at the age of 92.[7]

This Gottfried console featured a player mechanism in a drawer similar to that of a reproducing grand piano. It probably saw service in a funeral parlor, although perhaps some theatre instruments were so equipped. One can only speculate where the organist's knees were supposed to go!

The Gottfried company entered this float in Commodore Perry's Centennial Parade of 1913. This photo was taken outside the Gottfried factory at 19th and Myrtle Streets. The claim of the float's sign, "the largest organ pipe in the world," was a bit of Barnum-style hyperbole which undoubtedly impressed the residents of Erie. (Where, might one inquire, were larger pipes to be found in 1913? One example would be the 64' trombones in the Sydney, Australia Town Hall.)

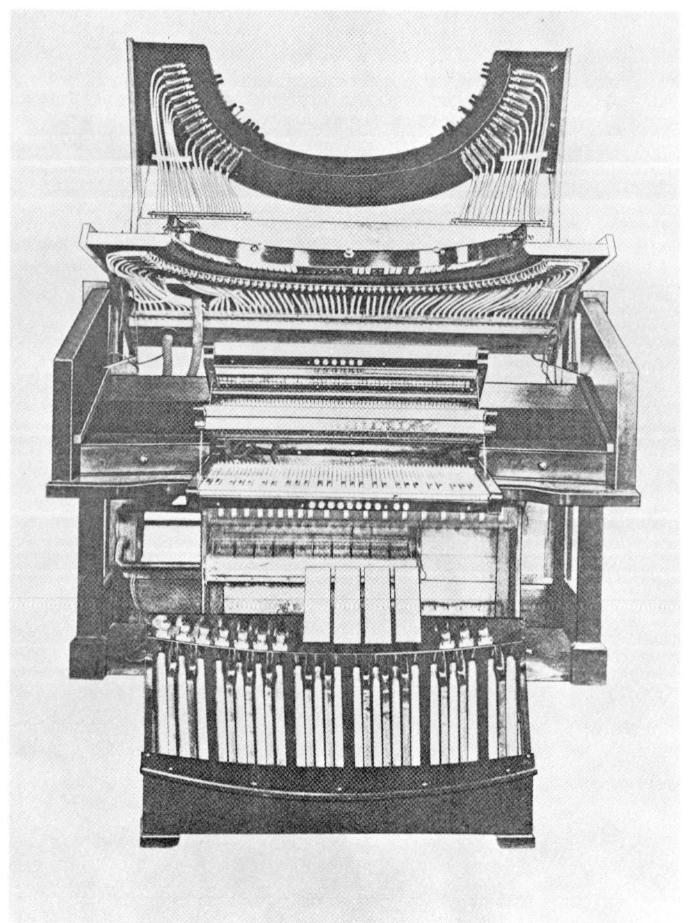

Gottfried horseshoe consoles were exceptionally easy to service: all parts swung out for ready access.

This large three-manual console was made by Gottfried for a builder who was not prepared to build his own. Considering the number of stops in this console, it probably controlled an organ of at least 15 ranks. Perhaps it was sold to the Griffith-Beach company for one of their theatre installations; certainly most builders who installed organs of this size would have constructed their own consoles.

This photograph of the pipe metal casting department in the basement of the Gottfried factory was taken c. 1909.

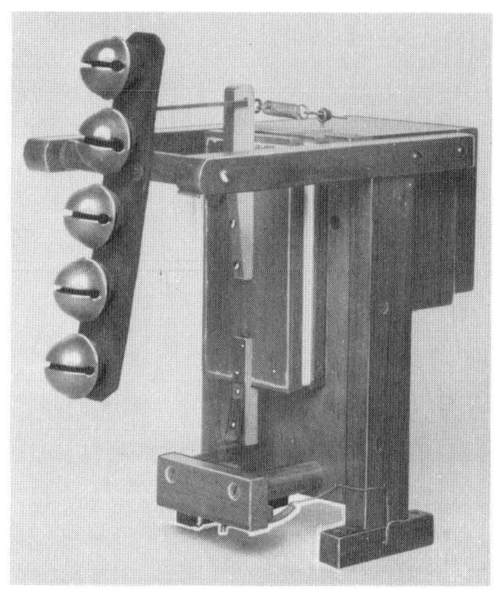

Gottfried trap actions were of modular construction allowing great flexibility in adapting to each customer's individual requirements. Beginning clockwise at the upper left, the instruments pictured on this page are the Chinese block, fire gong, tambourine, surf, castanets, triangle, train whistle, bird whistles, siren, boat whistle and sleigh bells. The surf effect consists of a valve which opens and closes slowly, allowing air to gush against a circular metal plate. The gradually rising and falling hissing sound thus produced is highly imitative of the actual sound of surf.

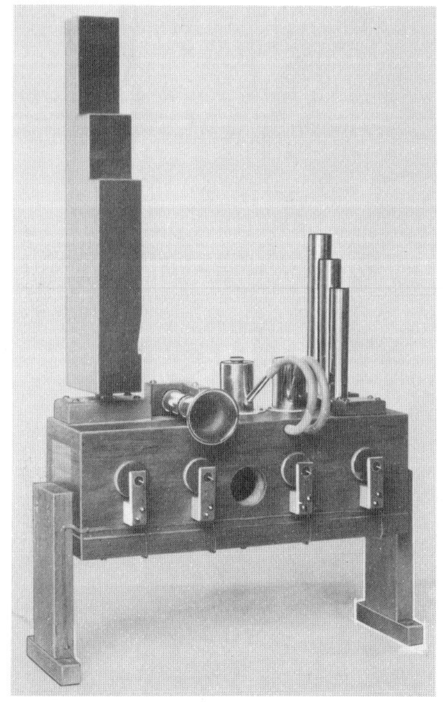

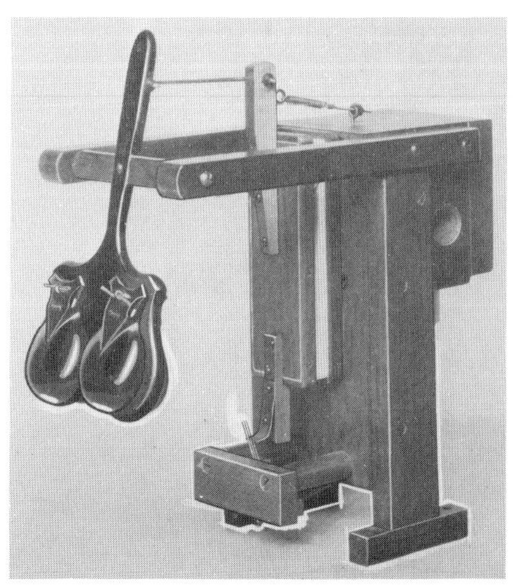

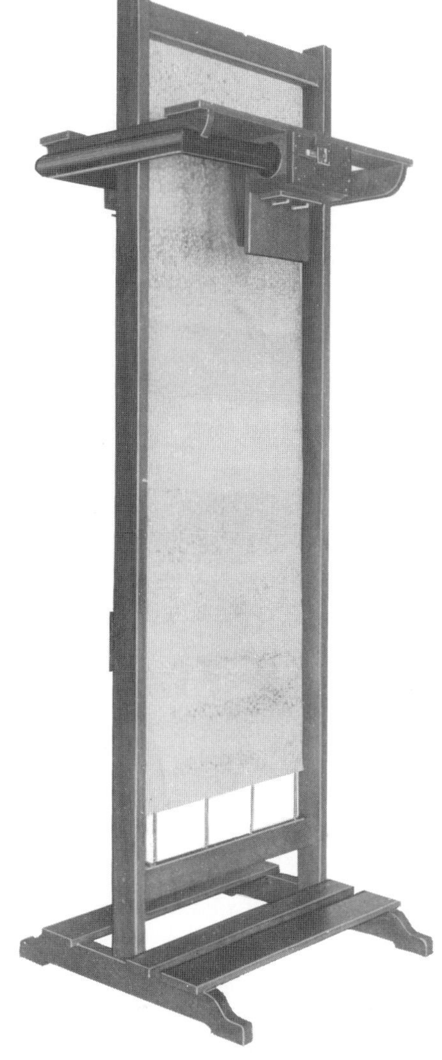

The traps on this page are, clockwise from the upper left, bass drum, thunder effect, rain effect, tympani and Chinese gong. Note the mechanical advantage of the strikers on the bass drum and Chinese gong, allowing these instruments to be struck with a real whomp!

Tympani, being tuned instruments, are rare in theatre organs because their pitch is quite unstable due to their heads being sensitive to temperature and humidity. They also consume a lot of space: just one or two of them would not be very useful musically; at least an entire octave of 12 would be required.

The rain effect consists of a revolving drum filled with pebbles, producing quite a realistic illusion. Motive power to turn the drum is provided by blowing a jet of air across fan blades in the cylinder below the revolving drum.

The thunder effect is achieved by large reiterating pneumatics which shake a piece of sheet metal. A similar effect can be achieved by playing several adjacent bass pipes simultaneously. Since this alternative requires only an inexpensive relay together with pipes which are already in the organ anyway, it is the method usually encountered in organs having a thunder pedal. Thunder sheets such as the one pictured here are quite rare.

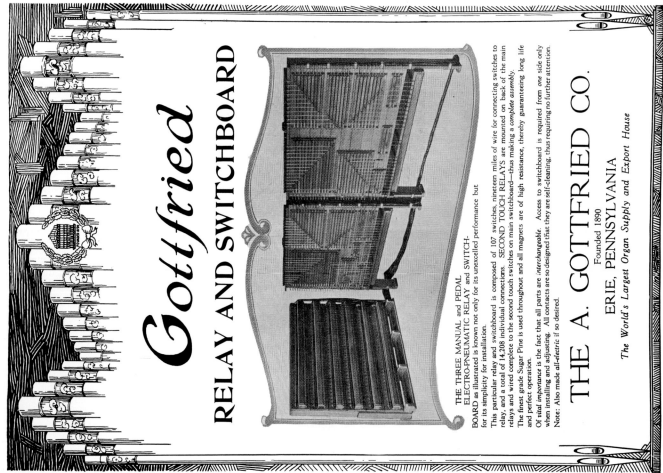

Gottfried

RELAY AND SWITCHBOARD

THE THREE MANUAL and PEDAL ELECTRO-PNEUMATIC RELAY and SWITCH-BOARD as illustrated is known not only for its unexcelled performance but for its simplicity for installation.

This particular relay and switchboard is composed of 107 switches, nineteen miles of wire for connecting switches to relay, and a total of 14,208 individual connections. SECOND TOUCH RELAYS are mounted on back of the main relays and wired complete to the second touch switches on main switchboard—thus making a *complete assembly*.

The finest grade Sugar Pine is used throughout and all magnets are of high resistance, thereby guaranteeing long life and perfect operation.

Of *vital importance* is the fact that all parts are *interchangeable*. Access to switchboard is required from *one* side only when installing and adjusting. All contacts are so designed that they are self-cleaning, thus requiring no further attention.

Note: Also made *all-electric* if so desired.

THE A. GOTTFRIED CO.

Founded 1890

ERIE, PENNSYLVANIA

The World's Largest Organ Supply and Export House

Gottfried

Marimba Harp and Action

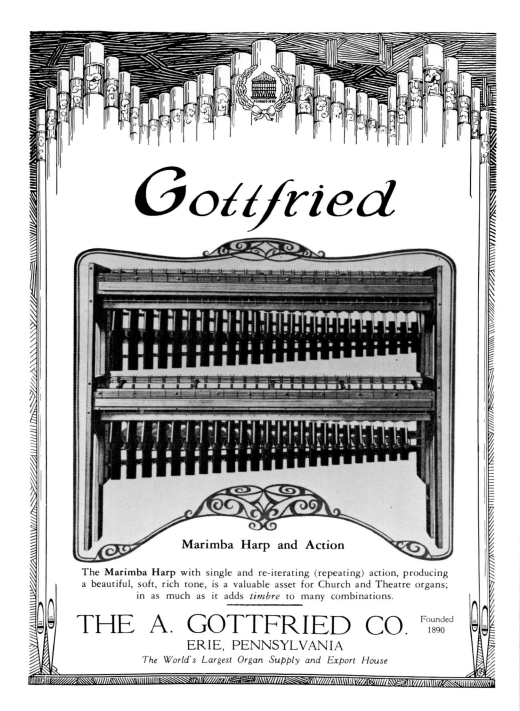

The **Marimba Harp** with single and re-iterating (repeating) action, producing a beautiful, soft, rich tone, is a valuable asset for Church and Theatre organs; in as much as it adds *timbre* to many combinations.

THE A. GOTTFRIED CO. Founded 1890

ERIE, PENNSYLVANIA

The World's Largest Organ Supply and Export House

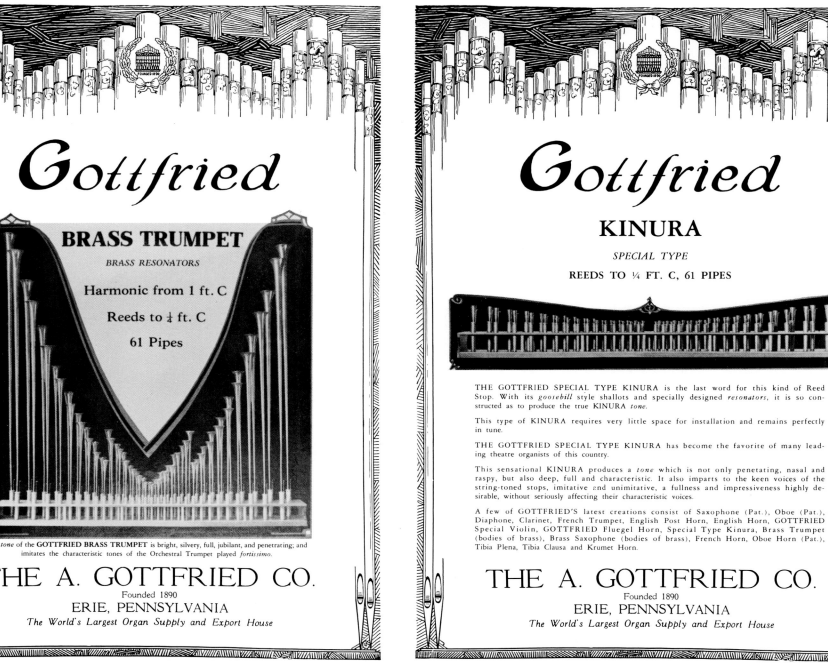

These ads, originally appearing full-page size in* The Diapason, *were composed by Anton Gottfried's son, Henry Gottfried,*[8] *who remained active in the organ industry until his death in 1986. Clockwise from the upper left, the ads appeared in* The Diapason *issues of May 1928, March 1928, December 1927 and November 1927.

CONSOLES
STRAIGHT CHESTS
UNIT CHESTS
RELAYS
SWITCHES
RESERVOIRS
PERCUSSIONS
TRAPS
SWELL SHADES

All types of Actions and supplies for the complete Organ.

Gottfried Five Manual Keyboard

PIPES

Gottfried pipes, both reeds and flues of wood and metal, are known the world over for their distinctive beauty and grandeur of tone. Years of constant research and experience, specializing in the art of organ tone, enable us to produce pipes of an unexcelled quality.

We invite
your inquiries — Quotations promptly given — Our prices are right

THE A. GOTTFRIED CO.

Founded 1890

ERIE - - - PENNSYLVANIA

The World's Largest Organ Supply and Export House

This ad in the September 1927 Diapason *was among the first composed by Henry Gottfried, Anton Gottfried's son, who had recently joined his father's firm following his graduation from business college. Before this ad appeared, the firm had been running the same simple ads for many years. Perhaps competition from the relatively new Organ Supply and Durst, Boegle firms helped prompt Gottfried's change in advertising tactics. The five-manual console featured in this ad was, ironically enough, made by Val Durst and Ignatz Boegle two years earlier when they were still Gottfried employees. It was made for organ builder S. H. Barrington who installed it in the Ardmore Theatre in Ardmore, Pennsylvania where it controlled 21 ranks of pipes.*

This ad was a staple in The Diapason *throughout the teens and mid-twenties.*

Gottfried's ad in the February 1929 Diapason *listed some of the more unusual ranks offered by the company. Several were unique creations of Anton Gottfried such as the American cornet and horn jubilanto. Neither of these ranks caught the fancies of organ builders, most of whom were suffering from a severe slowdown in business which began in 1928. As a result these stops are quite rare.*

ORGAN SUPPLIES

TO FILL ALL REQUIREMENTS

SUPPLIES	SPECIAL FLUE STOPS	SPECIAL REED STOPS
Actions	Tibia Clausa	French Trumpet
Chests	Tibia Plena	English Horn
Consoles	Tibia Minor	French Horn
Percussions	Stentor Gamba	Brass Trumpet
Swell Engines	Viol de Orchestre	English Post Horn
Tremolos	Magic Flute	Brass Saxophone
Traps	Nazard Gamba	American Cornet
Relays	String Celeste	Krumet Horn
Switchboards	Erzahler	Horn Jubilanto

WE MANUFACTURE AND CARRY IN STOCK EVERY PART WHICH IS NEEDED IN THE CONSTRUCTION OF THE PIPE ORGAN

"Over 39 years' experience"

THE A. GOTTFRIED CO.

Founded 1890

The World's Largest Organ Supply and Export House ERIE, PENNSYLVANIA

Anton Gottfried (right) watches Mr. Lasman (left foreground), his zinc pipe maker, preparing to solder the seams on some 8′ zinc basses.

A 1928 view of the Gottfried pipe shop at 25th and Ash Streets in Erie. On the table on the right are some 8′ oboe horn resonators which have just been soldered together. The upper ends of the resonators are covered with whiting which keeps the solder from adhering anywhere except the seams. The whiting will be washed off before the pipes are voiced.

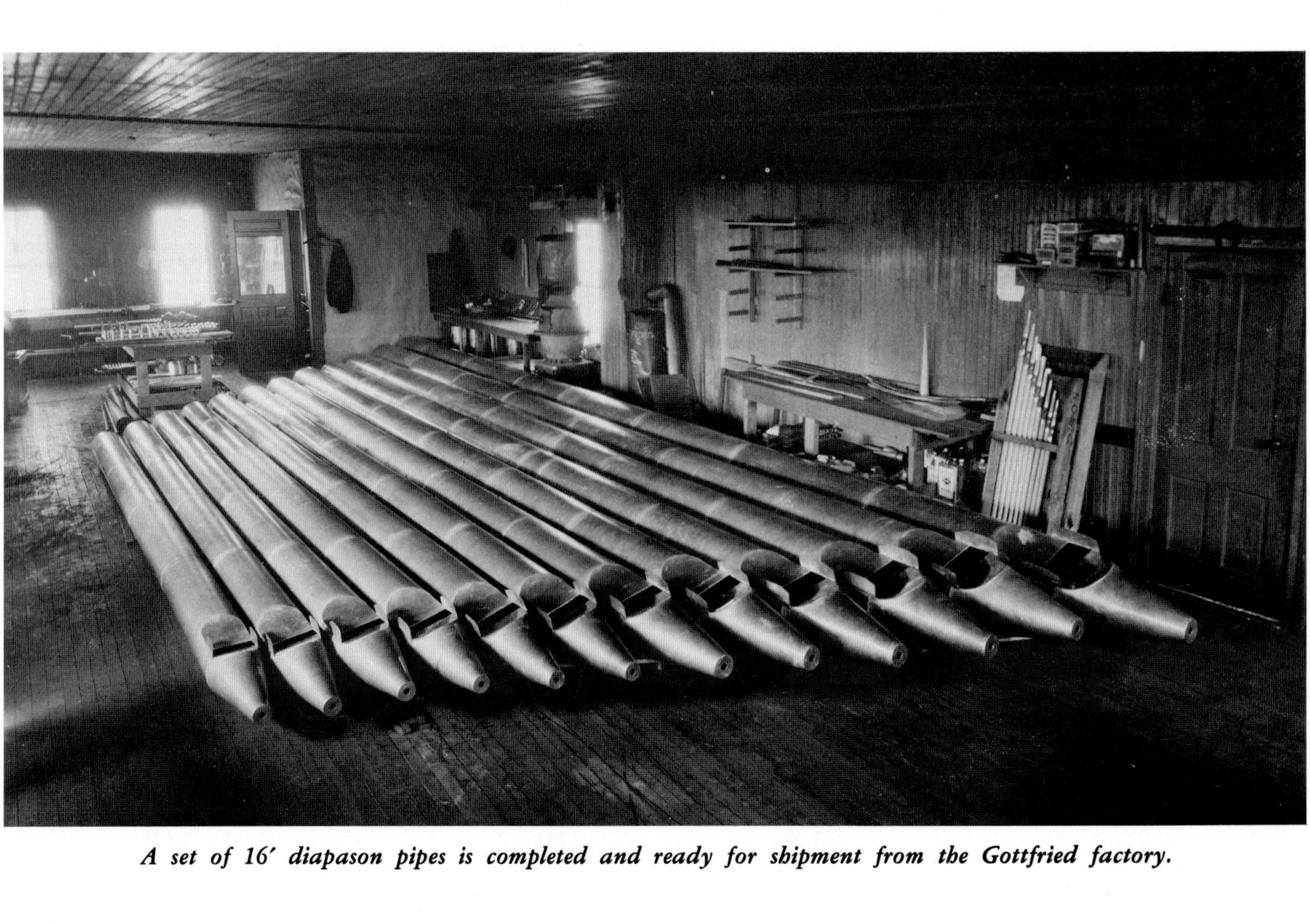

A set of 16′ diapason pipes is completed and ready for shipment from the Gottfried factory.

HAUSMANN & CO.

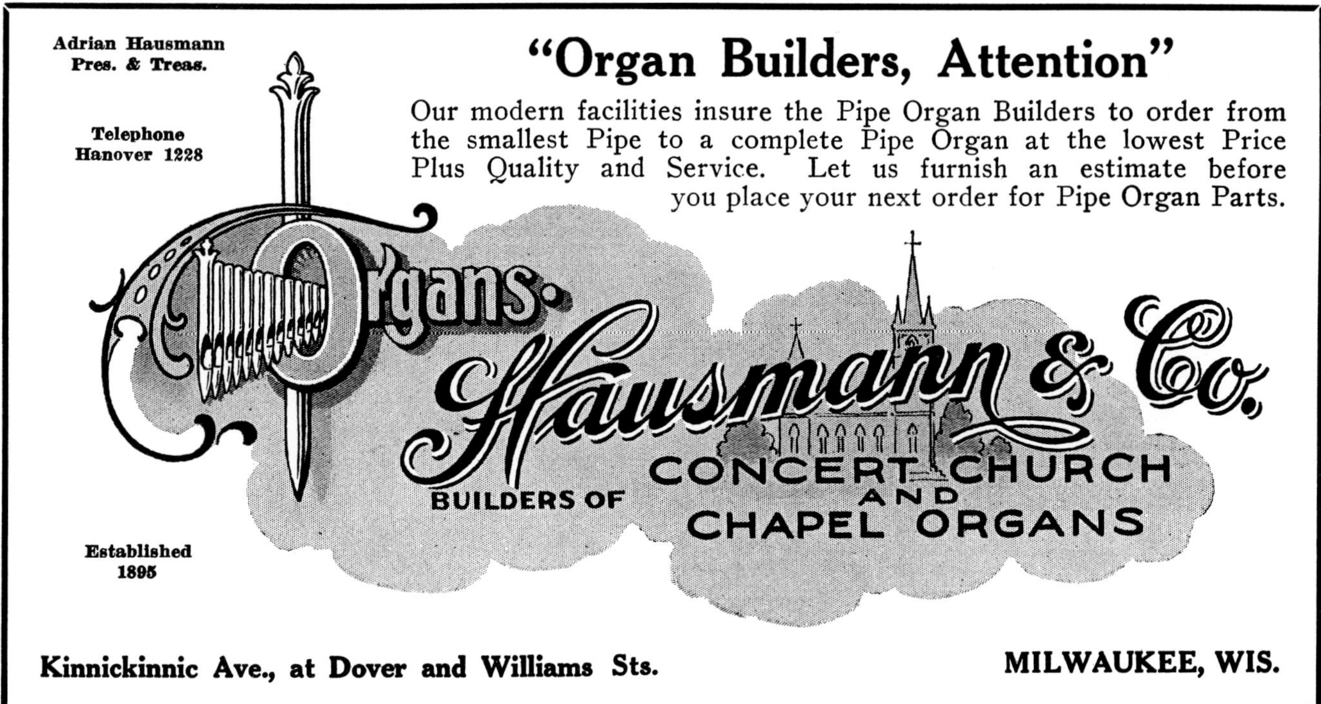

Despite elaborate advertising, Hausmann was a small firm which never really got off the ground. Organ historian Stanton Peters told the author that it was too bad the quality of Hausmann products didn't match that of their logo! This particular ad appeared in the May 1923 Diapason.

JARVIS ORGAN CO.

The July 1921 Diapason *advertised that the Jarvis Organ Co. supplied actions for small builders. Jarvis was itself quite a small—and ephemeral—firm.*

Bell Phone
Tioga 8402J

Factory and Office
605 West Erie Ave., Philadelphia

Jarvis Organ Co.

PIPE ORGAN BUILDERS

GET OUR ESTIMATE ON
REPAIRS - TUNING - ADDITIONS
REBUILDING, Etc.

Complete Electric Actions Made up and Supplied to Small Builders

Manufacturers of Percussions, Etc.

AUG. LAUKHUFF

Kirchenorgeln Fabrik aller Orgelbestandteil

Winderzeuger „Ventus" Klaviaturen

Church pipe Organs Manufactory of everything required for organ building Organ blower „Ventus" Keyboards	Orgues d'Eglise Manufacture de toutes les parties d'orgues Ventilateur électrique „Ventus" Claviers	Organi da Chiesa Fabbrica di tutte le parti d'organo Ventilatore elettrico „Ventus" Tastiere	Organos de igles Fábrica de todas p de órganos Ventilator eléctri „Ventus" Teclados

Weikersheim, ...

Württemberg

Telegramm-Adresse:
Laukhuff Weikersheim
Telefon Nr. 1

Giro-Konto
bei der Reichsbanknebenstelle Aalen
Postscheck-Konto Nr. 138 Stuttgart
Oberamtssparkasse Mergentheim
Zweigstelle Weikersheim
Giro-Konto Nr. 32

A. B. C. Code 5th und 6th Edition

Rudolf Mosse-Code

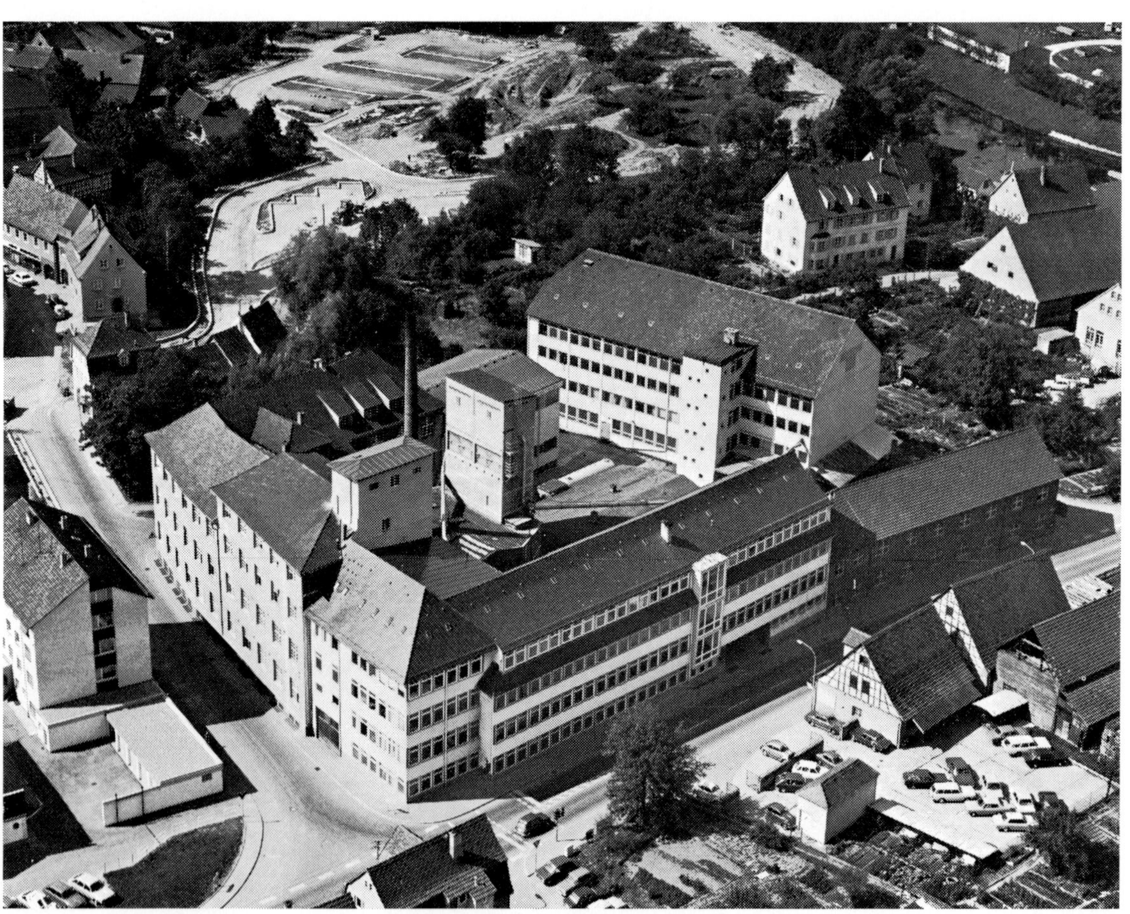

Laukhuff factory c. 1978.

Andreas Laukhuff, Sr. (1798-1871) learned organ building from Johann Eberhard Walcker in Cannstatt, Germany and later worked for Walcker's son in Ludwigsburg. Laukhuff married Walcker's daughter Katherine and in 1823 began his own organ business in Cannstatt. After Katherine's death he married Rosine Bernet in 1845 and had three daughters and three sons: August (1850-1886), Adolph (1857-?) and Andreas (1858-1933). August Laukhuff took over the business upon his father's death in 1871. He moved the firm to Weikersheim in 1877 and took his two brothers into the business.[1 2]

By 1880 the firm employed ten persons. By 1885 this figure had doubled. In 1886 August Laukhuff died at the young age of 36, leaving control to his brothers. When Adolph retired in 1903, over 100 people were employed. Andreas Laukhuff oversaw the further expansion of the firm to over 300 people by 1930. Upon the death of Andreas in 1933 his sons Otto and Wilhelm assumed control and in the 1980s their sons Hans Erich and Peter Laukhuff continue to direct a factory force of around 250 people who produce some of the highest quality organ parts in the world.[3 4]

Although Laukhuff has been a prominent European supplier for many decades, the firm didn't begin serious solicitation of American business until the 1950s. They did, however, sell a vox humana in the late 1920s to the United States Pipe Organ Company for one of their theatre instruments.[5]

Company-owned housing where many Laukhuff employees lived.

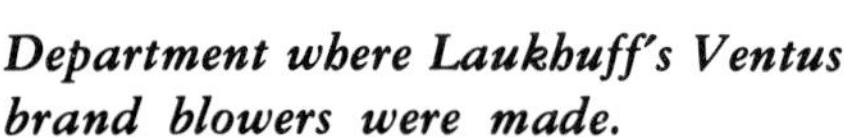

Department where Laukhuff's Ventus brand blowers were made.

Chest department of the Laukhuff factory c. 1928.

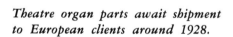

Theatre organ parts await shipment to European clients around 1928.

FRED R. DURST, PRES.
HARLEY L. SCOTT, VICE PRES.

HENRY KUGEL, TREAS.
REUBEN G. KUGEL, SECY.

Organ Supply Corporation

MANUFACTURERS OF

KEYS
WIRES
ACTION
LEATHER

PIPE ORGAN SUPPLIES OF EVERY DESCRIPTION

540-550 EAST SECOND STREET

CONSOLES
CHESTS
BELLOWS
WOOD PIPES

ERIE, PENNA.

NATIONAL ORGAN SUPPLY COMPANY

Manufacturers of

Reed Stops - Flue Stops - Front Pipes - Magnets
Stop Keys - Organ Hardware

ERIE, PENNA.

Organ Supply Corporation and National Organ Supply Co. were separate firms but because of interlocking directorates they were in the same "family." The two firms advertised separately until 1939 when a joint catalog was issued which advised that "Your order or inquiry directed to either company will receive prompt attention." In 1958 Organ Supply purchased the National pipe shop from the firm whose name had become Nosco Plastics, Inc.[1]

National Organ Supply Co. was the first of the two firms to be founded. It was begun in 1920 by Henry Kugel and his son, Harry Kugel, together with Harry Auch and John Hallas. Henry Kugel (1857-1936) had been in partnership with Anton Gottfried from 1892 to 1911 when he left to pursue non-organ related activities. Harry Auch was one of Anton Gottfried's original apprentices and John Hallas had been associated with the Haskell company.[2] [3] [4]

Organ Supply Corporation was founded in 1924 by Fred Durst, Harley L. Scott, Henry Kugel and his sons Harry H. Kugel and Rubin G. Kugel. Fred Durst (1883-1955) was born in Pomeroy, Ohio and began his career in the organ industry in 1906 with the Barckhoff Organ Company in his home town. He later worked for Wicks and in 1912 became superintendent of the Hinners Organ Company. In 1917 he moved to Erie to become superintendent of the Gottfried company. Anton Gottfried later joked that hiring Fred Durst was one of the worst decisions he ever made inasmuch as Fred and his brother Val Durst each formed competitive firms after being employed by Gottfried![5] [6] [7]

Following the death of Fred Durst in 1955 the presidency of Organ Supply was assumed by his son Carl F. Durst. In 1972 Erie businessman Fred Gluck purchased Organ Supply Corporation and merged it with Durst & Co., which he had purchased the preceding year. The Organ Supply factory building was sold and operations were consolidated at the Durst building at 32nd and Poplar Streets. The firm name was changed to Durst Organ Supply at that time. In 1978 the name was changed to Organ Supply Industries,[8] a name more reminiscent of the high quality for which Organ Supply Corporation had been so well known. Continued prosperity brought growing pains and in 1980 the company purchased the old Tellers Organ Co. factory and moved the metal pipe making and voicing departments there.[9]

An important personality at Organ Supply for many years, until his retirement in 1978, was Arthur E. Carr (?-1985). Art had married Fred Durst's daughter, Wilma, and joined the Organ Supply firm in 1945. He served as office manager and was the person responsible for taking telephone orders.[10] Art's cheery and friendly manner as the "voice of Organ Supply" won a warm spot for him in the hearts of the author and a number of other contemporary organ builders.

FRED R. DURST, Pres.
HARLEY L. SCOTT, V.-Pres.

HENRY KUGEL, Treas.
REUBEN G. KUGEL, Secy.

ORGAN SUPPLY CORP.

540-550 East 2nd Street
ERIE, PA.

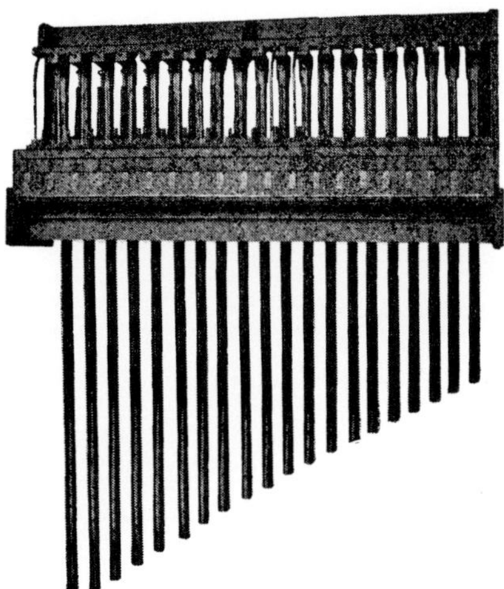

Chimes - -

and action, including hanging bar, dampers, assembled complete ready to install. A floor stand can be furnished if space is available.

Consoles - -

for theatre, auditorium, church and residence. Illustration shows console designed with setter boards accessible from organ bench.

Traps - -

mounted, wired, conductored, complete ready to install. Built according to customer's specification.

Manufacturers of complete organs and supplies of every description. We solicit inquiries from organ builders and repair men.

Organ Supply's May 1928 Diapason ***ad mentioned that the firm manufactured complete organs. Unlike the competing Gottfried company, Organ Supply did not sell complete organs under its own nameplate but instead furnished them to smaller builders who sold them under their own nameplates. The trap actions illustrated here were among the highest quality ever built, featuring extremely rugged construction to withstand the heavy use they received in accompanying silent films hour after hour.***

Dependable!

How many times do you return to a job after you have once thought it complete? These return trips are costly and eat into your profits.

By installing our dependable parts you can reduce these trips to a minimum.

Let Us Quote.

Organ Supply Corporation

540-550 East 2nd Street, ERIE, PA.

Consoles **Chests** **Actions** **Tremolos** **Pipes** **Wood Parts** **Swell Engines** **Supplies, Etc.**

This ad in the June 1925* Diapason *appeared early in Organ Supply's history. The horseshoe console pictured may have been built for a theatre but more likely was for a church.

Toned up to an Ideal---
Not down to a price

Nothing short of perfection satisfies this organization. Founded less than two years ago, the pipe organ world has granted enviable recognition to the "National's" ideal of true service.

While catering to organ supplies, in general, we are primarily specialists in organ pipes—and admittedly leaders in string-tone pipes. "National" string-tone, reed, and flue pipes are to be found in the finest organs in America.

In making any kind of a pipe, we cater to that discriminating trade which buys where the perfection of quality is the first consideration.

Our flue pipe organization is in position to give exceptional service on immediate orders.

NATIONAL ORGAN SUPPLY CO.

John H. Hallas, President — Henry Kugel, Treasurer
Harry F. Auch, Vice-President — Harry H. Kugel, Secretary

This National ad in the September 1921* Diapason *appeared just a year after the firm's founding.

Dependable--

Consoles Swell Engines
Chests Percussions
Actions Reservoirs
Tremolos Pipes
Traps Supplies

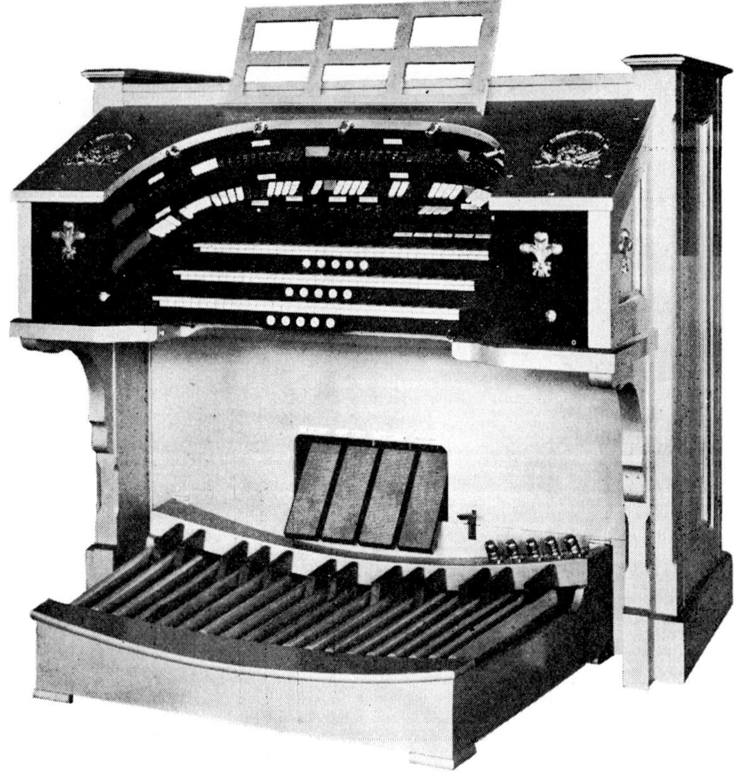

Write today for prices

Organ Supply Corporation

540-550 East 2nd Street

ERIE, PA.

FRED R. DURST, Pres.
HARLEY L. SCOTT, Vice-Pres.
HENRY KUGEL, Treas.
REUBEN G. KUGEL, Secy.

Organ Supply's ad in the January 1929 issue of The Diapason *featured a console which was probably built for organ builder Benjamin F. LeNoir of Philadelphia for one of the organs he installed in nearby New Jersey theatres.*

(opposite) One page of a National price list from the late 1920s. Wouldn't it be fun to turn back the clock and be able to order a new post horn for $145 or a brass trumpet for $350! The brass resonators for trumpets and saxophones were made for National in lots of six sets each by the H. N. White Company of Cleveland, Ohio, makers of band instruments.[11]

NATIONAL ORGAN SUPPLY CO.

ERIE, PENNA.

Reed Stops

	Compass	*Scale*	*Voiced*
32 ft. Bombard	cccc 32	20 in.	$
16 ft. Pedal Trombone	ccc 32	12 in.	
16 ft. " "	ccc 32	10 in.	
16 ft. " "	ccc 32	9x9 in. wood	291.25
16 ft. Ophicleide, Harmonic	ccc 73	10 in.	
16 ft. Tuba, Harmonic	ccc 85	8½ in.	375.50
16 ft. " "	ccc 85	7½ in.	362.25
16 ft. Contra Fagotta	ccc 32		
16 ft. " "	ccc 61	4⅝ in.	285.00
8 ft. Tuba, Harmonic	cc 61	7½ in.	
8 ft. " "	cc 61	6 in.	156.75
8 ft. " "	cc 61	5½ in.	151.75
8 ft. " "	cc 49	5½ in.	105.75
8 ft. " "	cc 61	5 in.	148.75
8 ft. " "	c 49	5 in.	103.25
8 ft. Cornopean	cc 61	6½ in.	159.00
8 ft. "	cc 61	6 in.	155.50
8 ft. "	cc 61	5½ in.	151.75
8 ft. "	cc 61	5 in.	147.00
8 ft. Trumpet	cc 61	5½ in.	148.25
8 ft. "	cc 61	5 in.	144.50
8 ft. "	cc 61	4½ in.	142.75
8 ft. "	cc 61	4 in.	139.75
8 ft. Fagotto	cc 61	Spec.	118.00
8 ft. "	c 49	Spec.	82.50
8 ft. Oboe and Bassoon	cc 61	Reg.	110.50
8 ft. Oboe	c 49	"	76.00
8 ft. Oboe, Capped	cc 61	"	115.50
8 ft. " "	c 49	"	79.25
8 ft. Orchestral Oboe	cc 61	"	116.50
8 ft. " "	c 49	"	77.75
8 ft. Clarinet, with sliding tops	cc 61	"	109.50
8 ft. " " " "	c 49	"	75.50
8 ft. Bell Clarinet	cc 61	"	124.50
8 ft. " "	c 49	"	85.50
8 ft. Vox Humana	cc 61	"	105.50
8 ft. " "	c 49	"	72.50
8 ft. Saxophone	cc 61	"	160.00
8 ft. French Horn	cc 61	"	157.00
8 ft. " "	c 49	"	112.50
8 ft. " "	cc 61	Spec.	172.50
8 ft. " "	c 49	Spec.	121.75
8 ft. French Trumpet	cc 61	Reg.	168.50
8 ft. English Post Horn	cc 61	Spec.	145.00
8 ft. English Horn	cc 61	Reg.	155.00
8 ft. Cor Anglais	cc 61	"	164.25
8 ft. Brass Trumpet, all brass resonators	cc 61	Spec.	350.00
8 ft. Brass Saxophone " " "	cc 61	"	340.00
8 ft. Kinura	cc 61	Reg.	93.75
8 ft. "	c 49	"	68.75
8 ft. Krummit	cc 61	"	128.50
8 ft. Mussette	cc 61	"	105.00
4 ft. Clarion	cc 61	"	107.75

Out of this facility at 540 E. Second Street in Erie came some of the highest quality components ever supplied to the organ trade.

A vox humana and chest furnished by Organ Supply Corporation to fit in a very small space.

The National Organ Supply Co. was located at Seventeenth and Cascade Streets in Erie and is shown here as it appeared in the 1930s.

Under the direction of superb craftsman Carl Durst, the chest department at Organ Supply was always busy supplying highest quality chests to organ builders in all parts of the country. These photographs date from the 1950s.

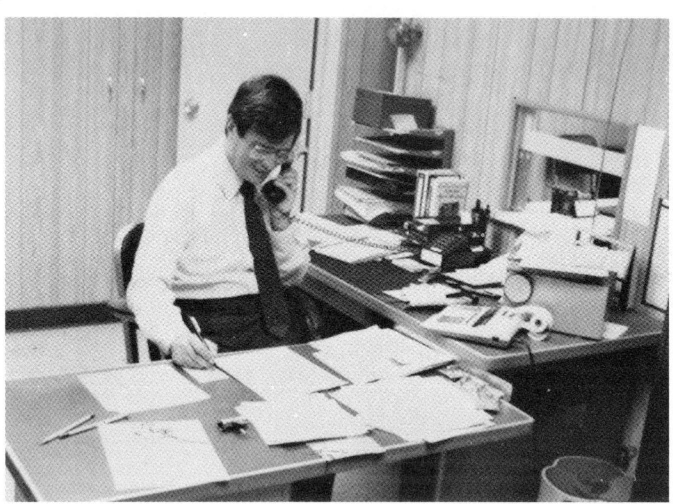

Jim Ivanoff handles the paperwork generated by customer orders and also accepts "rush" orders placed over the telephone. He joined the company shortly after Art Carr's retirement in 1978.[12]

Randy Wagner apprenticed with Homer Blanchard and worked several years at Holtkamp and Reisner before joining Organ Supply in 1976. In 1983 he was elected to the firm's board of directors and later became vice president. A man of many talents, Randy was a founding member of the Organ Historical Society and of the American Institute of Organbuilders. Having served as president of the latter organization, and as vice president of Organ Supply, Randy has had considerable influence on the course of contemporary American organ building. Fortunately for all of us, he is as skilled an organ builder as he is a genuinely nice guy.

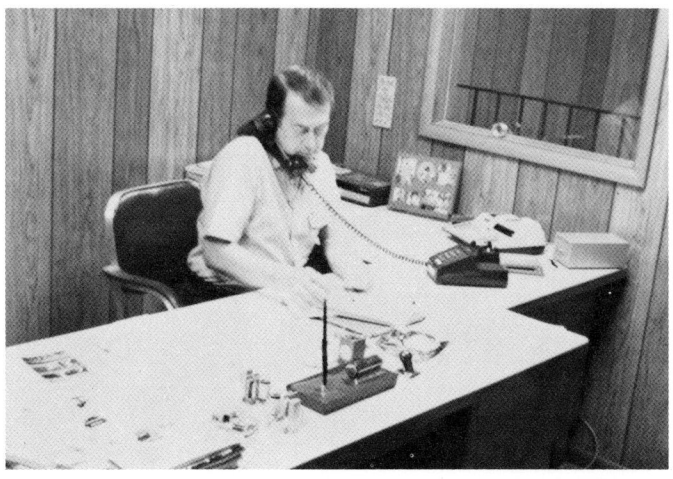

Dennis Unks became president of Organ Supply Industries following Fred Gluck's retirement in 1986. Reflecting the eclectic nature of the company, Dennis has assembled a three-manual theatre organ in his home. This is especially appropriate inasmuch as his father-in-law, Steve Bodman, installed most of the Wurlitzer theatre organs in Detroit.[13]

A PICTORIAL TOUR OF ORGAN SUPPLY INDUSTRIES IN THE 1980S

At left and below, scenes in the chest department.

Sherry Gregory deftly makes tuning slides using a hand-operated rolling machine. The diameters of the slides are determined entirely by the skill of the operator who varies the force which pinches the rollers together.

In this photo of the chest department a tracker chest awaits assembly on the right while an electro-pneumatic pitman chest is under construction to its left. Serving American organ building in the 1980s requires a firm of eclectic abilities!

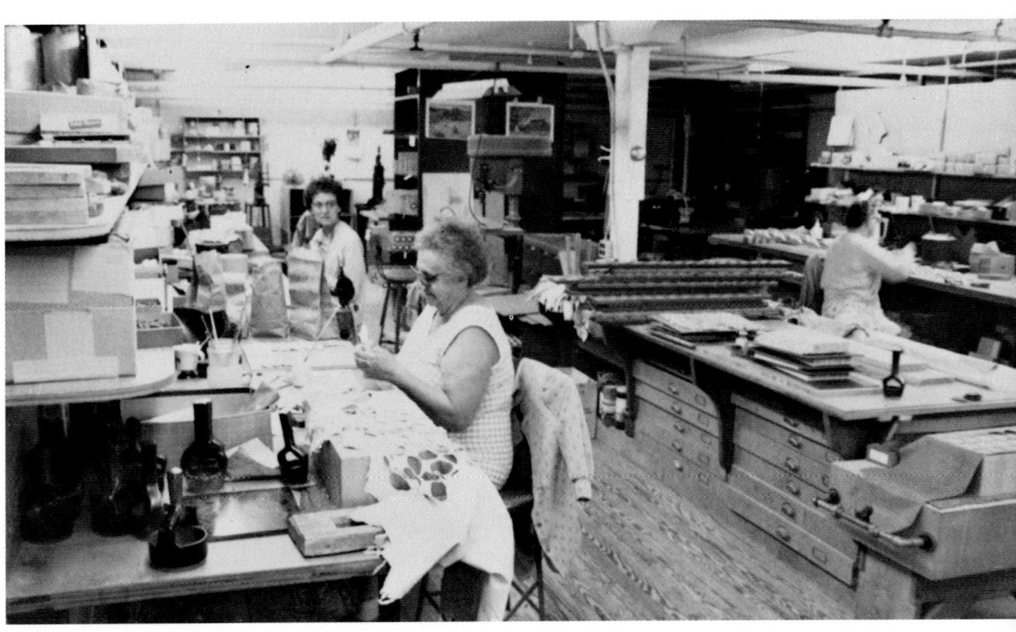

The small parts department on the second floor is where valves are assembled and chests are leathered. The machine in the center of the room which looks like a drill press is actually a clever vacuum-operated "pouch presser" which can leather a pouchboard in jig time.

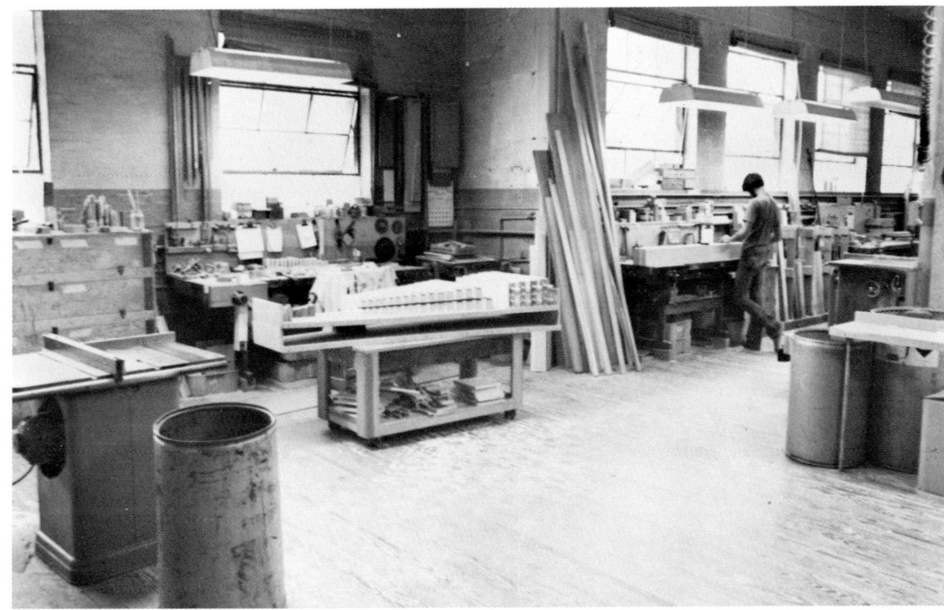

The wood pipe department is located separately from the metal pipe shop at the east end of the main Organ Supply factory. On a tray in the center of the picture is a replica of a Wurlitzer 10" tibia clausa nearing completion.

Thousands of dollars' worth of zinc is stored by thickness on these racks in the basement of the pipe shop.

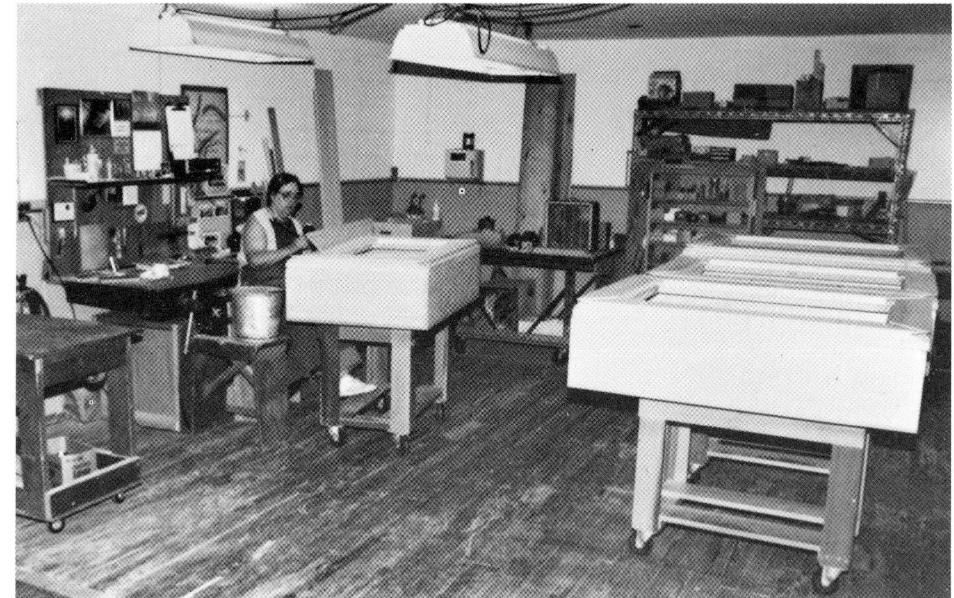

Patricia Wegner leathers reservoirs around the corner from the wood pipe department at the east end of the factory.

The former erecting room of the Tellers Organ Co. is now a storage and shipping area for Organ Supply Industries' pipe shop. The tall 16′ violin pipes awaiting repair in a bin at the center of the room are from a Kimball theatre organ.

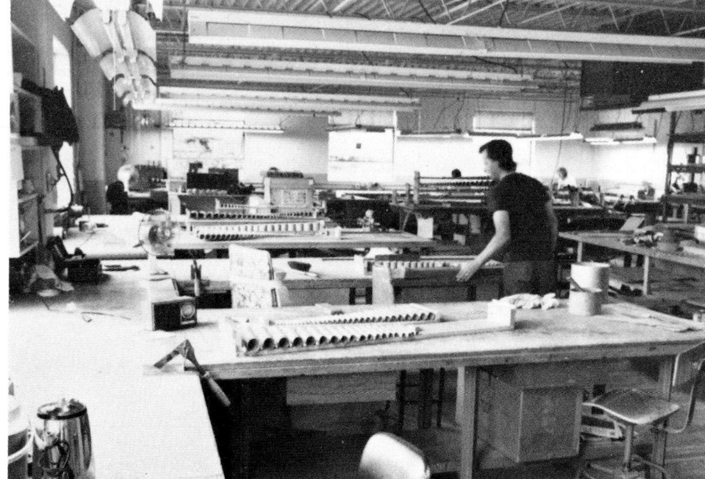

These are two of several large rooms where raw metal is cut, formed and soldered into completed pipes.

Console department.

Randy Wagner watches while Richard Lamberton, one of several flue voicers employed by Organ Supply Industries, prepares a rohrflote.

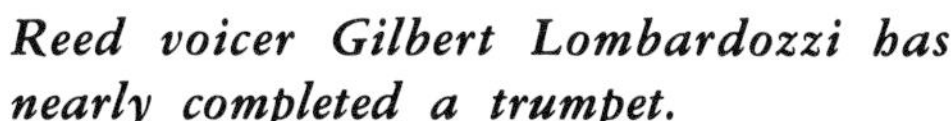

Reed voicer Gilbert Lombardozzi has nearly completed a trumpet.

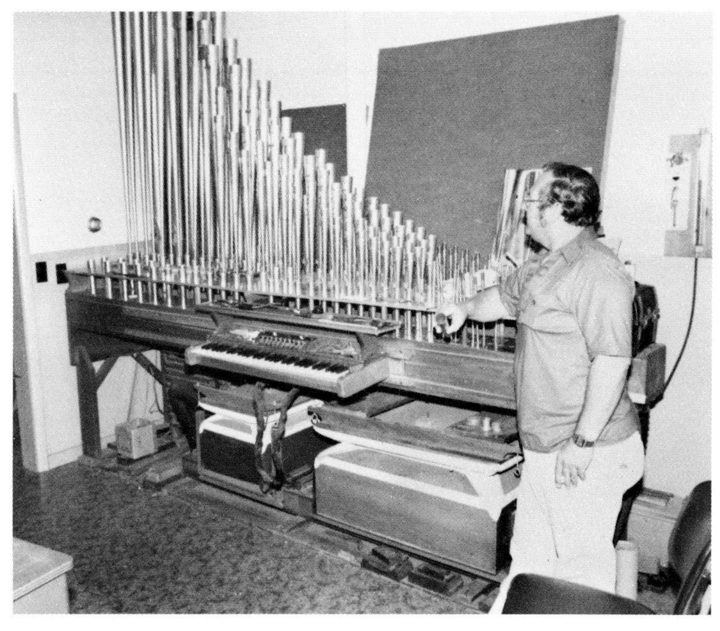

HERMAN STAHL

Organ Consoles?

Actions--Electric, Pneumatic?

Finished Products?

Wood-Pipes?

Generators?

To quote you, is a pleasure

Herman Stahl

209 W. 5th St. - ERIE, PA.

Mr. Stahl was one of many people in the organ business in Erie in the early 1920s. This ad appeared in the December 1920 Diapason.

COMSTOCK, CHENEY & CO.

Samuel M. Comstock was one of a number of men who entered the burgeoning ivory business along the Deep River in Connecticut in the early part of the nineteenth century. The community in which he settled eventually became known as Ivoryton in honor of the town's major industry. By 1860 George A. Cheney joined Mr. Comstock in the firm of Comstock, Cheney & Co. Another Cheney family member was a principal in the rival Pratt, Read firm and the competitiveness of these two businesses fanned the flames of a family feud for decades.[1]

The first piano ivories were cut by the Comstock firm in 1836 and by 1886 the manufacture of piano actions had begun. Comstock, Cheney and Pratt, Read challenged each other for industry dominance until 1937 when the firms merged. After the merger the Comstock, Cheney name was dropped and the new firm retained the Pratt, Read & Co. name. The former Pratt, Read factory was sold and manufacturing was consolidated at the Comstock, Cheney plant in Ivoryton.[2]

COMSTOCK, CHENEY & CO.,

IVORY CUTTERS AND MANUFACTURERS.

PIANO KEYS, ACTIONS AND HAMMERS.

Ivory and Composition Covered Organ Keys.

The only Company Furnishing the Keys, Actions, Hammers and Brackets Complete.

Telegraph and R. R. Station: **ESSEX, CONN.**

OFFICE AND FACTORY: **IVORYTON, CONN.**

Early Comstock, Cheney ad in The Musical Courier, *May 6, 1896.*

Pratt, Read plant c. 1950. The older buildings belonged to Comstock, Cheney & Co. which merged with Pratt, Read in 1937. In 1987 some of these buildings house Sohmer & Co., piano manufacturers, which Pratt, Read purchased in 1982.[3]

THE PIANO & ORGAN SUPPLY COMPANY

"PianO"
Actions and Keys

made the "P & O" way will be found in thousands of pianos throughout the west. Each year the percentage of pianos containing "P & O" actions and keys is growing proportionately larger.

The Piano & Organ Supply Company

Manufacturers of Piano Keys, Piano Actions and Organ Keys

Established 1898

2132 N. Racine Avenue Chicago, Ill.

This ad appeared in the February 1925 issue of Piano Trade Magazine. *The Piano & Organ Supply Company was absorbed by Pratt, Read in 1929.*[1]

In 1798 a clockmaker in Essex, Connecticut, Phineas Pratt, invented a saw for cutting ivory. The first use of this device was the manufacture of combs. Other ivory articles followed including book markers, letter openers, erasable memos, business cards, dominoes, toothpicks, cuff links and collar buttons.[3] Pratt's saw allowed the mechanization of a process which formerly had been carried on by manual labor. Ivory became a major business in the neighboring communities of Deep River and Ivoryton, the latter name itself a reflection of the importance of this industry to the town.[4]

In 1863 several local firms merged to form Pratt, Read & Co. In 1839 a predecessor company had cut its first piano ivories and in 1886 the manufacture of complete keyboards began, followed by piano actions in 1912. The aggressive Pratt, Read organization purchased a number of key and action companies over the years including Wasle & Co. in 1910, Strauch Bros. in 1912, Bransfield-Billings Action & Supply Co. in 1918, Sylvester Tower Co. in 1924 and The Piano & Organ Supply Company in 1929.[5] In addition to keys and piano actions, the firm was also a major supplier of player piano mechanisms.

In 1937 Pratt, Read merged with their major rival, Comstock, Cheney & Co., and the company name became Pratt, Read & Co., Inc. At the height of keyboard production, 1905-1912, the Pratt, Read and Comstock, Cheney firms were processing the tusks of over 4,000 elephants per year. An average seventy-pound tusk would supply ivory for about 45 keyboards.[6]

A number of other companies have been absorbed by Pratt, Read in the decades following the merger with Comstock, Cheney, not all of which are related to the music industry. One such firm was the Allen-Rogers Corp. of Laconia, New Hampshire which makes—no, not electronic organs—wood turnings! In 1968 Pratt, Read merged with Vocaline Company of America, Inc., the new firm assuming the latter name. In 1970 the name was changed to Pratt-Read Corp. The most recent acquisition was Sohmer & Co., piano makers, in 1982. In 1986 the keyboard and action division of Pratt-Read was sold to Baldwin, ending a century of involvement in that branch of the industry.[7]

Pratt, Read factory in Deep River, Connecticut. This building was erected in 1882, replacing an earlier structure which burned in 1881.[1] In 1986 the building, now on the National Register of Historic Places, was recycled as the Piano Works condominiums.[2]

Pratt Read Keys Solve the Problem

Manufacturers who produce fine pianos give attention to the interior as well as the exterior; but the appearance must be in keeping with the tone, the quality and the construction.

The keys are the first thing the customer uses, and the first thing he looks at. They must be made right in order to create the right impression.

Money spent for specially good keys is invested, NOT wasted.

Pratt Read Keys are Made Right and Look Right

Pratt Read & Co.

Established 1806 **Deep River, Conn.**

This ad originally ran full-page size in The Music Trades, *August 7, 1915.*

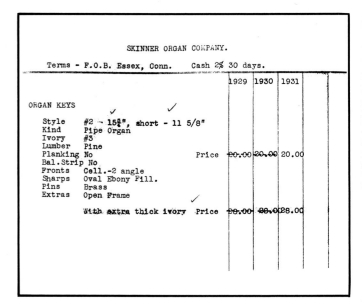

THE A. GOTTFRIED COMPANY.

Terms - F.O.B. Essex, Conn. Net Cash 30 days.

		1929			
ORGAN KEYS					
Style	Single - balanced per R.H.C.				
Kind	Pipe Organ				
Ivory	#3				
Lumber	Pine 17¾"				
Planking	No Price	24.00			
Bal. Strip	No				
Fronts	Cell.2 angle				
Sharps	Oval Ebony				
Pins	Brass				
Extras	Open Frame				

HINNERS ORGAN COMPANY.

Terms- F.O.B. Ivoryton, Ct. Net 30 days.

		1929	1930	1931
ORGAN KEYS				
Style	Single, 18 11/16", 22", 25 1/8" 28 3/8"			
Kind	Pipe Organ	GCS 4/18		
Ivory	#3			
Lumber	Pine- 17-7/16"			
Planking	No Price	~~25.50~~	~~25.50~~	25.50
Bal. Strip	No			
Fronts	Cell (same as Odell)			
Sharps	Oval Ebony			
Pins	Brass			
Extras				

MAXCY-BARTON ORGAN COMPANY, Successors to BARTOLA MUSICAL INSTRUMENT COMPANY.

Terms- F.O.B. Essex, Conn. Net Cash 30 days.

		1929	1930	1931
ORGAN KEYS				
Style	Single (14 1/8")			
Kind	Pipe Organ			
Ivory	#3			
Lumber	Pine			
Planking	No Price	~~26.00~~	~~26.00~~	26.00
Bal. Strip	No.			
Fronts	Cell. O-Gee			
Sharps	Oval Ebony Fill.			
Pins	Iron			
Extras	Open Frame			
	17 1/8" long	~~26.25~~	~~26.25~~	26.25

SKINNER ORGAN COMPANY.

Terms - F.O.B. Essex, Conn. Cash 2% 30 days.

		1929	1930	1931
ORGAN KEYS				
Style	#2 - 15¾", short - 11 5/8"			
Kind	Pipe Organ			
Ivory	#3			
Lumber	Pine			
Planking	No Price	~~20.00~~	~~20.00~~	20.00
Bal.Strip	No			
Fronts	Cell.-2 angle			
Sharps	Oval Ebony Fill.			
Pins	Brass			
Extras	Open Frame			
	With extra thick ivory Price	~~28.00~~	~~28.00~~	28.00

F. W. SMITH & SON.

Terms- F.O.B. Essex, Conn. Cash in advance.

			1930		
ORGAN KEYS					
Style	Single				
Kind	Pipe Organ		GCS 8/25		
Ivory	#3				
Lumber	Pine 16 9/16"				
Planking	No Price		28.00		
Bal. Strip	No				
Fronts	Cell. 2 angle				
Sharps	Ebony				
Pins	Brass				
Extras					
	No charge for boxing per	G.C.S.			

UNITED STATES PIPE ORGAN COMPANY.

Terms - F.O.B. Essex, Conn. Cash with order.

			1929
ORGAN KEYS			
Style	12", 16", 19"		
Kind	Pipe Organ		
Ivory	#3		
Lumber	Pine		
Planking	No	Price	
Bal. Strip	No	12"	26.00
Fronts	Cell.- 2 angle	16" &	
Sharps	Ebony Fill	19"	28.00
Pins	Brass		
Extras	Open Frame		

Pages from one of the few remaining Pratt, Read order books illustrate the diversity of products made by the firm. Nearly every customer had a unique requirement.

WOOD & BROOKS COMPANY

Wood & Brooks was founded in 1901 by Charles H. Wood, plant superintendent of Pratt, Read & Co., with the financial backing of the Brooks family, major Pratt, Read shareholders.[1] Their main plant was an enormous six-story building in Buffalo, New York, and a branch factory was operated in Rockford, Illinois, where piano action parts were made.

At the height of production Wood & Brooks used the tusks of 1,000 elephants per year for key coverings, approximately one quarter of that used by the Pratt, Read and Comstock, Cheney firms. In 1958 Wood & Brooks was sold to Sterling Precision Co. which in 1959 sold it to the Aurora Corp. of Illinois. In the wake of a declining domestic market for pianos, and hence for keyboards and actions, Wood & Brooks went out of business in 1970.[2 3]

LEATHER, FELT & CLOTH

GEO. W. BRAUNSDORF, INC.

This firm sought pipe organ business in the teens through ads such as this one which appeared in the December 1914 Diapason.

PHONE BEEKMAN 2359

THE CARLTON SALES CO.

LEATHER

12 SPRUCE STREET

G. KEARNEY, PROP. NEW YORK, N. Y.

This firm was not widely known in the organ industry although they did sell leather to the United States Pipe Organ Company.[1]

HAND & COMPANY

HAND & COMPANY

Successors to GEO. ALBRECHT

Manufacturers of

Leather for the Pipe Organ Trade

SEND FOR SAMPLES Phone, MAIN 1387

304 West Lake St., CHICAGO, ILL.

This firm advertised in The Diapason *throughout the 1920s. This particular ad appeared in the March 1927 issue. By the early 1930s the firm name had changed to George A. Hand and the company had relocated to 6808 Hilldale Avenue in Chicago.*

This firm advertised throughout the "golden age" of the theatre organ. The ad appearing here was originally in the December 1924 Diapason.

Mutty was a major supplier of rubberized cloth and tubing to the player piano and organ industries in the 1920s.

C. WEILBIER

BEG to announce to the trade that we are making a specialty of the manufacture of

"Zephir Leather"

Our product is made from Intestines, and is furnished in two thicknesses, one thin and the other slightly heavier, both absolutely air-tight and extremely pliable.

We have been supplying some of the more important Organ Builders and makers of Automatic Instruments throughout the world, who have used our Zephir Leather in the most costly and largest instruments.

On account of proven reliability, our product is given preference.

Orders promptly and carefully filled.

C. WEILBIER,
Hanover, Germany.

This ad in the July 1921* Diapason *makes a veiled reference to Wurlitzer, who used zephir in all their chests from the beginning of production through 1927.

WHITE, SON COMPANY

INCORPORATED

MANUFACTURERS AND IMPORTERS

FINE LEATHERS AND BOOKBINDERS MATERIALS

601 ATLANTIC AVENUE, BOSTON, MASS.

"COLONIAL" BINDERS BOARD
AGENTS
INTERLAKEN-WINTERBOTTOM
BOOK CLOTHS

CABLE ADDRESS
"WHITESON" BOSTON
CODES USED
WESTERN UNION-5TH EDITION-A. B. C.
BENTLEY'S COMPLETE PHRASE

SHIPPING AND RECEIVING AT
242-4 PURCHASE STREET

***This firm is still in business in the 1980s although sales to the organ industry now represent only a small portion of their business. This ad appeared in the March 1927* Diapason.**

WHITE, SON COMPANY

Announce the removal of their Offices and Warehouse to
601 ATLANTIC AVENUE, BOSTON
Specialists in the
Manufacture of Organ and Player Piano Leathers

TELEPHONE,
BEEKMAN 4408

WILLIAM A. WOOD
BERNARD A. WERNER

WOOD & WERNER, Inc.

Piano—Leather—Organ

83 GOLD STREET
Corner Spruce Street

New York, N.Y.

MANUFACTURERS OF
ORGAN LEATHERS
OUR SPECIALTY
WRITE FOR SAMPLES PHONE BEEKMAN 4408
WOOD & WERNER, Inc.
83 Gold Street, New York, N. Y.
Formerly connected with T. L. Lutkins, Inc., of New York

This firm was a relatively late entry into the organ industry. This ad appeared in the July 1928 Diapason.

MISCELLANEOUS PARTS

BILMER MFG. CO.

WOOD TURNINGS
FOR ORGAN BUILDERS
Stopper Handles and Rack Pins a Specialty
BILMER MFG. CO., 628 West 11th St., ERIE, PA.

This ad appeared in the January 1928 Diapason. *The firm advertised only briefly, no doubt discovering that most organ builders were basically woodworkers and could easily make their own stopper handles and rack pins.*

E. R. HOWARD

The Howard Organ Seat

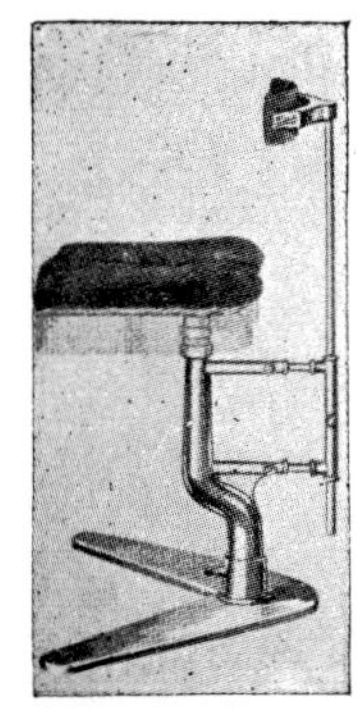

"Demonstrates its worth very effectively and I can't imagine myself doing without it." -JESSE J. CRAWFORD.

"I will never return to the old style bench. It is the most comfortable seat imaginable, actually adds to one's pedal technic, is perfectly adjusted and will be a revelation to those who use it.—LOUIS LOHMANN.

At last, perfect comfort on an Organ Bench! Contributes wonderfully to ease of pedal technic. Indispensable to the artist. Lasts a life-time and is your personal property; relieves the fatigue of steady hours of practise or playing. Gives unprecedented poise and buoyancy to the player. Perfectly adjusted *to every movement* of body and limb. Fully protected by patents.

ONE PERFECTED STYLE. TWO FINISHES.

Prices and terms on application.

E. R. HOWARD, Mfgr.

631 S. Grand View Ave. Dubuque Iowa.

The famous Howard seat sat in front of many hundreds of theatre consoles following its introduction in 1921. It was originally priced at $75 in aluminum finish or $85 in cast iron,[1] the latter being by far the more popular. The Howard seat featured divided pads which, swiveling independently, were supposed to provide freedom of motion to the organist's legs. Theatre organists were, and still are today, divided in their opinions about the desirability of Howard seats versus benches. Some, as did Jesse Crawford, adamantly insist on a Howard seat; others refer to them derisively, if not accurately, as "nutcracker seats"! E. R. Howard was himself a theatre organist, performing at the Strand Theatre in Dubuque.[2]

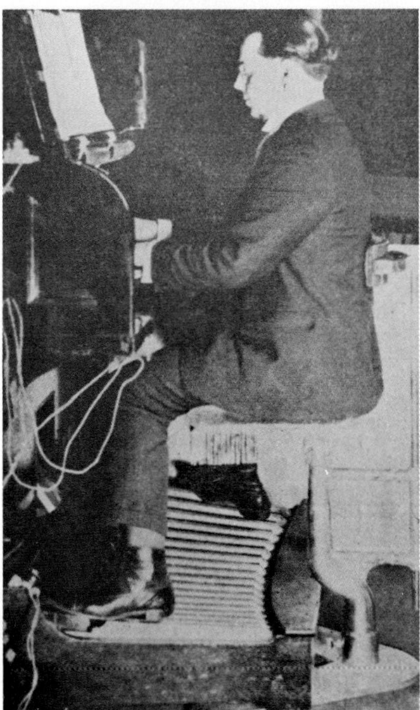

E. R. Howard sits on his famous invention.

THE JAMES P. McGREECE COMPANY

MANUFACTURERS OF

PIANO AND ORGAN HARDWARE

262 DOVER STREET

TEL. CON.

BOSTON, MASS.

McGreece was a supplier primarily to the piano industry although they did sell castings for swell pedals to the United States Pipe Organ Company.[1]

STANDARD ROLLING MILLS

When this ad appeared in the January 1914 Diapason, *the organ industry was in the throes of converting from tubular pneumatic to electric action, thereby severely curtailing the demand for this company's products.*

Standard Rolling Mills
INCORPORATED
363 Hudson Ave. Brooklyn, N. Y.
Organ Tubing
Lead, Tin and Composition
PROMPT SHIPMENT ON ALL ORDERS ASSURED

PERCUSSIONS

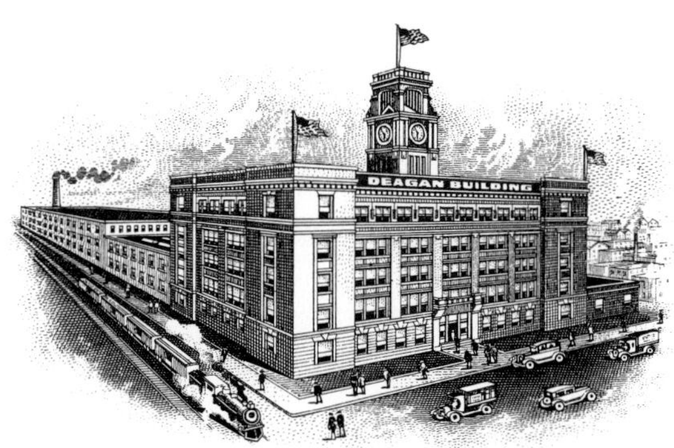

J. C. DEAGAN, INC.
Established 1880
OFFICE & FACTORY
1770 WEST BERTEAU AVENUE
TELEPHONE LAKE VIEW 4364
CHICAGO 13, ILL.
CABLE ADDRESS "DEAGAN" CHICAGO

John C. Deagan was a native American but received his higher education at the University of London. An accomplished clarinetist, he served as orchestra leader in such vaudeville theatres as Tony Pastor's in New York City and the old Opera House in St. Louis. While in England he heard a lecture given by the famous scientist Hermann von Helmholtz. This experience fueled a lifelong fascination with and study of scientific principles of acoustics and pitch on which, during his lifetime, Mr. Deagan was recognized as the leading authority. It was primarily though his efforts that A-440 was adopted as universal pitch.[1]

Deagan's first experiments with tuned percussion instruments centered around the glockenspiel. His perfected form of the instrument, which he called orchestra bells, raised it from being regarded as a toy to the status of a serious musical instrument worthy of inclusion in the modern orchestra.[2] In 1880 Mr. Deagan formed the J. C. Deagan Musical Bells Co. to manufacture his new product. By 1886 he had developed the xylophone and tubular chimes. In 1898 he moved to Chicago and abandoned his career as a professional musician in order to devote full time to the tuned percussion business. By 1912 he had prospered to the extent that a new 75,000 square-foot fac-

J. C. DEAGAN, INC. IS THE WORLD'S LARGEST MANUFACTURER OF
CARILLONS - TOWER BELLS - ORGAN PERCUSSIVES - MARIMBAS - VIBRAHARPS - XYLOPHONES - ORCHESTRA BELLS
CATHEDRAL CHIMES - TUNING FORKS - SCIENTIFIC TUNING DEVICES - ALTAR CHIMES - DINNER CHIMES - DOOR CHIMES

tory was constructed at a cost of nearly half a million dollars.[3] [4]

Deagan was continuously experimenting and introducing new tuned percussion devices. By the mid-teens Deagan catalogs listed over 600 items. Some of them were ephemeral novelties such as nabimbos and musical tomato cans. Many others, however, set industry standards. For many years the National Bureau of Standards used special Deagan tuning forks as their frequency references. Deagan dinner gongs announced meals in homes of the wealthy and Deagan Unafones and metal bamboos ("shaker chimes") were staples in the amusement business. Among later Deagan inventions were the vibraphone, introduced in 1927, and large-scale brass tubular chimes for outdoor use,[5] struck with enormous solenoids drawing 45 amperes at 45 volts DC. A process of tuning these huge chimes through the fifth harmonic, dubbed quintamonic tuning, was developed by Deagan engineer Henry Schlueter.[6]

The chime portion of the Deagan business was sold in 1972 to I. T. Verdin in Cincinnati, Ohio.[7] In 1978 the remainder of the Deagan enterprise was acquired by the Slingerland Drum Co., a division of C. G. Conn.[8]

John C. Deagan (1853-1934)[4]

Deagan's first factory.

DEAGAN

Pipe Organ Percussion Instruments

Are Used by All

Prominent Pipe Organ Builders

Write for Prices on

Chimes
Celestes
Marimbas
Pizzicato Nabimbas
Unatones
Xylophones
Parsifal Bells
Glockenspiels

ALL ATTACHMENTS PROTECTED BY LETTERS PATENT

Tuning, Workmanship and Material Guaranteed

J. C. DEAGAN

Deagan Building 4211 Ravenswood Ave.

CHICAGO, ILLINOIS

By the time this ad appeared in the September 1916 issue of The Diapason, *Deagan was already the industry leader in tuned percussions for pipe organ use.*

This 75,000 square-foot factory served Deagan from 1912 until the firm was sold in 1978. In 1987 the spirit of Deagan lives on, however, inasmuch as the building now houses the Century Mallet Instrument Service, specialists in the restoration of tuned percussion instruments. On an upper floor of the building the original Deagan carillon roll perforator still cuts rolls for Deagan carillon owners on special order.[10]

DEAGAN PERCUSSION INSTRUMENTS FOR PIPE ORGAN USE

INTRODUCTORY

THE instruments shown in the following illustrations and described herewith have been particularly designed for Organ Builders' use, and are the best. We have been manufacturing percussion instruments for Organ Builders' use for thirty-five years, and are the originators and introducers of every instrument which we list.

BREVITY OF DESCRIPTION

For obvious reasons, we have not gone into an extensive discourse regarding the merits of Deagan instruments, as they are too well known to require it. Neither shall we attempt to describe the tone of the various instruments in the specifications, but, in each case, shall confine ourselves to a brief technical description of the instrument itself.

However, it is a paramount fact that we are the pioneers in this line of work, and we believe it to be general knowledge that at no time have our instruments been equalled, either in a mechanical way or from the standpoint of tone and tuning.

ILLUSTRATIONS

The illustrations of the various instruments are from actual photographs. Where a number of instruments form a distinct group, being identical except as to register and widths of bars, only one, or at the most, two illustrations are shown depicting an average size instrument, taken at random from that group.

By referring to specifications and illustration, a comprehensive idea of the entire group of one particular kind of instrument can be quickly gained. It is thus the work of but an instant to secure a very clear idea of the various styles of instruments available.*

All Deagan instruments listed herewith are intended to be played with the bars in a vertical position, in which position they sound best. Any of the instruments, however, may be played from a horizontal position if desired.

*In addition to our regular standard percussions listed herewith we are also prepared to furnish instruments of special register and design to meet individual requirements. Prices on application.

MOUNTING

Some of the instruments are regularly mounted in two rows (two sections) while others are mounted in one row (one section). We mount each instrument in the way which experience has proven to be the most practical. However, at an additional cost of 10%, we can specially mount in double row formation any instruments which we specify in one row, and vice versa.

STANDARD MEASUREMENTS

All instruments as listed in this catalog are built with standard jigs and dies, and are thus made identical in measurements. The Organ Builder is, therefore, safe in making up a number of actions at a time, thereby greatly reducing their cost. We can positively guarantee to supply instruments which are absolutely uniform in every detail.

SCALE CENTERS

All Deagan instruments are made with 2¼" scale centers (or greater where bar widths require), thus allowing sufficient room for practically any type of action to be used. However, any instrument may be had with greater centers than those specified (or narrower where bar widths permit) at an additional cost of 10%.

ARRANGEMENT OF FRAMES

All frames have wooden end pieces, which greatly facilitate the fastening of the instruments into the Organ. They also simplify lining up the instrument in place, as when the end pieces are set perpendicular the centers of the bars (where the mallets should strike) are in one straight, continuous, horizontal row, thus making possible the use of actions arranged in the simplest manner. These end pieces also act as protectors for the instrument in transit.

Frames are made of well-seasoned solid quarter-sawed white oak, finished by hand in golden oak.

MITERED RESONATORS

Where, owing to lack of space it is desirable to miter resonators, same can be supplied on any of the instruments listed herewith at a slight additional cost per resonator.

It is not necessary to stipulate the number of resonators to be mitered. Simply specify instrument with mitered resonators and give the greatest depth permissible, i. e., from face of bar to back of resonator.

Instruments so ordered are, of course, entirely special and are not carried in stock, but can be shipped on very short notice.

MALLETS

Proper mallets are supplied with every Deagan instrument. The mallets which will be supplied are stipulated in each set of specifications. Some builders prefer to make up their own mallets, particularly for Cathedral Chimes. The instruments we list may be had without mallets if so desired, the price of the mallets in such cases being deducted from the price of the instrument.

MATERIALS USED

Metals used in manufacturing the vibrating or tone-producing parts are made in accordance with our own formulas and specifications. On the wood bar instruments the celebrated Nagaed wood is used. This wood has a clear musical tone and its seven-year seasoning insures permanence of tuning.

Our resonators are made of light-weight, seamless brass tubing, which will withstand every conceivable weather condition, and also the attacks of rodents.

OF DEAGAN MANUFACTURE THROUGHOUT

The fact that Deagan Percussion instruments for Organ use are made from start to finish in our own mammoth factory insures uniform and dependable quality at all times. We do not **"farm out"** any parts to job shops.

QUANTITY PURCHASES OF MATERIALS

Our adequate resources enable us to buy our materials in large quantities. Low prices thus secured are reflected in our low selling prices.* Large material contracts also enable us to specify the exact alloys in the various metals which we find best for our uses.

REGARDING SHIPMENTS

All Deagan instruments as catalogued are carried in stock, securely packed, ready for immediate shipment. All prices are f. o. b. Chicago.

*See accompanying list for prices.

PITCH

We advocate the use of A-440 (Universal) Low Pitch for organs for this reason:

An organ tuned to A-440 can be used with orchestra without any trouble. While the difference between A-435 and A-440 is so slight that it will not be noticeable to singers, there is, however, enough difference to make it impossible for orchestral musicians to play in tune with an organ in A-435 pitch, due to the fact that practically 95% of the orchestral wood winds are pitched in A-440, under normal temperature conditions. (A-440 is now the Official Pitch of the American Federation of Musicians. The U. S. Government has also adopted A-440 pitch.)

An organ tuned to A-440 can be used in any and every way that one tuned to A-435 can be, and in addition it is always in proper pitch for use in connection with orchestra in which capacity the A-435 instrument is useless. Most of the prominent organ builders realize the existence of this fact and have adopted A-440 as their standard pitch. The only possible reason for continuing to tune to A-435 is the following of a blind custom.

However, any instrument listed in this catalog may be had tuned to either A-435 or A-440 at the same price. In ordering, be sure to specify pitch desired. We can also tune these instruments to any pitch other than A-440 or A-435 at an increased cost of 10%.

REGISTER

The register of each instrument is specified according to the way in which it is usually connected up and used in the Organ. For example, where the actual pitch of the lowest tone of the instrument listed is "Tenor C" (one octave below "Middle C" of the piano) we term it "8 ft. C." Likewise "Middle C" is referred to as "4 ft. C," while the octave above "Middle C" we call "2 ft. C" and the "G" above that, "G in the 2 ft. octave," etc., etc.

FINISH

Deagan instruments are finished in the very finest possible manner. All metal parts are triple nickel plated in our own shops and by a special method which does not injure the tone in any way. All wood frames of our instruments are carefully finished with the best possible grade of varnish. Xylophone and Marimba bars are hand polished.

Deagan Bells, Xylophones, Marimbas, Chimes, etc., are finished products in every sense of the word, and the organ builder who installs them need never apologize for his percussion equipment.

On this and the next 20 pages are reproduced a c. 1916 Deagan catalog of percussions especially designed for pipe organ use. Also included are some later supplemental sheets such as the c. 1927 announcement of the vibraphone.

Deagan Organ Special Xylophone
No. 537

3 Octaves Chromatic, 2′ C to C
Length of Frame, 85½″

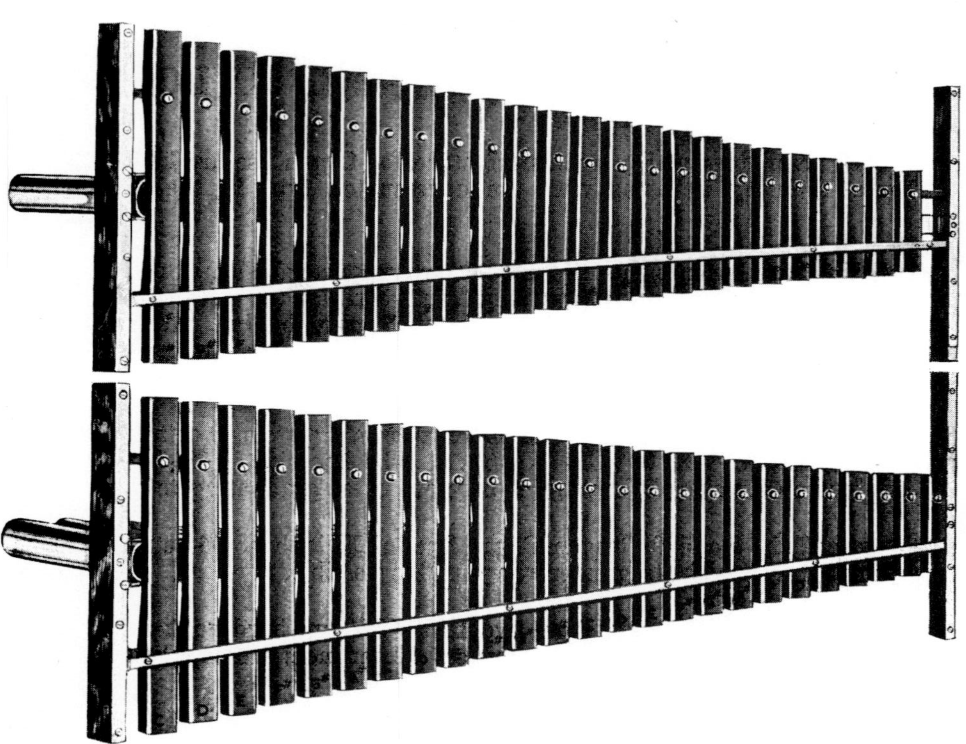

Deagan Organ Special Xylophone
No. 549

4 Octaves Chromatic, 4′ C to C
Length of Frames, 58½″ Each

THE DEAGAN ORGAN SPECIAL XYLOPHONE

Xylophones with resonators which we manufacture for Organ use are known as Deagan Organ Special Xylophones, differing in name with the unresonated type in the addition of the word "Special."

The bars used in these instruments are made of extra selected Nagaed which has been seasoned for at least seven years. These bars possess a naturally brilliant, musical tone and this quality is further augmented by the patent resonators (each tuned individually). We unhesitatingly recommend the use of the Deagan Organ Special Xylophone in every case where superior results are desired.

The Deagan Organ Special Xylophone is supplied in two registers, 3 octaves, 2 ft. "C" to "C" (No. 537), and 4 octaves, 4 ft. "C" to "C" (No. 549). The bar size is 1⅝"x$\frac{15}{16}$", although for the lower tones of the four octave size slightly wider bars are used, graduating to a width of two inches.

We urge the use of the No. 549 Deagan Organ Special Xylophone (4 octave size) on account of the better results musically which its greater range makes possible.

On all Xylophone registers ranging from two foot "C" up, hard rubber mallets are supplied, while below two foot "C" mallets of varying degrees of hardness are supplied, as the hard mallets do not give satisfactory results in this lower register.

A vibrating action is recommended in connection with all sizes. No dampers are required.

Specifications on page 15.

Illustration opposite shows No. 537.

Fully covered by Letters Patent

THE DEAGAN ORGAN SPECIAL XYLOPHONE

SPECIFICATIONS

DEAGAN ORGAN SPECIAL XYLOPHONE

No. 537

3 Octaves Chromatic (one section)

Range—37 tones, 2 ft. C* to C

Size of bars	1⅝″
Scale Centers	2¼″
Length	85½″
Height	17″
Depth	8¾″
Mallets	No. 2059
Pitch	A=440 or A=435

DEAGAN ORGAN SPECIAL XYLOPHONE

No. 549

4 Octaves Chromatic (two sections)

Range—49 tones, 4 ft. C* to C

Size of bars	1⅝″ to 2″
Scale Centers	2¼″
Length, each section	58½
Height, each section	21″
Depth, each section	15″
Mallets	No 2057; No. 2058; No. 2059
Pitch	A=440 or A=435

(See accompanying list for prices)

Illustration opposite shows No. 549

*See paragraph on page 4 under heading of "Register."

Fully covered by Letters Patent

Deagan Organ Xylophone
No. 3030

2½ Octaves Chromatic, G (in 2′ Oct.) to C
Length of Frame 69¾″

THE DEAGAN ORGAN XYLOPHONE

Where low price and minimum installation space are important factors, the Deagan Organ Xylophone is admirably suited. This instrument is made in two widths of bars, 1¼″ and 1⅝″, and in two scale ranges, 2½ and 3 octaves register, in each bar size.

While the Deagan Organ Xylophone is not equipped with resonators, the bars produce a brilliant tone, due to the long seasoning of the wood used and the careful mounting of the bars on the exact nodes. These instruments receive the same careful tuning and construction which is given to our higher grade Xylophones.

The Deagan Organ Xylophone, in all four sizes, is mounted in one row, which is the most convenient arrangement in an instrument of this type. Mounting in two rows can be substituted, however, at an additional cost of 10%.

The tone of the Deagan Organ Xylophone is snappy and brilliant, and no dampers are required.

SPECIFICATIONS

DEAGAN ORGAN XYLOPHONE No. 2930
2½ Octaves Chromatic (one section)
Range—30 tones, G (in 2 ft. oct. *) to C

Size of bars	1¼″x⅞″
Scale Centers	2¼″
Length	69¾″
Height	14½″
Depth	3¼″
Mallets	No. 2065
Pitch	A = 440 or A = 435

DEAGAN ORGAN XYLOPHONE No. 3030
2½ Octaves Chromatic (one section)
Range—30 tones, G (in 2 ft. oct.*) to C

Size of bars	1⅝″x 15/16″
Scale Centers	2¼″
Length	69¾″
Height	14½″
Depth	3½″
Mallets	No. 2059
Pitch	A=440 or A=435

DEAGAN ORGAN XYLOPHONE No. 2937
3 Octaves Chromatic (one section)
Range—37 tones, 2 ft. C* to C

Size of bars	1¼″x⅞″
Scale Centers	2¼″
Length	85½″
Height	17¼″
Depth	3¼″
Mallets	No. 2065
Pitch	A=440 or A=435

DEAGAN ORGAN XYLOPHONE No. 3037
3 Octaves Chromatic (one section)
Range—37 tones, 2 ft. C* to C

Size of bars	1⅝″x 15/16″
Scale Centers	2¼″
Length	85½″
Height	17″
Depth	3½″
Mallets	No. 2059
Pitch	A=440 or A=435

Illustration opposite shows No. 3030.

(See accompanying list for prices)

*See paragraph on Page 4 under heading of "Register."

Fully covered by Letters Patent

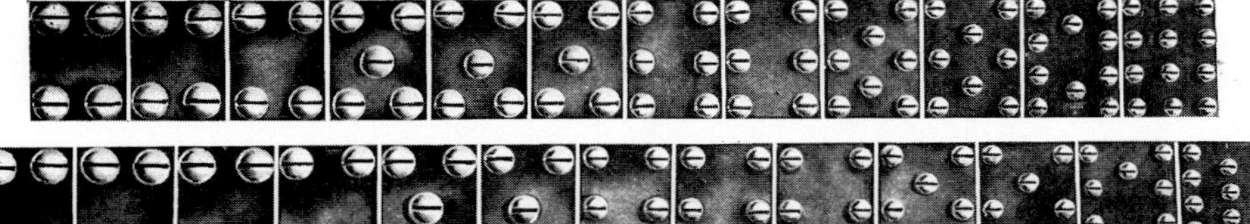

Deagan Organ Sleigh Bells
No. 625

2 Octaves Chromatic, 1-C to C
Mounts, 6″x 8″

Deagan sleigh bells are extremely rare. Two sets known to the author were in the Forum Theatre in Los Angeles (4/37 Kimball) and the Wisconsin Theatre in Milwaukee (3/17 Barton).

DEAGAN ORGAN SLEIGH BELLS

Organ Builders have only commenced to realize the effectiveness of Deagan Musical Sleigh Bells. They are especially recommended for use in theatre organs, as they are a most beautiful effect when properly used.

Deagan Organ Sleigh Bells are made of special formula bell metal which has exceptional musical and wearing qualities, and they are tuned with the utmost accuracy.

The Bells are attached to heavy sole leather mounts 6″ by 8″ in size, the number of bells varying from four in the lower tones to fourteen in the upper. By this ratio of distribution an even volume of tone is secured throughout the entire register.

Each tone unit should be mounted on a vibrating action of sufficient strength to insure a rapid and vigorous vibratory motion.

SPECIFICATIONS

DEAGAN ORGAN SLEIGH BELLS No. 620
1½ Octaves Chromatic (On Leather Mounts)
Range—20 tones, F (in 1 ft. oct.*) to C

Size of Mounts	6″x8″
Depth of Bells	2¼″
Number of Bells on each Mount	4 to 14
Pitch	A=440 or A=435

DEAGAN ORGAN SLEIGH BELLS No. 625
2 Octaves Chromatic (On Leather Mounts)
Range—25 tones, 1 ft. C* to C

Size of Mounts	6″x8″
Depth of Bells	3″
Number of Bells on each Mount	4 to 14
Pitch	A=440 or A=435

Illustration opposite shows No. 625

(See accompanying list for prices)

*See paragraph on page 4 under heading of "Register"

Fully covered by Letters Patent

DEAGAN "ONE-THIRTY-SEVEN" XYLOPHONE

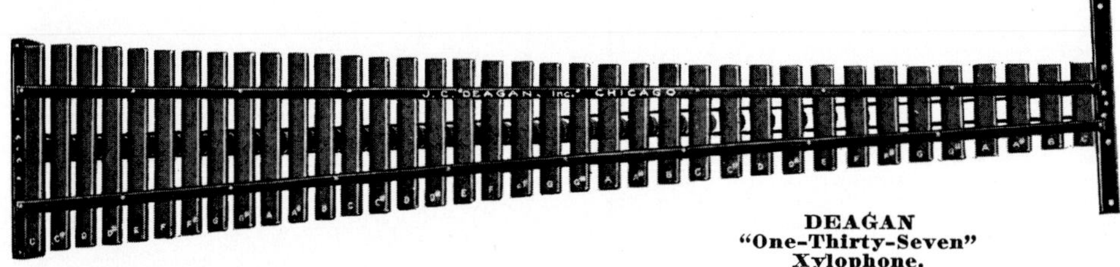

DEAGAN
"One-Thirty-Seven"
Xylophone.

Here is a genuine Deagan Xylophone with resonators that is low in price and so small that it can be used in installations where, owing to limited space, the larger Deagan Organ Special Xylophones could not be placed.

The volume and quality of tone of this little Xylophone will amaze you. It is already in use by a number of builders who have adopted it as standard equipment for some of their moderate priced instruments on account of its excellent tone, small size and low cost. Bars are of finest quality Nagaed and the finish throughout is first class. A Vibrating Action is recommended. No dampers are required.

SPECIFICATIONS

DEAGAN "ONE-THIRTY-SEVEN" XYLOPHONE (Cat. No. 137)

3 Octaves Chromatic (one section)

Range—37 tones, 2 ft. C* to C

Size of bars	1¼"x⅝"
Scale Centers	1¾"
Length	66½"
Height	13½"
Depth	8"
Mallets	No. 2065
Pitch	A-440 or A-435
Price	$90.00

* See paragraph on page 4 (of catalog proper) under heading of "Register."

Fully covered by Letters Patent

DEAGAN ORGAN CARILLON HARP

To supply the demand for a low priced instrument of the Harp Celeste type we brought out, a number of years ago, the Deagan Organ Carillon Harp. Through the use of a different alloy in the bars and by altering their dimensions somewhat we were able to produce an instrument with a slightly shorter tone than that of our regular Harp Celestes, thereby making the use of dampers unnecessary.

But one size is manufactured, four octaves, G in the 8 ft. Octave* to G, and while, in order to furnish it at a low price, we do not finish it as elaborately as we do our other instruments, tone quality—the important thing—has not been sacrificed.

Several prominent builders have used the Deagan Organ Carillon Harp (under various names) in their organs for years and with such excellent results that we have decided to catalog it and carry it hereafter as a stock item. Single stroke actions are, of course, recommended.

SPECIFICATIONS

DEAGAN ORGAN CARILLON HARP No. 2649

4 Octaves Chromatic (two sections)

Range—49 tones, G (in 8 ft. oct.*) to G

Size of bars	1⅛" to 2¼"
Scale centers	2" to 2¾"
Length, each section	55⅝"
Height, each section	11½"
Depth, each section	18½"
Mallets	No. 2045
Pitch	A-440 or A-435
Price	$200.00

Illustration opposite.

* See paragraph on page 4 (of catalog proper) under heading of "Register."

Fully covered by Letters Patent

The style 137 xylophone is the author's favorite because of its very bright tone when struck with the proper hard rubber mallet. Carillon harps were used as chrysoglotts by such builders as Barton, Wicks, Robert Morton and others.

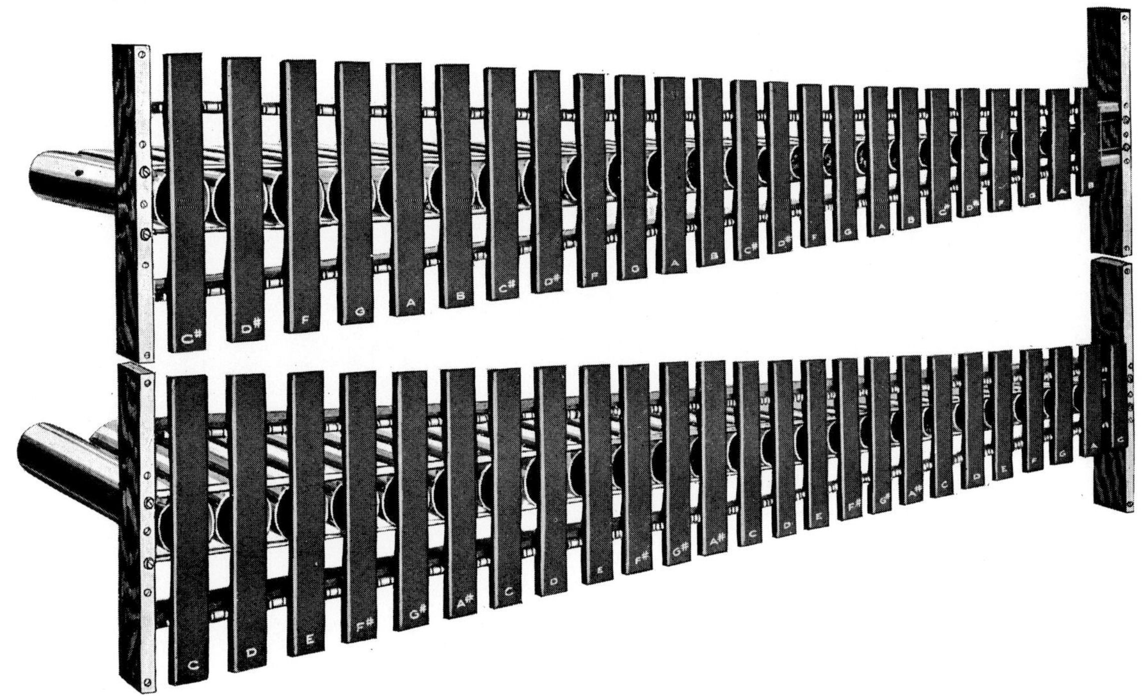

Deagan Organ Marimba-Harp
No. 349

4 Octaves Chromatic, 8′ C to C
Length of Frames, 84″ Each

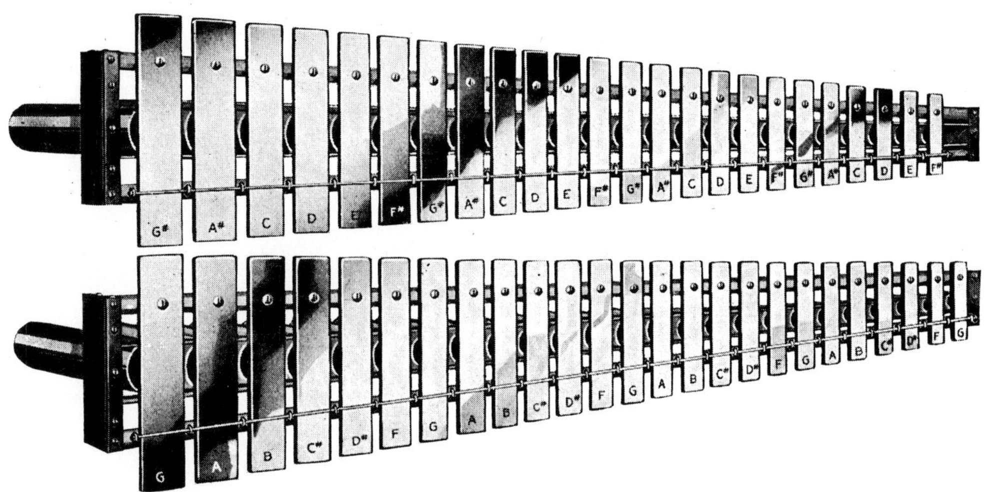

Deagan Organ Carillon Harp

No. 2649

4 Octaves Chromatic, G (in 8 ft. Oct.) to G

Length of Frames 55⅝″ Each.

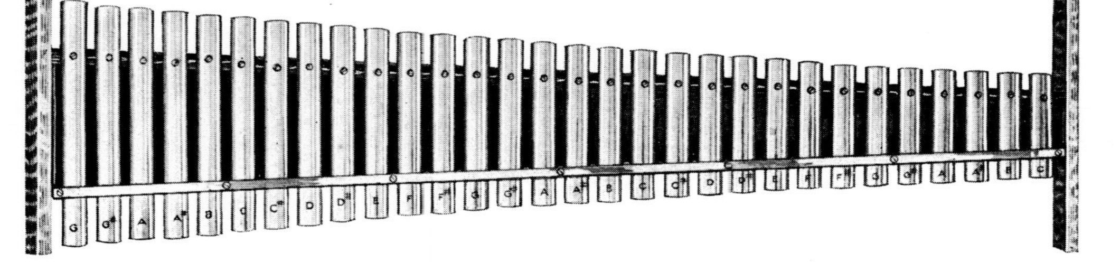

Deagan Organ Orchestral Bells
No. 2530

Round Top Model
2½ Octaves Chromatic, G (in 2′ Oct.) to C
Length of Frame 69¾″

THE DEAGAN ORGAN MARIMBA-HARP

(Nagaed Wood Bars)

We offer the Deagan Organ Marimba-Harp as the finest wood bar percussion instrument ever designed for Pipe Organ use. It gives a perfect Harp effect and as such we recommend it unreservedly. It has been adopted as Standard by many prominent Organ Builders.

The bars of this instrument are made from our very finest Nagaed wood, cut edge grain. Only selected bars are used. They are mounted by the suspended cord and post method over scientifically proportioned and accurately tuned Deagan patent resonators of seamless brass tubing.

This style of mounting allows the greatest possible freedom of vibration, the cord passing through the bars at the exact nodal lines. This cord, which is of heavy linen, is supported by metal posts, the holes in the latter through which the cord passes being machined perfectly smooth.

The Deagan Organ Marimba-Harp is supplied in two sizes, 4 octaves, 8 ft. "C" to "C" (No. 349), and 5 octaves, 8 ft. "C" to "C" (No. 361). The bars are 2 inches wide throughout except in the low two octaves (of each style) in which register they graduate to a width of 2½ inches.

Continued on page 19.

Illustration opposite shows No. 349.

Fully covered by Letters Patent

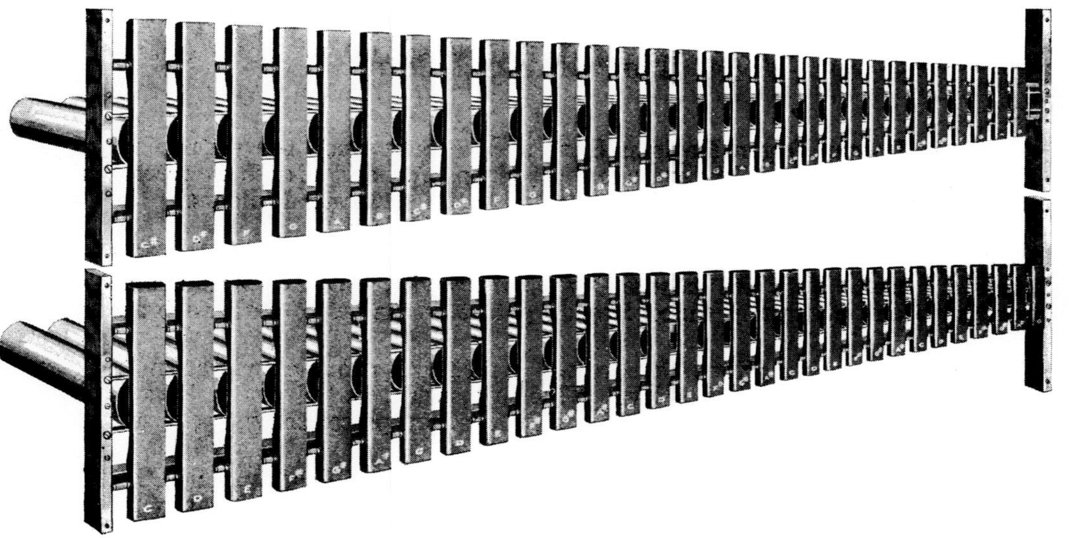

Deagan Organ Marimba-Harp
No. 361

5 Octaves Chromatic, 8′ C to C
Length of Frames, 102″ Each

THE DEAGAN ORGAN MARIMBA-HARP

(Continued)

It is in the Deagan Organ Marimba-Harp especially that the value of using Nagaed wood of many years' seasoning becomes quickly apparent. The beautiful, mellow tone which the instrument possesses is as much due to this condition as to the proportioning and tuning of the bars and resonators.

The Deagan Organ Marimba-Harp requires no dampers, the tone being of comparatively short duration, yet sufficiently long for the use of a single stroke action which is recommended.

SPECIFICATIONS

DEAGAN ORGAN MARIMBA-HARP No. 349

4 Octaves Chromatic (two sections)

Range—49 tones, 8 ft. C* to C

Size of bars	2″ to 2½″
Scale Centers	vary from 3″ to 4″
Length, each section	84″
Height, each section	19¼″
Depth, each section	28½″
Mallets	No. 2035
Pitch	A=440 or A=435

DEAGAN ORGAN MARIMBA-HARP No. 361

5 Octaves Chromatic (two sections)

Range—61 tones, 8 ft. C* to C

Size of bars	2″ to 2½″
Scale Centers	vary from 3″ to 4″
Length, each section	102″
Height, each section	19¾″
Depth, each section	28½″
Mallets	No. 2035
Pitch	A=440 or A=435

(See accompanying list for prices)

Illustration opposite shows No. 361

*See paragraph on page 4 under heading of "Register"

Fully covered by Letters Patent

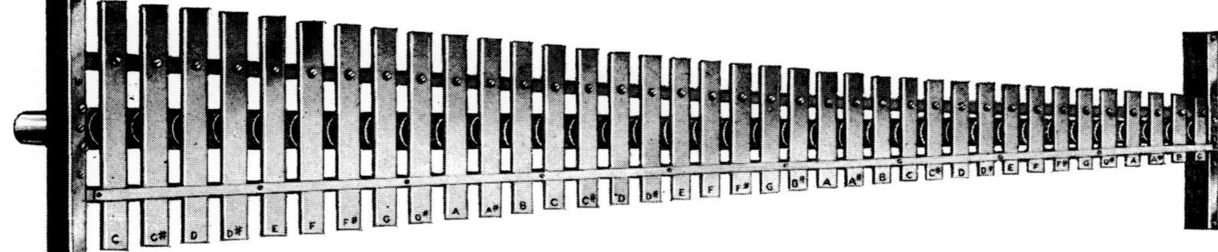

Deagan Organ Parsifal Bells
No. 637

3 Octaves Chromatic, 2′ C to C
Length of Frame 85½″

DEAGAN ORGAN PARSIFAL BELLS

The mounting of Deagan Roundtop Bell Bars over Deagan Patent Resonators results in a combination which gives the most pleasing Orchestral Bell effects imaginable. To this combination we gave the name of Parsifal Bells many years ago. They have constantly grown in favor, both as an orchestral auxiliary and for Organ use as well. These Bells are supplied in only the one scale range, 3 octaves, chromatic 37 tones, 2 ft. C to C.

The superb quality of tone possessed by Deagan Organ Parsifal Bells can not be duplicated, much less excelled by any other type of Orchestral Bells.

While Deagan Organ Parsifal Bells retain the Orchestral Bell characteristic of tone, there is an added color, especially in the middle and lower registers, due to the efficiency of the resonators.

Single stroke or vibrating actions can be used with equal success, dampers not being necessary, although recommended.

SPECIFICATIONS

DEAGAN ORGAN PARSIFAL BELLS No. 637
3 Octaves Chromatic (one section)
Range—37 tones, 2 ft. C to C

Size of bars.................1¼x7/16″ Roundtop
Scale Centers.................2¼″
Length.................85½″
Height.................13″
Depth.................8″
Mallets.................No. 2057-58-59
Pitch.................A=440 or A=435

Illustration opposite shows No. 637

(See accompanying list for prices)

*See paragraph on page 4 under heading of "Register."

Fully covered by Letters Patent

DEAGAN ORGAN ORCHESTRAL BELLS
(Mounted)

Deagan Organ Orchestral Bells (mounted) are furnished in two types of bars, the Standard Flat top and the patented Roundtop, both 1¼″ wide. Each type of bar is supplied in two scale ranges, 3 octaves, 2 ft. C to C and 2½ octaves, G (in the 2 ft. oct.) to C. Bars are mounted on beveled felt on white oak frames.

Both styles of Bells are manufactured from the very finest quality of alloy steel, made especially for Musical Bell purposes. The Flat tops have been on the market for more than thirty-five years and are too well known to require extended comment. They are the finest flat top Bells obtainable.

The Roundtop Bells, added within the past fifteen years, are the logical bell bar shape. They have a heavier and better tone than flat top Bells of the same comparative size and weight.

Either single stroke or vibrating actions can be used with equal success. Dampers are not necessary but can be used if desired.

SPECIFICATIONS

DEAGAN ORGAN ORCHESTRAL BELLS
No. 2230
(Flat Top Model)
2½ Octaves Chromatic (one section)
Range—30 tones, G (in 2 ft. oct.*) to C

Size of bars.................1¼x5/16″
Scale Centers.................2¼″
Length.................69¾″
Height.................10″
Depth.................3″
Mallets.................No. 2059
Pitch.................A=440 or A=435

DEAGAN ORGAN ORCHESTRAL BELLS
No. 2530
(Roundtop Model)
2½ Octaves Chromatic (one section)
Range—30 tones, G (in 2 ft. oct.*) to C

Size of bars.................1¼x7/16″
Scale Centers.................2¼″
Length.................69¾″
Height.................11″
Depth.................3″
Mallets.................No. 2059
Pitch.................A=440 or A=435

DEAGAN ORGAN ORCHESTRAL BELLS
No. 2237
(Flat Top Model)
3 Octaves Chromatic (one section)
Range—37 tones, 2 ft. C* to C

Size of bars.................1¼x5/16″
Scale Centers.................2¼″
Length.................85½″
Height.................12″
Depth.................3½″
Mallets.................No. 2059
Pitch.................A=440 or A=435

DEAGAN ORGAN ORCHESTRAL BELLS
No. 2537
(Roundtop Model)
3 Octaves Chromatic (one section)
Range—37 tones, 2 ft. C* to C

Size of bars.................1¼x7/16″
Scale Centers.................2¼″
Length.................85½″
Height.................13″
Depth.................3½″
Mallets.................No. 2059
Pitch.................A=440 or A=435

Illustration opposite shows No. 2530

(See accompanying list for prices)

*See paragraph on page 4 under heading of "Register"

Fully covered by Letters Patent

DEAGAN ORGAN ORCHESTRAL BELLS
(Unmounted)

In addition to furnishing Deagan Organ Orchestral Bells mounted, as described on page thirty-three, we also supply them unmounted, i. e., the bars only, as some Organ Builders prefer to supply the frames and mount the Bells thereon in their own factories.

The unmounted bells are supplied in the 1″ width as well as the 1¼″, in both the Flat top and Roundtop styles and are identical in quality with those which we furnish mounted on frames.

SPECIFICATIONS

DEAGAN ORGAN ORCHESTRAL BELLS
No. 3630
(Flat Top Model)
2½ Octaves Chromatic (Unmounted)
Range—30 tones, G (in 2 ft. oct.*) to C

Size of bars.................1″x5/16″
Length of longest bar.................9″
Length of shortest bar.................3¾″
Mallets.................No. 2059
Pitch.................A=440 or A=435

DEAGAN ORGAN ORCHESTRAL BELLS
No. 3730
(Flat Top Model)
2½ Octaves Chromatic (Unmounted)
Range—30 tones, G (in 2 ft. oct.*) to C

Size of bars.................1¼″x5/16″
Length of longest bar.................9″
Length of shortest bar.................3¾″
Mallets.................No. 2059
Pitch.................A=440 or A=435

DEAGAN ORGAN ORCHESTRAL BELLS
No. 3737
(Flat Top Model)
3 Octaves Chromatic (Unmounted)
Range—37 tones, 2 ft. C* to C

Size of bars.................1¼″x5/16″
Length of longest bar.................11¼″
Length of shortest bar.................3¾″
Mallets.................No. 2059
Pitch.................A=440 or A=435

DEAGAN ORGAN ORCHESTRAL BELLS
No. 3830
(Roundtop Model)
2½ Octaves Chromatic (Unmounted)
Range—30 tones, G (in 2 ft. oct.*) to C

Size of bars.................1″x7/16″
Length of longest bar.................10¼″
Length of shortest bar.................4⅝″
Mallets.................No. 2059
Pitch.................A=440 or A=435

DEAGAN ORGAN ORCHESTRAL BELLS
No. 3930
(Roundtop Model)
2½ Octaves Chromatic (Unmounted)
Range 30 tones, G (in 2 ft. oct.*) to C

Size of bars.................1¼x7/16″
Length of longest bar.................10¼″
Length of shortest bar.................4⅝″
Mallets.................No. 2059
Pitch.................A=440 or A=435

DEAGAN ORGAN ORCHESTRAL BELLS
No. 3937
(Roundtop Model)
3 Octaves Chromatic (Unmounted)
Range—37 tones, 2 ft. C* to C

Size of bars.................1¼x7/16″
Length of longest bar.................12″
Length of shortest bar.................4⅝″
Mallets.................No. 2059
Pitch.................A=440 or A=435

Illustration opposite shows No. 2230 (mounted)

(See accompanying list for prices)

*See paragraph on page 4 under heading of "Register"

Fully covered by Letters Patent

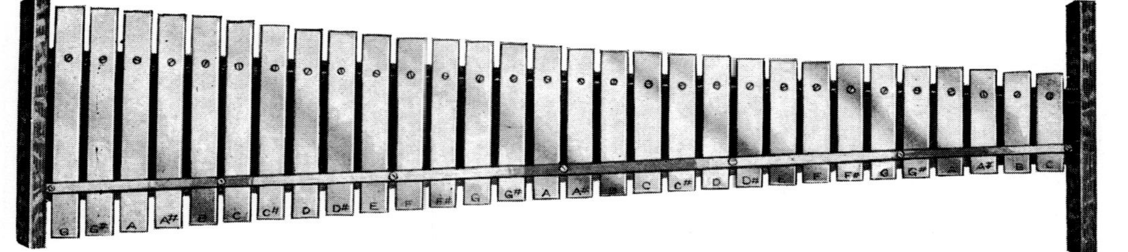

Deagan Organ Orchestral Bells
No. 2230

Flat Top Model
2¼ Octaves Chromatic, G (in 2′ Oct.) to C
Length of Frame, 69¾″

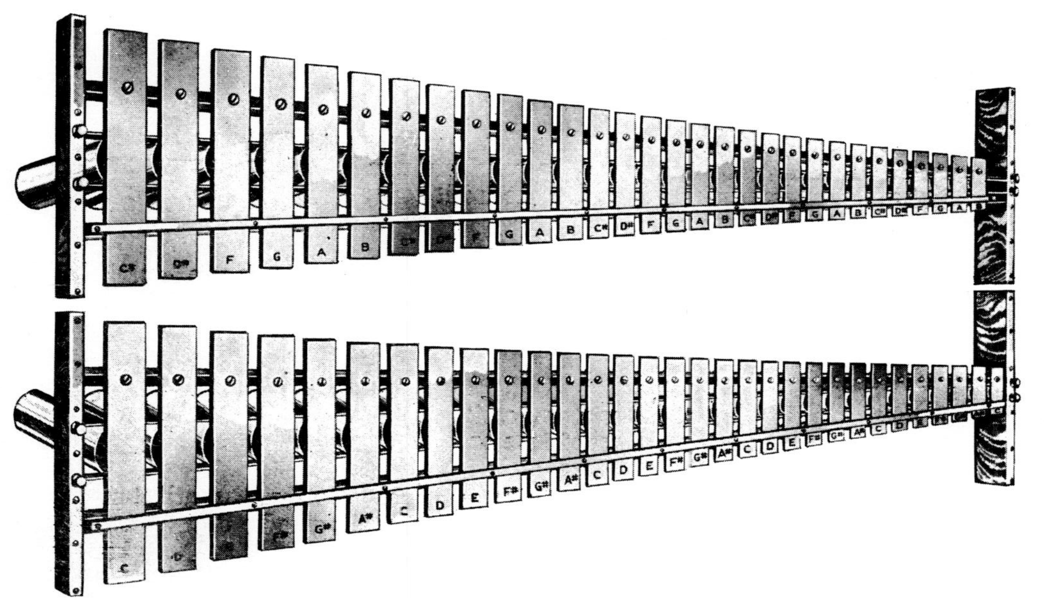

Deagan Organ Harp Celeste
No. 1661

5 Octaves Chromatic, 8′ C to C
Length of Frames, 80″ Each

THE DEAGAN ORGAN UNATONE
(Celeste)

This instrument is made with Roundtop steel bars of special alloy, ground very thin in the center, and mounted up over Deagan patent resonators of marked efficiency. The result is an exceptionally pleasing tone.

The bar centers are extremely sensitive and respond to a very light stroke of the mallet.

The Unatone is a very satisfactory and dependable instrument for Organ use and while it is one of our comparatively new effects it is already a prime favorite with Organ Builders. It is supplied in only the one size 3 octaves, chromatic, 4 ft. C to C.

The use of single stroke actions with dampers is recommended.

SPECIFICATIONS

DEAGAN ORGAN UNATONE No. 1737
3 Octaves Chromatic (two sections)

Range—37 tones, 4 ft. C* to C

Size of bars	1½″ to 2″
Scale Centers	2¼″
Length, each section	45″
Height, each section	11″
Depth, each section	15″
Mallets	No. 2045
Pitch	A=440 or A=435

Illustration opposite shows No. 1737

(See accompanying list for prices)

*See paragraph on page 4 under heading of "Register"

Fully covered by Letters Patent

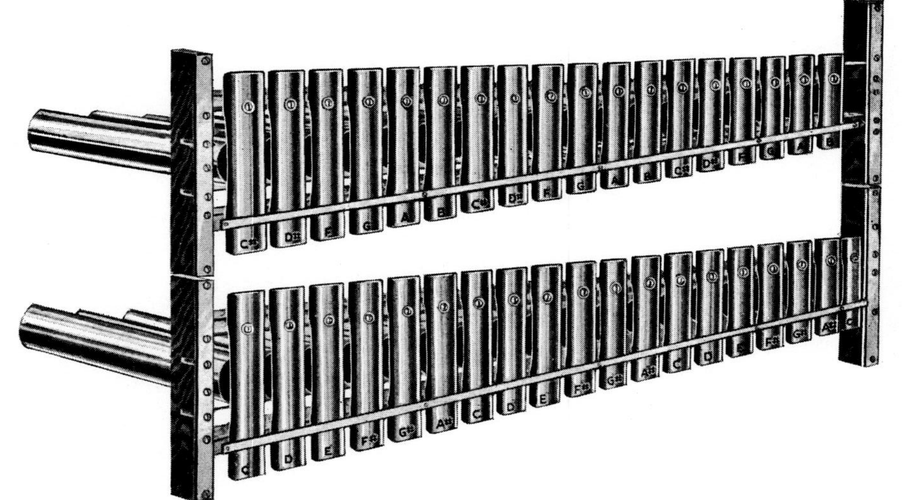

Deagan Organ Unatone
No. 1737

3 Octaves Chromatic, 4′ C to C
Length of Frames, 45″ Each

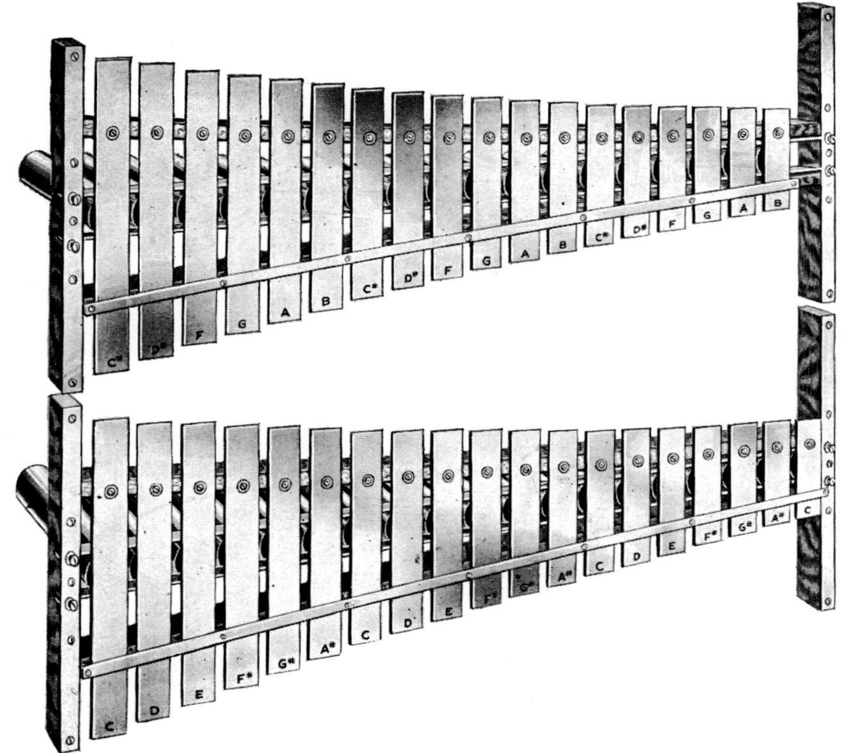

Deagan Organ Harp Celeste No. 1637

3 Octaves Chromatic, 4′ C to C
Length of Frames, 47½″ Each

DEAGAN ORGAN HARP-CELESTE

(Metal Bars)

The Metal Bar Harp-Celeste was one of the first percussions manufactured by J. C. Deagan for use in Pipe Organ. Since the first Deagan Harp-Celeste was introduced many years ago the popularity of the instrument has continued to increase until today it is specified as standard equipment by a number of well-known Organ Builders.

The bars of the Deagan Organ Harp-Celeste are of the finest quality of special alloy steel and are mounted on beveled felt which, on account of the narrow surface coming in contact with the bars, allows the greatest possible freedom of vibration.

The bars which vary in width from 1¼-inch in the upper register to 2¼ inches in the lower are augmented with Deagan Patent Resonators, each resonator being individually tuned in accurate register with its particular bar, as are all resonators on Deagan instruments.

We recommend the Deagan Organ Harp-Celeste unreservedly for a beautiful mellow-toned Harp effect and its use even in the highest priced Organs leaves nothing to be desired for an effect of this character.

The low prices at which the various sizes are offered are made possible by quantity production and place the Deagan Organ Harp-Celeste within the reach of every builder of up-to-date Organs. This instrument represents exceptional value in the Deagan line of Organ Percussions.

Continued on Page 27.

Illustration opposite shows No. 1637.

Fully covered by Letters Patent.

DEAGAN ORGAN HARP-CELESTE

(Continued)

The Deagan Organ Harp-Celeste is supplied in four different scale ranges, the largest size which includes the complete register obtainable in Deagan Percussions extending a full five octaves from Tenor (8 ft.) C to C, 61 tones chromatic. This size we catalog as No. 1661. No. 1649A consists of the lower four octaves only of the above 61 note range, No. 1649B the upper four octaves and No. 1637 the middle three octaves.

The use of single stroke actions with dampers is recommended.

SPECIFICATIONS

DEAGAN ORGAN HARP-CELESTE No. 1637

3 Octaves Chromatic (two sections)
Range—37 tones, 4 ft. C to C

Size of bars	1¼″ to 2″
Scale Centers	vary from 2¼″ to 2¾″
Length, each section	47½″
Height, each section	13″
Depth, each section	14″
Mallets	No. 2035
Pitch	A=440 or A=435

DEAGAN ORGAN HARP-CELESTE No. 1649B

4 Octaves Chromatic (two sections)
Range—49 tones, 4 ft. C to C

Size of bars	1¼″ to 2″
Scale Centers	vary from 2¼″ to 2¾″
Length, each section	61″
Height, each section	13″
Depth, each section	14″
Mallets	No. 2035
Pitch	A=440 or A=435

DEAGAN ORGAN HARP-CELESTE No. 1649A

4 Octaves Chromatic (two sections)
Range—49 tones, 8 ft. C to C

Size of bars	1¼″ to 2¼″
Scale Centers	vary from 3″ to 4″
Length each section	84″
Height, each section	17″
Depth, each section	27″
Mallets	No. 2035
Pitch	A=440 or A=435

DEAGAN ORGAN HARP-CELESTE No. 1661

5 Octaves Chromatic (two sections)
Range—61 tones, 8 ft. C to C

Size of bars	1¼″ to 2¼″
Scale Centers	vary from 3″ to 4″
Length, each section	102″
Height, each section	17″
Depth, each section	27″
Mallets	No. 2035
Pitch	A=440 or A=435

Illustration opposite shows No. 1661

*(See accompanying **list for prices**)*

Fully covered by Letters Patent

*See Paragraph on page 4 under heading of "Register"

DEAGAN ORGAN CATHEDRAL CHIMES

Deagan Organ Cathedral Chimes are too well known to require extended comment. Their use in thousands of Organs throughout the world and the fact that they are Standard equipment with the majority of Organ Builders indicate their standing with the trade.

THE PERFECT CHIME

Deagan Chimes have the true "Cathedral Chime" tone. This is largely due to the fact that they are of a Bell Metal composition after our own formula, the tubes being first cast and then drawn to size.

In the tuning, which is equally important, we exercise the most extreme care not only with respect to the fundamental tone but in the tuning of the partials as well.

VARIOUS TYPES

We list seven different types of Cathedral Chimes, designated as follows: Class A, Class B, Class C, Class K, Class M, Class R and Class S, respectively. All except the Class S Chimes are triple nickel plated, the latter being finished in burnished copper, lacquered.

Fully covered by Letters Patent

(Continued on next page)

OUR FINEST CHIMES

Deagan Class "A" Chimes are the one perfect Cathedral Chime. Graduating not only in length and diameter but in thickness of wall as well, they maintain the correct proportions throughout the entire scale, a perfect ratio existing between the various Chimes in the three dimensions. Thus any one Chime of a set is the exact counterpart of all the others except that as the scale ascends there is a proportionate reduction in EACH ONE of the three dimensions. Only in this way can absolute evenness of intonation be secured. This is an exclusive Deagan feature, not obtainable elsewhere. It is this scientific proportioning that makes Deagan Class "A" Chimes, far and away, the finest manufactured.

A SUPERIOR GRADE

Deagan Class "B" and Class "C" Chimes are alike except as to diameter, which, in each size, is uniform throughout the entire scale. Class "B" Chimes are 1½-inch in diameter and Class "C" Chimes 1¼-inch. The walls are of graduated thickness in both sizes. The Class "B" and Class "C" Chimes are second only to our Class "A" Chimes as to uniformity of tone value in contrasting registers.

MODERATE PRICED CHIMES

Deagan Class "K" and Class "M" Chimes, while medium priced, are far superior to the best Chimes offered elsewhere; that we guarantee. Class "K" Chimes are 1½-inch in diameter and the Class "M" Chimes are 1¼-inch, being of the same size as the Class "B" and Class "C," respectively, although not having the graduated wall feature.

ECHO ORGAN CHIMES

Deagan Class "S" Chimes are especially designed for Echo Organ use and give excellent satisfaction when so used.

These Chimes are distinctive from other Chimes inasmuch as the tubes are grooved with a series of rings which together with the special formula of metal used and their particular size bring out a different set of partials which give a distant Chime effect, exactly what is desired for Echo Organ use.

Deagan Class "S" Chimes vary in diameter from 1-3/64-inch to 1-5/16-inch. They are finished in lacquered burnished copper and will not tarnish.

Complete specifications will be found on pages seven and nine.

Fully covered by Letters Patent

DEAGAN ORGAN CATHEDRAL CHIMES

SPECIFICATIONS

CLASS "A"

No. A-20

Range—20 tones chromatic A to E

Diameter of longest tube	1⅝"
Diameter of shortest tube	1"
Length of longest tube	70"
Length of shortest tube	33"
Mallets	No. 2029
Pitch	A = 440 or A = 435

No. A-25

Range—25 tones chromatic G to G

Diameter of longest tube	1¾"
Diameter of shortest tube	1"
Length of longest tube	79"
Length of shortest tube	30"
Mallets	No. 2029
Pitch	A = 440 or A = 435

No. A-32

Range—32 tones chromatic F to C

Diameter of longest tube	2"
Diameter of shortest tube	⅞"
Length of longest tube	88"
Length of shortest tube	27"
Mallets	No. 2029
Pitch	A = 440 or A = 435

CLASS 'B"

No. B-20

Range—20 tones chromatic A to E

Diameter of tubes	1½"
Length of longest tube	69"
Length of shortest tube	38½"
Mallets	No. 2029
Pitch	A = 440 or A = 435

No. B-25

Range—25 tones chromatic G to G

Diameter of tubes	1½"
Length of longest tube	73"
Length of shortest tube	34½"
Mallets	No. 2029
Pitch	A = 440 or A = 435

CLASS "C"

No. C-20

Range—20 tones chromatic A to E

Diameter of tubes	1¼"
Length of longest tube	64"
Length of shortest tube	36"
Mallets	No. 2030
Pitch	A = 440 or A = 435

No. C-25

Range—25 tones chromatic G to G

Diameter of tubes	1¼"
Length of longest tube	68"
Length of shortest tube	32½"
Mallets	No. 2030
Pitch	A = 440 or A = 435

(See accompanying list for prices)

Fully covered by Letters Patent

DEAGAN ORGAN CATHEDRAL CHIMES

(Continued)

SPECIFICATIONS

CLASS "K"

No. K-20

Range—20 tones chromatic A to E

Diameter of tubes	1½"
Length of longest tube	69"
Length of shortest tube	38½"
Mallets	No. 2039
Pitch	A = 440 or A = 435

No. K-25

Range—25 tones chromatic G to G

Diameter of tubes	1½"
Length of longest tube	73"
Length of shortest tube	34½"
Mallets	No. 2039
Pitch	A = 440 or A = 435

CLASS "M"

No. M-20

Range—20 tones chromatic A to E

Diameter of tubes	1¼"
Length of longest tube	64"
Length of shortest tube	36"
Mallets	No. 2039
Pitch	A = 440 or A = 435

No. M-25

Range—25 tones chromatic G to G

Diameter of tubes	1¼"
Length of longest tube	68"
Length of shortest tube	32½"
Mallets	No. 2039
Pitch	A = 440 or A = 435

CLASS "R"

No. R-20

Range—20 tones chromatic A to E

Diameter of tubes	1"
Length of longest tube	56½
Length of shortest tube	32"
Mallets	No. 2040
Pitch	A = 440 or A = 435

No. R-25

Range—25 tones chromatic G to G

Diameter of tubes	1"
Length of longest tube	61½"
Length of shortest tube	30"
Mallets	No. 2040
Pitch	A = 440 or A = 435

CLASS "S"

No. S-20

Range—20 tones chromatic A to E

Diameter of tubes	1⅛" to 1$\frac{5}{16}$"
Length of longest tube	66"
Length of shortest tube	34¼"
Mallets	No. 2029
Pitch	A = 440 or A = 435

No. S-25

Range—25 tones chromatic G to G

Diameter of tubes	1$\frac{3}{64}$" to 1$\frac{5}{16}$"
Length of longest tube	72"
Length of shortest tube	32½"
Mallets	No. 2029
Pitch	A = 440 or A = 435

Illustration opposite shows No. A-20 Chimes.

(See accompanying list for prices)

Fully covered by Letters Patent

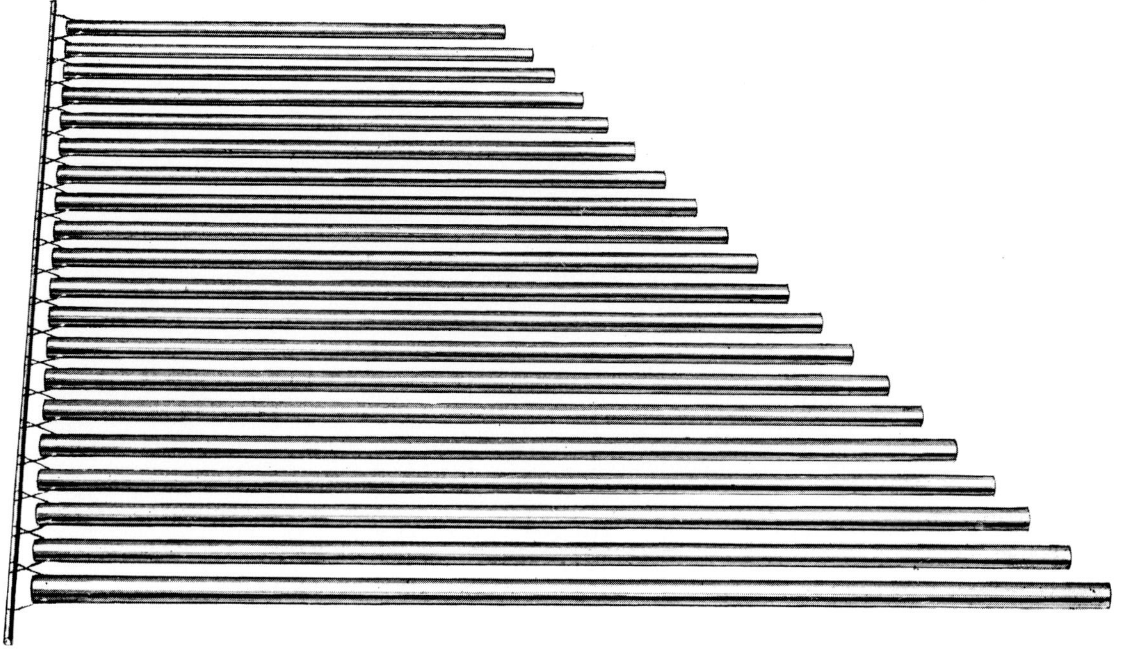

Deagan Class "A" Graduating Cathedral Chimes
No. A-20

20 Tones Chromatic, A to E

Deagan Electric Vibrating Action
No. 115

Length from Top of Action to End of Mallet 7 inches.

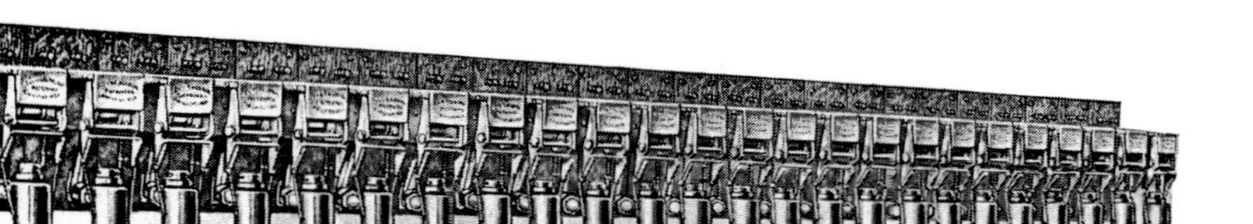

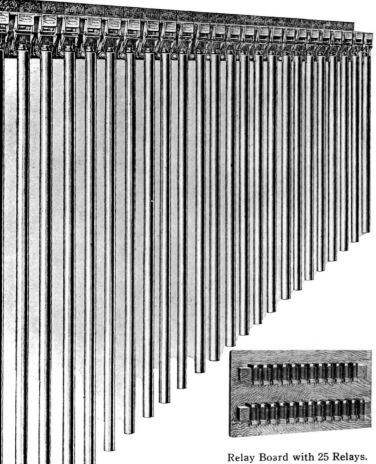

Relay Board with 25 Relays.

No. 900 Deagan Electric Chime Outfit

Total width of complete set of twenty-five Chimes and Actions mounted in one row as illustrated, 75 inches. Distance from bottom of longest tube to top of action, 74 inches.

DEAGAN TUBULAR TOWER CHIMES

ELECTRICALLY OPERATED

Played from Individual Keyboard or Organ Console

Though Church Tower Chimes may perhaps seem out of place in a catalogue devoted to Percussion instruments for Pipe-Organ purposes, the use of Electricity, which has enabled us to discard the antiquated rope-and-lever operated mechanisms and play such Chimes from either a Chime manual or Organ Console or both, prompts us to include them in this list.

Deagan Tubular Tower Chimes are a giant edition of our Cathedral Chimes. The same minute care is observed in the tuning and they possess a pure tone that is remarkably deep, resonant and sympathetic in quality—entirely free from the raucousness that is so dominant in Cast Bells.

Deagan Tubular Tower Chimes may be had in any scale up to a range of sixteen tones chromatic, E to G. Standard sets consist of ten, twelve, fourteen and sixteen tones. They occupy very little space, no derrick or hoisting mechanism is required to install them and the keyboard may be located at any distance up to five hundred feet from the Chimes.

A feature of paramount importance in the consideration of Deagan Tubular Tower Chimes is the fact that their music can, by the organist, be incorporated into the regular Church Services.

So low is the price of these Chimes that they are within the reach of every active Church organization or Philanthropy. They are "A Memorial Sublime" and any church equipped with such Chimes instantly becomes a landmark.

Correspondence solicited.

Fully covered by Letters Patent

DEAGAN ELECTRIC CATHEDRAL CHIMES

Deagan Organ Cathedral Chimes in combination with our Electric Chime Actions, in sets, and choice of individual keyboard or key contacts with Relay Assembly, comprise the Deagan Electric Cathedral Chime Outfit.

Our purpose in listing these outfits in complete unit sets is to bring to the attention of the Organ Builder the fact that our Electric Chime Actions are the logical and most satisfactory equipment for Deagan Cathedral Chimes.

Their combined use is not only conducive to best results, mechanically as well as musically, but their convenience of installation provides an added reason for their being used exclusively, whether Chimes are being installed in old Organs or included as standard equipment with new ones.

The use of the small individual keyboard is recommended only where it is desired to install Chimes with the least possible labor and expense. This keyboard can be attached to the console within convenient reach of the organist.

For standard installations the keyboard is omitted and light key contacts with Relays (the latter suitably mounted) are provided. See page 47 for description of single Relay.

Full description of Deagan Cathedral Chimes will be found on pages 5, 6, 7 and 9 of this catalog. See page 41 for description of the Deagan Electric Chime Action, also regarding Generators and Batteries.

No. 899—DEAGAN ELECTRIC CHIME OUTFIT:
Consisting of twenty 1¼" Deagan Class "M" Cathedral Chimes, A to E chromatic, twenty Electric Actions, twenty Relays, mounted, and twenty sets of key contacts with complete instructions for installing.

No. 900—DEAGAN ELECTRIC CHIME OUTFIT:
Consisting of twenty-five 1¼" Deagan Class "M" Cathedral Chimes, G to G chromatic, twenty-five Electric Actions, twenty-five Relays, mounted, and twenty-five sets of key contacts with complete instructions for installing.

Illustration opposite shows No. 900 Deagan Electric Cathedral Chime Outfit.
Complete descriptive pamphlet of these Chime Outfits sent on request.

(See accompanying list for prices)

Fully covered by Letters Patent

16 TONE SET

Deagan Electric Tubular Tower Chimes

HEIGHT 12 FEET

Deagan Electric Tower Chime Action No. 12 In Weather-Proof Hood

With Hood Removed

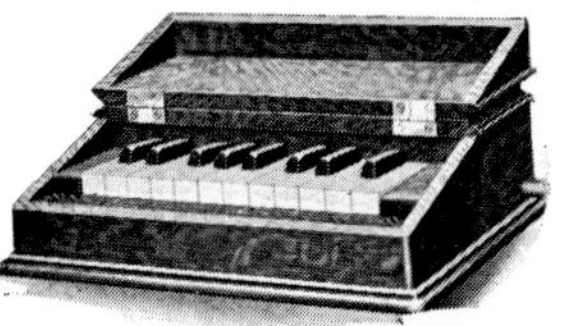

Electric Keyboard For Operating Chimes

DEAGAN ORGAN RELAY

No. 132

The Deagan Organ Relay has been designed especially for Organ use and is intended to relay the operating current for the No. 105 Deagan Electric Cathedral Chime Action and the No. 115 Deagan Vibrating Action.

It is wound to thirty-five ohms, draws about one-tenth ampere on ten volts and will operate on any direct current of from eight to fifteen volts.

This relay has many advantages, some of which are its small size and its adaptability to mounting in a continuous row. The contacts used are of a very high grade contact material and will last for years.

Illustration opposite.

(See accompanying list for price)

Fully covered by Letters Patent

Deagan Organ Relay No. 132

Actual Size

DEAGAN

Electric Cathedral Chime Action

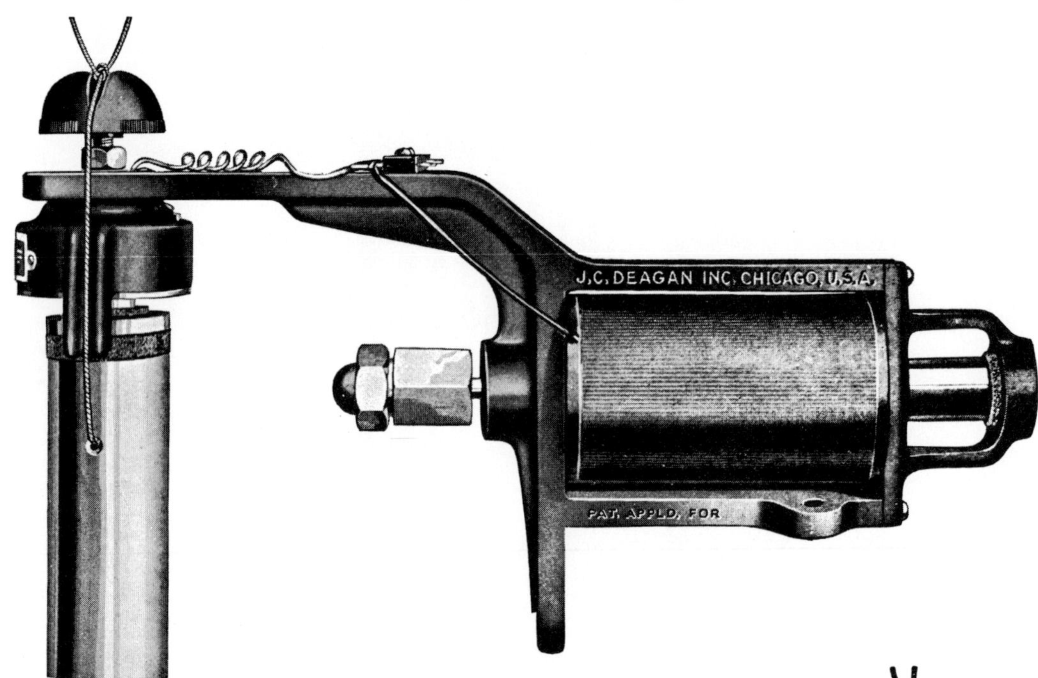

It's . . .

Rapid

Efficient

Easy to install

Practically indestructible

Equipped with a real damper

. . . . In short, it is exactly the sort of Electric Cathedral Chime Action you have always thought *could* be built.

Order a set and judge for yourselves.

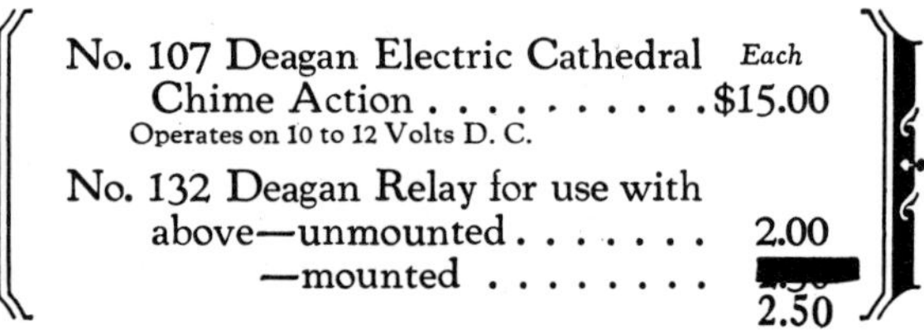

	Each
No. 107 Deagan Electric Cathedral Chime Action . . . . (Operates on 10 to 12 Volts D. C.)	$15.00
No. 132 Deagan Relay for use with above—unmounted	2.00
—mounted	2.50

When supplied in sets Actions are mounted on suitable wood base with substantial brackets for attaching to wall. . . . Complete wiring instructions accompany.

J.C. Deagan *Inc.*

Established 1880

The World's Largest Manufacturers of Percussion Musical Instruments.

DEAGAN BUILDING
Berteau and Ravenswood Avenues
Chicago, U. S. A.

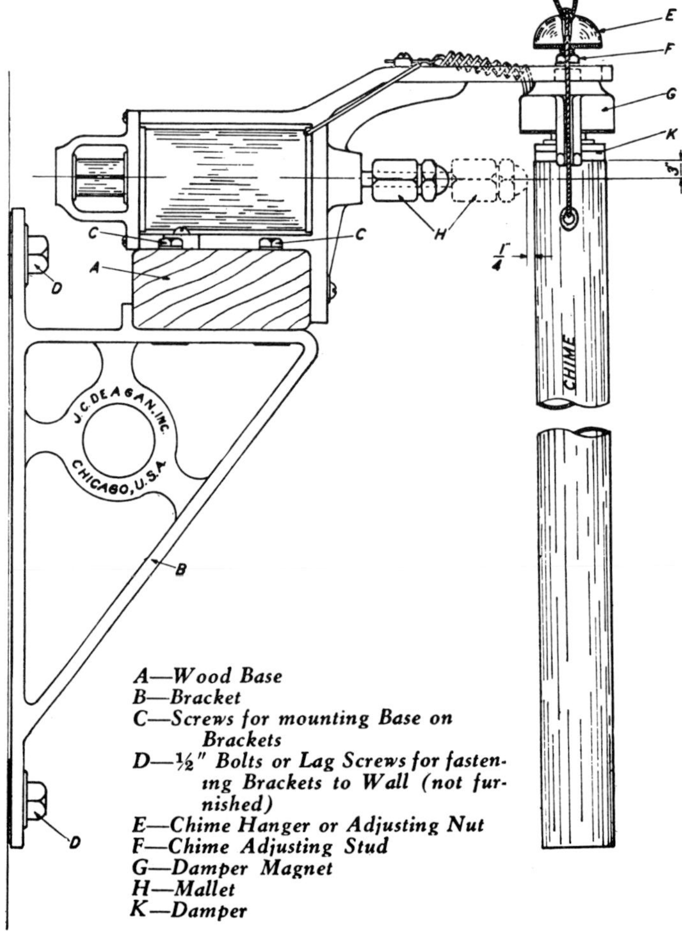

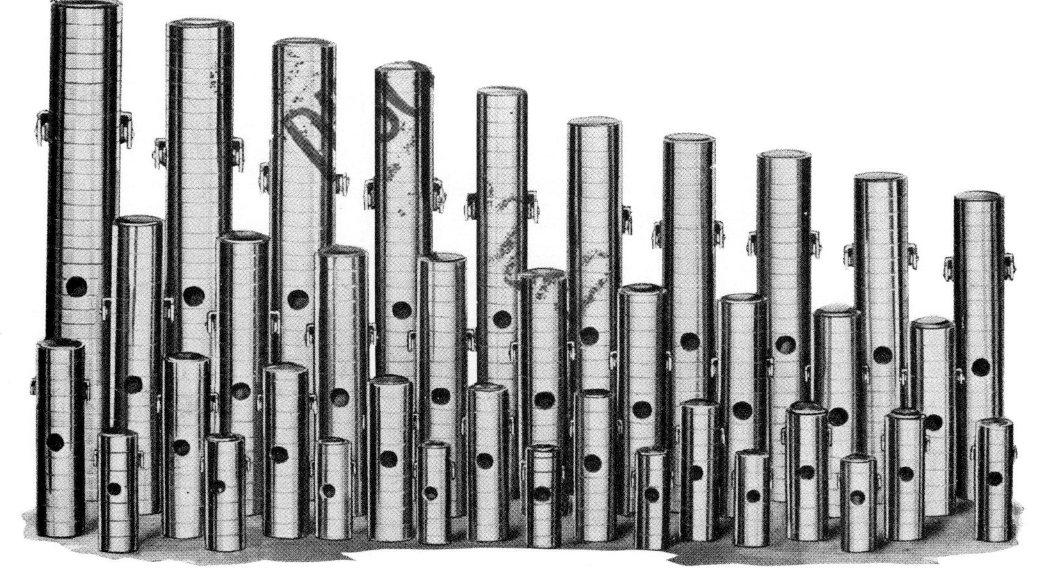

Deagan Organ Reveille Tubes
No. 2837

3 Octaves Chromatic, 4′ C to C
Diameter of Tubes, 2¾″ to 1⅜″

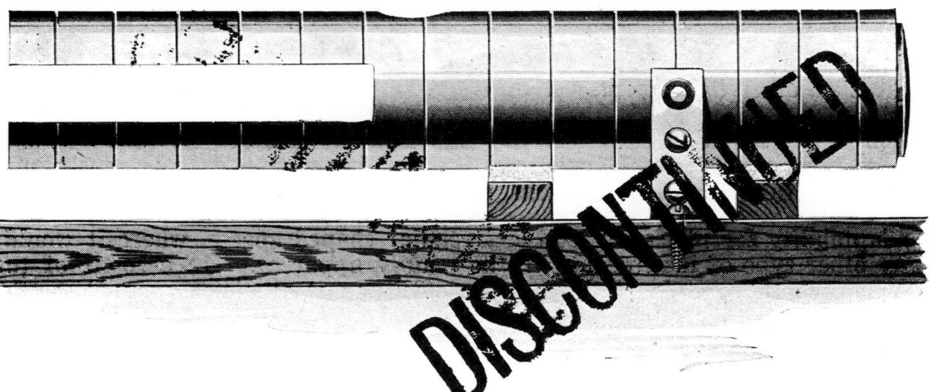

Single Deagan Organ Reveille Tube
Showing Method of Mounting, Etc.

DEAGAN ORGAN REVEILLE TUBES

Deagan Organ Reveille Tubes constitute, without a doubt, the finest Harp stop ever devised for organ use. They are made from a special alloy of Bell metal, the vibrant element and resonator being combined in each single slotted tube.

The tone which is of a beautiful, sonorous character will prove a positive revelation to the Organ Builder and a delight to hearers. The tone is entirely distinctive and the same effect can be secured from no other instrument.

By reason of the fact that each tone unit is absolutely complete in itself it is obvious that these tubes can be grouped as desired. If preferred they can be mounted promiscuously, without regard to regular order, each tube being independent of the other.

Their adaptability for placing in odd or irregular shaped spaces, where it would be impossible to mount any other type of instrument, will be readily apparent. On account of their peculiarity of construction each tube retains full resonator efficiency at all times, regardless of how it may be mounted.

Due to the sustained tone of Deagan Organ Reveille Tubes it is advisable to use single stroke actions and dampers with them. The type of damper we recommend is a wood disc slightly larger than the diameter of the tube and covered with felt or rubber and bushing cloth. The damper action should be so arranged as to press the disc squarely against the end of the tube, the movement being in the direction of the tube's length.

To secure perfect tonal results the mallet must strike the tube on extreme lower (slotted) end. Proper bracket for mounting is supplied with each tube.

Specifications will be found on page 23.

Illustration opposite shows No. 2837.

Fully covered by Letters Patent

DEAGAN ORGAN REVEILLE TUBES

We have divided the fifty-four tubes comprising the complete four and one-half octave scale range into six groups and priced them accordingly. We show below the tubes included in each group. By referring to the accompanying price list the price of any special scale range can be readily computed.

DEAGAN ORGAN REVEILLE TUBES
(Brackets for mounting included)

G in 8 ft. oct.

G G♯ A A♯ B C — Group 1
C♯ D D♯ E F F♯ — Group 2
G G♯ A A♯ B — Group 3
C C♯ D D♯ E F F♯ G G♯ A A♯ B — Group 4
C C♯ D D♯ E F F♯ G G♯ A A♯ B — Group 5
C C♯ D D♯ E F F♯ G G♯ A A♯ B C — Group 6

SPECIFICATIONS

DEAGAN ORGAN REVEILLE TUBES No. [illegible]
2 Octaves Chromatic
Range—25 tones, G (in 4 ft. oct.*) to G

Diameter of tubes .... 1½″ to 2⅜″
Length of longest tube .... 13⅝″
Length of shortest tube .... 4⅜″
Mallets .... No. 2035
Pitch .... A=440 or A=435

DEAGAN ORGAN REVEILLE TUBES No. 2837
3 Octaves Chromatic
Range—37 tones, 4 ft. C* to C

Diameter of tubes .... 1⅜″ to 2¾″
Length of longest tube .... 19⅞″
Length of shortest tube .... 3¾″
Mallets .... No. 2035
Pitch .... A=440 or A=435

DEAGAN ORGAN REVEILLE TUBES No. 2849
4 Octaves Chromatic
Range—49 tones, G (in 8 ft. oct.*) to G

Diameter of tubes .... 1¼″ to 3½″
Length of longest tube .... 26⅝″
Length of shortest tube .... 3⅛″
Mallets .... No. 2035
Pitch .... A=440 or A=435

DEAGAN ORGAN REVEILLE TUBES No. 2854
4½ Octaves Chromatic
Range—54 tones, G (in 8 ft. oct.*) to C

Diameter of tubes .... 1¼″ to 3½″
Length of longest tube .... 26⅝″
Length of shortest tube .... 2⅞″
Mallets .... No. 2035
Pitch .... A=440 or A=435

Illustration opposite shows single Deagan Organ Reveille Tube.

(See accompanying list for prices)

Fully covered by Letters Patent

*See paragraph on page 4 under heading of "Register"

DEAGAN PERCUSSION MALLETS

The importance of using the correct mallets in connection with Deagan Percussion Instruments cannot be overestimated, it being impossible to secure perfect tonal results with mallets which are improperly constructed.

The weights of the heads and the degree of hardness of the striking surfaces are carefully considered in making up Deagan Percussion Mallets.

If desired, we will, without extra charge, mount mallet heads on shanks furnished by purchaser.

SPECIFICATIONS

DEAGAN CATHEDRAL CHIME MALLET
No. 2029

Face adjustable.
Diameter of Head .... ¾"
Weight of Mallet .... 1½ oz.

DEAGAN CATHEDRAL CHIME MALLET
No. 2030

Face adjustable.
Diameter of Head .... ⅝"
Weight of Mallet .... 3½ oz.

DEAGAN CATHEDRAL CHIME MALLET
No. 2039

Permanent composition face.
Diameter of Head .... ¾"
Weight of Mallet .... 3½ oz.

DEAGAN CATHEDRAL CHIME MALLET
No. 2040

Permanent composition face.
Diameter of Head .... ⅝"
Weight of Mallet .... 2½ oz.

DEAGAN MARIMBA AND REVEILLE TUBE MALLET No. 2035

Various size rubber heads, padded and covered. Mounted on ⅜"x⅜" wood shanks. Length, 18 inches. Illustration shows two sizes of heads for 49 tone scale. These heads vary in size and hardness according to the register in which they are to be used.

DEAGAN PADDED MALLET No. 2045

Mounted on ¼-inch round wood shanks, 7" long. Otherwise same as No. 2035.

DEAGAN QUARTER HARD RUBBER HEAD MALLET No. 2056

Mounted on ¼" wood shanks, 7" long.
Diameter of Head .... 1¼"
Weight of Mallet .... 1½ oz.

DEAGAN HALF HARD RUBBER HEAD MALLET No. 2057

Mounting, dimensions, etc., same as for No. 2056.

DEAGAN THREE QUARTER HARD RUBBER HEAD MALLET No. 2058

Mounting, dimensions, etc., same as for No. 2056.

DEAGAN HARD RUBBER HEAD MALLET No. 2059

Mounting, dimensions, etc., same as for No. 2056.

DEAGAN HARD RUBBER HEAD MALLET No. 2065

Mounted on ¼" wood shanks, 7" long.
Diameter of Head .... 1"
Weight of Mallet .... 1 oz.

Illustration opposite.

(See accompanying list for prices)

Fully covered by Letters Patent

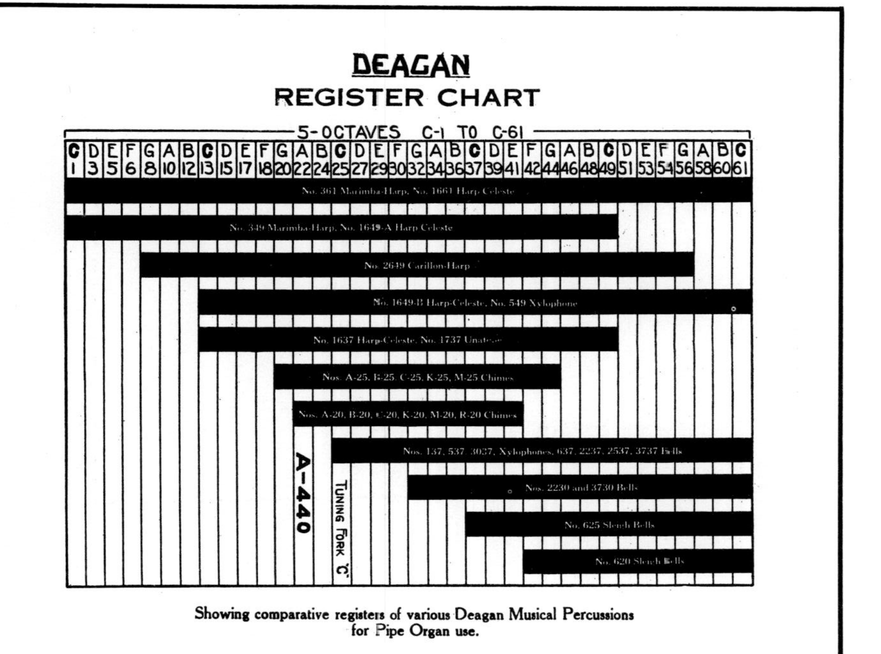

Showing comparative registers of various Deagan Musical Percussions for Pipe Organ use.

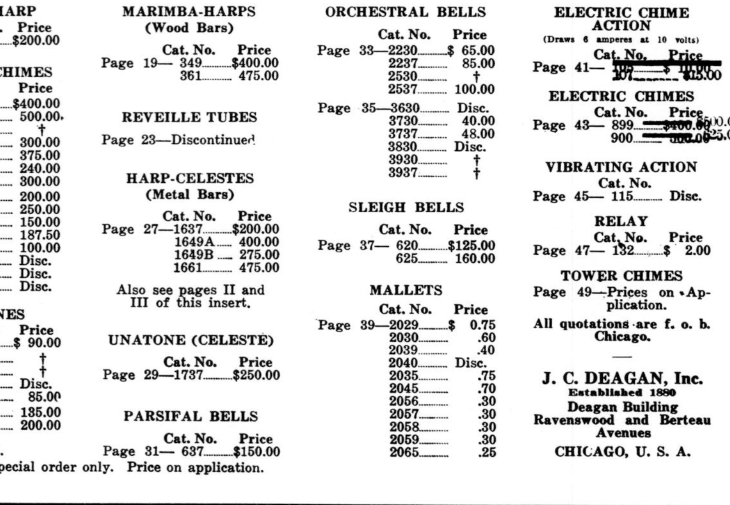

PRICE LIST

OF DEAGAN PERCUSSION INSTRUMENTS AND ACCESSORIES

FOR PIPE ORGAN USE

This price list, effective November 1, 1924, cancels all previous quotations. Please order by catalog number.

CARILLON HARP

	Cat. No.	Price
Page III★	2649	$200.00

CATHEDRAL CHIMES

	Cat. No.	Price
Page 7	A-20	$400.00
	A-25	500.00
	A-32	†
	B-20	300.00
	B-25	375.00
	C-20	240.00
	C-25	300.00
Page 9	K-20	200.00
	K-25	250.00
	M-20	150.00
	M-25	187.50
	R-20	100.00
	R-25	Disc.
	S-20	Disc.
	S-25	Disc.

XYLOPHONES

	Cat. No.	Price
Page IV★	137	$ 90.00
Page 11	2930	†
	2937	†
	3030	Disc.
	3037	85.00
Page 15	537	135.00
	549	200.00

★Of this insert.
†Supplied on special order only. Price on application.

MARIMBA-HARPS
(Wood Bars)

	Cat. No.	Price
Page 19	349	$400.00
	361	475.00

REVEILLE TUBES

Page 23—Discontinued

HARP-CELESTES
(Metal Bars)

	Cat. No.	Price
Page 27	1637	$200.00
	1649A	400.00
	1649B	275.00
	1661	475.00

Also see pages II and III of this insert.

UNATONE (CELESTE)

	Cat. No.	Price
Page 29	1737	$250.00

PARSIFAL BELLS

	Cat. No.	Price
Page 31	637	$150.00

ORCHESTRAL BELLS

	Cat. No.	Price
Page 33	2230	$ 65.00
	2237	85.00
	2530	†
	2537	100.00
Page 35	3630	Disc.
	3730	40.00
	3737	48.00
	3830	Disc.
	3930	†
	3937	†

SLEIGH BELLS

	Cat. No.	Price
Page 37	620	$125.00
	625	160.00

MALLETS

	Cat. No.	Price
Page 39	2029	$ 0.75
	2030	.60
	2039	.40
	2040	Disc.
	2035	.75
	2045	.70
	2056	.30
	2057	.30
	2058	.30
	2059	.30
	2065	.25

ELECTRIC CHIME ACTION
(Draws 6 amperes at 10 volts)

	Cat. No.	Price
Page 41	~~105~~	~~$ 10.00~~
	~~107~~	~~15.00~~

ELECTRIC CHIMES

	Cat. No.	Price
Page 43	899	~~$400.00~~ 500.00
	900	~~500.00~~ 625.00

VIBRATING ACTION

	Cat. No.	
Page 45	115	Disc.

RELAY

	Cat. No.	Price
Page 47	132	$ 2.00

TOWER CHIMES

Page 49—Prices on Application.

All quotations are f. o. b. Chicago.

J. C. DEAGAN, Inc.
Established 1880
Deagan Building
Ravenswood and Berteau Avenues
CHICAGO, U. S. A.

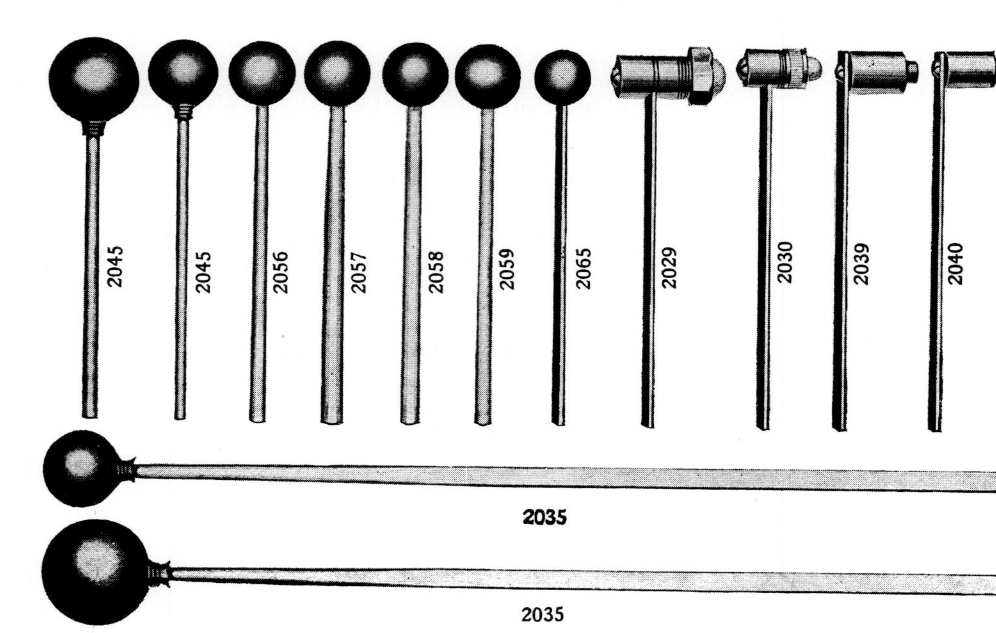

Deagan Percussion Mallets

No. 2055 DEAGAN
Felt Tipped, Wood Disc Harp Mallets

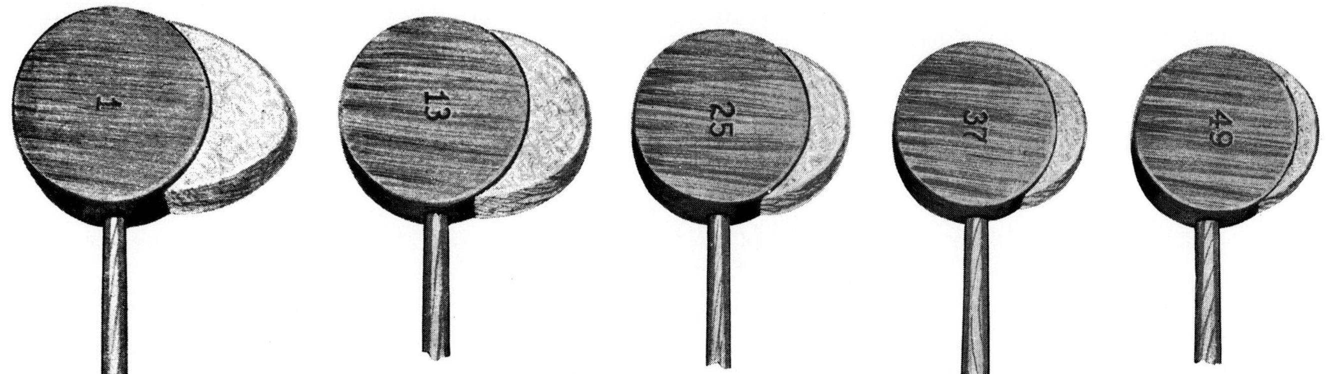

These Mallets will be supplied in place of regular Deagan Harp Mallet equipment when so ordered

---

The Harp Mallets Regularly Supplied

Deagan Harp-Celestes, Carillon-Harps and Marimba-Harps are regularly supplied with our No. 2035 or No. 2045 Mallets (as preferred) which differ only as to shanks, the No. 2035 having long, rectangular shaped shank and the No. 2045 short, round ones. The heads are of rubber, graduated as to size and hardness, and covered with black felt. We have always considered these Mallets to be best from the all important standpoint of tone, providing the felt covering is renewed from time to time as it wears through.

No. 2055 Deagan Harp Mallets Wear Better

However, the No. 2055 Mallets here illustrated give nearly as good tonal results as the No. 2035 and No. 2045 and have the added advantage of not requiring replacement of the striking tips. The five sizes of discs are illustrated but a still further graduation from 1 to 61 is provided by varying the thickness and degree of hardness of the felt tips. Where requested these No. 2055 Mallets (which are not listed in our Catalog) will be substituted with Deagan Harp instruments for either the No. 2035 or No. 2045 without extra charge.

If you want them be sure to so specify when ordering.

J. C. Deagan *Inc.*
Established 1880
DEAGAN BUILDING
Berteau and Ravenswood Aves.
CHICAGO

Factory and General Offices
J. C. DEAGAN, Inc.

These mallets were used to excellent advantage on Barton marimbas.

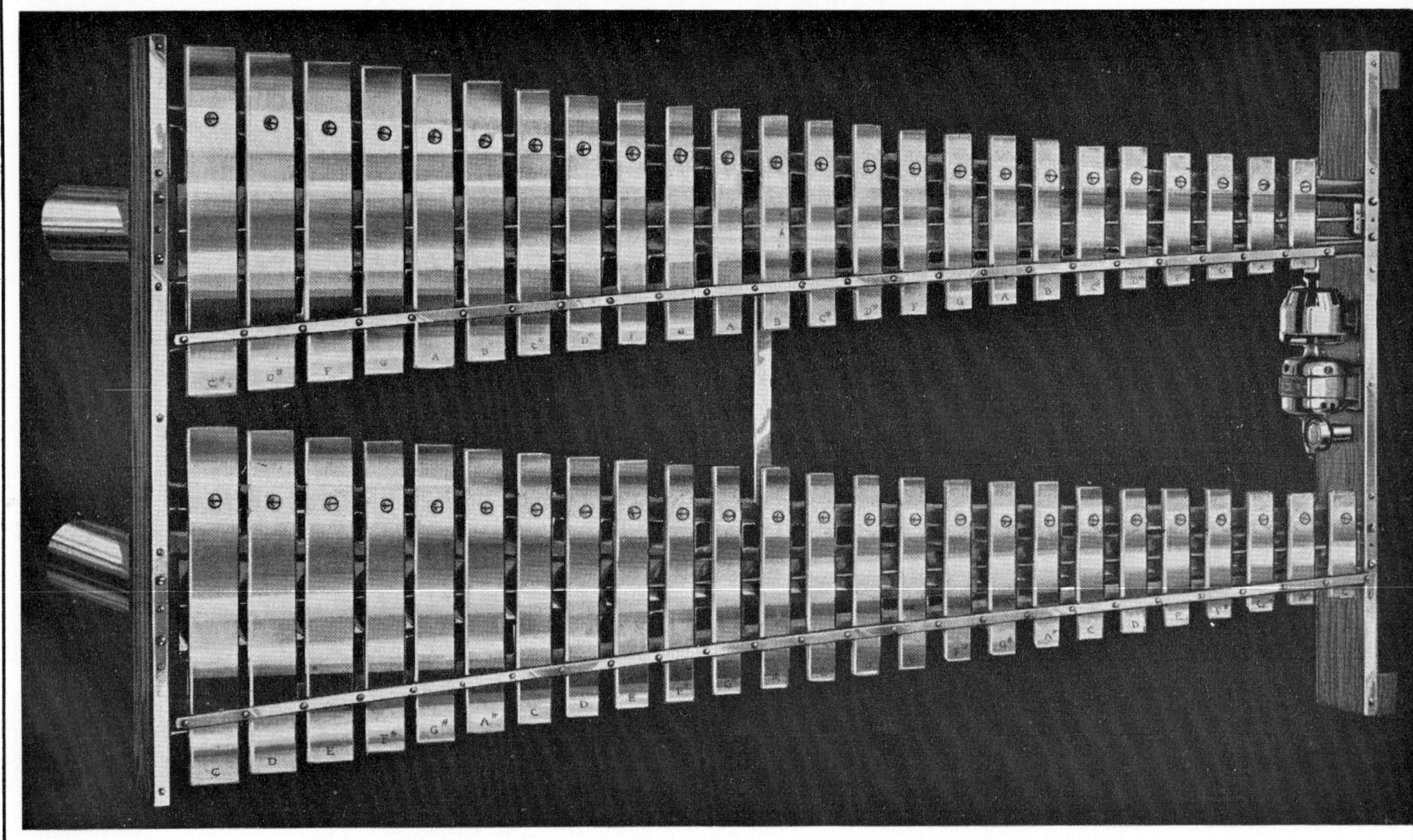

Illustrated is the No. 3149 Vibra-Harp. It is mounted as shown with the bars hanging vertically. The two rows of bars are assembled as one unit, in a single rigid frame.

DEAGAN VIBRA-HARP

A Glorious Golden Voice of Haunting Beauty

THE MODERN ORGANIST with a practically unlimited range of individual stops and an almost inexhaustible number of possible tonal combinations at his command might easily believe that even the most delicate and imperceptible differences in tonal shading must have been discovered and employed long ago. To this Organist the Deagan Vibra-Harp will prove nothing short of a revelation. A more distinctive, outstanding and totally different type of tone could scarcely be conceived—a type of tone that haunts the listener with its beauty.

The Deagan Vibra-Harp is a Percussion—that is, the tone is produced by striking the tone bars with padded mallets, yet its soft liquid song suggests anything but the Percussion idea. Many believe it suggests the human voice in a truer way than the Vox Humana.

Rich and colorful in tone the Vibra-Harp is appropriate for use in any organ, old or new. In the church it will add a new meaning to well loved hymns; under the finger tips of a concert master it opens up new avenues of exquisite phrasing and to all it is a pathetically lovely voice easily recognized and long remembered.

The Vibra-Harp Principle

BRIEFLY described the Vibra-Harp is a Harp-Celeste with a tremulant—hence the name Vibra-Harp (or Vibrato Harp). The very effective tremulant is secured by alternately opening and closing the resonators through the medium of pulsators or fans mounted on shafts and revolving in the tops of the resonator openings. Thus the tone of the bars is alternately weakened and strengthened. The principle is illustrated above. A short section of a pulsator shaft is shown in three successively ad-

Illustrating the Vibra-Harp principle. A short section of a pulsator shaft is shown in three successively advancing stages. The alternate opening and closing of the resonators thus produced results in the characteristic vibrato or Vibra-Harp tone.

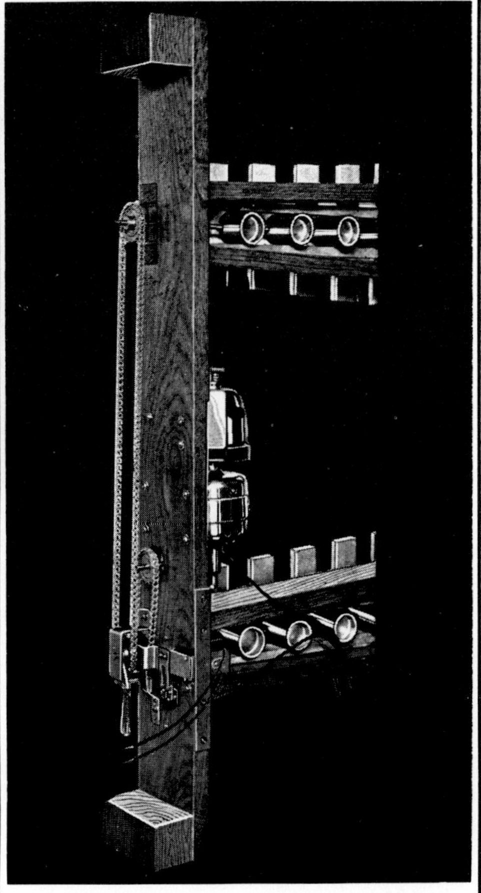

The Vibra-Harp viewed from the rear at the treble end, showing motor, driving chains, pulsator check and motor circuit relay. Relay cover is not shown.

vancing stages. The two shafts bearing the pulsators are rotated by a small 110 volt universal motor.

Dual Use— As Harp-Celeste and Vibra-Harp

THE DEAGAN VIBRA-HARP is in reality a most economical stop for it offers two distinct tonal effects for the price of but a single percussion viz.: Vibra-Harp and straight Harp-Celeste. We supply a simple and effective device known as a pulsator check which automatically brings the pulsators to rest at the point of maximum resonance (about 45° from vertical) when the Vibra-Harp stop tablet is thrown off. In this position the instrument is ready for use as a single stroke Harp-Celeste of unusual beauty and purity of tone. The pulsator check (illustrated at upper right) is a complete unit and no manufacturing is required on the part of the builder. By simply connecting up two wires to the 110 volt lighting circuit (A.C. or D.C.) and two wires to the organ circuits (10 to 15 volts D.C.) the instrument is ready for dual use. Complete instructions accompany each instrument.

DEAGAN Master Tuners are in daily use at the U. S. Bureau of Standards, Washington, D. C.

Actions and Dampers

A COMPLETE SET of properly graduated mallets is supplied but actions are furnished and installed by the builder. Due to the well sustained tone, individual dampers are necessary, one for each bar. These we do not furnish. It is also recommended that a master damper control be provided for releasing all dampers at will in the playing of arpeggios, etc. Some builders control the master damper release through a tablet; others prefer a pedal.

Prices and Specifications on last page.

Organist and Builder Praise the Vibra-Harp

Archer Gibson, eminent New York Organist says:

"The new Vibra-Harp has turned out to be a marvel—capable of new and unheard of effects—of the greatest practical use."

From the W. W. Kimball Company we have received the following:

" . . . We have come to the conclusion that they (Vibra-Harps) should be provided in large church organs and in organs intended for concert use especially, so long as this is not done at the expense of essential stops. We are specifying them in numerous instances."

A prominent Chicago Organ Builder says in regard to the Vibra-Harp:

" . . . The organist, pastor and congregation were overwhelmed by the beautiful tones that came forth. The Vibra-Harp is, without a doubt, the most beautiful stop addition than can be installed in any organ."

The Mudler-Hunter Company write in appreciation of the Vibra-Harp as follows:

"The other day the Vibra-Harp was played for the first time since the installation. Wish to advise that this is one of the most beautiful stops the writer has ever heard. It certainly is a credit to your Company."

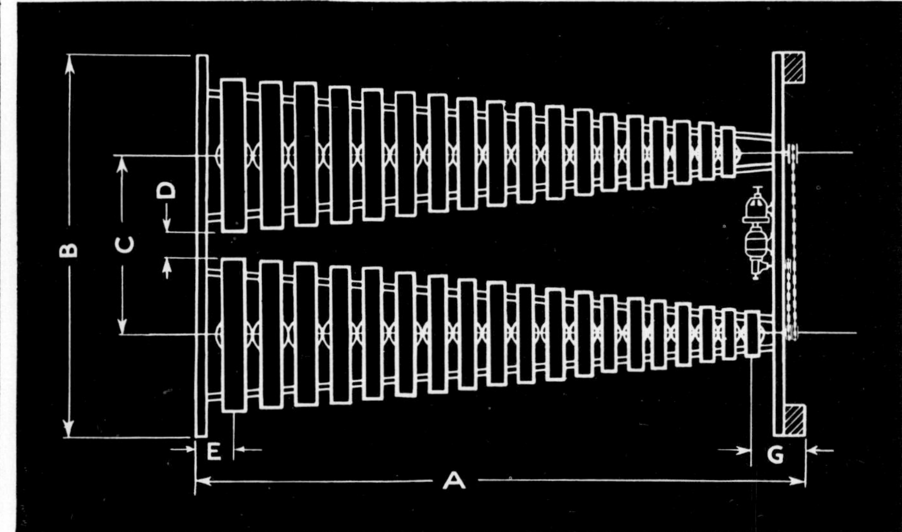

Complete dimensions (which refer to letters in blue print) and scale centers are shown below.

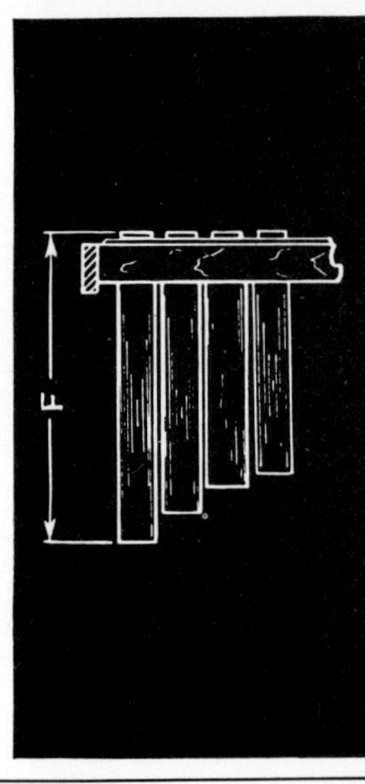

General Specifications

THE DEAGAN VIBRA-HARP consists of two rows of tone bars mounted over individual resonators, the two rows being arranged as one rigid unit (see blue print). In use the bars hang vertically. The two pulsator shafts traversing their respective resonator rows are driven by a small universal motor (110 volts A.C. or 110 volts D.C.). A small relay (a part of the pulsator check) operating on 10-15 volts D.C. serves to close the 110 volt motor circuit, thus avoiding the necessity of running conduit to the console.

Two types of tone bars are offered, viz.: tempered aluminum and steel. Because of its added limpid and flowing purity of tone the tempered aluminum model is recommended. Where funds are limited the steel bar still offers the entrancing and characteristic Vibra-Harp effect—plus the straight harp tone—at a somewhat reduced investment.

Prices

Aluminum Bars

Catalog Number	Number of Bars	Range	Mallets Supplied	Price
3149	49	8′ C to C	No. 2035	$750.00
3137F	37	F (in 8′ Oct.) to F	No. 2035	600.00
3137C	37	4′ C to C	No. 2035	550.00

Steel Bars

Catalog Number	Number of Bars	Range	Mallets Supplied	Price
S-3149	49	8′ C to C	No. 2035	$650.00
S-3137-F	37	F (in 8′ Oct.) to F	No. 2035	525.00
S-3137-C	37	4′ C to C	No. 2035	475.00

Dimensions and Scale Centers

Nos. 3149 and S-3149

						SCALE CENTERS									
A	B	C	E	F	G	C-D	D-E	E-F#	F#-G#	G#-A#	A#-D	D-E	E-F#	F#-G#	G#-G#-G#-C
81⅝″	36″	19″	3¾″	29″	2¼″	4⅜″	4⅛″	3⅞″	3⅝″	3½″	3¼″	3⅛″	3″	2⅞″	2¾″

Note: Dimension "D" is 3⅝″ on 3149 and 4½″ on S-3149.

Nos. 3137-F and S-3137-F

						SCALE CENTERS						
A	B	C	E	F	G	F-G	G-A	A-C#	C#-D#	D#-F	F-G	G-G-F
60⅜″	33½″	17½″	3⅛″	23½″	2¼″	3⅝″	3½″	3¼″	3⅛″	3″	2⅞″	2¾″

Note: Dimension "D" is 3⅛″ on 3137-F and 4″ on S-3137-F.

Nos. 3137-C and S-3137-C

						SCALE CENTERS				
A	B	C	E	F	G	C-D	D-E	E-F#	F#-G#	G#-G#-G#-C
57⅞″	29″	16″	2¾″	15½″	2¼″	3¼″	3⅛″	3″	2⅞″	2¾″

Note: Dimension "D" is 3½″ on 3137-C and $4\frac{11}{16}$″ on S-3137-C.

J. C. DEAGAN, Inc.
1770 Berteau Ave. - - Chicago

WALTER H. DURFEE & CO.

This ad appeared in the November 1919 Diapason. *Mr. Durfee was so anxious to sell chimes that he offered to ship them on approval! This sales tactic apparently did little good for this trade name is virtually unknown today.*

When Ordering Cathedral Chimes for Your Pipe Organ Specify

DURFEE TUBULAR CHIMES

The First in the Market

Sold on Approval

WALTER H. DURFEE & CO.
PROVIDENCE, R. I.

R. H. GEHRINGER, SECRETARY — CHAS. S. WALTON, PRESIDENT — WM. KOCH, TREASURER

EXCELSIOR DRUM WORKS

CHAS. S. WALTON CO., INC.

Manufacturers of
DRUMS
TAMBOURINES
and NOVELTIES

Manufacturers' Agents
DISTRIBUTORS OF
HIGH-GRADE
ACCESSORIES

200 SO. 10TH STREET, PHILADELPHIA, PA.

This firm sold percussion instruments to the United States Pipe Organ Company in nearby Crum Lynne, Pennsylvania.[1]

John B. Kohler (1874-1927) was born in Berlin, Germany and came to the United States as a boy of 16. After traveling all over the country he entered the employ of J. C. Deagan, Inc. in Chicago and was with that firm for 15 years, during which time he learned the musical percussion business. Desiring to seek his own fortune, he and Otto H. Liebich formed the business of Kohler & Liebich in 1912 and incorporated the business in 1915 under the name Kohler-Liebich Company, Inc.[1] In 1918 the firm inaugurated their trademark "Liberty Chimes," no doubt an attempt to capitalize on the patriotic spirit in the country following the Armistice. Their products were used by a number of builders of pipe organs and orchestrions but their sales were a distant second to industry leader J. C. Deagan.

The December 1918 issue of The Diapason *contained a full-page ad announcing the new Liberty Chime trademark. Earlier, a September 1916* Diapason *ad lists Kohler-Liebich's Chicago sales agent as J. G. Geagan. This name is incredibly—and perhaps not accidentally—similar to Kohler-Liebich's major competitor, J. C. Deagan.*

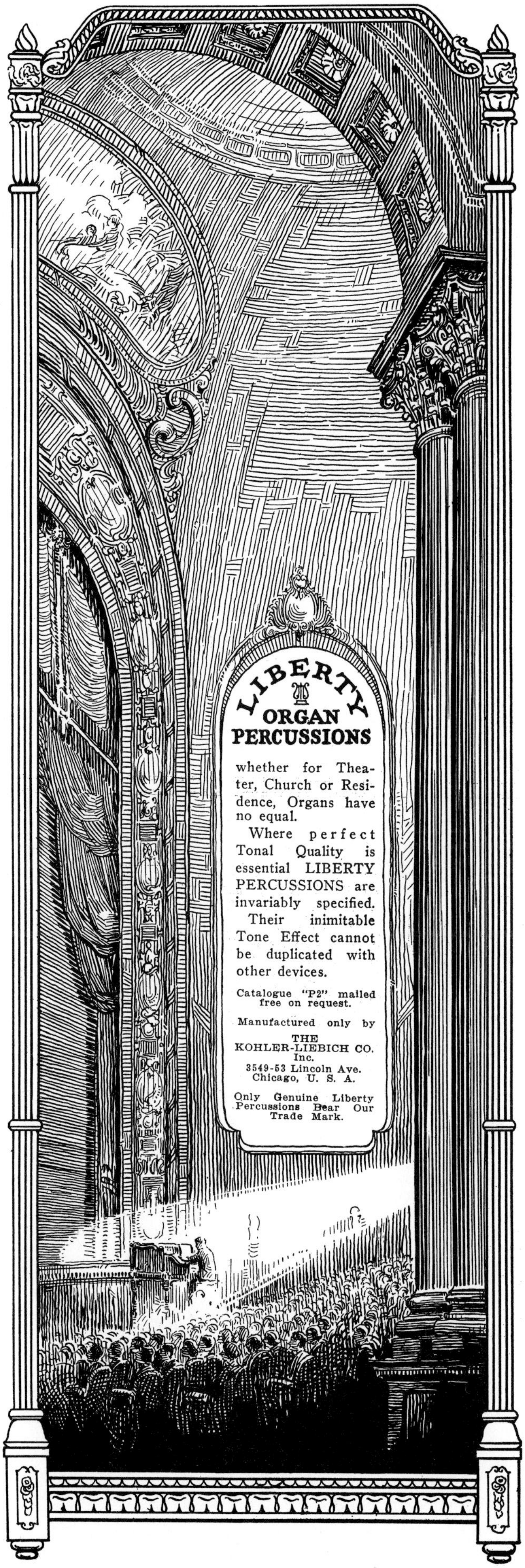

LIBERTY
ORGAN
PERCUSSIONS

whether for Theater, Church or Residence, Organs have no equal.

Where perfect Tonal Quality is essential LIBERTY PERCUSSIONS are invariably specified.

Their inimitable Tone Effect cannot be duplicated with other devices.

Catalogue "P2" mailed free on request.

Manufactured only by

THE
KOHLER-LIEBICH CO.
Inc.
3549-53 Lincoln Ave.
Chicago, U. S. A.

Only Genuine Liberty Percussions Bear Our Trade Mark.

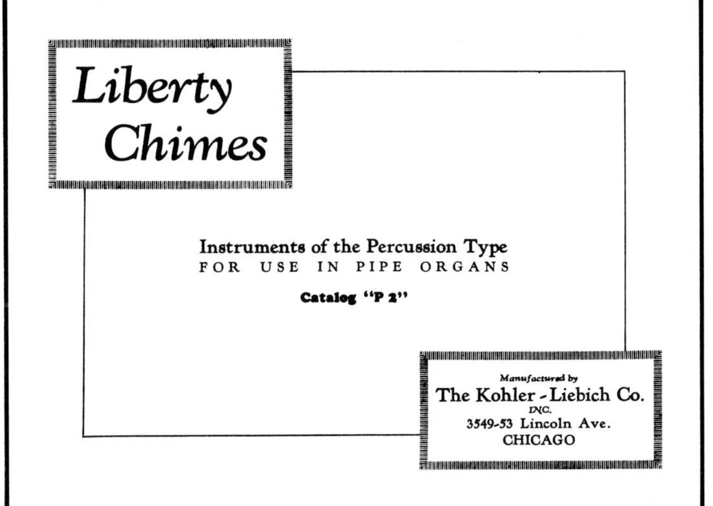

Liberty
Chimes

Instruments of the Percussion Type
FOR USE IN PIPE ORGANS

Catalog "P 2"

Manufactured by
The Kohler - Liebich Co.
INC.
3549-53 Lincoln Ave.
CHICAGO

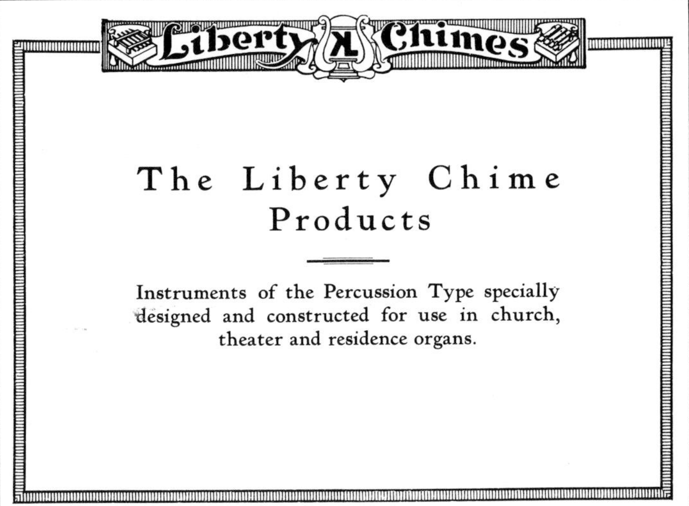

Liberty Chimes

The Liberty Chime Products

Instruments of the Percussion Type specially designed and constructed for use in church, theater and residence organs.

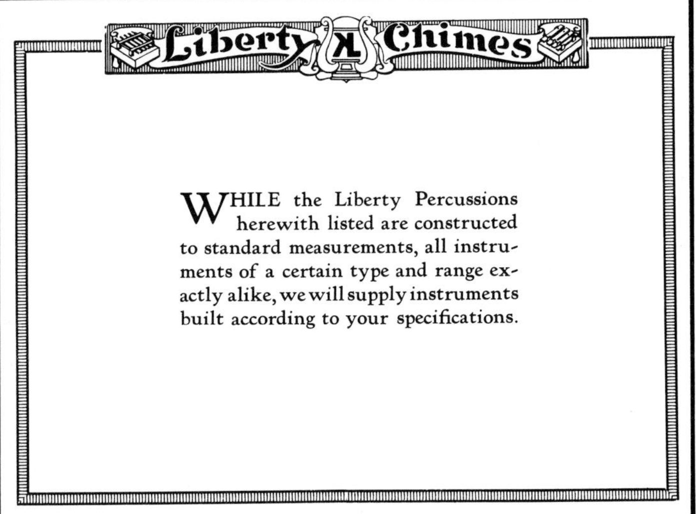

Liberty Chimes

WHILE the Liberty Percussions herewith listed are constructed to standard measurements, all instruments of a certain type and range exactly alike, we will supply instruments built according to your specifications.

Beautiful ad (at left) from the March 1927 Diapason *succinctly suggests that many Liberty percussions had theatre destinations. Above and on the following 14 pages is reproduced a rare Liberty catalog illustrating the wide range of instruments manufactured for the pipe organ industry.*

The Liberty Chime Products

Embrace the most popular tonal effects of percussion type instruments adaptable for pipe organ use.

These instruments are built up to a STANDARD and are guaranteed to be the best producible.

This guarantee means the use of the highest grade materials and expert workmanship.

In addition certain patented improvements embodied in the construction of the Liberty Chime Products are not obtainable elsewhere.

The constantly growing demand for the Liberty Chime Products is evidence of superiority.

Liberty Chimes means the utmost in Tonal Quality.

Liberty Organ

COMPETENT authorities on the peculiar tonal properties of tubular chimes have pronounced the Liberty Cathedral Chimes the best obtainable.

We can unhesitatingly recommend STYLE NO. 0—LIBERTY ORGAN CATHEDRAL CHIMES (graduated diameter, thickness, length) as the very finest toned chimes produced and STYLE NO. 1—LIBERTY ORGAN CATHEDRAL CHIMES (1½ inch diameter, extra heavy) by far the most perfect toned chimes of this size procurable.

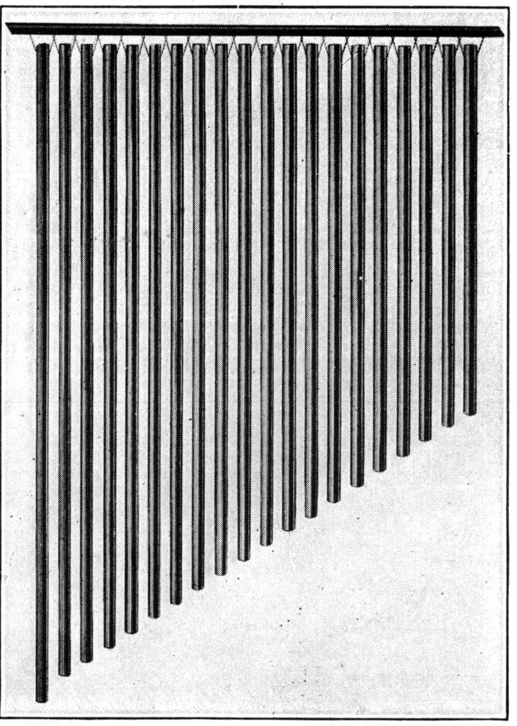

STYLE "1" No. 120. 20 Tubes, A to E chromatic.

Cathedral Chimes

ALL OTHER styles of the Liberty Cathedral Chimes listed while moderate in price, have the distinctive tonal superiority for which all Liberty Cathedral Chimes are noted.

Special care is employed in the construction of the hammers which are furnished with the Liberty Cathedral Chimes.

These hammers of the screw top type are equipped with special hide tips sectionally formed, the only perfect tip with which to obtain lasting and perfect tonal response.

All Liberty Organ Cathedral Chimes are supplied in polished nickel finish.

Liberty Organ Cathedral Chimes

STYLE "O" No. 020

20 Tubes, A to E, Chromatic

Longest Tube, diameter .... $1\frac{3}{4}$ inches
Longest Tube, length .... 73 inches
Shortest Tube, diameter .... $1\frac{3}{16}$ inches
Shortest Tube, length .... 34 inches
Screw Top Hammers .... No. 31
Pitch .... A-440 or A-435

STYLE "O" No. 025

25 Tubes, G to G, Chromatic

Longest Tube, diameter .... $1\frac{3}{4}$ inches
Longest Tube, length .... 81 inches
Shortest Tube, diameter .... $1\frac{3}{16}$ inches
Shortest Tube, length .... 31 inches
Screw Top Hammers .... No. 31
Pitch .... A-440 or A-435

STYLE "1" No. 120

20 Tubes, A to E, Chromatic

Diameter of Tubes .... $1\frac{1}{2}$ inches
Extra Heavy Wall ....
Longest Tube .... 69 inches
Shortest Tube .... 38 inches
Screw Top Hammers .... No. 31
Pitch .... A-440 or A-435

STYLE "1" No. 125

25 Tubes, G to G, Chromatic

Diameter of Tubes .... $1\frac{1}{2}$ inches
Extra Heavy Wall ....
Longest Tube .... 73 inches
Shortest Tube .... 34 inches
Screw Top Hammers .... No. 31
Pitch .... A-440 or A-435

Liberty Organ Cathedral Chimes

STYLE "2" No. 220

20 Tubes, A to E, Chromatic

Diameter of Tubes .... $1\frac{1}{2}$ inches
Longest Tube .... 69 inches
Shortest Tube .... 38 inches
Screw Top Hammers .... No. 33
Pitch .... A-440 or A-435

STYLE "2" No. 225

25 Tubes, G to G, Chromatic

Diameter of Tubes .... $1\frac{1}{2}$ inches
Longest Tube .... 73 inches
Shortest Tube .... 34 inches
Screw Top Hammers .... No. 33
Pitch .... A-440 or A-435

STYLE "3" No. 320

20 Tubes, A to E, Chromatic

Diameter of Tubes .... $1\frac{3}{8}$ inches
Longest Tube .... 67 inches
Shortest Tube .... 37 inches
Screw Top Hammers .... No. 33
Pitch .... A-440 or A-435

STYLE "3" No. 325

25 Tubes, G to G, Chromatic

Diameter of Tubes .... $1\frac{3}{8}$ inches
Longest Tube .... 71 inches
Shortest Tube .... 34 inches
Screw Top Hammers .... No. 33
Pitch .... A-440 or A-435

Liberty Organ Cathedral Chimes

STYLE "4" No. 420

20 Tubes, A to E, Chromatic

Diameter of Tubes	1¼ inches
Longest Tube	64 inches
Shortest Tube	36 inches
Screw Top Hammers	No. 33
Pitch	A-440 or A-435

STYLE "5" No. 520

20 Tubes, A to E, Chromatic

Diameter of Tubes	1 inch
Longest Tube	57 inches
Shortest Tube	32 inches
Screw Top Hammers	No. 33
Pitch	A-440 or A-435

STYLE "4" No. 425

25 Tubes, G to G, Chromatic

Diameter of Tubes	1¼ inches
Longest Tube	68 inches
Shortest Tube	33 inches
Screw Top Hammers	No. 33
Pitch	A-440 or A-435

STYLE "5" No. 525

25 Tubes, G to G, Chromatic

Diameter of Tubes	1 inch
Longest Tube	62 inches
Shortest Tube	30 inches
Screw Top Hammers	No. 33
Pitch	A-440 or A-435

The range from G to G, 25 notes, gives the most satisfactory results when 25 notes are required, while the most popular 20 note range runs from A to E chromatic. For 18 notes the usual scale is from C to F chromatic. Of course we can supply any scale within the 25-note range.

Liberty Organ Marimba Harps

The most perfect Harp Tone Effect as yet produced

ONLY the most select Honduras rosewood, the most musical tone-producing wood known, is used for the bars of the Liberty Organ Marimba Harps.

Mounted in the best known scientific manner, each bar over a correctly tuned and proportioned resonator, constructed of seamless brass tubing, finished in lacquered satin brass, the tone, construction and appearance of the Liberty Marimba Harps is unequalled.

We can unhesitatingly recommend the Liberty Marimba Harps as a fitting tonal effect in the most high grade and artistic organs.

Liberty Organ Marimba Harp No. 49

49 Notes, C to C, chromatic

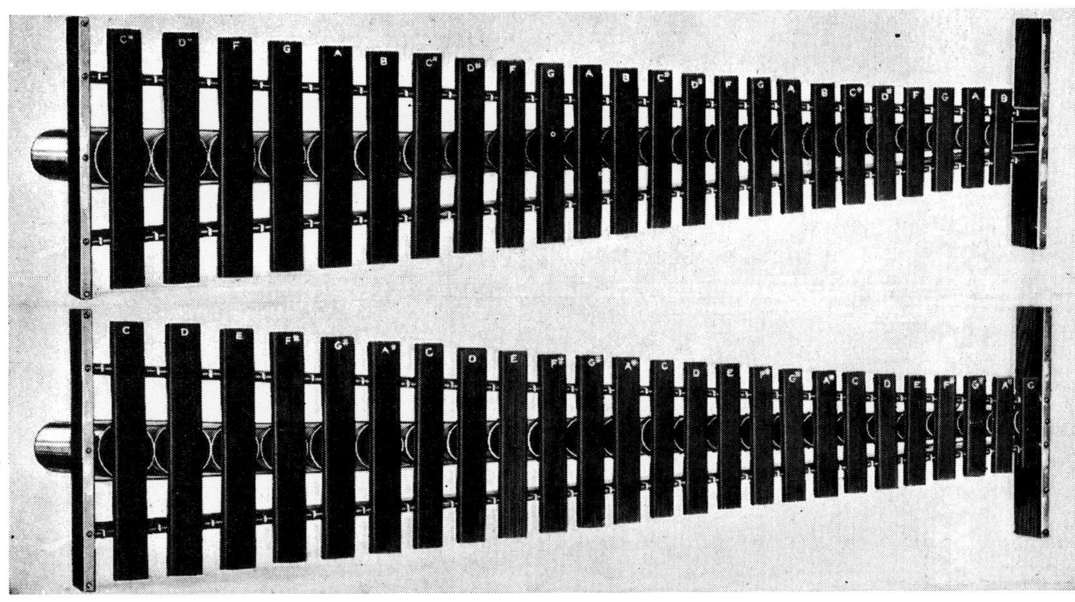

Liberty Organ Marimba Harps No. 49 and No. 61 are of exactly the same dimensions and spacings as Liberty Organ Harps (Metal Bars) No. 149 and No. 161 and are therefore interchangeable, the same action being suitable for either.

LIBERTY ORGAN MARIMBA HARP NO. 49

49 Notes—from 8 ft. C up
Mounted in two sections

Width of Bars...1⅞ to 2½ inches	Depth of Section........28 inches
Length of Section.......84 inches	Spacing, varied ......3 to 4 inches
Height of Section.......20 inches	Hammers, assorted.........No. 41

Pitch, A-440 or A-435

LIBERTY ORGAN MARIMBA HARP NO. 61

61 Notes—from 8 ft. C up
Mounted in two sections

Width of Bars...1⅞ to 2½ inches	Depth of Section........28 inches
Length of Section......102 inches	Spacing, varied ......3 to 4 inches
Height of Section.......20 inches	Hammers, assorted.........No. 41

Pitch, A-440 or A-435

LIBERTY ORGAN MARIMBA HARP NO. 1049

49 Notes—from G in 8 ft. octave up
Mounted in two sections

Width of Bars...1½ to 2½ inches	Depth of Section........22 inches
Length of Section.......84 inches	Spacing, varied ......3 to 4 inches
Height of Section.......20 inches	Hammers, assorted.........No. 41

Pitch, A-440 or A-435

FRAMES: Finished in ebony
METAL PARTS: Finished in tarnish and rust-proof enamel
ACTION: Single stroke, no dampers

Liberty Organ Harp [Metal Bars]

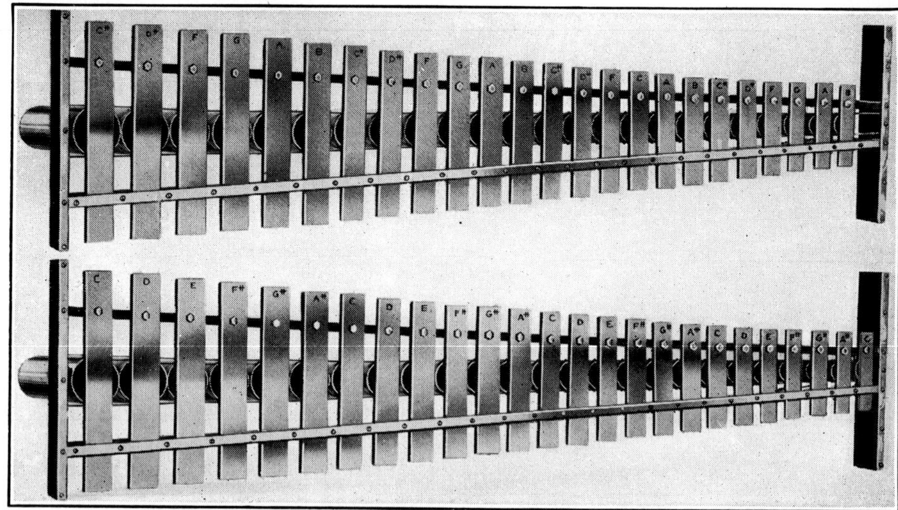

LIBERTY ORGAN HARP No. 149 (Metal Bars)
49 Notes, C to C, chromatic

These Metal Bar Harps produce a very sweet and mellow tone effect blending perfectly with other stops of the organ. ℂ Made according to our own formula the metal bars are mounted alternately on two frames in a manner so as to produce maximum tonal volume. ℂ The large resonators and perfect tone alignment of each bar with its corresponding resonator, result in perfect pure tone quality.

Liberty Organ Harp No. 149 [Metal Bars]

49 Notes—from 8 ft. C up—mounted in two sections

Width of Bars...1¼ to 2¼ inches
Length of Section........84 inches
Height of Section.......20 inches
Depth of Section.......27 inches

Spacing, varied.......3 to 4 inches
Hammers, assorted.........No. 41
Pitch ....A-440 or A-435

Liberty Organ Harp No. 161 [Metal Bars]

61 Notes—from 8 ft. C up—mounted in two sections

Width of Bars...1¼ to 2¼ inches
Length of Section......102 inches
Height of Section.......20 inches
Depth of Section.......27 inches

Spacing, varied.......3 to 4 inches
Hammers, assorted.........No. 41
Pitch ....A-440 or A-435

FRAMES: Finished in ebony
METAL PARTS: Finished in tarnish and rust-proof enamel
ACTION: Single stroke, dampers recommended

Liberty Organ Trinity Harp

THE Liberty Organ Trinity Harp has been specially designed for use where limited space and minimum cost are dominant factors.

Volume production allows us to offer these harps at an exceedingly low figure, the standard high grade tone quality, construction and finish being maintained throughout.

The bars of the Trinity Harps are specially ground and with the resonators tuned to the proper pitch, the tone of these harps has that pleasingly mellow richness so appealing to the listener.

Liberty Organ Trinity Harp No. 249G

49 Notes—from G in 8 ft. octave up. Mounted in two sections.

Width of Bars...1¼ to 2¼ inches
Length of each Section. 55½ inches

Height of each Section. 11½ inches
Depth of each Section. 18½ inches
Spacing ....2 to 2¾ inches

Hammers, assorted........No. 41
Pitch ....A-440 or A-435

FRAMES: Finished in ebony. METAL PARTS: Finished in tarnish and rust-proof enamel. ACTION: Single stroke, dampers optional.

Liberty Organ Celestes

THE Liberty Organ Celestes are without exception the very finest toned percussions of this type ever introduced.

The bars made of special alloy metal are mounted on sounding bases which contain individual compartments, one separate compartment of exact intensifying capacity for the vibrations of its respective bar.

For instance, the sounding bases of Liberty Celeste No. 349 contain 49 individual compartments, one compartment for each note.

The patented scheme of mounting the bars on the sounding bases, prevents the sound waves from interfering with one another and maximum tone volume of perfect clarity is the result.

The Liberty Celestes are the acme of tonal perfection and many builders are using these instruments under various names as standard equipment in their high grade products with gratifying results.

We cannot recommend the use of the Liberty Organ Celestes too highly, for their perfect adaptability as an organ unit of the highest caliber has been established for years.

Liberty Organ Celeste No. 349

49 notes C to C, four octaves chromatic, on two resonating bases as shown in illustration

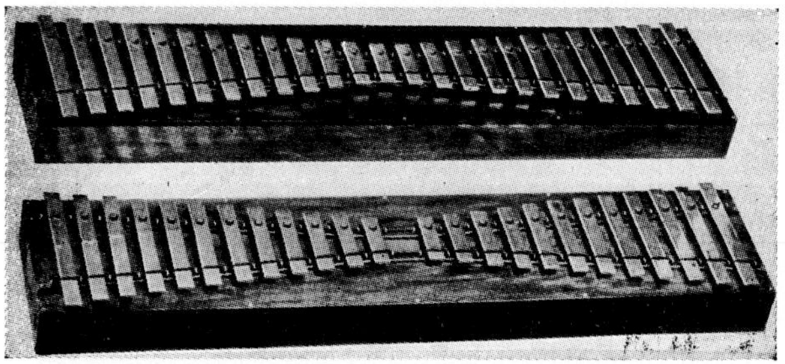

The dimensions of instrument shown are:

Sounding Bases. . . . . $58\frac{1}{2}$ inch long, 11 inch wide, $4\frac{1}{2}$ inch deep
Bell Metal Bars . . . . $1\frac{1}{4}$ x $\frac{3}{8}$ inch
Spacing . . . . $2\frac{1}{4}$ inch from center to center

LIBERTY ORGAN CELESTE NO. 337

37 Notes—from 4 ft. C up—mounted in two sections

Width of Bars.........1¼ inches	Depth of each Section..4½ inches
Length of each Section...45 inches	Spacing ....2¼ inches
Height of each Section...11 inches	Hammers, assorted.........No. 41

Pitch, A-440 or A-435

LIBERTY ORGAN CELESTE NO. 349

49 Notes—from 4 ft. C up—mounted in two sections

Width of Bars.........1¼ inches	Depth of each Section..4½ inches
Length of each Section.58½ inches	Spacing ....2¼ inches
Height of each Section...11 inches	Hammers, assorted.........No. 41

Pitch, A-440 or A-435

BASES: Finished in ebony.
METAL PARTS: Finished in tarnish and rust-proof enamel
ACTION: Single stroke, dampers optional

Liberty Organ Resonance Xylophones

Liberty Organ Resonance Xylophones are the very finest instruments of this type producible.

We are listing three different styles which we can heartily recommend for superior tone quality.

The bars for these instruments are made of specially selected and properly seasoned Honduras rosewood, the most musically toned wood known, and each bar is equipped with an individually tuned resonator correctly proportioned to the size and vibrations of its respective bar.

Mounted in the most scientific manner the result is snappy, brilliant, musical harmony.

The most perfect-toned xylophones obtainable, has been the verdict of critical users.

Liberty Organ Resonance Xylophone No. 437

37 Notes—from 2 ft. C up—mounted in one section

Width of Bars	1¼ to 1¾ inches	Depth of Section	9 inches
Length of Section	85½ inches	Spacing	2¼ inches
Height of Section	17½ inches	Hammers	No. 51

Pitch, A-440 or A-435

Liberty Organ Resonance Xylophone No. 449

49 Notes—from 4 ft. C up—mounted in two sections

Width of Bars	1¼ to 2 inches	Depth of Section	15 inches
Length of Section	58½ inches	Spacing	2¼ inches
Height of Section	21 inches	Hammers	No. 51

Pitch, A-440 or A-435

No. 437 Can also be furnished with 2-inch centers in which case the overall length of frame is 76 inches

FRAMES: Finished in ebony
METAL PARTS: Finished in tarnish and rust-proof enamel
ACTION: Vibrating, no dampers

Liberty Organ Resonance Xylophone No. 537

A small sized Tone Wonder

37 Notes—from 2 ft. C up. Mounted in one section.

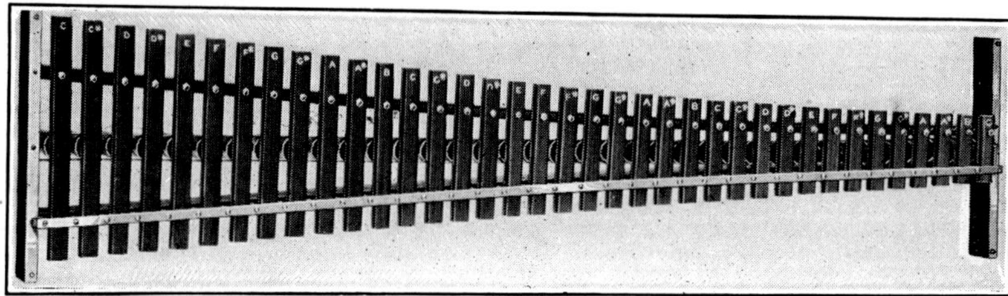

A tone wonder of the highest magnitude is this small-sized and low priced Genuine Liberty Xylophone.

Equipped with resonators throughout, bars of high grade Honduras rosewood, scientifically mounted and constructed, this Xylophone meets all requirements as to price, compactness and musical excellence.

Width of Bars	1¼ inches	Depth of Section	8¼ inches
Length of Section	56½ inches	Spacing	1¾ inches
Height of Section	13¼ inches	Hammers	No. 51

Pitch, A-440 or A-435

FRAME: Finished in ebony
METAL PARTS: Finished in tarnish and rust-proof enamel
ACTION: Vibrating, no dampers

LIBERTY ORGAN XYLOPHONE NO. 30

30 Notes—from G in 2 ft. octave up. Mounted in one section.

Made of selected Honduras rosewood, the bars are mounted on a sounding box frame and where low price and compactness are essential these xylophones will prove absolutely satisfactory.

Width of Bars	1¼ inches	Depth of Section	4 inches
Length of Section	54¼ inches	Spacing	1¾ inches
Height of Section	12 inches	Hammers	No. 51

Pitch, A-440 or A-435

FRAME: Finished in ebony
METAL PARTS: Finished in tarnish and rust-proof enamel
ACTION: Vibrating, no dampers

Liberty Organ Xylophone No. 937

37 Notes—from 2 ft. C up.
Mounted in one section on sounding box frame.

Width of Bars	1¼ inches	Depth of Section	4 inches
Length of Section	66½ inches	Spacing	1¾ inches
Height of Section	15 inches	Hammers	No. 51

Pitch, A-440 or A-435

Liberty Organ Xylophone No. 1030

30 Notes—from G in 2 ft. octave up.
Mounted in one section on sounding box frame.

Width of Bars	1⅝ inches	Depth of Section	4 inches
Length of Section	69¾ inches	Spacing	2¼ inches
Height of Section	14½ inches	Hammers	No. 51

Pitch, A-440 or A-435

Liberty Organ Xylophone No. 1037

37 Notes—from 2 ft. C up.
Mounted in one section on sounding box frame.

Width of Bars	1⅝ inches	Depth of Section	4 inches
Length of Section	85½ inches	Spacing	2¼ inches
Height of Section	17½ inches	Hammers	No. 51

Pitch, A-440 or A-435

Numbers 1030 and 1037 can also be furnished with 2 or 2⅛ inch spacing.

FRAME: Finished in ebony
METAL PARTS: Finished in tarnish and rust-proof enamel
ACTION: Vibrating, no dampers

Liberty Organ Orchestra Bells

WE ARE herewith listing two styles of the Liberty Orchestra Bells, mounted on frames and equipped with resonators.

The bars are of special alloy metal, and accurately tuned resonators, one for each bar, give these bells a tone amplification of great volume and purity.

The smaller bell No. 737 was designed to meet the demand for a high grade moderately priced bell, small proportioned, which can be used to advantage where lack of space prohibits the use of the larger type instrument.

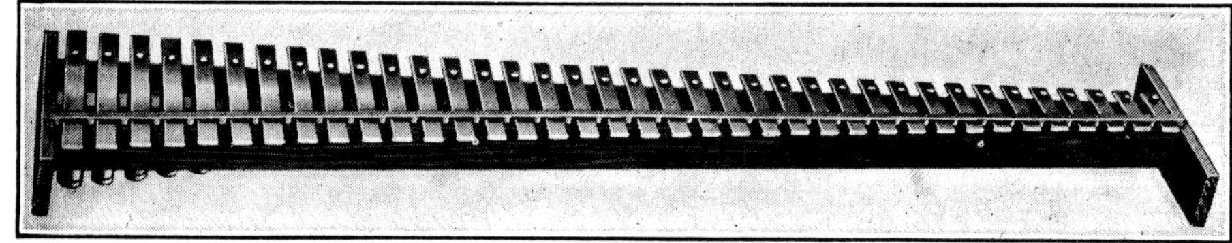

LIBERTY ORGAN ORCHESTRA BELL NO. 737

37 Notes—from 2 ft. C up—mounted in one section

Size of Bars............1⅛ x ⅜ inches
Length of Section...........66½ inches
Height of Section...........13¼ inches
Depth of Section........... 8¼ inches
Spacing .... 1¾ inches
Hammers ....No. 51

Pitch, A-440 or A-435

LIBERTY ORGAN ORCHESTRA BELL NO. 637

37 Notes—from 2 ft. C up—mounted in one section

Size of Bars............1¼ x ⅜ inches
Length of Section...........85½ inches
Height of Section...........13¼ inches
Depth of Section........... 8¼ inches
Spacing .... 2¼ inches
Hammers ....No. 51

Pitch, A-440 or A-435

Can also be furnished with 2 inch centers in which case the length of section is 76 inches.

FRAME: Finished in ebony
METAL PARTS: Finished in tarnish and rust-proof enamel
ACTION: Single stroke or vibrating, dampers optional

LIBERTY ORGAN ORCHESTRA BELL NO. 130 (Glockenspiel)

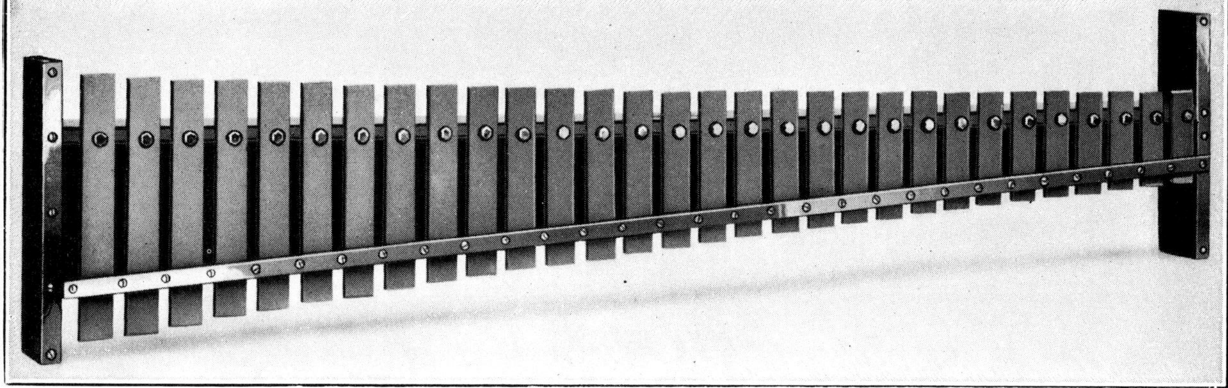

LIBERTY ORGAN ORCHESTRA BELL NO. 130

30 Notes—from G in 2 ft. octave up. Mounted in one section on sounding box frame

Size of Bars..... 1¼ x ⅜ inches
Length of Section..... 54¼ inches
Height of Section..... 11 inches
Depth of Section..... 4 inches
Spacing.............. 1¾ inches
Hammers............... No. 51
Pitch........... A-440 or A-435

LIBERTY ORGAN ORCHESTRA BELL NO. 230

30 Notes—from G in 2 ft. octave up. Mounted in one section on sounding box frame

Size of Bars..... 1⅛ x ⅜ inches
Length of Section..... 54¼ inches
Height of Section..... 11 inches
Depth of Section..... 4 inches
Spacing.............. 1¾ inches
Hammers............... No. 51
Pitch........... A-440 or A-435

FRAME: Finished in ebony. METAL PARTS: Finished in tarnish and rust-proof enamel
ACTION: Single stroke or vibrating, dampers optional

LIBERTY ORGAN ORCHESTRA BELL NO. 1137

37 Notes—from 2 ft. C up.

Mounted in one section on sounding box frame.

Size of Bars....... 1¼ x ⅜ inches
Length of Section..... 85½ inches
Height of Section..... 13¼ inches
Depth of Section....... 4 inches
Spacing.............. 2¼ inches
Hammers................ No. 51

Pitch, A-440 or A-435

LIBERTY ORGAN ORCHESTRA BELL NO. 1237

37 Notes—from 2 ft. C up.

Mounted in one section on sounding box frame.

Size of Bars....... 1⅛ x ⅜ inches
Length of Section..... 66½ inches
Height of Section..... 13¼ inches
Depth of Section....... 4 inches
Spacing.............. 1¾ inches
Hammers................ No. 51

Pitch, A-440 or A-435

No. 1137 can also be furnished with 2 or 2⅛ inch spacing.

FRAME: Finished in ebony
METAL PARTS: Finished in tarnish and rust-proof enamel
ACTION: Single stroke or vibrating, dampers optional

Liberty Organ Orchestra Bells

While the Liberty Organ Orchestra Bells on the preceding pages are mounted, we herewith list two sizes of Bell Bars which we supply unmounted (bars only) to accommodate the builders wishing to mount the bells to suit their own requirements.

Prices on other sizes and ranges on request.

Liberty Organ Orchestra Bells No. 330

(Not mounted)

30 Notes—from G in 2 ft. octave up

Size of Bars............1¼ x ⅜ inches
Length of Bars........9¾ to 4¼ inches
Pitch ....A-440 or A-435

Liberty Organ Orchestra Bells No. 430

(Not mounted)

30 Notes—from G in 2 ft. octave up

Size of Bars............1⅛ x ⅜ inches
Length of Bars........9¾ to 4¼ inches
Pitch ....A-440 or A-435

FINISH: Polished nickel or tarnish and rust-proof enamel

Liberty Percussion Hammers

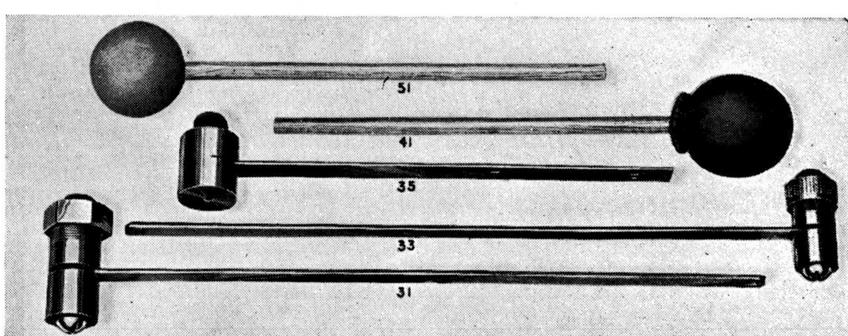

To obtain perfect tonal results the use of properly constructed hammers for playing the Liberty Percussions is absolutely essential.

Liberty Percussion Hammers are designed and constructed to produce pure tonal response of maximum volume.

Illustration shows five different types of hammers.

No. 31 and No. 33 are all metal hammers of the screw top type with removable tip. This tip which forms the striking surface is constructed of special sectionally formed hide, the one perfect tip with which to obtain uniform tonal response at all times.

No. 35 also all metal is equipped with flexible spring steel shank and a permanent sectional leather tip.

No. 41 and No. 51 hammers have ball shaped composition heads of various diameters and density to meet all requirements.

On the No. 41 hammers the ball shaped heads are padded and felt covered in order to procure a wide range of different tonal response when used with the instruments of large tone range.

Liberty Cathedral Chime Hammers
SCREW TOP TYPE, ALL METAL—NUMBER 31

Size of Heads...........¾ in. x 1¾ in.
Shank ....$\frac{1}{16}$ in. x ⅜ in.
Length ....10 in.
Weight ....4 oz.

Removable sectional hide tip.

Liberty Cathedral Chime Hammers
SCREW TOP TYPE, ALL METAL—NUMBER 33

Size of Heads...........⅝ in. x 1½ in.
Shank ....$\frac{1}{16}$ in. x ⅜ in.
Length ....10 in.
Weight ....3 oz.

Removable sectional hide tip.

Liberty Cathedral Chime Hammers
ALL METAL—NO. 35

Size of Heads.............⅞ in. x 1 in.
Flexible Steel Shank........½ in. x .020
Length ....7¼ in.
Weight ....3½ oz.

Sectional leather top.

Liberty Marimba, Harp and Celeste HAMMERS
Ball Shaped Type, Wooden Shank — No. 41

Size of Heads..............1 in. to 2 in.
Shanks ....¼ in. dia.
Length ....7 in.
Weight ....2 to 4 oz.

Padded and felt covered.

Liberty Xylophone and Orchestra Bell Hammers
BALL SHAPED TYPE, WOODEN SHANK—NO. 51

Size of Heads...1 in. to 1¼ in.
Shanks ....¼ in. dia.
Length ....7 in.
Weight ....1 to 1¾ oz.

Furnished in four different densities. Hard, medium hard, medium and soft.

PRICE LIST

Liberty Pipe Organ Percussions
FOR USE IN PIPE ORGANS

Effective April 1st, 1926

CATHEDRAL CHIMES

	Cat. No.	Price
Page 6	020	$400.00
	025	500.00
	120	300.00
	125	375.00
Page 7	220	200.00
	225	250.00
	320	180.00
	325	225.00
Page 8	420	150.00
	425	187.50
	520	100.00
	525	125.00

MARIMBA HARPS

	Cat. No.	Price
Page 11	49	$400.00
	61	475.00
	1049	350.00

ORGAN HARPS (Metal Bars)

	Cat. No.	Price
Page 13	149	$400.00
	161	475.00
Page 15	249 G	200.00

ORGAN CELESTES

	Cat. No.	Price
Page 18	337	$200.00
	349	270.00

ORGAN XYLOPHONES

	Cat. No.	Price
Page 20	437	$135.00
	449	200.00
Page 21	537	75.00
Page 22	30	48.00
Page 23	937	54.00
	1030	54.00
	1037	60.00

ORGAN ORCHESTRA BELLS

	Cat. No.	Price
Page 25	637	$150.00
	737	120.00
Page 26	130	60.00
	230	50.00
Page 27	1137	75.00
	1237	60.00
Page 28	330	40.00
	430	36.00

PERCUSSION HAMMERS

	Cat. No.	Price
Page 30	31	$ .75
	33	.60
	35	.60
	41	.75
	51	.50

All Prices are F. O. B. Chicago

THE KOHLER-LIEBICH CO., Inc.
Sole Manufacturers

3549-3553 LINCOLN AVENUE **CHICAGO, ILL., U. S. A.**

LEEDY MFG. CO., INC.

While working as a drummer at the Strand Theatre in Indianapolis, Indiana, Ulysses Grant Leedy (1867-1931) was becoming increasingly dissatisfied with the quality of the sound effects then available. Having a natural mechanical aptitude, he invented sound effects of his own and in 1900, with Samuel L. Cooley, launched the firm of Leedy & Cooley to produce them. Leedy became the sole owner in 1903, changing the firm's name to Leedy Mfg. Co. The incredible growth of the moving picture industry created a sizable demand for sound effects and by 1905 Leedy employed over 200 people.[1] [2] In the early days of silent films, the assemblages of sound effects used by theatre drummers were called "contraptions." This word was eventually contracted and the word "trap" came to mean any non-tuned percussion device other than a drum.[3]

Leedy's business gradually expanded to include drums and tuned percussions in addition to sound effects. As photoplayer and theatre organ manufacturers proliferated in the teens and twenties, Leedy became the primary supplier to that market. Leedy owned stock in the Wurlitzer company and as a result was the major supplier to the world's largest theatre organ builder, supplying most of the percussions Wurlitzer did not build themselves. Leedy and Ludwig were the two dominant firms in the percussion industry in the 1920s; other suppliers included Wilson Brothers in Chicago, the Duplex Manufacturing Co. in St. Louis, Fred Gretsch in Brooklyn, and the Yerkes Company in New York.[4]

In 1928 U. G. Leedy sold his company to C. G. Conn, band instrument manufacturers in Elkhart, Indiana, after learning that his sons had no interest in continuing to operate the firm. Conn continued manufacturing percussions under the Leedy name and, after 1930, the Leedy-Ludwig name until 1955. In that year Conn decided to divest itself of the percussion business and the Leedy name was sold to the Slingerland Drum Company who purchased it primarily in order to take the name off the market.[5]

12 PAGES IN COLORS

The New 1929

Leedy

CATALOG "R"

JUST OFF THE PRESS!

96 Pages Many New Numbers

A postal will bring one to your door---FREE

—All "Full Dress" Drums at Lower Prices

Leedy Mfg. Co., Inc.
Palmer St. and Barth Ave.
Indianapolis, Indiana
U·S·A

"The World's Finest Drummers' Instruments"

One of Leedy's last ads appeared in Melody *magazine.*

Ludwig & Ludwig
Drum Makers to the Profession
Ludwig
1611-1627 North Lincoln St.
(Wicker Park Station)
Phone Armitage 0080
Cable & Telegraph Address
"Ludrum-Chicago"
Chicago, Ill.

Ludwig was one of the two dominant companies in the drum business during the 1920s, Leedy being the other. Although Leedy numbered more theatre organ customers, Ludwig probably had the edge on quality as evidenced by their sales to Kimball and to Barton, firms not noted for using second-best materials.

William F. Ludwig (1879-1973) was born in Germany and came to America with his parents in 1887. Although his father, a professional trombonist, insisted that his son gain a broad musical education on a variety of instruments, it was the drum which most attracted young Bill Ludwig. He played a number of engagements as a professional drummer, including touring with the Wood Brothers Circus, and eventually found himself in the vaudeville orchestra at the Auditorium Theatre in Chicago in 1908. It didn't take long for Ludwig to realize that his old-fashioned mechanical bass drum pedal was too sluggish to keep up with the new jazz and ragtime syncopations the orchestra featured.[1] His solution was to invent a new drum pedal with a more responsive action.

Ludwig's new drum pedal was such a success that other drummers who saw it wanted one, too. With his brother Theobald (1888-1917), Bill Ludwig founded Ludwig & Ludwig in 1909 and the new company was off to a running start.[2] By 1925 the firm, which was to become the most famous in the drum industry, employed 300 persons. Sales were evenly divided between drums and sound effects for the accompaniment of silent motion pictures.[3] Unfortunately for Ludwig & Ludwig and for the theatre organ industry, movies learned to talk. The demand for silent movie drummers evaporated quickly and by the end of the decade Ludwig & Ludwig had only 35 employees.[4]

In 1930 Ludwig & Ludwig was acquired by C. G. Conn of Elkhart, Indiana, who in 1928 had already bought the Leedy Mfg. Co. Drum manufacturing was consolidated in Elkhart under the Leedy-Ludwig name with Bill Ludwig as general manager. Mr. Ludwig yearned to be his own boss, however, and in 1936 he resigned to form the W. F. L. Drum Company. When Conn decided to quit the drum business in 1955, Ludwig purchased his name back and changed W. F. L.'s name to Ludwig Drum Co. The name became Ludwig Industries, Inc. in 1968 following the acquisition of the Musser Marimba Company in 1966 and the Schuessler Fiber Case Company in 1968.[5]

After the death of William F. Ludwig in 1973, his son William F. Ludwig, Jr., acknowledged as the world's leading authority on the history of drums and the percussion industry, became president of the firm. In 1981 Ludwig Industries became a division of the Selmer Company (also in Elkhart, Indiana), another leading manufacturer of musical instruments.[6]

William F. Ludwig (1879-1973)

On the next three pages are reproduced excerpts from the elaborate 1927 Ludwig catalog.

Whistles and Imitations

Ludwig Three-in-One Whistle

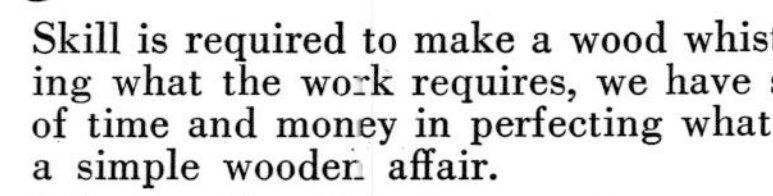

Skill is required to make a wood whistle. Knowing what the work requires, we have spent a lot of time and money in perfecting what looks like a simple wooden affair.

It is not. Excellent for steamboat.

We take special pride in the careful construction of our wood whistles. They are skillfully voiced and respond to the slightest breath. They will sustain a rich, full tone when blown hard for railroad effects.

Voiced by experts to blow very easy and will not overblow. 16″ long.
No. 521§ Price, each.................. **$3.00**

Snore Imitation

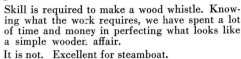

Very effective for comedy pictures.
No. 557—Snore Imitation. Length 6″........................... $0.30

Nose-Blow

A short, hard blast produces a regular "bandana" handkerchief effect. Will also produce an accurate imitation of fly buzz, bee hum and mosquito.
No. 556—Nose Blow Imitation.
4″ long....... **$0.20**

Ludwig Bell-Plate and Railroad Imitations

A steel bell-plate, $9\frac{1}{2}$″ wide by 7″ high, furnished with mallet. Not polished nor plated.
No. 531........ **$3.00**

No. 528—Ludwig Railroad imitation; effect is produced with heavy springs in box, stroked with a lever across the springs......... **$6.00**

No. 529—Complete bell and R. R. imitation—(a combination of Nos. 531 and 528) makes the complete outfit. **$9.00**

Ludwig Professional Bird Whistle

The best bird imitation on the market. Carefully voiced for accurate imitation. The effect is realistic and sure. Heavily nickeled and made of brass. Used with water and so designed that cover cap makes it leakproof.
No. 511—Ludwig Bird Whistle.
3″ high........................ **$2.00**

Bird Whistle

An inexpensive and popular bird whistle that will serve the purpose for the school and juvenile orchestra. $2\frac{1}{2}$″ high.
No. 512—Bird Whistle........ **$1.25**

No. 512

Bird Whistle

An economical water-carrying bird whistle. $3\frac{1}{2}$″ high.
No. 514§ Bird Whistle........ **$1.50**

No. 514

New Ludwig Three-Tone Boat and Train Whistle

You can dismiss all worry and anxiety from your mind when you use this new effect. Made of metal, highly nickeled and is a compact, sturdy trap that will give many years of service. More reliable than wood—and less bulky. Voiced just as the perfect whistle effect you have long wished for. It is without question the finest of whistle effects we have ever made. Drummers, we'll guarantee that you have never played a trap that will give you the satisfaction you realize in performing on this new whistle. It is three-toned and you get many variations of the standard steamboat and train calls. $7\frac{1}{4}$″x$4\frac{1}{2}$″.
No. 515§ Ludwig Three-Tone Whistle.................... **$3.00**

Ludwig Drum Major and Police Whistle

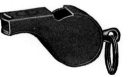

A shrill metal whistle that is used for commands and assembly calls in Drum Corps and Bands. Also used for trap work as a police traffic whistle, mailman, etc.
No. 524—Price, each..... **$0.50**

Ludwig Sand Blocks

Swish, swish, swish—for soft shoe dancing and nigger shuffle effects. Also used in the children's juvenile orchestras for rhythmical figures. 3″x 5″.

No. 752, pair............. **$0.50**

Ludwig Sleigh Bells

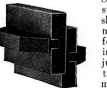

Still effective as ever. Used a lot on hand strap or for wrist similar to one pictured in juvenile orchestras. Good small trap for the drummer as well. Four (4) bells on wrist strap.

No. 419..... **$0.60**

No. 490—11 bells on strap........ **$2.50**

No. 491—20 bells on strap........ **4.00**

The Same Principle in the Victrola

We quote with permission direct from the Victor Company's catalog their method of building the finest cabinet work in their instruments:

"It should be noted that Orthophonic and Electrola cabinets are of veneered or laminated construction—the costliest and best method of cabinet making. When sound principles of construction require solid woods, we use solid woods, but since laminated construction permits the building of a cabinet that does not warp or shrink, the internal stresses being counterbalanced by alternate layers of wood; Victor builds exclusively with the finest and most expensive woods, cabinets of laminated construction."

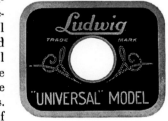

Photo by Inter. News Service

Superior Method of Bass Drum Construction

The Ludwig method of laminated shell construction is the most modern and improved form of building bass drums. Extreme strength of shell and ability to hold a perfect round are necessary to secure the best drum tone. Bass drum shells fashioned and built in accordance with the recognized correct principles used in the manufacture of aeroplanes are stronger and lighter. They will stand up longer under hard usage, maintain perfect round and are immune to climatic changes.

Government Test of Laminated Construction

According to U. S. Government Air Service Engineers in aeroplane construction the advantages of laminated or plywood construction over solid woods in report No. 84, N. A. for Aeronautics, Washington, D. C., is set forth:

In the first place, "strength with a minimum weight is required," and further, "It is not always possible to proportion a solid plank so as to develop the necessary strength in every direction and at the same time utilize the full strength in all directions. In such cases it is the purpose of plywood to meet this deficiency by cross-banding which results in a re-distribution of the materials."

Drops Ludwig Drum Shell from Aeroplane Nearly Two Miles

In an official test witnessed by Chicago newspaper representatives and International News Service photographer on June 5th, 1923, a Ludwig Drum Shell was dropped several times totalling a distance of 10,000 feet without showing signs of breaking or warping. The photo shows Mr. A. E. Davidson and the pilot Jas. Curran of Ashburn Field, Chicago, Ill., examining shell after the test.

The Trade-Mark on Professional Model Wood-Shell Snare Drums and Bass Drums

Trade-Mark

Registered

The above label is attached to all Ludwig "PROFESSIONAL" model wood-shell snare drums and Bass Drums. It is a bronzed metal nameplate that is fastened to the vent-hole with a brass grommet. This label is used to distinguish the "professional" highest quality models from the moderate priced line. It is emblematic of the World's Standard in Drums and Accessories. Only genuine Ludwig Professional models bear this mark.

The Ludwig "UNIVERSAL" Line

Trade-Mark

Ludwig TRADE MARK "UNIVERSAL" MODEL

Registered

The Ludwig line of "Universal" models fill the demand for a good substantial type of moderate priced drums adaptable to general practical needs. They are carefully assembled, and are built of high grade materials. The "Universal" models of wood-shell snare drums and bass drums are labeled with a white etched nameplate as shown above.

The Ludwig Inspection Tag

All Professional Model Ludwig Snare Drums are inspected under the direct supervision of Wm. F. Ludwig. They bear an inspection tag to that effect.

All Ludwig Products Are Marked

All metal traps and holders are stamped, cymbals, wood effects and all the various accessories bear the Ludwig label. Look for this mark of the genuine and highest quality on all Ludwig products.

Ludwig Imitations

Reed Effects

Ludwig reed imitations are remarkably true, they depict the genuine call or effect desired. Ludwig reed traps are a pleasure to use.

Rooster Crow

Perfect rooster effect—loud and lusty. Made of nickel plated brass tube with metal reed.

No. 501—Ludwig Rooster Crow, 8½″ long.... **$1.25**

Hen Cackle

Realistic effect for "cackle." Has durable brass reed. Made of brass tubing, heavily nickeled and polished.

No. 502—Ludwig Hen Cackle, 5½″ long.... **$1.00**

Baby Cry

Perfectly voiced imitation. Made of brass, nickeled and polished.

No. 503—Ludwig Metal Baby Cry. 5″ long.. **$0.75**

All-in-One Trap and Duck Call

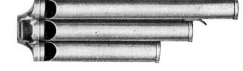

Combination Hen Cackle, Baby Cry, Duck Call, Jay Bird or Cow Bawl—all excellent imitations. The different effects can be obtained by simply shifting a small slide with your thumb or first finger. Use this once and you will never be without it again. Made of hard rubber; 4¾″ long.

No. 506§—Each **$1.75**

Allen's Duck Quack

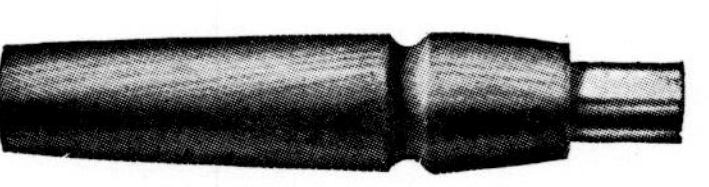

Made of wood and metal. A perfect imitation of duck quack. Can also be used as Hen Cackle, Rooster Crow, Pig Grunt and many other imitations. Every drummer needs one. Finely made and will last a lifetime. 5″ long.

No. 505§—Each **$1.25**

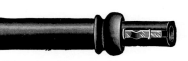

Ludwig Cow Bawl

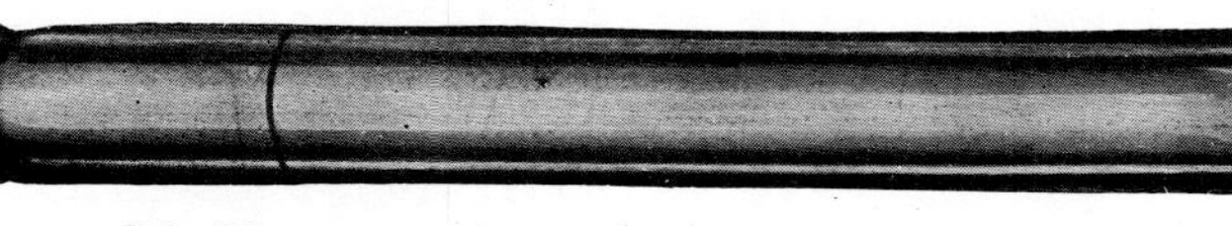

Strong, life-like tone. Made of nickel plated brass tubing, 15″ long. Detaches to 9″ for compact carrying.

No. 500—Ludwig Cow Bawl..................... **$1.75**

Three-Tone Interurban

A new three-toned effect for interurban train imitations and a variety of other calls. 5½″ long.

No. 523§—Interurban **$1.00**

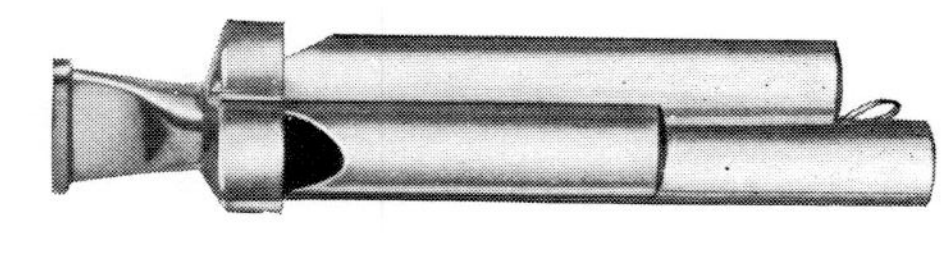

Ludwig Bell Mouth Wind Whistle

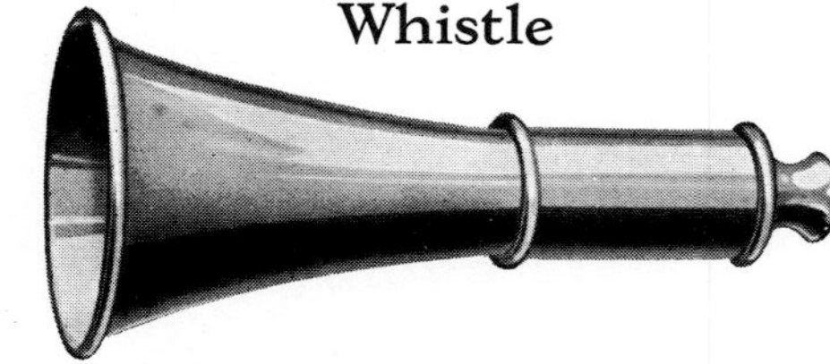

A metal wind whistle that is extremely powerful, ideal for cyclonic effects. Responds easily and quickly. 5″ long.

No. 549§—Ludwig Wind Whistle with bell **$2.00**

Cyclone Wind Whistle

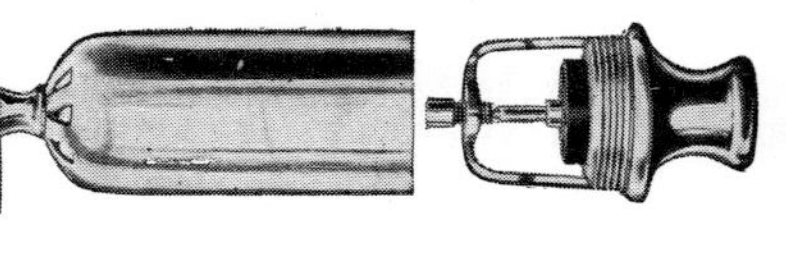

An imported whistle that responds to the slightest breath. No drummer can afford to be without a reliable wind whistle. 3″ long.

No. 513 .... **$1.00**

Ludwig Cuckoo

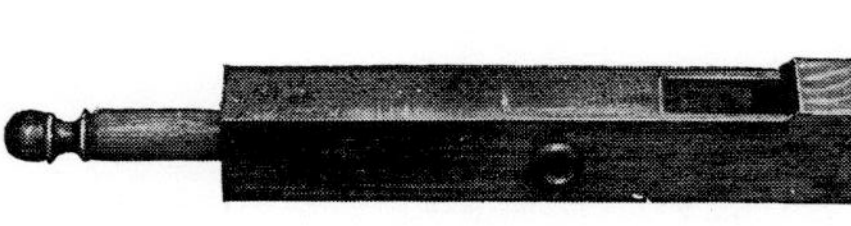

Single cuckoo, like illustration, made of same fine quality of hardwood. Skillfully voiced, perfect effect. 10″ long.

No. 526§—Price, each... **$1.75**

Three-Tone Metal Whistle

Nickel-plated, compact. Excellent imitation of small steamboat, launch, interurban electrics and motorcycles. A very effective, useful, inexpensive and durable little trap. 5½″ long.

No. 522§—Price, each **$0.75**

Ludwig's factory during the teens and twenties was at 1611 North Lincoln (now called Wolcott) Street in Chicago.

R. H. MAYLAND & SON

Electric Controlled Tubular Chimes
GIVING ANY DEGREE OF TONE DESIRED

Tubular Chimes, Harp Effects, Orchestra Bells
Xylophones, Electric Bells, Etc. for Pipe Organs

R. H. Mayland & Son
54 Willoughby St., BROOKLYN, N. Y.
Established 1866 SEND FOR CATALOGUE

Mayland is an old name in the tubular chime business as evidenced by this ad in the January 1915 issue of The Diapason. *Mayland brand chimes are still being sold in the 1980s, the Mayland name having been purchased by I. T. Verdin in Cincinnati in 1977.*[1]

MORRIS ELECTRIC ACTION COMPANY

The Morris Electric Action Company was another name used by the L. D. Morris Company in a not particularly successful attempt to become a supplier to the trade. The ad reproduced here appeared in the February 1926 Diapason. *For a history of the firm, see the Morris article on page 442 of this volume.*

PIPEWORK

GEORGE W. BADGER CO.

The following article appeared in the July 1921 *Diapason:*

NEW FACTORY OPENED BY BADGER COMPANY

IDEAL PLANT IS PURCHASED.

Business Founded in 1890 Now Has Excellent Facilities at Rockville Centre, L. I., a Suburb of New York

The metal organ pipe supply business founded in 1890 by the late George W. Badger is now operating in its new home in Rockville Centre, Long Island, having moved from Merrick to its present location on the thirty-first anniversary of its establishment. With the advantage of increased floor space and additional facilities this firm is now producing the largest volume of work in its history.

The main building is especially well adapted to the requirements of the organ pipe builder, being about 85 feet long and 35 feet wide, and consisting of two full-size working floors, a large cellar which houses the steam plant, blower system and other appurtenances, and a third floor front used entirely for storage purposes. The ample steam heating plant will insure comfort during the winter. An excellent electric lighting system has been installed, providing for the best light possible, an important requirement for fine work when the days grow shorter. These, with other improvements, prove a benefit to the working force. All machinery, including swing saw, turret lathe, drill grinder, etc., are motor driven, the light and power circuits drawing current direct from the main city power station. Wiring throughout the plant is in conduits and all switches are in safety boxes. A large duplex Kinetic blowing system furnishes the wind to the voicing machines in pressures up to thirty inches, two motors providing the motive power.

A large metal melting furnace with a powerful gas

This ad appeared in the April 1922 Diapason.

burner has been added to the casting equipment. A special gas annealing oven was also added for the purpose of efficiently annealing zinc with a minimum of labor. The unique feature of the annealing apparatus is the specially constructed six-wheel truck on which two casks of zinc may be easily wheeled into the oven and out of it to any part of the floor.

The office, shipping, zinc pipe, shallot, casting and annealing departments are on the first floor. The metal and reed departments are especially favored in a large light room on the second floor. The voicing rooms are also on this floor, and of construction that allows the vertical voicing of sixteen-foot steps. (sic)

The factory is in the central part of Rockville Centre, near the railroad station and all shipping facilities. Rockville Centre is one of those beautiful home towns which are characteristic of that section of Long Island within easy commuting distance of New York. Splendid train service connects with Manhattan and Brooklyn.

In 1890 George W. Badger severed connections with the Steere & Turner Organ Company of Springfield, Mass., to engage in the business of manufacturing metal organ pipes. On the solicitation of the Reuben Midmer & Sons Organ Company, he rented a part of their factory on Steuben street in Brooklyn, remaining there fifteen years and making all the pipes for the Midmer concern and supplying other builders throughout the country. During this time he earned an enviable reputation in the organ world for high-class workmanship and business integrity. When the Midmer Company built in Merrick, Mr. Badger was induced to accompany them, again renting a part of the Midmer factory. Here he remained another fifteen years, up to the time of his death in February, 1920. Since that time Mr. Badger's son-in-law, Walter V. Elliott, formerly associated with several large manufacturing concerns at Bridgeport, Conn., has carried on the business.

During the past year business increased to such an extent that much difficulty was experienced at Merrick through lack of available room for expansion, the Midmer Company having given up all the extra room it could without handicapping its own production. A separate building with greater floor space and especially adapted to organ pipe manufacturing was the only solution, and with that in view the factory in Rockville Centre, formerly occupied by the Kayser Glove Company, was secured by purchase.

The Badger Company is devoting its entire efforts to the manufacture of metal organ pipes, specializing, however, on voiced reed stops of every description and on all pressures. This concern has to its credit a number of splendid reed installations in churches, theatres and residences throughout the country. Two expert voicers are constantly engaged voicing reed stops. There are about a dozen employed in the shop at present.

The success of the Badger Company is attributed largely to its policy of service to the organ builder, cooperating in every way toward the development of scales and voicing to meet his individual requirements. The greatest discretion is used in not having the organ builder's name displayed in any advertising nor in any way indicating the buying for his organ of a product not his own make. To any builder requiring a highly specialized product, this factory becomes his individual pipe shop, eager to embody his ideas in materials and workmanship, working as his own employes (sic) and in the same manner as if the shop were in his own factory.

James Bolton was born into an organ building family in Liverpool, England c. 1884. His grandfather was an organ builder and his father worked for Willis. Bolton came to America around 1889 because his father had been hired to be shop foreman of the Samuel Pierce Organ Pipe Company in Reading, Massachusetts. Jim Bolton worked for Pierce, Farrand & Votey and Skinner before leaving for the west coast in 1916 where he landed a job with the American Photo Player Company in Berkeley, California. Eventually he established his own pipe shop and counted F. W. Smith, Artcraft, E. A. Spencer and Schoenstein as customers, among others. In 1927 he was persuaded to move to the new Artcraft factory building in Santa Monica, California where he made pipes for Artcraft as well as for other builders, particularly E. A. Spencer. After Artcraft folded in 1928, Bolton moved to a shop of his own in Santa Monica. In the late 1930s he moved to San Diego, California and operated an organ service business there well into the 1960s.[1]

Jim Bolton photographed c. 1963.

FREDERICK S. BROCKBANK

This ad in the March 1916 Diapason *announced the opening of a new pipe making business which was located adjacent to the American Master Organ Company factory in Lakeview, New Jersey. Frederick Brockbank was an Englishman who received his training in reed voicing from the Willis and Hope-Jones firms. After coming to America he was with the Skinner Organ Company for a number of years before establishing his own business early in 1916. Not meeting with financial success, Mr. Brockbank later worked for Aeolian, Odell and Frazee. He was in the employ of the last firm at the time of his death in 1929 at the age of 46.*[1][2]

Samuel Pierce (1819-1895) was foreman of the E. & G. G. Hook pipe department.[1] In 1846 he moved to Reading, Massachusetts and in 1847 began the manufacture of organ pipes in an ell of his home.[2] This was the first shop in America established to sell pipes to the trade. Because of his early position in the market and the excellent quality of his product, Pierce eventually became the country's largest pipe supplier. A 1922 article claimed that their factory contained "the greatest array of pipe scales ever assembled under one roof"[3] and the author doesn't doubt it.

In 1897, two years after Samuel Pierce's death, the firm was incorporated as the Samuel Pierce Organ Pipe Company. In 1900 management was assumed by William S. Dennison (1869-1946) who had joined Pierce in 1885. In 1917 Dennison became treasurer and in 1924 changed the name to the Dennison Organ Pipe Co.[4] Edwin B. Hedges, whose own pipe making firm Dennison absorbed in 1919, was head voicer for many years. Warren L. Fletcher (1875-1943) was another well-known Dennison employee. He learned voicing with Hutchings-Votey and joined Pierce in 1903, remaining nearly 30 years, during four of which he was superintendent of the factory.[5] Fletcher had a reputation for being the fastest reed voicer in the plant, completing stops in half the time as other voicers.[6] Nonetheless, his work was of excellent quality and he took pride in it as evidenced by a personalized stamp he used on low CC of each rank which read "W. L. FLETCHER, VOICER."

Reeds were a particular specialty of Pierce/Dennison. Many builders, even those who built their own flue pipes, such as Moller, Murray M. Harris, Bennett and a number of others, ordered many of their reeds from Pierce. The roster of Pierce customers reads like a directory of American organ building. Nearly every organ builder in America, including industry giants such as Wurlitzer, Robert-Morton, Austin, Kilgen and Aeolian-Skinner, purchased from Pierce at one time or another. All of these firms had their own pipe shops but turned to Pierce when their own production lagged or when they required a specialty stop of particularly difficult or unusual construction. Many of the larger firms such as Barton and Marr & Colton had no metal pipe shop at all so they relied heavily on trade suppliers such as Pierce not only for quality but also for timely delivery.

One of the most spectacular organs ever built, the 6/51 Barton in the Chicago Stadium, contains mostly Dennison pipework. There are two Meyer diapasons and one Gottfried tuba in the Stadium organ, orders no doubt placed by Dan Barton to honor those loyal suppliers by including their work in his magnum opus. But when it came to the 25″ strings, the 35″ double-languid diapasons, the diaphones and the specialty reeds, Barton knew the right place to go: Dennison. And his trust was well founded, as anyone who has experienced the magnificence of that instrument can attest.

Dennison continued in business through the 1970s although in later years production slowed to a trickle. Around 1976 Dennison was purchased by Harold Strand who wanted the buildings to house his surplus electronic parts business. Machinery and assets of the pipe making business were gradually sold and around 1979 Don Warnock purchased most of what was left and formed the Dennison-Warnock Company, which continues in business in a small way in the 1980s.[7]

Ad in the November 1924 Diapason.

The Home of
Pierce Organ Pipes
in 1910

Pierce Organ Stops

Are the Best

Tonal Qualities Unexcelled

SAMUEL PIERCE ORGAN PIPE CO.
READING, MASS.

"Pierce Reeds"

are the standard
for tonal quality.

Try a Stop and
be convinced.

Samuel Pierce Organ Pipe Co.
READING, MASS.

(left) Pierce ad in the November 1923 Diapason. *What appears to be a lawn is today Pierce Street. This building, already enlarged several times by the time this photo was taken, was further expanded later to handle the increasing business of the roaring twenties. The building barely visible on the left was the wood pipe shop. Another building, which long-time Dennison employee Sid Eaton called "the barn," was erected approximately where the photographer stood to take this picture. (right) A heavily mitred tuba has been voiced in one of the plant's fifteen voicing rooms as shown in this ad from the August 1924* Diapason.

SAMUEL PIERCE ORGAN PIPE CO. *List*

READING, Mass. *2/10-22*

REED STOPS, VOICED

Two-thirds of the trouble from reed stops is caused by dust or dirt. Do not unwrap the pipes until you are ready to set them in the organ. Hold the top of the pipes down while removing the wrappers allowing the dirt to fall away from the pipes instead of into them. Before placing on the chest, the wind should be put on, and each hole cleaned with a feather while holding the key down.

The above instructions are of the utmost importance for the best results.

	Compass	Scale	VOICED
32 ft. Bombard,	cccc 30	20 in.	
16 ft. Pedal Trombone,	ccc 30	12 "	
16 ft. Pedal Trombone,	ccc 30	10 "	$250.00
16 ft. Pedal Trombone,	ccc 30	XXX $7\frac{1}{2}$"	----- 225.00
16 ft. Pedal Trombone,	ccc 30	9 x 9 " wood	
16 ft. Tuba,	cc 61	special	
16 ft. Contra Fagotto,	cc 61	$4\frac{5}{8}$ in.	-------235.00
8 ft. Tuba,	cc 61	$5\frac{1}{2}$ "	
8 ft. Corncpean,	cc 61	$6\frac{1}{2}$ "	-------158.65
8 ft. "	cc 61	6 "	151.20
8 ft. "	cc 61	$5\frac{1}{2}$ "	140.90
8 ft. "	cc 61	5 "	-------136.15
8 ft. Trumpet,	cc 61	$5\frac{1}{2}$ "	
8 ft. "	cc 61	5 "	
8 ft. "	cc 61	$4\frac{1}{2}$ "	-------128.05
8 ft. "	c° 49	$4\frac{1}{2}$ "	
8 ft. "	cc 61	4 "	-------124.80
8 ft. "	c° 49	4 "	
8 ft. Oboe and Bassoon,	cc 61	reg.	-------109.40
8 ft. Oboe,	c° 49	"	
8 ft. Orchestral Oboe,	cc 61	"	-------120.00
8 ft. Orchestral Oboe,	c° 49	"	
8 ft. Bell Clarinet,	cc 61	"	-------117.70
8 ft. Bell Clarinet,	c° 49	"	
8 ft. Clarinet,	cc 61	"	-------112.00
8 ft. Clarinet,	c° 49	"	
8 ft. Vox Humana,	cc 61	"	-------107.00
8 ft. Vox Humana,	c° 49	"	
8 ft. Saxophone,	cc 61	"	-------118.50
8 ft. Saxophone,	c° 49	"	

PRICES SUBJECT TO CHANGE.

This 1922 price list is the latest so far discovered by the author. Not included are the diaphones, tibias, kinuras, post horns and keen strings which would figure so prominently in Dennison's sales later in the 1920s.

SAMUEL PIERCE ORGAN PIPE CO. *List*

READING, MASS. *2/10-22*

WOOD STOPS

	Compass		Scale	Price Unvoiced	Price Voiced
32 ft. Pedal Open Diapason	cccc 30				
16 ft. " " "	ccc 30		$11\frac{3}{4}$ x 14		
16 ft. " " "	ccc 30		$10\frac{3}{4}$ x $12\frac{7}{8}$		
16 ft. " " "	ccc 30		$9\frac{7}{8}$ x $11\frac{3}{4}$		
The following prices are for pipes boxed, F. O. B., Boston, Mass.					
16 ft. Pedal Bourdon	ccc 30	No. 1	$7\frac{5}{8}$ x $9\frac{1}{8}$	$162.00	192.00
16 ft. " "	ccc 30	No. 2	$6\frac{3}{4}$ x 8	150.00	175.00
16 ft. " "	ccc 30	No. 3	$5\frac{7}{8}$ x 7	136.00	161.00
16 ft. " "	ccc 30	No. 4	$5\frac{1}{8}$ x $6\frac{1}{8}$	128.00	153.00
16 ft. " "	ccc 30	No. 5	$4\frac{1}{2}$ x $5\frac{1}{2}$	124.00	149.00
16 ft. Open Pedal Violone (Tuning Slides)	ccc 30		8 x $5\frac{3}{4}$	380.00	420.00
8 ft. Pedal Stop Flute	ccc 30		$4\frac{1}{4}$ x $5\frac{1}{4}$	73.70	93.70
8 ft. Pedal Open Flute	ccc 30		$4\frac{5}{8}$ x $5\frac{3}{4}$	125.95	155.95
8 ft. Doppel Flute (upper octave metal)	cc 61	No. 2	4 x 5	82.95	122.95
8 ft. " " " " "	c° 49	No. 2	$2\frac{1}{8}$ x $2\frac{5}{8}$	51.75	81.75
8 ft. " " Widest depth	g°		$1\frac{5}{8}$ x $2\frac{7}{8}$		
16 ft. Manual Bourdon	cc 61	Ex.	$5\frac{5}{8}$ x $6\frac{3}{4}$	142.50	177.50
16 ft. " "	c° 49	Ex.	$3\frac{3}{8}$ x 4	58.00	83.00
16 ft. " "	cc 61	No. 1	$4\frac{15}{16}$ x $5\frac{7}{8}$	133.75	168.75
16 ft. " "	c° 49	No. 1	$2\frac{15}{16}$ x $3\frac{9}{16}$	54.80	79.80
16 ft. " "	cc 61	No. 2	$4\frac{5}{16}$ x $5\frac{1}{8}$	125.00	160.00
16 ft. " "	c° 49	No. 2	$2\frac{9}{16}$ x $3\frac{1}{16}$	53.00	78.00
16 ft. " "	cc 61	No. 3	$3\frac{15}{16}$ x $4\frac{3}{4}$		
16 ft. " "	c° 49	No. 3	$2\frac{3}{8}$ x $2\frac{7}{8}$		
8 ft. Stopped Diapason	cc 61	Ex.	$4\frac{1}{8}$ x 5	61.75	91.75
8 ft. " "	c° 49	Ex.	$2\frac{1}{2}$ x 3	34.50	54.50
8 ft. " "	cc 61	No. 1	$3\frac{3}{8}$ x 4	52.25	82.25
8 ft. " "	c° 49	No. 1	2 x $2\frac{3}{8}$	31.30	51.30
8 ft. " "	cc 61	No. 2	$2\frac{15}{16}$ x $3\frac{9}{16}$	49.65	79.65
8 ft. " "	c° 49	No. 2	$1\frac{3}{4}$ x $2\frac{1}{8}$	27.20	47.20
8 ft. " "	cc 61	No. 3	$2\frac{9}{16}$ x $3\frac{1}{16}$		
8 ft. " "	c° 49	No. 3	$1\frac{9}{16}$ x $1\frac{7}{8}$		
8 ft. Stopped Bass (for Dulciana, etc.)	cc 12		$2\frac{1}{2}$ x 3	22.00	32.00
8 ft. Gros Flute (Stopped Bass)	cc 61	No. 2	$3\frac{3}{8}$ x 4	72.10	102.10
8 ft. " "	c° 49	No. 2	$3\frac{1}{8}$ x 4	44.10	66.10
8 ft. Melodia (12 stopped)	cc 61	Ex.	$3\frac{3}{8}$ x 4	62.50	92.50
8 ft. "	c° 49	Ex.	$2\frac{3}{8}$ x $2\frac{7}{8}$	34.50	54.50
8 ft. " (12 stopped)	cc 61	No. 1	$2\frac{15}{16}$ x $3\frac{9}{16}$	58.00	88.00
8 ft. "	c° 49	No. 1	$2\frac{3}{16}$ x $2\frac{5}{8}$	31.35	51.35
8 ft. " (12 stopped)	cc 61	No. 2	$2\frac{15}{16}$ x $3\frac{9}{16}$	54.35	84.35
8 ft. "	c° 49	No. 2	$1\frac{15}{16}$ x $2\frac{3}{8}$	29.80	49.80
4 ft. Flute Traverso (upper octave metal)	cc 61	No. 1	$2\frac{3}{16}$ x $2\frac{11}{16}$	39.45	64.45
4 ft. " " " " "	c° 49	No. 1	$1\frac{5}{16}$ x $1\frac{5}{8}$		
4 ft. " " " " "	cc 61	No. 2	2 x $2\frac{7}{16}$	37.50	62.50
4 ft. " " " " "	c° 49	No. 2	$1\frac{1}{4}$ x $1\frac{1}{2}$		
4 ft. Wald Flute " " "	cc 61	No. 1	$2\frac{1}{8}$ x $2\frac{5}{8}$		
4 ft. " " " " "	c° 49	No. 1	$2\frac{3}{8}$ x $1\frac{3}{4}$		
4 ft. " " " " "	cc 61	No. 2	$1\frac{15}{16}$ x $2\frac{3}{8}$		
4 ft. " " " " "	c° 49	No. 2	$1\frac{1}{4}$ x $1\frac{1}{2}$		
4 ft. Flute D'Amour (2 upper octaves metal)	cc 61	Reg.	$1\frac{7}{8}$ x $2\frac{1}{4}$	34.70	54.70
4 ft. " " 2 " " "	c° 49	Reg.	$1\frac{1}{4}$ x $1\frac{1}{2}$		

PRICES SUBJECT TOCHANGE.

SAMUEL PIERCE ORGAN PIPE CO.

READING, MASS.

FLUE STOPS, METAL

	Compass	Scale	No. Zinc	Price Unvoiced	Price Voiced
16 ft. Contra Gamba,	ccc 61	45	24		
16 ft. Contra Dulciana,	ccc 61	44	24		
16 ft. Pedal Dulciana,	ccc 30	44	30		
16 ft. Pedal Violone,	ccc 30	42	30		
8 ft. Pedal Violoncello,	ccc 30	53	17		
16 ft. Open Diapason,	ccc 61	33	29		
8 ft. Stentorphone,	cc 61	38	17		
8 ft. Open Diapason,	cc 61	40	17	$155.10	$171.60
8 ft. " "	c° 49	40	5	68.30	80.55
8 ft. " "	f° 44	40		55.15	65.65
8 ft. " "	cc 61	42	17	134.70	151.20
8 ft. " "	c° 49	42	5	63.30	75.55
8 ft. " "	f° 44	42		51.75	62.25
8 ft. " "	cc 61	43	17	132.35	148.85
8 ft. " "	c° 49	43	5	61.25	73.50
8 ft. " "	f° 44	43		49.95	60.45
8 ft. " "	cc 61	44	17	124.15	140.65
8 ft. " "	c° 49	44	5	58.15	70.40
8 ft. " "	f° 44	44		47.30	58.75
8 ft. " "	cc 61	45	17	122.10	138.60
8 ft. " "	c° 49	45	5	55.15	67.40
8 ft. " "	f° 44	45		44.80	55.30
8 ft. Violin Diapason,	cc 61	48	17	100.90	117.40
8 ft. Violin Diapason,	c° 49	48	5	51.40	63.65
8 ft. Geigen Principal,	cc 61	50	17	94.10	110.60
8 ft. Geigen Principal,	c° 49	50	5	49.90	62.40
8 ft. Gemshorn (conical),	cc 61	4 in.	17	94.10	114.10
8 ft. Gemshorn "	c° 49	"	5	51.30	65.30
8 ft. Dulciana,	cc 61	55 to 58	12	76.30	93.30
8 ft. Dulciana,	c° 49	55 to 58		43.50	56.00
8 ft. Viola da Gamba,	cc 61	56 or 57	12	85.15	105.15
8 ft. Viola da Gamba,	c° 49	56 or 57		46.50	61.50
8 ft. Aeoline or Unda Maris,	cc 61	58 or 60	12	74.55	91.55
8 ft. Aeoline or Unda Maris,	c° 49	58 or 60		39.90	52.40
8 ft. Oboe Gamba,	cc 61	60	12	81.75	101.75
8 ft. Oboe Gamba,	c° 49	60		44.85	59.85
8 ft. Viole D'Orchestre,	cc 61	spec.	12	77.65	98.65
8 ft. Viole D'Orchestre,	c° 49	spec.		45.80	61.80
8 ft. Salicional or Vox Celeste,	cc 61	62	12	79.20	99.20
8 ft. Salicional or Vox Celesté,	c° 49	62		44.45	59.45
8 ft. Quintadena,	cc 61	reg.	12	64.15	82.15
8 ft. Quintadena,	c° 49	reg.		41.10	56.10
4 ft. Rohr Flute or Chiminee Flute,	cc 61	reg.	12		
4 ft. Rohr Flute or Chiminee Flute,	c° 49	reg.			
4 ft. Octave or Principal,	cc 61	56	5	55.90	67.90
4 ft. Octave or Principal,	cc 61	58	5	52.85	64.85
4 ft. Flute Harmonic,	cc 61	(large)	18	51.75	65.75
4 ft. Flute Harmonic,	cc 61	(small)	8	48.20	62.20
4 ft. Gemshorn,	cc 61	reg.		42.75	56.75
4 ft. Violina,	cc 61	67		51.30	66.30
4 ft. Violin,	cc 61	spec.		55.60	70.60
2⅔ ft. Twelfth,	cc 61	68		41.45	51.45
2 ft. Fifteenth,	cc 61	72		34.20	46.20
2 ft. Piccolo,	cc 61	70		34.20	46.20
2 ft. Flautina,	cc 61	75		34.20	46.20
2 ft. Flageolet (conical),	cc 61	74		33.20	47.20
2 ft. Piccolo Harmonic,	cc 61	reg.		38.90	51.90
8 ft. Stopped Zinc Bass,	cc 12	44	12		
8 ft. Stopped Zinc Bass,	cc 12	50	12		
8 ft. Stopped Zinc Bass,	cc 12	56	12		
3 rk. Mixture,	tc183	72 79 84	15th 19th 22d		
4 rk. Mixture,	cc244	79 84 91 96	19th 22d 26th 29th		
3 rk. Cornet,	cc183	72 77 83	12th 15th 17th		

PRICES SUBJECT TO CHANGE.

SAMUEL PIERCE ORGAN PIPE CO.

THE VOX HUMANA STOP

This beautiful stop is found in all modern Organs, even those that boast of but few stops.

The state of perfection it has attained thru our development is seemingly appreciated by the trade as is evidenced by the large output of these pipes in the last dozen years.

Opinions differ as to the proper quality of tone for the Vox Humana but as it is treated in our Voicing rooms on various pressures and in several scales, its qualities adapt it to the requirements of the Cathedral Organ, the exacting work of the Concert Organist and the sentimental pictures in the theater. Its various registers are pleasingly imitative of the human voice.

The regulating device of "canister top," as some call it, was first generally applied to this stop in our factory and has been widely copied by other makers. Thus equipped, the pipes are easily controlled for tone regulation and stand well in tune.

Order "Pierce Vox Humana Stops." They are the best.

In this July 1923 Diapason *ad Pierce touted their vox humanas and claimed to have pioneered the canister top which became nearly universal in most builders' voxes. Pierce/Dennison vox humanas have long been favorites of the author.*

Another page from the 1922 price list.

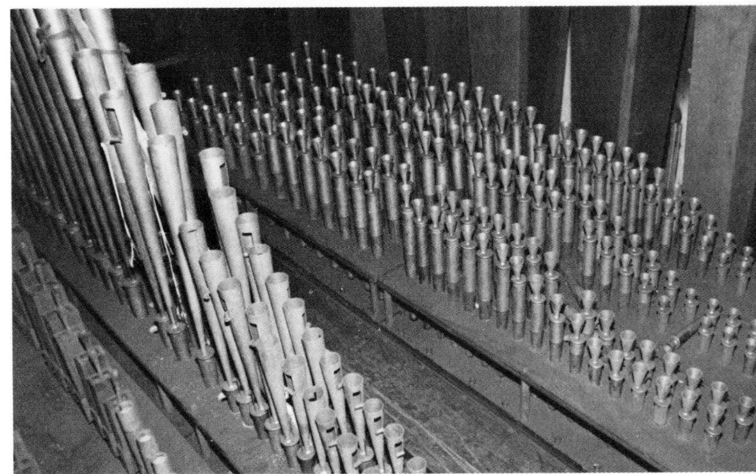

Dennison ranks abound in the Chicago Stadium's 6/51 Barton. At lower left is a saxophone of unusual construction. The two mitred pipes in the background are low CCC and CCC# of the 16′ English (post) horn. At upper left is one of the author's all-time favorite reeds, the Stadium's Dennison tuba mirabilis. What power and majesty are created by these innocuous looking pipes! A perfect acoustical impedance match is secured by having the resonator tips the same diameter as the shallots. Because the tips are thus so small only a minimal soldering surface exists to attach the resonator to the block. Hence a support rack is necessary for even the shorter treble notes lest their extra-heavy resonators fall over of their own weight. At upper right are boots for the 16′ octave of the tuba mirabilis, featuring wooden resonators. At center right is a sea of 183 Dennison kinuras on 25″ wind. What a squawk! To their left is English post horn I. At lower right is a view of Division II. From front to back the ranks are English post horn II, tuba celeste III ranks, the double-languid diaphone II on 35″ wind and its 16′ wood diaphone extension.

F. W. KREBS, PRES.
H. M. HEINTZ, VICE PRES.

E. WAMBSGANS, SECY-TREAS.
S. ROTH, MANAGER

The Erie Reed Pipe Company

SPECIALISTS IN REEDS

OFFICE AND FACTORY 26TH. AND CHERRY STREET

ERIE, PENNA.

The Erie Reed Pipe Co. was formed c. 1921 by three former Gottfried employees: F. W. "Willy" Krebs and Steve Roth, who made shallots and reed blocks and Ed Wambsgans, who was a flue and reed voicer. Working in cahoots with them was another Gottfried employee, a young fellow named Williams. Henry Gottfried, the son of Anton Gottfried and an officer of the Gottfried firm, recalls that "they left Williams in our reed department so he could steal materials and parts as well as data from our scales and patterns for their use. Well, Williams was caught and confessed and all four men were arrested and put in jail. One evening all their wives came to our house crying and begging Dad not to prosecute them. Dad, [who] was soft hearted, agreed not to prosecute their husbands and they were let out. All told Dad later on that he made a mistake as he could have got rid of a competitor."[1]

The first location of the Erie Reed Pipe Co. was at 28th and Parade Streets. By April 1921 they had moved to larger quarters at 26th and Cherry Streets.[2] The firm was in business until 1933 when they were absorbed by Durst & Company.[3]

Erie Reed Pipe Co.
Incorporated

Manufacturers of

REED and METAL PIPES

Artistic Excellence in Voicing

26th and CHERRY Sts.
Erie, Pa.

In early advertising the firm offered wood pipes in addition to reeds and flues but by the time this ad appeared in the February 1923 Diapason *the wood pipes had been discontinued.*

Firma Ernst Doelling Postfach 58 Markneukirchen i. Sa.

Spezial-Fabrik für Schallstücke und Bestandteile zu Messingblasinstrumenten

Stadtbank Markneukirchen, Konto Nr. 101 / Postscheck-Konto Leipzig 303 72
Telegramm-Adresse: Fedom Markneukirchen
Fernsprecher Nr. 2836

Markneukirchen, Sa., den
Postfach 58

The Ernst Doelling firm was a major supplier of brass resonators to the organ industry world-wide. A 1931 letter to American pipe manufacturers Gutfleisch & Schopp states ". . . I am since long years manufacturing bells for musical instruments as a specialty. My bells enjoy a very good reputation all over the world. In your country I have some customers who import bells of my firm in regular lots. Besides I am furnishing organ pipes (sic) makers in Germany with bells for their special purposes." The letter offers sets of polished brass resonators at the following prices: for brass 0.42 mm thick, 8′ octave of 12 pipes, \$41.00; upper octaves of 49 pipes, \$48.00; total weight of 61 pipes about 26½ lbs. For brass 0.55 mm thick, 8′ octave of 12 pipes, \$50.00; upper octaves of 49 pipes, \$54.00; total weight of 61 pipes about 36½ lbs.[1] How many of us would like to roll back the clock and place an order for a few sets at these prices!

9/6/1931

1 Set of bells for Organ Pipes, for upper octaves.

Made of brass, entirely polished.
One set consisting of 49 bells of the following dimensions:

Size:		length: inches:	length: millimeters	diameter of bell edge: inches:	diameter of bell edge: millimeters:
1	abt.	36.o	915	4. 8/16	115
2	"	34. lo/16	88o	4. 7/16	113
3	"	33. 4/16	845	4. 6/16	111
4	"	31. 14/16	81o	4. 5/16	1o9
5	"	3o. 8/16	775	4. 3/16	1o7
6	"	29. 2/16	74o	4. 2/16	1o5
7	"	27. 12/16	7o5	4. 1/16	1o3
8	"	26. 5/16	67o	3.15/16	1o1
9	"	25.o	635	3.14/16	99 97
1o	"	23. lo/16	6oo	3.13/16	
11	"	22. 4/16	565	3.12/16	95
12	"	2o. 14/16	53o	3.11/16	93
13	"	19. 7/16	495	3. 8/16	9o
14	"	18. 11/16	474	3. 7/16	88
15	"	17. 13/16	453	3. 6/16	86
16	"	17. 1/16	434	3. 5/16	84
17	"	16. 5/16	415	3. 4/16	83
18	"	15. 9/16	396	3. 7/32	82
19	"	14. 14/16	378	3. 3/16	81
2o	"	14. 3/16	36o	3. 2/16	8o
21	"	13. 7/16	343	3. 1/16	79
22	"	12. 13/16	326	3. 1/32	78
23	"	12. 3/16	31o	3.o	77
24	"	11. lo/16	295	2.31/32	76
25	"	11. 4/16	286	2.15/16	75
26	"	lo. 13/16	275	2.15/16	75
27	"	lo. 5/16	262	2.15/16	75
28	"	9. 14/16	251	2.29/32	74
29	"	9. 7/16	24o	2.29/32	74
3o	"	9.o	229	2.14/16	73
31	"	8. lo/16	22o	2.13/16	72
32	"	8. 3/16	2o8	2.25/32	71
33	"	7. 13/16	199	2.12/16	7o
34	"	7. 8/16	19o	2.11/16	69
35	"	7. 1/16	18o	2.21/32	68
36	"	6. 11/16	17o	2.lo/16	67
37	"	6. 5/16	16o	2.19/32	66
38	"	6. 1/16	154	2.19/32	66
39	"	5. 12/16	146	2. 9/16	65
4o	"	5. 7/16	139	2. 9/16	65
41	"	5. 3/16	132	2. 8/16	64
42	"	4. 14/16	124	2. 8/16	64
43	"	4. 9/16	116	2.15/32	63
44	"	4. 5/16	11o	2.14/32	62
45	"	4. 1/16	1o3	2. 6/16	61
46	"	3. 14/16	98	2.11/32	6o
47	"	3. lo/16	92	2. 5/16	59
48	"	3. 7/16	87	2. 4/16	58
49	"	3. 5/16	84	2. 3/16	57

Narrow bell end of all sizes is 15/32 " (= 12 millimeters) Ø

9/6/31

1 Set of Bells for Organ Pipes : for the low octave (8')

made of brass, fully polished,
one set consisting of 12 bells of the following dimensions :

		full length:		diameter of bell :		diameter of narrow end:
C	abt.	8o 9/16" (=2o4,5 cm)	abt.	5 11/16" (=14,5 cm)	abt.	9/16" (=14 mm)
C♯	"	75 3/16" (=191 cm)	"	5 11/16" (=14,5 cm)	"	9/16" (=14 mm)
D	"	71 5/16" (=181 cm)	"	5 11/16" (=14,5 cm)	"	9/16" (=14 mm)
D♯	"	66 11/16" (=169,3 cm)	"	5 4/16" (=13,3 cm)	"	8/16" (=13 mm)
E	"	62 14/16" (=159,3 cm)	"	5 4/16" (=13,3 cm)	"	8/16" (=13 mm)
F	"	63 8/16" (=161,3 cm)	"	5 4/16" (=13,3 cm)	"	8/16" (=13 mm)
F♯	"	55 1o/16" (=141,2 cm)	"	5 " (=12,7 cm)	"	8/16" (=13 mm)
G	"	52 14/16" (=134,2 cm)	"	5 " (=12,7 cm)	"	8/16" (=13 mm)
G♯	"	43 " (=1o9,2 cm)	"	5 " (=12,7 cm)	"	7/16" (=12 mm)
A	"	48 1/16" (=122,o cm)	"	4 11/16" (=12,o cm)	"	7/16" (=12 mm)
Bb	"	45 1/16" (=114,5 cm)	"	4 11/16" (=12,o cm)	"	7/16" (=12 mm)
B	"	41 14/16" (=1o6,3 cm)	"	4 7/16" (=11,3 cm)	"	7/16" (=12 mm)

These long bells are not made of one single piece, but the narrow half is joint by ferrule with bell piece.-

Dimensions of brass resonators offered by Ernst Doelling.

GUTFLEISCH & SCHOPP

MANUFACTURERS OF

Church and Parlor Organ Pipes

ESTABLISHED 1898

PATTERSON AND MECHANIC

ALLIANCE. OHIO

August R. Schopp (1869-1954) was born in Bad Orb, Germany. Coming to the United States in 1884, he began working for Hilborne L. Roosevelt in New York where he learned the trade of pipe maker. He subsequently worked for several other organ building firms including Haskell, Hook & Hastings, Jardine and Farrand & Votey. In 1898 Schopp and Leonhard Gutfleisch formed the partnership of Gutfleisch & Schopp[1] in Roselle, New Jersey. Their main customer in their early years was the Votey Organ Co. for whom they made not only organ pipes but hundreds of feet of metal tubing for Pianola player piano actions.[2]

Sometime after the turn of the century Gutfleisch & Schopp moved to Alliance, Ohio, the home of Hillgreen, Lane & Co. Not surprisingly, Hillgreen-Lane became Gutfleisch & Schopp's major customer. During the 1920s the firm's second largest customer was the Page Organ Company of Lima, Ohio. Gutfleisch & Schopp supplied copies of Gottfried ranks to Page and even copied Gottfried's elliptical logo which was, however, lettered "PAGE" instead of "A. GOTTFRIED."

In 1954 the Gutfleisch & Schopp partnership was dissolved and the firm of A. R. Schopp's Sons, Inc. was formed by Robert and Harvey Schopp. August Schopp worked six days a week in the firm he helped found and at his death in 1954 at age 85 he was believed to be the oldest active pipe maker in America.[3] After the death of Robert L. Schopp in 1968 control of the firm passed to his son, Bob Schopp, who continues to head the company of about 15 employees[4] who produce some of the finest reeds made in America. In the early 1970s, at the urging of the author, Bob Schopp resurrected the old dies for making goosebill shallots which hadn't been used since Page stopped ordering krumets and post horns in 1929. Since that time Schopp has made a number of kinuras, en chamades and post horns for the author and for other organ builders who desire the uniquely fiery tone goosebill shallots produce.

When Hillgreen-Lane went out of business in 1973 Schopp took over their woodworking department.[5] Schopp now furnishes chests, reservoirs and other wooden parts to the trade in addition to flue and reed pipes.

Advertisement in the May 1928 Diapason. *Even when business was decimated later in the Depression, Gutfleisch & Schopp realized the value of advertising. Their annual advertising bill from* The Diapason *in the 1930s was one of the firm's major expenses.*[6]

GUTFLEISCH & SCHOPP

MANUFACTURERS OF

Church and Parlor Organ Pipes

ESTABLISHED 1898

PATTERSON AND MECHANIC

ALLIANCE. OHIO

			Compass		Scale		
16	Ft.	Tuba Harmonic	ccc85	pipes	8 1/8	in.	375.00
16	"	" "	ccc85	"	7 [illegible]/8	"	362.00
8	"	" "	cc61	"	5 [illegible]/8	"	151.00
8	"	" "	c49	"	5 [illegible]/8	"	105.00
8	"	Cornopean	cc61	"	6 1/2	"	159.00
8	"	"	cc61	"	6	"	155.00
8	"	"	cc61	"	5 1/2	"	151.00
8	"	"	cc61	"	5	"	147.00
8	"	Trumpet	cc61	"	5 1/2	"	148.00
8	"	"	cc61	"	5	"	144.00
8	"	"	cc61	"	4 1/2	"	142.00
8	"	"	cc61	"	4	"	139.00
8	"	Oboe & Bassoon	cc61	"	Reg.		110.00
8	"	"	c49	"	"		76.00
8	"	" (Capped)	cc61	"	"		115.00
8	"	" "	c49	"	"		79.00
8	"	Orchestrial Oboe	cc61	"	"		116.00
8	"	" "	c49	"	"		77.00
8	"	Clarinet with Slides	cc61	"	"		109.00
8	"	" " "	c49	"	"		75.00
8	"	Vox Humana	cc61	"	"		105.00
8	"	" "	c49	"	"		72.00
8	"	Saxaphone	cc61	"	"		160.00
8	"	French Horn	cc61	"	"		157.00
8	"	" "	c49	"	"		112.00
8	"	Cor. Anglais	cc61	"	"		164.00
8	"	Kinura	cc61	"	"		93.00
8	"	"	c49	"	"		68.00
8	"	Mussette	cc61	"	"		105.00
4	"	Clarion	cc61	"	"		107.00

Gutfleisch & Schopp price list from the 1920s.

August R. Schopp and four of his employees, all of whom had been pipe makers for more than fifty years each, pose in front of the pipe metal casting table in 1952. From left to right are Schopp, Almer Wolpert, Frank Swain, John Wolpert and Frank Schuster.

Shop foreman Henry Wayne deftly solders a trompette resonator to its block.

Bruce Snyder, formerly with Hillgreen-Lane and now head flue voicer at A. R. Schopp's Sons, Inc., voices a koppelflote.

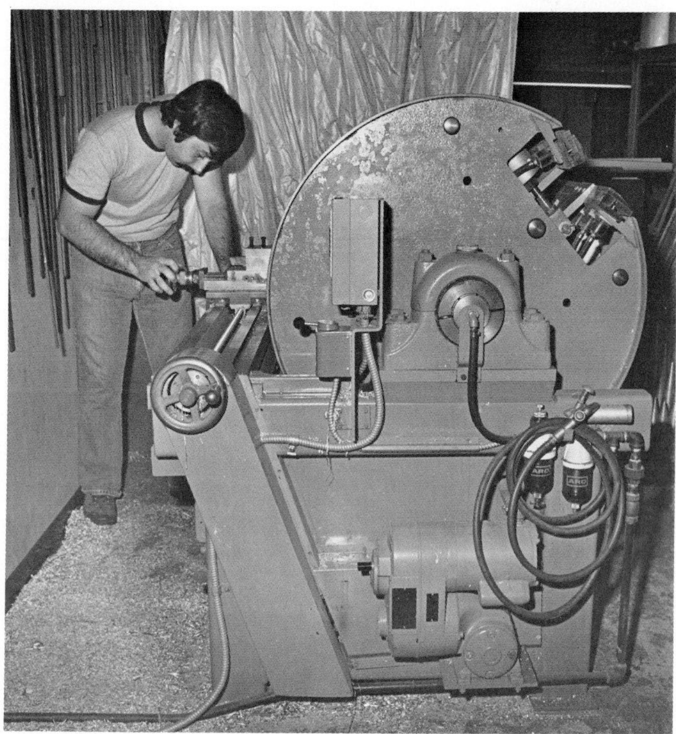

Joe Russo operates a pipe metal planing machine. In the early 1970s Schopp pioneered the use of the automated planer to insure absolute uniformity of pipe metal thickness.

An admirer of theatre as well as classic organs, Bob Schopp poses at the console of the 5/69 mightiest Wurlitzer in Wurlitzer Hall, DeKalb, Illinois.

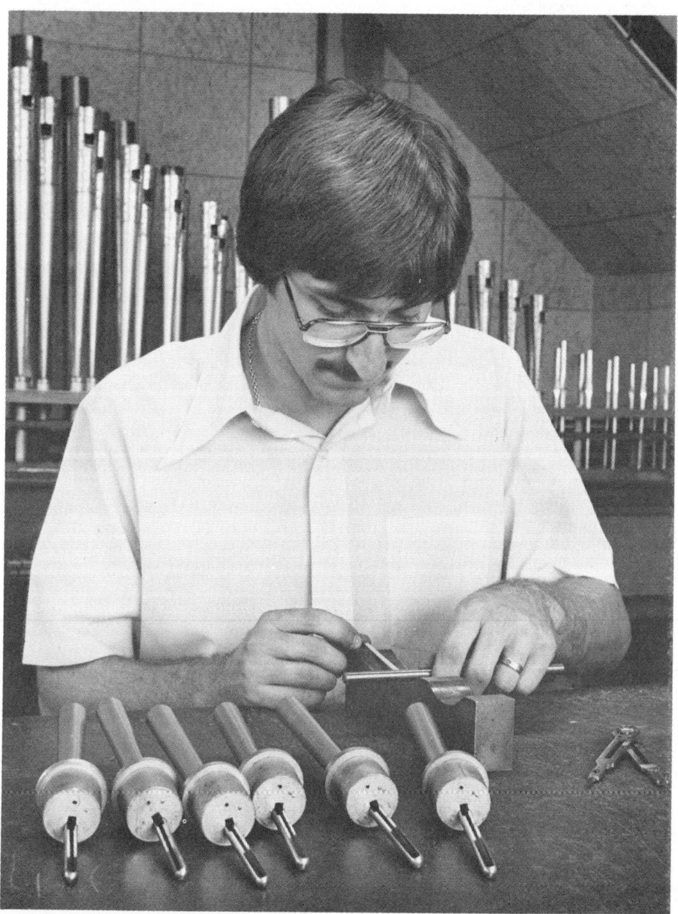

Fred Oyster curves a reed tongue for a French trompette. Mr. Oyster and Bob Schopp together voice some of the finest reeds made in America in the 1980s.

EDWIN B. HEDGES,

Metal and Wood Organ Pipes

KEYS, ACTION, WIRES, ETC.

Highest Grade Reed and Flue Pipes.
Artistic Excellence in Voicing.

WESTFIELD, MASS.

Edwin B. Hedges (1872-1967) was a gifted musician, a talent which no doubt contributed to his legendary ability as a voicer. As a child he played several instruments and earned extra cash by playing in theatre and dance orchestras. His father, Edwin Hedges, Sr., joined the Willliam A. Johnson company in Westfield, Massachusetts at the age of 18 and within three years became Johnson's head pipe maker. Eventually he went into business for himself, supplying pipes to other builders as well as to Johnson. Edwin B. Hedges grew up in his father's business and learned flue voicing from Edward Chaffin, Johnson's flue voicer, and reed voicing from Johnson's reed voicer, Thomas Dyson.[1]

In 1903 Edwin Hedges, Sr. died[2] and Edwin B. Hedges continued the business until 1919 when he merged with the Samuel Pierce Organ Pipe Company in Reading, Massachusetts.[3] He continued working at Pierce (which later became the Dennison Organ Pipe Company) until 1944 when he joined Aeolian-Skinner for three and a half years. In 1948 he went back to Dennison and worked there off and on until just a few years before his death in 1967 at the age of 95.[4]

Edwin B. Hedges
Manufacturer
Organ Pipes
Highest Grade of
REED *and* FLUE PIPES
ARTISTIC EXCELLENCE
in VOICING
Westfield, Mass.

Hedges advertisement in the July 1916 Diapason.

Edwin B. Hedges works in his voicing room at the Dennison Organ Pipe Company c. 1953.

HIRST ORGAN SPECIALTY COMPANY

Announcement

Special organ pipework to the scales used in the famous English Cathedral Organs and Modern Orchestral Organs.

Flue and Reed pipework for the Church, Concert and Theatre Organ. Estimates given on special work upon application.

HIRST
ORGAN SPECIALTY
COMPANY
INCORPORATED
WARSAW, N. Y.

Jack Hirst was foreman of the metal pipe shop at the Hope-Jones Organ Company in Elmira, New York. He retained this position after Wurlitzer moved the Hope-Jones operation to North Tonawanda.[1] Mr. Hirst apparently followed David Marr and John Colton, two other Wurlitzer employees who left North Tonawanda to form their own firm in Warsaw, New York. The Hirst company, whose ad in the September 1916 Diapason *is reproduced here, was a short-lived concern.*

Corner Court and North Second Streets

Illinois Organ Supply Co.

Manufacturers of Organ Pipes

Pekin, Illinois

Alfred Gautschi, an employee of Anton Gottfried, was sent in the early 1920s to call upon one of Gottfried's largest clients, the Hinners Organ Company of Pekin, Illinois. Mr. Gautschi must have liked Pekin because Hinners persuaded him to stay there and to establish his own pipe shop. The Illinois Organ Supply Co., although an adjunct of the Hinners factory, was operated as a separate business.[1] The reeds produced by this firm were of excellent quality. Their vox humanas are particular favorites of the author and are very buttery sounding, almost like brass saxophones.

Illinois Organ Supply pipes were sold to well-known firms such as Wangerin, Kilgen and Jerome B. Meyer. It is interesting to speculate why Meyer, another fine supplier to the trade, would have found it advantageous to order pipes from another firm.

HOYT METAL CO.

Save Money on Your Metal Bills

by using

Hoyt's Rolled 2-Ply Pipe Metal

Used and endorsed for following Pipes:—

Oboe—Trumpet—Cornopean
Open Diapason—Octave
Clarinet—Vox Humana

Rolled to any gauge.
Sheets of convenient size.
Information and sample on request.

HOYT METAL CO.
111 Broadway, New York

HOYT METAL CO.

NEW YORK N. Y. No. 111 Broadway — ST. LOUIS, MO. 300 No. Broadway

ORIGINATORS AND MANUFACTURERS OF

HOYT'S
Two-Ply Organ
PIPE METAL

Hoyt's Stringtone Pipe Metal
SATIN FINISH
Specified by Critical Builders

The Diapason *contained these Hoyt ads in February 1917 (left) and July 1923 (right). Hoyt's two-ply metal was basically lead with a thin coating of tin for a shiny appearance. The term "Hoyt metal" eventually became generic for this variety of metal whether actually manufactured by the Hoyt Metal Co. or not. Hoyt metal was very popular in the 1920s and was used by many builders in lieu of ordinary lead or common metal.*

F. W. KREBS
MANUFACTURER OF
ESCHALLETTS
2626 HAZEL ST. ERIE, PENNA.
UNIFORMITY GUARANTEED

"Willy" Krebs was a shallot maker at Gottfried who left that firm c. 1921 to become one of the founders of Erie Reed Pipe Co.[1] *He advertised his services as a shallot maker to the trade throughout the 1920s, beginning in the December 1922* Diapason. *Curiously, ads with nearly identical wording for the Titan Tool Company, another Erie concern, ceased after the November 1922 issue of* The Diapason.

ESCHALLOTS
For Reed Pipes
Manufactured in a way assuring uniformity throughout
F. W. KREBS, 2626 Hazel Street, Erie, Penna.

KAYLOR & CLARK

Kaylor & Clark and A. D. Kaylor were companies whose principals were undoubtedly former employees of M. P. Moller. The ephemerality of these firms is evidenced by the fact that long-time Moller pipe shop superintendent Howard Nalley recalled nothing about them, and Howard's memory was quite sharp! Another long-term Moller employee with an exellent memory, Harold Ocker, recalled that "During the period 1936 to 1940 it was not uncommon for some of the smaller organs to be sold with the use of reconditioned pipes. [Factory superintendent] Fred Carty and I selected most of the pipes from a substantial inventory of used pipes. I seem to remember Fred showing me several pipes that were scribed 'Kaylor' which would indicate the pipemaker."[1]

KAYLOR & CLARK

MANUFACTURERS OF

METAL
ORGAN PIPES

HAGERSTOWN, MD.

A. D. KAYLOR

MANUFACTURER OF

METAL
ORGAN PIPES

HAGERSTOWN, MD.

Ads appearing in The Diapason, *above, in December 1921, and right, in February 1923.*

MANSFIELD ORGAN PIPE WORKS

Established by McCollum Bros., 1841
Organ Pipe Works, 1871

Mansfield Organ Pipe Works

MANSFIELD DEPOT, CONN.

THE OLDEST WOOD PIPE MANUFACTURERS IN THE U. S. A.

PATENTEES AND SOLE MANUFACTURERS OF THE METAL TOE PIPE FOOT

The superiority of our goods speaks for itself. Eight out of every ten of our customers we have served for forty years or more. Also handles, rack pins, plain wood feet. Samples and price list gladly sent on request. Satisfaction guaranteed.

This ad appeared in the September 1927 Diapason. *This firm either directly or indirectly (through middlemen) supplied virtually every organ builder in the country with metal-toed feet for wood pipes.*

AMERICA'S HIGHEST STANDARD

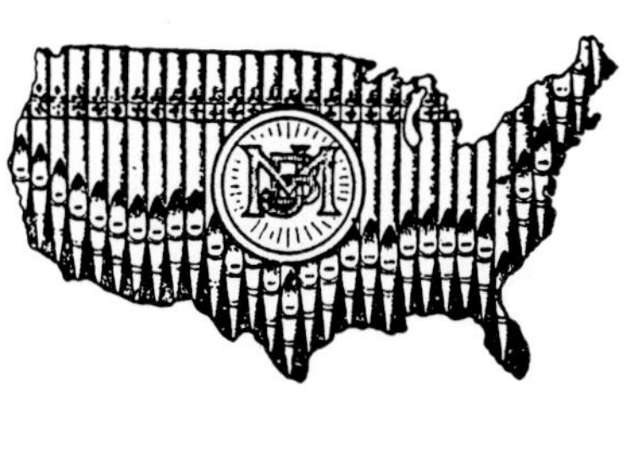

REPRESENTED THRUOUT THE WORLD

A FEW PROMINENT PIPE ORGAN SCREEN INSTALLATIONS

ST. MARY'S CATHEDRAL, MINNEAPOLIS, MINN.
ST. JAMES' CATHEDRAL, SEATTLE, WASH.
CONGREGATION BETH ISRAEL, CHICAGO
SACRED HEART SEMINARY, MILWAUKEE
MISSION COVENANT CHURCH, CHICAGO
OUR LADY OF SORROWS, CHICAGO
ST. PAUL'S, WASHINGTON, D. C.
UNIVERSITY OF SOUTH DAKOTA
ST. JOHN'S, TROY, NEW YORK
CHICAGO ORCHESTRAL HALL

JEROME B. MEYER & SONS, Inc.

MANUFACTURERS OF

ORGAN PIPES AND ORGAN MATERIAL

NATURAL ZINC - BRONZED AND TIN FRONT PIPES

SCIENTIFICALLY MADE :: ARTISTICALLY VOICED

SATISFACTION GUARANTEED

OFFICE AND FACTORY:
2339 SOUTH AUSTIN STREET
TEL. SHERIDAN 2741

MILWAUKEE, WIS.,

Jerome B. Meyer (1872-1949) was born in France. His older brother Frank was a pipe maker in the J. Rinkenback organ factory in their home town of Ammerschwihr. Frank Meyer emigrated to the United States in the early 1880s and found employment as a pipe maker with Carl Barckhoff in Salem, Ohio. In 1888 he persuaded his brother Jerome, then 16, to leave Europe to avoid military training and to join him in Ohio where he could learn the pipe making trade. Through the 1890s Jerome Meyer worked for Barckhoff and also for Wirsching. Around 1897 he accepted the position of pipe shop foreman for the Lyon & Healy plant in Chicago. When Lyon & Healy's pipe organ division moved to Battle Creek, Michigan in 1906, Jerome Meyer moved with them. Early in 1908 Lyon & Healy decided to discontinue organ production and Mr. Meyer purchased some of their inventory and went into business for himself.[1]

In 1909 Jerome Meyer accepted an invitation from the Hann-Wangerin-Weickhardt Co. in Milwaukee to take charge of their pipe shop. Under the terms of their agreement, Mr. Meyer was allowed to make pipes for the trade as well. By 1913 this business had grown to such an extent that Mr. Meyer decided to build his own shop on the lot just south of the Wangerin-Weickhardt factory.[2] Throughout the teens Wangerin continued to be Meyer's best customer although the Meyer roster of clients was continuously expanding. By 1920 the Wangerin company had established its own pipe shop and was no longer a Meyer customer. Its place was soon taken by the Bartola Musical Instrument Company, which became Meyer's best customer in the mid- and late 1920s. Barton purchased dozens of strings, diapasons and quintadenas from Meyer, as well as hundreds of flute and tibia treble octaves for the wood pipes Barton built themselves.[3]

Meyer also found customers outside the pipe organ industry: a number of automatic musical instrument manufacturers purchased their metal pipes from Meyer. Their major such customer was Operators Piano Co. of Chicago, makers of the Reproduco. From 1921 to 1930 Operators purchased 507 sets of pipes, 245 of which were

The Meyer factory looks the same in 1987 as it did in 1927, the year an addition housing the voicing room and offices was made to the front of the building. The only change is the address, which became 2339 S. Austin Street after Milwaukee streets were renumbered. The building barely visible at the right is a part of the old Wangerin factory.

Charles T. Meyer (right) and his son Gordon prepare to cast pipe metal in the basement of the Meyer factory in the 1950s. Note the necktie on Charles Meyer. He wore a tie to work every day until his retirement in 1984.

quintadenas. The National Electric Piano Company of St. Johnsville, New York purchased 40 sets of violins and flutes between 1922 and 1926. Other customers included Nelson Wiggen, who bought two sets of violins and four sets of flutes in 1923; Seeburg, who ordered seven sets of quintadenas in 1928; and the Marquette Piano Co., who purchased three sets of violins in 1921.[4]

When Jerome B. Meyer died in 1949 the firm was taken over by his son Charles T. Meyer (1900-1986). Charles' son, Gordon L. Meyer, is now president of the firm and is admirably carrying on the high quality standards set by his father and grandfather. Although his primary business is pipework for classical organs, Gordy Meyer has supplied the author with a number of new theatrical ranks, from 16′ solo strings to 2′ tibia trebles.

(opposite) Members of the Meyer family at work in their shop in the 1920s. From left to right are Charles T. Meyer, an unidentified man, Jerome B. Meyer, another unidentified man, Victor Meyer (nephew of Jerome Meyer) and another unidentified man.

At left, Jerome B. Meyer works at his voicing machine c. 1928. At right, in the very same voicing room, his grandson Gordy Meyer carries on the family tradition in 1986.

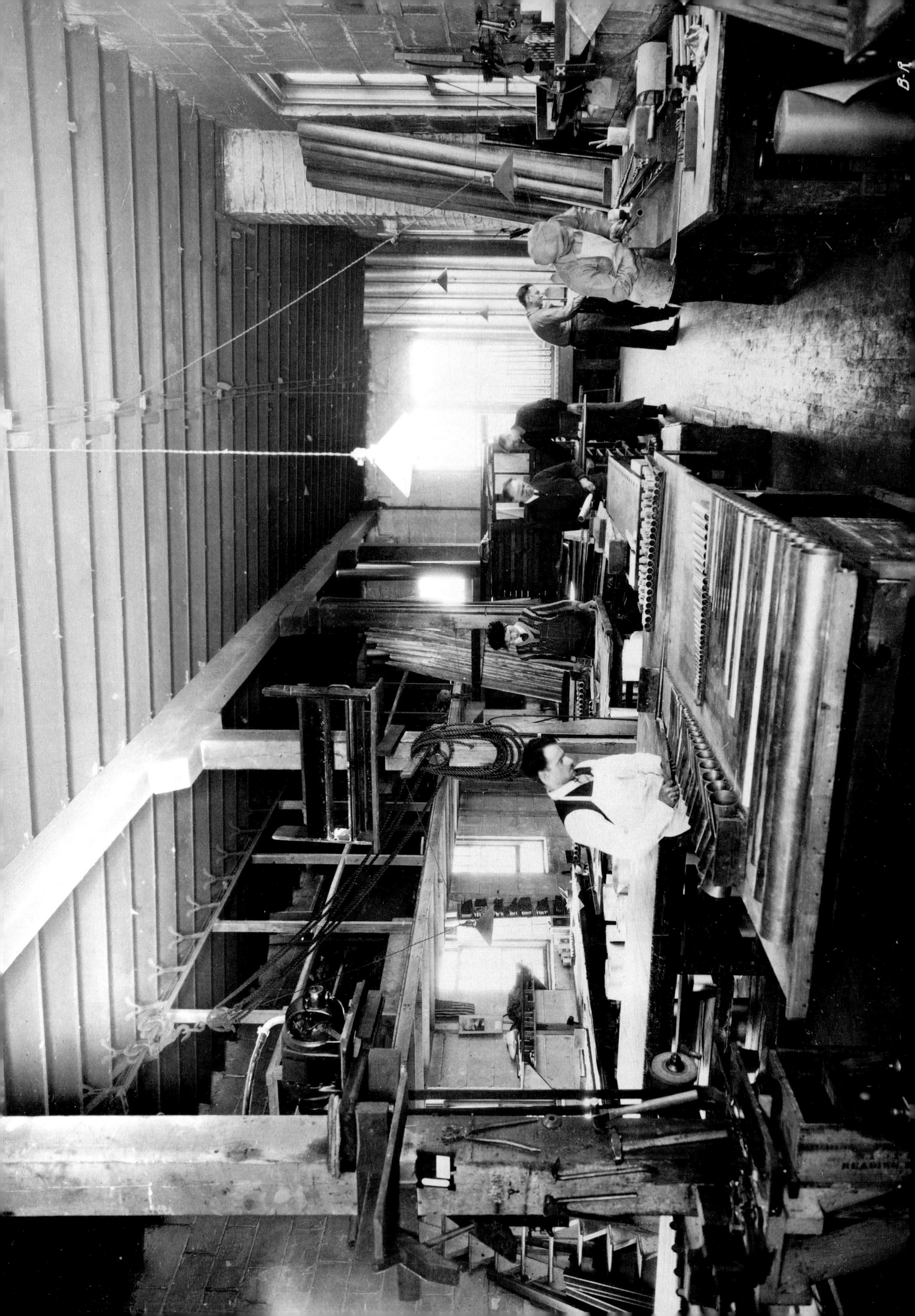

Meyer ad in the November 1923 Diapason. *Note the number of case pipes in production. Front pipes provided a large part of Meyer's business in its early years.*

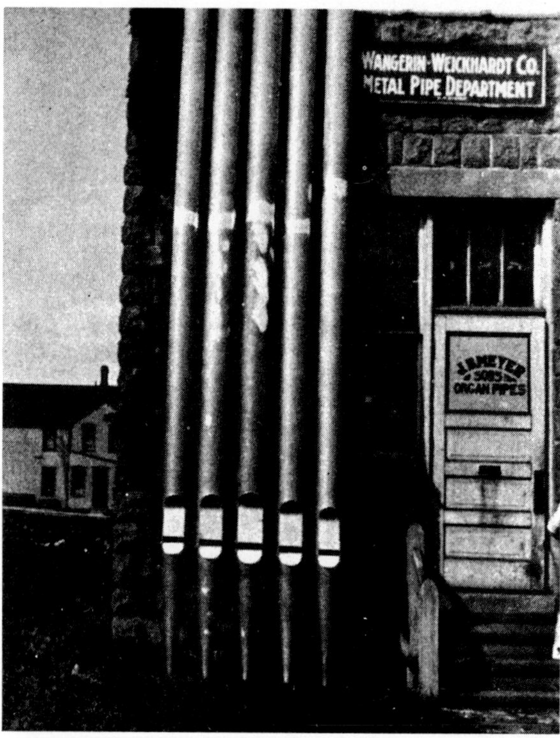

This photograph of the front of the Meyer factory was taken shortly after it was built in 1913. The sign proclaiming that it was Wangerin-Weickhardt's metal pipe department was removed soon thereafter. Wangerin continued to be Meyer's largest customer until they established their own pipe shop in 1920.

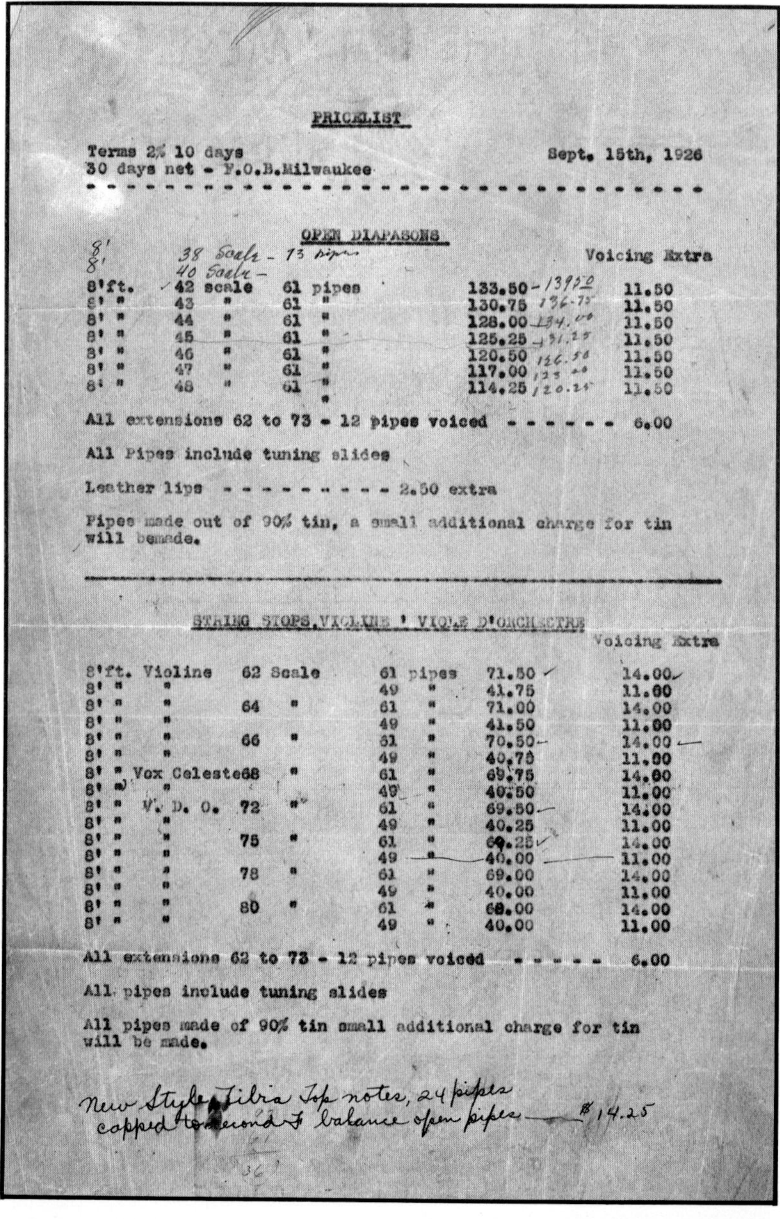

PRICELIST

Terms 2% 10 days
30 days net - F.O.B.Milwaukee
Sept. 15th, 1926

OPEN DIAPASONS

8' 38 Scale - 73 pipes
8' 40 Scale -

			Price	Voicing Extra
8'ft.	42 scale	61 pipes	133.50 - 139.50	11.50
8' "	43 "	61 "	130.75 136.75	11.50
8' "	44 "	61 "	128.00 134.00	11.50
8' "	45 "	61 "	125.25 131.25	11.50
8' "	46 "	61 "	120.50 126.50	11.50
8' "	47 "	61 "	117.00 123.00	11.50
8' "	48 "	61 "	114.25 120.25	11.50

All extensions 62 to 73 - 12 pipes voiced - - - - - - 6.00

All Pipes include tuning slides

Leather lips - - - - - - - - - - 2.50 extra

Pipes made out of 90% tin, a small additional charge for tin will bemade.

STRING STOPS, VIOLINE ' VIOLE D'ORCHESTRE

					Voicing Extra
8'ft.	Violine	62 Scale	61 pipes	71.50	14.00
8' "	"		49 "	41.75	11.00
8' "	"	64 "	61 "	71.00	14.00
8' "	"		49 "	41.50	11.00
8' "	"	66 "	61 "	70.50	14.00
8' "	"		49 "	40.75	11.00
8' "	Vox Celeste	68 "	61 "	69.75	14.00
8' "	"		49 "	40.50	11.00
8' "	V. D. O.	72 "	61 "	69.50	14.00
8' "	"		49 "	40.25	11.00
8' "	"	75 "	61 "	69.25	14.00
8' "	"		49 "	40.00	11.00
8' "	"	78 "	61 "	69.00	14.00
8' "	"		49 "	40.00	11.00
8' "	"	80 "	61 "	68.00	14.00
8' "	"		49 "	40.00	11.00

All extensions 62 to 73 - 12 pipes voiced - - - - - 6.00

All pipes include tuning slides

All pipes made of 90% tin small additional charge for tin will be made.

New Style Tibia Top notes, 24 pipes capped to second F balance open pipes — $14.25

One page of a Meyer price list c. 1926. The Barton company ordered scale 42 diapasons and scale 72 and 75 VDOs by the dozens from this list.

This page from an early Meyer catalog contains a really amusing line: "They will give that pipe organ effect!" Meyer sold display pipes to a number of theatres. Some of these, having one-manual Schuelkes or Bartola pit organs, for example, could certainly benefit from all the illusion Meyer could create!

ORGAN PIPES.

Genuine Pipe Organ Show Pipes or Dummy Fronts, as they are sometimes called, are made out of durable sheet metal, formed on mandrels and finished like a regular Pipe Organ Speaking Pipe.

The pipes are finished in a rich gold bronze and laquered so as to retain their luster.

Pipes can be placed artistically in any Theater. In Archways, former door openings, over exit doors, across corners or against flat walls. Can easily be attached. Anybody can set them in position. Have them put in your Theater—they will give that pipe organ effect.

We solicit your further correspondence.

DESIGN FOR SIDES OF STAGE IN THEATRES

In lower photos, at left, Doug McGee and several other shop employees roll stiff sheet zinc around a wooden mandrel to form a replica Wurlitzer 16′ solo string. At right, the completed pipe bodies await having their feet soldered on.

MID-WEST ORGAN SUPPLY COMPANY

THE MID-WEST ORGAN SUPPLY COMPANY

Manufacturers of

Metal and Zinc Organ Pipes

--::--

218 East Sixth Street

ALTON -- ILLINOIS

This firm, located just across the Mississippi River from St. Louis, was active throughout the 1920s. The above ad, appearing in the October 1921 Diapason, *mentions only metal pipes although in later years wood pipes were also offered. Firms such as Robert-Morton and Kilgen frequently ordered pipes from Mid-West when their own pipe departments fell behind production schedules.*

OLIVER ORGAN CO.

Oliver Lowe began his organ building business in the mid 1920s. He built a number of small theatrical instruments in the San Francisco bay area sporting tibias and horseshoe consoles with colored stop keys, although none is known to have been installed in a theatre. He was apparently proud of his wood pipes; one eight-rank organ he built contained four wooden ranks! Following his retirement in the early 1940s his business was absorbed by Schoenstein & Co.[1]

CALIFORNIA

Wood Pipes

8000 sq. ft. devoted to wood pipes alone. Artistic voicing. Immediate delivery. Write for our special introductory offer on 8 ft. Tibia, and price list.

OLIVER ORGAN CO.

BERKELEY, CALIF.

Oliver Lowe offered his wood pipes to the trade in this ad in the January 1927 Diapason.

TITAN TOOL COMPANY

Early in his career, the famous organ parts supplier Anton Gottfried engaged Fred Albrecht of the Titan firm to make tools and dies for the production of reed pipe parts such as blocks and shallots.[1] *Titan later offered shallots to the trade but discontinued advertising after the November 1922 issue of* The Diapason.

ESCHALLOTTS
for REED PIPES
Manufactured in a way assuring uniformity throughout
PRICES ARE RIGHT
TITAN TOOL COMPANY ERIE, PA.

The White System of Reed Voicing
Used Exclusively

Special Equipment for Heavy Pressure
and 32 ft. Work

FREDERICK I. WHITE

Reed Pipes

FOR CHURCH AND CONCERT ORGANS

IMPORTANT

WHEN ORDERING STATE PITCH, PRESSURE AND MITERING LENGTH. IF PITCH IS NOT INTERNATIONAL SEND PITCH PIPE.

Reading, Mass.

F. I. White was a reed voicer whose work spanned several decades. He learned his craft with Jardine and later worked for Samuel Pierce in Reading, Massachusetts.[1] His reputation must have been excellent even in the earliest days of his business; in 1903 he received an order for a 32′ bombard for the largest organ in the world, the Los Angeles Art organ at the 1904 St. Louis World's Fair. Low CCCC of this stop, pictured here outside Mr. White's shop, measured 24″ square and 33½′ long and was made from lumber 2″ thick. During the 1920s he voiced a number of reed ranks for Barton, Marr & Colton and other makes of theatre organs.

White's reputation in the trade was so well established that he rarely advertised. This ad in the May 1928 issue of The Diapason *doesn't even mention the reeds which were his specialty.*

PLAYERS & ROLLS

Automatic Musical Instrument Company

1500 Union Avenue, S. E.

Grand Rapids, Michigan

Office of Sec'y-Treas.

All communications should be addressed to the company and not to individuals, to receive prompt attention.

The Automatic Musical Instrument Company grew out of an idea that patrons of coin-operated pianos should be able to select which tunes they wanted to hear rather than to take potluck with their nickels, as had previously been the case. Patents for such a tune selecting device were applied for in 1909 and in 1910 the National Piano Mfg. Company was organized to make the instruments. The firm had another revolutionary idea—that the pianos should not be sold but should remain the property of the firm, sharing their receipts with proprietors where they were "on location." The National Automatic Music Company was organized to handle this aspect of the business.[1] In that period of the American economy it was not unusual for a business to be broken into several such operating companies even though they often shared the same ownership and/or management.

By 1925, 4200 National pianos were collecting nickels all over the country. Late in that year the two operating companies merged to form the Automatic Musical Instru-

The Grand Rapids factory as it appeared in its heyday. Its appearance has changed little in the 1980s.

ment Company. The coin-operated piano business was slowing down, its place being taken over by the radio and the phonograph. Sages at AMI Incorporated, as the firm eventually became known, had the wisdom to develop a coin-operated phonograph. By 1930, 8500 of them were in service, all company-owned as had been the pianos before them.[2] AMI eventually joined Wurlitzer, Seeburg and Rock-Ola as one of the big four juke box makers. In the late 1950s AMI was acquired by Rowe International, Inc., a major vending machine manufacturer. As of 1987 the AMI name is no longer a corporate trademark but the same factory which produced pianos and juke boxes in the 1920s is now making bill changers and video juke boxes.[3]

The Automatic Musical Instrument Company participated in the organ industry by supplying roll changing mechanisms to Welte, Estey, Artcraft and probably other builders as well. For another photo of such a unit see page 682 of this volume.

This Multi-Control unit, as the company referred to its roll changers, was sold to the Artcraft Organ Company of Santa Monica, California.

INVOICE

Automatic Musical Instrument Company
1500 Union Avenue, S. E.
Grand Rapids, Michigan

Date January 12, 1931.
Your Order No.
Our Order No.
Shipped Via
Date Shipped

SOLD TO Artcraft Organ Company,
Santa Monica, California

SHIPPED TO Automatic Musical Instrument Co.,
2608 So. Hobart Blvd.,
Los Angeles, Calif.

TERMS: Cash on delivery
F.O.B. Grand Rapids, Michigan

1	20 Roll Double Multi-Control complete with one control station, 25 ft. 30 conductor silk covered cable, and electrical equipment for 50 cycles, 110 Volt, A.C.	1,200	00		
5	Extra Control stations	125	00		
50 ft.	30 conductor silk covered flexible cable	12	50		
400 ft.	24 conductor rat proof cable for concealed wiring	53	00		
1	Contactor Mercury switch	2	91		
1	Epco Mercury switch	1	69		
1	Extra "V" belt 7'6"	1	13		
2	16 Tooth sprockets for #18 chain - 3/8" hole	No charge			
2	Belt Hooks	"	"		
2	Pulleys for 50 cycle motors	"	"		
	Freight prepaid Grand Rapids to Los Angeles	33	92		
				1,430	15
	Less Advance Payment			400	00
				1,030	15

Invoice for an elaborate Multi-Control system wherein twenty different selections could be chosen from any of six rooms of a large residence.

CLARK ORCHESTRA ROLL COMPANY

MANUFACTURERS OF

HAND-PLAYED MUSIC FOR REPRODUCING ORGANS, AUTOMATIC PIANOS AND ORCHESTRIONS.

Roll-Makers For 40 Years

DE KALB, ILLINOIS

The Clark Orchestra Roll Co. was formed in 1920 when Ernest G. Clark purchased the coin-operated roll division of the QRS company. The vast majority of the Clark business was in rolls for coin-operated instruments. Clark produced their last new "nickelodeon" roll in 1940 and were still in business as late as 1942.

A very small part of the Clark business was producing rolls for pipe organ players. Smaller organ builders, who couldn't afford to establish their own roll departments, used Clark organ rolls or, in many instances, ordinary 88-note player piano rolls. Clark made rolls only; the player devices were usually purchased from other suppliers. Such players offered by the smaller builders, rare in any form, are extremely rare on theatre organs. Mortuaries constituted most of what little market existed for them.

Clark organ rolls were of different scales from those of the major builders who offered organ players. Wurlitzer, Moller, Kimball, Welte, Skinner, Estey, Austin, Aeolian and Link made their own rolls which would fit only their own instruments.

The Clark buildings still stand in DeKalb as of 1985. Out of these doors rolled much of the toe-tappingest music ever perforated.

AND—

SPEAKING OF ORGAN ROLLS

we present

THE CONSOLE-ART
134 notes
15¼" wide

THE CONSOLETTE
98 notes
Standard 88 note width

THE CLARK ORGAN ROLL
90 notes
Standard 88 note width

Complete Player-units ready for installation may be procured.

THE CLARK ORCHESTRA ROLL CO.
DE KALB, ILLINOIS

Clark ad in the January 1930 Diapason. *The "complete player units" mentioned were actually made by Roesler-Hunholz, Inc. of Milwaukee, Wisconsin. Ernest Clark was a director of this firm.*

L. B. DOMAN CORPORATION

This brochure announced the Artona player in 1928. The first sale was made to Marr & Colton for the Reginald Webb studio in Detroit where Artona music rolls performed by theatre organists Carlton James and Paul Forster were broadcast over WJR radio. Marr & Colton purchased a second Artona player for a funeral home. Two Artonas were sold to Votteler-Holtkamp-Sparling, also for funeral homes. A fifth and probably last Artona was sold to Hinners late in 1933 for an Indiana residence. The Doman factory contained a recording organ of Doman's design controlled by a two-manual Marr & Colton console. A high-speed perforator connected to it cut rolls in real time as organists played. Lewis Doman died in 1935, the victim of a spider bite. The contents of the Doman factory, virtually intact after a half century, were rescued in 1988 by Ohio enthusiasts Roger E. Morrison and Dan Spies so it is possible that Artona music may once again entertain listeners in the 1980s.[1]

Theatre Organist

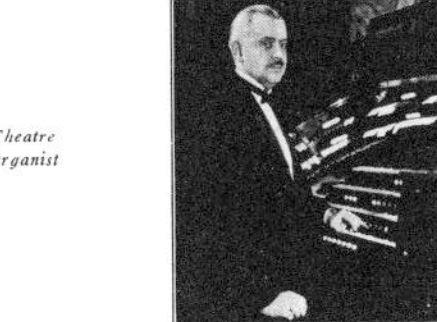

Studio 1924 E. Genesee St.

PAUL H. FORSTER

Syracuse, N. Y., Feb. 26, 1929.

L. B. Doman Corp., Camillus, N. Y.

Gentlemen:

It was a great pleasure to hear the actual reproduction of my playing at your place of business last week. When I played the organ to make the master roll you told me that I would have a thrill when I heard the roll and I can truthfully say it was a thrill of thrills. I could just imagine myself playing the piece, so accurate was the reproduction. The Player regulated the stops and the swell shutters along with playing every note just as I had played.

The capabilities of your Player are unlimited and I would recommend it to any one having an organ as it is so different from any other Player.

Wishing you the best of success, I am,

Cordially yours,

(Signed) PAUL H. FORSTER.

THE MARR & COLTON COMPANY, Inc.
Organ Builders

Warsaw, N. Y., Feb. 26, 1929.

Mr. L. B. Doman, Camillus, N. Y.

Dear Mr. Doman:

We are looking forward to a quick delivery on the recent orders that we placed with you for your Organ Player, as we feel that it reproduces the artist's playing in the finest manner possible.

We believe that if you can give us an early delivery we can send you in further orders, as your Player is the best we have heard reproduce.

Yours very truly,

(Signed) The Marr & Colton Co.

By DAVID MARR.

Historical

The mechanism of the Organ Player described hereafter is the invention of L. B. Doman, president of the L. B. Doman Corporation. Mr. Doman has had wide experience in the design and making of player actions. He was founder of the Amphion Piano Player Company, now part of the American Piano Company, and for thirty years its chief engineer. Mr. Doman was inventor and patentee of the principal controlling mechanism forming the expression control of the Ampico Reproducing Piano. A great many inventions in the player and music roll field have been designed and patented by him.

Out of the wide experience gained in this line comes the latest invention—A Player for Pipe Organs, reproducing with 100% fidelity the playing of any organist and also using orchestral arranged rolls giving effects far beyond those possible by any organist.

The Player

The Player mechanism is encased in a cabinet about 42 inches long, 38½ inches high, 17 inches deep. The power is provided by a universal motor operating on any 110 volt lighting circuit. This motor drives a small vacuum pump by which the pneumatic devices are operated. The Player may be placed in any position near or remote from the organ and is connected to the regular console (or to the organ) by a cable of wires such as is used for connecting the usual console with the organ proper. In the rear of the Player plainly marked terminals are provided to which the cable wires may be easily soldered.

The compass of the player is 61 notes Accompaniment, 61 notes Solo, 30 notes Pedal, 7 Degrees of Swell Crescendo.

Style A Player has twelve master combinations each controlling up to twelve stops, these combinations are recombined by the Player and music roll so as to give nearly 4,000 combinations in all.

Style B, intended for larger instruments, has 24 master combinations giving in all nearly 8,000 usable combinations. The same roll is used for both Players, a transfer switch controlled by music sheet operating the second group when used on Style B.

The take up spool, except while re-rolling a played roll is always moving in playing direction so that the music roll may be attached without waiting and turning the take up spool by hand.

All contacts of the Player mechanism are direct from the tracker. There are no lock-valves and no switches. Any part of any roll may be repeated without waiting for registration or other locking devices to act. The Player is controlled by two push buttons, "Play" and "Re-roll" and three levers, "Repeat—Stop", "Automatic Registration, on—off" and "Tempo, Slow—Normal—Fast."

The Music Roll

The rolls used on the Player are 11¼ inches wide, they have 112 working lines of perforations and a central line of perforation for controlling the tracking of the music properly.

All rolls are made at our factory by machines designed and built by L. B. Doman Corporation, especially for this work. The longest roll will play 15 to 20 minutes.

A Standard Player—A Standard Roll

In conclusion we desire to emphasize the fact that ARTONA is offered as a Standard Player—suitable for use on either large or small organs. With its adjustable registration, which can be set to suit the environment of any organ, it makes possible for the first time a Standard Organ Roll which in turn, on account of its large and varied field of usefulness makes possible a comprehensive library of Music Rolls available to the organ user at reasonable prices.

That, Mr. Organ Builder, is the story. If you can use a Standard Player and a Standard Roll we would be glad to have your co-opertaion.

L. B. DOMAN CORPORATION,
CAMILLUS, N. Y.

Camillus is the easterly entrance to the Finger Lakes Region of Central New York. It is eight miles west of Syracuse, directly on Genesee Turnpike, the main East and West highway through New York State. It is served by the Auburn Branch of the N. Y. C. R. R. and frequent Bus service is maintained to and from Syracuse, N. Y.

We extend a cordial invitation to anyone interested to call at our factory and hear ARTONA.

THE MOORE AND FISHER MANUFACTURING COMPANY

The author knows little about the Moore and Fisher firm, whose ad in the June 1931 Diapason *is reproduced here. Ernst D. Moore was manager of the player action department of Pratt, Read,*[1] *also located in Deep River, and it seems likely that he may have been a principal in Moore and Fisher.*

After graduating from grade school in 1911 Elmer Hunholz (1896-) began his career by working for the Edmund Gram Piano Company in Milwaukee. Working through all the departments, he eventually became assistant to factory superintendent Fred Roesler. When the Gram factory closed in 1923 Roesler and Hunholz formed a business which serviced pianos and all types of roll-operated instruments. In that line they realized profits in a relatively untapped area—but let's allow Mr. Hunholz himself to tell the story:

"We felt there was a need for a mechanism to play the pipe organ from a music roll for use in funeral parlors and even in large homes. The average organ builder knew nothing about players; therefore, we felt if our company built the player and kept a library of music we could sustain ourselves and supply a need in the trade. In our research . . . we found that the Clark Orchestra Roll Co. of DeKalb, Illinois had a small library of organ rolls which had been used for funeral homes . . . We contracted to buy the organ roll department of Clark . . . and took on their organ roll editor, Roy Holland, to handle the roll operation there. The rolls were cut in DeKalb and sent to Milwaukee where they were spooled up and boxed and put into stock.

"During the time that Mr. Holland was at DeKalb we developed a new roll which could play three manuals on an organ. We had a connection with George Kilgen & Sons of St. Louis, Missouri and put a recording mechanism on their studio organ and they got some recordings from some of the world's best known organists such as Pietro Yon . . . and Charles Courboin . . . Our market for rolls and players was slowly developing for residence organs; we sold to Wicks, Hook & Hastings, Hall . . . Pilcher and . . . Casavant . . . Then . . . the government instituted the income tax and large residences were out and that stopped the pipe organs for homes. About this time we had a disastrous fire in our factory and our music roll department with its master records was badly hit. Our music roll stock and masters were almost completely wiped out.

". . . The Playrite music roll company was in receivership in Milwaukee and . . . with our organ roll experience [we] took it over and started making music rolls for the home player piano. We made rolls for some five years or more and then business tapered off with the player piano . . . The Miesner Piano Co. closed up in Milwaukee. Mr. Hoskins, who was superintendent of Miesner, came over to work with us and took charge of the music roll department until it closed shop. About this time Mr. Roesler made up his mind to retire and moved to California for his health. Mr. Hoskins and myself carried on the piano and organ rebuilding operation through the years. Mr. Hoskins retired and moved to California also, leaving me alone with the operation and the building which we had purchased during our most prosperous times . . . I stayed to manage the building and did a little piano work on the side . . . This went on for ten years or more until February 1977 when I sold out and am now completely retired at 81 years."[1]

Artistouch player mechanisms, built by Roesler-Hunholz, were certainly inexpensive compared to prices charged by other manufacturers: in 1933 the wholesale price of a standard model, not including a cabinet, was $450.[2] This price would have allowed an organ builder a tidy profit; even with a 100% markup, the retail price was still below that charged by most other builders. Unfortunately, in the depths of the Depression, few Artistouch players sold at any price.

ALBUM
of
RECORDINGS
for the
ORGAN

ARTISTOUCH
ORGAN ROLLS
Standard Series

"Reproducing the Personality of the Artist"

MANUFACTURED SOLELY BY
ROESLER - HUNHOLZ, INC.
MILWAUKEE, WIS.

ARTISTOUCH *organ rolls are for use only with Reproducing organs using the* ARTISTOUCH *reproducing mechanism. The better known and responsible organ builders in the United States, Canada, and foreign countries are licensed to install and service* ARTISTOUCH *reproducing units, thus assuring a prompt source of supply for* ARTISTOUCH *rolls everywhere.*

1. All ARTISTOUCH rolls are made to a standard tracker bar width of 11¼ inches, and are manufactured from a high grade paper. They are free from atmospheric expansion and contraction.

2. ARTISTOUCH rolls render a true interpretation of the artist's recording, and make use of the full resources of even the largest organs. All control, including registration, swell expression, crescendo, etc., are cut into the roll, and are reproduced as recorded.

Order ARTISTOUCH rolls by catalogue number only.

3. Special attention is called to the fact that any number of single rolls totaling not more than a half hour of playing time may, upon request, be joined together to make a continuous roll, and that such roll may be obtained at the cost of the individual selections.

On this and the next four pages are reproduced a portion of an extremely rare Artistouch roll catalog c. 1930, omitting the funeral and sacred selections. An amazingly wide variety of music was available; it is regrettable that so few of these rolls were ever sold.

Classic and Popular Music

No.	Name	Composer	Price
S-644	Absent	Metcalf	$2.50
S-988	Absinthe Frappe (It Happened In Nordland)	Herbert	3.00
S-26	A Day in Venice 1. Dawn 2. Gondoliers 3. Venetian Love Song 4. Goodnight	Nevin	4.25
S-15	Adieu	Friml	3.00
S-516	Ah! Sweet Mystery Of Life	Victor Herbert	2.75
S-672	Alice Blue Gown (From "Irene")	Tierney	3.00
S-174	All For You	Bertrand-Brown	2.75
S-994	All For You (Princess Pat)	Herbert	3.00
S-83	Al Fresco	V. Herbert	2.75
S-217	Algerian Song	Ketelbey	3.50
S-1032	Aloha Oe		3.00
S-366	Alpine Storm	Kunkel	3.00
S-313	Among My Souvenirs	Nicholls	2.75
S-64	Amoureuse	Berger	2.75
S-1012	Anchors Aweigh	Zimmerman	3.00
S-767	Andante (From "Orfeo")	Gluck	3.00
S-528	Andante	Bartlett, Op. 205	3.25
S-782	Andante	Mendelssohn	3.00
S-768	Andante Cantabile (From Quartet In D Major)	Tschaikowsky	3.50
S-508	Angel's Serenade	Braga	3.25
S-264	1. Angelus 2. Symphonette	Massenet Berge	3.50
S-710	Artist's Life	Strauss	3.25
S-233	Ave Maria	Gounod	3.00
S-363	Ave Maria	Schubert	3.00
S-57	Badinage	Victor Herbert	3.00
S-417	Ballet Music From Faust	Gounod	3.50
S-755	Barcarolle	Reinecke	2.50
S-1037	Barcarolle (Tales of Hoffmann)	Offenbach	2.75
S-202	Barber of Seville, Overture	Rossini	3.50
S-184	Basket Of Roses	Albers	3.00
S-999	Bells Of St. Anne de Beaupre	Russell	3.50
S-459	Bells Of St. Mary's, The	Adams	2.75
S-78	Beneath a Balcony	Winne	3.00
S-130	Berceuse	Jarnefelt	3.00
S-785	Berceuse	Schytte, Op. 26, No. 7	3.00
S-977	Blest Christmas Morn	Wallace	2.75
S-140	Blossom Time, Selection	Romberg	4.00
S-108	Blue Danube	Strauss	2.75
S-194	Boccaccio, Overture	Von Suppe	3.25
S-322	Bohemian Girl Waltzes	Ascher-Mahl	3.50
S-4	Bowl Of Pansies	Reynard	2.75
S-181	Brown Bird Singing, A	Wood	2.75
S-418	Bubbling Spring	Rive-King	2.75
S-405	By The Waters Of Minnetonka	Lieurance	3.00
S-507	Call Me Thine Own	Halevy	3.25
S-68	Calm As The Night	Bohm	2.75
S-547	Can't Yo' Heah Me Callin' Caroline	Roma	3.00
S-116	Carissima	Penn	2.75
S-475	Carry Me Back To Old Virginny	Bland	2.75
S-12	Caresse de Papillon	Barthelemy	2.75
S-84	Carnations	Albers	3.25
S-187	Cavatina	Baron	2.75
S-369	Cavatina	Bohm	2.75
S-770	Cavatina, Op. 85	Raff	3.00

CLASSIC AND POPULAR MUSIC

No.	Name	Composer	Price
S-261	Chanson	Friml	2.75
S-149	Chansonette	Friml	2.75
S-71	Chanson Sans Paroles	Heller	2.75
S-115	Chanson Triste	Tschaikowsky	3.50
S-17	Chant d'Amour	Frommel	2.75
S-134	Chant Erotique	Berge	3.00
S-80	Chant Sans Paroles	Friml	2.75
S-769	Chant Sans Paroles, Op. 2, No. 3	Tschaikowsky	3.00
S-290	Chimes Of Love	d'Albret	3.00
S-649	Chloe (Song Of The Swamp)	Moret	3.25
S-595	Chocolate Soldier, Selection, Roll No. 1 1. That Would Be Lovely 2. Falling In Love 3. My Hero	Strauss	3.50
S-596	Chocolate Soldier, Selection, Roll No. 2 1. The Letter Song 2. The Chocolate Soldier	Strauss	3.50
S-711	Ciribiribin	Pestalozza	3.00
S-598	Cloister Scene, A	Alfred T. Mason	3.50
S-419	Cocoanut Dance	Herman	2.75
S-471	Come Where My Live Lies Dreaming	Dressler	3.00
S-107	Concert Valse	Friml	2.75
S-364	Consolation	Mendelssohn	3.00
S-387	Consolation No. 5	Liszt	3.00
S-260	Croquis et Silhouettes	Schutt	2.75
S-58	Cupid's Frolic	Miles	3.00
S-712	Danube Waves	Ivanovici	3.50
S-150	Dance Of The Woodnymphs	Fitzgerald	3.00
S-621	Danny Boy	Weatherly	3.25
S-145	Dancing Leaves	Miles	3.25
S-476	Darling Nellie Gray	Hanby	3.25
S-131	Dear Heart What Might Have Been	Spencer	3.00
S-677	Dear Love, My Love	Friml	3.00
S-607	Deep In My Heart, Dear	Romberg	2.75
S-553	Deep River	Rogers	2.75
S-306	Desert Song, The	Romberg	3.00
S-311	Djamileh, Overture	Thompson	3.00
S-602	Do You Remember?	Bond	2.75
S-120	Dream, A	Bartlett	3.00
S-713	Estudiantina	Waldteufel	3.50
S-60	Elegie	Massenet	2.75
S-824	Elsa's Dream	Wagner	3.00
S-744	Erotik	Grieg	3.00
S-407	Evening Hour	Hulten	2.50
S-645	Evening Star (From Tannhäuser")	Wagner	2.75
S-463	Eventide	Huerter	3.00
S-846	Fifth Nocturne	Leybach	3.50
S-777	Finale—Sixth Organ Sonata	Mendelssohn	2.75
S-199	Fingal's Cave, Overture	Mendelssohn	3.50
S-997	Fireside Fancies	Clokey	3.50
S-619	Firefly, The, Selection	Friml	4.00
S-987	Fleurette	Herbert	3.00
S-312	Flying Artillery, Overture	Bergenholtz	3.50
S-620	Fortune Teller, Selection	Victor Herbert	3.50
S-144	Fountain, The	Miles	3.00
S-157	From The Depths, Op. 55, No. 6	MacDowell	3.00
S-454	Funiculi-Funicula	Denza	2.75
S-21	Garden Dance	Vargas	3.00
S-201	Gavotte Moderne	Severn	3.25
S-100	Gippsland March	A. F. Lithgow	2.75

CLASSIC AND POPULAR MUSIC

No.	Name	Composer	Price
S-143	Glow Worm, The	Lincke	3.00
S-121	Good-Bye	Tosti	3.00
S-185	Gypsy Love Song	Smith-Herbert	3.00
S-1036	Hark, The Herald Angels Sing		3.00
S-1033	Hawaiian Medley		3.00
S-105	High School Cadets	Sousa	2.75
S-570	Holy City, The	Adams	3.50
S-624	Huguette Waltz, From Vagabond King	Friml	2.75
S-271	Hungarian Dance No. 5 and 6	Brahms	3.25
S-834	Hymn To The Sun	Rimsky-Korsakov	3.25
S-784	Idylle	Merkel	3.00
S- 77	I Know A Lovely Garden	d'Hardelot	2.75
S-416	Il Bacio (The Kiss)	Arditi	3.00
S-548	I Love You Truly	Bond	2.50
S-627	I'm Falling In Love With Someone (From "Naughty Marietta")	Victor Herbert	2.75
S-406	Im Herbste	Grieg	3.50
S-221	In A Chinese Temple Garden	Ketelbey	3.00
S-129	In A Monastery Garden	Ketelbey	3.00
S-216	In A Persian Market	Ketelbey	3.25
S- 2	In Arcadia	Sellars	3.00
S-124	Indian Love Call	Friml	3.00
S-408	In My Neighbor's Garden	Nevin	2.75
S-309	Intermezzo From Cavalleria Rusticana	Mascagni	2.75
S-375	In The Sweet Bye and Bye	Webster	2.75
S-993	Isle Of Our Dreams, The (Red Mill)	Herbert	3.00
S-308	Italian Nights	Lee S. Roberts	3.00
S-284	Japanese Sunset, A	Deppen	3.00
S- 24	June	Tschaikowsky	2.75
S- 8	June Breezes	Miles	3.25
S-180	Just An Ivy Covered Shack	Rupp	3.25
S- 76	Just A Wearyin' For You	Bond	3.00
S-984	Kamennoi-Ostrow	Rubinstein	3.50
S- 82	Kiss In The Dark, A	V. Herbert	2.75
S-557	Kiss Me Again	Victor Herbert	3.00
S-989	La Serenata	Herbert	3.00
S-175	L'Amour-Toujours-L'Amour	Friml	2.75
S-594	La Juive, Prelude	Halevy	3.00
S-848	Largo (New World Symphony)	Dvorak	4.00
S-467	Largo	Handel	3.25
S-210	L'Arlesienne, Prelude	Bizet	2.50
S- 3	Legend Of A Rose	Reynard	3.00
S- 33	Liebestraum	Liszt	3.25
S-102	Lights Out	Earl E. McCay	3.00
S-477	Listen To The Mocking Bird	Alice Hawthorne	3.00
S-123	Little Gray Home In The West	Lohr	2.75
S-295	Lotus Land	Scott	3.00
S-986	Love Is The Best Of All	Herbert	3.00
S-992	Love Is Tyrant (The Singing Girl)	Herbert	3.00
S-798	Love, Take My Heart	Joseph Meyer	3.00
S-132	Love Song	Friml	2.75
S-985	March Of The Toys	Herbert	3.00
S-213	Masaniello, Overture	Auber	3.25
S-473	Massa's In de Cold, Cold Ground	Foster	2.75
S- 16	Meditation	Cadman	3.00
S-111	Meditation (From Thais)	Massenet	3.00
S-288	Melody	Dawes	2.75
S-197	Melody	Friml	2.75

CLASSIC AND POPULAR MUSIC

No.	Name	Composer	Price
S-973	Melody In F	Rubinstein	3.25
S-510	Melody In G Flat	Cadman	2.75
S-776	Memories	Van Alstyne	2.75
S-307	Merry Widow Waltzes	Lehar	3.00
S-674	Message Of The Violet (From "Prince Of Pilsen")	Luders	3.00
S- 61	Mighty Lak' A Rose	Nevin	2.75
S-995	Moonbeams (Red Mill)	Herbert	3.00
S-1003	Moon Is Low, The		3.00
S-413	Morgenstimmung, Op. 46, No. 1	Grieg	3.00
S-628	Murillo	Terschak	3.50
S-391	Musetta's Song	Puccini	3.00
S-114	My Heart At Thy Sweet Voice	Saint-Saens	2.75
S-603	My Heart Stood Still		3.00
S-623	My Isle Of Golden Dreams	Kahn, Van Alstyne & Blaufuss	2.75
S-469	My Old Kentucky Home	Foster	3.00
S-278	Narcissus	Nevin	2.75
S- 97	National Emblem	E. E. Bagley	3.00
S-293	Neapolitan Nights	Zamecnik	2.75
S-766	Nocturne, Op. 9, No. 2	Chopin	3.00
S-489	Nola	Felix Arndt	3.25
S-195	Notturno	Grieg	3.25
S-274	Old Refrain, The	Kreisler	2.75
S-470	Old Black Joe	Foster	3.00
S- 28	Old Mother, The	Dvorak	2.75
S-478	Old Oaken Bucket	Sam'l Woodworth	2.75
S-103	Officer Of The Day	R. B. Hall	2.75
S- 23	Offertory In G	Loud	3.25
S-626	O Maria, O Mari	Capua	3.25
S-176	One Alone	Romberg	3.25
S-188	One Fleeting Hour	Lee	3.00
S-401	One Sweetly Solemn Thought	Ambrose-Gledhill	2.75
S-622	Only A Rose, From Vagabond King, Selection	Friml	2.75
S-122	O Sole Mio	Capua	3.25
S-559	Over the Waves	Rosas	3.00
S-420	Parade Of The Wooden Soldiers	Leon Jessel	2.75
S-222	Pastel Minuet	Paradis	3.00
S-211	Peer Gynt's Home-Coming	Grieg	2.75
S- 74	Perfect Day, A	Bond	2.75
S- 86	Pierette	Friml	2.75
S-779	Pilgrim's Song Of Hope, The	Edouard Batiste	3.00
S-629	Pink Lady, Selection	Caryll	3.50
S- 98	Pitt Panther March		2.75
S-403	Pique Dame, Overture	Von Suppe	3.75
S-783	Poeme	Fibich	2.75
S-118	Polish Dance	Scharwenka	3.00
S-249	Poupee Valsante	Poldini	2.75
S-164	Powder and Patches	Miles	2.75
S-1005	Prelude and Fughetta in C	Faulkes	3.25
S-991	Punchinello	Herbert	3.00
S-223	Pyramids (From Egyptian Suite)	Stoughton	2.75
S-246	Quartette From Rigoletto, The	Verdi	2.75
S-517	Ramona	Mabel Wayne	3.00
S-984	Reve Angelique (Kamennoi-Ostrow)	Rubinstein	3.50
S-404	Robespierre Overture	Litolff	3.25
S-388	Romance, Op. 44	Rubinstein	2.75
S-826	Romance, Op. 88	Williams	3.00
S-113	Rosary, The	Nevin	3.25

CLASSIC AND POPULAR MUSIC

No.	Name	Composer	Price
S-827	Roses	Weatherly & Adams	3.00
S-106	Rustle Of Spring	Sinding	2.75
S-270	Salut d'Amour	Elgar	3.50
S-411	Schubert's Serenade	Schubert-Liszt	3.00
S- 99	Semper Fidelis	J. P. Sousa	2.75
S-310	Semiramide, Overture	Rossini	3.75
S- 18	Serenade (Student Prince)	Romberg	3.00
S-247	Serenade	Drigo	3.00
S-842	Serenade	Gounod	2.75
S- 70	Serenade	Toselli	3.00
S-389	Serenata	Moszkowski	3.00
S-109	Skaters Waltz, The	Waldteufel	3.25
S-415	Sextette, From Lucia Di Lammermoor	Donizetti	3.00
S-1035	Silent Night		2.75
S-468	Simple Aveu	Thome	3.00
S-847	Sing Me To Sleep	Greene	3.25
S- 29	Smoke Wreaths	Friml	3.00
S-204	Sometime	Friml	2.75
S-458	Somewhere A Voice Is Calling	Tate	2.75
S-136	Song Of Love	Romberg	3.00
S-127	Song Of Songs	Moya	3.00
S-294	Sonata In G Minor	MacDowell	2.75
S-844	Song of India	Rimsky-Korsakov	3.00
S-386	Souvenir	Drdla	2.75
S- 65	Souvenir De Venice	Quinn	2.75
S-465	Spring Song	Mendelssohn	2.50
S- 96	Stars and Stripes Forever	Sousa	3.00
S-1000	Stein Song (University of Maine)		3.00
S-370	Storm, The	Weber	2.75
S-218	Stradella Overture	Flotow	2.75
S-138	Sunrise and You	Penn	3.00
S-474	Swanee River	Foster	2.75
S-214	Swallow, The	Serradell	2.75
S- 27	Swan, The	Saint-Saens	2.75
S- 11	Sweet Forget-Me-Not	Miles	3.00
S-625	Sweet Dreams	Friml	3.00
S-472	Swing Low Sweet Chariot		2.75
S-600	Symphonie No. 6 (Pathetique), Op. 74	Tschaikowsky	2.75
S-1010	Tannhäuser Overture	Wagner	4.50
S-714	Thousand And One Nights Waltz	Strauss, Op. 346	3.50
S-385	Titl's Serenade	Titl	3.00
S-289	To A Violet	Zamecnik	3.00
S-119	Toreador Song	Bizet	2.75
S-390	To Spring	Grieg	3.00
S-466	Träumerei	Schumann	2.75
S-996	Trois Chorals For The Organ	Franck	4.00
S- 13	Tulips	Miles	2.50
S- 25	Under The Leaves	Thome	2.75
S-151	Unfinished Symphony	Schubert	3.75
S-886	Vacant Chair, The	C. F. Roat	2.75
S-142	Vagabond King, The, Selection	Friml	3.75
S-829	Valse	Brahms	2.50
S- 22	Valse Charme	Roberts	3.25
S- 9	Valse Danseuse	Miles	3.25
S- 7	Valse Lucille	Friml	3.00
S-414	Valse Parisienne	Roberts	3.25
S-215	Vanity	Jackson	3.00
S-494	Vision	Rheinberger	3.00
S-365	Volga Boatman, The, Folk Song		3.00
S-786	Walther's Prize Song	Wagner	2.75
S-104	Washington Post	J. P. Sousa	3.00
S-558	Wedding Of The Winds	Hall	3.50
S-990	When You're Away (The Only Girl)	Herbert	3.00

CLASSIC AND POPULAR MUSIC

No.	Name	Composer	Price
S-135	Where My Caravan Has Rested	Teschemacher & Lohr	3.00
S-112	Where The River Shannon Flows	Russell	3.00
S-259	Whispering Hope	Alice Hawthorne	3.25
S-550	Will You Remember?	Romberg	3.00
S-998	Will O' The Wisp	Nevin	3.50
S-513	Woodland Echoes	Friml	2.75
S-676	World Is Waiting For The Sunrise, The	Lockhart & Seitz	3.00
S-549	Your Eyes Have Told Me So	Blaufuss	2.50
S-110	Zenda Waltzes	Witmark	3.50

CLASSIC AND POPULAR PROGRAMS

(These rolls play approximately thirty minutes)

S-5028

Intro.:

Name	Composer	Price
The Firefly, Selection	Friml	
Chocolate Soldier, Selection No. 1	Strauss	
Chocolate Soldier, Selection No. 2	Strauss	
Fortune Teller, Selection	Herbert	7.00

S-5038

Intro.:

Name	Composer	Price
Barcarolle (Tales of Hoffmann)	Offenbach	
Fifth Nocturne	Leybach	
Blue Danube Waltz	Strauss	
Andante Cantabile (Quartet in D Major)	Tschaikowsky	
Thousand And One Nights Waltz	Strauss	
Serenade	Gounod	
Andante (Orfeo)	Gluck	$7.00

S-5039

Intro.:

Name	Composer	Price
Largo (New World Symphony)	Dvorak	
Simple Aveu	Thome	
Vision	Rheinberger	
Andante (Violin Concerto)	Mendelssohn	
I Love You Truly	Bond	
Chant Sans Paroles, Op. 2, No. 3	Tschaikowsky	
Spring Song	Mendelssohn	7.00

S-5040

Intro.:

Name	Composer	Price
Salut d'Amour	Elgar	
Artist's Life	Strauss	
Dear Love, My Love	Friml	
Andante	Bartlett, Op. 205	
Sing Me To Sleep	Greene	
Estudiantina	Waldteufel	
Calm As The Night	Bohm	7.00

S-5041

Intro.:

Name	Composer	Price
At Dawning	Cadman	
Nocturne, Op. 9, No. 2	Chopin	
Absent	Metcalf	
Can't Yo' Heah Me Callin' Caroline	Roma	
Elegie	Massenet	
When You Look In The Heart Of A Rose		
A Cloister Scene	Mason	
Sometime	Friml	7.00

CLASSIC AND POPULAR PROGRAMS

(These rolls play approximately thirty minutes)

S-5042

Victor Herbert Favorites

Intro.:
March Of The Toys
Love Is The Best Of All
Badinage
Kiss Me Again
Fleurette
I'm Falling In Love With Someone
Gypsy Love Song
Al Fresco
Ah, Sweet Mystery Of Life 7.00

S-5043

Victor Herbert Favorites

Intro.:
Absinthe Frappe
Serenade
Because You're You
Punchinello
When You're Away
Love Is Tyrant
In The Isle Of Dreams
All For You 7.00

S-5044

Intro.:
Song Of India.......... Rimsky-Korsakov
Idylle .... Merkel
The Fountain .... Miles
Berceuse........... Schytte, Op. 26, No. 7
Good-bye .... Tosti
In Arcadia .... Sellars
Hymn To The Sun...... Rimsky-Korsakov
Cavatina .... Raff
Il Bacio, Waltz .... Arditi 7.00

S-5045

Intro.:
Message Of The Violet........... Luders
Ballet Music From Faust......... Gounod
Musetta's Song .... Puccini
To A Violet .... Zamecnik
Song Of Love .... Friml
Dawn .... Nevin
Will You Remember............ Romberg
L'Amour-Toujours-L'Amour .... Friml 7.00

S-5046

Intro.:
Song Of Songs.................. Moya
Nola .... Arndt
Huguette Waltz .... Friml
Cocoanut Dance .... Herman
Your Eyes Have Told Me So..... Blaufuss
Bubbling Spring .... Rive-King
Alice Blue Gown .... Tierney
Dancing Leaves .... Miles
Deep In My Heart, Dear........ Romberg 7.00

CLASSIC AND POPULAR PROGRAMS

(These rolls play approximately thirty minutes)

S-5047

Intro.:
Danny Boy .... Weatherly
Garden Dance .... Vargas
Kiss Me Again .... Herbert
Parade Of The Wooden Soldiers..... Jessel
Somewhere A Voice Is Calling........ Tate
Serenata .... Moszokowski
Zenda Waltzes .... Witmark
The World Is Waiting For The Sunrise.... 7.00

S-5048

Intro.:
Schubert's Serenade .... Schubert-Liszt
My Heart At Thy Sweet Voice.. Saint-Saens
Cloister Scene .... Mason 7.00

S-5049

Intro.:
Liebestraum .... Liszt
Evening Star .... Wagner
The Swan .... Saint-Saens
In A Monastery Garden......... Ketelbey 7.00

S-5050

Intro.:
The Old Refrain .... Kreisler
Träumerei .... Schumann
Reve Angelique .... Rubinstein
Meditation (Thais) .... Massenet
Angel's Serenade .... Braga 7.00

Special attention is called to the fact that any number of single rolls totaling not more than a half hour of playing time may, upon request, be joined together to make a continuous roll, and that such roll may be obtained at the cost of the individual selections.

DANCE MUSIC

The following rolls are specially arranged in waltz and fox trot tempo

No.	Name	Composer	Price
S-1017	Japansy, Waltz		$2.75
S-1018	The Skaters, Waltz		2.75
S-1011	Dancing With Tears In My Eyes		2.75
S-1012	Anchors Aweigh		2.75
S-1013	Humoresque	Dvorak	3.00
S-1020	Kiss Waltz		2.75
S-1021	Betty Coed		2.75
S-1022	Merry Widow Waltzes		2.75
S-1023	Blue Danube Waltz	Strauss	2.75
S-1024	Danube Waves	Ivanovici	2.75
S-1025	Missouri Waltz		2.75
S-1026	Over The Waves	Rosas	2.75
S-1027	Our Director, March		2.75
S-1028	The Invincible Eagle, March		3.00
S-1029	Spirit Of Independence, March		3.50

Denison Brothers (not to be confused with the Dennison Organ Pipe Company) supplied many of the stop keys used by organ builders in the first decades of the twentieth century. Most of the major builders, including Wurlitzer, were customers of this firm at one time or another. The company remained in business until 1943 when it was acquired by the Hagerstown Engraving Company of Hagerstown, Maryland. In 1950 the company became the Hagerstown Engraving & Stamping Co. and in 1954 the name was shortened to the acronym Hesco.

In the early 1950s the organ engraving portion of the business was taken over by Max Mogensen who today operates the business as Hesco, Inc. Mr. Mogensen's grandfather was born in Bornholm, Denmark, the home town of M. P. Moller, so there is a lineage of organ blood in the family.[1] The Hesco firm today, as did Denison in the 1920s, supplies many American organ builders with engraving work of highest quality. Mr. Mogensen's son Rick Mogensen manages the organ engraving department and has kept abreast of contemporary technology by installing computer-operated engraving equipment to enhance the quality of the company's products even further.

In 1970 Hesco made duplicates of the original templates used to engrave stop keys in the Wurlitzer factory.[2] Since that time, many contemporary enthusiasts have availed themselves of the opportunity to outfit their restored consoles with brand new stop keys having authentic Wurlitzer engraving. Although Wurlitzer engraving is still done by manual labor, most other work is now done on computer-controlled engraving machines.

This advertisement was a staple in The Diapason *for many years.*

THOMSON ENGRAVING COMPANY

MANUFACTURERS AND ENGRAVERS

STOP KEYS, NAME PLATES, TABLETS, PISTONS ETC.

NYACK, NEW YORK

The Thomson company was a small fish in a big pond dominated by larger firms such as Denison Bros., Gottfried and Organ Supply. One of Thomson's clients was the United States Pipe Organ Company, who purchased their stop keys. The Thomson business was acquired in 1929 by the W. H. Reisner Mfg. Co., Inc., of Hagerstown, Maryland.[1]

ADDENDA TO VOLUME I

This section contains material which came to light following the publication of *Encyclopedia of the American Theatre Organ*, Volume I.

AEOLIAN

This excellent series of photographs taken in the Aeolian factory came from the collection of Jim Crank.

(above) Engineering and drafting department. (upper right) Metal pipe shop. (right) Racking pipes.

Aeolian factory employees pose for a photograph in 1928.

Console assembly department photographed March 21, 1925. The four-manual console under construction was Aeolian opus 1542 for the Assa Candler residence in Atlanta, Georgia.

Wood pipe shop. Note that several of the same ranks were made at one time as a manufacturing economy.

Wiring the relay for a highly unified organ destined for a theatre.

Action assembly department.

BARTON

Warren G. Maxcy, financier and president of the Bartola Musical Instrument Company.

A very dapper Dan Barton photographed in 1929.

A fascinating view of the huge Chicago Stadium under construction shows the concrete pads in the ceiling on which the organ will be erected. The blower and relay rooms will occupy the center pad; the four organ chambers (only three of which are visible here) flank it on all sides. Concrete catwalks allow access to all parts of the organ—if one isn't afraid of 100′ heights!

The Chicago Stadium console opens for ease of servicing.

The world's largest organ blower begins its ascent into the loft of the Chicago Stadium. Standing on the far left is Ralph Waldo Emerson, the first organist at the Stadium. To his left is Walter Gollnick, Barton's chief of installations.

GSCHOFF

WILSON WILL BE AT THE ORGAN

This builder came to the author's attention over a year after the publication of *Encyclopedia of the American Theatre Organ,* Volume I. Mr. Gschoff apparently did some business in northern California in the early 1920s; further information concerning him has proved quite elusive. The author first saw the name Gschoff in a 1927 list of theatre organs maintained by the Schoenstein firm in San Francisco. This list disclosed Gschoff organs in the T&D (California) Theatre in Salinas and in the California (Fox) (U.A.) Theatre in Richmond.

California organ historian Tom DeLay produced a 1921 newspaper article with a photo of the Salinas T&D console. Mr. DeLay also recalled some details of the Richmond California Theatre instrument which had been inspected by a friend of his, Francis Aebi, some years ago. Mr Aebi confirmed that it was indeed a Gschoff organ. He recalled that the console was quite crude and that the chests were of both early Robert-Morton and early Wurlitzer manufacture, indicating that the instrument was assembled largely from parts of older organs.[1]

Historian Judd Walton next provided the author with a few more details including the builder's full name, Charles Gschoff (pronounced "chef"). Judd revealed that Leland Jacobus, one of the founders of the American Photo Player Co., was a friend of Gschoff and that he helped install the 2/14 instrument at the California Theatre in Richmond.[2]

Charles "Doc" Wilson opens the Gschoff organ in the T&D (California) Theatre, Salinas, in 1921. The photo's heading can be quite amusing; if read just right it says "Wilson will beat the organ."

LENOIR

SYMPHONIC ORCHESTRAL UNIT
BUILT BY
BENJ. F. LENOIR.
PHILADELPHIA, PENN.

Nameplate from the 3/10 LeNoir in the Lyric Theatre, Camden, New Jersey.

OPUS LIST CORRECTIONS & ADDITIONS TO VOLUME I

Most of the following entries represent additional information to the opus lists in Volume I of *Encyclopedia of the American Theatre Organ,* such as organ sizes, opus numbers and blower numbers which were not known previously. A few of the entries correct errors of fact, however. These have asterisks to assist those readers who wish to make corrections in the appropriate pages of Volume I. The author encourages all readers to correct these factual errors so that the record will be as historically accurate as possible for future readers.

AMERICAN MASTER

West Hoboken, NJ .... Now known as Union City.

ARTCRAFT

Pasadena, CA .... Washington (Cinema 21) Th.

AUSTIN

*page 46: Beverly, MA .... Larcom Th.
page 46: Boston, MA .... Park (State) Th.
*page 46: Kansas City, MO ... Liberty (Roxy) Th.
page 46: Kansas City, MO .... Newman (Paramount) Th.
page 46: Troy, NY .... Mark Strand (Troy) Th.
opus 539 .... Park (State) Th., Boston, MA .... See opus 708.
*opus 661 .... Larcom Th., Beverly, MA
opus 708 .... Park (State) Th., Boston, MA .... Additions to opus 539.
*opus 765 .... Liberty (Roxy) Th.,
opus 828 .... Newman (Paramount) Th.
opus 876 .... Ware (Cabot Street Cinema) Th.
opus 1065 .... Mark Strand (Troy) Th. .... 7" wind.

BALCOM & VAUGHAN

*Portland, OR .... KGW/KEX Radio .... Delete "destroyed by fire in 1946."
Portland, OR .... KOIN Radio .... Robert Morton from Olympic Th., Seattle, Washington.
Everett, WA .... Rollerfair Rink .... Moved from Playland Rink, Seattle, Washington.
Renton, WA .... Maple Leaf Tavern .... Kimball from Trianon Ballroom, Seattle, Washington.
Seattle, WA .... Playland Rink .... 2/5, moved in 1956 to Rollerfair Rink, Everett, Washington.

BARCKHOFF

*Pittsburgh, PA .... Delete entire entry.

BARTON

Champaign .... Rialto Th. .... Moved in 1986 to Tivoli Th., Downers Grove, Illinois.
*Chicago, IL .... Crystal Th. .... 3/?, 1920, not a divided manual console.
*Chicago, IL .... Riviera Th.
*Chicago, IL .... WBBM Radio .... 2/?, 192?, moved to new studio in 1926 with blower 18653.
*Chicago, IL .... WBBM Radio .... 3/10, delete "and enlarged to 3/14 . . ."
*Rockford, IL .... Orpheum Th. .... 192?
Springfield, IL .... 240 organ.
Cedar Rapids, IA .... Iowa (Cedar Rapids Community) Th.
*Detroit, MI .... Birmingham Th. .... Should be in city of Birmingham, Michigan.
Detroit, MI .... Add: Conservatory of Music .... 2/3, 192?, practice organ.
Detroit, MI .... Add: Olympia Stadium .... 2/8, 1925, blower 16737, 5 hp, 18" wp.
3/14, 1935, blower 22890, 7½ hp, 13" wp, additions from WBBM Radio, Chicago, Illinois.
*Flint, MI .... Ritz Th. .... Opened as Globe Theatre.
*Jackson, MI .... Delete entry.
*Kalamazoo, MI .... Bijou (Majestic) (Capitol) Th. .... 3/11, 1924, 108 organ.
*Kalamazoo, MI .... Capitol Th. .... Delete entry.
*Wyandotte, MI .... Delete entry.
*Ypsilanti, MI .... Delete entry.
*Dallas, TX .... Capitol Th. .... 2/?.
*Dallas, TX .... Midway Th. .... Moved in 1931.
*Denison, TX .... Delete entry.
Newport News, VA .... Moved in 1968 to Virginia Theatre, Alexandria, Virginia.
Baraboo, WI .... Ringling Th. .... 289 organ.
Janesville, WI .... Jeffery Th. .... 2/8.
Madison, WI .... Eastwood Th. .... Built by Wangerin—opus 369.
*Madison, WI .... Majestic Th. .... Second entry should be: New Madison Th., 2/?, 1923, blower 15158, 3 hp, 5"&10" wp, opened as Grand Theatre.
Milwaukee, WI .... Garfield Th. .... 253 organ.
Milwaukee, WI .... Hollywood (Coronet) Th.
Milwaukee, WI .... Idle Hour (Alamo) Th.
Milwaukee, WI .... Miller (Towne) Th.
Milwaukee, WI .... Murray (East) Th.
Milwaukee, WI .... National Th. .... Moved in 1984 to Wilshire Ebell Theatre, Los Angeles, California.
Milwaukee, WI .... Princess Th. .... Opened as Grand Theatre.
Milwaukee, WI .... Savoy (Oasis) Th.

Milwaukee, WI ....Studio (Ogden) Th.
*Milwaukee, WI ....Teutonia Th. ....Correct theatre names are: Milwaukee (Capitol) (Ritz) (National) (Apollo) Theatre.
*Milwaukee, WI ....WTMJ Radio ....2/7, 243 organ.
Racine, WI ....Crown Th. ....201 organ.

BENNETT

*Freeport, IL ....Correct theatre names are: Lindo (Freeport) (Lindo) Th.
Rock Island, IL ....Fort Armstrong (Fort) Th.
*Dallas, TX ....KRLD Radio

ESTEY

*page 128: Los Angeles, CA ..West Coast Th......................Delete entry.
page 128: Riverside, CA ......Loring Opera House (Golden State) Th.
page 128, add: Florence, KS ..Mayflower Th......................Unknown opus number.
*page 128: Boston, MA ....Dudley Th.........................Is actually in Roxbury, Massachusetts.
page 128: Boston, MA ....Modern (Mayflower) Th.
page 128: Boston, MA ....Add: Old South Th. ....Unknown opus number.
*page 128: Boston, MA ....Shawmut (Roxie) Th. ....Is actually in Roxbury, Massachusetts.
page 128: Boston, MA ....Star (Rialto) Th.
*page 128: Jamaica Plain, MA ....Jamaica Th. is correct theatre name.
page 128: Portland, OR ....Irvington (Do Thanh) (Irvington) Th.
opus 1241: ....Modern (Mayflower) Th.
opus 1525 ....Roxbury, MA
*opus 1600 ....Shawmut (Roxie) Th., Roxbury, MA
opus 1665 ....Loring Opera House (Golden State) Th.
opus 1777 ....Ontario, CA
opus 1789 ....Star (Rialto) Th.
*opus 1864 ....Correct entry is: Glendale Th., Glendale, CA, 3/27, 1920, blower 11454, 5 hp, 6″ wp.
*opus 1966 ....Jamaica Th.
*opus 2214 ....Delete second entry, "West Coast Th., . . ."
opus 2277 ....Irvington (Do Thanh) (Irvington) Th.
*opus 3037 ....Correct blower number is 24984.
page 131 ....Add: Florence, KS, Mayflower Th., 2/11, tubular pneumatic.
page 131 ....Add: Boston, MA, Old South Th.

FRAZEE

Boston, MA ....Fenway (Berklee Performance Center) Th.
Boston, MA ....St. James (Uptown) Th..............Add: 1915, blower 6697.
*Boston, MA ....South End (Loew's New Columbia) Th., 1917, blower 8213.
Roslindale, MA ....Rialto Th. ....Opened as Gorman's Theatre.

GOTTFRIED

*Chicago, IL ....Avon Th. ....Delete entry.
*Philadelphia, PA ....Bronson (Byrd) Th.

GRIFFITH-BEACH

Elizabeth, NJ ....Masonic Temple 3/22
Newark, NJ ....Shrine Auditorium (Mosque Th.) (Symphony Hall)
West Hoboken, NJ ....Now known as Union City.

HILLGREEN-LANE

page 165: Shreveport, LA .....Saenger (Capri) Th.
page 165: Detroit, MI ....Washington (Fox Washington) Th.
*page 166: Dallas, TX ....Columbia Th........................Opus 636.
*page 166: Dallas, TX ....W. D. Neville's Th. ....Correct name is Parkway Theatre.
*opus 309 ....Parkway Th.
opus 342 ....Saenger (Capri) Th.
opus 385 ....Washington (Fox Washington) Th.
*opus 402 ....Strand Th.
opus 551 ....Saenger (Capri) Th.
*opus 636 ....Columbia Th.
*opus 911 ....2/3

HINNERS

Aurora, IL ....Tracker action.
Springfield, IL ....Vaudette (Lyric) (Tivoli) Th.
Milwaukee, WI ....Princess Th. ....Opened as Grand Theatre.

HUTCHINGS

*Boston, MA ....Eagle Th. ....Is actually in Roxbury, Massachusetts.

KILGEN

*page 198: Birmingham, AL...Pantages Th. ....Opus 3934.
page 198: Chicago, IL ....Kenwood (Ken) Th.
*page 198: Brazil, IN ....Lark Th.
*page 199: Waltham, MA .....Embassy Th.
*page 199: Laurel, MS ....Strand Th.
page 199, add: Union City, NJColonial Th.........................Unknown opus number.
page 199: Portland, OR ....Capitol (Blue Mouse) Th.

page 200: Milwaukee, WI .....Ritz (Villa) Th.
opus 1628 ....Blower 6630.
opus 3054 ....Blower 11617.
opus 3126 ....Blower 13529.
opus 3515 ....Kenwood (Ken) Th.
opus 3615 ....Ritz (Villa) Th.
opus 3685 ....See opus 4145.
*opus 3742 ....Strand Th.
opus 3761 ....Taken in on trade from Janet Theatre.
opus 3915 ....With Mills violin.
*opus 3934 ....Pantages Th.
*opus 4007 ....Embassy Th.
*opus 4155 ....Lark Th.
opus 4157 ....Capitol (Blue Mouse) Th.
opus 5281 ....Blower 25296.
opus 5465 ....Blower 25433.
opus 5769 ....Blower 25559.
opus 6013 ....Blower 25777.
page 205: Minneapolis, MN ...Dyckman Hotel 2/4
page 205: Kansas City, MO ...Empress Th.........................Moved in 1922 to Empress Theatre, St. Louis, Missouri.
page 205: St. Louis, MO ......Old Grand Central Th..............Moved in 1924 to Cinderella Theatre, St. Louis, Missouri.
page 205: St. Louis, MO ......Pershing Th........................Moved in 1921 to Arsenal Theatre, St. Louis, Missouri.
page 205, add: Union City, NJColonial Th.........................1928.

KIMBALL

*Birmingham, AL ....Delete entry.
Los Angeles, CA ....Forum Th. ....Moved in 1931 to Western (Wiltern) Theatre, Los Angeles, California.
*Oakland, CA ....Franklin Th.........................Located at 1438 Franklin.
*San Francisco, CA ....Haight Th.
San Francisco, CA ....Silver Palace (Hub) Th.............Opened as Globe Theatre.
San Jose, CA ....T & D (California) (Mission) Th.
*Wilmington, DE ....Arcadia Th. ....3/10, 1921, blower 12188, 5 hp, 8″ wp, KPO 6585.
*Wilmington, DE ....Strand Th. ....Delete entry.
*Washington, DC ....Ambassador Th. 2/7
*Washington, DC ....Cosmopolitan Th....................Delete entry.
*Miami, FL ....Miami Beach Pier Th. ....KPO 6916.
*Chicago, IL ....Areon Th. ....Delete entry.
Chicago, IL ....Avon Th. ....2/7, 1914, blower C464, ½ hp, 5″ wp; new blower 5808, ½ hp.
Chicago, IL ....Add: Bugg Th.
Chicago, IL ....Add: Kenwood (Ken) Th. ....Moved in 1926 to Marlowe Theatre, Chicago, Illinois.
Chicago, IL ....Add: Milford Th.
Chicago, IL ....Regent Th. ....1926, KPO 6953.
Chicago, IL ....Wabash Th. ....KPO 6773.
*Chicago, IL ....WGN Radio ....1935, blowers 25407 & 25411, additions to 3/7 Wurlitzer.
Melrose Park, IL ....Melrose Park (Rose) Th.
Libertyville, IL...2/4
*Evansville, IN ....New Grand Th. ....1925.
*South Bend, IN ....Studebaker Opera House ....Correct name is Oliver Opera House.
*Pittsburg, KS ....Delete entry.
*Wichita, KS ....Delete entry.
Baltimore, MD ....New Belnord Th....................KPO 6504.
Baltimore, MD ....Rivoli Th...........................Opened as Wilson Theatre.
*Boston, MA ....Columbia Th........................Delete entry.
*Boston, MA ....Fenway Th. ....Delete entry.
*Boston, MA ....Globe (Center) (Pagoda Center) Th.
*Boston, MA ....St. James Th........................Delete entry.
*Salem, MA ....New Plaza Th. ....Delete entry.
Adrian, MI ....2/10.
Detroit, MI...................Add: Elks Temple 2/7
*Detroit, MI...................Loop Th.............................2/5.
*Jackson, MI, correct entry: ...Orpheum (Capitol) Th..............1916, blower D739, 1 hp, 5½″ wp.
2/7, 1928, blower 21564, KPO 7020.
Minneapolis, MN ....Auditorium (Lyceum) Th. ....4/58.
Minneapolis, MN ....Curtis Hotel ....KPO 6560.
St. Louis, MO ....Orpheum (American) Th.
Omaha, NE...................Sun (State) Th.
*Atlantic City, NJ ....Stanley (Roxy) Th. ....15 hp, 10″&15″ wp.
Newark, NJ ....Family Th. ....2/10.
Woodcliffe, NJ ....Broadway (Astor) Th................City now known as North Bergen.
Cleveland, OH ....Hilliard Square Th. ....Actually located in Lakewood, Ohio.
Marion, OH ....Marion Th...........................3/8, moved in 1930 to WAPI Radio, Birmingham, AL.
*Springfield, OH..............Unidentified theatre is indeed Sun's Regent Theatre.
Bristol, PA ....5 hp, 10″ wp.
*Bryn Mawr, PA ....Bryn Mawr (Seville) Th.
Lansdowne, PA ....5 hp, 10″ wp.
Philadelphia, PA ....Add: Amber (Castle) Th. ....1920, opened as Amber Pastime Theatre.
Philadelphia, PA ....Avon Th. ....1923, blower 15119.
Philadelphia, PA ....Bell (Benson) Th....................Located at 6338 Woodland.
*Philadelphia, PA ....Milgram Th.........................Delete entry.
Philadelphia, PA ....Regent (Film Guild Cinema) (Cinema Art) (Hollywood) (Europa) (Studio) Th., 2 hp, 5½″ wp, moved from Family Theatre, Newark, New Jersey.
*Philadelphia, PA ....Uptown (Nutec) Th. ....3/18, KPO 7048.
*Philadelphia, PA ....Wynne Th. ....3/?, 1927, blower 20674, 10″ wp, KPO 6966.
Pittsburgh, PA ....Stanley Th. ....KPO 6946; parts later appeared in Warner (Center) (Grand) Theatre, Mil-

waukee, Wisconsin in 1931.
Scranton, PA ....Strand Th. ....2/11, later moved to Binghamton (Capri) (Forum) Theatre, Binghamton, New York and enlarged to 2/12.
*Wilkes-Barre, PA ....Capitol Th. ....3/8, 1920, blower 11189, 3 hp, 8″ wp, KPO 6538.
*Wilkes-Barre, PA ....Metropolitan Th. ....Delete entry.
*Dallas, TX ....Delete entry.
*Houston, TX ....Delete entry.
San Antonio, TX ....Majestic (State) Th.
*Atlantic City, VA ....Delete entry.
Aberdeen, WA ....Moved in 1944 to Ice Arena Rink, Portland, Oregon, by Balcom & Vaughan.
Seattle, WA ....Arabian Th. ....KPO 6840.
*Seattle, WA ....Capitol Th. ....2/11.
Seattle, WA ....Grand Th. ....Moved in 1931 to KOL Radio, Seattle, Washington, by Balcom & Vaughan.
Seattle, WA ....Olympic (Woodland) Th. ....Moved in 1931 to Trianon Ballroom, Seattle, Washington.
*Seattle, WA ....Pantages Th. ....Delete entry.
Madison, WI ....Fuller Opera House (Parkway) Th.
Madison, WI ....Orpheum Th. ....KPO 6957.
Milwaukee, WI ....Warner (Center) (Grand) Th.

KOHL

Rochester, NY ....Lyndhurst (World) Th.
Rochester, NY ....Palace (Sun) Th.
Rochester, NY ....Princess (Rexy) Th.
*Rochester, NY ....Stanley Th. ....Correct name is Stahley Th.

LENOIR

add: Camden, NJ ....Lyric Th. ....3/10.

LINK

*Los Angeles, CA ....Rampart Th. ....Delete entry.

LOUISVILLE

*opus 532 ....La Rose Th., Jeffersonville, IN.
*opus 536 ....2/5.
opus 234x ....Later moved to Rivoli Theatre, Indianapolis, Indiana.

MAAS

Beverly Hills, CA ....Wurlitzer opus 473.
San Luis Obispo, CA ....2/7, Wurlitzer opus 260 plus clarinet, tibia and oboe horn.

MARR & COLTON

Fullerton, CA ....Alician Court (Fox) Th.
New Britain, CT ....3/?.
New London, CT ....Capitol Th. ....Moved in 1978 to Jane Pickens Theatre, Newport, Rhode Island.
Bethesda, MD ....Hiser (Baronet) Th.
*Roxbury, MA ....Puritan (Teatro Americano) Th. .....Actually located in Boston, Massachusetts.
Bay City, MI ....Add: unidentified th. ....2/7.
Bay City, MI ....West Side Th. ....2/4.
Charlotte, MI ....2/6.
Detroit, MI ....East End Th. ....3/9.
Detroit, MI ....Ferry Field (Beacon) Th. ....2/6.
Detroit, MI ....Gladwin (Booth) Th. ....3/8, opened as Gladwin Park (Aladdin) Theatre.
Detroit, MI ....Grosse Point Park Th. ....2/?.
*Detroit, MI ....Martha Washington (Campau) Th. ...Actually located in Hamtramck, Michigan.
Grosse Ile, MI ....Add: Myrtle E. Ubsell residence .....?/15, 1929.
*Minneapolis, MN ....McPhail School of Music ....Delete second entry; there was only one organ.
*Brooklyn, NY ....Dyker (RKO Dyker) Th. ....3/11, blower 0415B, 7½ hp, 12″ wp.
*Brooklyn, NY ....Shore Road Th. ....2/6, 1928, blower Q23B, 3 hp, 9½″ wp.
Rochester, NY ....Rochester Th. ....Later moved to Oriental Theatre, Sherwood, Oregon.
*Rochester, NY ....Strand (Happy Hour) Th. ....Enlarged to 4/18 and later moved to Family Theatre, Rochester, New York.
Syracuse NY ....Regent Th. ....Opened as Syracuse Theatre.
*Syracuse, NY ....Temple Th. ....Delete entry.
*Watertown, NY ....Strand Th.
*Bismarck, ND ....Eltinge (Bismarck) Th.
Toledo, OH ....Rivoli Th. ....4/23, moved in 1985 to Ohio Theatre, Toledo, Ohio.
Bellevue, PA ....Bellevue Th.
Nesquehoning, PA ....Newton Th.
Philadelphia, PA ....Rivoli Th. ....Opened as 52nd Street Theatre.
*Spokane, WA ....Hippodrome Th. ....Delete entry.
Wheeling, WV ....Capitol (Capitol City Jamboree Hall) Th.

MIDMER-LOSH

Hempstead, NY ....Rivoli (Adelphi-Calderone) Th.
New York, NY ....Adelphi (Yorktown) (New Yorker) Th.

MOLLER

page 402, add: Birmingham,
AL ....Temple Th. ....Opus 3939.
*page 402: Oakland, CA ......Fox Oakland (Orpheum) Th.
page 402, add: San Francisco,
CA ....Moller Studio ....Opus 5213.
page 402, add: Stockton, CA ..KGDM Radio ....Opus 5213.

page 402, add: Stockton, CA . .E. F. Peffer residence ....Opus 5886.
page 402: Newark, DE ....State Th.
page 402: Washington, DC ....Avenue Grand (Capitol Hill) Th.
page 402: Chicago, IL ....Commodore (Cine Oympia) Th.
*page 402: Richmond, VA ....Murette Th.
page 403: Boston, MA ....Loew's State (Donnelly Memorial) (Back Bay) Th.
*page 403: Boston, MA ....Olympia Th.........................Correct names are: Scollay Square Olympia (Scollay Square) Th., opus 1601.
*page 403: Boston, MA ....Rialto (Rivoli) Th. ....Actually located in Roxbury, Massachusetts.
*page 403: Cambridge, MA ...Central Square Th...................Opus 2566.
page 403: Detroit, MI ....Washington (Fox Washington) Th.
page 403: Flint, MI ....Globe (Ritz) Th.
page 403: Astoria, NY ....Steinway (Astoria) Th.
*page 404: Spartanburg, NC ....Actually located in South Carolina.
page 404: Ashland, PA ....Roxy Th............................Opus 5151.
page 404: Bristol, PA ....Forrest (Grand) Th.
page 405: Philadelphia, PA ....Belvedere (Chestnut Hill) (Hill) Th.
page 405: Providence, RI .....Strand (Paramount) Th.
page 405: Norfolk, VA ....Granby (Lee) Th.
page 405: Milwaukee, WI .....Parkway (Rock River) Th.
*opus 1601 ....Scollay Square Olympia (Scollay Square) Th.
opus 1939 ....Strand (Paramount) Th.
opus 2237 ....Granby (Lee) Th.
opus 2267 ....Strand (Paramount) Th.
*opus 2416 ....Belvedere (Chestnut Hill) (Hill) Th.
*opus 2548 ....See opus 2675.
*opus 2566 ....Central Square Th.
opus 2692 ....Forrest (Grand) Th.
opus 2739 ....Washington (Fox Washington) Th.
*opus 2741 ....Fox Oakland (Orpheum) Th. ....Located at 1730 Broadway.
*opus 2791 ....Murette Th.
opus 2888 ....See opus 4551 and 4318.
opus 2893 ....Globe (Ritz) Th.
opus 2921 ....Avenue Grand (Capitol Hill) Th.
*opus 2980 ....Loew's State (Donnelly Memorial) (Back Bay) Th., 3/16.
opus 3140 ....Later moved to Hippodrome Theatre, Los Angeles, California.
opus 3191 ....Parkway (Rock River) Th.
opus 3243 ....Commodore (Cine Olympia) Th.
opus 3450 ....Steinway (Astoria) Th.
add: opus 3939 ....Temple Th., Birmingham, AL ....4/46, 1924, $27,000.00; blower M107B, 7½ hp, 6"&10" wp for main organ; blower M108B, 7½ hp, 5"&10"&15" wp for solo/echo organ.
opus 3990 ....Strand (Paramount) Th.
*opus 4527 ....Roxbury, MA.
opus 5151 ....Roxy Th.
add: opus 5213 ....Moller Studio, San Francisco, CA ...3/7, 1928, blower Q418B, 7½ hp, 10" wp, style 70, sold in 1934 for $2,500 to KGDM Radio, Stockton, California.
opus 5337 ....State Th.
add: opus 5886 ....E. F. Peffer residence, Stockton, CA .2/8, 1931, $4,900.00, blower S619B, 1½ hp, 5" wp, with Artiste player and horseshoe console.
*opus 6184 ....Spartanburg, SC.
opus 11433 ....Resold to New Tokyo Beer Hall for $320,000!

ERRATA FROM VOLUME I

page 6: Here and throughout the book the name Vaughan of Balcom & Vaughan is consistently misspelled.

page 28: L. L. Alnett & Son is the correct full name of this builder.

page 51: Upper right photo caption should read: The Kimball console was originally in the WGN radio studios in Chicago.

page 76: In photo caption, 24 should be 25.

page 78: In photo caption, division III should be division IV; trumpet should be English horn; and tibia plena should be tibia molis.

page 79: In division III, the French horn has 61 pipes, for a divisional total of 706 pipes.

page 223: Lower right photo: The console is pictured as remodeled by Balcom & Vaughan.

page 234: Second column, line 10, "one" should be "a look-alike."

page 371: Upper right caption should read: Ray Sawyer plays the 3/18 Moller in the Los Angeles Hippodrome. In 1925 this organ was moved from Loew's State Theatre in Los Angeles when a new 3/11 Wurlitzer was purchased to replace it.

page 379: Upper left caption: Frederick Albert Hoschke should be Walter Smith.

page 383: Lower right photo caption should read: Ralph Barncord voices the Foort 16′ wood diaphone.

page 389: Left caption: John A. Davis, Jr. should be Frederick C. Mayer.

page 398: First line of caption should read: Fred Carty voices a 32′ violone for Trinity Methodist Church, Youngstown, Ohio.

page 429: Geneva: add page 421.

page 431: Smith-Geneva: add page 421.

page 431: Smith organs: add page 421.

FOOTNOTES

AUTOMATIC MUSICAL INSTRUMENT COMPANY

1. Automatic Musical Instrument Co., *History, Organization and Personnel of the Automatic Musical Instrument Co.* (Grand Rapids: Automatic Musical Instrument Co., 1930), p. 5.
2. Ibid., pp. 5-7.
3. Conversation with Hank Hoevenaar, March 5, 1986.

BAYLEY MANUFACTURING CO.

1. *The Diapason*, November 1919, p. 3.

B. F. BLOWER CO., INC.

1. *The Diapason*, November 1919, p. 3.
2. *The Diapason*, June 1921, p. 16.
3. B. F. company records.
4. Letter from Rosalie Luedtke, March 12, 1983.

JAMES H. BOLTON

1. Walter B. Trepte, "Jim Bolton, Organbuilder," *Post Horn*, Volume 4, #4, p. 20.

FREDERICK S. BROCKBANK

1. *The Diapason*, February 1916, p. 15.
2. *The Diapason*, May 1929, p. 10.

THE CARLTON SALES CO.

1. United States Pipe Organ Company factory records.

COMSTOCK, CHENEY & CO.

1. Conversation with Peter H. Comstock, September 17, 1987.
2. Ibid.
3. Ibid.

J. C. DEAGAN, INC.

1. *The Diapason*, June 1934, p. 4.
2. Ibid.
3. *The Moving Picture World*, April 27, 1912, p. 346.
4. *The New Grove Dictionary of American Music* (London: Macmillan Press Limited, 1986), Volume I, p. 591.
5. *The Diapason*, December 1927, p. 3.
6. Conversation with Kirk Collins, 1972.
7. Conversation with Robert Lent, February 1987.
8. *The New Grove*, Volume I, p. 591.
9. *The Diapason*, June 1934, p. 4.
10. Conversation with Lawrence Kerecman, January 1987.

DENISON BROTHERS

1. Conversation with Max Mogensen, July 1986.
2. *Theatre Organ*, August 1970, p. 24.

DENNISON ORGAN PIPE CO.

1. *The Tracker,* Volume 26, #1, p. 4.
2. *The Diapason,* November 1924, p. 36.
3. *The Diapason,* June 1922, p. 19.
4. *The Diapason,* April 1946, p. 2.
5. *The Diapason,* April 1943, p. 19.
6. Conversation with Sid Eaton, September 17, 1987.
7. Conversation with Don Warnock, September 17, 1987.

L. B. DOMAN CORPORATION

1. Conversation with Roger E. Morrison, December 19, 1988, quoting Doman factory records in his possession.

DURST, BOEGLE & CO.

1. *The Diapason,* November 1965, p. 34.
2. Organ Supply Industries, Inc., 1982 catalog, p. 3.
3. Personal notebook of Val P. Durst, dated 1912-1917.
4. *The Diapason,* April 1929, p. 10.
5. Organ Supply Industries, Inc., 1982 catalog, p. 3.

ERIE REED PIPE CO.

1. Letter from Henry Gottfried, August 31, 1983.
2. *The Diapason,* April 1921, p. 9.
3. Organ Supply Industries, 1982 catalog, p. 2.

EXCELSIOR DRUM WORKS

1. United States Pipe Organ Company factory records.

FIRMA ERNST DOELLING

1. Letter from Firma Ernst Doelling to Gutfleisch & Schopp, June 9, 1931.

A. GOTTFRIED CO.

1. Conversation with Henry Gottfried, March 31, 1983.
2. Robert Morton factory records.
3. *The Diapason,* November 1954, p. 4.
4. Letter from Henry Gottfried, August 31, 1983.
5. Conversation with Henry Gottfried.
6. Conversation with Randall Wagner, October 7, 1985.
7. *The Diapason,* November 1954, p. 4.
8. Conversation with Henry Gottfried.

GSCHOFF

1. Letter from Tom DeLay, October 21, 1986.
2. Conversation with Judd Walton, June 25, 1987.

GUTFLEISCH & SCHOPP

1. *The Diapason,* September 1954, p. 1.
2. Schopp factory records.
3. *The Diapason,* September 1954, p. 1.
4. Conversation with Bob Schopp, May 11, 1987.
5. Conversation with Robert Hillgreen, Jr., July 1982.
6. Schopp factory records.

EDWIN B. HEDGES

1. John Van Varick Elsworth, "The Story of a Great Voicer," *The Tracker,* Volume 16, #2, pp. 3-5.
2. Ibid., p. 5.
3. *The Diapason,* August 1919, p. 12.
4. Elsworth, op. cit., pp. 3-5.

HIRST ORGAN SPECIALTY COMPANY

1. *The Console,* November 1969, pp. 22-24.

E. R. HOWARD

1. *The American Organist,* April 1922, p. 146.
2. *The Diapason,* November 1921, p. 19.

ILLINOIS ORGAN SUPPLY CO.

1. Robert E. Coleberd, Jr., "Yesterday's Tracker: The Hinners Organ Story," *The American Organist,* September 1960, p. 11.

KAYLOR & CLARK

1. Letter from Harold Ocker to Peter Moller Daniels, December 3, 1983.

KINETIC ENGINEERING COMPANY

1. Laurence Elvin, *Organ Blowing, Its History and Development* (Lincoln, England: Laurence Elvin, 1971), p. 103.
2. Ibid., p. 104.
3. *The Diapason,* November 1941, p. 3.
4. *The Diapason,* August 1929, p. 6.
5. *The Diapason,* August 1919, p. 18.
6. Kinetic Engineering Company records.
7. Spencer Turbine Company records.
8. Conversation with M. P. Moller III, October 1982.

AUGUST A. KLANN

1. Letter from Paul Klann, July 6, 1981.
2. Letter from Robert G. Lent, August 1986.
3. *The Diapason,* February 1926, p. 4.
4. Letter from Robert G. Lent.
5. *The Diapason,* December 1928, p. 6.

KOHLER-LIEBICH COMPANY, INC.

1. *The Diapason,* September 1927, p. 8.

F. W. KREBS

1. Conversation with Henry Gottfried, March 31, 1983.

AUG. LAUKHUFF

1. 1928 Laukhuff catalog.
2. 1978 Laukhuff catalog.
3. Ibid.
4. 1928 Laukhuff catalog.
5. United States Pipe Organ Company factory records.

LEEDY MFG. CO., INC.

1. *The Music Trades,* October 1986, pp. 56-58.
2. *The New Grove Dictionary of American Music* (London: Macmillan Press Limited, 1986), Volume III, p. 24.
3. Conversation with William F. Ludwig, Jr., December 4, 1986.
4. Ibid.
5. Ibid.

LUDWIG & LUDWIG

1. William F. Ludwig, Sr., "The Ludwig Story," advertising pamphlet issued by Ludwig Industries, Inc., November 1984.
2. Ibid.
3. *The Music Trades,* October 25, 1986, p. 62.
4. William F. Ludwig, Sr., op. cit.
5. Ibid.
6. Ibid.

R. H. MAYLAND & SON

1. Conversation with Bob Lent, February 1987.

THE JAMES P. McGREECE COMPANY

1. United States Pipe Organ Company factory records.

G. MEIDINGER & CO.

1. Letter from U. P. Meidinger, November 1, 1984.
2. Ibid.

JEROME B. MEYER & SONS, INC.

1. Elizabeth Towne Schmitt, "Pipe Making—A Family Tradition," *The Tracker,* Volume 23, #2, pp. 18-20.
2. Ibid., p. 20.
3. Meyer factory records.
4. Ibid.

THE MOORE AND FISHER MANUFACTURING COMPANY

1. *Piano Trade Magazine,* February 1925, p. 61.

L. D. MORRIS & CO.

1. *The Diapason,* April 1945, p. 6.
2. *The Diapason,* August 1916, p. 1.

J. H. & C. S. ODELL & CO.

1. F. R. Webber, "A Century of Odell Organs," *The Tracker,* Volume 26, #4, pp. 8-12.
2. *The Diapason,* March 1920, p. 3.
3. Conversation with Anthony Meloni, December 11, 1985.

OLIVER ORGAN CO.

1. Conversation with Jack Bethards, June 4, 1984.

OPERATORS PIANO COMPANY

1. Q. David Bowers, *Encyclopedia of Automatic Musical Instruments* (Vestal, New York: Vestal Press, 1972), p. 542.

ORGAN SUPPLY CORPORATION

1. Organ Supply Corp. factory records.
2. Organ Supply Industries, 1982 catalog, pp. 2-3.
3. *The Diapason,* March 1936, p. 26.
4. *The Diapason,* November 1954, p. 4.
5. *The Diapason,* February 1955, p. 23.
6. Conversation with Henry Gottfried, March 31, 1983.
7. Organ Supply Industries, 1982 catalog, p. 3.
8. Ibid.
9. Conversation with Randy Wagner, October 25, 1983.
10. Letter from Fred Gluck, April 1985.
11. Letter from Harry H. Kugel to E. O. Shulenberger, July 27, 1938.
12. Conversation with Jim Ivanoff, March 31, 1986.
13. Conversation with Dennis Unks, October 6, 1985.

OTIS ELEVATOR COMPANY

1. Otis Elevator Company, *Tell Me About Elevators* (Farmington, Connecticut: Otis Elevator Company, 1974), pp. 7-8.
2. Ibid., p. 16.
3. Ibid., p. 37.
4. Ibid., p. 10.

PAGE ORGAN COMPANY

1. Conversation with Earl Beilharz, 1982.
2. *The Diapason,* March 1924, p. 7.
3. *The Diapason,* September 1924, p. 1.
4. Conversation with Earl Beilharz.
5. Ibid.
6. Ibid.
7. *The Diapason,* September 1934, p. 1.
8. Conversation with Roger Mumbrue, December 10, 1985.
9. Conversation with Earl Beilharz, October 7, 1984.

EARL D. PAVETTE

1. Balcom & Vaughan factory records.
2. Conversation with Bill Bunch, April 20, 1983.
3. Letter from Bill Bunch, Seattle, Washington, September 2, 1982.
4. Ibid.
5. Letter from Bill Bunch, July 5, 1982.

PELOUBET AND COMPANY

1. Robert E. Coleberd, Jr., "Philipp Wirsching, the Consummate Builder," *The American Organist,* October 1968, p. 29.
2. Conversation with Riley Daniels, October 1982.
3. Moller factory records.
4. Conversation with Homer Blanchard, December 1982.
5. Coleberd, op. cit.
6. Moller factory records.
7. Conversation with Riley Daniels, October 1982.
8. Moller factory records.

THE PIANO & ORGAN SUPPLY COMPANY

1. Conversation with Peter H. Comstock, September 17, 1987.

HENRY PILCHER'S SONS

1. *The American Organist,* August 1927, p. 200.
2. Ibid.
3. *The Diapason,* April 1946, p. 1.
4. *The American Organist,* August 1927, p. 200.
5. *The Tracker,* Volume 19, #2, pp. 12-16.
6. Pilcher factory records.
7. Letter from Harvell Mason, Tyler, Texas, July 11, 1982.

PIPE ORGAN SERVICE COMPANY

1. Letter from Randy George, Council Bluffs, Iowa, October 18, 1982.
2. *The Diapason,* February 1925, p. 8.
3. Letter from Randy George.
4. Conversation with Virgil Fox, August 1, 1987.

POWERS

1. *The Console,* February 1969, p. 3.
2. *The Tracker,* Volume 9, #3, p. 14.

PRATT, READ & CO.

1. *The Musical Age,* 1906, p. 588.
2. *The Day,* New London, Connecticut, March 27, 1986, p. D3.
3. *The Audubon,* July 1987, pp. 77-78.
4. Conversation with Peter H. Comstock, September 17, 1987.
5. Ibid.
6. Ibid.
7. Ibid.

CONRAD PRESCHLEY

1. *The Diapason,* September 1942, p. 14.

W. H. REISNER MFG. CO., INC.

1. *The Diapason,* July 1929, p. 8.
2. Reisner factory records.
3. *The Diapason,* April 1924, p. 18.
4. Ibid.
5. Conversation with Peter Wright, August 1986.
6. Letter from Kimber-Allen Ltd., November 21, 1986.
7. Reisner factory records.

REUTER ORGAN COMPANY

1. Philip M. Smith, "A History of the Reuter Organ Company, 1917-1975, An Evolution of Taste," University of Kansas master's thesis, April 1976, pp. 11-13.
2. Ibid., pp. 11-14.
3. Ibid., p. 14.
4. Ibid., p. 22.
5. Ibid., pp. 15-16.
6. Jack L. Sievert, "The Reuter Theatre Organ," *Theatre Organ,* Volume 4, #2, p. 4.
7. Smith, p. 17.
8. Ibid., p. 16.
9. Ibid., pp. 18-19.
10. Ibid., p. 13.
11. Ibid., p. 19.
12. Ibid., pp. 19-21.
13. Reuter factory records.
14. Conversation with Robert Vaughan, December 22, 1982.
15. Reuter factory records.
16. Conversation with John Selig, December 22, 1982.
17. Reuter factory records.
18. Conversation with John Selig.
19. Conversation with Durrell Armstrong, 1972.
20. Conversation with John Selig.
21. Reuter factory records.
22. Ibid.
23. Smith, pp. 14-15.
24. Ibid., pp. 15-21.
25. Ibid., p. 51.
26. Ibid., p. 15.

JAMES N. REYNOLDS

1. *The Diapason,* August 1944, p. 4.

ROBERT MORTON ORGAN CO.

1. E. A. Spencer factory records.
2. Tape recorded interview of John M. Ferris by Tom B'hend c. 1964.
3. Interview of R. P. Matthews by Tom B'hend, July 1, 1964.
4. Jim Lewis, "The History of the Murray M. Harris Organ Com-

pany, 1894-1913," *The Bicentennial Tracker,* 1976, p. 110.
5. Interview of Stanley Williams by Tom B'hend, May 22, 1963.
6. Interview of Arthur C. Pearson by Tom B'hend, July 20, 1963.
7. Ibid.
8. Ibid.
9. *The Diapason,* August 1922, p. 8.
10. Lewis, p. 110.
11. Ibid., pp. 110-112.
12. *The American Organist,* March 1926, p. 62.
13. *The Console,* May 1965, unnumbered page.
14. *The Diapason,* May 1971, p. 18.
15. *The American Organist,* March 1926, p. 63.
16. Ibid., pp. 63-64.
17. Lewis, p. 113.
18. *The American Organist,* March 1926, p. 64.
19. Lewis, pp. 113-114.
20. *The Diapason,* June 1940, p. 4.
21. Lewis, p. 114.
22. Williams interview.
23. *Cipher,* November 1964, pp. 12-14.
24. Williams interview.
25. Ibid.
26. *The Diapason,* August 1913, p. 1.
27. Pearson interview.
28. *Cipher,* November 1964, pp. 5-8.
29. Williams interview.
30. *Cipher,* November 1964, p. 9.
31. *The American Organist,* March 1926, p. 65.
32. *The Diapason,* December 1916, p. 1.
33. *The Console,* May 1965, p. 4.
34. Ibid., pp. 4-6.
35. Bowers, p. 381.
36. *The Console,* May 1965, pp. 5-7.
37. *Cipher,* November 1964, pp. 18-19.
38. Williams interview.
39. *Cipher,* November 1964, p. 26.
40. *The Diapason,* June 1917, p. 1.
41. *The Console* September 1966, pp. 3-4.
42. Williams interview.
43. *The Console,* September 1966, p. 3.
44. Williams interview.
45. *The Console,* September 1966, p. 3.
46. *The Console,* May 1965, p. 10.
47. *The American Organist,* March 1926, p. 67.
48. Interview of Asa Taylor by Tom B'hend, January 18, 1964.
49. *The Console,* September 1966, p. 16.
50. *The American Organist,* March 1926, p. 65.
51. Interview of Louis Maas by Tom B'hend, August 27, 1963.
52. Williams interview.
53. Tape recorded interview of Paul Carlsted by Tom B'hend, c. 1963.
54. Ibid.
55. Ibid.
56. *The Console,* September 1966, p. 21.
57. Wicks factory records.
58. Bowers, p. 293.
59. Ibid., p. 656.
60. Williams interview.
61. Matthews interview.
62. Form letter from J. A. G. Schiller to creditors of the American Photo Player Company, November 14, 1923.
63. Carlsted interview.
64. *The Console,* September 1966, p. 23.
65. *The Diapason,* March 1925, p. 1.
66. *The Diapason,* July 1925, p. 2.
67. Interview of Wilbur R. Bergstrom by Tom B'hend, July 31, 1963.
68. *The Diapason,* August 1927, p. 38.
69. Bergstrom interview.
70. Letter from R. P. Elliot to Lloyd M. Davey, October 10, 1929.
71. Matthews interview.
72. Pearson interview.
73. Ibid.
74. *The Console,* September 1966, p. 17.
75. Matthews interview.
76. Pearson interview.
77. Conversation with Tom B'hend, 1983.
78. Ibid.
79. Interview of Archie March, Jr. by Tom B'hend, July 10, 1962.
80. Matthews interview.

ROESLER-HUNHOLZ, INC.

1. *Amica Bulletin,* December 1977, pp. 255-256.
2. Letter from Leslie Hoskins to Jerome B. Meyer & Sons, August 7, 1933.

ROOSEVELT ORGAN WORKS

1. F. R. Webber, "Two Roosevelts Built Church Organs," *The Tracker,* Volume 10, #3, pp. 9-10.
2. Ibid., p. 9.
3. Orpha Ochse, *The History of the Organ in the United States* (Bloomington: Indiana University Press, 1975), p. 265.
4. Ibid., p. 209.
5. Webber, op. cit., p. 9.
6. Ibid.
7. Ochse, op. cit., pp. 263-265.
8. Ibid., p. 272.
9. *The Diapason,* September 1942, pp. 1-10.
10. *The Tracker,* Volume 27, #2, p. 10.
11. Letter from F. R. Webber to A. R. Schopp, September 12, 1952.

SCHAEFER ORGAN CO.

1. *The Diapason,* August 1921, p. 20.
2. *The Diapason,* April 1920, p. 24.
3. *The Diapason,* September 1924, p. 4.
4. *The Diapason,* August 1925, p. 10.
5. Schaefer factory records.
6. Ibid.
7. Conversation with Dave Broskowski, February 1983.
8. Ibid.

SCHANTZ ORGAN COMPANY

1. *The Diapason,* March 1925, p. 6.
2. Ibid.
3. Conversation with John Schantz, July 1982.
4. Ibid.

WM. SCHUELKE ORGAN CO.

1. Elizabeth Towne Schmitt, "William Schuelke, Manufacturer of Church and Chapel Organs," *The Tracker,* Volume 25, #1, pp. 52-53.
2. Ibid., pp. 52-59.
3. Ibid., pp. 55-59.
4. Ibid.
5. *The Diapason,* June 1913, p. 9.
6. *The Diapason,* October 1914, p. 1.
7. Schmitt, pp. 59-61.
8. *The Billboard,* May 20, 1922, p. 75.
9. *The Billboard,* May 1, 1920, p. 77.
10. Jerome B. Meyer & Sons factory records.

J. P. SEEBURG PIANO COMPANY

1. Harvey Roehl, *Player Piano Treasury* (Vestal, New York: Vestal Press, 1973, second edition), p. 104.
2. Len Ackland, "Decline of Seeburg a Genuine Capitalist Tragedy," *Chicago Tribune* Business Section, March 5, 1980, p. 1.
3. Bowers, p. 599.
4. Ibid., p. 497.
5. Ibid., pp. 598-599.
6. Ibid., pp. 600-601.
7. Conversation with Gene Skarda, February 27, 1986.
8. Ackland, pp. 1-9.

SKINNER ORGAN COMPANY

1. Skinner Organ Company, *Stop, Open and Reed,* Volume 3, #1 (1925), p. 5.
2. Dorothy J. Holden, *The Life and Work of Ernest M. Skinner* (Richmond, Virginia: Organ Historical Society, 1985), p. 44.
3. Conversation with Bill Bunch, November 5, 1986.
4. Holden, pp. 1-3.
5. Ibid., p. 75.
6. Ibid., pp. 5-7.
7. *The Diapason,* January 1956, p. 2.
8. Holden, p. 19.
9. Ibid., pp. 25-30.
10. Ibid., pp. 31-33.
11. *Rotunda,* March-April 1933, p. 31.
12. Holden, p. 77.
13. Ibid., p. 107.
14. Ibid., p. 65.
15. Ibid., p. 60.
16. Ibid., pp. 66-67.
17. Ibid., pp. 80-81.
18. Ibid., p. 124.
19. Ibid., p. 145.

20. Ibid., pp. 147-149.
21. Ibid., p. 156.
22. Aeolian-Skinner factory records.
23. Holden, p. 175.
24. Ibid., p. 180.
25. Ibid., pp. 210-212.
26. Ibid., p. 226.
27. William H. Barnes and Edward B., Gammons, *Two Centuries of American Organ Building* (Glen Rock, NJ: J. Fischer & Bro., 1970), p. 76.
28. Holden, p. 191.
29. Conversation with Bill Bunch.
30. Holden, p. 90.
31. Skinner Organ Company, op. cit., pp. 4-5.
32. Ochse, p. 356.

F. R. SMITH

1. *The Diapason*, February 1944, p. 4.
2. Conversation with David Dickson, October 2, 1982.
3. Ibid.

SMITH UNIT ORGAN CO.

1. Smith Unit Organ Co. catalog c. 1922, pp. 5-7.
2. *The Diapason*, December 1921, p. 17.
3. *Moving Picture World*, July 6, 1918.
4. Douglas Marion (alias of Judd Walton), "The Smith Unit Organs," *Theatre Organ*, Volume 2, #4, pp. 5-6.

E. A. SPENCER

1. Conversation with Ted Herman, 1982.
2. *Cipher*, November 1964, p. 5.
3. *The American Organist*, March 1926, p. 64.
4. *The Console*, September 1966, p. 3.
5. Ibid.
6. *The Console*, May 1965, p. 10.
7. *The American Organist*, March 1926, p. 67.
8. Conversation with George Wright, March 1983.
9. Ibid.
10. Conversation between Tom B'hend and Asa Taylor, January 18, 1964.

SPENCER TURBINE COMPANY

1. Conversation with David Hunt, August 2, 1982.
2. *The American Organist*, September 1928, p. 357.
3. Ibid., pp. 358-360.
4. Conversation with David Hunt.
5. Ibid.

J. W. STEERE & SON ORGAN COMPANY

1. Orpha Ochse, *The History of the Organ in the United States* (Bloomington: Indiana University Press, 1975), pp. 240-242.
2. Alan Laufmann, *Organ Handbook 1983* (Richmond, Virginia: Organ Historical Society, 1983), p. 27.
3. Ibid.
4. *The Diapason*, April 1921, p. 1.
5. *The Diapason*, January 1920, p. 19.

EDWARD STEIN

1. Hilborne L. Roosevelt catalog, December 1888.

STEVENS ORGAN COMPANY

1. *The Diapason*, April 1943, p. 7.
2. *The Diapason*, May 1913, p. 1.

SYMPHONY PLAYER COMPANY

1. Covington, Kentucky, City Directory, 1918-19 edition.
2. Bowers, p. 580.
3. Ibid., p. 600.

TELLERS-KENT ORGAN COMPANY

1. *The Diapason*, September 1920, p. 15.
2. Organ Supply Industries catalog, July 1982, p. 2.
3. *The Diapason*, April 1918, p. 8.
4. Conversation with Henry C. Tellers, July 1982.
5. William H. Barnes and Edward B. Gammons, *Two Centuries of American Organ Building* (Glen Rock, NJ: J. Fischer & Bro., 1970), p. 91.
6. Conversation with Herman Tellers, July 1982.
7. Letter from W. E. Biebel, Erie, Pennsylvania, 1983.

THOMSON ENGRAVING COMPANY

1. *The Diapason*, July 1929, p. 8.

TITAN TOOL COMPANY

1. Letter from Henry Gottfried, August 31, 1983.

UNITED STATES PIPE ORGAN COMPANY

1. Letter from Robert G. Lent, Bayville, New Jersey, August 1982.
2. Ibid.
3. United States Pipe Organ Company factory records.
4. *The Diapason*, March 1924, p. 15.
5. Letter from Robert G. Lent.
6. Ibid.
7. Conversation with Alan Lightcap, July 1982.
8. Ibid.
9. United States Pipe Organ Company factory records.
10. Conversation with Robert G. Lent, July 1986.
11. Ibid.
12. Letter from Robert G. Lent.
13. United States Pipe Organ Company factory records.
14. Letter from Robert G. Lent, September 19, 1982.
15. Letter from Robert G. Lent, August 1982.
16. Ibid.
17. United States Pipe Organ Company factory records.

CHAS. VINER & SONS

1. "Charles Viner Is Dead," *The Diapason*, 1919.

VOTTELER-HOLTKAMP-SPARLING ORGAN CO.

1. John Allen Ferguson, *Walter Holtkamp, American Organ Builder* (Kent, Ohio: Kent State University Press, 1979), pp. 1-2.
2. Ibid.
3. Letter from Walter Holtkamp, Jr., January 13, 1983.
4. Ibid.
5. *The Tracker*, Volume 23, #2, p. 20.
6. *The Diapason*, April 1943, p. 7.
7. Ferguson, op. cit., pp. 2-5.
8. Ibid., pp. 2-3.
9. Holtkamp factory records.
10. Ferguson, op. cit., pp 2-5.
11. *The Diapason*, April 1943, p. 7.

WANGERIN ORGAN COMPANY

1. *The Diapason*, March 1919, p. 1.
2. *The Diapason*, June 1925, p. 1.
3. *Bombarde*, April 1966, p. 21.
4. Wangerin Weickhardt theatre organ catalog c. 1916, p. 14.
5. Letter from Dave Broskowski, 1982.
6. Conversation with Stanton Peters, December 1982.
7. *The Diapason*, March 1919, p. 1.
8. *The Diapason*, December 1961, p. 30.
9. *The Diapason*, January 1927, p. 1.
10. *The Diapason*, February 1943, p. 4.
11. Conversation with Gordy Meyer, 1983.
12. Letter from Dave Broskowski, 1982.

WARSAW ELEVATOR CO.

1. *125th Anniversary Celebration, Warsaw, NY 1968*, pp. 11-12.
2. Ibid., p. 12.

WELTE-MIGNON CORPORATION

1. Q. David Bowers, *Encyclopedia of Automatic Musical Instruments* (Vestal, New York: Vestal Press, 1972), pp. 632-634.
2. Ibid., p. 336.
3. Ibid.
4. Ibid., p. 323.
5. Doug Hickling, "The Postwar American Welte Company," *The Console*, April 1972, p. 6.
6. Doug Hickling, "Lloyd Davey Recalls His Days with Welte-Mignon Corporation," *The Console*, May 1972, p. 9.
7. Conversation with Henry Gottfried, November 17, 1983.
8. *The American Organist*, July 1925, pp. 290-291.
9. Hickling, April 1972, p. 7.

10. Hickling, May 1972, p. 10.
11. *The Diapason,* July 1925, p. 3.
12. Hickling, May 1972, p. 9.
13. Ibid.
14. *The Diapason,* June 1927, p. 12.
15. Hickling, May 1972, p. 9.
16. Hickling, April 1972, p. 8.
17. Hickling, May 1972, pp. 13-14.
18. *The Diapason,* July 1926, p. 33.
19. Hickling, May 1972, pp. 10-13.
20. Ibid., pp. 13-14.
21. Ibid., p. 14.
22. Hickling, April 1972, p. 8.
23. Ibid., pp. 8-10.
24. Hickling, May 1972, p. 14.
25. Hickling, April 1972, p. 10.
26. *Cinema Theatre Organ Digest,* May 1, 1956, p. 14.
27. Hickling, May 1972, pp. 15-17.
28. Ibid., p. 19.
29. Hickling, April 1972, p. 10.
30. Ibid.
31. Hickling, May 1972, p. 10.
32. Welte-Mignon Corporation, *The Welte Philharmonic Organ* (New York: Welte-Mignon Corporation, 1927), pp. 2-10.
33. *The Diapason,* May 1926, p. 9.
34. Edward Jablonski, *Gershwin* (New York: Doubleday, 1987), p. 101.

WESTERN SERVICE CO.

1. Iowa City, Iowa *Press-Citizen,* January 29, 1926, p. 5.

FREDERICK I. WHITE

1. Conversation with Sid Eaton, September 17, 1987.

WICKS PIPE ORGAN COMPANY

1. *The Diapason,* December 1936, p. 7.
2. *Centennial History of Highland, Illinois,* p. 240.
3. Conversation with John Sperling, 1982.
4. *Centennial History of Highland, Illinois,* pp. 240-244.
5. Ibid.
6. Conversation with Sandy Balcom, April 19, 1983.
7. *The Diapason,* November 1917, p. 13.
8. Letter from Martin Wick, November 2, 1982.
9. *The American Organist,* October 1939, p. 338.

C. F. WINDER ORGAN COMPANY

1. Letter from Donald Traser, Richmond, Virginia, December 1, 1982.
2. *The Diapason,* March 1914, p. 3.
3. Letter from Donald Traser.
4. *The Diapason,* November 1914, p. 7.
5. Letter from Donald Traser.
6. *The Diapason,* December 1915, p. 1.
7. Artcraft factory records.
8. Conversation with Larry Abbott, June 1982.
9. Letter from Donald Traser.

WIRSCHING & COMPANY

1. Robert E. Coleberd, Jr., "Philipp Wirsching the Consummate Builder," *The American Organist,* October 1968, pp. 14-15.
2. Ibid., pp. 24-26.
3. Ibid., p. 26.
4. Ibid., pp. 28-29.
5. Ibid., p. 29.

WM. WOOD PIPE ORGAN COMPANY, INC.

1. *The Diapason,* September 1942, p. 14.
2. *The Diapason,* May 1923, p. 20.
3. *The Diapason,* September 1942, p. 14.
4. *The Diapason,* December 1924, p. 21.
5. Ibid., p. 30.
6. Bill Peterson, "The William Wood Pipe Organ Company," *Theatre Organ,* Volume 5, #4, pp. 28-29.
7. *The Diapason,* September 1942, p. 14.
8. Peterson, op. cit.
9. *The Diapason,* September 1942, p. 14.
10. Conversation with Dennis Hedberg, December 1982.
11. *The Diapason,* September 1942, p. 14.
12. Hedberg conversation.
13. Peterson, op. cit., p. 29.
14. Hedberg conversation.
15. Peterson, op. cit., p. 29.
16. Ibid.
17. Ibid., p. 28.

WOOD & BROOKS COMPANY

1. Conversation with Peter H. Comstock, September 17, 1987.
2. *Buffalo Courier-Express,* March 27, 1972, p. 5.
3. *Buffalo Evening News,* October 6, 1959, p. 23.

ILLUSTRATION ACKNOWLEDGMENTS

The author is grateful to the following individuals who enhanced the beauty of this book by contributing photographs and documents. Special credit is due Mr. Tom B'hend, for twenty years editor of *The Console,* who donated many halftones from that publication. All contributions are acknowledged by page number and, where appropriate, abbreviations of position on the page as follows: B, bottom; C, center; L, left; R, right; T, top.

FRONTISPIECE: 434, Michael Miller.

TABLE OF CONTENTS: 437-439, Mr. & Mrs. Gordon Meyer.

ODELL: 443, 444T, Anthony Meloni.

OPERATORS: 445T, 451, 452, Harvey Roehl. 445B, author's collection. 446, 447, Mr. & Mrs. Gordon Meyer. 448-450, Judd Walton.

PAGE: 454T, Earl Beilharz. 454B, 458B, *Theatre Organ.* 455-457, 459, B'hend & Kaufmann Archives. 458T, Bill Lamb. 453, Bob Schopp.

PAVETTE: 461, Bill Bunch.

PELOUBET: 462, Pete Daniels.

PILCHER: 464, Jack Bethards. 466, 467, 470T, Stanton Peters. 468, 469, 470B&LC, Organ Historical Society.

PIPE ORGAN SERVICE: 472, Mr. & Mrs. Gordon Meyer.

REUTER: 473T, Steve Adams. 473B, 474TR, 475, 476, 477TR&BR, 478-481, 482T, 483B, 484T, 485, 486, 487TL&BR, 488, 489, Franklin Mitchell. 474TL, *Theatre Organ.* 477TL, Bill Lamb. 474B, 477BL, 487TR&BL, author's collection. 484B, David McCain.

REYNOLDS: 490C, Mr. & Mrs. Gordon Meyer.

ROBERT MORTON: 491T, 511B, 512, 513B, 514B, 515B, 517B, 518-520, 523, Jack Bethards. 506R, Ron Downer. 491B, 492B, 495R, 496R, 497B, 498, 499T, 502-505, 507-510, 511T, 515T, 521, 522B, 524, 525, 527-530, 531B, 532, 533T, 534, 535, 536T&R, 538T, 540, 541, 551T, 552T, 553, 554B, 556T, 557T&B, 559TR, 560B, 561, 562BR, 564, 565TR&B, 566, 567T, 568, 569, B'hend & Kaufmann Archives. 506L, 517T, 537B, 552B, Clay Holbrook. 492T, 497T, Ed Crome. 493B, Ken Crome. 495L, Tom Harmon. 516TL, David McCain. 493T, 513T, 516TR, 526T&C, 551B, 554T, 556C&BL, 558, 559TL&B, 560T, 562TR&BL, 563, 565TL, 567B, Art Pearson, 496, 499B, 531T, 537T, author's collection. 522T, Bill Bunch. 514T, 526B, *Theatre Organ.* 516B, 556BR, 557C, 562TL, Ruth Kingsley. 533B, 538B, Alfred Buttler. 536BL, Nick Snow. 538C, Theatre Historical Society. 542-550, Stan Kann. 493C, Organ Historical Society.

ROOSEVELT: 583T, 584, 587B, author's collection. 583B, Organ Historical Society. 587T, David McCain. 585, Bob Schopp. 586, Theatre Historical Society.

SCHAEFER: 588T, 589TR, David Broskowski. 588B, author's collection.

SCHANTZ: 589B, Jack Sievert. 590T, Tom Harmon. 590B, 591-593, 594T, John Schantz.

SCHUELKE: 595T&BL, 596R, Organ Historical Society. 595C, Fred Dahlinger. 595BR, Mr. & Mrs. Gordon Meyer.

SEEBURG: 597, Harvey Roehl.

SKINNER: 598T, 605, 607-611, Allen Harrah. 599T, David McCain. 599B, author's collection. 600T, Tom Hazleton. 601, B'hend & Kaufmann Archives. 603, Gus Brummer. 604B, Bill Bunch. 598, 604T&C, Organ Historical Society.

F. R. SMITH: 612, Henry Gottfried.

SMITH UNIT ORGAN: 613, John Schelkopf. 614T&C, 616T, *Theatre Organ.* 628, author's collection. 614B, Bill Bunch. 616BL, 617B, Bill Lamb. 617T, Larry Broadmoore. 618-621, 622TR&B, 623-627, B'hend & Kaufmann Archives. 616BR, Bob Longfield.

SPENCER: 632, B'hend & Kaufmann Archives. 633TL, Bill Lamb. 633TR, author's collection.

STEERE: 634CR, Organ Historical Society. 635T, Irv Glazer. 634T, Steve Adams.

SYMPHONY: 637R, John Shanahan.

TELLERS-KENT: 639T, 641, Henry Tellers. 642, Randall Wagner. 639B, 640T&C, Stanton Peters.

UNITED STATES: 643, 644L, 646, 648 all but BR, 649T, Robert Lent. 644R, 645T, 647, 648BR, 650, Alan Lightcap. 645B, David McCain. 649B, B'hend & Kaufmann Archives.

VAN WYCK: 652, 653T, B'hend & Kaufmann Archives.

VINER: 653B, *Theatre Organ.* 654, Homer Blanchard.

VOTTELER: 655, 656, 658-661, Walter Holtkamp, Jr. 657TR&BR, David McCain. 657L, Tom Harmon.

WANGERIN: 662T, 663TR, David Broskowski. 667BL, 668B, B'hend & Kaufmann Archives. 662B, 663TL, 667T, 670T, David McCain. 663LC, Richard Sklenar. 664-666, 668B, 669, Stanton Peters. 667CR, *Bombarde.* 670B, author's collection. 670C, 671, Clarence Braun. 667BR, Mr. & Mrs. Gordon Meyer.

WELTE: 673T, 676B, Mike Ohman. 676C, Bill Bunch. 677, Ron Sanchez. 673B, 674, 675, 676T, 678, 679L, 682R, 683, 684, 685T, 686T, B'hend & Kaufmann Archives. 686B, 687, 688, 689T, David McCain. 681, author's collection. 682L, 689B, 690T, Tom Harmon. 685B, Harvey Roehl.

WICKS: 694, Mr. & Mrs. Gordon Meyer. 695R, Steven Goldstein. 696L, 698TL, 714B, 721, author's collection. 695L, 698TR&B, 720BL, David McCain. 703-705, 729T, Stanton Peters. 696R, 699-702, 709TR&B, 710, 711T, 712BL, B'hend & Kaufmann Archives. 709TL, 711BL, 713, 715, *Theatre Organ.* 697, 714T, 716-719, Martin Wick. 711BR, 720BR, Bill Lamb. 706-708, 720T, John Sperling. 712R, Faye Wheeler. 712T, Kay McAbee.

WINDER: 729B, David Barnett. 730, David McCain.

WIRSCHING: 731, 733T, David McCain. 732, B'hend & Kaufmann Archives. 733B, 734, 735, Organ Historical Society.

WOOD: 736, David McCain. 737BR, Dennis Hedberg. 737, 738TL, 739, *Theatre Organ.*

BLOWERS

B. F. BLOWER CO., INC.: 742T&BL, Mr. & Mrs. Gordon Meyer. 742BR, Chris Feiereisen.

KINETIC ENGINEERING COMPANY: 744, 745B, 746, 747T, Pete Daniels. 745TL, 747B, David McCain.

G. MEIDINGER & CO.: 749-754, Mr. & Mrs. Gordon Meyer.

SPENCER TURBINE CO.: 755T, Pete Daniels. 756BL, 767, B'hend & Kaufmann Archives. 755B, 756BR, 757, 766, 768-771, 772B, 774, 775, author's collection. 758-765, 773, David Hunt. 756TR, Stephen Pinel.

ZEPHYR ELECTRIC ORGAN BLOWER CO.: 776T, B'hend & Kaufmann Archives. 777, Stanton Peters.

CHAMBER HEATERS

BUFFALO GAS RADIATOR CORPORATION: 778, Tom Harmon.

CRAMBLET ENGINEERING CORPORATION: 779T, Steve Adams.

ELECTRICAL PARTS

ELECTRIC SPECIALTY COMPANY: 782B, 783, Bob Lent.

ELECTRIC VIBRATO CO.: 782T, Tom Harmon.

AUGUST A. KLANN: 784T&R, Bob Lent. 785TL, author's collection.

W. H. REISNER MFG. CO., INC.: 788T, Pete Daniels. 788BL, David McCain. 788BR, 789, Pete Wright.

TRIUMPH ELECTRIC CORPORATION: 792T, Tom Harmon.

ELEVATORS

CURTIS PNEUMATIC MACHINERY COMPANY: 794, B'hend & Kaufmann Archives.

OTIS ELEVATOR COMPANY: 795T, Jerry Hickey. 795B, author's collection. 796, Anne Millbrooke.

PETER CLARK, INC.: 797, B'hend & Kaufmann Archives.

GENERAL SUPPLIES

DURST, BOEGLE & CO.: 798T, Mr. & Mrs. Gordon Meyer. 798B, 799B, 800T, Randall Wagner. 800B, Henry Gottfried. 801-805, Pete Daniels.

THE A. GOTTFRIED CO.: 806T, Pete Daniels. 808T, B'hend & Kaufmann Archives. 809T, Randall Wagner. 809B, David McCain. 806B, 807, 808B, 810, 811, 815B, 816B, Henry Gottfried. 816T, Dennis Unks. 812T, 813, Tom Harmon.

AUG. LAUKHUFF: 818T, Bob Schopp. 818B, author's collection. 819, 820, Bob Lent.

ORGAN SUPPLY CORPORATION: 821T, Pete Howell. 821C, 826BR, Pete Daniels. 826BL, Bill Lamb. 825, 826T, 827C&B, 829-831, author's collection. 827T, David McCain.

KEYBOARDS

COMSTOCK, CHENEY & CO.: 833, Peter H. Comstock.

THE PIANO & ORGAN SUPPLY COMPANY: 834T, Peter H. Comstock.

PRATT, READ & CO.: 834C, 835, 836, Peter H. Comstock.

LEATHER, FELT & CLOTH

THE CARLTON SALES CO.: 838T, Bob Lent.

T. L. LUTKINS: 839T, Bob Lent.

L. J. MUTTY CO.: 839B, Bob Lent.

WHITE, SON COMPANY: 840C, Bob Lent.

WOOD & WERNER, INC.: 841T, Bob Lent.

MISCELLANEOUS PARTS

E. R. HOWARD: 842TL, B'hend & Kaufmann Archives. 842TR, Stephen Pinel.

THE JAMES P. McGREECE COMPANY: 842B, Bob Lent.

PERCUSSIONS

J. C. DEAGAN, INC.: 843C, Mr. & Mrs. Gordon Meyer. 844TR&BR, David McCain. 844CR, B'hend & Kaufmann Archives. 845-864, author's collection.

EXCELSIOR DRUM WORKS: 865C, Bob Lent.

THE KOHLER-LIEBICH COMPANY: 866T, Mr. & Mrs. Gordon Meyer. 867R, 868-881, Bill Lamb.

LEEDY MFG. CO., INC.: 882, Richard Groman.

LUDWIG & LUDWIG: 883, Bob Lent. 883B, 884-886, 887T, William F. Ludwig, Jr.

PIPEWORK

JAMES H. BOLTON: 890T, Jack Bethards. 890C, Stu Green.

DENNISON ORGAN PIPE COMPANY: 891T, Mr. & Mrs. Gordon Meyer. 893, 894L, Bob Lent. 895, author's collection.

ERIE REED PIPE CO.: 896T, Bob Schopp.

FIRMA ERNST DOELLING: 896B, 897, Bob Schopp.

GUTFLEISCH & SCHOPP: 898T&R, 899B, 900T&BR, Bob Schopp. 900BL, Fred Oyster.

EDWIN B. HEDGES: 901T, Mr. & Mrs. Gordon Meyer. 901B, Organ Historical Society.

ILLINOIS ORGAN SUPPLY CO.: 902B, Mr. & Mrs. Gordon Meyer.

F. W. KREBS: 903B, Mr. & Mrs. Gordon Meyer.

JEROME B. MEYER & SONS, INC.: 905B, author's collection. 905T, 906T&BR, 907, 908BR, 909, Mr. & Mrs. Gordon Meyer. 906BL, David McCain. 908BL, Organ Historical Society.

FREDERICK I. WHITE: 911C, Jack Bethards. 911B, Bob Schopp.

PLAYERS & ROLLS

AUTOMATIC MUSICAL INSTRUMENT COMPANY: 912C, 913, B'hend & Kaufmann Archives. 912B, John Perschbacher.

CLARK ORCHESTRA ROLL COMPANY: 914T, Harvey Roehl. 914C, author's collection.

L. B. DOMAN CORPORATION: 915, Mr. & Mrs. Gordon Meyer.

ROESLER-HUNHOLZ, INC.: 916C, Mr. & Mrs. Gordon Meyer. 917-921, Bob Lent.

STOP KEYS & ENGRAVING

DENISON BROTHERS: 922T, Mr. & Mrs. Gordon Meyer.

THOMSON ENGRAVING COMPANY: 923, Bob Lent.

ADDENDA

AEOLIAN: 924, 925, 926T, Jim Crank.

BARTON: 926B, 927T, John Fett. 927BL, author's collection. 927BR, Fred Gollnick.

GSCHOFF: 928T, Tom DeLay.

LENOIR: 928B, Paul Wasserman.

INDEX

Abel, Earl, 511
Abrams, Sylvain, 496
absolute pitch, 421
Academy Th., Lebanon, PA, 304
Adams, Steve, 5, 11, 441, 442
Ade, J. Fred, 644
Admiral Th., Chicago, IL, 300
Adolphson, Gustav, 159
Aebi, Francis, 928
Aeolian Co., 22-28, 50, 94, 132, 182, 223, 365, 492, 493, 598, 600, 601, 606, 682, 890, 914, 924, 925
Aeolian-Skinner, 12, 22, 51, 234, 378, 600, 601, 604, 606-608, 612, 788, 795, 891, 901
Aeolian-Votey, 132
aeroplane effect, 497
air flow regulator, 757
Aladdin Th., Denver, CO, 705-709
Alarçon, Ben, 714
Albertsen, U. J., 169
Albrecht, Fred, 911
Albrecht, George, 838
Alda, Frances, 681
Aldine Th., Philadelphia, PA, 209
Alien Property Custodian, 673, 685
Allan, B., 327
Allegheny Th., Philadelphia, PA, 367, 368
Allen air appliance blower, 321
Allen-Rogers Corp., 835
Allen Th., Cleveland, OH, 210, 212
Allyn Th., Hartford, CT, 41
Alnett, L. L., 740, 934
Ambassador (Rockne) Th., Chicago, IL, 142
Ambassador Th., St. Louis, MO, 702
Ambassador Th., Washington, DC, 210
American Bridge Co., 322
American Institute of Organbuilders, 454, 827
American Master, 28-30, 890, 929
American music rolls, 445
American Organ, 498
American Organist, The, 421
American Photo Player Co., 494-496, 499, 500, 503, 510, 531, 553, 632, 695, 890, 928
American Steel & Wire Co., 781
American Th., Norfolk, VA, 620
AMI Inc., 913
Amica Bulletin, 10
amplex, 421, 613, 615
analysis, 421
Anderson, E., 550
Anderson, Helen, 214
Anderson, William, 442
Andriesian, Dan, 70
Anglo-California Trust Co., 500
Apollo Th., Indianapolis, IN, 300
Apollo Th., Princeton, IL, 472
Arcada Th., St. Charles, IL, 139
Arcadia Ballroom, Chicago, IL, 70, 73
Arcadia Th., Dallas, TX, 478-481
Arcadia Th., Philadelphia, PA, 227
Arcadia Th., Windber, PA, 212
Ardmore Th., Ardmore, PA, 54, 800, 814
Arey, Duane, 268
Aristocrat automobile, 347
Arlington Th., Santa Barbara, CA, 286
Armstrong, Durrell, 475
Art Organ Co., 731
Artcraft, 31-33, 632, 729, 890, 913, 929
Arthur, David, 677
Artiste player, 363, 371, 374, 378-380, 399
Artistouch player, 917-921
Artona player, 915
Ascher, Nate, 62
Ascher Brothers, 62, 66, 210
Astor automobile, 347
Auch, Harry, 145, 821
Auditorium, Dallas, TX state fairgrounds, 64, 65, 68
Auditorium Th., Chicago, IL, 584-587, 883
Audsley, George, 366, 367, 583, 585
augmented pedal, 421
Aurora Corp. of Illinois, 837
Aurora Th., East Aurora, NY, 654
Austin, Basil, 33, 34, 39, 40
Austin, Donald, 33, 42
Austin, Frederick, 33, 38
Austin, Harry, 38
Austin, John, 33-35, 38-40, 208, 585
Austin co., 20, 33-48, 153, 565, 632, 677, 891, 914, 929
Automatic Musical Co., 265
Automatic Musical Instrument Co., 32, 676, 912, 913
Autovox, 270
Averbeck, Maximillion, 315
Awe, Harry, 58, 60
Aztec Th., San Antonio, TX, 533, 534

Badger, George, 316, 888, 889
Badger co., 195, 316, 644, 888, 889
Bagdad Th., Portland, OR, 246, 247
Baker Hotel, St. Charles, IL, 140
Balaban, Barney, 62
Balaban & Katz, 62, 66, 210, 213
balanced valve, 696
Balboa Th., San Diego, CA, 526
Balcom, C. M., 22, 49-51, 461, 695
Balcom & Provorse, 49
Balcom & Vaughan, 20, 49-53, 929, 934
Balcom, Vaughan & Chase, 50
Baldwin Piano Co., 835
Barckhoff, Carl, 54
Barckhoff co., 54, 99, 288, 473, 731, 821, 905 929
Barker, Charles, 583
Barker Bros., 677, 681
Barlow, Charles, 92
Barnes, William, 367, 421, 584, 606, 638
Barnes & Buhl, 97
Barrington, S. H., 55, 800, 814
Bartholomay, F. A., 56
Barth Th., Carbondale, IL, 705
Bartolas, 16, 57-60, 62, 66, 101, 663, 667, 909
Bartolina, 60
Barton, Dan, 57-62, 66-70, 72, 73, 77, 82-84, 663, 891, 926
Barton co., 2, 10, 12, 14, 20, 57-89, 172, 425, 472, 663, 666, 668, 671, 740, 742, 757, 779, 791, 793, 797, 847, 848, 861, 883, 891, 895, 905, 908, 911, 926, 927, 929, 930
Bayley Manufacturing Co., 741, 742
Beach, Earl, 154
Beacon Th., Boston, MA, 121
beard, 421, 422, 424
beater, diaphone, 338, 421, 422
Beatty, Ed, 62
Beatty, J. A., 678
Becker, Rene, 153
Beckwith Organ Co., 788
Bedstead Manufacturing Co., 795
Beethoven Orchestral Organ, 499
Begueline, Ed, 719
Beilharz, Earl, 11, 441, 454
Beilharz, Ellsworth, 453, 454
Beitel, E. G., 31, 32
Belden Manufacturing Co., 781
Bell, Alexander Graham, 598
Bell, P., 494
Belmont Th., Chicago, IL, 176
Beman, Frank, 90
Beman co., 90, 91
Bender, Eugene, 733
Bennett, James, 92
Bennett, Robert, 92-95
Bennett Organ Co., 20, 92-96, 99, 137, 284, 328, 472, 791, 891, 930
Benson, Carl, 208, 676, 681, 682
Bent, E. F., 546, 547
Benzeno, William, 11, 322
Berlis, Charles, 145
Bernet, Rosine, 819
Berrington, Ormond, 678
Berry, Howard, 400
Best Th., Parsons, KS, 709
Bethards, Jack, 511
Bewell, Arthur H., 147
Beyer, Max, 673, 676
B. F. Blower Co., 18, 19, 198, 693, 742, 743
B'hend, Tom, 11, 420, 441, 491, 501, 940
Bierck, H. A., 744
Bierck, J. G., 744
Bijou Th., Richmond, VA, 620
Bijou Th., Savannah, GA, 620
Bilgen, Albert, 714
Bilmer Mfg. Co., 841
Biograph Th., Chicago, IL, 668
Birkmaier, Arthur, 677
Bishop, Ronald, 30
Blanchard, Homer, 11, 441, 468, 827
Blank, Abe, 62, 66, 211
Blashfield, Frank, 97
blind combination action, 28, 421, 423
block, 421, 422
Blue, Alice, 514
Blue Light automobile, 347
Blunk, Bill, 739
Bockisch, Karl, 673
Bodman, Steve, 827
Boegle, Ignace, 147, 798, 800, 814
Boehm Th., Albion, MI, 69
Bohrer, Walter, 636
bolster, 421
Bolton, F., 492
Bolton, James, 31, 890
Bonawitz, Karl, 209
boot, 421, 422, 426
borrowed stop, 421
Bovard Auditorium, Los Angeles, CA, 516
Bowers, Dave, 12, 421, 441
Bowes, Edward, 107
Boyd, Alec, 243
Boyer, Conrad, 643, 649
Boynton, Harry, 531
Bransfield-Billings, 834
Braun, Eugen, 22
Braunsdorf, George, 837
Brenner, Jacob, 742
Brenner Tank, Inc., 742
Breu, H., 327
bridge, 421
Brinkley, John, 475
Brin Th., Menasha, WI, 69
Broadway music rolls, 445
Broadway Th., Boston, MA, 518
Broadway Th., Santa Ana, CA, 705
Broadway Th., Yonkers, NY, 29
Brockbank, Frederick, 890
Brockman, W. J., 666
Bronson (Byrd) Th., Philadelphia, PA, 146-148, 151
Brook, Arthur, 327
Brook, W., 327
Broome, Dave, 34, 35
Broskowski, David, 11
Brown, Albert, 141
Brown, Herbert, 744
Brown, John, 717
Bruns, William, 795
Bryceson brothers, 583
Bruder, Gustav, 378
Buchheim, Eugene, 719
Buchheim, John, 718, 719
Buck, George, 13, 14, 441
Buffalo Gas Radiator Corp., 778

Buhl, P. C., 97
Buhl & Blashfield, 97, 98
Buhler, Frank, 210
Bunch, Bill, 11, 51, 52
Burkhard, Henry, 676, 678
Burlington Pipe Organ Co., 99
Burnham, M. E., 676, 681
Butterfield, W. S., 62, 66, 83
Buttler, Biff, 11, 56, 441
Byington, John, 99, 176

Cadet Chapel, West Point, 389
Cadillac dealership, San Francisco, CA, 523
California (Fox) (U. A.) Th., Richmond, CA, 928
California Organ Co., 209, 493, 495, 496, 501, 506, 508, 548, 549, 555, 556, 564, 632
California Th., Santa Barbara, CA, 498, 507
calliope, 332, 421, 423
Cameo Th., New York, NY, 602
Cameron, J., 327
Campagnone, James, 322
Campbell, James, 316
Campbell, John, 682
Campkin, Frederick, 155
canceller bar, 39
Candler, Assa, 925
cap, 421, 422
Capitol Music Roll Co., 445
Capitol Roll & Record Co., 445
Capitol Th., Allston, MA, 607, 609-611
Capitol Th., Binghamton, NY, 268, 270
Capitol Th., Chicago, IL, 211
Capitol Th., Davenport, IA, 369, 711
Capitol Th., Detroit, MI, 164
Capitol Th., Kalamazoo, MI, 68
Capitol Th., Louisville, KY, 469
Capitol Th., Madison, WI, 68
Capitol Th., New York, NY, 107, 112, 114-116
Capitol Th., Rome, NY, 365
Capitol Th., St. Paul, MN, 185, 191
Capitol Th., Wheeling, WV, 183
Capitol Th., Wilkes-Barre, PA, 212
capture combination action, 421
carillon harp, 848
Carlsted, Paul, 491, 498, 500, 516, 557, 562
Carlsted chest, 496
Carlton Sales Co., 838
Carman Th., Philadelphia, PA, 147
Carney, Al, 176-178
Carr, Art, 821, 827
Carruthers, Harry, 248
Carruthers, Joseph, 208, 214, 229, 248
Carter, Gaylord, 541
Carty, Fred, 383, 388, 904, 934
Casavant, Claver, 100
Casavant, Joseph, 100
Casavant, Samuel, 100
Casavant co., 100, 101, 473, 806, 917
Casino Th., Avalon, CA, 457
Castillo, Lloyd, 118
Castillo Theatre Organ School, 118
Castro Th., San Francisco, CA, 528, 529
Cathedral of the Incarnation, Garden City, NY, 584
Cavaille-Coll, Aristide, 583
Cecile music rolls, 445
celesta, 423
celeste, 423
Central Park Th., Chicago, IL, 62, 66
Century II, Wichita, KS, 51
Century Mallet Instrument Service, 844
Century Pipe Organ Co., 139, 141
Century Th., Philadelphia, PA, 518
Chaffin, Edward, 901
Challenge music rolls, 445
Chant, W. H., 464
Chaplin, Charles, 545
Charles, Henry, 495, 496, 499
Charles, Milton, 541
Chase, J. Riley, 50
Chelberg, John, 159
Cheney, George, 833
chest, 423
Chicago Musical College, 366
Chicago Stadium, 2, 68, 70, 73-82, 84, 757, 791, 793, 891, 895, 927
Chicago Th., Chicago, IL, 66, 176, 178
Chinese gong, 235
Chinese temple blocks, 138
Chorophone, 39
Christian X, King, 346
chrysoglott, 368, 423
City Opera House, Frederick, MD, 704
Clancy, Tom, 82
Clark, Ernest, 914
Clark, Peter, 797
Clark, Theodore, 676
Clark, W. A., 552
Clark Orchestra Roll Co., 914, 916
Clark Th., Vacaville, CA, 739
Clark & Fenton, 101
Clark, M. A. & Sons, 101
classic organ, 423
Clemmer Th., Seattle, WA, 116
Clemmer Th., Spokane, WA, 212, 226
Cleveland Symphony Organ, 661
Clipp, Joseph, 367
Clough, James, 736
Clough & Warren, 33, 181, 736
Coburn, Walter, 102
Coburn Organ Co., 102
Coburn & Taylor, 102
Coinola pianos, 445
Coleberd, Robert, 93, 464, 731
Coles, Hubert, 29
Coliseum, Los Angeles, CA, 677
Coliseum Th., San Francisco, CA, 513
Collingswood Th., Collingswood, NJ, 644
Collins, Clyde W., 289
Collins, Kirk, 5, 10, 190
Colonial Th., Brooklyn, NY, 297
Colonial Th., Milwaukee, WI, 65
Colonial Th., Norwich, NY, 265
Colonial Th., Portland, OR, 246
Colonial Th., Seattle, WA, 223
Colony (Broadway) Th., New York, NY, 603, 607
Colton, John, 289, 290, 305, 902
Columbia Music Roll Co., 445
Columbia Th., Erie, PA, 638, 639
Columbia Th., Sharon, PA, 639
combination action, 423
combination piston, 423
Comerford Amusement Co., 210, 212
common metal, 423
Compensating Pipe Organ Company, 655
Comstock, Samuel, 833
Comstock, Cheney & Co., 833-835, 837
Conacher, Peter, 613
concert organ, 423
cone tuning, 423
Congress (Mexico) Th., Chicago, IL, 797
Conn, C. G., 844, 882, 883
Console, The, 10, 11, 420, 421, 491, 940
Convention Hall, Atlantic City, NJ, 319-343, 422-424, 426, 740, 744, 747, 784, 785, 791, 806
Convention Hall Ballroom, Atlantic City, NJ, 231
Cook, J. Lawrence, 378
Cook, Maurice, 538
Cooley, Samuel, 882
Coronado Th., Rockford, IL, 68, 71
Corsini, Andrew, 11, 441
Costello Th., New York, NY, 301
coupler, 423
Courboin, Charles, 388, 465, 682-684, 916
Cousans, L. B., 744
Cousans, R. A., 744
Cousans, J. R. Sons and Co., 744
Cove Th., Glen Cove, NY, 318
Cowham, Bernard, 58-60
Cox, Arthur, 441
Cozatt, Perry, 103, 104, 740
Cramblet Engineering Corp., 779
Cramers, Howard, 388
Crandall, H. M., 210
Crane, C. Howard, 210
Crank, Jim, 924
Crawford, Jesse, 16, 214, 226, 286, 496, 498, 509, 842
Crawford Automobile Co., 346
Cremona pianos, 597, 742
crescendo pedal, 423
Crentz, Otto, 636
Crome, Edward, 491
Crome, Ken, 28
Cronin, Francis, 176
Crystal Cathedral, Garden Grove, CA, 516
Curtis Pneumatic Machinery Co., 794
cutup, 423
cypherless device, 644

Dagmar automobile, 346, 347
Daly, William, 677, 678
Daniels, Mark, 548, 549
Daniels, Peter, 11-13, 347, 387, 390, 441
Daniels, Riley, 209, 214, 347, 383, 388
Dargis, C., 327
Davey, Lloyd, 214, 223, 233, 677, 679, 682-684
Davis & Ferris, 442
Day, Augustus, 736
Deagan, John, 843, 844
Deagan co., 171, 177, 211, 235, 244, 843-864, 866
death rattle, 423
Deck, William, 636
Decorators Supply Co., 193
Deerpath Th., Lake Forest, IL, 139, 140
De Grasse, Simon, 522
De Lay, Tom, 441, 928
De Luxe Th., Detroit, MI, 619
De Mello, John, 98
De Mille, Cecil, 522
Delft Th., Marquette, MI, 298
Denison Brothers, 922, 923
Dennison, William, 891
Dennison Organ Pipe Co., 55, 65, 68, 71, 73, 84, 182, 195, 197, 290, 307, 397, 424, 465, 643, 663, 677, 740, 891-895, 901
Dennison-Warnock Co., 891
Depue, Harold, 472
Derrick, Silas, 132
Derrick & Felgemaker, 132, 345
Des Moines Th., Des Moines, IA, 211
Dethier, Gaston, 674
Dewar, Robert, 316
Diapason, The, 11, 12, 174, 421, 681
diaphragm regulator, 321, 335, 337, 422
Dickinson, Clarence, 674
direct electric, 423, 694-698
Dirksen, Richard, 472
Discus blowers, 386
Dittes, Mr., 676
divided manual, 60, 61
Doelling, Ernst, 896, 897
Doering, G. A., 694
Doerr, Nicholas, 105
Dollinger, Malin, 441
Doman, L. B., 915
Dominique, G. A., 676
double languid, 321, 325, 331, 423, 424, 895
Dougherty Organ Co., 655
Douglas, R., 327
Dowling, Leonard, 31, 632
Draper, Alan, 714
drawl unit, 496
Dream Th., Seattle, WA, 119
Dreamland Ballroom, Chicago, IL, 70, 73
Du Bois, A., 678
Duci Bella, Joseph, 11, 441
duckbill shallot, 423, 424
Dudley Th., Boston, MA, 116
Dunstedter, Eddie, 185
Duo Art reproducing piano, 598

duplex, 423
Duplex Manufacturing Co., 882
Dupont, Dorothy, 14
Durfee, Walter, 865
Durst, Carl, 821, 827
Durst, Fred, 798, 821
Durst, Roland, 798
Durst, Val, 147, 800, 814, 821
Durst, Wilma, 821
Durst-Boegle, 55, 147, 261, 262, 740, 798-805, 814
Durst & Company, 798, 821, 896
Durst Organ Supply, 798, 821
Dyson, Thomas, 901

ear, 422, 423
Earle Th., Philadelphia, PA, 243, 249
Eastern Th., Columbus, OH, 730
Eastman, Electa, 736
Eastman, George, 42
Eastman School of Music, 41-45
Eaton, Sid, 892
Eberson, John, 456
Ebert, S. H., 744
echo organ, 220, 227, 423
Eddy, Clarence, 587
Edgewater Beach Hotel, Chicago, IL, 371
effect, 424
Effingham Th., Effingham, IL, 704
Egyptian Th., Milwaukee, WI, 69
Ehrhardt, Alfred, 11, 154, 441
Eilers Music Co., 49, 286, 495
electric action, 424
Electric Specialty Co., 782, 783
Electric Vibrato Co., 782
Electrolian Organ Co., 492-494, 501
electro-pneumatic, 424
Elgar, Charles, 70
Elks Temple, Los Angeles, CA, 527
Elliot, R. P., 22, 24, 33, 49, 156, 208, 209, 214, 223, 229, 233, 234, 348, 371, 421, 495, 496, 498, 599, 674, 676-679, 681-683, 685, 744, 745
Elliott, Walter, 316, 889
Elm Skating Club, Elmhurst, IL, 142
Ely, Augustus, 28
Elysee delivery car, 347
Embassy Th., Fort Wayne, IN, 454
Emerson, Ralph, 62, 70, 927
Empress Electric pianos, 445
Empress Th., Anchorage, AK, 210, 212
Empress Th., Cordova, AK, 210
enclosed, 424
Encyclopedia of Automatic Musical Instruments, 10, 12, 421
Endres, Anthony, 83
Engle, William, 33
erecting room, 424
Erie Burial Case Co., 798
Erie Reed Pipe Co., 147, 195, 644, 896, 903
Essex Institute, 174
Essex Th., New York, NY, 317
Estey co., 20, 105-132, 137, 153, 316, 337, 475, 494, 755, 913, 914, 930
Estey family, 106
Estey Piano Co., 673
Evans, John, 683
Evans, Roscoe, 332
Evans, Walter, 694
Evenheeter, 779
Everett Piano Co., 378
Excelsior Drum Works, 865
Exeter Street Th., Boston, MA, 117

Fabry, G., 327
Fagan, J. K., 741, 742
Fairchild Aviation, 400
Fair Park Auditorium, Dallas, TX, 64, 65, 68
fan tremolo, 35, 36, 424
Fargo Th., Geneva, IL, 137, 138
Fargo Th., Sycamore, IL, 137
Farnam, Lynnwood, 674
Farrand, William, 132
Farrand Organ Co., 22, 132
Farrand & Votey, 16, 22, 33, 132, 208, 322, 492, 584, 731, 736, 737, 748, 890, 898
Federlein, Gottfried, 28, 674
Feiereisen, Chris, 11, 18, 441
Felgemaker, A. B., 102, 132, 133, 145, 638
Fenton, Arthur, 101
Fenton Organ Co., 101
Ferris, John, 541
Ferris, Richard, 442
Ferris & Stuart, 315, 442
56th Street Th., Philadelphia, PA, 226
Fine Arts Th., Monmouth, IL, 104
finishing, 424
Firma Ernst Doelling, 896, 897
First Presbyterian Ch., Staunton, VA, 470
Fischer, J. & C., 206
Fischer Th., Fond du Lac, WI, 69
Five Boro automobile, 347
Flaherty, Charles, 179
Fleishacker, Mortimer, 500, 501
Fleming, William, 492, 493
Fletcher, Henry, 491
Fletcher, Warren, 891
Fletcher & Harris, 491, 501
Floyd, C. B., 155, 677
Floyd, Clifford, 155
flue, 424
flue pipe, 424
Fogg, Clarence, 565
Foort, Reginald, 381, 386, 388, 421, 744
Foort organ, 346, 365, 382-388, 390, 399, 806
foot, 424
Forest Hills Th., Long Island City, NY, 614, 615
Forster, Paul, 301, 915
45th Street Th., Seattle, WA, 226
Forum Th., Los Angeles, CA, 210, 214, 216, 218-222, 230, 243, 679, 847
Foto-Orchestra, 498, 510, 632
Fotoplayers, 16, 51, 495, 496, 498, 499, 503, 510, 524
foundation, 424
Fountain Square Th., Indianapolis, IN, 299
four-poster lift, 65, 69, 190, 300, 793
Fox, Virgil, 472
Fox, William, 348, 350, 371
Fox (Orpheum) Th., Oakland, CA, 368
Fox (Seventh Avenue) (Music Hall) Th., Seattle, WA, 501, 537
Fox Th., Atlanta, GA, 192, 360, 362, 375-377
Fox Th., Aurora, IL, 170
Fox Th., Detroit, MI, 15, 374
Fox Th., Philadelphia, PA, 351
Fox Th., St. Louis, MO, 374
Fox Th., San Diego, CA, 526
Fox Th., San Francisco, CA, 374
Fox Wilshire Th., Beverly Hills, CA, 108, 287
Francke, Hattie, 736
Frazee, H. Norman, 134
Frazee, Leslie, 132, 134
Frazee, Roy, 134
Frazee Organ Co., 134-136, 890, 930
free reed, 424
frein, 424, 425
Fridlund, J. Vern, 676
Friedrich, Ed, 718
Fruttchey, Frank, 162
Fuller, Frederick, 83
fundamental, 424
Funkhouser, J. O., 388

gabriel horns, 595
Gaiety Th., Trenton, NJ, 373
Garden Th., Davenport, IA, 211
Garden Th., Greenfield, MA, 302
Garrick Th., Winnipeg, Manitoba, 711
Gautier, Jacques, 678
Gautschi, Alfred, 169, 902
Geagan, J. G., 866
general cancel, 424
General Electric, 757, 782
general piston, 424
General Precision Engineering, 270
Geneva Organ Co., 20, 137-144, 177, 178, 613, 791, 797
Gerrard, C. P., 145
Gershwin, George, 677, 678
Giesecke, Carl, 806
Gilbert, Robert, 11, 441
Gillett, Don, 378, 606
Gittins, George, 673, 676, 677, 681, 682
glass crash effect, 228
Glatz, Rudolph, 676, 677, 681
Glazer, Irvin, 11, 441
Gleason, Harold, 42
Glen Th., Glen Ellyn, IL, 72
Gluck, Fred, 798, 821, 827
Goderich Organ Co., 655
Goldthwaite, Chandler, 223
Goll, George, 673, 676, 684
Gollnick, Walter, 58, 59, 78, 927
gong, Chinese, 235
Goodell, H. E., 649
Good Hope Lutheran Ch., Bucyrus, OH, 207
Goodrich, William, 174
Goodwill Th., Johnson City, NY, 91
Goodyear Rubber Co., 599
goosebill shallot, 145, 333, 423, 424, 807, 813 898
Gordon, F., 327
Gordon's Olympia Th., Brockton, MA, 176
Gottfried, Anton, 145, 147, 150, 151, 330, 676, 806, 807, 814, 815, 821, 896, 902
Gottfried, Henry, 11, 147, 441, 676, 807, 813, 814, 896
Gottfried co., 20, 49, 51, 55, 69, 71, 83, 84, 137, 138, 145-152, 169, 176, 178, 265, 315, 397, 454, 461, 588, 612, 613, 616, 660, 673, 676, 737, 738, 740, 791, 798, 800, 806-816, 821, 822, 891, 896, 898, 902, 903, 923, 930
Gould, C., 327
Grace Cathedral, San Francisco, CA, 12
Grace Lutheran Ch., Fargo, ND, 667
Gram, Edmund Piano Co., 916
Granada Th., Malden, MA, 134
Granada Th., Patchogue, NY, 319
Granby Th., Norfolk, VA, 620
Grand Riviera (Riviera) Th., Detroit, MI, 528, 529
Grand Th., Norristown, PA, 228
Grand Th., Wausau, WI, 184, 185, 190
Grant Union High School, Sacramento, CA, 51, 52, 807
Gratian, John, 153
Gratian, Joseph, 153
Gratian, Warren, 153
Gratian Organ Builders, 153, 154
Great States theatres, 62
Greeley, Mae, 716
Green, Stu, 11, 441
Greenbrier Hotel, White Sulphur Springs, WV, 371
Gregory, Sherry, 828
Gregory, S. J., 62, 66, 77
Gretsch, Fred, 882
Griffith-Beach, 154, 809, 930
Griffith Piano Co., 154
Grimmer, Hugo, 717
Gruenstein, S. E., 681
Gschoff, Charles, 928
Guilmant, Alexandre, 502
Gustafson, Harvey, 667
Gutfleisch, Leonhard, 898
Gutfleisch & Schopp, 145, 159, 454, 565, 896, 898

Hagerstown Engraving Co., 922
Hagerstown Engraving & Stamping Co., 922
Hagerstown Trust Co., 346

Haggarty, J. J., 549
Hagstrom, Oscar, 207, 214, 223
Haldeman, Clarence, 31, 32, 729
Hall, Ben, 421, 538
Hall, Harry, 155, 156
Hall, Thomas, 315
Hall & Labagh, 583
Hall Organ Co., 20, 155-157, 565, 677, 917
Hallas, John, 821
Haltnorth Th., Cleveland, OH, 265, 268-270
halving ratio, 383, 424
Hamel, Brink, 473
Hamilton, Wade, 536
Hampton, Hope, 296, 297
Hand, George, 838
Hand & Co., 838
Hann, Frederick, 662
Hann-Wangerin Co., 662
Hann-Wangerin-Weickhardt Co., 662, 905
Hanrahan, J., 327
Hanson, Eddie, 60
Hardy, Walter, 208, 223
Harmon, Paddy, 70, 73, 77
harmonic, 424
harp, 424, 425
Harrah, Allen, 11, 441
Harris, David, 196, 683
Harris, Edward, 92
Harris, Murray M., 491-493
Harris, Murray M. Organ Co., 491-494, 498, 499, 501, 504, 505, 507, 508, 551, 552, 632, 891
Harrison, G. Donald, 107, 365, 599, 606, 682
Harrison & Harrison, 365
Haskell, C. E., 157
Haskell, Charles, 157, 158, 264, 565
Haskell, William, 105, 107, 157, 337, 425
Haskell basses, 107, 109, 127, 425
Haskell co., 157, 158, 821, 898
Haslam, Edwin, 694
Hastings, Anna, 174
Hastings, Francis, 174
Hausmann & Co., 817
Hawaii Th., Honolulu, HI, 514
Heathman Hotel, Portland, OR, 614
Hedback Th., Indianapolis, IN, 458
Hedberg, Dennis, 738
Hedgeland, Frederic, 207
Hedges, Edwin Sr., 901
Hedges, Edwin B., 145, 565, 891, 901
Heinz Auditorium, Pittsburgh, PA, 232
Helmholtz, Herman von, 843
Hershey Community Th., Hershey, PA, 601, 795
Hesco, 922
Hess, Max, 182
Hettche, John, 655
Hickey, Jerry, 441
Highland Th., Chicago, IL, 66, 70, 83
Highland Th., Ft. Thomas, KY, 90
high pressure, 425
Hill, John, 139
Hillgreen, Alfred, 159
Hillgreen, Robert Jr., 11, 159, 160
Hillgreen, Robert Sr., 159
Hillgreen, Lane & Co., 20, 159-168, 453, 472, 784, 898, 930
Hillstreet Th., Los Angeles, CA, 370
Hillstrom, Nils, 22, 684
Hillstrom Reed Organ Co., 159
Hinners, Arthur, 169, 172
Hinners, John, 169, 172
Hinners & Albertsen, 169
Hinners Organ Co., 20, 31, 32, 95, 103, 169-173, 791, 793, 798, 821, 902, 915, 930
Hippodrome Th., Alton, IL, 153
Hippodrome Th., Los Angeles, CA, 371, 934
Hippodrome Th., Murphysboro, IL, 704
Hippodrome Th., Youngstown, OH, 656
Hirst, Jack, 902
Hirst Organ Specialty Co., 902
Hitchcock, William, 598
Hocker, Harry, 560
Hogans, Henry, 137, 613
Hogans, Walter, 613
Holland, Roy, 916
Hollingsworth, Mr., 94, 95
Hollywood Beach Hotel, Hollywood, FL, 227
Hollywood Th., Detroit, MI, 66, 69, 83
Holtkamp, Henry, 655, 660
Holtkamp, Mary, 655
Holtkamp, Walter, 655
Holtkamp, Walter Jr., 11, 441, 655
Holtkamp Organ Co., 655, 827
Holtzer-Cabot, 60, 782
Holycross, Larry, 454
Holycross, Tom, 454
Hook, E. & G. G., 174, 179, 891
Hook, Elias, 174
Hook, George, 174
Hook & Hastings, 134, 155, 174-176, 565, 673, 898, 917
Hoover, Earl, 388
Hope-Jones, Robert, 16, 33, 66, 154, 208, 492, 494, 496, 498, 599, 613, 615, 622, 623, 677, 729, 736, 758
Hope-Jones Organ Co., 209, 214, 229, 289, 290, 494, 498, 677, 744, 745, 890, 902
Hopkins, George, 113
Horsewhip co., 634
Hoschke, Frederick, 378-380
Hose, John, 378, 388, 390
Hoskins, L. J., 917
Howard, E. R., 842
Howard seat, 842
Howard Th., Atlanta, GA, 517, 519
Howell, H. A., 176-178, 791
Hoyt metal, 93, 425, 903
Hoyt Metal Co., 903
Huber, Carl, 718
Huber, James, 83
Huer, Mr., 494
Humphreys, Tink, 58-60, 62
Hunholz, Elmer, 916, 917
Hunt, David, 11-14, 441
Hurlbutt, Jay, 60
Hutchings, George, 92, 93, 132, 134, 179
Hutchings Organ Co., 132, 179, 180, 491, 492, 598, 729, 930
Hutchings, Plaisted & Co., 179
Hutchings-Votey, 132, 179, 891

Illinois Organ Supply, 195, 663
Imperial Roller Rink, Portland, OR, 737, 738
Indiana Th., Indianapolis, IN, 66, 67, 756
International Organ Supply Co., 145
Iowa (Cedar Rapids Community) Th., Cedar Rapids, IA, 72, 663, 671
Iris Th., Miles City, MT, 519
Iseminger, H. M., 394
Isis Th., Lynchburg, VA, 620
Isis Th., Richmond, VA, 620
Ivanoff, Jim, 827

Jacobsen, Norman, 174
Jacobus, Guy, 594
Jacobus, Leland, 928
James, Carlton, 915
James Th., Columbus, OH, 210
Jardine, George, 182, 462, 898, 911
Jarvis Organ Co., 817
Jefferson Th., Fort Wayne, IN, 210
Jefferson Th., Philadelphia, PA, 468
Jenkins Music Co., 694
Jensen & Von Herberg, 212
Johnson, A. F., 137, 138
Johnson, Albin, 676
Johnson, Julius, 679
Johnson, William A. Organ Co., 634, 901
Johnston, E. S., 494
Johnston Organ & Piano Manufacturing Co., 493, 501, 632
Jones, W. Meakin, 223
Jones, Linick & Schaeffer, 210
Jordan, James, 28
Jordan, Arthur Piano Co., 694
Jost, Edgar, 475
Jost, Frank, 473
Jost, Henry, 473, 475
Judkins, Laura, 709
Judkins, Phil, 709
Junchen, David, 8-10, 13, 190, 795
Junchen, Lawrence, 5
Junchen, Lucy, 795
Junchen-Collins Organ Corp., 10, 169
Junchen Pipe Organ Service, 169
junction board, 425

Kaimuki Th., Honolulu, HI, 98
Kantnor, Arnie, 716
Karlton Th., Philadelphia, PA, 212
Karn, D. W., 181
Karn-Morris, 181
Kast, Otto, 718
Katt, A. J., 694, 718
Katz, Sam, 62
Kauffman, L. E., 544, 547, 549
Kaufmann, Preston, 11, 441
Kaylor, A. D., 904
Kaylor & Clark, 904
Kayser Glove Co., 889
Keefe, Walter, 58-60, 62
Keith Memorial Th., Boston, MA, 134
Keith theatres, 212
Kelly, Thomas, 181
Kennedy, Stuart, 181
Kent, A. E., 132
Kent Th., Kent, WA, 461
Kerrisdale Th., Vancouver, BC, 100
Keswick Th., Glenside, PA, 24-27
Ketcham, O. W., 643
keydesk, 425
Keyser, Charles, 394
KFRC Radio, 632, 633
KGW/KEX Radio, 51
Kibbee, Gordon, 286
Kibler, W. C., 798
Kilgen, Alfred, 183
Kilgen, Charles, 182
Kilgen, Charles C., Jr., 183, 191
Kilgen, Eugene, 182, 183
Kilgen, John, 182
Kilgen, Louise, 191
Kilgen, Sebastian, 182
Kilgen Associates, Inc., 182
Kilgen co., 12, 18-20, 92, 105, 147, 177, 182-205, 271, 289, 474, 740, 742, 784, 797, 891, 902, 910, 916, 930, 931
Kilgen Organ Company, Inc., 182
Kimball, Henry, 134
Kimball, William Wallace, 206-208, 217
Kimball, William Wallace, Jr., 208, 234
Kimball co., 20, 22, 24, 49, 52, 66, 68, 82, 147, 182, 206-260, 286, 350, 371, 424, 427, 461, 498, 499, 531, 565, 676, 679, 681-685, 687, 731, 740, 742, 745, 772, 793, 797, 830, 847, 883, 914, 931, 932, 934
Kimball-Frazee Organ Co., 134, 135
Kimball, Smallman & Frazee, 134, 135
Kimball-Welte, 677, 684
Kimber-Allen, 788
Kindt Th., Davenport, IA, 24, 26
Kinema (Criterion) Th., Los Angeles, CA, 515
Kinema Th., Fresno, CA, 522
Kinetic Engineering Co., 13, 18, 19, 198, 209, 321, 382, 643, 741, 744-747, 755, 758, 776, 777, 888
Kingsley, Bert, 498, 501, 516, 521, 556, 557, 562
Kinsley, Bert . . . see Kingsley, Bert
Klann, August, 784
Klann, Paul, 784, 785
Klann co., 55, 159, 164, 784, 785
Klein, J. W., 496
Kline, Richard, 387

Kloehs, Gustav, 643, 644, 649
KMA Radio, 474
KMBC Radio, 536
KMOX Radio, 188, 190
KMPC Radio, 28
KNBC Radio, 682
Koch, Herbie, 190
Koehnken & Grim, 314
Kohl, Arthur, 261, 262, 740, 799, 800, 932
Kohler, John, 866
Kohler, Sylvester, 464, 470
Kohler Industries, 673
Kohler-Liebich, 866-881
KPO Radio, 682
Kraft, Edward, 223
Kramer Organ Co., 263, 613
Krebs, F. W., 147, 896, 903
Kreglo, Paul, 387, 388
Kreis, L. Alvin, 636
Kugel, Harry, 821
Kugel, Henry, 145, 147, 821
Kugel, Rubin, 821
Kugler Th., Philadelphia, PA, 209
Kuhlman, Harvey, 711
Kurtz, Kenneth, 60
Kurtz-Seeburg Action Co., 597

labial pipe, 425
Labor Temple, Louisville, KY, 284, 285
La Fayette Th., Batavia, NY, 653
Lake Th., Milwaukee, WI, 663
Lamb, Bill, 11, 15, 440
Lamb, H., 327
Lamberton, Richard, 831
Lamson, Dode, 453, 454
Lancashire, John, 92, 93
Lancashire-Marshall, 92, 159
Lancashire and Turner, 92
Landon, John, 421
Lane, Charles, 159
Lane, E. W., 179
Lane, Howard, 12
languid, 425
Lankershim family, 494
Lasman, Mr., 815
Lathrop, Capt., 210
Laukhuff, Adolph, 819
Laukhuff, Andreas, 819
Laukhuff, August, 819
Laukhuff, Hans Erich, 819
Laukhuff, Otto, 819
Laukhuff, Peter, 819
Laukhuff, Wilhelm, 819
Laukhuff co., 145, 644, 731, 818-820
Lawrence, H. A., 678
Leathurby, George, 613
Leathurby-Smith, 613, 614
leathering, 425
Leatherman, Frank, 271
Leedy, U. G., 882
Leedy & Cooley, 882
Leedy-Ludwig, 882, 883
Leedy Mfg. Co., 882, 883
Leibert, Dick, 535
Leicester Piano Co., 736
Leigh, Leonard, 171, 185
Lemare, Edwin, 516
LeNoir, Benjamin, 158, 264, 740, 824, 928, 932
Lent, Robert F., 644
Lent, Robert G., 11, 441, 643, 644, 784
Leonard, Laurence, 11
Levoy Th., Millville, NJ, 264
Lewis, Homer, 365, 367
Lewis co., 613
Lexington Th., Milwaukee, WI, 595
Liberace, 683
Liberty Chimes, 866-881
Liberty Th., Davenport, IA, 95
Liberty (Roxy) Th., Long Beach, CA, 508
Liebich, Otto, 866
Light, James, 322
Lightcap, Alan, 644
Lincoln Square Th., Decatur, IL, 62, 63
Lincoln Th., Lakewood, OH, 657
Lincoln Th., Lincoln, IL, 138
Link, Edwin, 265
Link, Edwin Jr., 8, 265, 270-272
Link, George, 265, 272
Link Aviation, Inc., 270
Link Piano Co., 8, 20, 265-283, 791, 914, 932
lip, 422
Lipes, Harold, 458
Liturgical Organ Co., 454
lobby organ, 67, 374
Lodes, Joseph, 716
Lodes, Kathryn, 716
Loew syndicate, 348
Loew's 83rd Street Th., New York, NY, 369
Loew's Jersey Th., Jersey City, NJ, 541
Loew's Kings Th., Brooklyn, NY, 434
Loew's Paradise Th., Bronx, NY, 539
Loew's Penn Th., Pittsburgh, PA, 534, 535
Loew's Pitkin Th., Brooklyn, NY, 538
Loew's State Th., Los Angeles, CA, 934
Loew's State Th., New York, NY, 354
Loew's State Th., Providence, RI, 538
Loew's Valencia Th., Jamaica, NY, 538
Logan, Jacqueline, 522
Lombardozzi, Gilbert, 831
Los Angeles Art Organ Co., 492, 501, 502, 551, 911
Losh, George, 101, 316, 317, 322, 328
Losh, Siebert, 101, 316-318, 320-322, 327, 348, 747
Louisiana Purchase Exposition, 502
Louisville Pipe Organ Co., 20, 284-286, 791, 932
low pressure, 425
Lowe, Oliver, 910
Luberoff, Louis, 209, 349-351, 360, 367
Lubliner & Trinz, 210, 213
Ludwig, Theobald, 883
Ludwig, William, 883
Ludwig Drum Co., 883
Ludwig Industries, Inc., 883
Ludwig & Ludwig, 244, 882-887
Lugwigtone, 657
Luedtke, Rosemary, 11, 18, 441
Lufkin, W. W., 207
luminous console, 105, 107, 112, 115, 120
Lutkins, T. L., 839
Luxor taxicab, 346, 347
Luz, Ernst, 348
Lynch, Mayme, 716
Lyon & Healy, 92, 655, 905
Lyric Th., Camden, NJ, 928

Maas, Louis, 286, 287, 498
Maas Organ Co., 286-288, 932
Maas-Rowe, 287
Mabel Tainter Memorial Th., Menominee, WI, 634, 635
MacClain, Leonard, 226
MacNeur, Robert, 161
Madison Th., Detroit, MI, 160
Madison Th., Peoria, IL, 169, 171, 793
Maerz, Dana, 718
Magnetic Organ Action Co., 786
Majestic (Perry) (Shea's) Th., Erie, PA, 639
Majestic Th., Detroit, MI, 162
Majestic Th., Grand Rapids, MI, 66
Majestic Th., New York, NY, 514
Majestic Th., San Antonio, TX, 537
Malarkey, E. C., 54, 288
Malotte, Joseph, 453
Malinjos Piano Co., 597
mandolin, 425
Mansfield Organ Pipe Works, 904
manual, 425
manual chest, 425
March, Archie, 286, 563, 565
March, Archie Jr., 563
marimba, 425
Marketplace (Markley) Th., Norristown, PA, 55
Marks, Arthur, 599, 606
Marks Th., Cleveland, OH, 592, 593
Marlotte, H. A., 394
Marquette Piano Co., 597, 742, 906
Marr, David, 289-291, 305, 902
Marr & Colton, 11, 14, 20, 102, 182, 183, 289-313, 350, 737, 740, 793, 797, 891, 911, 915, 932
Marr and Collins Co., 289
Marshall, Edward, 92
Marshall, George, 92
Marshall, Octavius, 92, 93
Marshall, Thomas, 92
Marshall Brothers Organ Co., 92
Marshall & Odenbrett, 92
Martin, A. Perry, 179
Martin, James, 679
Martinetti's Restaurant, Crystal Lake, IL, 713
Mason, Harvell, 467
master xylophone, 68, 425
Mathers, Alfred, 314
Mathers, Richard, 314
matrix relay, 183, 195, 373, 384
Matthews, R. P., 495, 500, 501, 533, 537
Maus, Harry Page, 453, 454
Maxcy-Barton, 84
Maxcy, W. G., 59, 82, 926
May, Eddie, 299
Mayer, Frederick, 389
Mayland, R. H., 887
McAbee, Kay, 67
McCain, David, 11, 12, 441
McComas, L. E., 346
McCourt, James, 636
McCurdy, Alex, 233
McGee, Doug, 909
McGinnis, Grace, 441
McGreece, James P. Co., 842
McLaughlin, Walter, 316
McQuigg, Charles, 493, 494
Mead, William, 268
Mechanical Orguinette Co., 22
Medinah Temple, Chicago, IL, 34
Meidinger, G., 748
Meidinger, U. P., 748
Meidinger, G. & Co., 748-754
Meisel & Sullivan, 315
Melgard, Al, 62, 65, 77, 82
melody coupler, 320, 425
Meloni, Anthony, 442
Memorial Auditorium, Worcester, MA, 233
Merrill Th., Milwaukee, WI, 668
Metropolitan Opera House, Philadelphia, PA, 350, 355-360, 378
Metropolitan Th., Boston, MA, 232
Metro Th., Johannesburg, South Africa, 796
Met Th, Philadelphia, PA, 350, 355-360, 378
Mettler, Rose, 716
Meurling, Emil, 787
Meyer, Charles, 906
Meyer, Frank, 208, 905
Meyer, Gordon, 11, 441, 666, 906
Meyer, Jerome, 60, 84, 145, 208, 445, 588, 594, 595, 663, 670, 891, 902, 905-909
Meyer, Victor, 906
Michel, George, 207, 208, 233, 248, 685
Michell, C. C., 33
Michigan Th., Ann Arbor, MI, 66, 68
Michigan Th., Chicago, IL, 228
Midland Th., Hutchinson, KS, 40
Midmer, Reed, 315, 316
Midmer, Reuben, 315, 316
Midmer co., 101, 315-317, 744, 889
Midmer-Losh, 20, 153, 315-344, 348, 384, 740, 784, 806, 932
Mid-West Organ Supply Co., 910
Miesner Piano Co., 917
Mignon piano, 673
Millbrooke, Anne, 441
Miller, Allen, 11, 35
Miller, Fred, 495

Miller, Jack, 399
Miller, Michael, 11, 441
Miller's California Th., Los Angeles, CA, 509, 512
Miller's Th., Los Angeles, CA, 510
Mills Violano, 531
Milner, F. T., 207, 209
Minor, C. Sharpe, 265, 267, 273-277, 541, 548
Minuette, 105, 107-110
Mitchell, Ron, 710
Mixsell, Dr., 548
mixture, 425
Mogensen, Max, 922
Mogensen, Rick, 922
Moline Pipe Organ Co., 92
Moller automobile, 347
Moller, George, 345
Moller, Kevin, 347, 388
Moller, Martha, 347
Moller, M. P., 132, 234, 345-347, 361, 366, 382, 390, 397, 744, 758, 788, 922
Moller, M. P. Jr., 234, 346-348, 367, 388
Moller co., 10, 12, 13, 20, 82, 99, 147, 156, 160, 192, 196, 209, 214, 233, 345-415, 424, 461-463, 467, 474, 565, 644, 693, 677, 689, 711, 740, 744, 788, 806, 891, 904, 914, 932-934
Moller Motor Car Co., 346, 347
Moller Piano Co., 316
Monarch Tool & Mfg. Co., 636
Monroe Th., Rochester, NY, 262, 799
Montauk Th., Passaic, NJ, 154
Moore, Ernst, 916
Moore and Fisher, 916
Morris, Leonard, 442, 888
Morris Electric Action Co., 888
Morrison, Roger E., 915
Morrison Th., Alliance, OH, 162, 163
Moser, Ira, 464, 465, 470
Mosque Th., Newark, NJ, 154
Moss, Tony, 441
Mother Church of Christ, Scientist, Boston, MA, 174
mouth, 425
Mozart Th., Elmira, NY, 619
MSR rolls, 616, 617
Mullaney, W. J., 694
Multi-Control player, 682-684, 913
Muri, John, 15
Musicalle player, 682
Musser Marimba Co., 883
mutation, 425
Mutty, L. J., 839

Nagel, Max, 11, 12, 182, 183
Nalley, Howard, 387, 396, 397, 904
National Automatic Music Co., 912
National Cash Register Co., 112
National Electric Piano Co., 906
National Organ Supply Co., 84, 137, 147, 195, 197, 307, 643, 660, 740, 821-826
National Piano Mfg. Co., 912
National Theatre Supply Co., 187, 198
neighborhood theatre, 425
Nelson Wiggen, 906
Neptune Th., Seattle, WA, 212
Netzer, Pat, 473, 718
New Era Organ, 289
New Fillmore Th., San Francisco, CA, 512, 520
New Grand Central Th., St. Louis, MO, 191
New Mexico Military Institute, 161
New Mission Th., San Francisco, CA, 519
Nichols, Glenn, 394
nicking, 401, 425
Niemann, Frank, 676
Nixon Grand Th., Philadelphia, PA, 243
Nixon-Nirdlinger, 210
Noble, T. Tertius, 674, 681
Nolan, Buddy, 454
Nordstrom, G. V., 179
Norman Bros., & Beard, 289
Norris, Lester, 139
Norris Th., Norristown, PA, 55
North, George, 155
North Center Th., Chicago, IL, 228, 248
Northwest Recording Studio, Seattle, WA, 51
Nosco Plastics, 821
nuancer, 378
Nuttall, James, 677, 682, 683, 729
Nyquist, Carl, 94

Oakland Th., Chicago, IL, 669
Oaks Roller Rink, Portland, OR, 739
Obeco blowers, 742, 743
Ochse, Orpha, 421, 607
Ocker, Harold, 904
O'Connell, Charles, 388
Odell, Caleb, 442
Odell, John, 442
Odell co., 442-444, 890
Odenbrett, Phillip, 92
Odenbrett & Abler, 92
Odeon Carlton Th., Toronto, Ontario, Canada, 160, 161
Odeon Th., Atlanta, GA, 620
Odeon Th., Richmond, VA, 620
offset chest, 425
Ohio Beauty, 589
Ohio Th., Columbus, OH, 528
Ohio Wesleyan University, 214
Old St. Louis Noodle & Pizza Co., 10
Oliver Organ Co., 910
Olympia (Paramount) Th., New Haven, CT, 635
Olympia Th., Lynn, MA, 179
Olympia Th., New Bedford, MA, 179
Olympia Th., New York, NY, 518
Operators Piano Co., 445-452, 597, 740, 905
opus lists, explanation of, 17-20
opus number, 425
Orange Th., Orange, CA, 710
orchestral organ, 423, 425
orchestrion, 425
Orcutt, O. W., 492
Organ Blowing Engineering Co., 742, 743
Organ Builders Association of America, 599, 662
Organ Historical Society, 11, 441, 468, 827
Organ Supply Corp., 147, 159, 171, 264, 265, 588, 740, 798, 814, 821-827, 923
Organ Supply Industries, 160, 642, 798, 821, 827-831
Organola player, 731
Organ Power Co., 755
Orgatron, 378
Orgoblo . . . see Spencer Turbine Co.
Oriole Terrace Dance Hall, Detroit, MI, 181
Oriental Th., Chicago, IL, 176
Oriental Th., Milwaukee, WI, 71
Orpheum circuit, 210, 213
Orpheum music rolls, 445
Orpheum Th., Jacksonville, FL, 620
Orpheum Th., Springfield, IL, 66
Otis, Elisha, 795
Otis Elevator Co., 601, 795-797
Outlaw, Jerry, 182
overtone, 425
Owl Th., Riverside, CA, 118
Oyster, Fred, 900

Pabst Th., Milwaukee, WI, 132, 322, 373, 748
Page Organ Co., 20, 66, 176, 189, 453-461, 788, 791, 898
Palace Th., Jamestown, NY, 296
Palace Th., Little Rock, AR, 188
Palace Th., Marion, OH, 456
Palace Th., New York, NY, 520
Palace Th., Philadelphia, PA, 229
Palace Th., Rockville, CT, 112, 113
pallet, 425
Palmer, B. J., 22
Palmgreen, Gustav, 316
Palm Th., Chicago, IL, 667
Palm Th., Philadelphia, PA, 513
Pantages (Orpheum) Th., San Francisco, CA, 528, 529
Pantages Th., Portland, OR, 528
Pantages Th., Salt Lake City, UT, 518
Pantages (Warner) (Warnor) Th., Fresno, CA, 536
Pantheon Th., Chicago, IL, 213
Paramount Th., Hamilton, OH, 82
Paramount Th., Kokomo, IN, 459
Paramount Th., Middletown, OH, 82
Paramount Th., Newport News, VA, 70, 82
Paramount Th., New York, NY, 51, 52
Paramount Th., Phoenix, AZ, 315
Park Th., Philadelphia, PA, 646
Parker, G. L., 694
Parmentier, C. A. J., 115, 674
Pasadena Civic Auditorium, Pasadena, CA, 10, 365, 399
Pastime Th., Iowa City, IA, 693
Pastor's Th., New York, NY, 843
Paterson, Geoffrey, 441
Pathe, 678
Pavette, Earl, 461
Payne, A. R., 643, 649, 694, 706
Pearson, Arthur, 501
Pearson, Carl, 551
pedal chest, 425
Pekin Th., Pekin, IL, 169, 172
Peloubet, Leonard, 378, 462, 733
Peloubet co., 462, 463
Pepin, J. E., 100
percussion, 425
Percy, Vincent, 40
perfect pitch, 425
perforator, music roll, 38, 379
Peters, Stanton, 284, 817
Peterson, Hjalmar, 159
Peterson, Oscar, 159
Peterson Electro/Musical Products, 10
Peters, F. A., 134
Petit Ensemble, 183
Pfeffer Organ Co., 182
Phillips, E. J., 400
photoplayers, 425
Photo Player Co., 500, 501
piano console, 425
Piano & Organ Supply Co., 834
Piano Player Manufacturing Co., 637
Pianola, 898
Piccadilly Th., Chicago, IL, 191-193
Piccadilly Th., New York, NY, 301, 303
Pierce, Samuel . . . also see Dennison, 145 594, 616, 660, 890-894, 901, 911
Pilcher, Gerard, 464, 466
Pilcher, Henry, 464, 466
Pilcher, Henry Jr., 464, 466
Pilcher, Paul, 464, 466
Pilcher, Robert, 464, 466
Pilcher, William, 464-466
Pilcher, William Jr., 464, 466, 467
Pilcher co., 20, 147, 464-471, 473, 917
Pilcher & Chant, 464
Pinel, Stephen, 441
Pipe Organ Service Co., 472
piston, 425, 442
pitman chest, 233, 375, 425
pit organ, 214, 426, 497, 506, 523, 524, 567
Pittsburgh Organ Parts Co., 787
pizzicato, 426
Plaisted, M. H., 179
Platt, Henry, 501
player, 426
Player Piano Manufacturing Co., 636
Playhouse Th., Atascadero, CA, 616
Playman, Glen, 616
Playrite music rolls, 917
Plaza Th., Kansas City, MO, 794
pneumatic, 426
pneumatic composition knobs, 442
pneumatic stack, 426

Poolshark, Mr., 182
Portnoff, Nat, 371
Posthorn, The, 11
pouchboard, 426
Powers, Hiram, 472
Powers co., 472
Prante, August, 284
Pratt, Alfred, 174
Pratt, Phineas, 834
Pratt Read, 740, 833-837, 916
Preschley, Conrad, 748
Price, Raymond, 464, 470
Priest, John, 602, 603
Princess Th., Bloomington, IN, 121
Princess Th., Honolulu, HI, 514
Proctor's Palace Th., Yonkers, NY, 29
Prometheus Electric Corp., 780
Provorse, Lloyd, 49
Purvis, Richard, 12
push-up player, 426, 427
Pyle, C. C., 60, 62

QRS Co., 445, 914
Quadruplex player, 38, 39
Quilty, W. T., 284
Quimby, W. C., 210
Quinby, E. J., 113
quintamonic tuning, 844

Radio City Music Hall, New York, NY, 17, 362
Rainbow Th., Milwaukee, WI, 589
rain effect, 811
rank, 426
Raymond, Chester, 145
recorder board, 426
Red Devil, 390
Redford Th., Detroit, MI, 71
Redmond, W. G., 475, 476, 483
Redoehl, Henry, 719
Redondo Rink, Redondo Beach, WA, 51
Red Seal music rolls, 445
Red Vest Pizza House, Monterey, CA, 714
reed, 422, 426
reedless reeds, 107, 111, 145, 426
Regal Th., Chicago, IL, 66, 68, 793
Regent Th., Detroit, MI, 223
Regent Th., Philadelphia, PA, 243
register, 426
register crescendo, 426
registrate, 426
registration, 426
regulator, 426
Reiling, Ann, 536
Reisner, Bill Jr., 788
Reisner, W. H., 788
Reisner co., 52, 137, 172, 271, 285, 321, 328, 384, 385, 453, 588, 617, 737, 788-791, 827, 923
Reisner Kimber Allen, 788
reiteration, 426
relative pitch, 426
relay, 426
Reliance Electric Motor Co., 782
Remsburg, Wilbur, 394
reproducing organ, 426
reproducing piano, 426
Reproduco organs, 445-452, 597, 905
reservoir, 426
resonator, 422, 426
Reuger, Cullie, 473
Reuter, Adolph, 473, 475
Reuter co., 20, 473-490
Reuter-Schwartz, 473, 482, 484
Reynolds, James, 490
Rex Th., Duluth, MN, 101
Rhapsodist pianos, 636
Rialto Th., Atlanta, GA, 620
Rialto Th., Butte, MT, 28, 30
Rialto Th., Des Moines, IA, 513
Rialto Th., Joliet, IL, 67, 68, 70, 83
Richards, Emerson, 231, 316, 320, 322, 324, 327, 336, 422
Ricksecker, Fred, 495
Ringling Brothers Circus, 183
rink organs, 50, 51, 737-739
Rinkenback, J., 905
Ritz (Manos) Th., Indiana, PA, 536
Riverside Church, New York, NY, 174
Riviera Th., Brooklyn, NY, 212
Riviera Th., Rochester, NY, 299
Rivoli Th., Philadelphia, PA, 296, 298
Rivoli Th., Rochester, NY, 261
Rivoli Th., Toledo, OH, 304
Roberson Center, Binghamton, NY, 270
Robert Morton co., 8, 14, 17, 19, 20, 49, 66, 82, 209, 286, 287, 384, 434, 491-582, 632, 663, 695, 731, 736, 740, 742, 806, 848, 891, 910, 928
Roberts, Oral, 712
Robbins & Myers, 782
Robyn, Alfred, 191
Rochester Th., Rochester, NY, 301
Rock Island Organ Co., 94
Rock-Ola, 445, 913
Rodocker, Roy, 445
Roehl, Harvey, 441
Roesler, Fred, 916, 917
Roesler-Hunholz, 914, 916-921
Rokus, Anton, 492
Rollerdrome Skating Rink, Culver City, CA, 737, 738
Rollerland Rink, Renton, WA, 50
rolls, music, 10, 38, 379, 380, 445, 914-921
roll top, 426
romantic organ, 423, 426
Roosevelt, Frank, 583, 584
Roosevelt, Hilborne, 157, 583, 584
Roosevelt, Theodore, 583
Roosevelt co., 16, 105, 132, 145, 196, 345, 492, 583-587, 617, 636, 729, 736, 898
Roosevelt Th., Buffalo, NY, 299
Roosevelt Th., Chicago, IL, 210, 213, 214
Rosen, Ken, 11, 441
Rosenthal, Jay, 11, 441
Rosewood Th., Chicago, IL, 618
Ross, Tommy, 492, 563
Rosser, William, 11, 337
Roth, Steve, 147, 896
Rowe, Paul, 287
Rowe International, 913
Roxy Th., New York, NY, 14, 214, 230, 772
Royal York Hotel, Toronto, Ontario, 806
Rubens, Jules, 62
Ruffu, Anthony, 322
Runge, Max, 716
Ruppert, Jacob, 681
Russell, C. B., 473
Russo, Joe, 900
Rust, Hielo, 169
Ryder, George, 598

Sabin, Bill, 265
Sabol, Albert, 473, 475
Saenger, Julian, 533
Saenger Th., New Orleans, LA, 533
St. Francis Th., San Francisco, CA, 506, 528, 529
St. John's Lutheran Ch., St. Paul, MN, 734
St. Louis Pipe Organ Co., 12, 182
St. Louis Th., St. Louis, MO, 217
St. Mary of the Lake Seminary, Mundelein, IL, 177
St. Matthew's Lutheran Ch., Medina, OH, 160
St. Paul's Cathedral, London, England, 806
Salem Church Organ Co., 159
Sandberg, Theodore, 94, 95, 328
Sartwell, C. B., 501, 556, 569
Satterwhite, Florence, 679, 681
Satterwhite, Preston, 679, 681
Savoy Th., Milwaukee, WI, 663, 669
Sawyer, Ray, 315, 371, 934
Saxe, Tom, 62, 66
scale, 426
Schaeble, Peter, 538
Schaefer, Bernard, 588
Schaefer Brothers theatres, 62
Schaefer Organ Co., 588, 589
Schaeffer, Jake, 473, 475, 488
Schaff Brothers Piano Co., 265
Schantz, Bruce, 589
Schantz, E. F., 589, 590
Schantz, John, 589
Schantz, O. A., 589, 590
Schantz, Paul, 589
Schantz, V. A., 589, 590
Schantz, Victor, 589
Schantz co., 18, 464, 589-594, 740, 776
Schick razor factory, 683, 686
Schiller, James, 500
Schillinger, Fred, 145
Schine theatres, 261
Schlueter, Henry, 844
Schmitt, Curt, 177
Schoenstein, Felix, 49
Schoenstein, Leo, 49, 286, 498, 499
Schoenstein & Co., 491, 511, 890, 910, 928
Schopp, August, 898, 899
Schopp, Bob, 160, 441, 898, 900
Schopp, Harvey, 898
Schopp, Robert, 898
Schopp's Sons, A. R., 898-900
Schuelke, Max, 594, 595
Schuelke, William, 594-596, 662
Schuelke, William J., 595
Schuelke and Steinert, 594
Schuelke Organ Co., 594-596, 638, 662, 909
Schulke, Wilhelm, 594
Schuessler Fiber Case Co., 883
Schuster, Frank, 899
Schwarz, Earl, 473
Scott, Harley, 821
Scott, Walter, 454
Scott, Walter "Scotty," 682, 683
Scotty's Castle, Death Valley, CA, 682-684
scroll tuning, 426
Sears Roebuck, 445
Seeburg, J. P., 597
Seeburg, Noel, 597
Seeburg Piano Co., 137, 271, 597, 613, 616-620, 628, 638, 906, 913
Seeburg-Smith, 137, 263, 597, 613, 616, 617, 619-621, 628, 742
Seifried, Leo, 718
Seifried, William, 719
Selig, John, 473, 474
Sellers, Preston, 176
Selmer Co., 883
Senate Th., Chicago, IL, 213, 248
Seng, John, 421
serpent, 34, 221, 228
Seth, H. P., 565
setterboards, 154, 215, 264, 426
shallot, 422, 426
Shawmut Th., Boston, MA, 116
Shea's Hippodrome Th., Buffalo, NY, 621, 627
Sherman Clay, 49, 286, 632, 694, 695
Shoninger pianos, 57
Shrine Auditorium, Los Angeles, CA, 370
shuffle effect, 228
Shulenberger, E. O., 234, 348, 388, 462
Simmons, A. A., 736
Simmons, Fred, 736
Simmons, Clough & Co., 736
Simplex blowers, 8, 19, 198, 693, 742, 743
Simplex Theatre Supply Co., 694
Simpson, Ken, 176, 177
single stroke, 426
Sjoberg, J. P., 597
Skinner, Ernest, 179, 223, 421, 425, 598-600, 603, 606, 607, 673
Skinner, Richmond, 606
Skinner & Cole Organ Co., 598
Skinner Organ Co., 20, 22, 182, 208, 232, 234,

289, 467, 598-612, 634, 673, 676, 677, 682, 687, 890, 914
Slingerland Drum Co., 844, 882
Smallman, Edward, 134
Smith, Charles F., 613, 614
Smith, Fred R., 612, 613, 740
Smith, F. W., 137, 494, 597, 613-617, 622-626, 890
Smith, H. D., 736
Smith, H. W., 736
Smith, Lester C., 11-14, 441, 756
Smith, Ray, 737
Smith, Walter, 379, 934
Smith-Geneva, 137, 613
Smith Unit Organ Co., 20, 51, 137, 142, 263, 613-631
Snyder, Bruce, 900
socket, 422, 426
Sohmer & Co., 833, 835
Solle, Otto, 693
solo ukelele, 95
Sommerhof, W. A., 132, 638
Sooey, Ray, 113
sostenuto, 426, 427
Sousa, John Phillip, 265
Southern Pipe Organ Co., 694
Southtown Th., Chicago, IL, 797
Sowada, Paul, 676
Sparling, Allan, 636, 655, 659
Spencer, E. A., 21, 315, 493, 498, 510, 511, 531, 632, 633, 890
Spencer, Ira, 755, 756
Spencer blower list, 12-14
Spencer-Dowling, 632
Spencer Motor Co., 755
Spencer Turbine Co., 12-14, 17-19, 198, 475, 675, 740, 741, 744, 755-777, 782
Sperbeck, Arthur, 284
Sperbeck, Ben, 284
Sperling, John, 11, 441
Spevere, Tony, 464, 470
Spies, Dan, 915
spotted metal, 424, 427
Spring, Joe Gibbs, 66
square bass drum, 533
Stack, Robert, 94
Stahl, Herman, 633, 832
Standaart, 147
Standard Rolling Mills, 843
Stanley Company of America, 210, 212, 225, 350
Stanley Th., Philadelphia, PA, 209, 212, 214, 215, 229
Stannke, Albert, 93
Starck music rolls, 445
State Lake Th., Chicago, IL, 213
State Th., Ithaca, NY, 265
State Th., Milford, MA, 134, 135
State Th., Minneapolis, MN, 185, 191
State Th., Roseland, IL, 372, 373
State Th., Seattle, WA, 95
State Th., Uhrichsville, OH, 612, 613
State Th., Westerville, OH, 658
Steele, Edith, 472
Steer, John, 634
Steer, Susan, 11
Steer and Turner, 634
Steere, John, 634
Steere Organ Co., 328, 565, 599, 634, 635
Steere & Turner, 441, 634, 635, 889
Stein, Adam, 636
Stein, Edward, 636
Steinert, Theodore, 594
Steinway (Astoria) Th., Astoria, NY, 442-444
stencil piano, 494
Sterling music rolls, 445
Sterling Precision Co., 837
Stevens Organ Co., 612, 636, 655
Stoll, Al, 83
stop, 427
Storf, Otto, 716
Strack, Otto, 322, 323
straight, 427
Strand, Harold, 891
Strand Th., Dubuque, IA, 842
Strand Th., Indianapolis, IN, 882
Strand Th., Niagara Falls, NY, 296, 297
Strand Th., Philadelphia, PA, 227
Strand Th., Richmond, VA, 620
Strand Th., Schenectady, NY, 297
Strand Th., Sunbury, PA, 364, 365
Stratford Th., Chicago, IL, 213
Strauch Bros., 834
Stuart, Levi, 442
Stuart, William, 442
Suburban Homes Co., 494
Sullivan, Louis, 587
Sunstrand brothers, 94, 95
Superior Th., Richmond, VA, 730
Super Paramount automobile, 347
Supertone music rolls, 445
Suttie, Jim, 11, 441
Sutton, Herbert, 563
Swain, Frank, 899
swell box, 427
swell shades, 401, 427, 568
swell shoe, 427
switchstack, 427
Sylvester Tower Co., 834
Symmes, D. D., 145
Symphonic Registrator, 290, 298, 304
symphonizer, 378, 379
Symphony Player Co., 637, 638, 742
Synchronized music rolls, 445
synthetic, 427

Taft, Frank, 22
Tally's Th., Los Angeles, CA, 504, 505
Tangley calliope, 423
Taylor, Asa, 31
Taylor, George, 102
T&D (Appleton) (State) Th., Watsonville, CA, 508
T&D (California) Th., Salinas, CA, 928
Tellers, Henry, 132, 638
Tellers, Henry C., 441, 638
Tellers, Herman, 638
Tellers, Ignatius, 132, 638
Tellers-Kent Organ Co., 638-642
Tellers Organ Co., 20, 132, 638, 821, 830
Tellers-Sommerhof Organ Co., 638, 640
Temple, Arthur, 102
Temple Organ Co., 102
Temple Th., McCook, NE, 517
tenor C, 427
tertiary action, 68, 427
Thayer, George, 265
Theatre Historical Society, 11, 441
Theatre Organ, 10, 11, 421
theatre organ, definition of, 16, 17
theatre organs, number installed, 20, 21
theatres . . . see individual theatre names
Themodist, 598
Thompson, Arthur, 22
Thomson Engraving Co., 923
thunder effect, 811
Thynne, William, 492
tibia clausa, 16, 17
tibia plena, 616
Tiffany, J. Burr, 731
Time-O-Stat Controls Co., 779
Tinker, Ralph, 563
Titan Tool Co., 903, 911
Title Insurance and Trust Co., 495
Tivoli Th., Aurora, IL, 141
Tivoli Th., Chicago, IL, 66, 83
Tivoli Th., San Francisco, CA, 511, 514
Tod, A. H., 284
Topp, James, 675
Toth, Louis, 660
Town Hall, Pretoria, South Africa, 232
Town Hall, Sydney, Australia, 338, 808
Tracker, The, 11, 421
tracker action, 16, 169, 170, 187
traps, 882
Traser, Donald, 11, 441
tremolo, 427
tremulant, 17, 35, 36, 427
Treul, Roland, 69
trick coupler, 427
Trinity Baptist Ch., Camden, NJ, 112
Trinity Episcopal Ch., Mattoon, IL, 484
Trinity Methodist Ch., Youngstown, OH, 934
Trio Roller Rink, Milan, IL, 10, 12
triple harmonic, 336, 427
Tripp, Donald, 683, 684
tripper combination action, 355, 427
Triumph Electric Corp., 792
Trivo Co., 365
Tschantz, Abraham, 589
tubular pneumatic action, 207, 427, 442
tuning spring, 422, 427
Turnbull Co., 793
Turner, George, 634
Turner, Harold, 232
Turner, William, 92
Twelfth Street Evangelical United Brethren Ch., Detroit, MI, 145, 146
20th Century automobile, 347

Uhl, Mrs. Mel, 546, 548
unenclosed, 427
unification, 427
United Artists Studio, Los Angeles, CA, 120
United States Pipe Organ Co., 20, 55, 643-652, 706, 784, 838, 842, 865, 923
United Technologies Corp., 795
unit orchestra, 427
unit organ, 427
universal windchest, 33-37
Unks, Dennis, 827
Uptown Th., Wichita, KS, 477

Van Nuys family, 494
Van Valkenburg, B. R., 495
Van Valkenburg, Harold, 495
Van Wart, Harry, 328, 634
Van Wyck, Bernard, 652
Varneke, W., 327
Varsity Th., Evanston, IL, 138, 143
Varsity Th., Lawrence, KS, 482
Vassar College, 677
Vaughan, Ernest, 49, 50
Velazco, Emil, 371
ventil chest, 119, 159, 164, 427
Ventus blowers, 819
Verdin, I. T., 844, 887
Verlinden, Edmund, 662, 663, 666
Verlinden-Weickhardt-Dornoff, 666
Verney, R. C., 99
Verney, William, 473
vibraphone, 427, 844, 862-864
Victor pianos, 445
Victor Talking Machine Co., 112, 113
Victoria Th., Mahanoy City, PA, 353, 357
Victoria Th., Mt. Carmel, PA, 352, 353
Victoria Th., Shamokin, PA, 350, 352, 353
Villard Th., Villa Park, IL, 149
Viner, Charles, 653
Virginia Th., Atlantic City, NJ 229
Vocaline Company of America, 835
voicer, 427
V'Oleon, 530, 531
Voris, William, 316, 322
vorsetzer, 42, 427, 685
Votey, E. S., 132, 736
Votey Organ Co., 22, 132
Votteler, Gottlieb, 655
Votteler, Henry, 655, 660
Votteler-Hettche Co., 636, 655
Votteler-Holtkamp-Sparling, 284, 636, 655-661, 915
VSM Abrasives Corp., 160

Wagner, Randy, 827, 831
Wakefield Th., Bronx, NY, 678
Walcker, Johann, 819
Walcker, Katherine, 819
Walcker, E. F. & Co., 145
Walcker & Son, 736
Waldrop, Uda, 682
Walker, Howard, 33
Waller, "Fats", 113
Waltham Church Organ Factory, 179
Walton, Judd, 441, 928
Wambsgams, Ed, 147, 896
Wanamaker's Department Store, Philadelphia, PA, 208, 502
Wangerin, Adolph, 662, 666
Wangerin Organ Co., 20, 58, 69, 72, 73, 84, 182, 301, 662-672, 791, 902
Wangerin-Weickhardt, 208, 662, 664-669, 733, 905, 908
War Memorial Auditorium, Worcester, MA, 233
Warner, Thomas, 677, 679
Warner Th., Hollywood, CA, 303
Warnock, Don, 891
Warren, Samuel, 181
Warren & Sons, 181
Warsaw Elevator Co., 793, 797
Wasle & Co., 834
Watson, E., 327
Watson, Reginald, 388
Wayne, Henry, 899
WBBM Radio, 65
WEAF Radio, 674
Webb, Reginald, 291, 915
wedge, 422
WEEI Radio, 118
Wegner, Pat, 830
Weickhardt, Fred, 588
Weickhardt, George, 588, 662, 666
Weickhardt, Joseph, 588, 666
Weickhardt-Schaefer Organ Co., 588, 670
Weilbier, C., 840
Weiss, Carl, 538
Wells, Jake, 619, 620
Wells Th., Norfolk, VA, 620
Welte, Berthold, 673
Welte, Carl, 673
Welte, Edwin, 673
Welte, Emil, 673
Welte, Michael, 673
Welte co., 20, 22, 155, 156, 182, 208, 214, 223, 233, 365, 673-692, 745, 913, 914
Welte-Mignon piano, 673, 675
Welte Multitone pianos, 445
Welte-Tripp, 686-690, 683, 684
Werner, H. J., 286, 495, 496, 498-500, 553
Western (Wiltern) Th., Los Angeles, CA, 214; also see Forum Th., Los Angeles, CA
Western Service Co., 693
Westhoff, Joseph, 726
West Point Military Academy, 389
W. F. L. Drum Co., 883
WGN Radio, 51, 232, 234, 934
WHA Radio, 83
WHAS Radio, 188, 190
WHDH Radio, 188
Wheelan, J. D., 694
Wheeler, Richard, 678
White, Frank, 28
White, Frederick, 145, 911, 912
White, H. N. Co., 807, 824
White, Son Co., 840
Whiteford, Joseph, 606
Whitelegg, Richard, 233, 348, 365-367, 378, 682, 684, 689
Whitely, John, 492, 493
Whiteman, Paul, 535
Whitham, Albert, 682
Whitney Organ Co., 132
Whitsett, W. P., 494
Whitworth, Reginald, 421
WHK Radio, 39, 40, 148
WHT Radio, 176, 189, 457
Wick, Adolph, 694, 718
Wick, Edgar, 718, 719
Wick, Edmund, 716, 717
Wick, Eleanore, 716
Wick, John, 694, 695
Wick, Louis, 694
Wick, Martin, 11, 441, 695
Wick, Victor, 718, 719
Wicks co., 20, 49, 102, 147, 153, 196, 322, 369, 423, 473, 499, 694-729, 740, 742, 786, 821, 848, 917
Widney Co., 792
Widor-Ronfort, Gustave, 28
Wilder Brothers shirt factory, 489
Willcox, J. H., 179
Williams, E. A., 454
Williams, Orville, 678
Williams, Silas, 159
Williams, Stanley, 494, 496, 498, 500, 507, 556, 557, 564, 731
Williams, R. S. Co., 736
Williams Master Organ, 454
Willis, Henry Vincent, 321, 327, 335, 677
Willis, Mrs. Henry Vincent, 327
Willis co., 92, 93, 365, 606, 806, 890
Willis weight, 422, 427
Wilshire Boulevard Temple, Los Angeles, CA, 214
Wilshire Ebell Th., Los Angeles, CA, 549
Wilson, Charles, 928
Wilson Brothers, 882
Wiltern Th., Los Angeles, CA . . .see Western Th., Los Angeles, CA
wind chest, 427
Winder, Charles, 31, 729
Winder Organ Co., 729-731
winker, 427
Winter, Elmer, 717
Winter, Florence, 716
Winter, J., 327
Winthrop Th., Winthrop, MA, 641
Wirsching, Clarence, 733
Wirsching, Phillip, 494, 662, 663, 731-733
Wirsching co., 462, 731-735, 905
Wirsching-Peloubet, 462, 463, 733
Wisconsin Th., Milwaukee, WI, 62, 66, 73, 83, 847
WJJD Radio, 141
WJR Radio, 291, 915
WKY Radio, 188
WLAC Radio, 188
WNAC Radio, 118, 606
Wolpert, Almer, 899
Wolpert, John, 899
Wood, Charles, 837
Wood, Granville, 132, 208, 736
Wood, Willet, 488
Wood, William, 132, 736, 737, 748
Wood, Wm. Pipe Organ Co., 20, 736-739
Wood & Brooks, 837
Wood Brothers circus, 883
Wood & Werner, 841
Woodberry, Jesse, 134
Woodlawn Th., Chicago, IL, 213
Woodley's Optic Th., Los Angeles, CA, 507
Woodstock Pipe Organ Builders, 181
Woolsey Hall, New Haven, CT, 634
WOWO Radio, 458
WQXR Radio, 234
Wright, Bill, 40
Wright, Charles, 93
Wright, Ed, 93
Wright, George, 16, 545, 632, 807
Wright, John, 137
Wright, Peter, 788
Wrigley, William, 457
Wurlitzer, Farny, 8, 223
Wurlitzer, Rudolph, 223
Wurlitzer co., 8, 9, 12, 17, 20, 21, 49, 51, 52, 66, 70, 82, 83, 134, 137, 147, 164, 171, 176-178, 182, 183, 185, 196, 209, 214, 223, 232, 286, 289, 332, 346, 350, 362, 390, 425, 427, 453, 498, 500, 517, 541, 565, 613, 643, 652, 653, 668, 677, 682-685, 693, 702, 740, 742, 766, 793, 794, 796, 797, 806, 827, 829, 840, 882, 891, 900, 902, 909, 913, 914, 922, 928, 934
Wurlitzer Hall, DeKalb, IL, 900
WWJ Radio, 606-608

Yakima Th., Yakima, WA, 116
Yerkes Co., 882
Yon, Pietro, 916

Zajic, Adolf, 365, 384, 387, 389, 401
Zephyr Electric Organ Blower Co., 18, 475, 588, 589, 741, 776, 777
Zeuch, William, 599
Zidlick, John, 327, 334
Zildjian cymbals, 244
Zimmerman, Harry, 176
Zimmerman, Walter, 717
Zwebell, A. B., 543, 546, 549
Zweifle, William, 473, 717